THE
DISAPPEARANCE
OF TOM PILE

www.randomhousechildrens.co.uk

IAN BECK has worked as a freelance illustrator for many years (including such notable artwork as the record cover for Elton John's Goodbye Yellow Brick Road album). Ian turned to writing and illustrating children's books when his own children were born.

THE
DISAPPEARANCE
OF TOM PILE

IAN BECK

CORGI BOOKS

THE CASEBOOKS OF CAPTAIN HOLLOWAY:
THE DISAPPEARANCE OF TOM PILE
A CORGI BOOK 978 0 552 56776 3

First published in Great Britain by Corgi,
an imprint of Random House Children's Publishers UK
A Penguin Random House Company

Penguin
Random House
UK

This edition published 2015

1 3 5 7 9 10 8 6 4 2

Copyright © Ian Beck, 2015

The Random House Group Limited supports the Forest Stewardship Council® (FSC®),
the leading international forest-certification organisation. Our books carrying the
FSC label are printed on FSC®-certified paper. FSC is the only forest-certification scheme
supported by the leading environmental organisations, including Greenpeace.
Our paper procurement policy can be found at www.randomhouse.co.uk/environment.

Set in Goudy Old Style

RANDOM HOUSE CHILDREN'S PUBLISHERS UK
61–63 Uxbridge Road, London W5 5SA

www.randomhousechildrens.co.uk
www.totallyrandombooks.co.uk
www.randomhouse.co.uk

Addresses for companies within The Random House Group Limited can be found at:
www.randomhouse.co.uk/offices.htm

THE RANDOM HOUSE GROUP Limited Reg. No. 954009

A CIP catalogue record for this book is available from the British Library.

Printed and bound in Great Britain by CPI Group (UK) Ltd, Croydon CR0 4YY

For Michael and Iris Holloway

PROLOGUE

'Tell us your story,' the voices said. 'We want to hear your story – all of it . . .'

That was when I started speaking out loud to the night stars all around me, and to the music, the voices in my head. They said, 'That's it. Go on . . . go on . . . tell us, tell us all . . .'

My mother died when I was seven. I remember so clearly the simple coffin box in our little cottage parlour. It lay there closed and screwed down, resting on trestles, and even then I knew that she was inside it. My father sat beside it with his head bowed, his mug of tea resting on the lid. The parlour was almost dark, with just a single lit tallow candle on the mantel, and still he sat there quietly all night.

She was buried in February – on St Valentine's Day, to be exact. The dark earth was tamped down hard and wet. The grave was dressed with greenery and one or two hothouse blooms from the Rectory. Mr Woolard had cut the grave and Mr Woolard's son had made the coffin. There was no stone or marker as yet, only the few pale flowers under the sleet and the ivy.

I stood at the grave while the Woolards lowered the coffin down on wide hessian straps. My father was standing at the graveside in his black Sunday best, one hand on my shoulder. He was the first to throw in some of the wet earth and flowers from the heap by the open grave. I looked around at the expectant faces: the Reverend Stone, Miss Gladwyn, my uncle and aunt, and then my father, who was hatless in the cold. His beard and side whiskers were grey, and his teeth were clamped together, making his cheeks look hollow. His hair was whipped by the wind that blew across Gallows Hill, where we would see the lights together for the first time, years from that night . . .

The Dorchester Weekly Courier & Advertiser

Friday 25th July 1890

Reports of shooting stars, falling meteors and unusual lights in the sky have been made from various towns and villages in the west of the county during the last week. The director of the County Historical and Archaeological Museum at Dorchester, Hector Brewer Esq., announced that he would be happy to receive and examine any pieces of fallen meteorite material that may be found at or near the area of the sightings. Falling stars were observed near the villages of Swyre, Puncknowle, Burton Bradstock, and on Gallows Hill at Litton Cheney. The sightings were reported over three nights, and alarm was caused when some residents reported sightings of what were described by some as 'angels' on Gallows Hill itself and in the surrounding landscape. However, no evidence of any such manifestation has been forthcoming.

Several of the witnesses have been interviewed by a representative of the London Scientific, Philosophical and Spiritual Society, a Dr Frobisher, who has been able to draw no firm conclusion from his findings.

He stated that, 'In such cases there can sometimes be in effect a kind of mass delusion or hysteria which can lead perfectly sane, level-headed and practical country people to conclude that they have seen supernatural apparitions such as ghosts, will–o-the-wisps and even serious religious manifestations such as sacred saints and angels and the like. In my own mind I am satisfied that what the witnesses observed was no more than a series of optical illusions brought on by the effects of the apparently unusually bright lights arising from the local meteor activity. In rural areas such events have throughout history been interpreted as signs and omens, and ideally we should not allow ourselves to be too troubled by them in our more scientific and rational age.'

Cover Note

I don't want to waste too much of your valuable time by telling you all about myself. I am not very important. You don't need to know much about me personally. I will simply say that I did something very secret during the Second World War. All that was, of course, some twenty four years ago now, although the results of our work are still very much with us.

What I did was rightly categorized as secret, for I was dealing with the mysterious and the unexplained – it would perhaps be better described as the inexplicable. I was always viewed with suspicion. Some thought I was wasting valuable war resources by looking, as I did almost daily, into reports of odd and unexpected things: sightings and events that were, in the majority of cases, the ravings of the deluded, the drunk and the insane. I was there to thoroughly investigate the five per cent or so of those reports which were not so easily explained away; those strange and deeply troubling events that happen all the time, whether there is a war on or not.

The idea of investigating such things made some of the high-up folk in the War Office very nervous indeed. Some of them found it almost laughable, and said so endlessly in circulated memos. In the end, of course, we were proved right, but our stories have remained secret and classified. The secrecy embargo has finally been lifted; I would suggest this is because the astonishing events of last July have finally made it unnecessary, hence this volume – the first, I hope, of a good few.

I am all too aware, however, that the licence to publish could be revoked at any point, so my concluding dateline below could, in fact, be out of date by the time these words reach the public.

I had actually been conducting these investigations since I graduated from university many years before the war. But when the conflict began, and the threat to our democratic freedom and our very way of life became ever more real, I gained the strong support of the highest authority, in the form of Winston Churchill himself. He was only too aware that in the 1930s the Germans had founded a secret department: the Office of the *Unerklärliche & Übernatürliche*, which roughly translated as the 'Unexplained and the Supernatural'. It was a subject the Nazis and Hitler took very seriously indeed, and Churchill knew that; he was of course unwilling to take the risk that the Axis powers might stumble on an advantage of any kind, however bizarre and remote, that might be denied to us, the Allies.

I was thus allowed to recruit my own small unit, with a very similar aim to our German counterparts. We were known as Department 116 – which was simply the number on our annexe door. We comprised a handful of technicians and research scientists, and one very bright young man from the East End of London. As a child he had shown a kind of genius for recognizing the mathematical patterns behind the seemingly random and disordered. He also had a strong – indeed, an almost uncanny – sense of intuition, which proved very helpful in certain circumstances. His name was Jack Carmody, and he was to become my man in the field, my special investigator; my 'go to' man, if you like. We were given offices close to Churchill in his Citadel and the Admiralty buildings, and more or less left to get on with it.

This, the first of our cases to be published, will be told partly in Jack Carmody's words, because he kept a detailed journal of our adventures, and partly in my own, because I did too – although of course it was not encouraged by the authorities. Now, in retrospect, I am glad that we did keep such detailed journals. With the help of these, and the other evidence, the whole story of Tom Pile can be told.

I have added in certain previously classified documents: direct transcripts of wire recordings, various intercepted messages and more, which all add their own layers of truth to the narrative. Some of the documents date back to long before the war; before the twentieth century, in fact. Each entry adds another little piece to the strange jigsaw puzzle of past, present and future which makes up Tom Pile's story. These events were so mysterious, and revealed something so huge and potentially dangerous, that they had an effect which went way beyond what might have been expected at the time.

So the roots of this story were laid down long before the war – and not just in these islands, but on the mainland of Europe too, as you will discover. I have tried not to interfere with the original testimonies, some of which I intend to present here in facsimile form. It will be up to the reader to read them carefully in order to see the big picture, which I hope will be revealed as each piece finally falls into place.

M. D. Holloway
(Captain, retired)
Glynde, Sussex

CHAPTER ONE

'Down to darkest Dorset today, then,' Captain Holloway said to me with a friendly wink. I was about to set off and was, you can bet, excited enough about what I might finally find there. Still, a tiny part of me wished I wasn't going away and leaving poor old London. There were too many things I had to leave behind – and who knew for how long? And it was not just that. I would miss the terror and drama of the Blitz. I was worried that, what with the bombs falling, and the destruction of dear old London, which seemed certain in those early days, I might never see the place the same way again. I couldn't let that stop me, though. Fear was a curse, and I wasn't about to give in to it. I could trust my aunt Dolly to look after herself, and she would look out for my own place too. Anyway, there I was, all ready to go. I was kitted out in my very stiff and uncomfortable new uniform, and I felt not only self-conscious, but a bit of a twerp too, to be honest.

'That's right, sir,' I said, looking down the length of my new and very itchy khaki strides (that, by the way, is slang for trousers in these parts).

'You might remember to return a salute to an officer, by the way, Carmody. You may be a pretend soldier and I might be one too, but we must at least play the part for our lords and masters.'

'Yes, sir, sorry, sir,' I said, and brought my hand up beside my forehead in what I hoped was a correct salute, as fast and as smartly as I could without laughing.

'Better,' he said, and he smiled his smile, and I could see that he wasn't taking it all that seriously after all. The bluster and noise was for the sake of the others who might be listening in the outer office of the Citadel annexe.

'Now, you've got the camera, plenty of special film and everything else?'

'All packed, sir.'

'Then good luck. Remember, anything you can get of these lights – the more the better. Of course, you know what else to look out for?'

'Yes, sir,' I said, grinning again. 'An actual live

person, if I can manage it.' Another smart raising of the hand.

'That's right, Jack. The real thing, and remember to get into the saluting habit and stay in it. You're supposed to know how to salute. You're meant to have gone through all that in basic training.'

'Right, sir.'

Viktor Prejm, a tame Polish airman who is said to be 'walking out' with our general office assistant and copy typist, Miss Greville, was perched, as casually as ever, on the edge of her desk while she tried to work. She was giggling when I reached the office.

'What's funny, then, Ruth?' I said.

'Nothing funny about you, Jack,' she said. 'Mr Prejm here just said he wanted to whisk me away to a romantic hideaway like one of these.' She gestured to the frosted glass panel to one side of her work area, over which she had taped dozens of picture postcards. There were sunny seaside and cottage scenes and the like, making it her own personal blackout area, shielding her from the worst of the bustle in the big office. 'Fat chance, I told him,' she added. 'I was laughing at his ruddy cheek, that was all.'

'I was only asking Ruth to file a translation document for me.'

'Dear Viktor,' Ruth said. 'Look, it's already done. I do know how to file – and I don't mean my nails. I used to be an archivist, don't forget. I know my way around all kinds of files.' She smiled.

Viktor raised his hands in mock surrender and shrugged, as if to say, *English girls*, and then gave me an ironically appraising look as I turned to struggle up the stairs and out of our inner sanctum, all crouched over (we have a low ceiling) and weighed down with the army kit bag over my shoulder and an overstuffed army-issue suitcase in each hand.

'Take care now, young man,' he said, helping me up the steps and along the corridor. 'Where are you off to? Somewhere more exotic than I was proposing to take your Miss Greville, I trust?'

'Can't really tell you that, now, can I, Viktor?'

'No, of course not, er, Corporal,' he said, his eyes widening a little as he took in my smart uniform. 'Well, now, look at you. Whatever else you do, just mind out for the girls, looking like that, eh? What would your girlfriend say if she were to find out?' And then he laughed.

I laughed too, but the joke was on me. Unlike Viktor, I didn't have a girlfriend.

It wasn't until I had struggled off the dingy train at Dorchester South and had been standing for a while in the poorly lit, bone-damp, cold station forecourt, waiting for the army truck from Burton Bradstock to come and collect me, that it properly hit home.

I was in the army, and I was in 'darkest Dorset' all right, just as Captain Holloway had said.

Standing there shivering on that late afternoon made me feel homesick for life in the good old smoke. I had no idea how long I was likely to be stuck down here on what might be just another wild-goose chase. We'd had plenty of those to contend with in our time.

There was one tiny saving grace, though, at that moment. The station was near a brewery, and that telltale warm, malty smell drifted over occasionally on the wind. It was almost as good as standing near Truman's in Brick Lane.

CHAPTER TWO

I have to admit something. There's no getting away from it. I'm a London boy through and through. There were times during those first few quiet days down in the country when the thought of a nice warm picture house – like the Sphere on Tottenham Court Road, or the Rialto on Coventry Street – showing a good old horror picture or a Marx Brothers comedy, and sharing it with a crowd of jumpy, laughing Londoners, was like a vision of heaven itself. After all, the deep dark countryside wasn't meant for everyone, but in the end that wasn't the point. I should at least have brought my travelling telescope with me for those rare clear nights. My army-issue binoculars had to stand in for my stargazing (and by that I don't, of course, mean looking at Miss Greta Garbo), but they just weren't as good.

It's hard to say exactly when everything started for me; hard to date when my path in life was suddenly clear. It was long before I first met up with Captain Holloway, in any case.

I was born in August, so I was always the youngest in my class at the local school. School didn't last long. Not that being the youngest held me back at all, as it is meant to – far from it, in fact. I was always a bit of a whizz. I could read almost anything before I ever went to school. I surprised the teachers with my abilities right away, especially for my age, and with my background. I was part of the dirt-poor but very respectable London working class, and I still am in a way. I'm not saying I was especially proud of it, but I certainly 'wasn't ashamed neither', as my aunt Dolly would have said, and did say, over and over, to anyone who would listen.

She brought me up on her own, Dolly did. She was my father's sister. Salt of the earth, and a bit more besides. She was fierce in her determination to look after me. I was, after all, her brother's only son. She was fierce too in her ambition to get me properly educated. Dolly had enough drive, pride and loyalty for about ten people. She was a force to be reckoned with.

I never knew my parents. To me, growing up in the streets of Hackney, Aunt Dolly had to be both mother and father. She saw my promise early. She moved heaven and earth and worked the system sideways, backwards and upside down for me. She applied for scholarships. When my abilities really started to show, I was tested and probed and questioned so often it felt normal to me. I suppose it must have been some of the strange things I did when I was very young that alerted her. First there was the thunder, and then there was the lady in grey.

She never tired of talking about the incident with the thunder. Aunt Dolly didn't like thunder. I noticed it once in a storm. There was one of those particularly loud claps of thunder overhead, the kind that almost shake the room, and she went all to pieces. I suppose I was about four years old, and her fear must have made a big impression on me. A year or so later, I was sitting in the back garden with her on a warm afternoon when I suddenly went and stood right in front of her and pressed my hands very tightly over her ears.

'Whatever are you playing at, Jack?' she said.

A moment or two later there was a huge and terrifying clap of thunder overhead. I saved her from hearing it: I just knew it was coming. Even at that age I could read the seemingly random patterns in the sky and the atmosphere. Aunt Dolly couldn't get over it. She told the neighbours, she told Lew the barber, she told everybody. They mostly looked at her like she was a bit touched. It just served to further convince her that her late brother's son, her only nephew, her Jack, was 'special'. It was quite something to live up to. Every time I got my hair cut – and in those days it was pretty often – Lew would tell all the customers, 'This little boy 'ere knows when the thunder's going to bang off before it happens. How about that, then? 'E ought to go on the halls.' I blushed with embarrassment as I looked at myself in Lew's mirror while he laughed and rinsed out his comb in a cup of white liquid.

I would have liked to go on the 'halls', as he put it, but not in variety. I wanted to be up on the silver screen. I wanted to be a Hollywood actor, like Ramon Navarro or Douglas Fairbanks. I suppose what I have done since has involved acting at various times; playing a part to deceive.

My childhood bedroom was at the back of the house overlooking the garden patch. Dolly slept in the middle room. She had the big front bedroom with the two windows all kitted out as a study for me. I would sit up there working even on bright summer's evenings. The other kids would all be out playing street cricket or generally roughhousing about while I sat there and read my books and solved things. I didn't mind. I didn't feel deprived. Sometimes I roughed it up with the best of them. I wasn't weak or scared; I had my share of fun and games. I played knock-down ginger and the like, and generally annoyed the neighbours from time to time like all the local kids.

'It's only natural, after all. Boys will be boys, you know,' Dolly would say, arms folded across her wide shelf of a bosom, head nodding in apparent sympathy with whoever had banged on the door to complain.

Every year I enjoyed our little backyard blaze

on Bonfire Night. Aunt Dolly let me set off bangers and jumping jacks and sky rockets out of our Brock's selection box, just like everybody else. However, I didn't much care for the stuffed homemade Guy Fawkes that kids used to wheel around in old prams, collecting 'pennies for the Guy' long before November the fifth. When I was very little, my overactive imagination gave those poorly stuffed straw men life. I felt them watching me from behind their papier-mâché masks, which I saw hung in rows on string in the local paper shop. I knew they weren't real, but once they were put on the dummies, I believed in them.

I wasn't like everybody else. I don't say that to show off. It is the simple truth.

I saw things.

I saw the bones behind the mask.

I saw the structure under the surface.

I also saw the patterns in large groups of numbers. I could pick out the connections and links between seemingly random events. I could see the core shapes in apparently formless things – like cloudscapes, for instance, or crashing waves and rushing water torrents. I could decode almost everything, or at least it seemed that way. I saw these patterns and connections fast, and I saw them clearly and simply; I didn't have to think or try or struggle. I solved things.

And I suppose you might say I even had visions of a kind; the sort of thing people referred to as 'being psychic' or having 'second sight'. I couldn't predict the Derby winner or anything like that, but I had something else. It was a kind of sixth sense, if you like, for odd and unexplained things. If predicting the thunder wasn't enough, there was the other incident; the one Aunt Dolly *didn't* tell everybody about. The woman in grey.

My aunt Dolly supplemented her income by doing bits and pieces of fine needlework, dressmaking and knitting for people. She was very skilled at it, and often made things for the locals who were that bit better off, too busy or too idle to make their own. Sometimes she took me to their houses to show me off. One of her 'ladies', Mrs Burtenshaw, lived a bus ride away, up in Hampstead. She had a large house with railings around it and a big gate. I had to be on my best behaviour. After we were given tea, with tiny triangle-cut sandwiches and fruit cake ('Only one slice now, Jack, and don't ask for another!'), I needed to go to the lavatory. I put my hand up and asked as if I were still at school.

'Please may I use the lavatory?' I said, and I saw Aunt Dolly beam at my polite approach.

'Of course,' Mrs Burtenshaw said. 'Just go out of here and turn left, keep on down the passageway, and there is a door on your left, and that is the cloakroom. Inside there is another door, and that leads to the lavatory.'

The hallway had a shiny marble floor with black-and-white squares like a chessboard. I could easily imagine big scaled-up pawns lined up along one side protecting the knights and bishops. I dawdled along, counting the squares to see if there was an even number between the front parlour and the cloakroom. Then I smelled something very sweet. I looked up, and saw a woman in the hallway looking at me. She was dressed in a long grey dress and a straw hat with a wide brim. Over her arm was one of those trug gardening baskets, full of cut roses.

'I was just going to put these in water,' she said, opening the cloakroom door and letting me pass by. It was the roses that smelled so sweet. 'There ought to be a suitable vase in here somewhere. You carry on, young man, don't mind me.' She looked down at me and smiled, then turned her back and began rummaging on a shelf. I went through the door to the lavatory.

After I had finished I went back out into the cloakroom. The roses had been arranged in a china vase. The lady's straw hat was hanging from a peg behind the door. I was careful to wash my hands because I knew Aunt Dolly would make very sure that I had.

When I got back to the parlour, Aunt Dolly said straight away, 'I hope you washed your hands, Jack.'

I held them out for inspection, back and front.

'Good boy,' she said.

'You found it all right, then?' Mrs Burtenshaw asked.

'Yes, thank you,' I said. 'The nice lady showed me.'

'Nice lady?' she repeated, a frown creasing her brow.

'What nice lady?'

'The one I just met; the one with the roses,' I said.

There was a silence after I spoke, and I knew I'd done or said something wrong; I had somehow upset this woman.

'Roses?' she said, quietly and intensely. 'How was she holding them?'

'In one of those flat-bottomed trug baskets. She was looking for a vase to put them in.'

The colour drained out of the woman's face. She looked like a sheet of paper. 'You saw her?'

'Yes, Mrs Burtenshaw.'

'She spoke to you? You spoke to her?'

'Yes. She said something like, "Don't mind me, you carry on."'

'Are you all right?' Aunt Dolly said.

The woman was staring at me in shock, her hand to her throat. 'No, I'm not,' she said. 'He says he's seen her.'

'Who's he seen?'

'My sister. What was she wearing?'

'A long grey dress and a hat.'

'It really was her . . . My God. Did you put him up to this, Miss Carmody? Have I ever spoken about her to you?'

'Of course I didn't, Mrs B., and I swear you have

never mentioned your sister to me, not once. Have you fallen out with her or something? Is she not meant to be here?'

'My sister used to wear a straw hat and an old grey day dress. She wore them for gardening. Tell me again what she said to you.' She seemed even more intense now, and she leaned forward and held my wrist hard, as if to stop me getting away, or daring me to be wrong.

'She said, "I was just going to put these in water," and then, "There ought to be a suitable vase in here somewhere," and after that, "You carry on, don't mind me."'

'There was no message for me? Nothing at all except talk of the flowers?'

'No,' I said.

'Has he done something wrong?' Aunt Dolly said, putting her hand on my shoulder.

'Not as far as I know. He is the first to see her. I hoped I might; I felt something once in that hallway, not long after she died, but I never saw her.'

'Died?' Aunt Dolly whispered.

'I never saw her,' Mrs Burtenshaw continued, almost to herself. 'And we had such a strong connection too. Surely she would have shown herself to me . . .' She shook her head then and let go of my arm.

'I can show you the flowers,' I said – even then,

young as I was, aware that none of this was normal. It was almost as if there were a charge of electricity in the air, as if a thunderclap were imminent.

'Flowers?'

'The roses she had. They are in the cloakroom, in a vase.'

Mrs Burtenshaw took my hand in hers and held it slightly too hard. 'You are not teasing me, are you?'

'No, Mrs Burtenshaw,' I said.

'He wouldn't do that, Mrs B. Jack's a good boy, bright as a button. Gets up to larks like any other boy, but he's not cruel.'

'Show me the flowers.' Mrs Burtenshaw led me back out into the tiled corridor. We all three stood just inside the door frame looking down the empty space. The polished floor, the rugs, the wood-panelled walls. I sniffed the air, and there was still the sweet rose smell.

'I smell the roses,' Mrs Burtenshaw said, and her voice, I remember, was quavery and suddenly nervous. She led the way down the passage. Aunt Dolly had her hand on my shoulder. The silence in the hall was deafening. It was quiet and calm, but it seemed to me that everything around us was screaming, there was so much tension, such a strange force of veiled energy in that house. I didn't experience that kind of pent-up and hidden force again until one night many years later, on a hilltop in West Dorset.

Mrs Burtenshaw closed her eyes and quickly opened the cloakroom door. The roses were there, neatly arranged in a white vase on an old sideboard below a row of shelves. White and sweet smelling, they were, at least a dozen of them. We stood huddled together in the doorway, just looking at them.

'Perhaps you put them there and forgot,' Aunt Dolly said, doing her best to be helpful.

'Oh, no,' said Mrs Burtenshaw quietly. 'That bush has long gone over. Madame Hardy, a damask rose – the old kind. They only flower once or twice a season.' She leaned forward, picked one of the roses out of the bunch and brought it up to her face. 'It ought to be a comfort,' she murmured, 'but I can't help feeling cheated.'

She turned to Aunt Dolly. 'I think you arranged this to trick me. I don't know why, but you hid those flowers somehow, and then the boy put them in there and made up that story. I think you had better leave.'

Aunt Dolly frowned. 'I'm sorry, Mrs B., but you're quite wrong. I told you before that this boy is special. You remember, I said he could tell when it was going to thunder, and he covered my ears to protect me from it? Well, now he's gone and properly seen a ghost, by the sound of it.'

'I shall pay you for your work and that will be that. Just be thankful I haven't called the police.'

'How ridiculous!' Aunt Dolly protested. 'Call the police! He's not a liar and nor am I. We are respectable, honest folk.'

'That may be. I would still like you to leave, thank you.'

On the way home we stopped off at a café. Aunt Dolly bought me an ice cream. 'I could do with a brandy after that. Always said you were special, Jack. You weren't scared, were you?'

'No,' I told her honestly. 'She seemed a nice lady. I didn't know she was a ghost before.'

It was one thing to see the patterns in things, to see through them. That was all connected to links and fast thinking. I suppose I was a bit like one of those adding machines most of the time. Seeing that lady in grey, though, was very different. Part of me sensed something about that hallway before I saw her. I knew there was something up: some part of my inner antennae told me. It was as if I had opened another undiscovered part of myself that afternoon. I realized, almost with a shock, that there were unexplained things, deep mysteries just at the edge of my understanding. I had somehow lifted a curtain on a new world.

Aunt Dolly drank her tea, but I could tell she was troubled. What had just happened had scared her, and she wasn't someone who scared easily. It hadn't scared me, though – quite the opposite. I was excited by what else might be behind the curtain. Aunt Dolly never mentioned what I saw in that house in Hampstead. She didn't tell Lew the barber or anyone else – it worried her too much. I think she thought that I had somehow conjured up the lady in grey.

As I got older, I developed a keen interest in astronomy, and in the worlds beyond our own – which is how I came to be taken up by Captain Holloway.

When they discovered what I could do, I was soon whisked away from my local infant school. I was tutored at home instead, and that's when all the testing started. Aunt Dolly would regularly take me in to appointments in the West End. We went to impressive but fusty offices in places like Russell Square, where I was set difficult theorems and mathematical problems. We would visit various institutes where my intelligence was tested. It was all very friendly, but it involved us both getting dressed up and me having my hair strictly parted and smarmed down with horrible brilliantine, which Dolly bought at Lew's.

I had to be polite, and hang my gabardine raincoat up on the hook, and sit at a desk in a plain brown varnished room all on my own. Then I would have to answer the questions.

'Just do your best, Jack,' Dolly said. 'You can't be expected to do more than that.'

I was asked by a friendly examiner after one of the tests if I 'had an ambition at all'.

'I would like to look at the craters on the moon through a proper big telescope, sir,' I said. I was just fourteen at the time.

A week later we got a letter.

Dear Miss Dorothy Carmody and Master Jack Carmody,

Allow me to introduce myself. My name is Michael Holloway and I have been told by an examiner friend of mine, Mr Anthony Paine from the College of Preceptors in Russell Square, that following a very successful recent mathematical examination Jack expressed an ambition to observe the moon through a proper telescope. I have a private observatory in my garden near Lewes on the Sussex Downs. I would be delighted to welcome you both here for just such an observation. I would suggest a date in mid March when the moon will be at the half phase, which allows for better viewing of the craters, etc.: March 19th would seem to be the best date. We must pray for a clear sky. If you are agreeable, a car will be sent to collect you from your home and will also take you back again. There will of course be no charge for this. I look forward to hearing from you both and very much look forward to welcoming you here.

Yours faithfully,

M. D. Holloway

(Captain – ret'd)

We were collected by a uniformed driver. He was behind the wheel of a Humber 12. I had never ridden in such a car before, and nor had Aunt Dolly.

'My word,' she said, 'this is a very nice car. I hope her at number fourteen saw us getting in, Jack, toffee-nosed old cow – pardon my French.'

We were driven to Mr Holloway's house high on the South Downs. Luckily it was a rare clear night. The sky was cloudy over south London as we drove out. The ground was still white after the late snowfall. Even though the car had a heater, Aunt Dolly sat with a heavy picnic blanket over her lap all the way down. The weather had been overcast and cold for most of the year. That night, though, away from the city, the moon was clear. I could see it as the car climbed the hill up to the house, which was hidden in a copse of trees.

Mr Holloway was a tall man. He came out to meet us with his pipe clenched between his teeth; he waved, a broad smile on his face. His hair was thin at the front and swept back over his ears. He had a high forehead and looked like the kind of professor you might see in a film. He stooped forward a little to shake my hand. 'Welcome, Jack,' he said. 'And you, dear lady, must be Jack's aunt Dolly. Well done, both of you, for getting here.'

'We ain't done much,' Dolly said. 'Your driver fetched us here; we just sat.'

'I meant partly in regard to Jack's education. It's you we all have to thank for encouraging his great talents, I gather?'

'I do my best. You have to, don't you? Always knew he was a clever boy.'

'More than clever.'

I liked Mr Holloway right away. He was friendly and engaging; a bit like some of the examiners I had met, but more jokey. I felt comfortable with him. Later, when I came to know him better, I realized that whenever he said something, it was with a special kind of authority, a certainty; it seemed that he knew everything about whatever the particular subject was. It was as if somehow he carried with him, all hidden away, the contents of a huge electric brain, which, like the nine-tenths of an iceberg, was floating under the water. In his case the waters of the everyday.

'Anyway,' he said, 'the moon is our business this evening. Come on – we've no time to waste.'

Aunt Dolly sat it out in the kitchen, chatting to the driver over a pot of tea.

Mr Holloway had a big wooden shed on a circular set of rails in the garden behind the house. The roof had a sort of dome, which could open in half, allowing for a view of the night sky.

There was a big refractor telescope set up.

'You see, Jack, I use this place as a summer house in daytime and good weather. I can move it around along the rails to follow the sun. At night it becomes my home observatory like it is now.'

Mr Holloway pointed to a chair set up under the eyepiece of the telescope. 'Park yourself there, Jack,' he said.

I sat down in the chair.

'Now, on the side there you will see the small sighting scope – got it? Good. Now line up the visible edge of the light and shadowed area on the moon with the cross hairs. When you move that small scope into place, it moves the big scope as well – that's it. Now look through the eyepiece of the big scope.'

There it was. My first view of an alien world. I could

see details of the craters on the defined edge between the light and the dark area. They were thrown into sharply detailed relief. I probably said something stupid like, 'Cor,' or 'Blimey.' Something uncouth anyway.

'Never fails to impress, does it?' Mr Holloway said. 'Think how far away it is. It's about 238,900 miles from Earth on average. At its closest approach, which is called the lunar perigee . . . I bet you know that word too.'

'Yes,' I agreed.

'The moon is 221,460 miles from us here on Earth. At its farthest approach—'

'That's the apogee,' I said.

'That's the one, well done – *then* the moon is 252,700 miles away.'

'It's moving,' I said.

'Of course, and it looks fast through there, doesn't it?'

I spent a happy hour examining the edge areas. I checked the details of crater names against the moon map – the Plato crater, and the Mare Imbrium.

'I am certain that one day we will settle a colony on the moon,' Mr Holloway said.

'I want to go and live there,' I told him.

'Maybe you will, Jack. It's not entirely impossible, you know.'

He settled himself on an old sofa which was pushed up against the back wall under the moon map. He lit his pipe. 'So you have two more years of study – although looking through some of your results, I can't imagine what they are finding to teach you any more.'

'You've seen my exam results?' I said.

'I see everything, I'm afraid. I'm a very nosy person, and because of my job I'm allowed to do and see all sorts of things that most people can't. What would you like to do after your studies are over, Jack?' he said.

I turned from the eyepiece. 'I don't know – find a job, I suppose.'

'What kind of job would you like to have?'

This was where I always came unstuck. The jobs I wanted to do either didn't exist, or were impossible for someone like me. First off I had always wanted to be an actor in the pictures. Aunt Dolly took me twice a week to the Dalston Odeon. I loved films. Secondly, but most of all, I wanted to be a detective who could solve mysteries through making all the odd connections that only I could see. A kind of clairvoyant secret sleuth operating on the edges of instinct and science. How could I, a fourteen-year-old boy with brilliantined and badly cut hair, explain that to anyone older, anyone in charge? How could such a job exist? It was mad.

'It's hard to explain to anyone,' I said, my confidence

rising just a little as I looked over at Mr Holloway, who seemed to be willing me on. I felt I could confide in him and it would be all right. 'I think, sir, that most of all I would like to be a kind of detective,' I said awkwardly, both expecting and fearing that I would be laughed at.

'That's very interesting,' he said, not laughing at all. 'What kind of detecting? Do you mean criminal stuff – fingerprints and all that?'

'No, not really that. Like I said, it's hard to explain. It's more to do with the mysteries of science; more to do with unexplained things – finding out about them and investigating.'

'What you mean is: are there little green men on Mars, and what really happened to the *Mary Celeste*, and is there a spirit world – and all the time pretending that you are not doing it and keeping it all secret; that sort of caper?'

'Something like that, yes,' I said.

'Well, then, it looks like you have come to the right place.' Mr Holloway cheerfully banged the arm of the sofa so that a cloud of dust rose up in the lamplight. He reached out his hand. 'Shake that, young man,' he said. 'I think you and I are going to work well together in the not-too-distant future, because, you see, the job I just described to you – that is exactly what I do.'

CHAPTER THREE

As far as I could see, as I sat there hugging my knees under the dripping wet tarp in the back of the lorry, looking out at all that gloom on the way over to my billet, Dorset was just a lot of bare wet trees and cold-looking hills. There were some buildings, I grant you – farms, barns, cottages, and I don't know what, all clinging to the round hillsides for dear life. It was all very Thomas Hardy and bleak and doomed-looking in the November dusk; and romantic, I'm sure. There wasn't much in the way of actual pavement, though. There weren't too many shops, either, and no picture houses – at least where I ended up. Just a lot of cows and sheep, and noisy cockerels, and all of them started making their big racket well before dawn.

Oh, and another thing: it was bloody freezing cold too.

The village where I was billeted, Litton Cheney, was in the Bride Valley in West Dorset. Not much of a centre to it, not many houses; a tiny place really. You could walk the length of it and hardly notice you had come out the other side. There were two ways into the village proper. It was as if one half was attempting to make its way up Gallows Hill, and the rest was content to stay in the flat valley. One road snaked its way down gradually from the main top road that eventually led to Honiton via Bridport. The other way in was from the same main road but was much steeper. There was a fine view of the valley and the sea from the top. This route ran directly into the village all the way down Gallows Hill. Litton Cheney had a church, and there was a pub, the White Horse, off to the south – where I had my rooms. There was one general grocer's and tobacconist's shop.

The church was north of the main route through the village. You could reach it in two ways. One was along a narrow track called Church Path. There were half a dozen labourers' cottages on one side looking out over the valley, with the Rectory at the far end behind its iron gates. Then there was another path that led up from the lower edge of the village past the steep border of the Rectory garden, where there was a spring which bubbled out and ran back down the side of the path. A corrugated-iron 'tin tabernacle' club house with a pitched roof, which looked like a cricket pavilion, was set at the very top of this path, and this was my main office. I shared it with the officer of the local centre for Air Raid Precautions – or ARP, for short – Mr Feaver.

Almost every day there was some new fear or alarm in the village. As soon as I started on my regular patrol, villagers either came running up to me with some story or other, or went and reported to Mr Feaver in the tin hut. They were all full to bursting with panicky rumours and stories.

For instance, a Mrs Hinde-Smith claimed that the German invasion had started already: her maid had spotted some Hitler youth spies near the village. Turned out to be just some Boy Scouts out camping in what was called Rocks Field, looking after a few evacuees.

There were constant rumours of Nazi landings too. One morning Mr Fry, a particular nuisance, and a bugbear of mine, swore he had seen dozens of parachutes dropping down onto Gallows Hill in clear daylight. When the ARP warden went up there to investigate, the parachutes turned out to be nothing more than an innocent flock of sheep.

With more than one aerodrome based around Dorchester, just a few miles from us, the whole village, and even those further west, had witnessed the recent Battle of Britain. This had lasted from July until October. I think this had set the mood of panic up nicely, because the villagers went on about it all the time.

When I was first stationed there, I just about saw the tail end of it all. At least, I saw a skirmish – a bit of action in the sky. I noticed some Spitfires and Hurricanes just after takeoff from the hills above Dorchester, and soon after that I heard the air-raid sirens. None of it seemed to be real at first. The planes were all so high, they were just little silvery dots; they looked like toys. Though toys would never have left the distinctive white vapour trails that everyone in London had got used to seeing. There was the distinctive droning sound of the engines too. Then I heard distant ack-ack guns. I saw the shells explode with those soft-looking puffs of dark or light smoke. They drifted in a fixed velocity pattern which I could read clearly against the background colour of the sky. The vapour trails crisscrossed each other, and I heard the machine-gun fire, both from our planes and from the Germans'. Once shot down, the planes fell quickly, spinning and turning, the vapour trails echoing the seemingly chaotic patterns of the falling craft – which of course were not chaotic to my eye. I noted a number of parachutes. More than one surely meant that the crew had baled out of a German bomber. The distant siren sounded the all clear. I was lucky that day: one of our fighters flew low over the village and went into a victory roll as he barrelled out over the top of Gallows Hill, which was exciting to watch. I heard no more about any arrests or the survival of the parachutists. Life at Litton Cheney was mostly aggravation, routine and tedium.

As my cover was to be the local support service to the ARP office, I heard all the rumours of invasion and tales of hidden spies – and worse.

There was a group of London evacuees who played in and around the village. They upset some of the villagers one Sunday morning by jumping out of the bushes at them, holding wooden rifles and shouting out in what they thought was German. All of this was reported to our office with a straight face.

The fear and panic was everywhere, and it was mostly irrational. If one of the locals saw a piece of broken glass or mirror, or even a bit of shiny tin, by the roadside, it was seen as a possible signalling device put there to alert enemy aircraft. If someone hung out their washing on a Tuesday, when on the Monday morning the weather had been good for drying, some of the villagers found it deeply suspicious, and would report the possible signal to us very seriously.

All sorts of strange advice and rumours circulated about what to do if anyone actually found a possible invader or spy. In the White Horse pub one evening, I heard the theory that you should go up to a suspicious person and ask, 'Excuse me, sir, but how tall are you, if you don't mind my asking?' If the suspect answered in metres, then they were plainly the invading enemy.

The other option offered up in the bar was that you should suddenly stamp on a suspect person's foot and see what language they swore back at you in.

Mrs Gladwyn's unmarried sister Ada told me once that she carried a brown paper bag full of pepper in her handbag at all times to 'throw into the invader's eyes should they get near enough'.

I will admit it was hard to picture poor little Miss Ada throwing her bag of pepper over a hulking great storm trooper.

The night things kicked off properly, it was not only freezing cold, it was raining too. Well, actually, no . . . sorry . . . start again – let's be more accurate here. It wasn't *exactly* rain. You see, back in London, rain was rain, and fog was fog. We had plenty of both, but we kept them apart. We wouldn't allow them to muddle themselves up and get mistaken one for the other. It was not the same, though, down in the country. For a start, it was so close to the sea; within hearing distance on a windy night. The rain down there was sometimes really more of a heavy sea mist – a 'precipitation', I suppose it would be termed officially (I might be a cockney lad, but I am, as you can tell, well educated). It was more of a 'soak you right through' sort of a fog. You could smell the salt water and the acrid engine oil and that rank whiff of seaweed; they were all mixed up in it as it rolled in off the sea – that is, if you could bring yourself to breathe it in at all.

That night I was on my 'reassuring presence' rounds, walking my preferred circuit of the village not far from my billet. There were no stars to be seen, nothing much to look up at, just low cloud and the general cold wetness. I stopped in the most sheltered corner I could find on my regular beat.

I had a decision to make.

I stamped my army boots (have you ever tried on a pair of army boots? They don't bend at all), just to try and get the blood flowing again. Anything to warm up my poor cold feet.

I had been doing my level best to look and behave like a regular soldier; of course, I wasn't one at all, just acting the part. I saw myself as a plucky young soldier in a propaganda film. The others weren't meant to know about me, which is why I had to work extra hard on my act.

I pushed myself further in under the high overhanging bushes to get out of the wet stuff, and tried my hand once more at rolling a blessed cigarette.

It seemed to me that the British army ran on Naafi tea and hand-rolled cigarettes. Nearly all the other soldiers in the barracks over at Burton Bradstock 'rolled their own', and whenever I went over there, I felt like the odd one out for being unable to do it properly. I never even had any cheap Woodbines to offer round like everyone else.

I was under Captain Holloway's strict orders to do my best to fit in. I had to try and be like all the other regular soldiers. So I practised rolling rotten filthy fags. I did it again, and for the last time, on that fateful evening.

I held up the thin paper tube, already stuffed with Gold Flake tobacco, and sealed it, as I had seen the other soldiers do, by running my tongue along one edge. I turned so I was facing out of the wet as much as I could, and tried to light it – and then that was it.

I'd had enough.

I made my decision.

I threw the horrible soggy thing away among the

tree roots. Who was I trying to kid? Smoking wasn't for me, Jack Carmody.

'That's it. Enough is enough. It's finished, Jack,' I said out loud in my very best Leslie Howard voice to the wet leaves pressing in all round me. Even though no one but the leaves was listening, it somehow had to be said, and out loud too. I was giving up smoking, and the idea of smoking, and anything to do with smoking, for ever and ever amen. And that was before I'd even got properly started on it.

Everybody in the regular army smoked like chimneys. Captain Holloway had his pipe. But I didn't like it, and I couldn't get the hang of it anyway, even though I knew it would make me look older and more like a proper soldier if I could. Part of me enjoyed that aspect – the pretending. As I said before, it was like being an actor in a big film. I played my part. The only problem was, it went on all day. I wasn't like the rest of the soldiers: I was undercover, and when I was with them, I think they sensed something about me; something a bit off kilter. Anyway, since I was posted to the village, away from the main barracks, the smoking didn't seem so important. There was no one around here to impress or notice in any case.

'No more fags ever, ever, ever,' I said out loud to the dripping leaves. 'Decision made. Good boy,' I added.

To someone who'd spent as much time as I had skiving off to old horror films in the picture houses of the West End, the whole village looked like a properly haunted place. The odd bit of light that got through the wet fog only made it look worse. All that was needed to make the setting perfect was the jagged silhouette of a ruined castle looming up on Gallows Hill above the village; now, that would have really completed the picture.

The heavy fog (the locals called it a 'sea fret') had been rolling in all afternoon from the nearby Chesil Beach – a weird-looking place where they carried out practice bombing runs . . . but that's a whole story in itself.

The fret masked the full moon. I have studied the moon; I know the moon. I could look up at the moon and identify all the so-called seas, and the craters too; the larger ones are all named. The Sea of Tranquillity didn't seem to fit any more, though, what with the bombing raids and the Blitz. A bomber's moon, it was called now. There were so many new words and phrases with the coming of the war. Just like the rumours – and not just of the approaching German invasion. There were rumours of secret bombing raids too. Mr Feaver told me last week that a stick of bombs had been dropped from a German plane near Bridport. 'Just to soften us up for when they land,' he said.

I suggested to him that it was most likely on its way to attack the naval docks down at Plymouth, further west, and 'Jerry just let some go for the hell of it.'

'I heard that the only casualties, Jack, were an outhouse roof that lost all its slates, and two rabbits – and luckily one of those was still edible and some clever beggar put the poor thing straight into a pie and baked it,' he told me.

All this might have been true; then again, it might not. There were so many stories and rumours flying about then, most of them best taken with a pinch of salt (rabbit pie . . . pinch of salt . . . ha ruddy ha) – like the one about German paratroopers dressed as nuns. There were rumours, and there were counter-rumours, and there were straight out lies.

I had been billeted in the White Horse 'Hotel' (so called). I had two rooms upstairs, which were cushy enough compared to an army barracks. I was forced to spend some time down in the bar, obviously, and the locals wasted no time in bending my ear with all their tales about this and that. One or two of the older ones remembered the stories about the 'lights in the sky' from way back in the 1890s, which of course interested me, though I couldn't really let on how much.

'The newspaper sent a man down here from London

back then in the old days, when it was happening before. He sniffed around and interviewed all the local folk who had seen them and all. Now some say the lights they have seen, 'tis the Germans and their planes and parachutes and all that. Well, answer me this: what about back then in 1890? Where were *those* lights from? It weren't no Germans then, was it? They never did find out.'

'Was no one there at all; was the beer talking,' seemed to be the popular view about the reported lights seen above the village in the distant past.

Of course, I knew a lot more than that, but I couldn't tell them. I was on special, 'need to know only' secret duties for Captain Holloway, but as far as anyone else was concerned, I had been sent down to help out with the local ARP.

I'd been teased all the time back in the outer office before I went off to Litton. 'Too scared and skinny to load mines and too young to play with the big boys, eh, Corp? You might as well enjoy cream teas with the farmers' daughters down in that village of yours.'

I only wished some of that had been true, but things were not like that in the deathly quiet village of Litton Cheney, I can tell you. Nothing much happened that wasn't ancient history or panicky ill-informed rumour; at least, not until that evening.

Communiqué 1

Translated from the <u>GERMAN</u> original
(Cl./Capt Holloway office 116 title for future use)
December 1939

Greetings from the other side. I am now in place, 'old chap', and am of course fully trusted. In fact, it is all better than we could have hoped for. There are some limits, and we shall soon no doubt be suffering from some of what you might call privations, 'old bean'. The English, though, have already been lulled into calling it the 'Phoney War', as if nothing else were going to happen to inconvenience them but another pile of sandbags heaped up outside the office and the 'terrible bore' of carrying a gas mask with them at all times. I shall report again when and if. Until then I am lying as low as I did before; as low as it is possible to lie. I am not to be disturbed; indeed, I am lying so low, I might as well already be forgotten and forlorn in my own grave, such is my silence and my deep overhead cover. I do remember one thing, though, from my earliest days – an old soldier saying: 'Cover from view is not necessarily cover from fire.' I always keep it in mind.

CHAPTER FOUR

I knew that there would be no sign of my friend Mr Feaver, the fussy ARP warden, before it was fully dark and the start of his official rounds. 'Finishing up his cooked tea, no doubt, in his nice cosy cottage,' I said to the wet bushes next to me, and they shivered a sort of reply at me, and we all waited together while my watch ticked.

I wondered what he would be eating. I could imagine his plate only too well. Whatever was on it would be swimming in flour-thickened gravy, which would cover most of the blue and white pattern. There would be a couple of nice big boiled spuds and some carrots sliced in rounds, topped by a meat pie – pigeon or rabbit, I guessed – and maybe some boiled cabbage on the side. Sort of thing my aunt Dolly would have set in front of me before the war, except her pie would have been steak and kidney. Things weren't in such short supply in the country.

There was something about that evening, something odd in the air, and not just the sea mist and the smell of diesel oil. I felt little ripples of apprehension, shivers and gooseflesh across my neck. It was what I would describe as my 'thunder' feeling, and it meant something was up. I walked the length of Church Path. Most of the old labourers' cottages were closed off and in darkness. Some evacuees and land girls were expected to be using them soon. Now they looked forlorn and doubly neglected in the dark. I finally saw our ARP headquarters through the fog. By the time I reached the corrugated-iron hut, it was properly dark. That real-country, no-light-at-all dark. The rooks (I was actually getting to know the names of birds and trees) were squawking and calling out as they settled for the night in the tall beech trees (see?) that skirted Gallows Hill and the edge of the big Rectory garden.

Mr Feaver would surely be in there by now, fussing about and getting all his fire buckets and stirrup pumps lined up nice and ready, just in case, along with our three chairs, a table, a telephone and a tea urn sitting together in the dingy tin tabernacle.

'Such a ruddy depressing racket those birds make,' I said as I went in, rubbing my hands. 'Give me the shivers, they do.' In fact, the whole winter countryside either gave me the shivers or bored me rigid; it was all pretty depressing and bleak. Warden Feaver nodded at me, his finger to his lips. He was standing bolt upright listening to someone on the telephone, looking as official as he could manage. He wore his navy blue siren suit tightly buttoned up. I am sure he thought it made him look like Winston Churchill himself. In one respect he was right: they were about the same size around the waist.

His tartan muffler was tied under his chin and then stretched up over the top of his carefully but oddly hand-lettered ARP tin helmet, which was perched squarely on top of his head. Even inside his own village hall, he was taking no chances. However, to be fair to the old chap, he had already brewed up some very welcome tea in the big brown teapot.

He nodded his head again and pointed at two enamel mugs steaming nicely on the trestle table next to the lamp and the regulation issue field telephone (official use only). 'Nice and fresh brewed, mind,' he said quietly, his hand over the mouthpiece.

'Won't say no, Mr Feaver,' I mouthed. 'It's brass monkeys out there tonight, and it's that damp cold too – seems to get right through to your bones,' I added in a whisper. I held my hands out to the paraffin stove.

'We've had a report,' the warden said as he put the receiver back, picking up his clipboard. 'That was local area command on the telephone, and our old friend Mr Fry was up at my cottage earlier too. Said he saw something as well – I've noted it all down here for you – "Odd-looking lights in the sky up over the top road," and then he says he saw a strange low-flying aircraft when he was out on Gallows Hill, walking his dog. He reckons he's seen these things more than once. Says he's reporting it direct to someone he knows in higher authority, if we can't be bothered to do anything about it. Says we ought to "go and have a look for ourselves instead of drinking tea in here all night" – damn cheek. Oh, here y'are, then – I did sweeten it, Corporal.' And he pushed one of the mugs across the table at me. 'Two lumps.'

'Two lumps.' I nodded my appreciation and gratefully swallowed some of the hot sweet tea. I kept my cold hands wrapped around the mug.

'Damn cheek is right,' I said. 'When was this all supposed to have happened?'

'Not half an hour ago. Mr Fry said he *heard* something too – sounded like low-flying aeroplane engines; the kind, he said, that land Nazi parachutists.'

'How would he know that?' I wondered. 'I ask you – it'll be another flock of sheep, no doubt.'

The mysterious lights were in fact the very things I had been sent down to investigate; those and the possible sighting of an actual person of interest, of course. I couldn't share any of that with Mr Feaver, though. It was all I could do to mask my rising sense of excitement. 'Strange I didn't hear anything while I was out on my patrol. Tell you what,' I said, as casually as I could, 'we'll satisfy Mr Fry for once: we'll go up Gallows Hill in a minute and have a little poke about. That'll shut him up for a bit – but only when I've finished this cup of tea.'

I hoped I had remembered to put film in the camera. My real job, my secret job, after all, was to faithfully record and report such things to the captain, not clump around the village listening to rumours about people signalling to the enemy by leaving bits of shiny tin or broken mirrors by the road, or hanging their bloomers out on a Tuesday morning instead of wash-day Monday.

CHAPTER FIVE

The sea fret had grown even thicker by the time we left the hall. The top of Gallows Hill had almost vanished into a vague dark cloud. Warden Feaver went ahead, holding up his home-modified version of a blackout lantern. We would have looked like a couple of those protesting villagers in *Bride of Frankenstein*, if I'd only been holding a pitchfork instead of a rifle. The lantern gave out such a faint beam of light across the chalky ground that it made the surroundings look more like a horror film setting than ever.

Mr Feaver had a first-aid box ('just in case, Corp'), attached to an old Sam Browne belt left over from his Great War service. I had my rifle and the camera strap across my back and round my neck. I had put my heavy army greatcoat back on before we left the hut. For once I was glad of my stout boots as we clumped our way up the chalk road surface.

'Shouldn't want to climb this just after it's snowed,' I said. Gallows Hill had a gradient of one in four.

'Snow don't come very often down here,' Warden Feaver told me, 'but when it do, the whole village might be cut off. You can't get any sort of lorry up or down this road. Snow has been known to lie as high as the tops of these hedges so that you can walk over them. No deliveries get through – nothing.'

We carried on up until, looking back down the hill, we could just make out the very faint shimmer of the golden cockerel on top of the church weather vane, down among the bare trees of the churchyard. We stopped to catch our breath and listened. At first all I could hear was the faint roar of the sea four miles to the south. There was another sound, though, in the background; it could have been a low-flying aircraft, but it was hard to gauge which direction it was coming from.

'That might be it,' the warden said. 'The aircraft Mr Fry said he heard. What should we do now?'

'Wait,' I said. 'We don't even know if it's anything at all yet. Let's just give it a moment, shall we?'

We waited, and as we listened, the sound, whatever it was made by, came and went, as if it too were being momentarily blurred and then magnified by the swirls of wind and sea fog.

Then a bright shaft of light appeared some way higher up the hill and touched the white roadway. There were others too, but further away, near the crest of the hill.

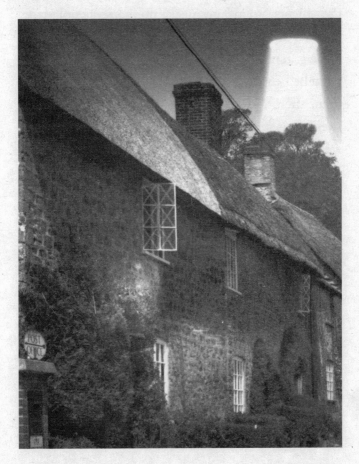

I got the captain's camera ready at once. Luckily I had already loaded it with special-issue extra light-sensitive film. 'It might just pick up something,' I said, and I clicked and wound through a couple of times, and then the light moved off. My own 'thunder meter', as before, was properly clicking into place. I was getting the shivers around my neck, the goose pimples too, and one further thing: whenever I reached this state of heightened awareness, ever since the lady in grey, I smelled the sweetness of those roses. I could smell them then, out on that bleak wintry hill. My inner needle was spinning around the dial. Something really was up.

'Can't see why you'd want to *photograph* them; shoot at them maybe. What on earth could they be anyway?' Mr Feaver said.

The lights showed again, a little higher up the hill: one was a shaft of pure white like a sudden searchlight turned on the road out of the clouds above. There was sound now too – a faint rippling thud like a giant footstep.

'Sounds like they could be laying mines or even dropping incendiaries,' I said, clicking off two or three more hopeful shots. I knew that this was certainly not the case, but I couldn't risk letting Warden Feaver know what was really happening. I ran further up the

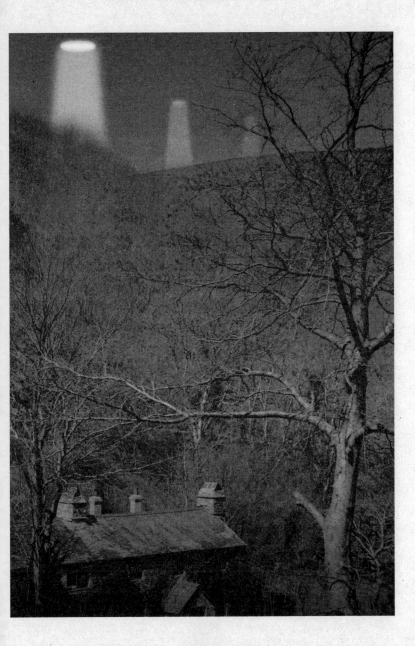

hill. 'Could even be parachutists, I suppose,' I called back to him, for he was struggling to keep up.

'Can you see them, then?' he shouted breathlessly.

'I can see something,' I said. 'Though God knows what.'

We were nearly halfway up the hill when the lights came again, only now they were directly over our heads, and dazzlingly bright for just a second or two.

'The aircraft noise is stronger too,' I said, 'although it doesn't have the distinctive rumble of a Heinkel or a Junkers.'

The line of lights moved on, like lightning, further back down the hill. They touched the ground on the way, one after the other.

'Damn,' I said. 'Back down there, Mr Feaver – look.'

Above the church, somewhere among the tangle of shrubs and trees, the lights appeared again in a blinding flash. I photographed what I could manage in a rush, and then raced past old Feaver back down the hill again. 'Wait for me,' he called out, and ran after me, his dim lantern light waving about in the fog.

CHAPTER SIX

I stopped in my tracks, hesitating near the steps that led up to the churchyard. The sweet smell had come again out of nowhere: somewhere nearby there was something strange. I knew the signs by now . . .

The lantern on the iron arch over the gates was switched off, but bright light suddenly flooded out of the open door of Mr Fry's house. He was standing on his porch in a grubby old dressing gown, with a broom raised above his head.

'Now you've heard them and seen them,' he said, 'perhaps you will believe me. Invading Germans, you see, just as I told that fool Feaver earlier. Now perhaps you'll believe what I saw and heard – and not for the first time.'

'Please close your door at once, sir, and respect the

blackout,' I said. 'And please keep it closed. We are dealing with this now.'

'Why would I take orders from you? You look like a ten-year-old. Answer me that,' Mr Fry said.

I was used to this sort of thing.

'It has nothing to do with my age, sir, which I assure you is not ten. It is a question of the law. We are at war and the blackout must be respected, and you surely know that.'

He glared at me, then turned on his slippered heels and slammed the door shut. His dog started barking loudly from behind it.

The warden arrived, out of breath, still holding his helmet onto his head. He put the lantern down on the ground and stayed bent low for a moment with his hands on his knees, getting his breath back.

'You all right, Mr Feaver?' I said.

'I'll be right as ninepence in a mo', young Jack,' he said, straightening up and holding the lantern high above his head. 'Just not used to running at my time of life. I'm guessing, from all the noise, that Mr Fry's been on at you?'

'Yes, he has,' I said. 'I put him straight.'

'What should we do now, then?' Mr Feaver asked.

'I think we should go up into the north churchyard.'

'You sure, Corp?' he asked. 'Looks empty to me –

nothing there but sleepers, if you catch my drift.'

'I agree, Mr Feaver, but I have a strong feeling that someone or something is hiding there.'

I had a real horror of treading on the grass humps and mounds of earth above the dead. I've never liked cemeteries much – who does? – especially in the dark, and especially after some of the things I've seen. It was like the game we used to play back in the smoke when I was a really little kid: avoiding the cracks between the paving stones – except now I knew that it was all real. It couldn't be helped. To go any further we had to clamber over the ancient green mounds of the village dead. It had to be done; the sweet smell was calling to me and I had to act on it.

The place looked abandoned and haunted on that wet November night. The older monuments and high gravestones loomed up out of the pitch darkness, dull-white and grey. The rusty iron gate was half pulled open, and it was covered in drops of water which caught the low light from Mr Feaver's lantern. Ragged swirls of sea fog floated all around it. We went up the steps side by side: Mr Feaver held the lantern out in front of us, and I pointed my rifle forward with the bayonet, my 'pig sticker', fixed in army regulation fashion.

We crossed the wet grass over the sleeping mounds and went up the second short set of steps into the higher, north part of the cemetery. The next instant, I heard the same throb of aircraft noise, somewhere in the fog right above our heads, and then there was another blinding flash of light, which dazzled me as it hit the ground, accompanied by those thumps – which felt loud and deep enough to wake the sleepers under our feet.

The sea fret had somehow gathered here in this corner too, and had grown even thicker. When my eyes had recovered from the light, the darkness seemed extra dark again and the lantern was having little effect.

There was no aircraft sound anywhere now, just an uneasy silence.

It was then that something large and white rushed out of the darkness at us.

I already had the camera raised in case, and I clicked just the once before I had to sidestep. A terrified-looking albino stag with large antlers leaped straight at us out of the fog. I could read the fear in its glaring eye as it rushed past, and then careered off through the tangle of bushes. I watched it clear the steps in a single bound, and then it dashed off to the side in a swerving panic. It was soon galloping up the chalk road of Gallows Hill.

'Good God!' Mr Feaver shouted. He had fallen back in shock, and was leaning against one of the taller gravestones. 'What the bloody hell! Where did that come from? I've never seen the like – nearly gave me a ruddy heart attack, it did.'

'I thought they lived wild in the forest, not here,'

I said, only just regaining my own balance.

'They do,' he replied. 'They do, Jack. I've never seen anything like that here, ever – not a white hart, not here in the village like that.'

We waited, recovering from our shock in the uneasy quiet. 'Not even those awful rooks are squawking now, and they're never quiet,' I said. I breathed in deep draughts of Dorset air, cold and damp, but overlaid with that sweet rose smell. I looked around carefully. I was sure that the deer was not the only living thing in the churchyard.

'Wait a moment,' I said. I set off further in among the tombs, aware of something just out of reach.

'Shouldn't we get back inside, Corp?' Mr Feaver called out to me. 'There's nothing left for us here.'

I was soon in total darkness: the light from the warden's lantern was so weak it had no effect at all if you stepped just a few paces away from it. The churchyard was almost completely silent now; I could only detect one sound – of something or someone breathing heavily among the shadowy gravestones.

'Who goes there?' I called out suddenly, as loudly as I could, into the quiet air.

'Is that . . . is that you, reverend sir?' a voice called back to me fearfully from among the graves. 'I didn't hurt it – I couldn't do it, not with that knife – it didn't seem right. I was trying to save it, honest. I promise I was.'

'No,' I called back, my heart pounding, 'it is not the reverend anybody. It is Corporal Carmody of the Ninth Essex Regiment. I am patrolling here with Air Raid Precautions Officer Feaver. I should warn you now that we are armed. Who might you be, friend or foe? Step forward slowly now and show yourself.'

A shadow emerged and took a nervous step forward.

'Mr Feaver, your lantern up here please,' I called out.

The warden was soon next to me, puffing and wheezing. 'What is it, Corp?'

I took the lantern and held it out at arm's length. Standing in front of us was a boy of about thirteen or fourteen, not so very much younger than myself.

'Well, look at that,' Mr Feaver said.

'Do you think we have found a parachutist?' I asked, doing my best to play along and so keep Mr Feaver in the dark. I knew that this boy was no German paratrooper.

'I thought you m-might be the r-reverend,' the boy suddenly said haltingly, ignoring what we had just said. His teeth chattered – I presumed from the cold. He stood stock-still and shivered. He was wearing a rough-looking dark waistcoat and breeches and a dirty white shirt. He was shaking all over and wide eyed, apparently with fear.

'Was that animal anything to do with you, then?' I said.

'I didn't hurt it, honest, sir. It was old Gawen's idea – he wanted it and promised me a share, but I changed my mind, and now I don't know where he is.'

'Right,' I said, pulling myself together and sounding as convincingly official as I could manage. 'Warden Feaver, sir, if you wouldn't mind just looking behind all these stones here for anything that may have been hidden – a discarded pack, weapons, parachute, anything at all.'

'Right you are,' he said and moved away, taking the lantern light with him.

The darkened shape of the boy stood staring ahead and not always straight at me. His face was deathly pale. He looked dirty too, and the whites of his eyes were just visible in the gloom as he flicked his gaze right and left, then back to me. He was clearly terrified of something.

'First thing now,' I said. 'Please put your hands up high above your head where I can see them.'

The boy obeyed at once, lifting his arms straight up into the air.

'Where are you from?' I asked.

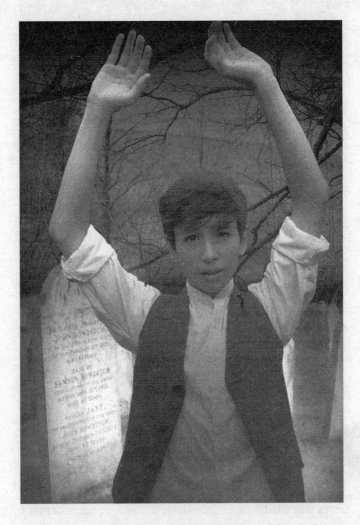

'From round here, course,' the boy said in what I recognized as the local accent.

'You sound as if you might be, but then accents can be learned and faked, and you Germans are clever devils, aren't you,' I said, keeping up the pretence that I thought the boy might be just that.

My feelings about this boy being there had been correct. Once again there was a stirring, a quickening of something around my sixth sense, my thunder meter. Something was wrong with all this. The boy didn't fit; my readings were, as they say, 'off the scale'. Here was the very thing – the 'person of interest'. I had to dampen my excitement down in front of Mr Feaver, but there was something distinctly odd and at the same time familiar about everything that had happened.

Warden Feaver returned from his search behind the graves. 'Nothing there,' he said, and moved closer to the boy. 'I don't know this lad by sight at all.' He shook his head. 'Certainly not local to us.'

'You're not from this village, then?' I asked.

'I am, though. I live very close by – just down the path there.' The boy lowered his arm and pointed. 'I live at the cottage down there, the first one past the steps on Church Path.'

'No one lives there – it's boarded up, and has been ever since the last tenants left. It's up for requisition for possible evacuees,' the warden said.

'But I live there with my father,' the boy insisted.

'I think you'd best come with us,' I said. 'Slowly now – come forward. You look frozen, and the least we can do is get you into the warm.'

The boy was shivering violently, as if he had just been pulled out of freezing water and saved from drowning. He came into the dim circle of lantern light, and I saw that he had a tangle of dirty-looking dark hair.

'*Woher kommen Sie, junger Mann?*' ('Where are you from, young man?') I asked suddenly, as if trying to trick him and catch him out with my best LCC-board school-certificate German.

The boy just looked back at me; his face was a complete blank. Not a flicker of recognition at the German.

'All right, come on, then.' I waved my rifle, the bayonet pointing up the slope back towards the tin tabernacle.

The boy walked hesitantly between me and Warden Feaver. Mr Fry appeared again, scuttling out of his now darkened doorway. In one hand he was holding a threatening garden shovel instead of the broom, while in the other he held his muzzled dog, which growled and strained against the lead.

'So you actually caught the little Nazi swine,' he said. 'The first of many, I'm sure. Why not let me at him?'

'Step back, please, sir,' I said.

'Not much to look at, is he? Some soldier *he* is – not

much to worry about if they are all like that. Looks more like a damned gypsy.'

'Back inside please, sir. We have this under control now.'

The boy broke away and blundered ahead for a few feet in a sort of panic.

'He's escaping now,' Mr Fry said. 'Fat lot of use you are. Shoot him, man.'

'No, sir. He has not escaped, sir, if you look properly. There will be no shooting.'

Warden Feaver had hold of the boy by the scruff of his shirt.

Mr Fry went reluctantly back into his cottage, grumbling to himself.

Communiqué 2

SECRET
WAR DEPARTMENT
CLASSIFIED MESSAGE CENTRE

Translated from the GERMAN original
(C2./Capt Holloway Office 116)
Undated – filed early 1940

I have met someone. They think I am 'quite the thing'. In turn they could in fact be quite the useful thing too. I need someone like this – a natural cover. Couples can do things and go places here in London with more ease; the individual cannot wake up without suspicion. The idea of a romance is a pleasant distraction in itself.

They work for one of the War Office Ministries – nothing too sensitive. I was told there were bombing raids on the cities outside London, although the newspapers here are censored. They fear a coastline invasion. I have joy to determine that the submarines can now operate out of Brest.

CHAPTER SEVEN

Mr Feaver pushed the boy gently over the threshold of the hall. He stood blinking in the sudden brighter light and I gestured for him to sit down at the warden's table. I moved the black Anglepoise lamp up and round a bit so that I could get a good look at him. The boy watched me, shivering in silence. It was a fearful silence rather than a sullen or defiant one.

'You look like you could use a cup of tea,' I said, as casually as I could manage.

The boy nodded a yes while he continued to stare straight ahead at the upturned electric light bulb. He reached his finger out suddenly, and before I could stop him he touched the bright glass. The bulb seemed to react. It brightened momentarily, and the boy pulled his finger back as if he had been stung.

'Careful now, lad, you'll burn yourself,' I said. 'You

should know better than that – or are you playing the simple card now, I wonder?' It was an interesting moment. It seemed that a surge of something had passed through the light filament when he touched it; as if he himself were charged with energy in some way.

I moved the base of the lamp back to keep it away from him, and then picked up the camera.

'Look at me,' I said. The boy stayed still and I took a photograph of him and then wound the film on and took another.

'What you doing?' he asked.

'Taking a photograph,' I replied.

The boy said nothing; he just stared back into the camera lens.

Warden Feaver slid a mug of tea across the table, along with a tin bowl with three or four sugar cubes rattling around in it.

'Sugar?'

The boy said nothing, so I stirred two of the cubes into the tea for him.

'Steady on now – our sugar is in short supply,' the warden said.

'I think he needs it more than us, Mr Feaver,' I said.

'Lucky to get it at all, if you ask me, Corp.' He shook his head.

The boy picked up the mug and held it up as if for

an inspection. He looked at it in wonder, as if he had never seen anything quite like it before. He put it to his lips and carefully drank some of the tea with his eyes tightly closed. He kept the mug up close to his mouth, as if he were savouring the heat and steam from it as much as the tea itself.

'Time to ask you some questions, I'm afraid,' I said. 'You must understand our position here,' I added. 'We have had several reports of low-flying aircraft, and then you and some unlikely wild animal suddenly turn up in the local graveyard together straight afterwards.'

'I live here,' the boy said quietly. 'This is my home and we were going hungry. I didn't want to hurt it.'

'So where did that deer come from? You know, you shouldn't be out at this time of night. You were obviously up to no good. There's a war on, and a strict blackout and all that.'

'Obvious to me, Corp,' Mr Feaver said.

'Go on,' I told him.

'He's most likely one of those badly behaved London evacuees and he's been sneaking out with this mate of his, Gawen, from wherever they're billeted – over at Burton, most likely, or I hear there are some at Puncknowle. They've been doing a bit of venison poaching and we caught this one. The others ran off.'

'Is Mr Feaver right? Are you from London – is that

it? Grabbing some free venison off the ration?'

'No, I live here, in this village. I was born here and my poor mother is buried up in the churchyard, may God rest her soul.'

'I see. Well, we can check up on all that later. What is—'

I was interrupted by the field telephone ringing suddenly and shrilly into the quiet. The boy jumped forward off his chair as if in terror of the phone. He lunged forward to touch it and knocked the receiver off its cradle. I watched as it fell awkwardly to the floor.

It was as if, for just a split second, an invisible hand had steadied the receiver as it fell.

It visibly slowed in the air.

The warden didn't notice anything because it was on the far side of the table from him, but I did, and my interest in the boy was suddenly doubled. A tinny voice came floating up out of the fallen receiver. The boy, startled, backed away from the table.

'What's that?' he said.

'Now, you shouldn't have done that, should you? That belongs to the WD, that's Government property, that is,' Warden Feaver said, bending down and scrabbling awkwardly under the table for the telephone receiver.

'WD?' the boy asked, looking at me with a blank

expression on his face. 'WD?' he said again.

The warden picked up the receiver and spoke quietly into it. 'Yes, sir, as a matter of fact we *are* aware of it. Yes, we saw it ourselves. Yes, sir, I'm sure someone will be looking into it.' He put the receiver back.

'Someone has reported seeing that white stag,' he said. 'Been running wild up on the main road over to Honiton.'

I said to the boy, 'WD means War Department. We have that telephone in here because it is the year 1940 and we are at war and we are keeping a lookout for enemy aircraft. Now, come on, calm yourself and sit back down.'

He looked at me with a frown on his face, as if he was working something out. He closed his eyes and mumbled something which I didn't catch.

I took a pen from the table and a sheaf of Captain Holloway's incident report sheets.

'Have the Boers won, then?' the boy asked. 'Is that what you mean?'

'The Boers?' I said. 'No, that all ended in – ooh, what was it? – 1902. We are at war with Germany now, of course.'

'We are at war with Kaiser Bill as well now?'

'Kaiser Bill? Where have you been living? It's 1940,' I said, carrying on with the standard question and response for the benefit of Mr Feaver.

'No,' he said under his breath, his head shaking from side to side. 'No, no, no – can't be.'

'We're at war with Herr Hitler, of course. You know, the one who looks like Charlie Chaplin but is not at all funny.' I touched my index finger to my upper lip in an attempt to look like a caricature of Hitler and his moustache.

The boy continued to shake his head slowly. He certainly wasn't faking his ignorance.

'First things first,' I said, opening the pen. 'Let's start as we mean to go on. Your name?'

'My name is Tom – Tom Pile,' the boy answered, staring ahead past my shoulder into the darker part of the hall.

'And how old are you, Tom?'

'I'm fourteen – in any case, that's what I was told last birthday.'

'Why were you out in the churchyard this evening?'

'I started from there with old Gawen this evening, but I don't know how I got back there. I can't seem to remember anything much about tonight.'

'Were you sent here from Germany?' I said for Mr Feaver's benefit. I knew full well that Tom might well have come from a lot further away than Germany.

'No, course not. Like I said, I'm from here. I'm

from this village. I've lived here all my life . . . all my life . . .' His voice trailed off and his eyes lowered, and he suddenly looked very sad and young and dirty and bewildered.

'All your life, you say . . . But,' I pointed out, 'the warden here doesn't know you at all, and he knows everyone in this village and hereabouts.'

'Well, I don't know him,' the boy said, shaking his head wildly. 'I don't know anything or anyone any more.'

CHAPTER EIGHT

It was late when I finally led Tom off to my billet in the White Horse. I took full responsibility for him. Warden Feaver made me sign a letter to that effect, which he folded into his report ledger.

'Just in case, Corp, you understand.'

I understood all right. It was called 'covering your back'. Everyone official seemed to do it – must have orders in triplicate, must keep flimsies, must have letters and files all backed up with carbons, responsibility shifted far away down the line. That was how everything worked now with the war.

We didn't go in through the public bar. I didn't want to draw too much attention to the boy. If word got out that we had found a possible German invader in the local churchyard, then I might have a lynch mob of Dorset peasants on my hands, all carrying flaming torches and pitchforks, and we would soon be back in the churchyard burying him. I was sure that this boy was no German. I could see it clearly enough. He was not part of some pre-invasion force. If he was – if this was the best they could come up with – then it was surely all over for Hitler, and no mistake.

Luckily the upstairs rooms had their own side entrance. I took him up and sat him down by the table and told him to stay there. Then I locked him in from the outside and went to find the landlord.

The bar was full of the usual locals – though it was not a place frequented by Warden Feaver. He was church warden as well, and would have considered himself a cut above the public bar at the White Horse. The news about the boy wouldn't have come through yet, but it would only be a matter of time.

'Evening, Corporal,' said the landlord, Mr Cox.

'Evening. A half of bitter, please, squire – and is there anything to eat?'

'Could get the wife to make you up some sandwiches. Nothing hot left tonight, I'm afraid.'

'Sandwiches will do well enough. Two, if you could. I have an extra mouth staying tonight.'

'Oh, I don't know if I can allow—'

'Yes you can,' I interrupted, tapping the side of my

nose. 'It's an army matter. Very strictly hush-hush,' I added.

'Understood,' he said, and handed me a dimpled glass.

Mrs Cox came through from the kitchen and said, 'I can do cold lamb and mustard piccalilli – that do?'

'Very nicely,' I said.

One of the older villagers, Mr Gladwyn, who was always to be found sitting by the big fireplace in the public bar, called me over.

'Any chance of a bitter, Corporal? Only I've got something to tell you, just between you and me, mind.'

I was used to this. No doubt he had seen one of his neighbours signalling to the Germans by putting a mirror in the hedgerow or heard someone in the village speaking German. After all, I was down there to dig around and find things out, so I shelled out for a pint of the finest and took it over to the fire. He drank a good quarter of it off and then spoke to me quietly.

'Post office van driver from Bridport was just in 'ere earlier, Corporal. Said he saw some low aeroplanes. Well, he said there were bright lights up in the sky. Says he saw them, and then, after that, on his way 'ere, he saw a white stag running free and wild up on the Honiton road. Nearly forced him off the road, it did. Gave him a shock. He said it looked like a ghost creature out in the fret like that. Never 'eard the like. Rum things happening round 'ere all over again.'

'All over again?' I said.

'Aye, it's not the first time for seeing the lights hereabouts and more. Ask any of the older folk: they might remember it – lights in the sky and all, 'bout forty years ago.'

'I'm sorry,' I said, playing dumb. 'I'm obviously missing something here. What exactly do you mean?'

'Look it up, lad – must be records of it all somewhere that will tell yer. I don't know much about it, only heard the stories. My old father – God rest his soul – told me he had seen them, but then I never did. The post office man was all shaken up by it too – 'ad to 'ave a brandy and water, not like himself at all – 'e's a cider man normally. I say it means invasion for sure. Bad omens, I reckons they are. We'd best brace ourselves for it – looks like Ada might need her bag of pepper after all.'

Back in my room I found the boy slumped down on one of the single iron beds which had been pushed up under the window. He had fallen asleep. His position and his pale colour reminded me of that old painting, *The Death of Chatterton*; the boy looked dead too. I went over and felt for his pulse. He wasn't dead, but he was dead to the world. I covered him with a blanket and let him be.

The landlady brought the sandwiches up. I opened the door just enough to allow her to get the plate through. They would see the boy soon enough at breakfast time; I didn't want to fuel their curiosity just yet.

I ate one of the lamb sandwiches. It was good, as far as it went, but I already had strong yearnings for a fried fish-and-chip supper, all sprinkled over with salt and malt vinegar. After seeing a film in Leicester Square. That wouldn't happen any more – not for now anyway. I saved the boy one of the sandwiches in case, and finished up my report for Captain Holloway. I had set up a film-developing tank in the cupboard, and I loaded the film from the camera onto the holder in the pitch dark, closed it off and set the crucial timer. When the negatives were dry, they would go up to London in the pouch, to be printed up along with my notes for Captain Holloway. We would see then if I'd managed to get anything of the lights.

CHAPTER NINE

The boy slept right through, past breakfast time. I wondered what dreams were spooling through his mind, if any, while I enjoyed a good rasher or two of bacon and a fresh egg on a fried slice down in the public bar. One saving grace of the Dorset countryside: there was not so much evidence of shortages and rationing at that time.

'Your, er . . . companion not up yet, then, Corporal?' Mrs Cox asked.

'No, Mrs Cox, he's not.'

'Not one of your soldiers, then?'

'Not really, no. We found him hiding in the churchyard. We think he might have been out poaching. He seems lost.'

She looked startled at this. ''E's more of a prisoner, then, is he?'

'In a way, I suppose he is, for the moment, yes,' I said. 'Nothing to be frightened of, missus. He's very low risk. He's only a boy – no more than fourteen or so. He looks worn out and harmless enough. Might even be a bit simple-minded. He says he lives in the village, but the house he claims to live in is apparently all boarded up – has been for some time.'

'You sure 'e's not a German spy, then? He could be fooling you?'

'No,' I said, 'I'm not sure of anything at all, and that's why I'm taking him over to the barracks later for proper questioning. He seems confused to me. I would like to give him some breakfast, though, later on, if I may.'

I took a cup of strong tea up with me. The boy was sitting on the edge of the bed looking out of the window at the road below.

'The road is black,' he said to me in a puzzled tone, almost as if he was asking himself a question, as if he had only just noticed it.

'Yes, it is. The grass is green too, when you can see it,' I added, trying to make light banter with him.

'Road wasn't that colour yesterday.'

'No? What colour was it, then?'

'The usual colour, of course,' he said defensively. 'Someone's painted it all over black since yesterday.'

I put the tea down for him. 'Cup of tea for you there,' I said. 'Tell me some more about what happened last night before we found you.'

'Can't remember much of anything.'

'All right,' I said, as breezily as I could. 'We'll be off soon. We're going into Dorchester to see if we can find out a little bit more about you.'

'I live here, though. My father will be wondering where I am. I ought to go and see him.'

'Tell you what: you drink that tea, and there's a sandwich I saved for you, if you want it, and we'll go and see if we can find him.'

I used the bar telephone to warn Dorchester barracks that we would be coming over later, and also to ask for a delivery driver to go to the station with an urgent package by rail for Captain Holloway in London.

I also checked if there was enough hot water for the boy to have a bath. He certainly needed it.

'I suppose so, Corporal,' Mrs Cox said grudgingly. 'Here's the key. Keep an eye on things, mind.'

I ran some hot water and encouraged the boy to get in. He smelled like an old tramp – as if he hadn't washed in weeks.

'We might find you some better clothes too, or at least get these cleaned.'

His clothes stank as badly as he did. I had my suitcase of civvies in the room, and as I wasn't much taller than him I thought I could kit him out until his stuff could be washed and possibly even de-loused.

I locked him into the little bathroom on the landing. I sorted his clothes out and took the chance to feel inside his pockets. A penny and a farthing, dating from 1882 and 1883 respectively, a rough linen handkerchief and a bone-handled folding fruit knife in one. Not much to carry about – wouldn't get very fat on that. A penny farthing wouldn't buy you much nowadays, I thought.

What I found in the other pocket was something else altogether, and it set my pulse racing. It was a thin square, apparently made of metal. It weighed next to nothing, almost as if it were cut from a bolt of fine silk, and yet it was hard and felt very dense. The intense colours shimmered, even in the dull light of my bedroom. The effect was similar to the rainbow patterns you see in a puddle under a car when the oil or petrol has leaked out. The whole metal surface looked like that, and as I stared down at it, the colours actually seemed to shift and glow, move a little and then settle. I had never *seen* the like before, and yet I looked at it with a shock of recognition. I then realized that I had read a *description* of it. It was in a secret file document, one of the many copied and smuggled in from Germany before the war. The evidence had been found and examined by the German security office – their own secretive Department X, which is a close equivalent to what we are doing. Captain Holloway showed me that particular file, and I remember we went through it carefully because it contained a description of the only piece of hard evidence.

I had a spare WD evidence envelope, and I prepped it ready but I couldn't let it go. The little square of metal (if that is what it was) sat there like a spell. Studying it for any length of time was like looking into the burning coals of a fire. I remembered feeling that same lost sensation on winter nights while Dolly toasted a slice of bread in the flames on a long-handled toasting fork. I saw a sudden expansion. It was as if the tiny crags and fissures among the flames and the red-hot embers of coal had grown, filled my field of vision and become a real and huge landscape. It was hypnotic, and so was this strange sliver of rainbow. I could feel my concentration slipping, and the little pulsing square of colours seemed to be getting bigger as I looked at it. I quickly turned away and broke the spell, but I had to force myself to do it. I quickly opened the despatch bag and put the shimmering metal square very carefully into the WD envelope. I included my notes from the night before and the negatives, adding a note to explain that the boy had actually had the square of metal in his pocket when found. I added the words *Günzburg Clinic File*, and a big exclamation mark, knowing – hoping – that Captain Holloway would pick up on it at once and realize and understand.

I hurried back along the corridor to the bathroom. I didn't want to say anything about the small scrap of metal to the boy. I unlocked the door. He was sitting on the edge of the bath, wrapped in a towel. He seemed almost cheerful.

'I bet you feel a lot better now,' I said.

'I would do,' he said, 'except for this.' He showed me his upper arm, where there was a neat scar and evidence of what looked like a bullet wound.

'How did you manage that?' I asked.

'Wasn't there before,' he said. 'I've never seen it in my life. I never been wounded there.' He pulled and stretched out his pale, almost blue-white skin.

'Maybe it happened when you were very young,' I suggested. 'You have just forgotten.'

'No,' he said.

'Well, it's very well healed and neatly done.'

He shook his head. 'Don't understand,' he said, and

then added, 'Never had a bath in one of these before,' patting the enamel rim of the bath tub. 'We use one o' them metal tubs. Dad keeps it in the outhouse at the back.'

His bath water looked like dirty river water. I pulled the plug out and allowed it to flow away.

'They got a bath just like this up at the Rectory. The Reverend Stone has one in there.'

'That's nice for him,' I said. 'I've laid out some clothes of mine. They should fit you all right – they're good, and clean too. My Aunt Dolly in London looks after me very nicely. I'll get your clothes washed meanwhile – they certainly need it.'

The boy dressed himself in a pair of my old grey flannel trousers, a striped work shirt with no collar, and a sleeveless Fair Isle patterned pullover that Aunt Dolly had knitted for me a while ago. I watched him test the scar on his arm again before he rolled down the shirt sleeve; the wound plainly bothered him. He had to pull the belt buckle up to its tightest notch to keep his trousers up, but all in all it wasn't too bad a fit.

Mrs Cox tapped on the door. 'A messenger's here for your London parcel, Corporal,' she said. 'Oh, and there's a policeman wants to see you too.'

'All right, Mrs Cox. Thanks.'

I went downstairs with the WD package and gave it

to the messenger. The boy followed me down hesitantly and hovered somewhere behind me. The copper stood to attention, all official, upright and ready in the dingy snug bar, with his notebook out, waiting.

'Good morning, Corporal,' he said with a formal nod. 'Now, Warden Feaver over by the church tells me that you personally took charge of a possible vagrant or suspected poacher – perhaps even a German agent – last night. Is that correct?'

'As far as it goes, in a way, yes.'

'Is that him, then?' He indicated to somewhere behind me with his pencil. ''Cos I need to ask him a few questions.'

'There's no need, Constable. I will be taking him to Dorchester with me in just a mo for that very purpose. This is an army matter now and I have taken full responsibility.'

'Is that so?'

'Why, yes, I am afraid it is,' I said.

I tugged at the copper's sleeve and pulled him away, out of hearing of the boy, further down into the gloom at the end of the bar. I grew up in the East End of the smoke, after all, and I knew how to talk to coppers.

'Between you and me,' I said, in a hushed, confidential tone, 'I think this boy is in need of all sorts of help.' And I winked, as if to say he was sixpence short of a shilling, which at that moment was, after all, still a possibility. 'Before I get him over to army HQ at Dorchester, I thought I would take him up to Church Path. He claims he lives there. It shouldn't take a moment to sort out. Perhaps you would like to come with me, sir?' I said, gushing with extra respect.

'Do you know, I think I should do just that,' he said, closing his notebook.

'Thing is,' I said, 'the boy needs a bit of breakfast first – he looks half starved. He refused a cold lamb sandwich earlier – can't say I blame him for that, but I think he needs something hot on a morning like this, don't you? I should think you could do with a cuppa too,' I added, sensing his weakness.

We sat in a corner of the snug. The boy ate eggs and bacon; actually, he more like wolfed them down. The copper watched him, plainly suspicious.

'You a Romany, then, lad?' he said. 'Look like a traveller – are you?'

'No,' the boy said between mouthfuls, shaking his head vigorously. 'Ask the Reverend Stone, if you don't believe me,' he added, pushing away his empty plate.

I had met the local vicar during my first week in the village and he wasn't called Stone. I said nothing.

'I haven't made the acquaintance of the local reverend yet,' the copper said, 'but then, I've only been down at the Burton station for a couple of weeks. I seen your regiment down there, though, Corp.'

'I can't say anything about that, Constable, obviously.'

'No, of course not,' he said, looking over at the silent boy, who watched us seemingly with no understanding at all, holding onto his mug of tea with both hands.

'Come on, then,' I said.

The boy put on my old civvy overcoat and scarf, and we set off to walk through the village back to the church.

The boy looked around as if puzzled by almost everything we passed.

'Whole road has been painted black,' he said as we turned onto the main village street. I felt like saying that it wasn't paint, just the natural colour of the tarmac, but held back.

The grocer's shop was open, and there were some vegetables in boxes outside the door. The shopkeeper came out in an apron and added some potatoes to one of the boxes from a sack. The boy stopped and watched him as he filled the box.

'What is it?' I asked.

'New grocer,' the boy said.

I stepped up to the man, a ruddy-faced figure wearing a cloth cap and a muffler. I had been in his shop more than once.

'Mornin', Corporal,' he said. 'Some Gold Flake for you at all?'

'No thank you, never again,' I said. 'Given it up for good. How long have you run the shop here, if you don't mind my asking?'

'Let's see – we first came over from Honiton in early thirty-four, I think – so six years, give or take.'

'Do you know this young man?' I asked, indicating the boy.

'Can't say I do,' the grocer said. 'What's he supposed to have done?' he added, noticing the copper standing a few feet further off.

'Doesn't matter,' I said.

I turned to the boy. 'He's not the new grocer. He's been here in the village for six years, he says.'

'I've never seen him until today,' the boy said. 'He wasn't here yesterday.'

'He was, though, because I bought some tobacco from him yesterday afternoon.'

The boy looked back at me, mystified. He just stood hunched and huddled up in my old coat. I could see that he was feeling out of his depth, out of his life, out of his mind, out of something. If he was acting, then this was first-rate stuff and he should have been in the pictures.

We soon arrived at the small farm cottages that lined the path up to the church. We went up to the one closest to the church itself. A fence, once painted white, now patchy with lichen and the wood mostly rotten, ran along the narrow front garden. It was deep enough for a couple of overgrown, tangled hedges and not much else. The same fencing also ran along the front of the twin cottage next door. Both places were boarded over. The doors were sealed off with crossed planks. The upstairs windows had curtains in them but they were filthy and torn. The downstairs ones were boarded up like the door. The boy looked at the house, and his face set at once in a strange rictus of both agonized shock and disbelief. He walked up to the door and banged on it and rattled the handle.

'Dad!' he called out. 'Dad, what's going on?'

I watched him carefully for any sign of acting or overacting, but there was none. He seemed genuine. It gave me goose pimples just to watch him.

Then he pulled at the planking that was nailed across the door as hard as he could. 'No,' he said. 'No.'

'You claim this is where you live, then?' the copper said in his official voice.

'Yes, I do. I *do* live here, I've *always* lived here. I've lived here since I was a baby,' the boy said, his voice cracking.

There was no doubt in my mind that he was telling the truth as he saw it. The agony of disbelief on his face was too real. It was the kind of weird grief that would be impossible to fake. It came from the heart; from inside; from his soul. He had it, he felt it, and to him it was real.

'I think it's clear,' the copper went on, 'that no one lives here and no one has lived here for quite some time, by the look of things.'

'I'm afraid he's right,' I said quietly, putting my hand on the boy's narrow shoulder. 'Just look at it.'

'I have gone quite mad, then,' the boy said, equally quietly, 'and will surely be up in the Herrison Asylum before long.'

He turned his back to us and looked down from the front of the cottages back over the sloping landscape as it fell away to the sea. Above, there were ragged scraps of darker grey clouds chasing after each other on a westerly wind. I followed the boy's gaze, and saw the pattern in the clouds as they rolled together. I could clearly picture the opposing air currents and wind pressures that had made them form these particular shapes at this particular moment, in terms of equations and the subtle application of various elements.

My thoughts were interrupted by the boy saying, 'This is all the same as it should be, all of this,' and he raised his hand as if to trace the areas that remained familiar to him. 'Nothing else is,' he added, his voice flat. He continued to look out at the unchanged landscape and the not so distant sea.

'Last night,' I said, 'when I first called out to you, and this morning, you mentioned the Reverend Stone.'

'Yes, my dad does jobs for him around the big garden. The reverend knows me well enough. He lives up at the Rectory, just through those gates there.'

'Let's go and see him, then, shall we?' I said, turning away from the sky and the shabby, dismal-looking cottage.

CHAPTER TEN

From Captain Holloway's journal

My morning started badly. I left the house without my gas mask and its accompanying and very annoying square bulky case. I hadn't got very far when I realized. An office girl wearing a bright yellow scarf walked past me. I noticed her gas-mask case swinging from her shoulder. She wore it casually, almost jauntily, like a fashionable handbag. I automatically reached for the empty space where my own usually hung. I knew that they were a nonsense, a kind of placebo to reassure a frightened population. As far as intelligence was aware, there would be no gas bombs. However, I had no wish to draw attention to myself or risk a fine or a court appearance. I like to stay nicely anonymous; in the shadows, as it were. I groaned to myself and ran back up to Adur Terrace. My landlady was already out on the step polishing her brass door furniture.

'You've forgotten it again, haven't you, sir?' she said, shaking her head.

'Yes, of course I have,' I said.

I wore a captain's uniform. I was, of course, a captain in the first show, but had no real regiment now. Mine was a token posting – a camouflage, if you like – enough to stop anyone wondering what I was up to. As far as my landlady and neighbours were concerned, mine was a dull but vitally necessary job in army and navy administration. My very close friends knew little better. I lived 'out' – that is, away from any form of barracks. It was just a short suburban railway ride to our office, which was housed in a deep and secure underground annexe somewhere near the Admiralty building.

I was forty-seven years old, and as yet unmarried, and not likely to be. I was wedded to the work, I was wedded to the idea. I was in many ways the keeper of the biggest secret. Pursuing the truth of that secret was what I actually did for the war effort. It was a far cry from administration – that at least I can tell you.

I waited with the other commuters on the platform at Putney station. There were a scattering of uniforms among the business suits; I even caught a glimpse of the girl with the bright yellow scarf again. She added a welcome touch of colour on a cold November morning. Everyone had their gas-mask box with them. Some stood awkwardly reading the morning paper, trying not to let it get in the way. Others tapped on the outer case, drumming their fingers while they waited impatiently for the train. I doubted I would get a seat – I rarely did: by the time the Waterloo train reached Putney on the Kingston loop line, it was pretty full.

I looked out of the train window. The glass, like most other windows all over London, was partly obscured, crisscrossed with anti-shatter tape. As we rocked slowly past Battersea and the river, I could make out through the drifting steam and flying smuts the barrage balloons floating on their tethers high above the chimneys of the big power station. They shone silver in the cold sunlight.

I finally got a seat after Queenstown Road and found that, by chance (in my experience, few things are down to mere chance; there is usually the hand of a designer there somewhere), I was sitting opposite someone I recognized. It was Viktor, the Polish beau of Miss Greville, who worked in the outer front office. He had apparently been among the first wave of refugees who saw just what was looming from Herr Hitler and his crew, and fled to Britain long before the actual war. He was often called into the outer office to act as a linguist on translation questions. There was inevitably a lot of chatter and traffic now from occupied Eastern Europe. He had some unpronounceable-looking surname . . . Prejm. Viktor Prejm.

He nodded politely and said, 'Good morning, Captain,' with a faint apologetic smile.

'Morning,' I said. 'It is Viktor, isn't it?'

'Indeed, Captain, it is,' he said, and made a slight bow of acknowledgement, then quickly turned away, indicating his book.

I had my own reading matter in my attaché case, but it was not something I could take out and read on a public train. All my documents were marked either TOP SECRET or MOST SECRET. I only read them in my rooms on Adur Terrace or in my chilly brick-lined tunnel of an office.

The set of offices that made up Department 116 were to be found in a very low basement not far from the so-called Citadel near Admiralty Arch. They were not marked at reception, and any visitor was always there by appointment and certainly always expected. The rooms were safe enough from any air raids, but they were cold and damp in the winter, being far below river level, and stiflingly hot in the summer, when you couldn't even crack open a window. Part of me envied my young protégé, Jack Carmody, and his outing down to Dorset: at least he was in the open air, and would have a chance to look at the stars now and then. In fact, I hoped there might be a pouch report from Carmody waiting for me when I got in; one was certainly due.

In the event I had to wait around for the delivery until late lunch time. Finally a motorcycle courier was announced in the outer office. Miss Greville had already signed for the pouch by the time I reached the office. I took it back to my desk and opened it.

CHAPTER ELEVEN

All three of us walked up the curving drive from the gates. As we rounded a bend in the drive, the Rectory came into view. It was an old house surrounded by a wild and overgrown garden. There were tall beech trees to our left, and the gloomy rooks were at their business as usual, cawing and cackling in the cold air.

A gardener with his back to us was raking up leaves from the front lawn. They were being heaped up on one side – I supposed for a bonfire.

The boy broke away from us at that point and ran forward up the drive.

The copper moved to stop him but I held his arm.

'No,' I said. 'Let him go.' I wanted to see how this would play out.

Tom called out, 'Dad, are you all right there? What happened to the . . . ?'

The gardener straightened up and turned round at the commotion, and the boy stopped dead in his tracks.

'What is it, lad?' the man said, shielding his eyes and looking over at him.

The boy had his back to us, and I saw his shoulders slump, and then he just fell forward as if in a faint, down on the grass beside the driveway.

At once there was chaos and confusion. The gardener shouted out for help, and both the copper and I ran forward. A man in army uniform came out of the house. I noticed that he was an officer, and luckily enough I remembered for once that I was in uniform too, and saluted him as smartly as I could before kneeling down and cradling Tom's head.

'What on earth is going on here, Corporal?' the officer asked.

'Sorry, sir,' I said. 'I had no idea the house was an official billet.'

'Oh no, this isn't a billet. I am just here on a private visit to my parents.'

'Would your father by any chance be the Reverend Stone, then, sir?'

'No, I am afraid he would not, Corporal,' the officer said.

The boy struggled to sit up, and looked at the gardener standing over him, and then at the officer, and then at the copper, and then finally at me.

'It can't be true,' he said. 'None of it – it's not possible.'

'I imagine this might be the young poacher, then,' the officer said. 'The one who was arrested last night. Mr Feaver was telling me about him earlier. I'm Captain Boulter, by the way . . . And you are . . . ?'

'Corporal Carmody, sir. Ninth Essex. This was the boy we found after the deer escaped, yes. I'm not entirely sure he is a poacher, though, sir.'

'Sounded pretty straightforward to me. Seems like he was caught red-handed with the animal.'

'In one way it does, sir, but the boy seems genuinely distressed and very confused.'

'Of course he does. He was caught, wasn't he? No doubt just playing for sympathy.'

'Maybe, sir, but I was bringing him up here to the house to find his father or the Reverend Stone. He says they can vouch for him.'

'The Reverend Stone,' the gardener said. 'I remember him all right – tall, skinny, pinch-faced man with not much hair on top. He was the vicar here, and over at Puncknowle as well. Mind you, this was a very long time ago – forty or so years. When he finally retired, I was still in the choir, but only just. He must have died a while back. He was one of the last vicars to have the living here at the Rectory.'

'My mother is buried just up there,' Tom said quietly.

'Show me,' I said.

He got up without brushing the leaves and mud off my old trousers. There was a set of steps that led from the east side of the lawn up into the churchyard. We followed him. He held on tight to the rickety rustic hand rail as he climbed the steps, and then, once he got in amongst the tombstones, he slowed down. He went a few paces further down the path, and stopped before a simple headstone as if he couldn't bear to go any further.

'My dad's brother – my uncle – is a mason at Bridport,' he said. 'He cut the stone for her. It's all wrong – it shouldn't look like that.'

We gathered around it. There was a mass of lichen and moss across the surface. I knelt down and brushed it away so that finally the deeply cut letters were legible.

From my kneeling position I read the inscriptions quietly; there were four of them.

I stood up and turned to face Tom. I spoke gently. 'It says here that Thomas Pile went missing or died in 1900.'

He had already stepped backwards onto the path. He shook his head from side to side and stood there trembling, with a bewildered expression on his face.

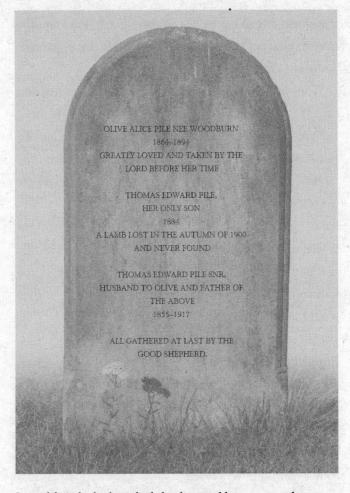

OLIVE ALICE PILE NEE WOODBURN
1864–1894
GREATLY LOVED AND TAKEN BY THE
LORD BEFORE HER TIME

THOMAS EDWARD PILE,
HER ONLY SON
1884
A LAMB LOST IN THE AUTUMN OF 1900
AND NEVER FOUND

THOMAS EDWARD PILE SNR,
HUSBAND TO OLIVE AND FATHER OF
THE ABOVE
1855–1917

ALL GATHERED AT LAST BY THE
GOOD SHEPHERD.

I couldn't help but feel for him: if he was mad, it was tragic; if it was all true, it was equally sad for him, however exciting it might be for me.

'No,' he said suddenly. 'No – someone's playing a terrible trick on me. It's not true, none of it – the house, the stone. It can't possibly be true! Look, I'm standing here in front of you. This is all a terrible dream, and in a minute I'll wake up in my bed.'

Tom wasn't acting any kind of part; this was real and raw.

'You'd better bring the boy into the house,' Captain Boulter said. 'He looks all in. He'll collapse in a minute.'

'His name is Tom, sir,' I said. 'I think we should use it, don't you?'

It was warm inside the house, and Tom sat awkwardly perched on the edge of a sofa, looking around the large L-shaped front room. It was a cheerful place, with a good log fire burning.

'It's all wrong here too. It's all been changed since the last time,' Tom said. 'There's different colours on the walls, and there wasn't never a fire laid in here in this room. No, it was always cold in here. The reverend only kept the back kitchen warm, not this room here. This was all covered in books on shelves, all the way round from top to bottom.'

'When do you think you were in this room here before, then?' Captain Boulter asked.

'Just a week or two ago. I came up and was told to wait in here for my father to finish up his work in the garden. It was raining hard, you see, and it was proper cold in here then.'

'What if I was to tell you that my parents have lived in this house since 1933, when my father retired from his office in London, and that Mr Legge here has been the only person working in the garden for them since then and that he works for nobody else?'

'Then I would say you were surely mistaken, begging your pardon,' Tom said, now almost defiant, looking around at us.

'I was taking Tom in to the Dorchester barracks, sir, as I said, to question him properly. Nothing he says seems to make much sense,' I said.

'I'll take you in my car, if you like. It'll save time,' the captain said, rubbing his hands. 'I'll admit I'm intrigued – I can't deny it. I'd like to help you interview him, then I can get a recording done. I'm very keen to try out one of our new machines. Would you mind at all?'

'No,' I said. How else could I have replied?

'I think you can safely leave this boy with the army now, Constable. We'll get him to Dorchester, I can vouch for it.'

'If you're sure then, sir,' the copper said.

'I'm very sure.'

CHAPTER TWELVE

Captain Boulter drove us into Dorchester. I was a bit worried by what he said about helping with the interview and recording it. That was my job; well, at least, it was Captain Holloway's job, and I needed to get that done, not this Captain Boulter. How was I supposed to pull rank on a ruddy captain?

Tom sat next to me in the back of the car. He pressed himself hard against the seat and stared straight ahead. Every now and then he looked out of the side window at the scrolling grey winter countryside. He looked as if he were in a trance, almost completely mystified by everything he saw and felt. He had surely never travelled in a car before. Every time we picked up speed and there was that slight lurch forward, he grabbed hold of my arm.

'It's all right, Tom,' I said. 'We are in a car – perfectly safe. It's just fast.'

He shook his head and looked down at the floor. Captain Boulter said, 'I don't know why you are humouring him like this. Surely he's seen a car before?'

'I honestly don't think he has, sir,' I said.

'Where has he been then? On a ruddy desert island all his life?'

'In a manner of speaking, I think he has, sir.'

Tom seemed especially puzzled by the tops of the surrounding hills. I noticed that there were now tall poles on some of the higher fields – I presumed to prevent enemy gliders and planes from landing.

'What is it?' I asked finally. 'You look like you're seeing ghosts.'

With his face pressed close against the window he said quietly, 'I am the ghost. It's all changed, all of it, everything I see.'

He stared out of the window as we approached Dorchester. He looked at everything as if he had never seen anything like it.

Finally Captain Boulter parked at what had been the old castle prison and was now Garrison HQ.

A sentry at the gate saluted him sharply.

'Can you find an interview room for us?' Captain Boulter said. 'And can you bring one of the new wire recorders and a mike down from the ops room?'

The sergeant showed us into a room on the ground floor and then left us. It was near the back of the building, and I guessed it might have been a cell or the warder's office originally. The bricks were painted in that same sickly, pale-green, almost shiny distemper that the army always favours. There was a glossy darker green line halfway up the wall under the one window, which was partly covered with a green holland blind and which looked out on a far brick wall and not much else. There was a basic table, a few canvas and metal hall chairs, a black Anglepoise desk lamp, and a notice board with a big map of Dorset pinned to it, but no telephone.

'This do you, sir?' the sergeant said when he came back with a recorder and microphone.

'Perfect,' Captain Boulter said.

After the sergeant had left, the captain set up the machine on the table. He plugged in the mike and switched on.

'Now then, testing . . . testing,' he said. 'One, two, one, two, testing.'

He played the recording back, and Tom looked startled. I ignored it. I was still working out how I could put a fly in the captain's ointment without arousing too much suspicion.

Boulter offered me a cigarette from a smart silver case.

'No thanks, sir, I don't,' I said.

'You sure?' he said, nodding. 'I find it calms the nerves.'

He lit up a cigarette and said to Tom, 'Why don't you take your coat off, lad?'

The boy didn't reply, but just sat where he had been put. He had hunched himself down as far into my overcoat as it was possible to go without disappearing. He looked on the verge of collapse. It was as if he were trying to crawl inside himself and vanish.

'I don't quite get your role in all this business, Corporal,' Captain Boulter said, blowing out a long stream of smoke. 'If this boy has gone in for a bit of petty larceny and poaching, why didn't you just leave him with the police? Why bother?'

I saw my chance. I decided to go public, just slightly. 'I'm not at liberty to explain my position fully, sir,' I said, with just a note of defiance, eyeballing him directly.

'Ah, I think I see,' he said, looking down at his watch. 'Cloaks and daggers, eh? I thought you were billeted in the village to help Mr Feaver with his ARP duties, but there's more?'

'Officially I am just that,' I answered, keeping up the

defiance. 'But yes, there is more.' If the worst happened, I would at least get a chance to let Captain Holloway know, and rank and strings and all else would surely be pulled then.

He sighed and nodded, and looked at me through his smoke as if he heard that sort of evasive answer all the time. First of all I explained what had happened. I was careful not to say too much about the lights in the sky and the photographs, and all the while Tom just sat there staring at the dull green wall.

'Old Feaver told me much the same story,' Boulter said when I had finished. 'Only he said you were taking some photographs out in the dark. Is that right?'

'That is right, yes.'

'I see. Some new kind of film, then, I imagine. One thing you can say for war time, it certainly increases the pace of invention. This recorder is a big improvement over the old ones, but there we are. I imagine that is all I'm going to be told about it, isn't it? This is all a bit of a hush-hush effort.'

I didn't reply. I just looked back at him.

'I didn't hear any aircraft at all last night, but then the Rectory walls are thick and I was dog tired. I went to bed early and slept like a baby.'

The sergeant bustled in with some mugs of army tea and a bowl of sugar laid out on an old tin tray.

'Very thoughtful indeed. Thank you, Sergeant,' Captain Boulter said, stirring his tea.

'Now, as far as I'm concerned personally, I think this boy's just a poacher and a bit of a nuisance,' he went on. 'I'm guessing that he is most likely an evacuee from the city. And certainly a good and well-practised liar. I suppose you think he's some kind of fifth columnist or something, or has a secret agenda. My advice normally would be to take him down to the police station here in Dorchester, get him charged with poaching, and then leave him there. We aren't in normal times, though, are we, Corporal?'

'No, sir.'

'So, assuming that whatever your other duties are, they include secret photographs and all, I think we should let this boy talk and see what he has to tell us.' He drank off his tea and stubbed out his ciggie.

'I'll let you ask the questions. I'll just work the recorder. Good luck, Corporal,' he said and switched on.

At first I encouraged Tom to drink his tea, but he just stared at it.

'Come on, it's all calm now. Perhaps you can tell me where you are really from,' I said.

'From Litton Cheney,' he said after a silence. 'Like

I keep saying, I was only out last night to get us some meat. I was helping old Gawen and he tried to get me to shoot at . . .' He faltered and looked up, and then closed his eyes. 'I remember one thing: there was a bright light in the woods like I seen twice before, ages ago. Then I don't remember anything else.'

'Try talking it all through from the beginning, Tom. Tell us all about yourself. By doing that you might be able to remember more. Who is old Gawen, for a start?'

'Gawen were testing me. He were getting me to shoot it – it was to see if I had the guts. See if I could do it. My dad and me, we needed the meat, see.'

'Where is this Gawen person now?'

Tom looked down at his feet and mumbled his answer. 'Don't know.'

Captain Boulter asked, 'Which woods were you in, then, exactly?'

'We was up somewhere near the village of Powerstock,' Tom said.

The captain went over to the map. He found Litton Cheney and marked it with a pin, then followed the line of Gallows Hill with his finger up to the old Honiton road. The village of Powerstock was up beyond that, north of the main road by a long way; among other things, I noticed that there were some new airfields marked there. 'It's a long walk,' he said.

'How did you get that stag all the way down to Litton from there with just two of you?' I said.

'I don't know how we got back to Litton at all. I just seemed to wake up, to come to there.'

'Did this Gawen have a light with him of some kind? Was that what you saw in the woods and what I saw in the churchyard?'

'Only had my dad's rifle and a knife and some sacks, that was it.'

'Start again, then. Tell me about your life, Tom,' I said. 'Take your time, don't rush. Tell us everything about yourself and all the people around you.' I sat back in my chair.

Tom leaned forward, his arms on the table top, and started talking quietly into the microphone. His testimony sounded almost as if he had said it all once before, to a room full of strangers perhaps. His voice was hushed, controlled and monotonous, almost as if he were in some kind of trance. He hardly drew breath . . .

My mother died when I was seven. I remember so clearly the simple coffin box in our little cottage parlour. It lay there closed and screwed down, resting on trestles, and even then I knew that she was inside it. My father sat beside it with his head bowed, his mug of tea resting on the lid. The parlour was almost dark, with just a single lit tallow candle on the mantel, and still he sat there quietly all night.

She was buried in February – on St Valentine's Day, to be exact. The dark earth was tamped down hard and wet. The grave was dressed with greenery and one or two hothouse blooms from the Rectory. Mr Woolard had cut the grave and Mr Woolard's son had made the coffin. There was no stone or marker as yet, only the few pale flowers under the sleet and the ivy.

I stood at the grave while the Woolards lowered the coffin down on wide hessian straps. My father was standing at the graveside in his black Sunday best, one hand on my shoulder. He was the first to throw in some of the wet earth and flowers from the heap by the open grave. I looked around at the expectant faces: the Reverend Stone, Miss Gladwyn, my uncle and aunt, and then my father, who was hatless in the cold. His beard and side whiskers were grey, and his teeth were clamped together, making his cheeks look hollow. His hair was whipped by the wind that blew across Gallows Hill, where we would see the lights together for the first time, years from that night . . .

The church and churchyard of St Mary's stands a third of the way up the hill above the valley. The beech trees march up the hill beside the churchyard. They are always full of rooks cawing in the wet air.

My uncle had arrived by trap from Bridport, where he

worked as a stonemason. He stood on the other side of me, his hand resting on my other shoulder. He was older and taller than my father, and he stood with a bowed head. His wife, Anne, was beside him, a handkerchief held to her eyes and her head lowered and turned from the biting wind, which I remember sounded like the sea on the pebbles on Chesil Beach as it ripped through the beeches.

My father spent much time there at that grave, and would talk to my mother when he used his scythe on the grass which, if left, grew long among the headstones. The same long grass where later I lay sometimes near my mother's stone on a hot summer afternoon, hiding. My mother was a 'gentlewoman', so said my father, whom God had 'taken to his bosom too early', she being young herself at the time. His name was Thomas and, yes, I was named for him, and he was commonly called Tom, just as I am. He was old; I should say at least thirty-five years at the time of our loss. All the hair had gone from the top of his head, on which, of custom, he wore – no, he wears, he wears . . . he is not dead – he surely lives. All of this is a bad dream. It is me, rather: I am the one who is most likely to be dead, shot down in the woods by old Gawen. So my father wears an old battered hat made of soft felt. He used to wear high boots, and a pair of well-polished leather gaiters, or leggings. He also used to maintain the woods and copses, and he even grew fruit and vegetables for the reverend. That was in the good time when he worked hard every day, excepting, of course, Sunday. Once he even sang in the choir, and was, I think, well enough liked by all. Miss Gladwyn, a woman of the village, gave us the balsam for my chest in winter and was always polite and kind with me.

When I was younger, on certain nights of good weather my father would take me on the long walk to the Chesil Beach, to night fish, or perhaps up Gallows Hill and on over to Bridport. The beach was a wild place, long and flat with the deep water right close to the shore. Father said that some of the Popish sailors from the armada of Spain were washed ashore there hundreds of years ago, and how even some in our own village, those who were darker of skin and hair, owed them their origin, and how some were like as to a Spaniard or Turk.

That was when we saw the lights in the sky. That was before my father took to drinking in the White Horse most every night and 'pissed away his wages', as old Gawen said.

Father once said that 'God and the angels would perhaps take me as well', as he eased my misery of cold nights when I couldn't breathe too well, and needs must hold my head over a pudding basin and breathe in the fumes from Miss Gladwyn's dark liquid balsam which steamed there. My father would hold a cloth about my face and pray for me. He was a bear of a man, with much of the outdoors about him. He would say that I was a good boy, and that I was all he had left, and that I was so like my mother. The angels came for her, and then they came for me . . .

Our own house was – no, not was, is – old, but it is still there; it endures. It is a cottage, not a house – don't run away with that idea – and it is made of stone, and is Church property. It stands halfway up a steep hill, the Gallows Hill, and looks down over the Bride Valley. It lies between the towns of Dorchester and Bridport, of which Bridport is the nearer place, and where there were boats, and ropewalks where rope is made.

When we had done our chores, and on days when my father didn't need me, I walked over to the village schoolhouse. A mile or so directly across the fields, though I followed the route around the village, which is formed by the natural lie of the water that flows out from the Rectory garden, where there is a spring. The water was always cold, even on the hottest summer day, and in the good weather of early summer we would come back from the schoolhouse wading in the stream against the flow. Now and then a dark spotted trout would dart between our legs.

With no mother, I needs must help my father at home, and often made his evening meal. Miss Gladwyn showed me how I must wash and prepare the vegetables, and I was soon in the habit of it. In the good days we had cheese in a steady supply from the rector, who allowed his field to be used for the grazing of sheep and cattle, in return for fresh milk, butter and cream, and meat. Miss Feaver would on occasion deliver us a good pie, and there were our chickens, which I fed and cleaned, and collected the eggs, Mr Fox permitting. That was in the good time before Father took to drinking in the daytime, and fell out with the reverend, and we went hungry, always hungry.

My father saw them . . . saw strange things when he saw the lights. Twice he was with me; once, though, he was on his own. He was fearful of what he had seen. He supposed the drink had made him mad, although he didn't tell me about it at the time. No, he waited until we were both filthy and starving and it was the bad times, and he was drunk on cheap cider and was threatening to hit me, and sitting in the cold and dark with no fire in the grate, with no meat, nothing to eat – that was when he told me about it. He told me that he had seen Heaven itself, and angels, and my late mother's face up in the sky. She was looking down on us. Others had seen the lights too, and he said that he had seen my poor mother as a ghost. He said a man came all the way down from London. A doctor, he was. He came down to interview those that had said they had seen the lights. All those in our village were interviewed, including my father, and they were also investigated for insanity. No one heard any more about it after the doctor had gone away. When I saw the lights, I didn't tell anyone else I had seen them . . . not until now.

The first time was one summer night when I was walking along the top road with my father. I was about ten years old and we were going towards Bridport. It was the full dark, and a sky full of stars, when the white light came. The light fell slowly, like a distress rocket as you might see off the beach from a ship in trouble, but this was bigger. It fell close to us, down into the dark copse of trees beside the road. We heard a single loud thump on the ground somewhere in among the trees. This was near Walditch, just south of the main Bridport road. We left the thoroughfare and went to see what had fallen. He thought it might be a piece of shooting star or meteor or similar, and so might fetch money from the museum at Dorchester, if it could be retrieved whole or in large part. Once we were beyond the road we tried to find an area that would show damage from a falling weight, or perhaps burns, as the rock – if that is what it was – must have some weight and the light must also have some heat. I was worried about my father, and was afeared we might face danger from the lights. Despite the darkness, it did not take us long to find damage. There were scattered branches along the ground in the centre of the copse, and then a light shone down on us, and where it touched the ground it made a deep booming sound such as might be made by the striking of a bass drum in a silver band. I looked up into the light. It was brighter than day in that one place just above the trees. I found myself unable to move, but just stared upwards, and at that moment I fancied I saw a figure somehow from within the sphere of light. Then it went dark. We looked around the area but could find no trace of any burned rock. We quickly rejoined the road, but said nothing one to the other; nothing of what we had seen or thought we had seen. I especially did not wish to upset or trouble my father.

On the second occasion we were returning to our cottage. My father had been in the White Horse public house and I had gone to fetch him home. He was not intoxicated, having, as he said, 'drunk little but had mostly stayed there at the inn to be by the fire and to be in good company'. As he neared the area of the church, we saw a bright light, and then another up on Gallows Hill. Strong beams of light striking the ground as if in a lightning storm. There was no sound this time, but the lights were not falling. They stayed in one place, high above the chalk roadway. We passed our own dwelling and made our way up the hill towards the lights. My father was frightened then, and he admitted it to me, and he wished he had his hunting rifle about him as we approached the place of the lights. There were two distinct ovals of light above the roadway. One was beside the other; we stood below them, alone on the road. We looked about us, but there was no one else to be seen. The flock was higher up the hill, but we could see no sign of a light in the shepherd's bothy, not even a wisp of smoke from the chimney. We were the only living things on that steep *road. Then my father said, 'Look,' and he pointed to the light. 'An angel, boy, and it has the face of your poor dead mother, and she's smiling on us.' I couldn't see it.*

My father was never the same after that night. That was when he started drinking all the time, and not working so much, and we went hungry for days at a time and we stayed hungry. Being hungry was my doom and my downfall . . .

Tom was suddenly quiet after that, and after a moment or two he slowly moved further forward across the table and rested his head on his arms. He went into a kind of sleep.

'Poor boy's a deluded faker, I'm afraid, just rambling on like that. I shouldn't wonder if he isn't some sort of Romany. Perhaps he's taken opium or laudanum or something,' Captain Boulter said.

'You may be right, Captain,' I said. 'It was all very odd. Might I have that recording, though, please?'

'Hmm, I suppose it will be all right. If I don't give it to you, you'll just request it through official channels, if I'm any judge. Well, all right, but let me just check that it worked first.' He rewound the spool. 'You haven't fallen for any of that desperate nonsense, have you?'

He played a fragment back. It had worked.

'All the evidence needs evaluating,' I said. 'I wouldn't want to jump to any conclusions. Is there a secure telephone I can use?'

'Yes, of course. The sergeant will show you. After that I expect you will be off with your prisoner. Take my advice, Corporal. March him down to the police station and hand him over. He will, I am sure, turn out to be a waste of your valuable hush-hush time.' He clapped me on the shoulder and handed me the recording.

'Thanks, sir,' I said.

CHAPTER THIRTEEN

From Captain Holloway's Journal

The whole thing was laid out in front of me, and for the first time I felt a kind of shiver of certainty. We had a real breakthrough, and there were pieces of physical evidence too. This could turn out to be the definitive test case. I read young Carmody's report through quickly, and then read it again while I waited for the negative roll of his photographs to be printed up. Reading between the lines, I sensed Jack's excitement at what had happened.

I was called to the dark room about twenty minutes later. The red light was on inside and there was the pervasive smell of Hypo.

Our technical whizz, Staff Sergeant Martin, had pinned a series of images up on the softboard cork wall that ran down one side of the darkroom. As soon as I was in and the door was secure, he switched from the red to the white light and produced a linen tester glass.

'I think we've got something – look,' he said.

The photographs were in a numbered sequence. At

one end of the wall were images of the lights. I could see the crest of a steep hill, and at the top a shaft of light beaming down from a cloud and lighting part of the roadway and a STOP sign.

'This fast film still gets enough detail, then,' I said. There were more of the lights in the sky – blurred oval-shaped discs, just above the low cloud layer. Then came the fourth picture, taken down the slope of the hill. Something solid could be seen through the ragged edge of cloud and fog. It was metallic looking, a sweeping curve – perhaps part of a wing formation, but with no markings visible, German or otherwise. And then the shafts of light were shining in a churchyard, and the shapes of the tombstones were clearly visible, and the true intensity of the beams of light seemed clear as well, incandescent and very strong. It would be hard to determine exactly what kind of aircraft would produce such a beam, and also why. Then came the startling picture of a white stag caught by the camera, a gleam of terror in its eye. And then pictures of the boy, at first out among the tombstones, a pale and overexposed face with eyes wide. Then one of the same boy sitting at a table, his expression inscrutable, but at the very least bewildered.

'Jack did well,' I said. 'Is there anything we can do to make that section there bigger, clearer?' I indicated the wing edge in the fourth picture.

'I can try,' Sergeant Martin said. 'I'll keep enlarging, but in the end all we'll get is the grain of the film itself.'

'Agreed, but I would like you to try, if you would, please.'

I let myself out, secured the darkroom door behind me, and went back to my desk. Among Jack's notes and reports there was a single WD envelope that I had yet to open. I tipped its contents out onto my desk.

Something astonishing sat there on my official WD blotter. I had seen a similar thing described just once before – in a smuggled and translated document from a restricted German scientific journal of 1936. It was one of the key pieces of evidence that I longed to see with my own eyes, and here it was in front of me on my own desk, safely gathered in, deep in the bowels of the Admiralty. A little shining trinket, roughly three inches square – slightly smaller than a postcard. A souvenir, perhaps, but a souvenir of where exactly? It certainly wasn't Skegness.

I sat down and moved it a little with the tip of my pen until it was under the direct beam of my desk lamp. It sat there, pulsing and glowing. I looked carefully at it; watched the colours cross its surface. I fumbled for my lower desk drawer and pulled out a magnifying glass of the sort that would not have shamed Sherlock Holmes in his heyday. It was limited in its magnification, but it was enough.

I studied the surface, and after a minute or so became almost hypnotized by the shifting patterns and colours. I found myself drifting a little. I pulled my eye away from it and put the lens down. Maybe that was the point: perhaps it was some kind of beguiling device; a hypnotic. The thing seemed alive. I sat up straight and shook my head. I picked up the surprisingly light, dense square and tucked it back into the envelope that Jack had put it in. He must have realized the significance of what he had found; we had been through all the various reports from our German counterparts together a year or so ago.

I went at once down to our file system, which was awkwardly placed high under the curved vault of our inner office ceiling. I pulled out the relevant file, took it back to my desk, and sat and read through it all over again. I put in a call to Jack Carmody. There was no time to lose.

NOT FOR CIRCULATION
Translated from the GERMAN original
From BERLIN Registry File
Department 116

MOST SECRET
From: The desk of the Chairman of Regional Special
Intelligence Investigations Authority
BERLIN September 1936
CLASSIFIED AND CONFIDENTIAL

Following on from a series of interviews (transcripts
supplied, see APPENDIX B — not for release) carried out at
the isolation clinic of Günzburg Sanatorium soon after the
discovery, arrest and protective custody of suspect A:
Fräulein V—

In summation I found the girl claiming to be V— (Warrant
No. 17847) of a reasonable educational standard and of some
school learning, although she was suspicious and evasive
and apparently ignorant of any recent history. She claimed
to know nothing of the Führer, for instance, which would
seem at the very least a foolish position to pretend to, and
a very dangerous game to play in the circumstances.

The girl showed some intelligence and a very thorough
and unlikely knowledge of the period of history that she
claimed to be living in. She also claimed that I was an evil
spirit; some sort of chimera conjured by angels to torment
her. She communes with angels, apparently. She is also oddly
consistent and convincing in her false world-building. She
says that she was apparently well enough thought of by
the town of —, which she claims to come from, and named
several residents who might vouch for her and prove her
claim. Even on a cursory investigation it was easily
discovered that all the persons she named were long dead.
However, from census records it was clear that each and
every one of those persons she mentioned had indeed lived
in — at the time she said they did.

There are two possible explanations:

1. At first the girl was believed to have developed some sort of obsession with a very old missing persons case from —, which happened sixty or more years ago. It was thought that she had somehow identified herself with the girl who was originally reported missing (according to the local police ledger, believed murdered) and was playing the part of the same missing person in that case – see original warrant. Incidentally, I strongly recommend sending someone to conduct a thorough search and literally dig around in the place and facts of that original case, all documentation from local records, burials, etc. However, judging from the ignorance, naivety and youth of the girl in question, the ability to come up with such an invention and identification, let alone all the simple fact-checking and collating involved seems highly unlikely.

2. In my opinion it is more likely that this girl is the third one so far to be found — and indeed as yet only surviving example — of the so-called disappeared. It would, of course, be more convenient for all to put her firmly in the former group. However, for me all evidence points to this second explanation. Her persistence of belief and her self-identification show her as one of the missing/returned, and the fact that she seems to be honestly telling the truth as she sees it demonstrates that my position may be upheld.

ADDENDUM

Fräulein V— later demonstrated the ability to move objects independently by mind, demonstrating under laboratory supervision the trait known as telekinesis. The Soviets have been secretly trying to develop this for some time. Her power manifests itself mostly through stress. One such demonstration proved fatally dangerous, and details were sent at once to BERLIN. (See attached Note C.)

However, there is of course still a strong possibility here not only of power, but also of a disturbed and unsound mind, and I would recommend that the continued complete protective custody order be kept enforced, along with supervised detention in a secure asylum and the administration of drug therapy, followed by a series of further interviews and investigations in order to discover her true identity and, indeed, the truth.

She had a bag with her on arrest, and among the contents was the item described in the attached APPENDIX D document.

NOTE C
April 1937

After much coaxing and not a small number of threats, the
girl was taken to a secure space, the abandoned aerodrome at
(B). A plane was loaded with explosives and flown in a circuit.
She was tasked with the job of bringing it down from the air
and onto a specific target, a complex of old buildings. The
pilot knew nothing of the test and was in any case
expendable. She was set to work, and after twenty minutes she
had worked herself up into an odd state. She first of all
destroyed the buildings on the ground. They were FLATTENED,
just as if a hurricane had passed over. Then she brought the
aeroplane down directly onto the ruins in a huge fireball.
She then proceeded to destroy two of the doctors who were
supervising and recording. The results of this may be seen in
the sealed can of film logged in the evidence file depository.
This film is to be viewed on a strict need-to-know basis only
and is not for general distribution within the department.

It was necessary to restrain her after the test. The girl
known as V— shortly afterwards _died_ in protective custody in
April 1937.

Müller, H.
Here signed ....

APPENDIX D
CONFIDENTIAL

Among the items found on the detained girl V— was something
which was at first thought to be some broken item, a shard of
cheap jewellery. Closer examination and analysis of this item,
however, have revealed it to be something else altogether,
and so far it is of unknown origin. A more detailed analysis
is contained in a further APPENDIX E (not released).

CHAPTER FOURTEEN

We locked the sleeping Tom in the interview room, and I was taken to another office. By using combinations of numbers and certain key code words, I was immediately put through to Captain Holloway's office. The army could be efficient when they needed to be.

'Carmody, where the hell are you? I've been trying to get you since the courier turned up with your envelopes.'

'I'm at army HQ in Dorchester. Been recording an interview with the boy in question.'

'Get on down to the station and take the next London train, and bring him with you. And go now, this very minute.'

'So do you think that this is what we have been looking for? That this might be it, sir? And by the way, this recording is something you need to hear.'

'I am quietly optimistic,' he said. 'Actually, I'm a lot more than that, but that's enough said on an open line. Now come on – jump to it and get weaving.'

It was hard not to show too much excitement or even to think straight after that. It looked like we had finally found our evidence. Early days, though, and I didn't want to get too excited. I went back down to the interview room, and the sergeant unlocked the door.

The boy was gone. The window was fully open and the blind pull was tapping against the windowsill.

At first I panicked, I will admit. I ran out into the corridor and charged up and down a couple of times like a headless chicken. The kind sergeant saw me and calmed me down.

'He looked harmless enough, that lad. What's the panic?'

'He's a security risk, and much more,' I blustered.

'I'd better fetch the captain then,' he said.

'No,' I said. 'Don't bother him. This is my responsibility.'

'He can't have got very far,' the sergeant said. 'Not if he got out of that window. It doesn't really lead anywhere – just to a closed-off yard and a high wall. I doubt he will have got over that.'

We went out through a side door into what used

to be the exercise yard for the Napoleonic prisoners who were once held there. The boy was tucked as far into the corner of the square as he could get. He was hunched down into my overcoat as if he were inside a tent.

I sat down next to him, pressed my head back against the flint wall and said, 'Look lively. I'm taking you up to London. There is a man there who wants to meet you. He's a good man too – kind, and not any sort of policeman.'

'Why would you want to do that?' the boy said, his head bowed, his mouth pressed into the collar of the coat.

'You're not in any trouble, Tom. You're of interest to us,' I said. 'Both you and your situation – your story.'

'I've got no situation. I'm a ghost, I am. I'm nothing but a will-o'-the-wisp.'

'You are as real as me. You are awake and I am awake.' I turned to him and shook him by the shoulders. 'Feel that? You are alive, and we are both sitting here in this old prison yard in the year 1940. The world is spinning away on its axis and getting further and further into trouble.'

'I don't know what you're talking about,' he said, looking at me with real fear in his eyes, like a trapped animal.

'We can do this calmly. I'm here to look after you, Tom. I can understand what you are going through. First we are going to stand up. Then we are going to leave here and walk down to the railway station. Then we are going to get on a train and travel to London to meet this kindly man who wants to talk to you. That is all,' I said, as slowly and matter-of-factly as I could.

He looked doubtful, but eased himself up, keeping his back against the wall. The sergeant stood a few feet off, plainly puzzled by the odd transaction and my tone.

I turned to him. 'It's all right, Sarge,' I said, tapping the side of my nose with my index finger, implying that I was dealing with a loony. 'We'll be off in a minute. He's coming back to London with me.'

'You have the authority, do you, Corp?' he said, his eyebrows raised.

I pulled my warrant card out of my field jacket pocket. 'Special operations,' I said.

'Fair enough,' he said. 'I can organize a car for you, if you want.'

'No thanks,' I said. 'We'll walk.'

Communiqué 3

SECRET
WAR DEPARTMENT
CLASSIFIED MESSAGE CENTRE

Translated from the <u>GERMAN</u> original
(C3./Capt Holloway Office 116)
Undated - filed late 1940

I have noticed a rise in activity. Something has happened at
the office. An AGENT (A) was sent off. I later found it was to
the WEST country. He sent something back which caused, in
the colloquial words of hereabouts, 'A FLAP', which is slang
for great <u>excitement</u>.
  'A' was called back.
  I am on alert for anything which is let drop. It is a tight
ship now, however, and I cannot force anything or I will
risk complete exposure. I shall keep a close eye and prepare
for the capture and flight option if necessary.

CHAPTER FIFTEEN

There was no time to go back to the White Horse and collect my stuff. We just left the barracks and set off on foot for the railway station. I wanted to get moving before Captain Boulter decided to interfere again. The high street was busy with army and civilian traffic, and even here, down in the country, there were sandbags around the shops and anti-shatter tape on the windows.

Dorchester was a garrison town, and as we walked through the centre, there was evidence of soldiers everywhere. I knew that the Parachute Regiment was based just outside the town at Piddlehinton Camp. I was told there had been extensive work in Dorchester preparing for the expected invasion. I could see signs of it everywhere in the town. There were concrete blocks set up near the roads and on the surrounding hills.

The locals called them 'dragons' teeth'. Squaddies had been hard at work digging anti-tank ditches, and there were pillboxes set up on main junctions; we were told that the bridges had been prepared with explosive charges for when the invasion started. There were rolls of barbed wire across the side roads, especially near the railway station. I half expected to see a German armoured car followed by a marching division of the Wehrmacht turn into the road outside Dorchester station.

Tom Pile trudged along beside me. His hands were pushed deep into the coat pockets. He made no eye contact with anyone, just shuffled along, occasionally looking up at a building or sentry post or installation.

'I never been on a train before,' he said as we waited on the station platform. There were other soldiers there too, a dozen or so of them at the far end of the platform. After a few minutes the London train up from Weymouth chuffed round the curve and into view. The engine must have been green originally, but it was so covered in mud and dirt that it looked almost khaki, as if it were in some way an official army engine. Wartime meant dirt and neglect, along with everything else. Resources were stretched, jobs were skimped; no one there to polish up the engines. Standards were slipping, or had already slipped. The shirker's phrase was:

'Don't you know there's a war on?'

I got us a good compartment to ourselves by flashing my special travel warrant card at the ticket inspector and saying that Tom was my security prisoner. We sat facing one another on the window side. It soon darkened as we travelled through the afternoon. I had to pull the blinds down and secure them when the lights finally came on. The bulbs were very dim in any case. I might as well have left the blinds up as far as any enemy aircraft were concerned. It was so dim in the carriage it would have made little difference.

'It'll be dark by the time we reach London,' I said.

'This is the way to Hell, isn't it?' Tom Pile said. 'I know it is. It explains everything to me. We are being taken there now. I know it. That tombstone said I was dead, along with my mum and dad, and I suppose you are dead too, and now I am being taken there with you and them, and all those dead soldiers on that platform. We are going all the way to Hell. The angels showed us the way last night. Old Gawen must have shot me instead . . . and I – I heard the bang and then . . .'

His eyes widened even as he said the word 'angels'. Then he fell silent, and pushed himself back in the seat as if he were struggling to dig himself into the springs and fabric.

I thought of the secret report I had read – the one

smuggled out of Germany; the one in our files which described the 'self-belief' of the found girl. Here was Tom displaying that selfsame conviction and complete self-belief. He believed everything that had happened to him. He was not pretending and nor was he mad. He was the real thing.

'It was them – the angels, the bright light, it was them. I saw them. I don't want to go.'

'Who did you see, Tom?'

'The angels – they came for me, and here we are now, all on our way.'

I leaned forward in my seat and took his hand. He looked back at me, puzzled.

'Tell me what they looked like, then,' I said.

He pulled his hand free, stood up quickly and stretched both his arms up towards the ceiling. The four lights in the carriage just below the string lattice of the luggage rack brightened and burned with a sudden fierce intensity. They gave off a kind of tungsten white heat, like the flash gun of a Speed Graphic press camera, just for a second or so, and then they all blacked out altogether. The carriage was plunged into total darkness.

'That's what I see. That's what they looked like,' he said.

The compartment door slid open and the ticket

inspector blundered in.

'Did your lights just flare up before they blacked out?' he said.

'Yes,' I said. 'What was it, then?'

'How many in here now? Just the two of you?'

The lights flickered back on, but if possible they were even dimmer than before.

'Yes,' I said. 'Myself escorting my prisoner,' I added quickly.

'I was worried about sabotage, you see. Lot of military on this train.'

'Should you even be talking that way?' I said. 'Careless talk, and all that.'

'You're quite right. Could I see your warrant once more, then?'

He took the paper from me but hardly looked at it. Instead he seemed more interested in Tom Pile.

'What's this one supposed to have done?'

'I can't discuss that, obviously,' I said.

'Couldn't he get to a barber's shop, then?' the inspector asked.

It was true that Tom Pile had longer hair than most, like a painting of a gypsy horse dealer.

'He's been living rough,' I said. 'It'll be cut soon enough when we get to London.'

The soldiers left the train at Southampton. I went

out into the corridor and watched them disembark on the steamy darkened platform. I beckoned for Tom to come and join me, and pointed them out as they shuffled into line.

'They are not dead, you see, Tom,' I said, 'and nor are you and nor am I. We are alive, and in an hour or so we will be in old London town, which to me is a kind of Heaven. To a country boy like you, I suppose it might seem like Hell, but let's wait and see, shall we?'

We settled back in the dimly lit carriage, and Tom nodded off for a while with his head tucked down against the stale velvet moquette of the seat rest. A framed photograph of Durdle Door rattled loose in its frame above his head. I dozed for a bit myself, but not for long.

CHAPTER SIXTEEN

I was jerked from sleep and woken up by a loud clanking noise, the squeal of metal brakes on metal, and a reverse thrust as the train shuddered to a sudden halt and then seemed to slide back on itself. I also heard the newly familiar wail of an air-raid siren somewhere in the distance over the chuffing of the engine. I knelt on the floor of the carriage, shuffled over to the side window and lifted just a corner of the blind. I could see the beams of gun emplacement searchlights piercing the dark. I could hear the drone of aircraft too, passing somewhere overhead. I guessed we were near London and there was a raid on. I shook Tom awake and let him look out at the scene. There was a sudden thump, and the ground shook, making the train shift back, and I heard more clanking. Another thump followed the first. Then the familiar deep crump of a distant explosion, a mile or more ahead of us.

'What is it? What's happening?' Tom said, gripping me by the arm.

'It's an air raid somewhere over West London. I told you before, we are at war now. Those are German aircraft. They are most likely bombing a factory, or it might be Isleworth Dock, west of London proper. I don't know, but I expect we are stopped here until the all clear. Might even be here all night.'

Tom stayed crouched, peering out through the crack in the blind, watching everything.

'I suppose that really does look like a vision of Hell to you, doesn't it?' I said. 'Are there flames now?'

'I can see a big fire over there,' he said. 'I don't understand.'

'Incendiaries,' I said. 'Those are bombs that cause fires. They start the raid by dropping a run of the incendiary bombs which mark the target with fire, and then they follow that up with the high-explosive run.'

'Where are they coming from, though?' he asked.

'From the sky, of course. From a formation of aircraft – bombers. That's why the lights are shining up: to try and isolate them so that the ack-ack guns can pinpoint them and shoot them down.'

Then, as if on cue, the guns started up with regular deep bangs.

'Keep looking – you will see the tracer fire up in the sky in a moment.'

'I do see something up there,' he said.

At that point there was a loud shout and a whistle blast outside our window.

'Put that damn blind down in there! Are you mad? There's a raid on. Do you want to alert the enemy, for God's sake? Respect the blackout!'

'ARP,' I said. 'Just like Mr Feaver back in Litton. You'd better get back over here, Tom.' I tucked the blind strap back into place. After that we sat in the dull amber lamplight, facing one another across the carriage, listening to the nasal drone of the aircraft engines overhead, the thump of the falling bombs, and the pounding of the anti-aircraft fire. Tom looked wide eyed but calm, considering what he had just seen.

'Welcome to London,' I said.

CHAPTER SEVENTEEN

By the time our train limped into Waterloo with a final loud sigh and release of steam, it was early morning. Outside the busy station there were signs of the recent air raids everywhere. 'We can walk from here,' I said. 'It's not far to the office.'

A pall of smoke and a smell of burning and ruptured gas mains and worse hung over the city as we walked across the river on the west side of Waterloo Bridge. The pavement was crowded with Londoners on their way to work. There was that 'business as usual' spirit about; a kind of drab, resigned cheerfulness in the face of misery, as if to say, 'Well, at least we survived another night.' People picked their way through bits of shattered glass and rubble, nodding politely and making way for one another. It was hard for the British not to be polite. I had to pull Tom away from the edge of the bridge and the view of the river. He seemed to want to stand and gawp at the dirty water traffic under the drifting fog and smoke.

'*Old London can take it* is what they kept telling us on the newsreels. I'm not so sure,' I said.

'Are we really in London now, then?' he asked.

'Course. Where did you think we were?'

'My dad went up to London once with his brother, my uncle, the one who is the stonemason,' Tom said. 'They had to deliver a memorial stone somewhere – came up in a horse and wagon. Took them a long time.' He fell silent, and I saw a horse and cart making its way across Waterloo Bridge on the other side, behind a tram.

'You still see horses and carts around town even now,' I said. 'Usually brewers' drays and the like – especially with the petrol rationing,' I added.

It was painfully obvious that none of my attempts to distract Tom with cheery chatter or interesting facts were getting through to him. The boy still walked along beside me obediently enough, but he was all hunched up, still lost in my civvy overcoat like a sleepwalker or someone in a daydream.

After crossing the bridge we turned left on to the Strand. A policeman was directing the busy traffic from the middle of the junction with the bridge. There were sandbags piled outside the bigger shops, and barbed wire was laid in rolls across dangerous sections of road and pavement where there was obvious damage.

'This is the result of the sort of thing we could see and hear from the train last night. Blitzkrieg, the Germans call it. Total war – that's what we are experiencing here: total war. The whole city could be reduced to a pile of rubble, like all that lot over there, if this goes on for much longer.'

'How long has it been going on, then?' the boy said. Perhaps he was waking up after all.

'Just started last year. We had a few months when everyone thought the worst was going to happen, and it didn't, and then all of a sudden it really did. Some would say I've been lucky – I've been and missed most of it down in Dorset. Part of me thinks that I ought to have been here, lending a hand to poor old London. But then, I've been doing my bit looking out for the secret enemy, and also I found you.'

'You think I am the enemy, then?'

'That's a good question, and that's what we are about to find out. If it's any help, I don't think you are an enemy at all. I have a sixth sense about things. I have hunches and intimations, and I've got a good one about you, Tom.'

There were gaping holes in one of the buildings tucked behind the Strand. It had taken a direct hit. I could see exactly how it had fallen too. How it had collapsed in on itself, leaving the back wall that faced the river intact while the front was a neatly stacked pyramid of shattered bricks and broken and charred timbers. There was sure to be a mathematical equation explaining the pattern in the seeming chaos and the way all the bricks had ended up in relation to one another, and the force of the high explosive used, and the angle at which the bomb had hit – but I couldn't even begin to tackle thoughts of that. I wasn't in the mood.

'Are we safe?' Tom said, looking around at all the shattered glass on the pavement and the gully of rubble and pools of water from the fire-fighting.

'They usually come at night,' I said. 'There have been some daylight raids, but not many. It's much easier to shoot them down in daylight.'

'What are those?' he said, pointing up to a line of silver barrage balloons floating over Charing Cross station.

'Barrage balloons,' I said. 'They confuse and damage the low-flying dive bombers. Well, that's the idea. Trouble is, Tom, there haven't been any low-flying dive bombers like there were on the beaches at Dunkirk or over Guernica in Spain a few years ago. The Germans use their high-altitude bombers to pound poor old London – Heinkels and so on, not Stukas.' I might as well have been speaking Serbo-Croat as far as Tom's reaction was concerned. I guessed he just couldn't take it all in.

We passed a barber's shop that was open for business, even though the shop window was all taped over. I persuaded Tom in and told him to sit in the barber's chair.

'He's had a bit of a shock,' I said to the barber. 'He was shipwrecked. Just got picked up off the coast. He can't talk at the moment.'

Tom was given a good, almost military haircut. It looked like he hadn't had one in months.

'That's better,' I said to him after I had paid the barber. 'You'll blend in more easily. We won't get so many looks now.'

We walked under Admiralty Arch and then turned off to the steps down to the Citadel annexe.

An MP stood guard at a sentry post outside the door among a tower of sandbags.

'Corporal Carmody and suspect to see Captain Holloway. We are expected,' I said, and remembered to salute smartly.

'Wait here please.'

There was a constant stream of people in and out of the bunker below us. Our offices were deep down at the end of a long low corridor. We were not first priority, but we had our place; according to the good captain, this was because we had Churchill's interest and blessing.

Miss Greville escorted us once we were past the guard. Viktor passed us in the corridor. He doffed his trilby at me and winked – I presumed at Miss Greville. We went down the staircase to the outer office, and the captain was already there, beaming out one of his smiles.

'Well done, Jack,' he said. 'Mind you, you look like Hell. A tiring journey and a rough night, I imagine.'

'Very much so, sir,' I said, saluting again.

'Come through into the inner sanctum, both of you. It's been a long time coming, but I have been looking forward to meeting you, young man,' he said, extending his hand to Tom and smiling from ear to ear, just as he had when I met him for the first time.

'We have a lot to talk about, but first I think a cup of strong, sweet army tea.'

CHAPTER EIGHTEEN

'I imagine that all of this, every last bit of it, is a puzzle to you, if my hunch is correct,' the captain said.

He sat down behind his desk with his back to the wall – a wall which was painted that same drab institutional green as the army office in Dorchester. I sat to one side of the desk, and Tom, the boy from forty years away, sat facing Captain Holloway. A set of my photographs was pinned to a framed cork board stretching behind the captain's head so that the boy could not fail to see them. There were the lights on Gallows Hill, and the boy's own face staring back, starkly lit by the Anglepoise lamp. There was the stag, much enlarged, the terror evident in its eyes.

'Quite a gallery, isn't it?' the captain said in his

best friendly uncle voice. 'Take us through it, would you, Jack?'

'Yes, sir,' I said, and got to my feet. I picked up a pointer from the desk and went through the images one by one.

'These are the bright lights I saw on the hill near the top. They moved very quickly: here they are directly over us, and here below us, down the hill near the churchyard. This is just at the northern part of the churchyard, and here is the stag that rushed out at us.'

'I didn't hurt it,' Tom said, staring at the photograph. 'I couldn't. It wasn't right.'

'No, you saved it, I think, Tom,' the captain said.

'Can't say I did – I saw it shot. Saw it fall down, shot. I was meant to go and finish it off. I couldn't do it, though, and I threw old Gawen's knife away, far as I could. Then the light came, and next thing I knew, the poor creature was on its feet again, racing past me.'

'You say it was shot?'

'Yes, it was Gawen shot it.'

'Where did the bullet strike – did you see?'

'Creature turned its chest to us, and the bullet struck it there, over the heart.'

'I see.' The captain stood up and tucked his chair under the desk. He took the pointer from me. 'If I may, Jack,' he said. He went close to the enlarged picture of the stag, and tapped the pointer on its chest.

'If you look carefully, you can see there is a scar that has been left by a line of tiny neat stitches. So, you see, the stag was indeed shot, and then there was time for someone to stitch its wound and help the healing process. Who was that? Did you do it?'

'No,' Tom said. 'No.'

'Who did, then? This Gawen character, perhaps, took pity on the animal.'

'No, sir. He wanted it dead. He wanted the meat, the venison. Must have been them, the angels, that healed it.'

'When did all this happen?'

'The day before yesterday – but then things have changed since then. It's all gone mad. I can't explain it.'

'Have you ever been to Germany, Tom?'

'No, never. Never been to London before, let alone Germany.'

'Something happened to a girl once in Germany very like what I think has happened to you down in Dorset. It has happened more than once or twice. I think it has happened many times. I doubt you have ever heard of the Office of the *Unerklärliche & Übernatürliche*, which roughly translates as "The Unexplained and the Supernatural". In fact, I would be very shocked if you had, because very few people, even those inside the

German Reich itself, know about it.'

'No. What does any of that mean, then?'

'No matter, for the moment. What do you make of this?' The captain picked up the little piece of metal I had found in Tom's trouser pocket. He held it out so that it shone and glowed in the lamplight.

The reaction was instant.

Tom stood up and said, 'The angels gave it to me. I must have it back.' His voice was blank, almost impersonal.

'They gave it to you?' Captain Holloway handed the little fragment over, and Tom took it quickly and put it in his trouser pocket.

'Yes, they gave it to me.'

'Who exactly are they, Tom?'

'Hard to say,' he replied. 'I can't describe them. I don't really see them, but I hear their voices when I have that with me. I haven't heard their voices, their music, for a while now, and I need to. They love me – they love me like . . . like a parent.'

'This is really the heart of the matter,' Captain Holloway said. 'The nature of these creatures and what they want with you or feel for you, Tom.'

'Don't follow you.'

'Your manner has changed since you took possession of whatever that little thing is.'

I had noticed the change too. Tom seemed confident now. He was standing upright, not slumped or slouched, burrowing into my old coat as if trying to hide himself.

'It's true, Tom,' I said. 'You have. It's as if you've had a sudden burst of energy; of confidence in yourself. Do you remember the lamp in the ARP office in Litton Cheney? Do you remember what happened when you touched it?'

'Like this, you mean?' he said, and he stretched out his finger to the lamp on Captain Holloway's desk. There was a sudden intensity to the light from the bulb, and from the ceiling lights as well. Instead of their usual underpowered yellowish glow, they went through white to a kind of dazzling tungsten silver blue; I had to turn my head away, it was so bright.

'Yes,' I said. 'I mean just like that.'

'Remarkable,' Captain Holloway murmured. 'Quite remarkable.'

Miss Greville burst through the door. 'What on earth—? Is everything all right in here?' she said, plainly out of breath. 'We thought there was an explosion or a fire . . .'

'Nothing to worry about, my dear,' the captain said. 'Just a little power surge in the system.'

She looked over at Tom and frowned, as if uncertain,

and then back at the captain. 'Well,' she said, 'if you're sure, sir?'

'I am perfectly sure. Really, Ruth. Thank you.'

She left then, but I could see she was puzzled – worried, even, by what she thought she had seen. After all, it wasn't every day that lightning appeared to flash in our dingy basement offices.

'That was a truly remarkable demonstration. I imagine you might be able to do much more if you put your mind to it.'

'I'm not . . . certain,' Tom said in his broad Dorset accent. 'But if the voices tell me how, then I might.'

'Sit down, Tom. Relax,' the captain said, and I sensed he was nervous now, as if the boy had suddenly become unpredictable; a ticking bomb or some other unknown deadly weapon that might suddenly go off without warning.

Tom sat back in the chair, but he was alert now, sitting up straight like an eager pupil.

'I'd like to tell you what we know, Tom. Are you comfortable? You look tense.'

Tom just sat quietly, expectant.

'Now, Jack Carmody here and I have worked together for a number of years. We investigate things, Tom. We dig and see what is what. We investigate odd things that no one else takes very seriously, like ghosts and séances, like apparitions and spirits, automatic writing – all of that and more. I suppose we are, for want of a better phrase, detectives of the supernatural or the paranormal. Does that make any sense to you, Tom?'

'No.'

'I think your experience comes very much into our remit. You have had a very strange experience, Tom, haven't you?'

'I can't make much sense of it.'

'You must be in a very disorientated state at the moment. Your confusion is understandable. Here is what I think has happened. You have met with some kind of non-human creatures of considerable power, and this meeting has happened more than once in your time. Now, I suspect through their agency, you have been brought to our time. There is a big missing piece of this jigsaw puzzle. How many years have elapsed? As far as you are concerned, you went out poaching a night or two ago, and then Jack here found you in the churchyard – found or disturbed you maybe – because of course, there was this animal with you which ran off before you could shoot it.'

'I saved it. I don't remember getting back there,' Tom said.

'I know you don't, Tom, and at some point I want to help you to remember. The thing is, forty years have passed between your time and our time, and you are still just about – what . . . fourteen, Tom?'

'I don't understand,' he said. 'I feel like I am dreaming all the time, or like I have died and come to life again, or I'm just in Hell. That's what I think.'

'My opinion is that your memory has been closed to you by these – for want of a better word – angels; these non-terrestrial beings. I want to find a way to open it all up to you and to us. I think that there is a deep dark secret locked away there. You see, I've been digging around a bit, Tom, in the newspaper archive. That's a place where very old newspapers are kept in big bound volumes. I found many things of interest, but mainly this . . . Here, read it – no, better, I'll read it out to you. It's from your local newspaper . . .'

Captain Holloway read the piece aloud. Tom looked shocked. He asked to see the paper, and Captain Holloway handed it to him. He looked down at it. 'I used to read little bits of the *Illustrated London News* out loud to my father of an evening. He used to bring it back from the Rectory sometimes when they had finished with it. Never thought I would be in a newspaper.'

He looked up. He suddenly seemed defeated again,

The Dorchester Weekly Courier & Advertiser

Sunday 16th December 1900

The hunt for the missing youth, one Thomas Pile, a labourer's son, aged 14 years approx, of Litton Cheney in the Bride Valley, continues. The boy has been missing without trace for a month. A gamekeeper recently handed in a discharged rifle to the police. It was found in the forest near the village of Powerstock, along with some discarded poacher's sacks.

The rifle was licensed to the boy's father, a garden labourer, who claimed to have no knowledge of where his son was or how his own rifle came to be where it was found. He said he had last seen his son into bed, and that in the morning when he went to wake him he was gone, and the bed cold. Police have searched and dug extensively in the area near where the rifle was found, so far with no result. Foul play cannot be ruled out.

slumped and even paler, if that was possible. 'My father really is dead now, then, along with my mother?'

'Yes, Tom,' the captain said quietly. 'I'm afraid so. This must be very hard for you. You see, Tom, you went missing forty or so years ago, and then suddenly you have turned up again. If you really *are* you, and we think you are, you are not the first. It has happened before. In Germany, for instance, this girl disappeared, and then, many years later, a confused girl was found wandering in a forest not far from the remote village where the original girl disappeared. She claimed to be that same missing girl from all those years before. *Impossible*, you will cry out in common sense. I might have agreed with you at one time. You are no Rip Van Winkle, Tom. You haven't been asleep in a hollow for forty years, but you have been somewhere else, and I don't think it was here.

'I think you are just one of many people who, over the years, have been abducted by – for want of a better word – some sort of aircraft, but one not of this earth. There, I've said it. The beings you call angels are, I believe, extra-terrestrial alien creatures from another world or universe who would appear to you – and, indeed, to most people – to be just that: angels. It is perfectly possible that these "angels" have been visiting this planet, our earth, among others, over many centuries. This would account for the old descriptions, and the fear and wonder that accompany such sightings. A few years before your disappearance the local paper reported sightings of lights in the sky. The very same lights which Jack here managed to photograph so recently.'

'I saw the lights before when I was little – same lights. Later on I saw them again: falling, they were, into the woods near Bridport.'

'That's right. Several locals saw the lights in about 1890. There are two reports – one in the paper, and one written by an investigator from London, who went down to interview the witnesses. It was seen then as a mass delusion, a kind of hysteria. At some point we need to get to your closed-off memories and unlock whatever it is that is inside you. Don't worry – I'm not suggesting we do anything now.'

'No need, Captain,' I told him. 'Like I said before, we have just such a recording: I made it in the garrison at Dorchester.'

'Good,' he said. 'I shall of course listen to it at once, but you need to rest, Tom. Jack will take you to a safe house for today and tonight. Back here bright and early tomorrow, and we will talk again. Take it easy, Jack. No doubt there will be more air raids tonight, so be careful. No risks, remember.'

CHAPTER NINETEEN

'First of all,' I said, once we were back outside, 'a good breakfast, and then the Underground home.'

We went to a Lyon's Corner House café north of the Strand.

Tom hardly spoke. I'm not sure how much he had taken in of Captain Holloway's theories.

He was soon wolfing down a plate of sausage, bacon, grilled tomato and fried bread, washed down with a cup of strong tea, and all for 10d. I had poached eggs on toast for 8d. SAVE FOR VICTORY, BUY WAR BONDS was printed across the bottom of the menu – as was the following, which made me laugh: *Notice is hereby given that margarine of the finest quality will be served with all goods except bread and butter.*

'Tom,' I said, 'when we were in the hall at Litton Cheney, you knocked the telephone off the table onto the floor. Do you remember that?'

'No,' he replied, 'not really.'

'Well, I do, because I noticed that you stopped it hitting the ground too quickly. You controlled it in the air – well, that's what it looked like. Do you remember that?'

'Not sure,' he said.

'Do you think you could do it again?'

He looked across the table at me, and for the first time, he smiled just a little. The metal milk jug rose off the tray and travelled the few inches over the table to land gently next to my china mug of tea.

'I see. Clever stuff, Tom.'

I looked at the table next to us. A woman in a hat with a raised netting veil was looking at Tom, open-mouthed. I wiped my mouth with a napkin and said, 'All a trick – 'e's a conjurer, you know.'

She nodded, but her mouth stayed open.

After that we walked along the Strand the other way, through the Aldwych and up to Holborn. Tom was still looking around as if he were in a dream. To be fair to him, after the quiet of Dorset it was rough, chaotic and smelly. Before we descended into the Underground, we went to Lincoln's Inn Fields. We just sat together quietly and watched some office girls out playing netball in the cold. What with the girls and the busy crowds on the pavement, I doubted whether Tom had ever seen so many people in his life.

'What do you make of it all?' I said.

'I can't make sense of anything,' he replied. 'All the carriages with no horses, and the train we were on . . . All so fast – and everything has changed, everything is so different, I don't really know what's going on. I feel like I am suddenly going to wake up and have to collect the eggs from our little henhouse. I'd like that to happen, to tell the truth.'

'I don't think that will happen, Tom,' I said. 'I think you are here with us in our time now, and you are here for good.'

I was worried what his reaction to travelling in the Underground might be. If he found the busy streets disturbing, what would he make of that?

Holborn is a frighteningly deep station, with especially steep escalators, or so it seemed to me, suddenly looking at it through Tom's eyes. The place stank of cheap fags and the body odour of people more or less living down on the platforms during the air raids. I doubted whether the smell would bother him as much as the dark and the chaos.

I had to encourage him to get on the moving staircase, because of course he had never seen anything like it before. He stood one or two steps below, looking up at me like a worried pet. He gripped the moving handrail with both hands while people hurried past us on their way down to the trains.

Even though I called out, 'Watch out for the last treads,' he panicked at the sight of them folding down into the dark space under the grille, and he tripped over his own feet at the bottom and sprawled across the floor. People tut-tutted and skirted round him as if he were a drunk.

'Come on,' I said, helping him up. 'I did try to warn you.'

'I thought I was going to be pulled down under there,' he said.

'I know,' I said. 'I should have warned you sooner. It's my fault. Children always think that the first time.'

'Yes, but I'm not a child, am I?' He was red-faced with embarrassment, brushing down the front of his trousers.

'In a way, though, Tom, you are. All this is as new to you as it would be to a seven-year-old on his first trip.'

'I suppose,' he agreed.

The platform was crowded with busy, hurrying people, though there were others who were already making space for themselves on the platform for later in the evening, hanging clothes from the pipework and generally settling in. The telltale rush of warm stale air came flooding out of the tunnel.

'Here comes a train,' I said. 'Hold on.'

It rattled towards us in a rush, pushing more foetid air ahead of it. I heard it as I imagined it might sound through Tom's ears now, and it really was unbearably loud. I saw him flinch beside me. He turned his head away and brought his arms up as if to shield his body.

'It's all right,' I shouted over the racket of the squealing brakes. The doors slid open with a whoosh, and a crowd of people left the train, pushing and barging carelessly past us. Then I had to push and shove to get us on, and of course there were no seats. I put Tom's arm up and got him to hold onto one of the straps above the seats.

'You're a straphanger like the others now, Tom,' I said. 'Like one of the daily commuters. A proper Londoner.' I tried my best to make light of things as the train lurched forward. I could see that he wasn't paying any attention to what I said. There was just that unmistakable look of panic in his eyes.

The carriage was very crowded. There were a lot of tired and worried Londoners, all squashed in tight, together with their awkward hard-edged gas-mask holders, with me and Tom. I was used to it, but he wasn't. At the next stop, Chancery Lane, more people got on, closing in on us even further. We were heading east on the Central Line, and at the Bank interchange, things got really bad. A whole crowd surged onto the train.

'Move right down inside the cars please. Make room now,' a voice called out from the platform. We were soon backed up hard into the corner near the doors on the other side of the carriage. I could see an almost mathematical pattern in the flow of figures pushing forward. There was surely a formula, an equation describing the way in which people tried to edge themselves into the remaining spaces by turning and squirming, as if the fit were almost preordained. I did my best to shield Tom from the worst of the pressure, but I could sense that the panic was rising in him.

"S all right, Tom,' I said, now having to turn my head awkwardly to be able to see him at all. 'Only one more stop.'

The pressure was unlikely to be relieved until we reached Liverpool Street. Everyone would get out there. But among those who had just joined the train at Bank were firemen, nurses and ARP auxiliaries, fresh from the horrors of the bombings, by the look of them. We were now under the worst of the blitzed areas at the centre of the city, and near the docks too. I could smell the smoke on them; their faces were soot-streaked, and they all looked drained and exhausted.

The train set off again, and the lights in the carriage flickered on and off for a minute. For a whole stretch the carriage was in total darkness. Then we just ground to a halt in the tunnel.

There were coughs and throat-clearings, and even some nervous laughter. Someone shouted out, 'Be a pal and turn 'em back on, would you, Adolf,' which was followed by more nervous laughter and another cry of 'Put that ruddy light out,' which was the kind of thing the ARP wardens would shout out to hapless folk who left their curtains open. More laughter gave way to groans and mutterings of displeasure.

'This is all we need,' someone near to us said.

This was a common occurrence – a train stuck at a signal in a tunnel. The lights stayed off. I was getting my approaching-thunder feeling.

'We'll be off again in a minute, Tom,' I said, as reassuringly as I could. It was not enough. If I felt the hot and oppressive sense of suffocation and burial, then what was Tom feeling? Someone struck a match to light their cigarette, and I saw that Tom had his eyes tight closed.

'Put that light out,' someone said in a mock posh voice. 'Don't you know there's a war on, old chap, what, what?'

More nervous, edgy laughter from the rest of the

passengers, all squashed up tight together in the carriage, breathing each other's body odour and anxiety. Death, after all, could come roaring down out of the sky at almost any moment.

Tom wasn't laughing. He still had his eyes shut. Indeed, he looked as if he was in terrible pain. I could do nothing. We were too tightly squashed in to even try to move, and in any case the train was between stations and in a tunnel and in the dark.

'Your mate all right, is he, son?' someone close to me said out of the muddle of shapes surrounding us.

'He's not used to all this,' I said, as cheerily as I could manage. I felt Tom's other arm moving out and up beside me. A harsh, low hum started up, and then an electrical buzzing and crackling sound, which rose through the carriage, along with Tom's arm. I was worried about what he might do, or be able to do, or be doing. According to her file, the German girl had been able to bring down an aircraft out of the sky.

The lights in the carriage suddenly sparked back into life.

''Bout time,' someone quipped. 'Thanks, Winston.'

The lights came on again all right, only now they were suddenly much brighter, and then they were brighter still; unnaturally so. The bulbs glowed tungsten blue-white bright, and the carriage was lit up as if by a lightning bolt, and everyone was picked out in alarming frozen detail. The train lurched forward suddenly too, and then, one by one, all the way down the carriage, the light bulbs blew out, one after the other. They shattered explosively, showering bits of super-heated glass down among the crowded passengers.

There was immediate chaos and panic. It was clear that everyone thought we had been hit during a daylight bombing raid or a previously unexploded bomb. The train moved on, building up speed as it rattled and swayed along the tracks in the now pitch dark, while the passengers also crashed back and forth and into one another as their terrified voices called out above the train noise.

'What the hell?'

'Help!'

'For God's sake!'

'Oh, help, please help me. I'm bleeding. There's glass in my hair . . .' and so on.

Trapped in the corner, I could do nothing to help them, and besides, I had a good idea of the cause of all the chaos.

'Let go now, Tom,' I said close to his ear. I held onto his arm and tried to calm him as best I could. 'Enough – let go. It'll be all right.' I could feel the tension in him; the stiffness in his bearing and all through his body, as if his nerves were strung out like wires.

The train seemed to gather speed. The rocking motion got worse. Some people stumbled into one another and even fell to the floor.

'Calm down now, Tom. That's enough,' I repeated.

He finally slumped back against the door and I felt the tension leave him like the air out of a punctured tyre. The train returned to its normal speed too. We finally pulled to a sudden jolting halt at Liverpool Street station, and that was when pandemonium broke out. In the light filtering in from the platform I could see that several of the passengers were covered in cuts from all the flying glass. The doors slid open and everyone fought to get off the train. Those who had been injured, the walking wounded, were helped off our carriage, and from all the others as well. Tom looked paler and more exhausted than ever, as if he had been drained of all his energy.

There were policemen on duty at points along the platform, and the train driver was reporting to one close to where we stood.

'It happened after Bank,' he said. 'I thought we must have hit a mine or an incendiary. The whole train seemed to get away from me at one point.'

'No explosions – nothing like that reported to us,' the copper told him.

People were milling all around us. Some were being treated by nurses for minor cuts and abrasions. The train doors were stuck open and the carriages gaped all the way down the platform.

The policeman turned to me. I suppose I must have stood out among the mostly civilian crowd in my uniform coat.

'See anything unusual, Corp?' he said.

'Only the same as everybody else here, mate. Not sure what happened really. One minute we were barrelling along as usual. Then we stopped, and the next minute the lights went out; then they came on again, really bright; then they shattered all over everybody – bulbs, glass, shades, the lot.'

'No explosions? No fire? No external intrusion? Nothing like that?'

'Not as far as I could see. Seemed, if anything, like an electrical fault to me – a surge in the system.' I shrugged. 'Sorry I couldn't be more use.' I turned and started to walk off, only to find that Tom was no longer beside me. I couldn't see him anywhere in the muddle on the platform – but I did see Viktor Prejm, some way back along the platform, looking over at me.

'Tom,' I shouted out. 'Tom Pile, where are you? You all right?'

There was no sign of him on the platform. I looked

back to where Viktor had been standing, but there was no sign of him either. At that moment I was more worried about what Tom might do, but an alarm went off somewhere in my system at seeing Viktor there. Surely that was more than a coincidence?

A NO EXIT sign led down a long twisting tiled corridor, and I just caught sight of a figure I thought must be Tom, running away ahead of me. I dodged through groups of injured people.

'Tom,' I called out. 'Tom, it's me, Jack. Stop!'

Halfway down the tunnel-like corridor, he stopped and turned to face me, and then raised his arms. The lights around him flared bright, then shattered, one after the other, and I was plunged into darkness.

CHAPTER TWENTY

I made my way along the dark corridor, back out to the ticket hall, where passengers were being treated. A ticket inspector blocked my way out.

'Can't any of you read?' he said. 'This is an entrance, not an exit. You're the second one to try this trick.'

'Where did he go?' I said.

'Who?'

'The first bloke – the one who came through here just now.'

'Oh, him. He pushed past me like you just tried, and then he ran off through there, and he didn't show no ticket neither.' He pointed to the street exit.

'He was my prisoner,' I said.

'Well, if that's the case, you should have taken better charge of him, then,' the inspector said.

I pushed past him myself, and set off running across the forecourt.

'Oi,' he called out. 'Where's your ticket, mate?'

'Don't need one,' I shouted back without even turning. I ran outside and joined the stream of people walking up the incline below the station spire and clock tower. Finally, out of breath, I reached the street. Tom had apparently vanished: there was no sign of him. I had lost him, and I had lost Viktor too.

I found a telephone box and gave the correct coded combination and got through to Captain Holloway in his office.

'I've lost Tom,' I said. 'He got away from me.'

'How?' The captain's voice was suddenly brisk and no nonsense. 'What happened?'

I told him. I also mentioned seeing Viktor on the platform. 'I think he must have been following us.'

'Seems that way. Hmm . . . Wait exactly where you are in that telephone box – I'll be with you soon.'

Communiqué 4

Intercepted radio message
Translated from the <u>GERMAN</u> original
(C4./Capt Holloway Office 116)
November 1940

The required parcel has been safely taken.
I will arrange collection and delivery at
the earliest.

CHAPTER TWENTY-ONE

We spent a fruitless hour and what must have been a whole tank of precious petrol driving around those streets that were still passable, looking for Tom Pile and Viktor. We must have gone into a dozen Lyon's Corner Houses and ABC Cafés; nothing much else was open.

We had a contact address for Viktor so we drove out towards Newington Green. Viktor lived in a tall run-down boarding house in Mildmay Park, overlooking the North London railway lines. A few cars were parked along the road close to the house. No one used their private cars much any more, what with the petrol rationing. I noticed a gap in the line of cars like a missing tooth, just outside the house.

'That's where Viktor kept his car, I'll put money on it,' Captain Holloway said, pointing to the gap.

The landlady was eager to help after we showed our special warrant cards. She took us up to Viktor's room, and then stood at the doorway jangling her ring of keys.

'Is he in trouble? I do hope not. He has such lovely manners – a proper gent. Nice looking too. I shouldn't like to think he had done anything *wrong*.'

'I'm sure we all feel the same,' Captain Holloway said with a smile. 'When did you see him last?'

'He was off earlier today, and all of a rush. He packed a suitcase, but left most of his things behind, far as I can see – even his overcoat and the rest.'

I searched Viktor's wardrobe. It was full of good suits, and racks of shoes, all neatly lined up. There were good cotton shirts neatly folded in drawers, and a selection of silk ties hung from the brass rail attached to the inside of the door.

There were two suitcases in the wardrobe.

'Look at these,' I said.

'Better open them, Jack,' Captain Holloway said. 'Carefully, mind.'

'It isn't going to be a woman's body, is it, all cut to pieces, in that case?' the landlady said, putting her hand up to her chest and fluttering her fingers.

'No, nothing like that – at least, I don't think so.'

'Only you hear of these things, don't you – what with all the terrible bombings and the blackout? It seems a person can easily get away with murder these days.'

I flicked the locks on first one, then the other, and lifted the lids.

'No dismembered ladies,' I said.

'Oh . . . thank God,' the landlady said with just a hint of disappointment in her voice.

Both cases were stuffed full with what looked like sheets cut or torn from old newspapers, and even some hardbound clerk's ledger books.

'What shall I do with this lot?' I said.

'We'll take them with us. I'll go through it all at some point. He must have had all this stuff here for a reason.' Captain Holloway turned to the landlady. 'I doubt he left you a forwarding address, did he?' he said.

'No. He'd already paid for another two months in advance, in cash, like he always does; he said he would be in touch with me later. What's he done, then?'

'We don't know yet. Could be anything. We just get sent to check on these things,' Captain Holloway said with a smile and a shrug.

'Murder?' she said.

'I'm sure you will be safe enough here, but if he should come back, please telephone me at this number' – he handed her a card – 'at once.'

'I will. I can't believe anything bad of him, a nicely

mannered man like that, though – not murder, surely?'

'Most likely they just want to talk to him because he's involved in some petrol coupon swindle, something of that sort. I don't really know why we were brought in on this at all. Bit of a sledgehammer to crack a nut, if you ask me,' the captain said reassuringly. 'He has a motor car, though, doesn't he?'

'Yes – it's gone now. It was always right outside. A black Austin Six, it was. He must have gone off in it.' She gestured to a photograph on the bedside table: it showed Ruth Greville and Viktor standing in bright sunlight in front of the same car.

'I took that picture for him with one of his girls,' she said.

'I doubt he used it much, did he, what with the petrol rationing. Oh, and just look at that – now we have the registration number.'

Once we were outside, a train rattled past from Canonbury station, sending plumes of white steam across the road.

'Travel by car or by train, I wonder?' Captain Holloway said as the steam billowed and cleared. 'What would you do, Jack?'

'Tom is in a very odd, fragile state,' I said. 'He hardly knows what he is doing. He's like a mine. He could go off at the slightest thing.'

'I wouldn't risk taking him on public transport. Not after what happened on the Underground. And as it turns out, it seems that our tame Nazi friend Viktor was there, so he surely knows that.'

'I find it hard to believe that Viktor is a Nazi,' I said. 'I wonder if he realizes that Tom's power is growing . . . I swear, from one light bulb to a whole train full in just a day!'

'I suspect Tom has no real idea of what he could unleash if he wanted to,' Captain Holloway said. 'Trouble is, the Germans already know very well what someone like him might be capable of if handled properly. They had one of their own, after all, until they lost her. She pulled an aeroplane down right out of the sky, if we are to believe their reports. They pushed her too far, and it killed her, I suspect. That worries me.'

'Worries me too.'

'Car it is, then,' he said, ushering me back into our unmarked staff car. 'But where would they go?'

'Either get him over to Germany somehow, or to some place here in England where he could do some serious damage to the Allies; to our war effort?' I said.

'An even more worrying thought,' the captain murmured. 'Take him, hide him away, win his confidence, train him up. The poor boy is a bit of a lost soul, after all, and our Viktor is a charmer, if nothing else. Then let him loose on one of our valuable targets – makes horrible sense to me. If you were looking after him and you knew he could inflict serious damage on your enemy, that's just what you would do. They don't care about him; to them he is a human weapon, no more. All they have to do is wind him up and watch him go. He'll only be kept alive as long as he's useful to them.'

'Poor boy has no idea,' I said.

'I'm not sure he has no idea at all. From what you said, he's finding out what he is capable of, and that could possibly play into our hands.'

CHAPTER TWENTY-TWO

Back in the office, while we waited for any news of sightings of the car, radio intercepts or short-wave chatter, I looked through all the file material on the German girl, poor little Fräulein V——.

I wondered what she made of her angels experience. It hadn't taken the Nazis long to realize that her 'power' or 'gift', if that was what it was, could be used as a weapon. She had, it seemed, died in some mysterious way after unleashing some of her power – or whatever she, like Tom Pile, was blessed or cursed with. Perhaps they had simply disposed of her as being no longer required, which was hard to believe; or perhaps just using her powers to the extreme had killed her . . .

It meant that Tom Pile was in danger in more than one way. It made me even more determined to find the poor boy before it was too late. Where would Viktor take him?

An impression of laughter came to my mind: it was a woman's laugh, and I remembered something that Ruth Greville had said:

'Mr Prejm here just said he wanted to whisk me away to a romantic hideaway like one of these.' She gestured to the frosted glass panel to one side of her work area, over which she had taped dozens of picture postcards. There were sunny seaside and cottage scenes and the like.

I went out into the office, where she was normally plugged into her earphones. She wasn't there. Her desk was piled up with all the usual paper traffic, but there was no sign of her. I went through to the outer area. 'Anyone seen Ruth – Miss Greville lately?' I said.

'She left shortly after you did this morning,' one of the photographic technicians said. 'Heard her speaking to someone on the phone first. Assumed she was off to meet her Viktor.'

'Oh, right,' I said, and went back to her desk.

It was neatly arranged. Her typewriter had the cover pulled over it as if she wasn't expecting to come back that day. Her coloured marking pencils were all lined up on a sheet of corrugated cardboard – 'Keeps them from rolling around on the desk,' she once told me.

I noticed a break in the pattern. One pencil was out of place, a black one. It was under the mounted desk sharpener, next to a mound of fresh shavings, and I noticed a broken lead. Her spiral-topped shorthand notebook was open and slewed across the desk on top of a confidential file which had not yet been returned to the registry. I picked up the notebook. The indented marks of what she had last written were visible. I lifted the page and held it at an angle under the desk lamp, then rubbed the black pencil lightly across the ghost letters.

She had written: *Gallows Hill Litton Cheney.*

Captain Holloway had a map of Great Britain pinned up on the wall; it showed, among many other things, all the secret locations of new airfields and military installations.

I went over and studied the Dorset section. There weren't many bases to choose from. There was an airfield at Warmwell, and there was a bombing target run base near Chesil Beach. Captain Holloway was in his office, with the contents of the suitcases taken from

Viktor's room spread out across the two desks and on a trestle table as well.

'Bad news,' I told him. 'Ruth went off to meet Viktor. He called her out earlier – she wrote *Gallows Hill Litton Cheney* on her notepad afterwards.'

'Looks like he's taken her there too. Now, why would he do that? Bit risky.'

'Maybe he's using her as cover. A couple looks less suspicious travelling with a boy than a single man would.'

'Tricked her into a romantic weekend, you mean,' Captain Holloway said. 'How would he explain it to her, poor girl?'

'He'll tell her it's official, hush-hush . . . Department wants a test run of Tom's powers,' I suggested. 'There's even a glider base somewhere up on Gallows Hill, above Litton Cheney, of all places – near where I found Tom.'

'Makes some sort of sense now,' the captain said. 'Odd thing is, there was a label in the lid of one of the suitcases – sort of thing you put your possessions in when you are sent away to school. Just had *R. Greville* written on it in blue ink, so Viktor must have got it from our Ruth to keep all this stuff in. Poor girl, she's in for a shock, I'm afraid, after all this.' He indicated the papers scattered across the table. 'Someone's been on to all this for a while now, Jack,' he said. 'Look, just sit here for a moment and read this. Just as I was saying, the German Office of the Unexplained and Supernatural have obviously been covertly trawling for cases of what they call "the disappeared" like this for years. Gathering and collating the evidence, just like Herr Viktor – or whatever his name is really. He's been doing a lot too, judging from all his loot here. It looks to me like he has been quietly stealing ledgers, police records and the like from reference libraries, and ripping pages from the newspaper archives, among other things. Read the section I have marked there, and you will see that young Tom Pile has been telling us a blinding truth in his halting way, just as we thought he was. It makes those pictures you took all the more remarkable – as you will see when you read the evidence in this ledger which our friend Viktor has so usefully marked and flagged.'

I sat down. The ledger was open on the desk; the entry was halfway through it, the place kept with a bookmark, which was itself part of a book dust jacket. It was neatly torn down the middle and had been cut from a library copy of H. G. Wells's novel *The War of the Worlds*. Viktor had a sense of humour all right.

This was what I read:

Transcribed from the third evidence ledger 1900 - 1902

Originally taken at Dorchester Police Station & subsequently
at Herrison Asylum for the Insane
Spoken by the accused-witness under oath over a two-day period.
Faithfully recorded by Mr Alfred Stevens Esq.,
Clerk/Recorder to the Court.

Disclaimer

I, Gawen Dilke, unemployed farm labourer of the County of Dorset,
do swear by this as a true account of the events of the night of
November 15th in the year of our Lord 1900, God Save the Queen.

I here add my mark in confirmation.

X

I have known the boy Thomas Pile for some time – not
since his birth, mind, but not long after. I know his father,
the sometime gardener at the Rectory, who is also called
Thomas. I have supped ale – well, more usually cider – with
him at the White Horse on many an evening. Seemed to me
lately like he was drinking away his pittance, was guzzling
all his hard-earned money up in the cider after his poor wife
passed and he saw the lights. The boy and him was going
hungry. I made the boy an offer. I'm not getting any younger
– thought I might need a young body to help me cut and
carry, help me tote the sacks of a night on occasion; share
the spoils too. I meant no harm to him. Folk in that village

have a grudge agin me a mile wide, and would say anything to watch me swing on the end of the rope out in the yard there. I know 'em all well enough to know they hate me, sinner that I am, may God forgive me, but they hate me no more than I hate myself.

I arranged to meet the boy in the cursed village of Litton Cheney, and well after dark. Church clock struck the half-hour after ten just before I found him. He was waiting below Church Path playing silly beggars on the cart tracks at the bottom end of Gallows Hill. Poked him in the back with this same finger.

(Prisoner held up his right index finger.)

'Move along, then. Come on,' I said. 'Quick as you like.'

Made him jump like as if the Devil hisself had touched him. Well, maybe he had, poor child, wretch that I am. Made him slip his foot in a puddle along the cart track.

'Been here long enough. I thought you weren't coming,' he dared say back to me, quick as you like and sharp as a tack.

'I said I would come, didn't I,' I said, 'you ungrateful whelp, and here I am. I ain't no clock watcher, no time keeper to you, and you can scram off back where you came from, quick as you like, if you want to. It'd be no skin off my nose, young Tom Pile.'

That shut him up.

We set off up the steep path beside the precious reverend's garden. We went past the cottages, which were all dark. We walked together uphill onto the white chalk road that is Gallows Hill.

''Tis a long walk, 'bout as far as Powerstock over the top road – that's where he last saw it,' I said.

'He?' the boy asked, still sullen.

'Aye, 'twas Ruben the shepherd who saw it, large as life, and he says it's a fine big beast too.'

He had promised to help me for a share. I didn't doubt that meat was rare on their table, and a good haunch of venison would keep for weeks, hung up in a cold scullery.

'Here, you can carry these sacks. 'Tis a steep walk too.' And God forgive me if I didn't lump those heavy sacks, those very ones (Prisoner indicated sacks among the evidence pile on table), across the boy's shoulders. Sacks that was stiff and crusted and smelled, even in that cold air, of blood and stale meat.

'We shall 'ave to lug the best of him back between us. You prepared for that, boy?' I said.

'Course I am,' he said.

'No one knows you are out, do they?'

'No,' he said.

'Good,' I said. 'Behave yourself tonight – do as you're told when I tell you, and I might, just might, take you with me again. I en't getting any younger and I could maybe make something useful out of a wet-behind-the-ears pup like you.'

We crossed the top road, and then, after a while, we walked downhill again, this time on the single track – the one that winds through the woods. We was surrounded by trees, and it was all darkness, and we was near that ruined chapel – the place they all say is haunted, where everyone died from the plague hundreds of years before. A properly haunted place, even on a good day in bright sunshine. I never felt anything strange there before, but I would allow it now, believe me.

The boy slowed his pace, seemed afeared and stumbled along behind me.

'What is it?' I said, turning. 'Walk steady, now. Keep up and keep quiet. We could be on him anytime from now.'

We walked together side by side after that: a boy of fourteen, a garden hand's son, you would say, and he was of previous good character too. And me with him, old Gawen, sinner, drinker, poacher. I wonder what you would say of me? 'Previously known very bad character', no doubt.

We neither looked at the other as we walked through those dark trees.

There were all the usual rustling noises from either side – twigs snapping. 'An old brocky badger sniffing about, most like,' I said. 'Or it might be a dog fox. Could be anything. He'll be more scar'it of us than we should be of 'im, so don't worry yourself.'

'I'm not worried,' the boy said, all defiant, furious that he should even be thought to be worried, as if he had been out in the surrounding woods on his own every ruddy night.

'This is where Ruben says he saw the white hart,' I said, 'so go carefully now. Nice prize that. Good bit of gravy he'll make to stick your bread in, eh?'

The boy said nothing.

Suddenly there it was in front of us. It stood all on its own. The white hart. It was ghostly white in among those dark trees. It was sniffing the air and listening and its ears were forward. I gripped the boy's arm and stopped him in his tracks. Then, quiet as a church mouse, I took the rifle from across the boy's chest.

'Go on,' I whispered, placing the gun in his hands and – oh, may God forgive me – I said, 'Here's your chance . . . prove yourself.'

The boy quietly shouldered his father's rifle, and he sighted right enough and careful down the barrel.

The stag stood still.

'Go on,' I whispered. 'Time is a-wasting – gently now.'

The boy lowered the rifle. 'No,' he mumbled to himself.

I waited a moment – couldn't believe he would be so stupid – then I snatched the rifle from him. 'Coward . . . useless puppy,' I whispered, and I steadied the gun against a tree.

I waited, lining up for the kill shot. The animal shifted slightly and presented a good view of its chest. Even the boy held his breath. The animal breathed out as I watched it. I marvelled at its strength and its whiteness, and then the boy suddenly went mad and shouted out loud at the stag.

'Go on!' he cried.

And I fired my kill shot just as he shouted.

I was sure I had hit it. The creature's legs buckled under it and it slumped down to the ground.

'You little fool,' I whispered, and I sincerely pray that the Lord may save me for saying this; for doing what I did. 'What were you thinking of? You put me off my aim, and now it's mortal wounded and suffering. You'll have to go and finish it off now.'

The stag was lying down, still alive. I could see its breath. I pushed my sharp hunting knife, handle first, into the boy's hand.

'Quick blow to the heart now and I'll let you off. Then we can cut it up and take it back.'

'I won't do it,' the boy said.

'Then you'll get none of it,' I said, 'and 'tis the last time you come out with me to line your larder, young Pile.'

The boy stepped away from me and let those there very sacks fall from his shoulder.

'Give me the knife,' I said. 'I'll do it, you useless—'

'No,' he shouted out, loud enough to wake the dead,

and then he threw the knife away, somewhere among the trees.

'You ungrateful little idiot,' I called out in my anger, and then he suddenly sprinted off like a roebuck, away into the darkness, as far from me as he could get. He ran towards the stag.

And then it happened . . .

(The prisoner collapsed at this point. The interview resumed the following morning.)

It was a blinding light and it came suddenly from deep in the trees near the ruins of the chapel; from the graves of the dead. I had heard about the lights. People in the village had seen them off and on a few years before, and now here they were again, right in front of me.

I can see him now. The boy just stood there for a moment, haloed by the light. It was like looking into the noon sun on a bright July day. I squinted my eyes tight shut and shielded my face with my hands.

'What the—?' I cried out suddenly, mostly fearing to have been caught in the act.

Then a second light moved across the ground in bright shafts from above. I looked up. I could see a strange shape moving back and forth somewhere high above the trees.

The boy moved further off towards the light. I thought, 'Tis the keepers, and that means prison for sure. Forgive the thought, but then I raised up the rifle again, and forgive me again if I didn't say out loud to the trees, 'May as well be 'ung for a sheep as a lamb. I'll leave no witness anyway,' and I sighted the rifle right over to where the boy was standing.

I watched him walk steady through the trees for another few yards beyond the stag towards the light.

I had no idea what kind of machine could be giving such a fierce light on a cold winter's night. I couldn't let myself think that the lights were those lights. My hand worked the trigger, and without thinking I found I had let off a shot directly at the boy. The bang was deafening. There was a roaring noise, followed by a kind of wailing scream, and the light went out at once, and darkness fell suddenly.

Then I had the unbidden thought. It was as if it had been suddenly planted there in my head. I were being punished. The light was from above, and it was God punishing me for poaching the squire's livestock. I were being punished for even thinking of shooting that white deer and then killing the boy.

I trembled then. I knew what those lights were – I couldn't fool myself any longer – and I felt such fear deep in my bones. Here was an apprehension of angels, of God in Heaven's own judgement on a miserable sinner like me . . . just as the others had seen them all those years ago. I fell then, right down onto my knees on the cold ground, and

I clasped my hands, these very hands, like this together in prayer.

'Forgive me,' I said out loud, my voice sobbing out into the cold over and over – and it was then that I saw it: the angel. It was like nothing I had ever imagined an angel to be; perhaps it was even . . . God himself?

I tried to call out for forgiveness, but my tongue felt as thick as an ox tongue and it stuck suddenly, and my mouth was dry and no sound would come. It was as if all my breath had been suddenly sucked from me. I remember crying, though. I remember my tears falling like a newborn. My tears flowed as I tried to look at the light; at the angel, which was made of light.

A cold wind blew then between me and where the angel of the Lord stood. I fell forward onto the cold mud and leaves. I pressed my face hard into the dirt. I thought of a rabbit and I pushed myself down. I tried to burrow into the Earth itself for safety. I heard more noises now, and was sure they were the agonized cries of the damned as they waited to welcome me down in Hades. 'Spare me, Lord. Spare me, spare me,' I cried out into the freezing dirt.

I stayed with my face pressed hard down into the filth and the darkness. There was a kind of whispered wailing noise, which was high pitched and went right through me; it hurt my ears and made me feel sick to my stomach. I lifted my head up and looked along the ground. The light *had brightened again, more so than ever, and the heaps of fallen leaves and the now upright body of the stag were all suddenly lifted, as one, into the air by the power of the Lord, up over the mud, just a yard or so from the ground.*

I floated up too, and I was held there among the leaves which all spun around me, and I was sure now that it was God himself made real. I clasped these hands tighter together in prayer as the noise got worse. It was like a police whistle blowing right in your ear. The ground rumbled and shifted below, and my eyes seemed to give out at that point. I sensed the lights rise up above the trees. I fell back to Earth with a bump. There was nothing after that but silence and complete darkness. After a minute or two, with my face pressed to the ground in fear, I dared look up. Where the boy Pile had stood there was nothing at all. I looked at the mound of bloodied sacks on the ground. I stood up, expecting to be struck down at any moment, either by armed keepers or by the angel of the Lord come to smite me.

Young Pile was gone, and the white hart was gone too. I staggered off then in fear, into the darkness towards Powerstock. I never saw Tom Pile again.

(Testimony ends.)

CHAPTER TWENTY-THREE

It was all there: the white hart, old Gawen – everything just as Tom had said and I had seen. The poor boy and the stag had leaped through time by forty years or so; no wonder he was so disoriented.

I looked again at the line of photographs I had taken down in Dorset. I was haunted by both Tom's face and the expression of the stag, the glint of terror in its eye. What had the poor dumb animal made of the angels who had so suddenly and mysteriously abducted it and so perfectly tended its gunshot wound?

'Right,' Captain Holloway said. 'We have no choice. We are driving down to Dorset and we have to go this minute. It'll take a while. We'll stay at your billet, and we will hopefully track down Viktor before he gets up to anything.'

'In my experience down there,' I said, 'they will be reported to the ARP authorities if they so much as hang a pair of underpants out on the washing line on the wrong day, or open a shiny tin of marrowfat peas in the open air.'

We left London in a fog. It was early evening, and as yet there were no air raids. Our progress was slow. There was less inessential traffic on the roads, but the dimmed and semi-obscured headlights of our staff car combined with the fog to make the going slow and potentially dangerous. Our conversation on the way down through the western suburbs and out was about the nature of the 'angels'.

'I wonder which part of the solar system or beyond they are from,' the captain said.

'Nowhere that can be seen even through your telescope,' I replied. 'Further – much further.'

'Yes,' he agreed. 'How do such beings, if that is what they are, even choose their subjects – victims, if you will? A girl in rural Germany, a boy out in the woods in Dorset and a shot stag, and who knows what else? Why them? It's all very rum; no one else will believe it.'

'The Germans believe it,' I said, 'and that is surely the point?'

'Indeed it is, Jack. Indeed it is. If we were at peace,

just think of the possibilities: we could share and pool our intelligence, but . . .' There was no need to say more.

We made such slow progress that by the time we reached the White Horse at Litton Cheney, it was closed and in darkness. There were, of course, right on cue, trailing wisps of a sea fret swirling round the building in proper Dorset fashion – wouldn't have been right if there hadn't been. I banged on the door at the side, and one of the upper windows opened and a cross voice called down in a loud and worried whisper, 'Who's there, and what the hell do you want at this time of night, may I ask?'

'Sorry, Mr Cox,' I called back. 'It's Jack, Corporal Jack Carmody, here with my superior officer, Captain Holloway. We just drove down from London. Took us longer than we thought.'

'Hold on, then.'

I pointed out Gallows Hill to Captain Holloway while we waited to be let in. 'That's the place,' I said.

'Looks bleak enough on a November night for anything,' he muttered.

CHAPTER TWENTY-FOUR

By morning Captain Holloway had already commandeered the telephone at the White Horse and was busy arranging for the intercept and triangulation of any odd shortwave traffic via the coastguard listening stations, and for searches of unoccupied buildings – or at least those known to be empty in and around the Chesil Beach area. Later that morning I took him up to meet Mr Feaver at the ARP hut.

'What happened to the poacher lad?' the warden asked us over a cup of ARP tea.

'Well, that's the thing,' Captain Holloway said. 'He was a bit more important than a poacher, and that's why Jack's come back here with me. We need everyone to be on the lookout for him. Any sighting of him, any rumour – anything at all, however trivial, however unimportant seeming it may be – call me at the White Horse.' He handed him a card with the number.

'What's he done, then?' Mr Feaver said.

'It's not so much what he's done; it's what he might do that worries us – can't say any more than that.'

'Oh, I see.' The warden nodded knowingly at me.

'I was never here just to assist the ARP,' I told him. 'Sorry about that – and leaving you with no warning or message. Couldn't be helped.'

''S all right, Jack – no harm done, though Mr Fry was up here earlier with the local paper. Seems some others have noticed those lights we saw up on Gallows Hill the other night. They been seen again – look there.'

I picked up the newspaper from the trestle table. There were two eyewitness accounts of the strange lights on Gallows Hill.

'Well, would you Adam and Eve it,' I said, trying to make light of it and handing the paper to Captain Holloway.

'Better take this outside, I think, Jack,' Captain Holloway said. 'Excuse us, Mr Feaver.'

We went and stood outside the tin tabernacle. The rooks were exchanging their gloomy sharp cries in the tall beeches of the Rectory garden, as usual.

'It's at times like these that I feel the need for my pipe,' Captain Holloway said, absently fumbling in his battle-dress pockets while reading the newspaper account. 'You've never gone in for the tobacco habit, have you, Jack?'

'Tried it – gave it up straight away. Not for me.'

'Helps me think straight; at least I tell myself that. Now, we are assuming that Viktor is somewhere in this area because he found out where Tom was from, and that he dragged his girlfriend, poor Miss Greville, into all this to give him some cover. It's all a bit thin, but we thought he might let that poor boy Tom loose on a remote air base just to see what he can do . . .'

'Fine – as far as it goes,' I said. 'Now we have a complication – the lights in the sky – and he will surely have seen this article or heard about it.'

'Exactly,' Captain Holloway said. 'It seems to me that Viktor will be tempted by that prospect far more than the chance to destroy a glider base or a bombing-run practice station. Here is his chance to get to the source, and as a good Nazi he will take it on, as sure as eggs are eggs.'

'So what do we do: stake out Gallows Hill and see what happens?'

'In the first instance, yes. If the lights really *are* back, we might just get lucky.'

'Just the two of us?'

'Good point, Jack. We could get some of our Essex

Regiment friends over at Burton Bradstock to lie in wait and surround the area, but my feeling is that: a) they wouldn't thank us in this lousy weather, and, b) the fewer people who witness what might happen, the better; if nothing happens, we would be seen as timewasters. What with all the invasion panic, we don't need to stoke up the rumour engine any further.'

'We'll manage, then,' I said, 'with just us and a camera.'

'We'll need more than a camera.'

'I have my rifle and Mr Feaver will have his stirrup pump.'

'Well, that's a comfort,' the captain said, and folded the paper. 'Give this back to him and say we'll return once it's dark.'

'Won't be long now,' I said.

CHAPTER TWENTY-FIVE

I had my army-issue rifle, of course – my Lee Enfield, the soldier's friend. I had fired a similar model a few times a year or so ago on a TA firing range. That was with 2.2 ammo, so effectively I was a novice at anything involving guns or fighting, but I had been accurate. Who knew what sort of force we would be up against later on Gallows Hill? I knew that Captain Holloway had his service revolver, which was a far less accurate weapon than my rifle, especially over any distance, so between us and Mr Feaver's tin hat and stirrup pump, what sort of a chance did we have? It was better not to think about it too much. We had Viktor's car registration, and I suggested that we send my new friend the local constable off noting cars around Langton Herring.

The evening bloomed with enough damp sea fret to hide a whole shipload of invading Nazis. I wondered what the real chances of the lights returning on a second evening were. I supposed that the odds were at least good enough to tempt Viktor to bring Tom out into the landscape – at least, if he was here somewhere.

The constable cycled up to the ARP hut at about seven in the evening to report, and he had a big smile on his face.

'Odd thing is,' he said between sips of Mr Feaver's eternally ready tea, 'I had a report from round there just yesterday. A woman came into the station – a regular visitor to us; sees a lot and hears a lot, if you know what I mean. She said a foreign voice, a German, had been heard thereabouts calling out from behind a hedge, and there was obviously a spy in the place. I said to her, *Are you sure it was German? Could have been a Czech or Polish voice, not German necessarily.* No, she was fairly sure it was German. This happens at least twice a day, I don't need to tell you, Mr Feaver. Folks are very jumpy, so I confess I ignored it. Then, when you asked me to look for a particular car, I remembered what she'd said, and so I went down there first. I checked the number plate, and blow me, there it was, large as life, in the driveway behind a closed five-bar gate. I noted it but did nothing.'

'Oddly enough,' Captain Holloway said, 'the nosy woman wasn't so far wrong, Constable. You have just made our job a lot clearer, if not any easier. We won't require any arrests – or, indeed, any intervention at all, at least not yet. We now have to spool out a little rope and let the suspect hang himself with it. There are others involved; we can't put them at risk so we don't want to spook him just yet. You did the right thing in leaving well alone. I assume you weren't seen?'

'Oh no, I was on my bicycle and the car was a way down the driveway from the farmhouse itself; didn't take me but a minute to spot it. Most of the locals thought the place was closed up and not used any more.'

'That all makes sense. I doubt it has been for a while.'

'Will you need me any more today?' the constable asked.

'I am afraid you are a luxury we can't afford, Constable. What we have to do we have to do alone and in secret. This is all strictly hush-hush, but by all means stay alert.'

'Right you are, Captain.' He put down his cup. 'Thank you, then, Mr Feaver, for the tea. I suppose this is all to do with those lights people been seeing?'

'Something like that,' I agreed.

'Well, you know where I am if everything gets out of hand, don't you,' he said. 'I can handle myself in a fight, you know,' he added, almost cheerfully.

'I'm afraid for security reasons we will just have to manage by ourselves for now. Thank you anyway – and, of course, not a word about it to anyone.'

The constable was soon away on his bike. I watched his dimmed rear light snake off back down to the main village street.

CHAPTER TWENTY-SIX

By seven the captain and I were setting off up the strange white surface of Gallows Hill. Mr Feaver stayed back in the ARP hut 'just in case', his buckets and stirrup pumps at the ready. We had briefed him to expect an arrest later and that was all. We took his dark lantern with us, and his first aid kit. I had my rifle slung over my back and Captain Holloway had taken charge of the camera. About halfway up the hill that led to the main Honiton road there was a passing place; a kind of lay-by with a gate in the hedge and access to a field. On the higher part of the field, a few yards from the road, stood an old stone shepherd's bothy, from which we would easily hear any motor cars coming up or down the hill – and any other kind of traffic. We went inside and settled down to wait.

'I've been thinking about where in the solar system these angel beings might come from, if at all?' the captain mused.

'I have too,' I said. 'Whatever craft they are travelling in seems to have been well hidden. Perhaps that's why they only appear at night, when there is a sea fog and overcast skies.'

'The only physical evidence we have is the lights. If we get Tom back – and it's a big *if*, I know,' Captain Holloway said, 'we must try and get him to remember what happened when they took him.'

'Most likely the experience has been hidden, either because it was too traumatic or because they wanted it that way.'

The captain went outside and looked up the hill towards the top road and the sky above. I followed him, and he turned to me.

'I've just remembered something. Tom took that little square of material he had with him. He put it back in his pocket. He's still got it.'

'We might discover what it was for, at least,' I said.

'Look,' Captain Holloway said, staring past me. 'Lights.'

They were over the crest of Gallows Hill: oval-shaped lights moving down towards the field. The captain got the camera out of his rucksack and started to take photographs. At the same time I heard a car climbing the hill. I heard the stop-and-start grinding of gear changes; the rumbling of the motor suggested it was having problems with the gradient.

'Car,' I said, and crossed over the wet grass to the gate. I watched it pull into a passing place on the other side of the road, just a hundred yards or so below us. The headlights were masked by the regulation slotted grille covers so that only just a little light escaped onto the the road itself.

The car sat there, just visible in the fogged dark. The engine was idling, coughing out smoke from the exhaust. I pushed myself up against the wet hedgerow as cover and used my army binoculars. The interior of the car was dark, but I could read the number plate clearly enough: NV 4103. It was Viktor's car all right.

'It's them,' I said.

The captain joined me among the wet leaves. I handed him the binoculars.

'The door's opening,' he said. There was a sudden rise in the light levels. The engine stopped running and I heard the car door slam shut. A shaft of light suddenly descended onto the roadway.

'Here they are,' the captain whispered, looking up.

The lights had appeared above us, and they were bright, but static overhead, just as they had been that first night on the hill. It was impossible to make out anything beyond the substance of the light itself, which was a bluish white, diffused and milky through the fog. The strange whining noise of the angels' engine was back too – and then there was the shuddering bass-drum thump as a shaft of light suddenly fell through the air and picked out the parked car. I could see three figures in the road close to the car. One was Viktor; the others were Tom Pile and Ruth Greville.

'Wait,' the captain said quietly.

The light was very strong, directly above them now. Viktor was wearing a raincoat with the collar turned up and a trilby hat. He looked like a plain clothes policeman. Tom was still wearing my overcoat, and his head was tipped back as he looked up into the light. Ruth Greville had her hands protectively on his shoulders. I studied the dynamic between all three of them; their posture and attitude to each other. Something troubled me. Tom suddenly raised both his arms, pointing upwards, and I saw that in each hand he was holding something that glowed bright.

I heard the camera click and roll on, click and roll on as the captain tried to document what was happening.

'Do you see,' he said. 'Look at his hands: he now has two pieces of that strange material. Viktor must have brought the piece the Germans found all that time ago.

They really have been planning for this. I suppose it summons them or something.'

I looked at Tom's hands through the binoculars. The pieces of metal were pulsating, and I could see traceries of their colours leaching up towards the light, which suddenly shut off, plunging the hill into darkness again.

'Blast,' the captain said. 'What now?'

The shaft of light appeared again briefly, only higher up the hill towards the main Honiton road this time. I heard the car door slam and the engine kick in, and within a few seconds the car had driven slowly past us up the hill in pursuit of the lights.

We had left our staff car back down in the village. We had little choice but to follow as best we could on foot. The car was struggling so it was not hard to keep it in sight. The shaft of light seemed to be leading the way up to the main road and beyond. We kept close to the hedges by the side of the road.

'I doubt they can see us,' I said, leading the way up. There was no traffic at all on the top road, and I watched the car sail across the gap and up onto the crest of the hill on the other side, where it turned off into a field.

CHAPTER TWENTY-SEVEN

In the fog and cloud above the top road there was now a huge pale oval of light. The effect was of veiled moonlight, as if the moon itself had come down close to the Earth on a clouded night. The light was an intense blue white, oddly cold looking. Two or three shafts of it suddenly came down onto the field behind the main road at the highest point of Gallows Hill.

We could see the car in the middle of the field. It was parked at an odd angle, with all its doors wide open, as if the driver had been in a great hurry. Viktor was standing beside Tom, and Ruth Greville was partly hidden on his far side. From Tom's hands, two strong beams of red light answered the white light coming from above.

'Time we did something,' Captain Holloway said. He pulled out his service revolver and walked quickly forward through the gap in the hedgerow and into the field.

'Wait,' I said. 'I don't think . . .'

Too late. He pointed the gun straight up into the air and fired it once. Viktor turned, and at once ran towards the car. Ruth Greville stepped back a few paces. I had only a half-second or so. I had already tucked the Lee Enfield against my shoulder. The light was perfect and the slewed angle of the car meant that I had a good view of the target. It only needed the one bullet fired into the petrol tank to set it all off. The fireball leaped upwards and the car lifted a little from the ground as it exploded. Viktor threw himself down on the ground, and Tom and Ruth turned towards us. Captain Holloway crossed the field with his revolver held out towards Viktor.

'Stay where you are,' he called out.

Viktor kneeled up on the grass, his hands high in the air, a grin on his face. 'Thank God,' he called out.

Tom's hands were up anyway, each one pumping more light up into the sky. The noise of whatever it was above the fog and cloud was louder now. There was a downrush of air too; I could feel it on my face. When I looked up, I saw that the fog was blowing away and the lights were getting lower and brighter, moving down towards us.

'Get up,' Captain Holloway called out to Viktor, who was now lit by both the overhead lights and the burning car.

'Are you all right, Tom?' I called out.

He said nothing; he just continued to hold his arms up towards the sky and the lights.

'The boy is capable of anything now,' Ruth shouted, a big smile on her face. 'And I really do mean *anything*.'

I looked over at her; she was still tucked just behind Tom. I saw that she was holding a service revolver out at arm's length and it was aimed directly at Captain Holloway.

'God, Captain, watch out – she's got a gun!'

'If I you have any sense,' she shouted out over the noise of the machine in the sky, 'you will go back to London and leave all this to me.'

'What on earth are you doing, Ruth?' Captain Holloway shouted back at her.

'I've been on to her for ages, Captain,' Viktor called out. 'She only took up with me as cover. I found a whole case full of evidence she had stolen. I followed her onto the Underground, and then I tracked her and the boy here – there was no time to alert you—' There was a bang as Ruth fired the revolver, and Viktor sprawled forward onto the ground.

I had no clear shot at her. She was so close to Tom, I couldn't risk it.

'I can make so much better use of this boy and his talents,' Ruth yelled over the noise. 'I'm sure you know that his abilities are growing all the time. Of course, at the same time I will encourage his friends up there to join us down here.' She waved her pistol up towards the oval of light above us. 'To join us in other ways too. Never mind getting the Americans into your war – what about us getting *this lot* onto our side? Think of that – imagine an army of Toms and an army of *them*.' She raised her head and smiled. 'Even better, I think, than having God on your side.'

'I don't think so,' Captain Holloway called back. 'I'm afraid that your sorry game is up.'

'Oh no, Captain, I'm sorry to say that my game is only just beginning. Yours is the one that is up. You really have no idea.'

With her free hand she quickly reached into her coat and pulled something out of the inner pocket. Before either of us could respond, she aimed it vertically up and fired what looked like a bright signal flare towards the centre of the light. There was a hush, a half-second or so of nothing, and then the light flared into an intense blue white. There was a deep low growl, and the angle of the light shifted as one edge of the oval dipped down towards the ground. There was a huge rumble, and a groaning sound, and I felt the air press down on me, as if a giant hand were forcing me to the ground.

'What the hell have you done?' the captain called out as he fell forward along with Ruth Greville. Only Tom was left standing. As I hit the ground, held down by the sheer weight of air pressure, I saw him still standing there, silhouetted against the intense light and the cascade of sparks falling from whatever it was above us.

There was an earthquake underneath me, and I felt myself being picked up and thrown down again. My rifle fell away across the ground, and then I saw it actually rise up into the air and hover there, suddenly freed from gravity. I saw part of a huge disc edged with intense white light slice into the ground. Huge chunks and clods of earth were thrown up into the air. The groaning metal noise continued, and a high-pitched scream was added to the rumble as more and more of the disc buried itself into the crest of Gallows Hill, as if it were burrowing down into the centre of the Earth.

The bright light suddenly went out, plunging the

hill into almost complete darkness. Chunks of earth, tree limbs, rocks and who knows what else tumbled down all around me. The burning black Austin, which had been lifted clear of the ground, crashed back to Earth on its side. Tom Pile was still standing with his arms held out and his head bowed. Halfway across the field I saw bits of the wreckage of what had once been above us scattered across the ground.

Ruth Greville staggered to her feet and set off towards the wreckage, where some light still glowed.

Tom Pile pointed at her, and I saw her sprawl headlong, three feet in the air, hovering above the ground.

As I stumbled over the churned-up ground towards Tom, I saw the captain on his knees, rubbing the back of his head. I called out to him, 'Are you all right, Captain?'

'Fine – just had a bit of a whack from a rock or something, that's all. Go and see to Tom. I'll check on poor Viktor.'

Tom turned to me. 'She killed them,' he said quietly. 'She's killed the angels. I can't hear their music.' He had tears coursing down his face.

Large chunks of twisted metal lay scattered all around, their surfaces rippling with colours that echoed those I'd seen on the little fragment

Tom had originally had in his pocket. Even as I looked at them, they faded to a nondescript grey. There was movement under the ground – rumblings and quiverings through the Earth itself. I could feel the tremors reverberating underneath me like echoes; a shifting pattern that I could almost track in my mind as the disc rolled on down through the layers of the hill.

'Were the angels in there, Tom?'

'They were,' he said. He turned to Ruth Greville, still hovering on her front, paralysed, three feet above the ground.

'Perhaps we can rescue them,' I said.

'No,' Tom said. 'I think they're gone now.'

There was a final seismic shift under our feet, and I staggered and saw Ruth fall back down to the ground.

Captain Holloway came and stood next to me. 'Viktor has a wound on his shoulder – it knocked him out, but I think he'll be all right. My revolver's gone, though – lost somewhere in all this. We need to restrain our Nazi friend here.'

'My rifle's gone too,' I told him.

A voice called out of the darkness at the roadside, 'Is everything all right here?'

It was Mr Feaver and the police constable.

'There's been a plane crash,' the captain said. 'We'll

need some help from the garrison to clear all this. We also have a Nazi spy to place under arrest – but not a word of this must get out, mind.'

'Sounded like a bombing raid,' the warden said.

'Well, in a way it was,' Captain Holloway explained. 'The woman over there was signalling to the enemy. I think they were trying to attack the base at Warmwell. Could one of you get over to the garrison at Burton Bradstock and rouse my old friend Colonel Gauntlett and see if he can spare us some men and a large vehicle to clear this at first light? We also have a brave man down with a gunshot wound – he's in urgent need of medical attention. Oh, and before you go, handcuffs and key please.'

'Right you are,' the constable said, rummaging at his belt and handing them over before setting off at once.

Tom Pile was sitting on the ground next to the now slumped and oddly stilled figure of Ruth Greville.

'Arms behind your back please, Miss Greville,' the captain said.

She looked up at him with a blank expression and indicated that her arms were already locked.

'Let me handcuff her, Tom.'

Tom nodded, and suddenly Ruth's body jerked in spasm, as if it had been suddenly shocked awake. The captain wrenched her arms round behind her back and locked the cuffs in place.

'How did you manage to bring that thing down? What was that you fired?' Captain Holloway asked.

She looked back at him, her mouth clamped shut in a thin line, and shook her head.

'I see you want to play the silent game, eh. Well, it's your funeral, Miss Greville, or almost certainly will be. Sadly, I doubt if we will ever know how that happened. Looked like a standard flare. What a terrible waste. Just look at all this.'

Mr Feaver stood looking around at the lumps of scattered wreckage. 'Is this all there is of it, then?' he asked.

'This is all that's left after the explosion, yes,' the captain said. 'By the way, I think we should wait here and guard the wreckage until the army comes.'

'Oh,' said Mr Feaver. 'That won't be until nearly seven tomorrow. I ought to get back in case of more raids.'

'Yes, you are certainly free to go. Not a word about what has happened here to anyone. What we have is the remains of an experimental German aircraft, which will need to be kept secure. They will have heard it all over the county, of course. All you need tell them is that a bomber was brought down on its way to destroy Warmwell base.'

'Understood.'

Mr Feaver set off back down Gallows Hill to the village.

The captain pulled his pipe out of his battle-dress jacket, struck a match and, cupping the bowl, lit it. He walked over and kicked at one of the lumps of grey metal. 'I suppose we have to hope that the soldiers will accept these as bits of a downed Nazi plane. It all looks nondescript enough now.'

He crouched down next to the boy and asked, 'What happened, Tom?'

'I can't rightly say. I was in a terrible pickle after that Underground train ride and I ran off. Anyway, he saw me at the station, that man there. He was nice and he tried to help me – said I was in danger and I had get away. Then she caught up with us and she threatened him with a gun and said she understood all about the angels; said she was sent by them to help and all; said she knew all about me, and told me other things too.'

'I think she did know, Tom. She dug out the old newspapers and files about you, and Viktor found the evidence she'd collected and took it from her – silly, brave man.'

'She said the angels wanted to see me again, and we came here and you saw what happened.'

'Oh yes, we saw all right – what a terrible waste!'

It was then that the Earth rumbled again, deep under our feet, as if an underground mine had exploded. I found myself swaying, and saw one of the trees in the hedgerow simply topple over. Ruth Greville sprang to her feet as, from the other side of the field, a bright light burst upwards from the ground. There was more rumbling below, like an earthquake, and then something burst up out of the field. It was almost too bright to look at: a shining disc much smaller than the one that had ploughed down into the ground earlier. It leaped up and then hovered about twenty feet in the air, spinning and sparking out light. We all stood and looked up at it. It was in its way a thing of rare beauty. Here was an object from far beyond the moon or the rings of Saturn, hovering in the air above our heads. Tom walked forward and held his arms out to the spinning silvery disc. Two great beams of white light shot out from his hands, and as if in answer, a burst of coloured light like a spinning rainbow enveloped him. Then, after a momentary pause, the disc shot upwards and vanished behind the rolling fog bank. We could just see a trail of light as it streaked upwards, like a shooting star in reverse. And then there was darkness and silence.

'Looks like your angels said goodbye, Tom,' I said.

'I know,' he said with a grin. 'I heard their music again.'

And then we were left standing in the cold field, surrounded by extra-terrestrial wreckage, waiting for the sunrise.

CHAPTER TWENTY-EIGHT

A small force from my supposed regiment, the Ninth Essex, appeared at around seven a.m. There was a covered lorry, and an army ambulance. They were led by the captain's old friend, Colonel Gauntlett. The men were soon at work clearing the few scattered lumps of twisted and half-melted grey matter that remained, along with the burned-out Austin.

'I feel I ought to tell you, Colonel, that this is a strictly secret operation connected to a secret weapon. No word of the nature of this clear-up must reach anyone at all, no matter what. As far as anyone else is concerned, we brought down a bomber here, a fluke event. This is a top priority.'

'Fully understood, Captain,' the colonel said. 'The man Viktor has only a superficial wound, I am told.

The bullet passed through the muscle and tissue of his upper arm and came out again. Luckily your Mata Hari over there turned out to be a bad shot,' he said, indicating Ruth with his cane.

'Incidentally,' he added, 'you might remind your corporal here to salute an officer from time to time.'

By eight o'clock the soldiers had collected up most of the metal lumps and put them in a trailer attached to the back of the lorry. Apart from the gaping crater and churned earth, there was not much to show for the downed aircraft – though they had found my rifle and the captain's pistol and the very pistol Ruth Greville had used among the debris.

She stood watching it all, her arms cuffed behind her back. Her coat flapped in the wind, along with her normally perfectly brushed hair. As the soldiers were packing up, she suddenly shouted out, 'Heil Hitler!' Though of course, she couldn't salute the way she would have liked.

'You think that was a bomber,' she called out again, 'brought down here? Well, I can tell you it was not any sort of bomber. Where are the bodies of the crew? Were there any German markings on those bits of wreckage? No, of course not, because that craft was not of this world at all, but from another planet far from here, and soon the Reich will join forces with the beings from that place, and together we will conquer the world.'

'You tell 'em, Eva,' one of the soldiers shouted back at her. 'Look out, it's the Martians coming – oooh.' The other soldiers laughed.

'She's mad, of course,' Captain Holloway said. 'A Nazi spy and a fanatic. Put her in the back with the rest of the rubbish.'

Ruth was quickly manhandled into the lorry.

'Who's the boy?' the colonel asked, pointing at Tom. 'A local?'

'In one way, yes; now he's more of an evacuee,' Captain Holloway said.

Who knew where Tom was from now? It was impossible to let on that he was from this place, but forty or so years ago. It was also impossible to know the extent of his powers yet.

The captain turned to him. 'When we get back to London, Tom, I want you to talk about everything that has happened to you; everything.'

The craft, or the parts of it left behind, were of course already securely buried deep underground on top of Gallows Hill. Once the surface wreckage had been cleared, there was little to show for the extraordinary events of just a few days before. The grass surface was torn away in areas, and deeply scarred, but most of the disturbed earth had fallen back into the crater when the smaller craft took off. Once the grass had grown over the scar again, there would be almost no trace of the crash. The official version was that an experimental enemy bomber had been brought down and destroyed before it reached Warmwell aerodrome. The crash site was classified, and no news of the incident was ever published. Those locals who had seen the lights or heard the explosions that night had their own theories. After all, it was not the first time that unexplained events of this kind had occurred on Gallows Hill.

Tom Pile accompanied us to London for extensive questioning. He came to stay with my aunt Dolly, who welcomed him as the orphan that he was, and lavished her own brand of kindness on him, so that he soon blossomed. We still had no idea of the extent of his abilities or how the 'angels' had been able to modify and mutate his nature. By December he was feeling well enough to submit to new and more extensive interviews on what he remembered of his abduction.

Tom was seconded into Department 116 as an operative, along with Viktor Prejm, who happily made a full recovery. After all, the war wasn't won yet, and someone with Tom's abilities was a more than useful addition to Captain Holloway's roster. Of course, we knew that the Germans knew we had him, and they would surely try to get at him again. That was for another time; for the moment he was as safe as anyone could be in the middle of the Blitz.

Ruth Greville was the daughter of a Nazi sympathizer among the upper echelons of the aristocracy. There were many who played that game in the early days but saw sense when war came. He was interned, and she was eventually tried in secret for treason. Normally in wartime this carried the death penalty. However, with all her ramblings and testimony about beings from another world, she was certified insane and detained in a maximum security institution at Herrison in Dorset – the same place where old Gawen ended his days all those years before.

Tom Pile's verbal testimony

Excerpt from a wire recording made at Department 116
Thursday 14th December 1940

*'Tell us your story,' the voices said. 'We want to hear your
story – all of it.'*

*That was when I started speaking out loud to the night
stars all around me and to the music, the voices in my head.
They said, 'That's it. Go on . . . go on . . . tell us, tell us
all.'*

*I couldn't bring myself to shoot the stag. Something
stopped me. I don't know what it was. The animal stood
there, shining white in the darkness. It was alert too; it
knew something was up. Maybe it had the smell of us, of
old Gawen and me. He certainly smelled bad enough, did
Gawen, and even the stiff old poacher's sacks we had with
us stank of rancid meat and old blood. Surely a white hart
could sense that in the air; could sense us and our intention
to kill . . . Old Gawen took the gun from me.*

*'Go on,' he whispered to me with his rotten breath.
'Go on,' and he pushed the gun back at me, all fierce, and
said under his breath, 'Here's your chance, boy,' and he
spat that word fiercer than the rest. 'Go on, you damned
boy . . . prove yourself.'*

I looked down the barrel and the stag stood there, still.

'Go on,' he whispered at me. His chin was dug in hard on my shoulder. 'Time is a-wasting. Nice and gently now.'

I lowered the rifle and said, as quietly as I could, 'No.'

He snatched the rifle away from me again and spat out, 'Coward! Useless-arsed little whelp!' and he steadied the gun against the side of a tree.

The stag shifted, turned almost as if it wanted to present itself as an easy target. Its chest was now square on to us. Everything was quiet. The stag's breath misted out. I realized I couldn't let it happen, no matter how hungry we were for some decent meat. This just wasn't right – I knew it, and I had to stop it then and there. I broke the strange hush, I broke the silence, and I shouted out loud right at the stag.

'GO ON.'

Gawen fired the shot at the very moment I cried out, and the shot deafened me for a second. My ears sang and I heard a whistling noise.

The stag's front legs folded under it and it fell to the ground.

'You little bastard,' Gawen shouted harshly, right into my ear, and he struck me across the back in anger. 'What in Hell were you thinking of? You put me off my aim, and now that thing is mortal wounded and suffering. You'll have to go and finish it off, and right now.'

The stag was down but still alive. I could see it was

breathing 'cos its chest was rising and falling and its hot breath was still misting. Gawen came and stood in front of me and pushed an antler-handled knife hard into my hand.

'You'll go over there now, you little turd,' he said, spitting his words out at me in a fury. 'You'll deliver one quick blow to that thing's heart right now. Do it and I'll let you live. Do it and I'll let you cut it up and carry it back over your shoulder in sacks. Fail, and I will shoot you dead without a thought. What do I care for you! Not a whit, not a farthing.'

'I won't bloody do it,' I said.

'Then you'll get nothing but a bullet,' he said. ''Tis the last time anyone sees you, young Pile.'

I didn't care; I didn't believe he would do it. So I walked away from him, throwing his filthy sacks down on the ground.

'Give me the knife,' he shouted out, 'you useless—'

'No,' I screamed at the top of my voice, and then I threw the knife with its rough-edged antler handle. I threw it away as far as I could among the trees.

'You ungrateful little swine,' he screamed back at me in a fury. I shouldn't have thrown the knife away. Part of me knew that in one way he was right. I should have gone over and put the poor beautiful animal out of its pain and misery, out of its death agony; I should have killed it clean. But I ran off as fast as I could before Gawen could get a bead on me and shoot me, because I really thought that he would. So I ran towards the stag. I didn't care any more – not about being hungry or working for old Gawen or killing, or being killed even. It all drained away from me. It was as if there was a voice in my head, a gentle voice, though loud in my mind – a gentle, loud, whispering, shouting voice telling me to walk forward, to come on into the light.

Then there was the light.

The light was suddenly there – like the one my dad and me saw, only this was the brightest light ever. It was white or silver, and it filled the trees and the spaces between the trees. I was walking now. I couldn't run any more. I was walking into a wholly silver and white place which hurt my eyes, but I couldn't turn away. It was as wide as the sky and as high as the sky, which was not dark any more, and the white stag was somehow beside me, up on its feet, all mended. The light dazzled my eyes, but I could see that the stag was walking quietly beside me as if it were my own pet dog or something. I heard a shot from the gun that Gawen had taken from me – at least, I think that's what it must have been. It sounded like that gun, but it seemed loud and far away at the same time. Something hit me then, and bored into me. It didn't hurt, but I felt a hard tug at my upper arm. Then I felt a gentle sensation, but I couldn't tell what it was or what had made it. There were shapes moving: a darker – a very slightly darker white shadow against the brighter white. There were tall shapes, and they were like walking trees, and the shapes were talking to me. They were telling me to keep walking, and I did. The forest had gone away, and there was just this bright space which stretched all around me now, from side to side and from top to bottom. I could see nothing but the silver and white light. It was all around me, shining down in beams like you sometimes saw in those pictures we were given in Sunday school. Those special beams of light all around the halo on the head of Jesus. I knew then that these were the angels from Heaven, and thought that perhaps old Gawen really had killed me with my dad's rifle because he was that cross because I wouldn't let him kill the white stag.

I didn't feel dead, though.

What would being dead feel like anyway?

I could still feel the solid ground under my feet, even though it was white now, and brighter than the big snowfall of last January. That was when the snow came in the night, and the next morning, why, it was up as high as the tops of the hedges. That was when the white snow was as high as the hedge tops and you could walk on the hedges all the way up and down Gallows Hill if you dared to. If you fell, it was only into the soft cold blanket of snow in any case. Out in the woods near Powerstock it was even brighter than that snow had been under the most glaring noonday sun.

The voice in my head told me to be calm, but it didn't

say any words. The voice in my head wasn't really a voice; it was like a piece of music, but I knew what it meant without hearing any words. I knew that I was meant to keep walking until I was in the middle of the light; where it was at its very brightest, shining like a star, but a star that was somehow in the fallow field below the Rectory garden. If you were up in the tree in that field on a clear day, with no sea fret, you could see the sea itself in the distance – and, if you were lucky, the sun sparkling on the sea too. Now the centre of the white light looked like the sea sun sparks had landed in that fallow field. That is how bright it was.

I put my arm over my eyes and looked away from the light and at the stag instead. The poor animal was standing right next to me, and one of the angels was touching it or stroking it. Well, I thought it was an angel, but maybe it was just me talking to the beast and stroking its hot rough coat. In any case the light made it hard to see clearly what was happening, but the animal was calm enough, and it moved its head in turn towards me. I could look right into its big brown eyes. I could see how the whites were creamy and slightly bloodshot as its eyes rolled back a little in its head. It looked at me, and I understood then that it didn't understand me at all. It might look into my eyes, but it wasn't thinking about the whites of my eyes. It wasn't thinking at all, it was just . . . being.

I don't know how I understood or even thought about

that. The angels must have told me or helped me to think it.

I kept my arms across my forehead, shielding my eyes, trying to look away from the brightness. I felt a movement under my feet, as if I were being lifted high up into the air. In that moment the white light, the silver light, the brightness suddenly snapped off into complete blackness. I felt the stag buck under my hand. 'Whoa,' I said. 'Whoa. Gentle there,' as if it were the Reverend Stone's dear little trap pony instead of a lost and frightened wild thing. It backed away, and I felt the sharp antlers against my hand as it lowered its head.

I looked up and saw all the stars.

All of them.

I saw other things. I saw a blackboard with white letters, white words. The words were calling out to me. I knew then that there were others like me. Some might be out there, among the stars. Others were down on the ground. I wondered if I would ever meet them.

All the stars – so many stars, and all bright and shining clear. They were in a great arc shape over my head. The stars were clearer than I had ever seen them, even from Gallows Hill on a clear night, and they were all around me; not just above me, but below me too, and beside me and behind me. The angels had taken me floating in the sky on my way to Heaven with the white stag, which was healed now – there was no blood on its chest. The music in my head was gentle, like a lullaby that you might sing to a baby to get it to sleep. I felt sleepy too. My arms and legs were heavy. I wanted to lie down next to the stag, which was curled up next to me with its legs folded under it, asleep among the stars.

I thought that if I did the same thing as the stag, I would never wake up again; I would really be dead and asleep for ever under a mound of grass and cowslips in the churchyard at Litton Cheney, so close to our own little house. I might wake up in a wooden box like the one my mother was put in. Then I saw the grass on the tombs so clearly, all grown long, and I saw my father cutting it, heard the whisper of his scythe, all busy in the good days; and the voice music of the angels in my head told me now to go on, go on, talk . . . talk to us. Tell us your story – we want to hear your story, all of it . . .

AFTERWORD

I actually started writing this book some time in the 1980s. I had imagined an adventure where mysterious unexplained lights are seen on the Dorset hills by a labouring boy in the 1900s. As is the case with many ideas, I didn't finish it, and the notes and jottings were put aside in a drawer, only to be developed much later.

I had the initial idea after I got to know the real village of Litton Cheney in the mid 1970s. My wife's parents lived there. The village is in the Bride Valley in West Dorset. There really is a steep hill that runs from the village up to the A35, which is the main road between Dorchester and Bridport. In real life this hill is called Whiteways; in my story I called it Gallows Hill instead. There is a Gallows Hill in Dorset, but it is nearer to Corfe Castle, in the east of the county. Things and people from real life often get switched around in made-up stories. My book is wholly a work of fiction, but bits and pieces of fact and history and real people have been smuggled in.

There was a real Tom Pile. He lived in the cottage described in the story. He was an agricultural labourer and gardener. He had fought in the First World War, which was the only time he ever left the village. In his later years, still living in the cottage on Church Path, he worked for my parents-in-law, who in the early 1950s had bought the nearby old rectory, with its big wild garden. I was struck by Tom Pile's name and wanted to use it, and so in my imagination I kidnapped him in his fourteenth year and took his alternate self on a whole new and divergent path. I have, of course, invented the big adventure that befalls him on that dark night in the woods near the village of Powerstock – which, by the way, also exists. A good friend was out in the woods near Powerstock and actually saw a white hart on one occasion, and so that too was filed away and finally entered the story.

There really was a Michael Holloway too, but he was not a special investigator into the unexplained. He was in fact an oil company executive, and along with his lovely wife Iris did much to encourage and enlighten me when I was a callow young art student. They pressed books and gramophone records into my eager hands – 'You must read this; you must listen to this,' and so on. My fictional Captain Holloway has, I hope, absorbed some of the real M. D. Holloway's generous and sterling qualities.

Jack Carmody is an invention, as is his aunt Dolly, although he shares my taste for old horror films and she shares my own late mother's brisk matter-of-factness.

I don't know if strange lights have ever been seen over the hills of Dorset, but at certain times of year it certainly seems possible: standing in the high churchyard on a clear winter night and looking at the stars, free of light pollution, is to properly experience the numinous and the transcendental.

Ian Beck

ACKNOWLEDGEMENTS

I am more than grateful to Natalie Doherty and Annie Eaton for their enthusiasm, encouragement and patient editing. To Laurence Beck for calm assistance with making the images. To the special qualities of the village of Litton Cheney in West Dorset. Finally, special thanks to Toby Robson and the staff of the Royal Ballet School at White Lodge Richmond Park, Surrey.

Read on for an exclusive extract
of the next story about Captain Holloway,
Corporal Carmody and Tom Pile:

THE
MIRACULOUS
RETURN OF
ANNICK GAREL

Author's Note:

Adolf Hitler's forces invaded France in the early summer of 1940. They swept through Belgium and the Netherlands. The German attack surprised the French, coming, as it did, through the forests of the Ardennes, and bypassing the strong French defences of the Maginot Line.

The French surrendered in June 1940, and France was occupied by German forces for most of the Second World War.

CHAPTER ONE

Douarnenez Fishing Port
Brittany, occupied France
Friday October 24th 1941

It was not the usual kind of storm.

There was no rain, for a start. Pierre Bouchard, skipper of the fishing boat Le Sillon, would have expected rain. The wet slate colour of the upper sky certainly promised it. There were lower clouds, too. They were a darker grey and they were stacked up well out beyond the harbour wall. There were flashes of lightning inside the lower clouds, but there was no thunder and, as yet, no rain. The granite of the loading dock was relatively dry.

There was another brightly explosive but silent flash of dazzling light over the sea.

'Sacrebleu! Did you see that?' the skipper said to his son, young Pascal.

'Ball lightning,' Pascal said.

The skipper spat onto the ground. 'Either that, or the Germans are up to something.'

'Should we be taking her out at all?' Pascal said, jumping down from the harbour onto the deck.

'It's always worth a try,' his father said, scanning round the harbour. Most of the fleet boats were still tied up, waiting out the weather. 'Chance to get a head start on the others, at least. I heard a rumour that the Germans caught a whole boatload trying to cross over to England. If it's true, old Morvan said they might ban the fishing altogether. Even close to shore fishing.'

'They couldn't do that, could they?' Pascal said.

His father shrugged. 'They're capable of anything, if you ask me. It'll be cutting off their nose to spite their face, though. Where will they get their fish from then? Spain, at twice the price? It won't last. Where's our friend Madec, by the way? As if I didn't know.'

The skipper gestured to Pascal, who reached up beside the cabin window and pulled on the rope which operated the hooter. A single fierce blast echoed around the Quai du Grand Port. It was not long before a small man could be seen emerging at speed from the Atlantic Café on the quayside. He was holding his beret onto his head as he ran towards their mooring.

'Let her go now son, take her out,' the skipper said. 'Be good running practice for Madec.'

The rope was uncoiled from the bollard and pulled down onto the deck, and the skipper jumped down after it.

'Here he comes,' Pascal said while the skipper coiled the rope up against his elbow.

'There will come the day,' the skipper said, 'when he will make the leap and miss altogether. I certainly won't be the one to fish him out.'

Another bolt of silent blue white lightning lit up the sky behind Madec as he too jumped down onto the deck of Le Sillon. Madec always had a yellow Caporal cigarette stuffed firmly in the corner of his mouth, and it was always unlit. 'Morning, skipper,' he said, picking himself up and dusting down his overalls. 'Bit close that time.' He patted young Pascal on the shoulder. 'All right, lad?'

'Yeah, fine,' Pascal said, busying himself with the ropes.

They chugged out a kilometre or more from the harbour, until they seemed to be almost directly under the eye of the storm. It still raged, strangely silent, overhead. Pascal had never seen a storm quite like it. Great flashes of ball lightning exploded, a quiet blue-white behind the clouds. The sea itself, though, remained almost calm. There was a swell, but that was to be expected in late October.

The air felt charged with static electricity. The hairs on Pascal's arms stood up and he shivered inside his slicker. They set the nets and waited alone on the sea. There were no other boats to be seen, as yet.

The cork floats bobbed and Madec finally lit his filthy Caporal cigarette.

'Hear about Malboeuf?'

'What about him?' the skipper answered.

'Arrested and held in the town. German patrol caught him with two English airmen in his boat. He picked them up off a rescue buoy.'

'What can I say?' the skipper said. 'Times are hard, and we must all be very careful.'

The heavens opened an hour or so later. The rain poured down. It fell almost vertically from the rolling dark clouds. The lightning flashes pulsed again. One or two shafts of light hit the surface of the sea, one after the other. Pascal looked up and scanned the sky.

'Those look like searchlight beams, but shining downwards. I thought a plane was out looking for something, but there's no plane up there at all. There's no sound either,' Pascal said, shielding his eyes. 'How can it all be so quiet?'

'I wouldn't know, son,' the skipper said. 'Come on, time to earn your soup.'

The skipper had tacked in a half circle. Now it was time to start hauling in the nets. Cascades of thrashing silver sardines flowed out and onto the deck. Madec and Pascal swept them down into the hold with their hands.

The second net yielded an even bigger haul.

There was something else as well.

Among the flickers of silver there was a darker shape. A slumped body. It lay face down, tangled among the netting and the flickers of gleaming fish.

'Look at this!' said Pascal, waving over to his father. He struggled forward against the rolling wet deck and did his best to untangle the body from the netting.

Madec joined him. 'It's a girl!' he called.

He took a knife from his belt and cut at the tangle of netting wrapped round the body. Once she was cut free, he turned the girl over, onto her back. 'Looks to be about his age,' Madec said, shaking his head and indicating young Pascal.

The girl wore a long dark dress with a rust coloured apron tied over it. She was as pale as the fish bellies all around her. Her head was haloed with a tangle of long blonde curls, and her eyes gazed, apparently sightless, up into the rain.

'A proper mermaid,' Pascal said.

'Looks like it,' the skipper said. 'We've finally gone and fished one in.'

'Poor drowned child,' Madec said, and lifted the girl's hand away from the side of her body. He felt her wrist. Then he lowered his head down to her breast. It was at that point that she suddenly coughed and sprayed a mouthful of seawater out into his face.

'It's a ruddy miracle,' the skipper said, crossing himself. 'She's alive!'

'She is that,' said Madec. 'I can feel a pulse, but the poor thing's very cold.'

'We must turn back,' the skipper said. He took off his waterproof and laid it over the girl.

'Question is, skipper,' Madec said, 'where did she come from? There's no trace of another boat out here.'

'Submarine?' the skipper suggested.

'Maybe she just fell out of the sky,' Pascal said. 'She looks like an angel with that hair.'

MAP

The Green

Patrus City

Veil River (aka Suicide Stretch)

Matrus City

PATRUS

MATRUS

N
W E
S

The Outlands

Not to scale

NIGHTLIGHT PRESS

First Edition

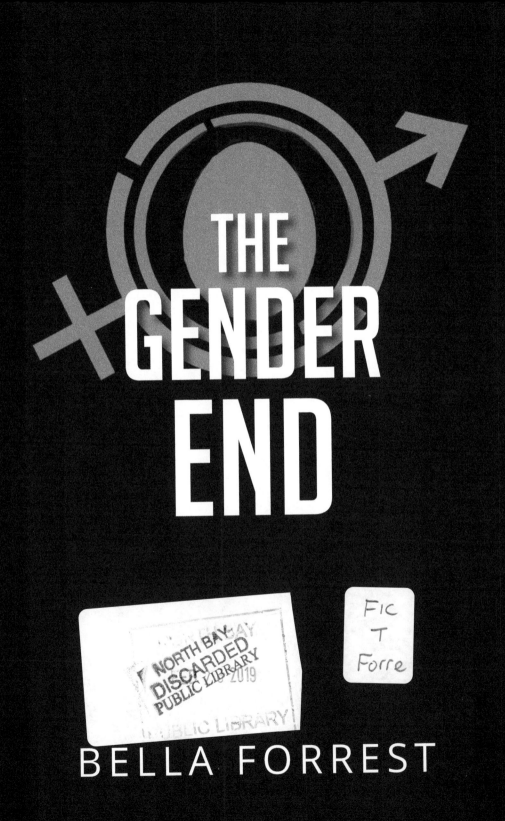

THE GENDER END

BELLA FORREST

CHAPTER 1

Viggo

Exiting the plant was surreal. What had been a cacophony of noise and chaos barely an hour ago was now replaced with the loud yet final roar of the fires that still burned on either side of this entrance. The rest of the noise consisted of muted sounds, sounds that I immediately gravitated toward—soft chatter, boots falling on the ground, and the groans of the wounded. Some people were crying, but quietly. Most simply stood around, vacant expressions in their eyes.

I recognized the look because I understood the feeling. It would be so easy to fall into that shelter of numbness, push away all that I had seen. The thought was tantalizing. I wouldn't have to think about Gregory, how small the bullet hole that had ended his life really was. Or the women I'd killed. Justified as I had been, it still didn't change the fact that I had erased people from existence today. None of them would ever feel the sun on their faces or the touch of someone they loved again.

There was guilt. I was alive, whole, save for a scraped shoulder and a few aching ribs. So many others had died. What made me special? Why was it their time and not mine? Where was the justice in any of that?

Alejandro's grip on my vest tightened, the fabric bunching uncomfortably around my neck. I adjusted my grip under his arm and glanced over at him. The older man was pale and his jaw set, determination stamped on his weathered face. I guided him around the corner to the wall, easing him down to the ground to keep from jostling his mangled hand. His good hand patted my shoulder as he leaned back, his breath coming in sharp gasps.

I squatted next to him as Tim helped Mags to a position leaning next to her uncle. The young woman still looked dazed, her blue eyes glazed and unfocused. As soon as her back touched the water treatment plant's wall, she jerked around, blinking as if she couldn't understand how she'd gotten there.

"Sit down, Mags," Alejandro grunted up at her, and she looked down at him, equally surprised to see both of us there.

"What? No, I can't." She looked up, biting her lower lip for a second. Shaking her head, she squared her shoulders. "I need to find Amelia," she said after a moment, referring to her third in command. She seemed as though she were grasping at straws, trying to stay in control when she really just needed to rest. I knew the feeling, and that only made it more painful to watch. "We need to be on cleanup and—"

"Sit down," ordered April, rounding a car, a first-aid bag already in her hands, and I started. The last time I had seen her she had been flying into a water vat, one continually churned by a massive arm used to keep the liquid moving.

"April! How did you—"

"I'm an excellent swimmer," she replied curtly, meeting my gaze. "And I promise to tell you all about it later. Right now, you have to let me check you out." She looked at me and frowned. "Who's in worse shape?"

I straightened up, my left side aching hard enough for me to reach out and use the wall as support. "I'm not sure. Alejandro's hand is pretty bad, but Mags is acting a bit dazed. She was lucid minutes before, but…"

Before I could finish the sentence, April had the scanner out, running its beam over Mags' face. Mags raised her hands, swatting lightly at the scanner, but April reached out and grabbed the woman's wrists, pinning them together almost effortlessly. I stared in surprise as Mags hissed in pain. April cocked her head, and moved the scanner down to Mags' shoulders and arms. She released her grip almost immediately, scanning the rest of her body while Mags massaged her shoulder.

"Mild shock, but likely because of a simple dip in endorphins due to adrenaline leaving the system," April told her. "Water and food for you, and you need to be checked out again for that shoulder. It's partially dislocated, but it can wait for a few hours. Alejandro?"

Alejandro looked up at her, his blue eyes already swimming with reluctance. "There are worse cases," he insisted, but April ignored him, squatting down. If the condition of his hand caused her any emotional discomfort, April didn't show it, which impressed me. I couldn't look at it without getting queasy—the fingers were bent at unnatural angles, like a glove had been shoved onto him all wrong, thanks to an enhanced woman crushing it with one hand.

"Viggo!" I looked up to see Tim pointing behind me, and turned in time to see Morgan and Cody moving toward us, awkwardly supporting Jay's weight between them. All three of them were wet, as if they had been swimming with all their clothes on. For all I knew, they had been. Cody was shivering violently in the chilly night air, but he looked like he was not physically damaged. Emotionally, I couldn't say. Morgan looked fine, thanks to the Liberator suit she was wearing; it was Jay who had my heart pounding with worry.

Even though he was wearing black, I knew he was bleeding. A torn blue scrap of fabric had been tied around his midsection, the front saturated with blood. I was moving before I could even register it, my hands going out to take the young man's weight off Morgan and support him.

"April!" I shouted over my shoulder as I gently turned him over.

Jay's wide blue eyes looked up at me, his lips quivering. Sweat and water droplets streaked his face, and I could see how much pain he was in by his intense grimace and labored breathing. Worse than that, though, was a kind of numb, dejected, absolute misery in his eyes.

"She shot me," he whispered hoarsely, and I could see how much effort it was taking him just to talk. My stomach churned seeing the young man so pale and hurt… and I felt a wash of rage coming over me, as well as ice-cold fear. Where was Violet?

"Who did?" I asked. "What happened?"

I looked up at Morgan for an answer; her mouth was pinched, her green eyes hard and angry. "Desmond shot him. It was a mess." She met my gaze and faltered for a moment. "She and some wardens captured Violet and took her onto a heloship. But Solomon was following us. I saw him jump onto the heloship from the top of the plant. He's… He's been helping us, so maybe he's helping Violet? I-I hope he's helping her. I couldn't, I didn't have time, I was fighting my—uh—" She faltered again, her head shaking.

Jay coughed, and I looked down at him as he took in another shuddering breath. Tim was kneeling next to him, holding his hand over Jay's wound, his silver eyes worried. "Tell him who you are," Jay said, addressing Morgan. "Trust him."

I looked from Jay to Morgan and back again, but Jay was focused solely on Morgan. Despite the severity of his injury, his face was firm—and dead serious. A small hand pressed insistently on my shoulder, and I gently lay Jay down as April pushed me out of the way. She ordered Jay not to move as I stepped back a few feet and looked at Cody and Morgan.

"What is Jay talking about, Morgan?"

It was Cody who answered, his voice oddly hollow. "She's… a princess from Matrus. She killed her twin sister."

I looked down at the young boy, and back to Morgan, wondering if it could possibly be true. It was all so very much to take in. Violet was either in enemy hands or Solomon was on board—and both ideas were awful for completely different reasons. Morgan was a princess… and had killed her twin? I was going to need the story on that. But there were so many things that needed my attention. Jay was wounded, Cody looked lost and broken, Alejandro and Mags were injured, and… My mind kept going to sickening places, where Violet was already dead. I had to go after her.

"I'm nothing like my sisters," announced Morgan flatly, interrupting my thoughts. The look of sheer disgust on her face made it hard for me to believe she was lying.

Blinking at her, I nodded, and then turned away, needing a minute to sort through what I could do something about and what I couldn't. The injured were going to be cared for by people more qualified than me, so that was off my list. Morgan could wait. We just needed to notify Ms. Dale and Henrik about who she was, but if what Cody was saying was true—and at this point, I doubted the kid was cogent enough to think of a lie—then that meant that whatever her background, she was definitely on our side. So she could stay.

"How long ago did they take Violet?" I asked, turning around.

Morgan's brows drew together over her green eyes, and she checked her watch, her mouth moving slightly. "About… I don't know, twenty, twenty-three minutes ago?"

"Okay." I squeezed my fingers together, activating my microphone. "Jeff, how much fuel is left in the heloship, exactly?"

There was a pause, and then Jeff's voice filled the line. "The readout says five percent, Viggo, but I'm not quite sure what that means in terms of flight time."

"It means about twenty minutes of flight, probably less," supplied Amber's voice in our ears, a strange reminder that half of what I was saying was still being broadcast to members of all our teams. "What's going on?"

"Violet was taken by Desmond on a heloship, heading…" I looked at Morgan expectantly, and her frown deepened, her eyes anxious.

"East," she supplied.

"East," I repeated into the comm. "Solomon was seen on the helo-ship as well, so there's a chance he got in and caused some damage. We need to get to a Patrian airfield, and find some fuel, so we can track the heloship down."

"You can't," replied a rich masculine voice, and I recognized it as Logan Vox, one of the rebel leaders we had recruited to take out the soldiers at the plant. "It's the reason I went into hiding and started re-cruiting for the rebellion. The Matrians started collecting pilots and dismantling aircraft. Our storehouses for parts—fuel, tools, munitions... they were all cleared out. It'll take at least a few days to repair the heloships, if we can even find the parts we need to repair them. It'd be too late at that point."

"Well," said Ms. Dale imperiously, her voice firm and commanding. "We'd better figure something out. Violet Bates is the reason we're all here and in this fight, boys and girls. She's the one who cracked this conspiracy wide open, and we owe it to her to go after her. So let's think of a way."

As if on cue, a car roared up toward us. Alarmed, I turned and yanked my gun around, my heart pounding uncomfortably, only to relax my aim when I saw Owen throwing open the door. Blood streamed from a small cut over his eyebrow, but the rest of him seemed relatively unscathed.

"Viggo," he shouted when he spotted me. "There's something I have to—"

"Madre de *dios*!" I looked past Owen to see Cruz standing on the other side of the car, his uninjured hand covering his mouth. My small amount of relief that Cruz had escaped further injury was overwhelmed by concern over what he was looking at. "What is that?" he demanded.

"Desmond," Owen replied grimly.

I quickly crossed the twenty or so feet that separated us and threw open the rear door. I immediately had to look away. If it weren't for the hair and the eyes, there would be no way of discerning the identity of the... well, pulpy remains of human lying in the backseat, clumsily thrown atop what looked to be some kind of tarp. I was surprised her eyes were still intact, given the remains of her face alone. I doubted I'd ever be able to forget the image of an exposed and broken jaw pushing through her flayed skin like that, while her still-open eyes stared vacantly at the seat ahead. I took a closer look at Owen and realized he was covered in blood, likely from carrying her.

"You moved her?" I asked him, still not comprehending why he would bring us such... decimated remains.

"Yeah, well..." He met my gaze, his eyes hard. "It seemed like the right thing to do. After all, people should see that even monsters can be killed."

The queasy feeling in my stomach remained. "It's true. But that's pretty, uh, gruesome." In truth, it was hard to connect that broken, mutilated body to the woman who had orchestrated so many of the awful plans that had changed the face of Patrus—and Violet's and my lives—forever. I found it hard to feel the anger, hard to feel that she was really gone. I knew this had been more merciful than the end she'd deserved, but it didn't make me feel anything at the moment other than disgust.

Owen's eyes glinted, and the hard look didn't fall from his face. "Look, I didn't bring her here for your approval. I brought her here because she fell—she almost fell *on* me—from the heloship that escaped the plant. I thought it was important for people to see, and it might be useful in dealing with the Matrians... but more importantly, I marked the coordinates where she landed. Maybe Thomas can triangulate the starting location from where the body landed. *We could track Violet.*"

The thought sent a pulse of energy through me. I immediately stood up and moved over to one of my men, asking him to give me his comms. Within seconds, I was back to Owen, holding the equipment out to him. He quickly slipped it on.

"Thomas," his voice buzzed in my ear. "I found where Desmond hit, and marked the coordinates. Do you think you can—"

"Are you sure she's dead?" Ms. Dale demanded. "We need proof. This is something we can't leave to chance—"

"I'm sure," I replied, cutting her off. "Owen brought her corpse back. She's definitely dead."

If Thomas had any triumph or sorrow over Desmond's death, his voice didn't show it. "Give me the coordinates, Owen."

I moved back over to Morgan as Owen began listing off the coordinates, questions burning through my mind. How had he and Violet gotten separated? "Morgan, why wasn't Owen with you?"

Morgan blinked at me, and then seemed to sag in relief as she noticed the blonde man by the car. I could tell by her expression that she was in shock... or maybe just drained. It was hard to tell the difference these days.

"Thank God he's okay," she muttered, pushing some of her hair behind her ear. "He drew off several of the enhanced Matrians. We were hopelessly outnumbered, and he shot at them and distracted their attention."

I made an instant decision not to be mad about Owen abandoning his post as Violet's bodyguard. I was sure he had done his best to keep Violet as safe as he could, all things considered. Besides, the man had been given an impossible task. The only way to keep Violet safe was to lock her up and throw away the key, and I would never ever let that happen to her, so it looked like a lifetime of reckless adventures for me. Not that I would complain—if we could just get her back from this latest one alive. I felt like praying to whatever was out there to keep her safe, but I felt even more like rushing after her as fast as I possibly could.

First things first. "They found Desmond's body," I informed Morgan quietly. "She was thrown from the heloship."

"Good," she replied, crossing her arms across her chest.

Cody started to cry quietly, and Morgan's face went from satisfied to mortified. Immediately she knelt down and pulled the boy into her arms, holding him and whispering softly to him. I watched them both as I waited for Thomas' analysis on the radio, listening to her tell him that it was over, and by picking up bits of their conversation I caught on to the fact that Desmond had fired at Cody, turning the entire boy's world upside down. My heart ached for him, but deep down, I was glad he had seen that darkness in Desmond before she had died. It would be good for him in the long run.

It was finally starting to process—like waking up and realizing the last night hadn't been a dream, but a memory. God, I was so happy she was dead. Now that I'd had a taste of a moment of thinking of the world without Desmond Betrand's evil schemes, I wouldn't apologize for that happiness. That woman had been the source of all my troubles since I'd met Violet. Well, one of the sources—the other was still at large. I just hoped Violet was all right.

I also hoped Desmond had been bluffing about her threat with the boys, because if she wasn't, we would have less than a week to find a way to rescue them or break Elena's hold over them before her "people" started executing them. It had sounded like an absurd plea that she'd made when we'd kidnapped her, just to force us not to execute her—but with Desmond and Elena, we could never really be certain.

"I have a trajectory mapped out," Thomas reported after a few long moments, snapping my attention back to the task at hand. "According to my calculations, if the ship was still flying on the heading Morgan pointed out, and using Desmond's body as a reference… as long as the trajectory hasn't changed, it would cross over a small part of the city in Matrus, and then… just keep going. Into The Outlands."

The pit of my stomach dropped. I fought the urge to collapse. I couldn't afford to—there was still time, either to stop Violet from getting out there… or just to follow her into it. There was still hope, too: Desmond's body confirmed that Solomon had gotten on board, or at least that there had been struggle enough for someone on our side to get rid of her once and for all. The fact that nobody had reported a ship going down, and Owen hadn't seen it either, meant they could still be flying. And even if we would have no way of knowing what was happening with the ship once they were past Matrus City, I had to go after her.

"Great," I said. "Now what do we do about our gas problem?"

"Well, I have an idea," said Henrik through the comm, and something in his tone hooked me immediately. His voice practically exuded the level of confidence I needed for this mission to succeed.

"I'm all ears, Henrik," I replied, trying to keep the impatience from my voice.

"We can get it from the Matrians."

"That's brilliant, Henrik," transmitted Ms. Dale. "The airfield is just over the river, so it should be within range of the fuel we have left, near the border between the city and The Green. It's also more isolated, so it's perfect."

I paused, and then felt the corners of my mouth pull up, even as Vox came back on the line. "You're insane!" he said. "That's a suicide mission."

"Not if it's done right," replied Amber calmly over the line. "Actually, I think it's genius. Elena certainly wouldn't see it coming, not so soon after we stopped her again. She'd be expecting us to try and put out fires here—"

"Something we should be doing," added Drew, one of the other rebel leaders, into the comms. I looked over and saw him leaning against a truck sixty feet away, his arms crossed over his barrel of a chest.

"And we *will* be doing that," said Henrik without worry. "We only need a small force of pilots to double as our assault force. Think about it, Logan. While we're at it, we could steal some of their heloships and cripple the rest. That'll keep Elena out of our hair for a little bit, and get us a bigger advantage for the next engagement."

"My pilots are ready for this," said Amber. "And I can get us to their airfield on the fuel we have left."

"Like hell I'm going to let some amateur pilot who thinks she knows best assume command over this thing," thundered Vox.

"Considering you taught me everything you know, I think you better just sit down and shut up right now, *Logan*," Amber snapped waspishly back, and I blinked. Was Logan Vox the heloship pilot who had taught Amber how to fly, ultimately setting off the chain of events that had caused her father to decide to marry her off to repay his gambling debts? If so, that was… a remarkable coincidence. And also odd. After all, Logan was an heir to the Deepvox legacy, or he would've been, had things not gone to hell in a handbasket. Why wouldn't Amber's father have just tried to pressure Logan *himself* into marrying her to help cover his debts?

There was a stretch of silence, followed by, "Amberlynn?"

Amber really hated that name, so I doubted very much that she would respond to it. But this time I was wrong—which meant something. Like she'd had more of a relationship with this guy than I'd imagined.

"Oh, have you finally realized it's *me*, you thick-skulled moron?"

There was another pause on the line. Then Vox's voice came back. "Of course I knew it was you. But it didn't seem like the kind of thing to discuss over the comms during the *mission*, thank you very much. I didn't think you'd remember me, anyway."

"As if." Amber's voice was deeply scornful, making it clear to all that the memories she was discussing weren't pleasant. "Whatever. I have bigger fish to fry than dealing with your spoiled butt. Viggo, I'm rounding up my pilots and heading to Jeff's location. Meet me there."

"Dammit, fine! My men will be there too," declared Vox, his irritation evident.

I exhaled. Any other moment I would have been floored by the amount of hidden drama between these two, but right now, I couldn't keep my mind on anything but getting to Violet. I pressed my fingers together. "Henrik, Ms. Dale? Can you—"

"Keep things together until you get back?" asked Ms. Dale dryly. "Do you even have to ask? Go get our girl and get her home. And give Elena a black eye for me while you're at it. I'm going to be restructuring command anyway, taking those still willing to fight and hitting the posts leading out of the city. We've already got groups heading out to check the known contaminated water sources. And some people who drank the tainted water to catch up to as well. We're going to try and round them all up to keep them from hurting anyone, maybe even stop them from hurting themselves, if we can. That'll take some time, but those heloships will make it faster, so hurry up and get out of here, boy. Us old-timers have got this."

"And I've got their backs while you're gone," added Owen.

I found the thought of all of them handling it comforting, even after everything that had happened, and I confirmed their transmission, already heading to a nearby vehicle. Tim followed me, his eyes wide.

"You coming?" I asked as I slipped into the driver's seat and turned over the engine. Tim hesitated, and then shook his head, looking back at where Jay was still lying on the ground, April working on him—her expression grim.

"I stay. Jay needs help. Henrik and Ms. Dale need help. You find Violet—bring home. I help here."

Pride burst from my chest, and I reached out and gently took the young man's shoulder. "Take care of them while I'm gone, okay?"

Tim nodded, his dark curls bouncing. "Be careful."

I waved a hand at him, dismissing the thought. If Violet was heading to The Outlands, then there was no telling what dangers we would come across. After all… nobody who had gone there had ever returned.

CHAPTER 2

Violet

"**Y**ou know, the next time you want to save my life, could you please avoid getting twenty thousand bullet holes in the process?"

I was back to talking to myself. Solomon was still unconscious, but was also still breathing, no thanks to my considerable efforts. Well, possibly thanks to my considerable efforts, but not if I couldn't get us back to Matrus in time for him to be saved. I had no idea whether he was bleeding internally, although I had accounted for each bullet's entrance and exit in my very thorough but nowhere near professional first aid.

"I just wish I could remember if exit holes were good or bad," I said, completing the thought out loud. I ripped off another long length of electrical tape using my teeth, and then carefully attempted to drape it over the cotton pad I had fixed to his shoulder. Placing it was tricky—with my right hand still in this stupid cast, it was a painstaking labor. I'd already lost several pieces of tape as the wind caught them and made them stick to themselves.

The wind was still screaming through the bay, and I shivered in the heloship's glacial temperature. My jacket helped me shrug off some of the cold, but my fingers were slowly going numb and my teeth chattered from time to time. Even though the cargo door was now closed, Solomon had definitely destroyed whatever seal there had been before, allowing the wind in.

Carefully, I applied the strip of tape, using the wind to sort of catch the end and keep it from dragging against anything until I had it where I wanted it. I worked quickly—periodically yawning as my body reminded me of how long it had been since I had slept, or even rested—pressing the tape down and then smoothing it over the contours of Solomon's chest, collarbone, and neck. I slid my cast against the tape as well, trying to create a seal around the white cotton pad, enough to put pressure on the wound, helping the blood to clot and stop the bleeding.

"See, I know what you're asking me," I said conversationally to the unconscious man. "Why didn't I attend Dr. Tierney's medical training when I had the chance? Well, I didn't have the chance, thank you very much! I was busy with planning a move, and, well, you know what? It's a pretty crappy excuse, and honestly... I'm sorry, Solomon. For... For everything."

Tears welled in my eyes unexpectedly when I got to the apology, and I quieted, trying to quell them, tamping down another piece of tape with shaking hands. I couldn't cry right now. There was too much to do. I just had to keep doing one thing at a time, as though this were all normal. That was what talking to Solomon had been about—keeping things light, keeping my mind off everything—but maybe it wasn't helping.

I sniffed hard once and leaned back to examine my work, sighing. It wasn't pretty, but it would hold. Leaning over the large man, I grabbed two packets out of the first-aid kit, examined their insignia, and then ripped the foil linings open. I had to use my mouth to peel away the plastic tabs on the back, but as soon as I managed it, I affixed one of the blood rejuvenation patches to Solomon's neck, as close to the carotid artery as I could manage. Then I placed the other on the opposite side.

It would have to do for now. I needed to remember to check on him in thirty minutes and apply another blood patch if his color wasn't any better, or if it had gotten worse. "I gotta go check on the flight path," I told him. "And see if I can get the pilot up. If I can't... Well... Let's not think about that."

I stood up, grabbing the pistol and the first-aid box. I had made Solomon the priority, reasoning that the geography east of Matrus was just deep canyons and gullies, supposedly like "up north" beyond The Green, where the boys who had failed the Matrian screening for aggression were sent to labor in the "mines". All lies.

Below us, there was actually nothing but rocky wasteland. At least I hadn't been forced to let my friend bleed out while I tried to steer a broken ship around a massive mountain range. However, there were no guarantees how long that would last.

Tucking the pistol into my pants was awkward, but I managed it as I turned and made my way back toward the cockpit. The other guns I had found were secured in the bathroom, on top of a panel that was clearly intended for some sort of ship maintenance. It wasn't the best hiding place in the world, but it would have to do. The other guard was unconscious and handcuffed to a part of the heloship's frame—I doubted she would be able to do a very thorough search at the moment.

I looked down at my watch as I passed her, which was good, because it meant my eyes happened to be looking in the right direction to see the "unconscious" guard's foot whipping sideways. I sidestepped, hopping up on the opposite bench and back down again, over her leg. I yanked out my gun, as casually as I could, as I looked at the larger woman, my exhaustion disappearing behind a rush of adrenaline and caution.

Her eyes opened to slits, and she sat upright, using her cuffed hand as a brace to pick herself off the ground. "It doesn't matter that you escaped," she said, smoothing back the wisps of hair that had slipped free of her neat bun with her other hand. "We'll catch you again, and this time you'll pay for your crimes."

I gaped at her. Was she slow, or just that determined? Either way, I wasn't having it. "Before you get all high and mighty issuing threats, I encourage you to think about the position we're in."

The warden—her sky-blue uniform marked her as a royal guard—looked around the bay, seemingly seeing it for the first time. My eyes drifted to the patch over her breast pocket, where the surname *Carver* was embroidered. The insignia above it marked her as a lieutenant.

"What happened?" she asked.

Glancing at the cockpit, or rather, the damaged remains of the cockpit, I sighed. "Desmond is dead. The controls to the ship are damaged, and we're flying into the middle of nowhere, and have been for the last"—I consulted my watch, trying to remember the last time I had looked at it—"hour or so. I'm on my way to wake up the pilot, hopefully, so that she can help us get out of this mess."

The woman squinted up at me, a frown line creasing the space between her thick eyebrows. "You're lying."

I resisted another sigh, unsurprised by her mistrust, and considered my options. Frankly, they all sucked. Tucking the gun back into the band of my pants, I pulled a tiny silver key out of my pocket—the one I had gotten out of her pocket a few hours earlier, while she was truly unconscious—and tossed it at her. She made no move to catch it, and it bounced off her chest and landed with a ping on the hard metal floor of the bay.

"I don't have time to earn your trust," I politely informed her. "So that's the key to your handcuffs. Use it or don't, I don't care, but if you become a threat to me or make this mess worse, I will shoot you." I made to leave, and then paused, as if a thought had occurred to me. Honestly, I was playing with dramatic timing on this one, but hopefully it would garner me a small amount of support from a woman who was, for all intents and purposes, an enemy. "Oh, and I tossed the rest of the guns overboard, so feel free to waste your time and search for one. Or don't. I really don't care."

Indifference would work, or at least I hoped it would. With luck, it would make her more likely to believe the severity of our situation, but also make her cautious about trying to attack me. Truth be told, I didn't want to have to kill either of the women on board. It wasn't their fault they viewed me as a criminal—they'd been fed nothing but lies. Not that it bothered me how they looked at me. I had been a criminal before. But it was much harder to take knowing that this time, they were condemning me for crimes I *hadn't* committed.

Anyway, none of that mattered now, and I needed to show them that it didn't, that we had to put aside our politics and differences to get a grip on this situation. We were going to have to work together. I didn't know much about heloships, but I damn well knew there was no way it was flying, landing, or *anything* as it was. I needed Lieutenant Carver to be up and walking. I needed her to not be a burden, but to actually help me of her own free will, because I wanted to get home alive. That meant I had to give a little early on, so that when things got hard, she'd hopefully be more willing to work with me.

I left the warden to her own devices and finished making my way into the cockpit. The pilot was where I had left her, still belted into her seat. Her seat, however, was lying opposite of the cockpit, just a few feet from the bathroom door, tipped on its side. The back of it was to me, but I could see her legs sticking out from the seat cushion, and they didn't seem to have moved.

Carefully and cautiously, I stepped around her. Her eyes were closed, but the warden in the cargo bay had been pretending before. Yet she hadn't been injured, and the pilot undoubtedly was—her left forearm was clearly broken, and there was a gash in her forehead. It had stopped bleeding some time ago, but dried blood was caked to her forehead, trailing down her nose and under her eye. The patch on her chest revealed her last name to be Durnell.

Reaching out, I took her pulse, relieved to find it still beating strongly, and then opened the first-aid kit. I sifted through the packets, and found the one marked with a hollow red square. Checking the list on the back of the lid, I confirmed it was the ammonia inhalant, and then cracked it open. Immediately a smell that reminded me of feline urine hit my nose, and my eyes began to water.

I held the packet under the pilot's nose, and her eyes twitched, and then snapped open. She jerked against the belt buckling her in, and then cried out in pain as she jostled her arm.

"Easy," I said soothingly, placing the opened packet into the box. The ammonia smell was still heavy, but it would fade quickly. "Take it easy."

"What happened?" she asked, panic thick in her voice. "Ah, God… My head."

"Wait, I have something for that." I consulted the itemized list on the back of the lid, and then pulled out a purple packet with a black circle in it. Opening it up, I pulled the backing off with my teeth and applied the adhesive side to her right temple, the one pointed at the ceiling. She winced—I wasn't gentle, but I wasn't being intentionally rough, either—and then a second later sighed in some relief.

"Thank you. That's better." She kept her eyes closed for a moment more, and then opened them again. "You're Violet Bates."

"I am, although if I were you, I wouldn't believe anything you've heard about me. But we don't have time to go through the rumors. The controls to the ship are busted, and we have been flying straight for the last hour."

The pilot frowned, and then her right hand began fiddling with the buckles keeping her in the sideways seat. I noticed immediately that several of the fingers on that hand were swollen, and I held up my hand, stopping her. "Your hand is hurt as well," I pointed out to her, and she stared at it as though she hadn't noticed earlier, her hazel eyes wide.

"I can't even feel them," she whispered, as if that thought frightened her, and I immediately empathized, while recognizing I didn't have the time to really show it.

"I'm sorry for that," I said. "But I need you to focus. Let me help you out of this."

The pilot nodded, but her gaze was still fixated on her hand. I reached for the buckle, and her head snapped over at the movement, her eyes bulging. "You can't! What if I can't feel my hand because I have spinal trauma? You could make everything worse!"

I hesitated, and then nodded. "Wiggle your toes?"

She blinked, and then her booted feet began to twitch slightly. "Are they working?" she asked, her voice barely a whisper.

Smiling in what I hoped would be interpreted as a reassuring way, I nodded. "They are. I doubt you have spinal damage. Can I undo this?"

"Can't you move the chair first?" she pleaded. "Stand it up?"

I shook my head. "The chair is too heavy." It really was. It was a monstrous frame of metal and padding that was meant to be welded into the ship. Amber had once told me it was supposed to keep the pilots safe in the event of a crash, but that meant the thing probably weighed several hundred pounds. "We have to do this now. The ship is flying on an unknown course into unknowable terrain."

She nodded, and I reached out to undo the clasp still holding her. I tried to break her fall, but the space was tight and one hand was essentially useless thanks to the cast. She dropped roughly, and unexpectedly, the last few inches to the ground, and gave an agonized cry as she landed on her hand.

"At least you can feel it?" I asked gently, trying to bolster her spirits as I helped picked her up.

It didn't work at all. The look she gave me was two parts anger, one part agony, and three parts revenge, but it couldn't be helped. I needed her help, and I felt a stab of irritation. I was literally the only one of the three of us doing anything to help her. I ignored the feeling, knowing that the way she felt about me didn't matter, as long as we could work together.

She leaned heavily on me, tears streaking down her cheeks. "It's really hard not to believe what they've said about you right now," she whispered accusingly, and I suppressed another surge of resentment, clenching my teeth together to prevent myself from saying anything too inflammatory. *Keep the peace*, I reminded myself. I was better than this. And I was beyond my long history of brawling for petty reasons, too… I hoped.

"I'm sorry that you're in pain," I said as I gently guided her around. "Just look at this place."

Her eyes narrowed as she surveyed the damaged remains of the cockpit. "Sweet mother. That monster gutted it!"

I bristled. Let her think whatever she wanted about me, but Solomon was a victim in all this. "He's not a monster. His name is Solomon, and he's my friend. If you want to blame anyone for what happened here, blame your precious Desmond. It's her fault he is the way he is, and I'm glad he threw her out of the cargo bay."

I wasn't surprised to find that I was glad she was dead. Well, relieved, anyway. Glad in the way that it felt like a great weight I'd been carrying around, a cloud of worry, nightmares, and fear, had suddenly evaporated, leaving the way clear for me to go on to other things. My hatred of her would take longer to cool and leave my body, but it would heal in time.

The pilot's face went pale at the mention of how Solomon had killed Desmond, and she looked at me with a healthy dose of panic in her eyes. "Is he still onboard?"

Nodding, I moved her forward a few steps, taking it slow for her. "He is, but he's unconscious. Desmond shot him a few times."

"He shouldn't still be... Belinda?"

I looked up and saw the warden who'd tried to trip me earlier ducking down to avoid hitting the overhanging ceiling as she stepped through the door, her brown eyes taking in the damage. She glanced over at the pilot and took a step forward.

"Kathryn, you're alive."

The pilot—Kathryn—groaned, but nodded. "Painfully so, but yes. Let me see what I can make of this mess."

Kathryn's arm pressed insistently on my neck and shoulder, but I didn't want to move any closer to Belinda—not with my gun in my pants. "Stand on your own. Belinda will help you, if need be."

Belinda gave me an incredulous look, but I gave Kathryn a moment and then stepped away from her, pulling my gun. Kathryn wobbled for a second, before Belinda moved in to take my spot supporting her. "We're not going to accomplish anything with a gun held on us," Kathryn announced softly.

"I'd agree with you," I replied coolly, "but there are two of you, and Belinda is much bigger than I am, *and* uninjured. I'm not certain I can trust you enough to work with you, but I need your help to repair the ship and get us back home."

"It seems you have an important decision to make," said Belinda, helping Kathryn to move forward so she could peer out the bubble window that made up the nose of the cockpit.

"Well, she'd better make it soon," whispered Kathryn, and I focused on her, noting her wide eyes and stiff spine. "Because I think I'd rather take the bullet than fly into that."

I stepped forward, keeping my gun trained on them both, and peered through the dark window, searching for the familiar sight of stars. They hung just as normal in the top half of the sky, but on the horizon, barely visible in the moonlight, a swirling black and gray wall of storm clouds in the distance blotted out the stars, growing larger as we hurtled toward it.

CHAPTER 3

Violet

We were soaring toward a cloud bank. It was still far away, but lightning flashed behind it, and the ominous clouds seemed swollen and turbulent, as if their thin mass were barely containing the storm raging within. Without the use of most of the instruments, not to mention the ability to control the aircraft, we would be completely unable to avoid any solid formation obscured by the storm, with no way to even tell there was an obstacle until the heloship hit it. Or lightning struck it. Or the violent winds tore it apart.

My heart thudded against my ribs, once, twice, even a third time, before my mind kicked itself awake, pushing through the uncertainty that had gained temporary control over my body. I looked at Kathryn and Belinda, and saw they were both looking at me. It took me another heartbeat to realize why.

The gun. Of course—it was ridiculous to think we could work together as long as they perceived I held the power. I looked down at it and then back at the pilot. "What do we do?" I asked as I ejected the magazine onto the floor and pulled back the slide to release the round in the chamber. The bullet and clip clattered to the floor, and I doubled over to pick them up. "You keep the bullets," I muttered, pushing them into Belinda's hands as I moved past her, shoving the now-useless gun into my pants. I still had the backup stash in the bathroom, so if worst came to worst, I could still resort to violence—right now it was merely a gesture. Although, from the gleam in Belinda's eyes, I knew she was considering taking the gun and the power, right now.

Unfortunately for her, we didn't have time for that. I looked over at Kathryn, who had gone back to staring frozenly out the window. "HEY!" I shouted, stomping loudly on the floor. Kathryn whipped her head back round to look at me. "We need to get this thing out of the way of that storm. You're the pilot. What. Do I. Do?"

Her terrified eyes blinked, and she took a deep breath, seemingly pulling herself together. "Right," she said, her gaze going back to the bubble window and the wall of storm clouds looming ever closer, her tongue darting out to swipe at her dry lips. "Right," she repeated, her eyes tracing the lines of damage.

"There's a panel there," she said, pointing to just behind where her uprooted seat used to be. The panel was clearly delineated in the floor, with some sort of chrome around the edges and a half-ring handle sitting on its side in a slotted space, so it lay evenly on the floor.

I slipped my fingers under the ring, prying it up so I could get a better grip. At the same time, Kathryn began to speak. Even though her voice was loud, her words seemed more directed at herself. "No displays. The column is heavy, indicating loss of hydraulic fluids. No response in over half the controls. How's it coming on that panel?"

Grunting, I pulled at it with my left arm, which was considerably weaker than my right, and began to lift the dense panel up, coming around it so that I was directly behind it and pulling. "It's been better! Belinda!"

Belinda was still standing there, her hands loosely clutching the magazine and single bullet I had handed her. "What's the point?" she asked numbly, her brown eyes staring out the window. "We're in The Outlands. Nothing ever comes back from The Outlands. We're screwed."

"Excellent defeat story, but I'm shooting for a happier ending. So get your butt over here and help me. RIGHT. NOW!" I wasn't sure how I managed it, but for an instant, my voice sounded exactly like Ms. Dale's—firm, uncompromising, and filled with an edge of superiority that surprised even me. It seemed to jolt Belinda from the fugue she had fallen into, and she moved toward me, a bit robotically.

I almost sagged in relief as she took some of the paneled door's weight from me. We heaved it over and looked down into the cavity we had opened up. Four blue glowing cables as thick as my wrist ran through it, held in by steel brackets. Dozens of other wires shot off from them, and an array of buttons, levers, and switches decorated all four sides.

Belinda and I exchanged looks, and she gave me a wide-eyed head shake. "This wasn't in the field manual," she said shakily.

"It's open," I shouted at Kathryn, ignoring Belinda, dropping to my belly and pointing over at where I had left the toolkit earlier—on the holotable in the center of the command deck. Belinda stood laboriously with a defeated sigh, but went to fetch it as Kathryn turned and examined it.

"Pull the red wires, and tell me what happens to the third cable from the left," she ordered, and I began yanking the wires from the plugs on the panels.

"The cable is flickering," I said as I finished. "It's rhythmic… What is that…?"

"It's the heart of the ship," Kathryn supplied, squatting down awkwardly. "It's the computer, or part of it, and if it's flickering, it means we have more control than I thought. If we can interface with it. I'm glad we got a response, but that's not super critical right now." She sounded relieved—well, as relieved as could be expected. "Now that you've pulled the red, flip those two switches—*those* two—the green and the yellow."

I followed her instructions, and something clicked overhead. The pilot stood up, wobbling slightly, and nodded up at a square panel that had just dropped from the ceiling. "Hydraulic hoses are going to be in there. I need you to pull that panel down so I can check the pump."

I stretched for it, but it was just out of reach. Looking around for something to stand on, I was rudely pushed out of the way as Belinda shoved me to one side. I balled up my fist and whipped around, expecting her to go for the gun, but she just rolled her eyes at me and reached up, easily pulling down the panel I needed. Four square metal rods extended from it as it came down. Inside were several thick plastic tubes attached to a cylindrical black metal device. The tubes were clear, save for several large dots of bright green liquid, clinging to their insides.

The pilot stared at the tubes, her eyes moving, and she cursed. "The pump is cracked. It must've happened when that *thing* yanked out the seat."

"His name is Solomon," I said sharply.

She gave me a hard look. "Your friend broke my arm and my hand and is responsible for this mess," she reminded me coldly, but I didn't feel ashamed for defending him. He wasn't fully in control of his actions. I fought off the urge to inform her of that, knowing we didn't have time. It wasn't relevant—but if they tried to hurt him, I'd throw them off the ship faster than they could say *what*.

Kathryn continued. "Belinda, there's a can of hydraulic fluid in the back. You, Violet, I need you to manually feed the fluid in. You're going to have to pour some into the tube and then blow, so we can get it into what's left of the steering column."

I nodded, a flash of lightning out the window catching my attention. "Awesome," I replied dryly, turning away from the storm and directing my attention back to the pump. Thunder clapped, and the entire heloship shuddered with it, setting my teeth on edge.

I yanked the feed tube, as Kathryn called it, off of the spout leading to the pump, and turned to the bay, watching Belinda as she effortlessly dangled from one of the cargo bay's roof beams, extracting a can from the red netting strung up over the bay. She dropped down with a clang and raced toward us.

"Excellent, Belinda," said Kathryn. "Grab a funnel from the tool kit and give it to Violet, then take what's left of the steering column and pull hard, to the left. It's going to fight you, so you have to keep pulling."

Belinda nodded. "Keep pulling," she repeated as she stooped over to grab the funnel. She helped me place the tip of the funnel into the tube and open the can of hydraulic fluid. If she felt any resentment for having to help me in my one-handed state, she managed to keep it to herself.

She moved around me to the column, and I began to pour, using the two most mobile fingers on my casted hand to carefully hold the tube. My fingers were freezing in the cold whistling in from the cargo bay, but I maintained my grip, knowing that dropping them right now could mean the difference between life and death. The can glugged as the green liquid shot out in jerky little spurts, beginning to fill the tube. I held it as high as I could, trying to get more in and keep air out, then set the can down, removed the funnel, and pressed my lips to the end of the tube, trying not to think about the chemicals I was about to put right next to my mouth. I hoped they weren't *that* toxic.

Kathryn shouted, "Now!" and I began to blow, hard, as Belinda grunted and heaved against the broken remains of the column. There was a metallic grating sound, and Kathryn looked up. I kept blowing until my lungs refused to expel any more air, and then quickly replaced the funnel, filling the tube up while trying to wipe my mouth on my shoulder. Kathryn stepped closer to the window—so close that the toes of her boots were hanging over the edge of the metal flooring and onto the glass.

"Again," she said, a sharp edge in her voice.

I glanced up as I lowered the can back down and saw only the cloud wall. We were turning, and there was still clear sky in the direction we were heading, but if we couldn't get the angle of turn sharper, then we wouldn't make it. I placed the tube to my lips, and when Kathryn shouted "Go!" I blew as hard as I was able to.

Belinda strained, and there was another metallic grinding noise overhead. "It's the rudders," Kathryn informed us. "They're squeaking because there isn't enough fluid. Just ignore it for now."

"Are we good?" asked Belinda, sweat dripping down her forehead as she struggled against the column. I studied it and her. She was strong, her biceps straining against the tight fabric of her uniform, but the black tube that jutted from the ceiling had only moved a few inches.

Kathryn shook her head as she continued to peer out of the window. "Not yet... But I think we're going to make it. One more time."

I sucked in yet another huge breath and blew for all I was worth as Belinda tugged the column toward herself, using her bodyweight to leverage it over as far as she could. The heloship shuddered slightly, but nothing else broke—and then Kathryn gave an excited whoop.

"We did it!"

I scrubbed my mouth against the sleeve of my jacket again, the strange mix of chemicals clinging to my lips, and moved up next to her. The arc of the turn was swinging us widely, but as more and more of the dark, starry night swung into view, I felt confident in Kathryn's assessment.

"Great, so now all we have to do is figure out where we can turn ourselves around, and..."

Kathryn noticed it just as I did. The jagged piece of rock—the edge of a cliff—appearing just to the left of the window. It was jutting out of the wall of storm clouds, dizzyingly close. Too close. We were going to hit.

I abandoned the hydraulics and simply threw myself into the steering column, pushing on it from the opposite side. Belinda grunted, looking up at me from her tilted position. "What is it?" she demanded, her eyes wide.

"Rock!" I shouted, as Kathryn pushed against me, trying to add to the weight we were putting onto the column. I felt the thick bit of metal shift, just a bit, underneath, and then there was a sharp jerk that pushed me farther forward before tossing me back. Kathryn fell, screaming in agony, as the whole ship bucked.

There was an awful scraping sound, and I felt certain half the ship was going to come off. And then, just as suddenly as it started, it stopped.

I was on the floor, Belinda's heavy legs on top of my chest. I pushed them off and picked myself up as Kathryn continued to wail in agony. I moved over to her. She rocked back and forth on her side on the floor, shakily holding her arm and hand out in front of her.

"Wait," I said, looking around the room for the medkit.

"Are we safe?" she whimpered, her voice fighting through the agony she was experiencing. I found the medkit on the floor and moved over to it, taking a moment to check the window.

"We are," I replied. The cloud bank was curving off to the right, rapidly giving way to the dark sky and a narrow ribbon of pink beginning to creep into the sky over the horizon. I scooped the medkit off the floor and headed back over. I could appreciate the view later. Kathryn was in serious pain.

"Here." I took another of the packets out and placed it on her neck. She was sweating, so the adhesive didn't immediately stick. Sighing, I carefully wiped down her neck with my sleeve, and then put it back down.

If she found me cleaning her neck odd, she didn't comment on it, and I didn't feel the need to either. She also didn't say thank you, even after I helped her sit up and move over to one of the seats bolted on the side of the wall. It wasn't worth commenting on, and maybe it was a bit petty of me to expect thanks in the first place. Besides, Kathryn was in pain, and I of all people knew how much that changed what came foremost in one's brain.

"Rest a minute," I ordered her, suddenly feeling bone-weary. "Belinda? You still with us?"

Belinda groaned and sat up, shaking her head. "What did we hit?" she asked, rubbing a growing dark spot just above her eyebrow.

"The rock," I retorted sarcastically, then got ahold of myself and toned it down to something slightly more civil. "You okay?"

She gave me a confused look. "What do you care?"

I gave her an incredulous look and put my hand on my hip. "I care because you represent two of the three functional hands on this helo-ship, and I very much like being alive."

The frown that seemed to perpetually be on Belinda's face deepened, and I resisted the urge to mention that it was not going to make for attractive wrinkles later in life. "We're just going to hang you when we get back to Matrus," she said. "You know that, right?"

"We can cross that bridge when and if we come to it. For now, all I care about is getting us back, and in order to do that, we're going to need each other."

"Or I could kill you now," she retorted. "Every second you're alive represents a threat to me and Kathryn."

"Oh, get off your high horse, *Belinda*," I grated out. "You both needed me just as much as I needed you back there. Kathryn's arm and hand would've made what we just managed impossible, and you'd both be as dead as I would. I gave up the gun, and I'm willing to do the work, so get over it." *Liar, liar,* I chided myself, thinking of the hidden guns, but I couldn't do this without safeguards. I couldn't trust these women as far as I could throw them.

Kathryn sighed and shifted her shoulders slightly, her face looking less strained than earlier. "She's right, Belinda. We need her too."

Belinda made an irritated noise, and then nodded. "Fine," she said. "But you stay where I can see you."

I chuckled and shook my head at her, moving past her toward the bay and taking the medkit with me, just in case. "I'm going to check on my friend," I informed her. "Feel free to follow, or not, but afterward, we need to figure out our next move."

CHAPTER 4

Violet

Solomon's condition remained unchanged, but I added another blood patch to be sure, and on impulse, a sedative. I hated doing it—I knew there was a possibility of side-effects that could push him into shock or even kill him—but if he woke up before we could find a way to get back, he could do more damage to the ship, or himself.

"Please don't die," I whispered to him as I slapped the sedative patch on his bicep. "I don't think I could bear it if I killed you trying to keep you safe from them…"

"You really talking to that thing?" Belinda asked, and I turned and saw her leaning against the doorframe separating the bay from the cockpit. "Seems to me like he can't hear you."

"You don't know that," I shot back as I straightened up and grabbed another blanket from under the nearby bench seat, draping it over him. The bay was still cold, and it felt like it had gotten colder in the last half hour. I considered asking Belinda to help me move Solomon to the cockpit, but I knew she would refuse, so I didn't waste the breath. "Besides, it's Desmond's fault he is how he is."

"Mm-hmm." I didn't react to the skepticism in Belinda's voice, although it made me wonder if there would ever be any future in which I wasn't looked upon by a Matrian woman with doubt and disgust. Probably not.

I knew I needed to get myself out of this mess, but all I could think about for a moment was the fact that Viggo was falling farther and farther away from me each moment that went by. I wasn't there to watch his back, which meant that when Elena came for our little resistance group—and she would—I wouldn't be there to fight beside him.

He was probably so worried about me.

I sucked in a deep breath, trying to quell the rising sadness. This entire thing sucked, but it mostly sucked because, deep down, *I* wasn't even sure we could get back. Belinda was right. No one had ever come back from The Outlands, not once, not any expedition Matrus, Patrus, or both had ever sent. And that thought sickened me, made me feel queasy any time it crossed my mind.

Which was why I had to keep busy. I wasn't about to give up, even with the certainty of death. I couldn't stop fighting, because I had something worth fighting for. Viggo. Tim. Owen and Ms. Dale. Amber. Henrik. Solomon. Morgan. Thomas. Quinn. Cad and Margot. Mags and Alejandro. Jay.

Oh God, Jay, I thought to myself, my heart aching. *Please let Morgan have fished him out of the water... and the wound be a simple fix for Dr. Tierney.*

It had been less than a year since Queen Rina had sent me on that mission to steal back the egg, and somehow I had gone from being completely and utterly alone, to having a family larger than I could ever imagine. And I couldn't abandon them.

"Ladies." Kathryn's voice carried in from the cockpit, loud and urgent enough to catch my attention. I turned, and saw her once again peering out the window, her body blocking most of the view from my limited angle through the narrow hall connecting the cockpit to the bay. More light was creeping in, though. A glance at my watch through tired and dry eyes revealed that it was almost six in the morning.

I moved toward her, pausing as Belinda slowly turned in the

narrow hallway formed by the bathroom on the left. She stepped aside as we drew near, revealing… Nothing.

And by nothing, I meant an absence of something. The ground below was colorful—I could admit that—the earth a blend of purples and blues I recognized, but on the ever-brightening horizon, I saw a contrast of golden and ochre hues, bright, richly striped, and alien.

But there was nothing else. No trees, no creatures, no water. Nothing but never-ending earth touching the never-ending sky. There weren't even hills. The land was as flat as it was desolate.

"There's nothing for us to orientate ourselves against," Kathryn said softly. "Just a few stars in the sky, but once they're gone…"

"What about the computer?" I asked, turning. "You said it was still there, we just had to interface with it. The holotable—"

"It's the first thing I checked," she said, shaking her head. "It's damaged."

I frowned, and then looked around. "How about a handheld? Surely you've got one of those."

"Protocol says we leave them in Matrus. After *your group* managed to get your hands on some, we made certain… changes."

"Oh." I wasn't sure why that surprised me; I just hadn't considered that they had developed countermeasures after we had gotten ahold of a few and hacked into them. Well, I assumed they would've changed frequencies and codes… but to eliminate an important piece of equipment? That seemed a bit of an extreme response.

Then again, maybe it was clever, and I was just being bitter that neither of them had one. Or me, for that matter. But I hadn't thought to take ours out of the car after it had been flipped over by an enhanced woman.

A thought occurred to me, and I looked around again. "Did Desmond have a bag or something?" I asked. "She went through one of the guard posts we had taken. Maybe she took one of our handhelds."

Belinda made a face like she had swallowed something sour, and gave me a hard look. "Which guard posts?" she demanded.

I looked at Kathryn and back to her, warning signals sounding in my head to proceed with caution. "Why?" I asked.

"My sister was at one of those stations," Belinda thundered. "So which one did you—"

"I would have no way to know that. I'm not sure how you classified your bases." I cut her off. I had to, or else this would escalate.

Belinda's neck began to grow red, and she took a threatening step forward. "You murderous cow, you don't care who you kill for your little war, do you! You don't know what you're taking from us, and all we were trying to do was help the Patrians!"

Kathryn stepped in front of her, awkwardly trying to soothe her while simultaneously backing up to keep Belinda from slamming into her and her broken limbs.

I wished that would stop me from running my mouth, but it didn't. Belinda had just hit one sore spot too many, and I would be damned if I was going to take that sort of comment at the expense of someone too ignorant to know what she was talking about.

"Maybe your sister and all of those soldiers shouldn't have been posted all around the city to keep people trapped while your *homicidal* queen had even more soldiers *poisoning* the water supply. Maybe then, she'd still be alive—she might anyway! My people don't particularly enjoy killing." I knew I shouldn't have said it as soon as it came out of my mouth, but being tired and angry was making my mouth move faster than my brain could keep up.

"You are just like those women, those Porteque women we read about in the files," Belinda hissed. "Trying to serve your Patrian man on his mad little conquest and stop us from helping those people!"

I faltered, surprised at the sick and disgusting comparison—one so disgusting that it made me pause and consider, for a fraction of a moment. What if I was? I shuddered, remembering the one who had taunted me so long ago, and met Belinda's gaze with a fury.

"Never compare me to those women," I said stonily, a violent rage blossoming to life under my skin. "You have no idea what you're talking about."

"ENOUGH!" Kathryn shouted. "Belinda, I'm sure Francis is fine. Violet... I'm sure you feel you're on the right side of things. But neither of those things matters right now! What matters right now is that we need to turn this bird around, and get home!"

Her words—the same words I had been trying to get into them both not too long ago—slammed into me. Belinda and I had baited each other, and I'd lost sight of the big picture in the process, letting my pride get the better of me.

Not that I regretted saying it. Nor did it stop me from wanting to plant a boot in her face. But at the same time, I hated all the death on my hands. As much as I blamed Elena, I also blamed myself. I had pulled the trigger. I had used grenades. I had pushed a man off a flying motorcycle, and I had set a woman on fire... every time making a choice—them or me.

And I had nightmares. Awful, terrible things. And I knew I would carry them with me forever. Yet if that was the price I had to pay to put an end to the madness Elena had caused, then so be it.

"I'm sorry," I said, after taking a long moment to calm myself. "I sincerely hope we did not kill your sister."

Belinda's mouth tightened, and she nodded. "I'm not sorry, but I'll... try not to bring up the war."

It would have to do. Kathryn nodded to us both, and then sighed. "Now that's over with, let's see what we can do about that interface."

CHAPTER 5

Violet

Twenty minutes of brain-wracking later, I stood over Belinda as she carefully peeled away a wire's plastic casing, using a knife I had provided from my boot. Belinda clearly hadn't been happy about that, but hadn't commented. I was trying to keep myself awake as we went through the mind-numbing task of attaching the multitude of wires to the handheld. Silence seemed to be the best way forward after our brush with violence, and I, for one, was grateful to contribute.

She carefully pulled the wire, freeing a bit more slack from the panel it ran on, and then began to twist the exposed wire around a metal contact under the handheld's hard plastic case. I dutifully held out the wire solder tool—a white tool with a metal ball at the end that emitted heat when the button was pressed, warming the metal end and melting the wire to the contacts on the back of the handheld.

I was glad I had thought of it. Kathryn said otherwise the only option would've been to land manually (something she had added she wasn't sure she could do without the computer to read elevation), but it had taken some time to find it. And now, it seemed it was going to take time to get the computer interfaced with the handheld.

"Violet, I need you to flip the page." It took a moment to register, but I leaned over to flip the page on the flight manual lying in front of Kathryn, ignoring the small stab of anger at how surly her tone was. Maybe it was petty, but it wasn't like I liked this situation any more than she did.

I looked up at her and realized she was sweating again, and I could tell the pain was beginning to overcome the patch I had given her. She fought through it, so I had to give her some respect—which meant I needed to let this irritation go. It could be that she was so focused on trying to carry through that she didn't have time for politeness. And I would almost buy into that, too, if she weren't giving the instructions to Belinda with all sorts of polite words, like "please" and "thank you."

As she began to read the next bit of instructions out loud to Belinda, prefacing them with a "can you," I refrained from rolling my eyes in annoyance and moved away a few steps.

A part of me was just frustrated that I wasn't doing anything at the moment. We needed two good hands to get the handheld interfaced, which meant Belinda, and Kathryn was the only one who could quickly decipher the more complicated terms in the manual and deliver the instructions in a clear way. So until they were finished, I was sort of a third wheel. I had managed to do a quick inventory of our food, water, and any other supplies that might be useful, which had been frustratingly small, and then checked on Solomon. His condition was the same, as best as I could tell. God, I wished Dr. Tierney was here.

Scratch that—I wished *we* were back *there*. Belinda and Kathryn included, if it came down to that. Sighing, I moved over to the window and stared out. The sun was now over the horizon, rising up over the edge and brilliant yellow in color. The light was so intense that I had to shield my eyes to block it out. The area below revealed itself under the growing dawn—bright yellow dirt, cracked and dry, like a mosaic on the floor. I'd never seen the earth such a color, so raw and naked.

How could anything survive out here? Was this what we had sent all those explorers out to—bone-dry wastes where nothing seemed to move? I shuddered, thinking about what it might be like down there.

I searched the wide expanse of the horizon and frowned when I saw a slim green line shimmer into sight just off to the right. Leaning toward it for a better view, I squinted and watched it approach, trying to decipher what it was as we drew closer to it.

After a few minutes, I stepped back into the cockpit and away from the bright light streaming through it. "Hey, Kathryn, can you take a look at this?"

"Uh, yeah. One sec. Just strip the wire and attach it to the third prong to the right. I'll be right back."

I shifted to one side as the pilot moved into the window, her hazel eyes searching. "What is it?" she asked.

"On the right. Is that a river?"

She craned her neck, squinting and awkwardly holding up her hand to block the incoming sunlight. "Looks like it. So?"

"Look at it. It's heading in the direction that cuts farther north… What if that's the beginning of Veil River?"

She gave an incredulous laugh and leaned back, her laugh dying when she saw I wasn't joking. "There's no way that could be Veil River," she said, her brow furrowing.

"Why not? Maybe it feeds into it, or connects to it. It's at least a landmark."

Kathryn bit her lip, her eyes staring out the window. "You're suggesting we try to turn this thing toward the river?"

I nodded, and she tilted her face up toward the ceiling, her eyes and lips moving silently as she performed some unexplained calculation in her mind. "We can only move at a fifteen-degree rate of turn right now," she said after a pause. "We'd need to start turning now, but I'm not sure if we should prioritize it over the handheld."

"If we don't do it now, we lose any chance of doing it after the handheld comes up. It's a source of water—"

"Which is probably toxic," Belinda interjected, having climbed up off the floor to squint over the top of Kathryn's head. "*Especially* if it leads to Veil River."

"It's not," I insisted. "I've been to The Green, where the toxic water is even more concentrated, and it glows blue. An unnaturally vibrant blue."

Belinda and Kathryn both exchanged surprised looks. "You've been to The Green? I mean, you've seen the river up that far?"

I nodded and then shrugged. "It's sort of a long story, and since it contains elements that will make Belinda angry, suffice it to say I sort of crash-landed there, got bitten by a centipede and chased by red flies, and nearly died a handful of times."

"Sweet mother," Kathryn whispered in horror, and no small amount of awe. I had to admit, it was kind of gratifying. If she was impressed by my survival abilities, then maybe she would be more inclined to continue advocating to Belinda for my continued place in the heloship's confusing chain of command. She looked back out the window, and then gave a tight nod. "Let's do it."

I quickly moved over to where the hydraulic pump and tubes still hung from the ceiling and began the process of pouring in more fluid. Belinda began unbuttoning the front of her uniform, shrugging out of it and revealing a thermal shirt, which she then stripped off, leaving a white tank top.

The light pouring through the window was generating a lot of heat, and even I was beginning to feel the room warm up, but for now, I ignored it, keeping my layers on—they felt like my armor. Once the line was full, I nodded at Belinda, and began to blow as she pulled on the steering column.

We repeated the procedure three times, just like last time, and each time Belinda was able to pull the column a few more inches over. The heloship deck tilted up slightly as she continued to hold it. I moved over to help her, the metal column vibrating with the strain of trying to hold the rudder and flaps without any hydraulic fluid to lubricate the mechanical gears.

Kathryn peered out the window, and after several long heartbeats, she finally shouted, "We're good!" and Belinda and I slowly eased off the column. The deck tilted back down as the turn evened out, and I moved over to the bubble. The river was now almost below us, to our right, as we hadn't quite crossed it during our slow turn. It curved back and forth, cutting a wide, winding path through the yellow earth. Nothing grew next to it, but still it churned below, sometimes smooth, other times violent, almost white, but flowing with strong currents northward—the same direction in which we were now traveling.

"I'll keep an eye on it," Kathryn said, and I turned, noticing that rivulets of sweat were pouring down her forehead. "I'm... I could use some water and a bit of a rest."

I nodded wordlessly and then went to retrieve her some water from the bay, unscrewing the lid of the bottle and holding it out to where she was now sitting on the floor, her back to one of the dead control boxes. Her cheeks flushed red, but she tilted her head back, and I carefully poured some into her mouth. She made a sound in the back of her throat, and I stopped, giving her a chance to swallow.

"How much fuel do we have?" I asked, fighting back another yawn as I poured some more water into her open mouth.

Behind me, Belinda tossed something metallic onto the floor, giving an irritated grunt, but I ignored her. It was an important question.

Kathryn swallowed the mouthful and exhaled. "It's hard to say for certain. I can't really tell how fast we're going, and have no idea if we're flying against the wind. At top speed with the hardest headwind we could actually continue moving against, we would've been halfway through our supply an hour ago. But since we are moving quickly, it's hard to say."

"How much time with no headwind?" I asked, and Kathryn crunched the numbers, then looked at her watch. "Two more hours? Maybe a little bit more. But again, there's no telling what speed we're moving at, not without the handheld."

Another metallic clang came from behind me, and I turned to see Belinda looking over her shoulder at us, the manual on the other side of the gap in the floor. "A little help." It wasn't a question.

I looked at Kathryn, and she gave me a little shrug as I recapped the water and sat it next to her. "Let me know if you want more," I said as I moved over to the manual. Picking it up, I stared at the first few dozen words on the page, trying to decipher the images and words there.

"Read it to me," Kathryn instructed as she gave a groan and slid down a few inches.

I repeated the words, skipping down a few lines as she told me they'd finished that part, and then listening closely. She took a minute, and then quickly explained the next batch of wires for Belinda to work on.

We were just on the last few wires—thank God—when Kathryn sat upright with a jerk, dragging my attention from Belinda, who was carefully soldering another wire to a metal contact. "What is it?" I asked, immediately alarmed.

I was already standing up and moving, even as she breathed, "What is *that*?"

As I looked out the window, I also found myself viewing the scene with confusion.

"I got it, if either of you care?" grumped Belinda from behind us.

"You see that, right?" asked Kathryn, looking up at me as I gazed at the massive gray and black structure that rose up from the desert at a ninety-degree angle, shooting up into the sky. The structure was so massive that the river that flowed by it seemed to disappear behind it. The walls were perfectly flat, the structure angled in an almost hexagonal shape, with strange black wings jutting out from the sides near the top.

"This might mean people!" I gasped, trying to resist the urge to press my nose against the glass, desperate for a clearer look. "Maybe they could help us. Maybe we could land there!"

"Are you crazy?" asked Kathryn, just as Belinda said, "There's people?"

"Look for yourself," I told her, stepping back from the window. Belinda set the handheld down and moved over to the window, looking at the structure as it continued to grow in our view. The platforms jutting off the side revealed themselves to be thicker than I'd first thought, and as it continued to draw nearer, it was clear that they were bigger than I could've imagined.

"Oh my God," said Belinda, her eyes growing wide. "It's so big. How can it be so big? It looks… sinister, like something from my worst nightmares."

"You have some pretty tame nightmares, then," I retorted, perhaps a touch bitterly, under my breath.

If Belinda heard me, she gave no sign of it as she continued to gape out the window. "It's so big," she repeated in awe. "It has to be at least a *mile* tall. Maybe more."

"Actually, I should be able to tell," said Kathryn. "Violet, the handheld."

I moved over to it, sitting down on the floor in front of it. The thing had dozens of wires jutting out of the back, and moving it too much could cause any one of them to disconnect—better just to go to it rather than attempt moving it. I clicked the screen on and immediately paused at the sight of the flashing red alert that popped up.

"Kathryn, you may want to get over here and look at this," I called over my shoulder.

"Belinda, help me up," she ordered, and I watched over my shoulder as Belinda bent over her, gently hoisting her up. Kathryn sagged heavily against the larger woman, and moved over, her legs almost giving out on her. Belinda helped lower her to the floor next to me, and she peered over my shoulder at the screen, reading the display. She spat out a curse and looked out the window. "I guess you're going to get your wish, Violet. We need to land now."

"What's wrong?" I asked, and she licked her lips nervously.

"The problem with the hydraulics is worse than I thought. All of the flaps, the blades, everything mechanical needs some of that fluid, and the system is bone dry. If we don't stop now to fix it, then the entire thing will lock up, and this thing will be about as movable as a flying brick. Then it's just a matter of time before we hit something, or run out of fuel."

"We could land on the ground," insisted Belinda. "We shouldn't land on that… *thing*! If there are people inside—"

"Then hopefully they'll be curious first," I cut in.

"It doesn't matter, Belinda," Kathryn replied tiredly. "The ground is too far below us. Trying to take it that far down with the hydraulics like this will only make everything worse. That tower is our only chance."

I looked over at Kathryn. "What do I do?"

"Push that button there, and then pull up the index. Go to the flight readout, then add a window for the controls. You're going to have to input my numbers precisely here. This is a more... mathematical way of landing."

I gave her an alarmed look even as my fingers danced across the screen. "You have done this before, right?"

The look she gave me told me all I needed to know. This landing was not going to be easy.

CHAPTER 6

Violet

I had braced myself as much as possible from my spot on the floor, but when the heloship hit the platform jutting out from the tower with a hard jolt, it still threw me to one side. My casted arm broke the fall, and from the bottom of the ship there came an awful grating sound, like glass being cut or nails being dragged down a chalkboard.

The noise stopped for another moment where we went weightless again, and then we landed with another hard jolt and it came back worse than before. Kathryn cried out. Even though we had taken great pains to strap her in using the remains of the harness, it was probably still hard to control both her arms beneath the elbow without being able to brace them on anything. I felt her pain—I knew what it was like to have most of my body unable to function. I'd made sure to strap Solomon down as quickly as I could before we impacted the tower, too. I didn't want him to be in any more pain, either.

The grating sound slowed to a stop, and the heloship shuddered before going still. I sat up and cut the engines the way Kathryn had instructed me to before we'd strapped her down. The subtle vibrations beneath me stilled, and I slowly extracted myself from the complicated mess of wires and equipment on the floor, gently setting down the hand-held that now controlled the heloship's engines. It had been difficult to hold during the landing with all the wires jutting from its back, and we still couldn't move it very far—hence why I was sitting on the floor to begin with.

I breathed in and climbed to my feet, taking a moment to carefully release Kathryn from her straps. Sweat continued to pour from her face, and she was growing paler. I knew that wasn't a good sign at all, but I couldn't be sure whether it was just from pain, or from some internal bleeding I knew nothing about.

"Give her some more water," I said to Belinda. "And check her stomach and chest for any dark bruises. I don't like her color."

"As if you care," said Belinda, unhooking herself from her own chair and moving forward on shaky legs.

"Oh for heaven's sake, Belinda." My legs were also shaky, but I was determined not to show them that. She looked at me, and I looked straight back into her eyes. "She's in pain. I'd have to be a monster not to care."

"Aren't you?" gasped Kathryn from between us.

Something inside me must have snapped a little at that—less anger, and more the sheer pain of being called something terrible, a word I hadn't heard in a long time. I heard my own voice crack. "A monster? Did I call Belinda a monster when she told me to my face that you were taking me back to execute me? No, she's just trying to do her job, and so are you, and I get it, I really do. But Kathryn, just because you view me as your enemy, it doesn't mean I can't understand, I can't *feel*, the fact that you're in pain. I'm a criminal, I won't deny that. But I'm not *inhuman*."

I ran out of breath and pressed my lips tighter together. Kathryn and Belinda didn't answer me, just stared at me with hard eyes, and I reminded myself again that it was pointless to try to get them to empathize with me.

Instead I moved back into the bay and knelt down next to Solomon. His body had shifted even under the straps—likely from the rough landing—but after my inspection of the bandages and the patches, everything still looked about the same. His color was darkening, finally, which was good, but it might not last long.

"I wish you were awake," I whispered as I inspected his wound. "I wish I could trust you to be awake… But please, just stay asleep for a little while longer."

Kathryn groaned loudly, and I turned to see Belinda helping her move through the narrow hallway that separated the cockpit from the cargo bay. "You were right," Belinda grunted. "She's got some really bad bruises on her chest and stomach."

"I'll be fine," Kathryn gasped, and I heard the wheeze in her voice. "We need to get out there and fix this ship."

"I need the bullets," I said, pulling out the gun.

Belinda and Kathryn froze.

"For all we know, this structure is abandoned," Belinda said, taking a step forward. "But why do *you* get the bullets? *I* should have the gun. I'm probably a better shot than you."

"That's true," I acknowledged. "Especially considering that my broken arm is my dominant one. But that just adds to the fact that Kathryn knows this ship, and you have the working appendages. The only thing I can do is play guard duty—so on the off chance there are people, I can defend us, although I hope they'd rather talk than fight."

Belinda snorted. "Someone like you trying *diplomacy*? Please."

"I seem to have inspired the three of us to work together." I held out my hand, looking at her expectantly.

Belinda just glowered at me, and yet again it was Kathryn who broke the stalemate. "Just do it, Belinda," she grated out harshly. "You're wasting time, and if I die because you two can't get along, at least I'll die knowing I took you with me."

Gallows humor. Maybe Kathryn and I could get along after all. I kept my face neutral, however, waiting for Belinda's reaction. She squinted at me, and then shook her head, her free arm reaching into her pocket and pulling out the clip. "You better keep us safe," she warned.

"I'll do my best," I replied, reaching out to take the clip. I slid it into the slot at the bottom of the handle and chambered a round, a process that required me to use my armpit and pray that no flesh or fabric got caught in the grooves. Belinda watched the process with a wary look on her face, but I ignored it and turned toward the door.

Stepping around Solomon's still form, I hit the button to open the bay doors. There was an odd grinding sound, and then the door jolted forward a few feet before stopping and slowly lowering down.

Immediately, bright yellow light streamed in, carrying with it a dry and dusty heat that blasted the atmosphere inside from warm to just plain hot. I had shrugged out of my jacket and sweater earlier to reveal the short-sleeved shirt I was wearing beneath—the cast made regular long-sleeved shirts difficult to wear, and for once that was to my benefit.

The door continued to open painfully slowly, the gears groaning loudly, before it settled with a clang on the hard shell of the platform of the building we'd landed on. I stepped out first, using my cast to shield my eyes from the bright sunlight. The burning ball of light was fully over the horizon now, steadily climbing up toward its zenith, but still hours away from noon.

The light created long shadows, and luckily, a portion of the tower blocked the bulk of it, creating more shade. We were just shy of being sheltered by the shade created by the tower; however, any remaining darkness would shrink away, rather than stretch toward us, as the sun climbed up into the sky.

I crept out of the ship, my eyes searching for any sign of movement.

The air seemed to ripple, and I realized it was from the heat—sweat was already beginning to collect at the base of my spine. I continued forward down the ramp, blinking furiously against the intensely bright light.

I paused when I came to the end of the ramp created by the door and bent over, examining the surface of the tower wing we'd landed on. What had appeared from far away to be a solid black thing was actually a deep rich brown, almost the color of earth that had been brought up from deep below. It also wasn't metal, as I had expected, but made up entirely of glass. And it wasn't like any glass I had ever seen before. For one thing, I couldn't see any sign of cracks or damage, even though an object of great size and weight had just crashed into it. For another thing, the glass itself was lined with small, perfect circles, black in color, running in tidy rows across it.

On impulse, I knelt down on the edge of the ramp and pressed my face to the pane of glass, doing my best to cut out the ambient light to see if I could peer through it. I couldn't, and didn't dare hold my face to the panel for too long. It was already hot from the sun's rays. After a little while, who knew how hot it would get outside of the ship? I was beginning to worry about the weather being as dangerous as anything else out here. We needed to move fast.

I stood up and stepped off the ramp, my gaze immediately going to the spot where the platform attached to the tower. If anyone were to come for us, I suspected it'd be from there. It was some hundred feet away, so it would be easy to see if anyone was coming, though there was no way to know that there weren't hatches elsewhere too.

"Is it clear?" Belinda called from behind me.

Stepping around the far side of the ship, I exhaled and lowered my gun. The platform in my view was still empty. "It's clear," I called back to her.

I hurried back into the ship as Belinda slowly helped Kathryn down, and I headed for the toolkit to make their jobs easier. Tucking my gun back under my armpit, I hefted it up and headed back out, following Belinda and Kathryn as they made for the nose of the ship.

Now we were on the shaded side of our ship, and the contrast between the sun and the shade was startling. Without the blazing rays beating down, I felt almost a touch too cold in my t-shirt. Still, I knew that would change soon enough—as soon as the rising sun reached its peak. Just one more reason to do this as quickly as possible.

I set down the toolkit and proceeded to help Belinda unscrew a panel under the wing, taking it off. All too soon, however, there was little for me to do, as the job really required the use of two arms—and Kathryn's expertise.

So I resigned myself to guard duty, and walked a path, sometimes slow, sometimes fast, but decidedly non-elliptical around the heloship. Patterns made it easier to make plans, and whoever was inside the tower had to be watching. I wasn't sure how, yet, but they would be.

If there was anyone in there, that was. Minutes had already ticked by since our landing. Almost half an hour, in fact. Granted, the place seemed huge, and perhaps traveling across it would be difficult, but that still seemed odd. Wouldn't anyone inside be able to see us through the panes of glass? But what if the odd platform structures didn't have anyone inside? For all I knew, they could be filled with machines that performed some important function. Nobody had ever talked about something that could sustain life inside The Outlands. Nobody had ever come from here, despite the close flying distance, and there had never been any reports of such a tower in Matrus... Though, knowing the higher-ups as I did now, I realized that even if there had been such reports, they might never have shared them with the public.

This place was a complete mystery to me, and the truth was that there was no way to know what was happening inside until someone chose to come out. If there was anybody there. And that uncertainty was weighing heavily inside my stomach. Sometimes I felt sure this structure was made for human uses; the next moment, I would feel equally sure there could be nobody out in this barren place, and I was guarding pointlessly. It made me twitchy and nervous, in spite of the heat trying to suck the energy away from me.

Smacking my lips together to try to generate a little moisture, I once again changed my orbit, moving closer to the edge that sat some sixty feet from the nose of the heloship. It was a bit far, but the area was so wide, I figured I would be able to see anything before it got too close.

As I passed by, I looked under the heloship's wing to see Kathryn leaning heavily against the side of it, and Belinda's legs sticking out from the hole we had opened up on the side. I drew nearer to the northern edge of the platform, trying to ignore the feeling of vertigo as the expansive wasteland opened up below me. It did not escape me that we were standing extraordinarily high, but... it also didn't bother me as much as it normally might. The platform felt sturdy under my feet, and it helped to steady me.

As the expanse grew, I frowned when I saw a splash of blue appear, and moved forward a little faster. The blue—a slim line initially—broadened and grew as I drew nearer, until I realized that what I was looking at was the river. I drew to a stop, sweat trickling down my back and my skin already feeling tighter and hotter than it should.

Turning back, I confirmed what I already knew: the river on the south side of the tower was still there, and still *green*. Then I turned back again to confirm the other truth: the river I could make out there, flowing north, was clearly blue—and not a natural shade. In spite of all of the ambient light and direct sunshine, the river still managed to glow an unhealthy hue.

Had there been any moisture in my mouth, it would've evaporated instantly. I raced over to the edge, slowing to a stop and then kneeling down next to it. I braced myself, and then, ever so slowly, began to peek over the edge.

I had to stop as a wave of dizziness engulfed me. Leaning back, I exhaled, trying to calm the queasy twisting of my stomach, and then sucked in a deep calming breath, steeling myself. Then, leaning forward, I started with my eyes glued to the building, allowing them to slowly drift up and then over as I continued to lean forward.

They traveled down the side of the platform—it was hard to tell how thick it was without any frame of reference, but I guessed the entire thing had to be at least twenty to thirty feet. Below it, the yellow-orange earth stretched out, and alongside that, just next to the tower, flowed the river, glowing that same eerie blue. I lifted my head and felt a sick churning sensation in my gut.

There must be people inside this tower. Because they were somehow responsible for the toxicity of the Veil River.

But how, or why? Were they aware they were doing it? Maybe they merely didn't care. What were they doing inside to produce that level of pollution? And why wasn't there any sign of a toxic zone like The

Green—could it be that nothing could grow out here, even with water?

If so, that meant there might not be people inside, and—

A sudden movement behind me caused my muscles to react instinctively, and I dropped low. I felt something impact my hip, heard a small noise of surprise, and felt more than saw a would-be assailant tumble over me and start to pitch over the edge. On impulse—I wouldn't have been able to do it if my rational mind had thought about it—I reached out and grabbed a handful of the white fabric suit the person was wearing and yanked with all my might.

We both tumbled back onto the relative safety of the platform, but I was still mostly upright. He landed on his backside, giving me my first look at him. Or her. It was hard to tell under the white biohazard suit that seemed to encase them, including little booties over their feet. They were wearing a mask with a filtration device, but the visor was tinted to block out the sun.

Reaching forward, I snatched the hood off, revealing a man with a round face and black, pencil-thin mustache. He blinked up at me, clearly surprised.

"Who are you?" I asked, and his eyes grew wider. He reached for something on his belt—a black stick with a rounded top—and I scrambled back to put some distance between us, keenly aware of the edge behind my back.

Then something jabbed me in between my shoulder blades, and the muscles in my body seized up as wave after wave of electrical energy was pushed through them. I recognized the feeling from the Liberator suit I had worn, only this charge was stronger and far more painful. For a horrible moment, I couldn't breathe, couldn't move, couldn't do anything save feel the agony. And then, all at once, it stopped, and I fell to the floor.

I lay there, my muscles twitching violently and pain still coursing through my nerves, making my body tremble and my breath come in sharp pants. I looked around and realized another figure had joined the first, their white-clad legs now coming into view. They must have been the one who had hit me with… whatever that was. Just beyond them, I made out three more white-clad figures, heading toward Kathryn and Belinda.

Somehow, I mustered up enough energy to stand, yanking my gun out. They hadn't even tried to take it, but I couldn't think about that too hard as I regarded the two people from behind it.

"Enough of this," I said, trying to keep the nervousness out of my voice. "I'm sorry we crashed on your tower, but we needed to or we would have died. Please, we only need a small amount of time to fix our ship, and I really don't want to kill anyone if I can avoid it."

The two closest to me stared at my face. Then Pencil-Mustache looked up at the second person, and gave a little shrug, looking exceptionally baffled. I glanced between the two of them, noting the second person was grasping a similar black stick to Pencil-Mustache. A horrible thought suddenly occurred to me.

"You guys speak English? Right?"

There was another pause, and then Pencil-Mustache looked at me and nodded. "We do at that," he said, slowly picking himself up off the ground and dusting off his suit.

The other figure took off his mask, revealing a rather handsome blonde-haired man with a strong chin and surprisingly hard look in his ice-blue eyes. "Knight MacGillus, shut up."

"Well, we have to talk to her," *MacGillus* whispered as he climbed to his feet. "The council will want a meeting with her. This is the first contact we've had with anyone from the outside."

"For all we know, they're all pirates and thieves, come to rob us of our technology."

"Sir, it is not our *jurisdiction*," MacGillus stressed, his eyebrows leaping into his receding hairline. "The law clearly states that the solar panels are under the jurisdiction of the—"

"Farmers," the other man finished with a sigh. "Although an argument could be made that jurisdiction has never had to be stretched out externally, so the purview of the outside could be seen as our concern, but…"

He trailed off as he noticed me watching. I gave a polite little smile, and he held off saying anything more.

"Violet!" shouted Belinda angrily from behind him, and I leaned to peer over his shoulder at where she and Kathryn were standing, encircled by the three other figures in white.

"Call them off," I said, looking at MacGillus' superior. "Please. You're the first intelligent life my people have met, too. I really don't want any hostility to start because of a misunderstanding."

The man blinked, and then rolled his lips tight over his teeth, emitting a shrill whistle that was exceptionally loud. The figures in white stopped their advance, and I eased up on the gun a little, lowering it a few inches. His eyes tracked the progress, but he made no reaction to the gun either way. His indifference was surprising, but maybe he was that unfazed by violence. Viggo had seemed weathered like that, when I first met him.

"My name is Jathem Dreyfuss, Knight Elite," he said after a long moment. "You may refer to me as Jathem. You and your companions will accompany me inside the tower, so that we may get to the bottom of who you are and what your intentions might be."

I shook my head immediately. "No way. My people stay out here and continue their work. I'll be the only one heading inside, and if they don't hear from me in one hour, they will be instructed to leave."

"I would need permission from my superiors before I could agree," Jathem said, his voice sounding almost tired.

"Then get it."

Jathem turned his head and closed his eyes. After a moment, he opened them and then nodded. "Very well, the council has agreed."

I frowned, my eyes flicking all over him, trying to figure out how he had managed to communicate without at least moving his mouth. His neck didn't seem to have anything on it, but... Maybe there was something under the skin? It was deeply unnerving, either way. For all I knew he could be talking to voices that didn't exist anywhere but in his head, and I had stumbled onto some sort of prison where insane people were kept.

I shuddered at the grim depths my imagination would go to as

Jathem lifted his arm. "Shall we?"

"Not just yet," I reminded him. "I still need to relay my instructions to my people."

He said nothing as I moved between them, heading over to the heloship like my pants were on fire.

CHAPTER 7

Violet

"What is going on?" Belinda demanded as I made my way toward where she was standing. Kathryn was awkwardly trying to stand next to her, although her legs didn't look like they were cooperating.

"These are the residents of the tower," I said, looking at the three other white-clad figures, those same black rod things clutched loosely in their hands. The tip of one glimmered blue, and I realized that those must carry the electrical charge that had dropped me a few minutes ago. "They've invited me inside to, uh, meet their leaders. The excellent news is that they speak English."

Belinda's eyes grew wide, and I motioned her toward the rear of the ship. She pondered me for a long moment, and then straightened up. "I'll be right back, Kathryn," she said, rising to her full, impressive height. She stood a handful of inches over the tallest person in white, which I hoped intimidated them slightly, although it was hard to tell behind the reflective face plates on their masks.

"It's all right," called Jathem to his people from behind us, and I turned to see him and MacGillus drawing nearer. "Let them talk."

The group collectively took a step back, solidifying my impression that Jathem was definitely in charge. He was already waving them over into a quick conference. I followed suit, and led Belinda around and into the cargo bay. "You're going to go with them?" she asked as soon as we were inside.

"I have to. There are far more of them than us, and we have no idea how lethal their weapons are."

"Those stick things?" She squinted at me. "What do they do?"

"They deliver some sort of electrical shock," I said, my shoulders twinging in memory of the experience. "I already got hit once, and I don't want to feel that again. Listen, we don't have much time. I lied about the other guns. They're above a panel in the bathroom."

Belinda immediately looked confused. "Why are you telling me this?" she asked, bewildered.

"Because I don't want to leave you here without any protection. And I'm hoping that will mean that if something happens and I don't make it back but you do… You'll take Solomon back to my people and tell them what happened. And… give Viggo Croft these."

I opened my bag and pulled out the wooden box Henrik had given me. Taking a minute to savor the smooth feel of the patterns, I felt the muffled clink of the wedding bands inside hitting the sides. I knew it wasn't, but it felt like… like this was the end. I couldn't shake the feeling that once I went inside that building, I would never get back out.

It took a moment to summon up the courage to straighten my spine and turn back to Belinda, holding out the box. "Tell him I'm… I'm sorry we didn't have enough time to get married first." My voice broke slightly at the end, and I hated myself for feeling the overwhelming urge to cry. I was being ridiculous, I knew it, but I couldn't take the chance of not leaving a message of some sort.

Belinda stared at the box, her face suspicious. "What is it?"

"Oh, for crying out loud, Belinda, it's a pair of wedding rings. They were a gift from a very dear friend of ours. When all of this stupidity was over, Viggo and I were going to get married. Will you please do this if I don't come back? Please?"

Her frown deepened, and, after a teeth-gratingly long silence, sighed and shook her head. She reached out, and I flinched back, but all she did was push the box back to me. "You should keep it with you," she said after a moment. "If he loves you, he'd want them with you. Then he could imagine you were actually married." She blinked in surprise and then flushed, the sharp edges of her high cheekbones turning a mottled red. "Sorry. Besides, it is stupid for you to wait until this is over… We caught you, and we'll catch your boyfriend soon and execute you both. Maybe if you're lucky, the queen will allow you to get married before we hang you."

My throat seized up, uncertain of how to even process her remark. On the one hand, I wanted to laugh—right in her face. On the other, that was a shockingly morbid thought, one that made my stomach feel as if a massive lump of ice had just formed inside it, chilling me to my core in spite of the sweltering heat outside.

I didn't want to die not having married Viggo first. I didn't want to risk another single moment of not having him be mine, forever. Even though we had discussed it, decided to wait, I realized I was tired of waiting. I wanted it, right then and there if he'd have me. Only he wasn't here. He was back home, and I was determined to get back to him, no matter the obstacles set in front of me.

I withdrew the box and tucked it back into my bag. "You're right. I was being silly." Shouldering the bag, I turned around and gave her a look. "I told them if I'm not back here in an hour, you're going to leave without me. Can you do that?"

Belinda gave me another suspicious look, and then nodded, but I wasn't finished. "Can you also promise to wait an hour, just in case you finish the repairs before I get back?"

She hesitated, and then nodded again. "The queen wouldn't like hearing that we left you behind. She really wants to execute you. Like, very badly."

"I'll bet she does," I replied dryly. God, I hoped I could kill that woman one day.

"Excuse me, ma'am?" called Jathem's voice from down the ramp, and I stepped to one side to see him and MacGillus standing there.

My hand tightened around the strap, and for a moment, I felt a deep heartsickness.

"Promise you won't leave without me?" I asked, and she nodded.

"I'll give you one hour exactly, but after that, we're gone."

It would have to do. I exhaled softly and moved down the ramp.

Jathem greeted me with a polite smile, but it came off more as menacing, given that his eyes were squinting against the bright sunlight and the goatee he wore around his mouth somehow had a sinister tilt. He led the way, moving across the platform toward the base of the column. I lagged behind, wondering how I hadn't seen them until they were almost on top of me, and then realized that the white suits used the waves of heat that made the air ripple, practically disappearing as they moved through them.

Not wanting to lose them, I sped up, my boots thumping loudly against the glass beneath my feet. As we neared the wall, it rose to even greater heights over my head, making my head spin with the implications of just how massive it was. I dragged my gaze down as we stepped into the sliver of shade cast by the edge of the building, the temperature dropping a few degrees.

Jathem approached the wall, confident and not the least bit confused as to his surroundings, in spite of the rows and rows of identical glass panels in front of him. He pressed on one, and it and the one above it popped open a few inches. Jathem gripped the side of it and hauled it back a few feet, revealing a dark corridor with a catwalk leading out from it, into the dark depths.

Hesitating for a second, I stepped inside, moving forward as MacGillus crowded in behind me. The door closed with a slow hiss, and Jathem let out a breath of relief. I turned, and realized both men were quickly stripping out of their suits. I didn't have time to feel alarmed, because even as they undressed, I realized they were wearing identical crimson uniforms underneath, resplendent with shiny black knee-high boots.

"Is a knight like a warden?" I asked, suddenly curious.

MacGillus looked over at me, his mustache twitching as the corner of his lip curled up. "I'm not sure what that is," he admitted honestly.

"A, uh, guard," I stuttered as I tried to find an accurate analogy. "An organized force that helps catch criminals?"

"Oh. In that case, yes, a knight is very much like that."

"You shouldn't tell her that," Jathem chided sternly, and I looked up to meet his eyes, suddenly feeling hesitant about even using the term "warden." Still, that didn't give away our location or surroundings—as long as I kept quiet about that, I couldn't imagine what I might say about our social customs that could give anything away. But I needed to be more careful in the future. It was probably best not to concede anything. Viggo had shown me how a cunning investigator could gather information from almost nothing, and Jathem could have that talent as well.

"Okay, well, if we can't talk about that, can you at least tell me about your council? How many people are on it? And are they elected, or is it an aristocratic system that you must be born into to rule?"

"How are leaders in your culture determined?" Jathem shot back, and I frowned.

"Look, Jathem, I'll be more than happy to answer your questions, but in my defense, we're not going to be meeting with my leaders. We're going to be meeting with yours. Any info would help. I mean, I don't want to disrespect your leaders by doing something stupid like speaking without being spoken to or some other tradition I don't understand."

Jathem frowned as he stepped past me, heading down the narrow passage. The tunnel was cramped—Jathem and MacGillus had to duck down to move through it—but my head barely brushed the top of the tunnel. It moved down about ten feet, and then opened up onto a landing. The wall was directly in front of me, and as I looked around, I realized we were standing on a set of stairs. There was a door directly across from me, with a hatch marking it 97-E-12. I noted it as I continued to marvel at the length of the stairs. There were no switchbacks that I could see, but rather a steady, fixed incline running along the width of the tower. I could see where it turned ahead, and there were dozens of landings with doors on either side running left to right.

"Wow," I breathed, looking up. "This is incredible."

"This is the shell," Jathem said, already beginning to climb the seemingly endless stairs. "I don't mind telling you this, as it relates to our defensive capabilities. If you do turn out to be some spy or nefarious individual, I want you to realize the frivolity of your cause before you even attempt it."

I couldn't help but smile at that as I trailed along behind him. "Seems fair. So the shell does what, exactly?"

"It protects and braces the area inside, keeping it environmentally sound. But more than that, it acts as a deterrent for any and all outside who might harbor ill intentions. Whole sections can be closed off at a moment's notice, long before anyone could get inside."

"So it's kind of like a beehive?"

"Do your people keep beehives to help pollinate your crops?" asked MacGillus from behind me, and I paused in my march up the stairs to look at him.

"Actually, I'm not sure. I'm not a farmer."

"Neither is he," said Jathem from ahead. "But MacGillus just married one, and now he thinks he's an expert. Although why he'd ever want to farm is beyond me."

"You know that farming was my first choice. I just have a black thumb is all."

"Your first choice?" I asked, not wanting to stall their flow of conversation, but also too curious to resist.

"Everyone in the tower has a task, a purpose, Miss..." Jathem paused and cocked his head, slowing on the stairs. "I never caught your name," he remarked.

"Oh, I'm sorry. I'm Violet. Violet Bates."

He inclined his head and then began to march again. I sucked in a breath, already cognizant that my ribs and thighs were aching, and followed suit. I hated that I was still injured—now, more than ever before, was a time when I most needed to be fit, and it just wasn't possible.

"As I was saying, everyone has a purpose, and is allowed to apprentice in whatever department he or she feels best suited to. Sometimes they are accepted, but other times they must find a different department, as their skills are not up to par."

"Ah. That's interesting," I replied. "I guess we do things similarly, but... enterprise makes it possible for anyone to do or be anything they want." *Depending on their gender and which side of the river they live on,* I would have added if I'd wanted to be completely accurate.

"Provided they have the mental capacity for it, I assume," he mused.

I frowned at the dryness in Jathem's voice, and then shrugged. It was accurate.

We finally reached the corner of the building, and turned. My breathing was coming in sharp bursts now, the ache in my ribs spreading. While my bruised ribs had seemingly settled down, the stairs were providing a unique set of challenges that they did not agree with.

Neither did my thighs or my calves, for that matter. The steps just seemed never-ending, and there was no way of knowing how much higher we would have to climb before we reached our destination. I felt a deep yawn coming on, the exhaustion of the past few days really starting to take its toll. The multitude of steps ahead of me were calling for me to sit down and find a way to catch at least a few minutes of precious sleep, as well as catch my breath.

MacGillus seemed to note my flagging strength first; after a few moments of my panting and wheezing, he said, "Miss, are you all right?"

"I'm fine," I insisted as I took a few more steps up, ignoring my aches and pains to prove my point.

Jathem turned and looked at me, his eyes taking in the cast and some of the still-visible bruising on my scalp and face. "You were injured recently?"

I gave a bitter chuckle and nodded. "You could say that." *You could also say that I went on an almost suicide mission to save my family and kill an insane princess with a grudge. I killed her, but I almost died in the process, so...*

"Change of plan," the man announced suddenly. "We're going to have you looked over by a member of our medical staff. We need to wait here while they clear the appropriate halls. We aren't prepared to alert the rest of the tower to your existence. Take a moment to catch your breath."

Blinking, I came to a staggering stop. "That's a very kind offer," I replied. "But it's unnecessary." He shrugged, and I felt a thrill of excitement, even through my feigned indifference. Could they be able to help me mend a little sooner?

"It's clear that your medical practices are rudimentary at best, and we are not a people who like inefficiency. You'll be met by two councilors after you have been examined by one of the Medica."

"The Medica?" I asked, trying to quell my excitement. "Is that what you call your doctors?"

"That is how we refer to the department of doctors," Jathem corrected, tugging his shirt down and smoothing it out. I noticed MacGillus was similarly making a point of straightening out his uniform, and frowned.

"And one of the councilors coming to meet us is *your* leader, isn't it?" I surmised out loud, and it really wasn't much of a question, but by the look in Jathem's eyes, he was at least a little impressed by my deduction.

"Indeed. Knight Commander Devon Alexander." There was a reverence in how he spoke Devon's name; I would have found it almost amusing if it weren't also a bit nerve-wracking. That level of devotion to a person made warning bells go off in my head as I recalled the Liberators' blind devotion to Desmond.

"I see. Who's the other one?"

"Raevyn Hart. She's Head Farmer."

A woman working with men? Maybe Matrus and Patrus' problems were not endemic to all human beings. That was… a nice thought. It meant we could grow and better ourselves, overcome the genderism that had separated us for all of recent history.

"She could coax an apple tree from used soil," MacGillus said. "Under her, her department's efficiency has gone up a whole percentage point!"

"MacGillus, shut your hole," Jathem barked, and MacGillus immediately turned contrite.

"I'm sorry. I didn't tell her how much we produced, just the stats."

Jathem sighed and pinched the bridge of his nose. "It's fine. We're all… a bit unsettled by all this. Let's just keep quiet until we get you checked out by the medics."

I exhaled and shoved my hand into my pocket. My questions would have to wait for a bit, it would seem.

CHAPTER 8

Violet

Several minutes of waiting on the same steps later—an eternity during which thousands of questions churned inside of me—Jathem, at some unseen signal, gave a nod and speared me with a look. "The way has been cleared. We need to climb up three more levels though. You ready?"

I nodded and ran a hand nervously over my scalp. The hair was growing back in quickly, but it still felt weird under my hand. I wiped my palm on my t-shirt and began to climb once more, following Jathem. We soon reached the correct level. According to the numbers, now we were at 124-N-43. He turned the wheel on the door to the inner wall and swung it outward, toward us.

He stepped through, leading me into a narrow hall with a long sheet of glass paneling one side of the wall. As he moved on down the corridor, my steps slowed to a halt, and I openly gaped at the enormity of the sight on the other side of the pane.

Just past it, I could see three giant structures hanging from the ceiling. Thousands of feet below, around the base of the tower, were lines of green vegetation, bisected by straight white lines that were probably footpaths. The three buildings were arranged in a rough triangle—the two closest were cylindrical in shape, and glowing, while the one farther away, at this angle framed perfectly by the white ones, was cone-shaped and so dark that the light reflected off of it, giving the illusion that it was glittering.

Bridges ran from structure to structure, and periodically, every hundred feet or so, a flat pavilion stretched in between them, seemingly suspended between all three, much like a hammock suspended in the air. The ones I could see looked very much like public parks. I could see people wearing uniforms similar in cut for the most part, but in different colors—mainly white, black, crimson, green, gray, and blue— but it was hard to discern much beyond that; that's how far away we still were.

"You built this?" I whispered in awe, my eyes tracking up to where filtered sunlight seemed to radiate out into the tower from all levels, illuminating it as if it were a warm summer's day and the inside was shaded by branches from dozens of trees.

"Our predecessors did," Jathem replied, his voice carrying from ahead. "Come along, Miss Bates."

"You better go, miss," MacGillus said as I lingered, and I reluctantly tore myself from the view. It was mesmerizing how... strange and beautiful it was. How could they have achieved all this? It was mindboggling.

I walked slowly after Jathem, following him down the hall while my eyes continued to slide all over the incredible sight out the window, drinking it in. The sheer manpower alone... If this tower were to be filled to its maximum capacity, I'd bet there could be more than three times the number of humans here than there were in Matrus and Patrus combined. At least. That was a staggering thought.

The windowpane ended as we neared a junction, and I looked back to note how many turn-offs we'd passed to get there. The uniformity of the shell made it all too easy to get confused. I didn't want that happening to me if I had to make a run for it.

"This way," Jathem said, pointing to the left. I turned the corner and saw a door with a white, glowing section of wall just above it. I couldn't grasp how they'd made the wall do that—but the sign at least was recognizable, a glowing red cross set in the center of the white panel. I pointed at it and looked back at Jathem, and he nodded.

This door, unlike the one before, was simple and had a flat-hooked handle. I followed MacGillus and Jathem through it, then blinked at the sudden expanse of whiteness that I saw. This entire area seemed to be white walls on white ceilings on white floors, all blending together. I focused dizzily as the two men in front of me led on. We seemed to be following some kind of glowing line in the floor, and I put my mind to memorizing that, too, as we went through several atrium-looking rooms and to another door marked with a glowing panel. With no people anywhere inside, the strange atmosphere of the area was only increased, and I felt more tense than I'd been since I'd gotten them not to fight me.

When we went through the door, a bald woman with dark tattoos on her scalp looked up from a petri dish she held in one hand, a dropper in the other hand hovering over it. She frowned when she saw us, and then sat down the petri dish and the dropper on the clear table in front of her.

Her eyes were dark brown, as were the strong eyebrows over them, and her mouth was like a tight rosebud.

"Knight Elite Jathem," she greeted formally, shooting me and my cast a curious look. "I assume this is what the level was cleared out for?"

"It is indeed, Medic Selka." He pronounced her name oddly, elongating the "s" and putting an emphasis on the "ka," and I wondered how the group knew English but spoke it differently than we did. Now that I noticed it, they all said some words differently, though not enough that I couldn't understand it.

The medic blinked coldly and looked me over, her curiosity replaced with professional aloofness.

"Come here," she ordered, moving to a wall. She pulled a panel out of its side, revealing a plush-looking bed, and patted it. "Please sit down."

I approached it and sat. It took a small jump to do so, given its height above the ground. Medic Selka pressed a few panels on the wall next to me, and the next thing I knew a flat beam of light had turned on and was moving over my head. I felt a tingle where it hit me, but nothing else. The medic reached out and grabbed my cast, looking at it with disdain and alarm, her brows furrowed tightly together.

"What is this thing?" she sniffed, her nose crinkling.

"I broke my arm not long ago," I replied, suddenly feeling self-conscious about the cast.

She looked over at Jathem and MacGillus, disbelief stamped over her face. "What is going on?" she demanded. "Who would've done something this... this cruel to another human being?"

I blinked and pulled my cast out of her grasp. The machine overhead whirred loudly, and I looked up to see the light retract back into the wall as the section below it lit up, the words "Image Generating" scrolling across it.

"Relax, M. Selka," Jathem soothed, his hands going up. "She's an undoc. Her family kept her well-hidden for years."

"Wow," she said with a surprised blink. "There hasn't been an undoc in, what... two years?"

"Not that we've heard of," MacGillus replied. "But you can see why the council wants it kept quiet. Bad for order."

"Especially given how old she is," replied Selka in a conspiratorial whisper.

Jathem frowned and crossed his arms. "This is classified protocol ten, M. Selka. Don't let your curiosity get you in trouble."

The woman frowned, a flash of irritation passing over her features, and then turned back to the screen. "Her arm was broken," she said, and I looked back up to find an incredibly realistic view of what was presumably my arm on the screen. The definition and detail in the picture was amazing, and it was completely colored in, but the outer layers of the flesh were translucent frames atop the picture of my bone. It was all there—skin, muscles, tendons, and veins. I'd known basically how bodies worked, and learned more from working with the experienced medical personnel in our group, but I'd never expected to see a picture of the inside of my own body. It was fascinating.

From the image, even I could see the break. It was partially healed, delicate little strands of bones slowly reaching out toward each other, some of them already connected with more on the way. It looked like it felt—painstakingly slow. It was mind-blowing that they could see into my body so vividly.

"These injuries are weeks old. Did she get caught in a gear?" M. Selka asked, her eyes moving as the images moved, following her fingers as she dragged them across the wall. She pinched them together over my shoulder and chest, the image shooting in, and then drew them apart, the image drifting down to my ribs. "Her ribs are still bruised from whatever happened, and she experienced some first- and second-degree burns. Her head…"

She trailed off then, her mouth working as she stared at the hole in my skull. I touched the scab that was still thick from the procedure, and looked up at her. M. Selka looked like she couldn't decide whether to be sick or not; her face was pale and disturbed.

She quickly collapsed the image and whipped around. "Who are you trying to kid, KE Jathem? There is no way anyone could have performed surgery like that. She would've died! The sheer *obscenity* of the harm it could do is beyond words! Who is she, and where did she come from?"

Jathem sighed heavily and touched his earlobe with a finger. "M. Selka, you are relieved of duty. Report to your superior and speak of nothing you have seen here until you are debriefed."

"Now you can't expect me to—" M. Selka fell silent, her head tilting to the side as if she were listening to something. After a moment, she pulled her top down with a yank at the bottom, smoothing it out, and then tapped her wrists into an x in front of her face. "*Wahela,* and my apologies, Knight Elite."

"*Tahatlana,* Medic. May your waters run clear and cold."

She nodded and moved quickly for the door, leaving in a hurry. The entire exchange left me baffled, and I looked up at Jathem. He turned from the door and saw me staring at him.

"You have questions," he said, his voice resigned.

"A billion," I replied, shifting excitedly.

He sighed. "I'll give you an answer to three, but if there is one I feel I shouldn't answer, I will skip it. Deal?"

A stupid one, but it would have to do. I gave him a nod, and started with the first one I could think of. "What's an undoc?"

"Undoc is short for undocumented. Population is strictly controlled and enforced in the tower—we are a completely balanced system. Too many people and the entire thing comes tumbling down. However, that doesn't stop some people from accidently conceiving, and then deciding to keep their child a secret."

"Interesting," I replied, because it was. The implications of it all, strict population control and secret children... This place had to be carefully monitored and observed to maintain order. It made me want to ask a dozen follow-up questions, like what happened to an undoc after it was discovered. I hated to think they might kill them just to keep the population under a certain number.

"We don't execute undocs," Knight Elite Jathem said tersely, and I realized I had spoken the last bit out loud. I shook my head to clear out some of the spider webs as he continued to speak, mumbling an apology. "We educate them and try to put them back into the system."

"The biggest problem is getting them placed," continued MacGillus. "Lots of departments won't take them, as they... represent a certain amount of controversy and shame."

I blinked at that. I knew they were trying to explain things to me, but it was clear they were things they took for granted, and even though I had gotten some good information out of that, a lot of it seemed implied, which meant it flew right over my head.

Sighing, I leaned back. "Second question. With Medic Selka now dismissed, does that mean I won't get to see how you guys could fix my arm faster?"

Jathem stared at me, and then smiled for a brief second. "We would never dream of that. It was just decided that you would be attended to by the Chief Surgeon. He'll be down in a few minutes."

"If we're lucky and he's feeling spry today," MacGillus mumbled, and Jathem reached out and smacked him loudly in the shoulder, making the other man yelp.

"Be respectful," Jathem said, just as the door swung open, and a man and a woman entered.

CHAPTER 9

Violet

The woman entered first. Something about her posture and physicality immediately made my hair stand on edge, it reminded me so much of Tabitha. However, as she drew closer to me, pushing deeper into the room, I could see subtle differences that clearly distinguished her from the now-deceased Matrian princess and psychopath.

For one thing, her hair was jet black, with clearly premature whitening occurring at the roots. It was collected and woven into an elaborate braid encircling the crown of her head, making it look like a dark, shining tiara. There were smile lines around her mouth, and a worry line seemed to be permanently indented between her thick, generous eyebrows. As she moved deeper into the room, I caught the smell of rich soil and vegetation, and noticed that the knees of her forest-green uniform were stained with dirt, as were her fingertips, and there was a smudge on her cheekbone as well.

Behind her came a tall, lanky man with long brown hair gathered in a tie at the base of his neck. He wore a goatee, like Jathem, but it was longer than Jathem's by half an inch. His face was narrow, his cheekbones high, with slight hollows underneath. An aquiline nose, thin and straight with a hooked end, added another angled element, making him seem almost stern, with the narrow countenance of a hatchet.

His eyes—a strange combination of one blue eye and one brown eye—blazed as they looked over me, and an all too vulnerable feeling crept over me as he took me in, like he could drink up all my secrets. He stepped in behind the woman, and stopped as she stopped, just a few feet away.

"I'm assuming this is Raevyn Hart and Devon Alexander?" I said, after the silence had grown unbearable. I kept my tone light, hoping to put the two newcomers at ease.

"Head Farmer Raevyn Hart and Knight Commander Devon Alexander," MacGillus said nervously, clearly correcting my bad manners, and I nodded, deciding not to speak for a minute.

"You're certain they landed on top of the Green?" the woman, Raevyn, said after a moment, turning her head toward Jathem. She didn't even seem to notice my blunder.

"Wait, you have *The Green* here?" I asked, blinking in surprise.

MacGillus blinked at me, confused. "I'm not sure—'the Green' refers to the Greenery, a place where—"

"Do not address her," Devon commanded in a stern voice. "And answer HF Hart's question."

There was a small pause as Jathem seemed to collect himself. He and several others reported the same occurrence.

"HF Hart," said Devon, his voice flatly stating the fact. "There is no reason to doubt the claim."

"They could be undocs," she retorted. "Very smart undocs, from Mechs, or possibly the Loaners. They could've built a ship... It was an oversight not to have surveillance outside of the tower."

"Scipio reports that it's not an oversight. The heat outside is too severe and would burn out the cameras by the hundreds. Daily."

"Who's Scipio?" I asked, and everyone stopped and looked at me, as if suddenly remembering I was in the room. I looked at Jathem and added, "That's my third question, but if you don't want to answer it, then my next one is: are the colors you're wearing to identify your role in the tower? Is it crimson for knights, green for farmers, white for medics... oh, oh... are the Mechs and Loaners other... departments, or whatever you call them?"

"Dear lord, KE Dreyfuss," breathed Raevyn at Jathem. "Whatever did you tell this girl?"

"Madam Councilwoman," said MacGillus, his voice humble and soft. "She asks a lot of questions, too many to be an undoc. And I was with KE Dreyfuss. I can testify that he did not give any answers that might put the tower at risk, only ones that might increase her understanding of our defensive capabilities."

"But not our offensive?" asked Devon, his voice holding a note of warning.

"Never, sir." Jathem's voice held a note of mortification.

I sighed and leaned back against the wall, folding my arms across my chest. It was difficult with the cast, but I managed. They were bound and determined, it seemed, to ignore me, and it was a little frustrating. I mean... I was the newcomer amongst them. Why weren't they as curious about me as I was about them? I'd figured at least one of them would have a little less self-control, or something.

A sharp rap sounded on the door, interrupting the argument. Knight Commander Devon stepped out of the way just as it swung open, admitting an elderly man wearing a white uniform.

"Chief Surgeon Sage," Raevyn said, inclining her head.

Chief Surgeon Sage was in his sixties, if I had to guess, and had snow-white hair and a bushy white mustache. In spite of his age, he stood tall, and his physique was surprisingly muscular, as if he could go out jogging at any moment. He smiled at Raevyn, a dimple forming in his cheek, and his eyes danced around the room until they landed on me.

"Is this our little alien girl?" he asked, stepping into the room.

"I have doubts about the assertion that she is an outsider, Marcus," Raevyn said bluntly, folding her arms across her chest. "She could be part of an undoc cell trying to leave the tower."

The older man's smile broadened as he stepped around her, drawing closer to me. His eyes were a dark green, and crystal clear. "Well, young alien woman, what's it to be—alien or undoc?" He sat down on a stool and rolled over a few feet, coming to a stop beside me. "Personally, I'm hoping for alien."

Immediately his eyes went to my cast. He examined it closely, a wild grin on his face. "My father told me this was how our great ancestors healed broken bones, but never in a million years did I think anyone would still implement it. Isn't that nifty!"

"Wait, you're saying *that* was the technique for setting bones in the past?"

Sage nodded at Raevyn's question, rotating my arm so he could examine the cast further. "Indeed. If she is an undoc, someone has access to old medical books or journals that are extremely out of date. I want them."

I smiled, unable to stop myself at the hungry quality to Sage's voice as he laid claim to some imagined medical documents. He pressed something to my finger, scraping gently, and then moved it away, inserting the narrow device into a port in the wall. The panel glowed white, and then faded. He leaned forward and tapped the screen, and the next thing I knew it showed blood cells, flowing their way through my body. He tapped another button, and I saw a double helix sitting there, sections of it automatically lighting up with flashing text. Looking down at my finger, I realized he must have taken a sample of my genetic material.

"Well, forget about the texts. She's definitely not from around here!" Sage announced with a clap of his hands. "We've got ourselves a genuine alien girl!"

I knew the way he kept calling me "alien" should've bothered me, but for some reason, it was hard to be upset by the cheerfully pleasant man. His eyes twinkled like he was in on some joke that he wasn't sharing with the rest of us, and I found it both enigmatic and intriguing. Maybe he would be someone I could glean some answers from.

"That's not possible," Raevyn exclaimed, taking a step forward. "Nothing can sustain life outside this tower. The ecological reports alone tell us that!"

"Hey, that's what our people thought too," I said. "You're the first sign of human life we've ever encountered."

"Young lady," said Knight Commander Devon, his gaze falling squarely on me. "You *will* tell us where you come from, and how your flying... gyroship works."

I swallowed and looked around the room. "Um, sorry, but I'm not so sure I want to tell you that, just like I'm sure you don't want to tell me if I called it on the uniforms." I leaned over and stage-whispered to Sage, "But I totally called it on the uniforms." The old man gave a bark of laughter, his shoulders shaking, and he looked around the room, grinning broadly.

"She's funny," he announced cheerfully to the otherwise somber room. I couldn't help but smile as he tugged my cast over.

I shifted a little as Devon crossed his arms, his eyes disapproving and dark, and I sighed. "Look, all jokes aside—and let me have that, I'm a little nervous—I have every reason to consider you all as big of a risk to my people as you are assuming I am to yours. This is the first contact any one of my people have had with anyone in The Outlands, and I'm also in uncertain waters. I definitely didn't think I'd be meeting other humans this morning."

"The Outlands? Is that what you call the Wastes?" asked Raevyn.

I opened my mouth to reply, just as Devon asked, "So your people have explored *The Outlands* before?" and I nodded.

"Yes to both questions. Parties have gone out... They haven't come back. No one ever comes back from The Outlands. But honestly, our coming out here wasn't even intentional. Our ship was damaged, and we're... we're just trying to make our way back home."

"I'm sorry, but that's not good enough, Miss..."

"Bates," Jathem supplied for Raevyn, and she nodded absentmindedly.

"Bates. We have no guarantee that you won't return with your people in a whole fleet of those gyroships with who knows how many weapons. Frankly, for you to think we can allow you to—"

There was a sharp crack, cutting Raevyn off, and I looked down to see CS Sage pulling the sides of my cast open. Immediately I felt the urge to gag as the smell of unwashed, dirty skin and old sweat wafted out from under the cast, my face flushing with embarrassment.

Sage wrinkled his nose, clucked his tongue, and pulled a small silver spray can from his pocket, spraying it all over my arm. The mist was cool, but not uncomfortable, and my skin began to tingle as the smell all but evaporated. He took a tissue out of a box and wiped at the skin, the white material quickly turning black, and my blush deepened.

"Sorry," I mumbled, and he shook his head.

"Not at all, but that is why these are more primitive methods. Your skin can mold or get an infection or irritation. I bet it has been itching a lot too."

"It really has," I replied, thinking of all the times I had almost lost a pen trying to use it to scratch under the cast.

"Not surprising," he said, tossing the tissue aside. My arm continued to tingle, the aching pain of the break fading away, and I gave it a considering look.

"Is that it?"

"Ha! Hardly. I think we can do a bit better than that."

He reached up and pressed something on the screen. Immediately a small section of the wall opened, and a thick plastic sheet came out, feeding through some kind of dispenser. Sage let it run and then tore it off. Indicating for me to lift my arm, he carefully wrapped the plastic sheet around it, looping it around and pressing it down against itself. He held it in place for just a moment, and then let go.

Amazingly, the plastic stayed in place, and I almost sagged in relief at how much better my arm suddenly felt. What was more interesting were two things: the first was that it was incredibly lightweight and left my hand completely free and useable. The second thing I noticed was that the plastic was actually comprised of dozens of hexagonal shapes, seemingly filled with some sort of gelatinous substance.

My hand still had stitches in it from where Tabitha had driven a knife through it, but the skin was almost completely healed, and CS Sage was already snipping and pulling the stitches out—after giving the area a quick blast with that silver canister again. I gasped involuntarily as he yanked at the thread, but the expected pain didn't come. Maybe the silver canister contained a pain reliever as well as a disinfectant? It seemed to do everything at once.

"The material will allow your skin to breathe while simultaneously pumping in the necessary ingredients for rapid bone growth and recovery," CS Sage said, noticing my scrutiny of the plastic wrapping. "On a fresh break, it would take about twenty-four hours, give or take the severity of the breaks. Since this is older, it should take less time."

He finished the stitches and placed a bandage over both sides of my hand to absorb the blood. "This is a knife wound," he stated flatly. "Easy enough to spot, and even easier to heal, but I'm a little curious as to how you came to get it, young lady."

"Someone stabbed me," I replied dryly, and he grinned, showing no sign of annoyance at my sarcasm. "Listen, I really appreciate you taking a look at me, but would you mind also taking a look at my friends? A few of them are in even worse shape than I was in, and it would really mean the world to me if you could help them."

CS Sage was now *tsk*ing over the scab covering up the hole in my head. He moved so quickly for such an old man, it was hard not to be impressed with just how filled with vitality he was. Soon another piece of that gelatinous material was pressed against my head, and immediately the dull ache I had been carrying there for weeks was gone. I hadn't even been aware it was there until it disappeared.

"Before we can even begin to discuss what to do with your shipmates," announced Raevyn matter-of-factly, her arms still crossed over her chest, "we have to decide what to do with you."

CHAPTER 10

Violet

"She'll have to remain here," Devon announced casually, his hands clasped in front of him. He looked around at the other councilors and shrugged. "She and her companions both. We'll have to... *integrate* them into our society. They'll be given the net, of course, but after that we'll be able to begin dissecting their gyroship. The ability to achieve flight would be of... great use to us."

I felt a trill of alarm at the hungry tone of his voice, like he was excited by the prospect of kidnapping three women in order to get his hands on the heloship. In fact, we were obstacles to his goals. I could tell he thought he was being gracious by even offering us a life inside the tower, and who knew if he was even telling the truth about that? I didn't like the way he'd said "integrate;" what did that even mean? What *net*?

I, for one, was not grateful, and, as CS Sage let go of my arm, I slid my right hand down to my pants, where my gun was still tucked.

Sliding it out, I settled it on my lap and kept a tight grip on the stock. It felt amazing to be holding it in my right hand again, but there wasn't any time for me to savor that feeling of rightness.

"My friends and I are not going to agree to that," I announced softly, and the Knight Commander looked over at me, his brows drawing tight over his mismatched eyes. I met his gaze head on, my jaw going up a few inches. "I have a family and a fiancé back where I came from. They have families as well. So we will not be staying with you. We won't be getting *integrated*—whatever that means—and we won't be letting you touch our... gyroship."

"You really aren't in a position to argue," Devon sneered, and I lifted the gun, pointing it right at his head. For once in the past few weeks, the movement was smooth, as if I had practiced it a dozen times just moments before, and I felt myself start to smile at how perfectly aimed I held it. It was solid, steady, no tremors.

His eyes took in the handgun, but he made no other reaction to it. "Is that supposed to scare me?" he asked, his hand already reaching for the black baton dangling through his belt.

"Enough, Alexander," spat Raevyn. "You know that I, WTS Callahan, and CS Sage won't agree to integration anyway. It's too big of a risk to the tower. She would inevitably talk—they all would."

"There are ways to prevent people from talking. IT Sparks and CL Mueller will back me," Devon calmly replied.

"Which means it will be up to Scipio to break the tie," Raevyn shot back smugly. "And per protocol—"

"It's all moot. We are still waiting on Scipio to formulate an opinion as to whose jurisdiction they fall under," announced Sage, his eyes completely on my gun.

His fingers reached out toward the gun, and I pulled it away, dropping my bead on Alexander and giving him a confused look. His eyes twinkled merrily as he took in the device, even going so far as to turn on the scanner and attempt to scan us both. His frown indicated that he hadn't succeeded, but it didn't seem to stop him from wanting to inspect it from all angles, coming around me to stare at it curiously.

"You don't have anything like this, do you?" I asked, as Raevyn continued to argue with Devon behind them. I kept an ear to their conversation, but they were heavily debating some sort of sub-sub-section of a charter to each other, and it was enough to make me want to cross my eyes.

"What does it do?" he asked, nodding at it.

"It…"

I trailed off as I saw the Head Farmer puffing up her form, getting nose to nose with the Knight Commander. She was not intimidated by him at all, and, given the red in her cheeks, she was furious.

"Just like a Mech to only see the immediate problem and not understand the big picture," she argued, her hands clenching. "You keep treating her like an isolated problem—she's not. Her people are out there; they might come looking. Oh, sure, she says that they're alone and isolated, but for all we know this could be a scout ship, or they could all be some sort of royalty! Regardless, the possibility exists. How do you want to greet a potential threat to the Tower? By treating their people with respect and some civility, and not getting caught with our hands in their cookie jar."

Sage followed my gaze and chuckled, crossing his hands across his chest. "Cogs and Hands do not get along," he whispered conspiratorially to me. As if I understood what that meant.

"Are they going to hurt each other?"

"Oh no, too proud to throw the first blow, those two. It's a shame, the damned Cog should know better—he's in an entirely different department now."

He said it so chidingly, like a disapproving grandfather, that I couldn't help but smile. "You know half the things you said are complete nonsense to me, right?"

"I know, hopefully it confuses our little alien girl. Do you have any words that might defuse the situation? They are discussing what to do with you, after all."

"Just that my people aren't likely to come after me," I said after a moment. I had contemplated a lie, weighed and measured it, but decided it was better to come clean. They wouldn't appreciate threats, and I had nothing to back them up with.

"Raevyn? Devon?" Sage's voice carried over the argument with a politeness that abbreviated the harshly hissed syllables coming out of Devon's mouth. I wasn't even sure when he had started speaking—I was too wrapped up in the oddity that was CS Sage.

Devon dropped back in his wheeled stool with a whoop, rolling away a few feet before using his feet to pull himself back over. Raevyn turned fully toward us, a tired expression on her face.

"What, Marcus?" she asked heavily.

"The alien girl has something she wishes to say," he announced cheerfully.

Raevyn seemed to sigh, and then looked over at me expectantly. "Yes?"

It occurred to me to lie yet again, even though I had just told Sage the truth less than a minute ago. And yet, I couldn't justify it. Odd as these people were, they were also the only contact with another civilization that my country had ever had. It was exhilarating, as well as terrifying, but more than that, it meant that we could start forming a relationship with this civilization. We could learn each other's cultures… histories… maybe even piece together whatever information they knew about the Fall.

"No one is coming for me," I finally said, just as Devon stepped out farther from behind Raevyn. "I don't tell you that as permission to keep me or my people here, just that you don't have to worry about any more of us. I could've lied, maybe used it as a threat to get us out of here."

"Why didn't you?" asked Devon sharply, his long arms folding across his chest.

"Because I think there is more that we could offer each other than that. I mean, I'm only speaking for myself, but I'm sure my people would love to meet your people."

"Come *here*?" Raevyn exclaimed, her eyes going wide. "Oh no, we don't have the resources to support any more mouths."

"Oh yes, *that* will certainly happen," added Sage, his sarcasm a touch more somber than before. He carefully adjusted a few instruments on a nearby tray, his mouth turned downward a little bit before ticking back up slightly. "You should just get back in your air canoe, and float away." He reached up abruptly, and I ducked down reflexively, watching as he tore off several sheets of the same kind as the one now encasing my arm.

He dropped them in a white bag, as well as the scanner and a few more items. "Are you going somewhere?" I asked.

A dimple appeared in his cheek as he smiled, and he nodded. "I am indeed. We have finally heard from the mysterious Scipio. He's allowing me to go tend to your friends!"

I stared as he hopped around to fully face me, his arms spread wide and an enthusiastic grin on his face. He seemed to be waiting for something, but I didn't move, uncertain as to what was even happening. After several long heartbeats, he sort of... deflated, although he still stood tall and proud. But there was a disappointment in the lowering of his hands and the slow deconstruction of his smile.

"Thank you?" I said, after a moment, looking at Raevyn and Devon for any sign of... something. That this was normal? I wasn't even really sure at that point.

"You're quite welcome, Miss Bates," he rumbled almost petulantly. "But the time for hugs has ended."

"I'm so—"

"I said good day, Miss!" His tone was curt, as were his motions as he snatched up the bag and marched off, placing what I assumed was an invisible hat on his head. Devon pushed the door open for him as he strutted by, and then he disappeared, Devon pulling the door closed behind him.

"There is something very terrifying about that man," breathed MacGillus, and Jathem reached over and smacked him lightly on the back of the head.

"Don't say that about him," the Knight Elite chided softly.

"You really shouldn't," added Raevyn. "You try getting to be ninety-two years old without having a few screws knocked out."

"He's ninety-two years old?" I exclaimed, my breath escaping from me. "Seriously?"

Raevyn turned, her face immediately turning red as she realized her mistake. She crossed her arms and gave an imperious shake of her head. "We are going to have to take extra care with what we say in front of her from here on out."

"Indeed." Devon's eyes had returned to me, and I shifted, suddenly feeling self-conscious. The gun was still in my hand, although it was resting in my lap now. I had stopped pointing it long ago, but the urge was back. "Knight Elite Dreyfuss, what is your assessment of Miss Bates?"

"Sir?" Jathem seemed surprised, and Devon turned, his hands going behind his back and clasping at the wrist.

"Not the report. I understand the question is vague. But just… her. What can you tell me through observation?"

"She's curious, sir," Jathem said without hesitation. "But she talked first, even after I had zapped her."

"She also stopped me from going over the edge, sir," added MacGillus. "I was racing right for her, and she could've let me fall, but she didn't."

"She wanted to know how to avoid any offense in her actions and deeds," Jathem cut back in smoothly over MacGillus. "She kept up with us on the stairs for a while, but she must have been in a lot of pain and clearly exhausted, which means she's strong-willed." I yawned at that, and then smiled at him, grateful he had noticed.

"She'd make a good knight," finished MacGillus, his eyes darting over to look at me.

I watched the exchange with no small amount of amusement. It was clear they were new to working together, but it reminded me a little bit of when Viggo and Owen bickered. It wasn't exactly the same dynamic, but the feeling was still there, and it was enough to send a pang of longing through me.

"Did she use the thing in her hand at all?" Devon prompted. "Can you even be sure it's a weapon?"

"What are you getting at, Devon?" asked Raevyn, leaning a hip against a wall and crossing her arms.

"There doesn't appear to be any power source on that thing. For all we know she's wielding a tool, Raevyn, and trying to keep the threat on us. We can seize her, and her weapon, and take that flying thing apart. And we should. Just see reason here."

"Devon, the girl has given us no cause to disbelieve her. She has actively reacted to threats to her person, and even then has chosen talk over violence. And your obsession with that flying contraption is just from being cog-bred. You know that..."

She trailed off, a frown passing over her face. I watched as the four other humans opposite me all went still, as if listening very intently. One by one their eyes dragged over to me, and there was suddenly caution there, and, clearly, in Devon's, downright anger.

Before any one of them could take a step toward me, I raised the gun toward the ceiling and squeezed the trigger.

The gunshot sounded loud in the small room, but I was ready for it, as I was for the small spark the bullet made as it hit the ceiling. The remains of the slug fell down with a sharp ding, and I lowered the gun to aim it at the others, who were flinching, their hands cupped over their ears. Devon's baton was in his hand, even cupped over his ears, while Raevyn was looking at me with alarm. Jathem openly gaped at me, his eyes wide, while MacGillus, sadly, cowered behind him, looking shaken and downright terrified.

I waited until they were looking at me, until they slowly lowered their hands, patiently counting the seconds in my head. At thirty-two they were ready to listen, so I spoke.

"This is a gun. I don't know all the components on it, but I do know that inside is a ball of metal sitting on top of a small amount of explosive powder. When I fire it," I gestured gently with the gun and was pleased to see them all flinch, "the explosion makes the piece of metal—we call it a bullet—move faster than sound, at speeds high enough to tear through human flesh and bone. Some guns are weaker, and that means the bullets might get stuck inside a person, sometimes even bouncing around and causing multiple injuries. Others are so powerful that they can leave a hole in you, sometimes so big that you can see right through it."

I scanned the room as I spoke, keeping my tone clinical and light. "I have seen, firsthand, the damage these things can cause, and I know all too well what it feels like to be the one who has caused it." I cleared my throat, suddenly dry-mouthed, and Raevyn slowly crossed her arms over her chest.

"What do you want?" she asked carefully.

"What I want is to know what message you just received that seems to have swayed your opinions against me. I guarantee if something is going on at my gyroship, then I have no previous knowledge of it. To be honest, those women and I aren't even that close."

"You aren't?" asked Devon, his eyes blazing with curiosity and malice, and I nodded.

"We really aren't. That being said, if you try to hold me accountable for something they did, I will be forced to defend myself."

"You'll never make it out of here in once piece," sneered Devon.

I let him have a moment in which he felt he had the upper hand, and then smiled. "Maybe not, but I'd kill all of you in the attempt, and at least… as many more as I could before you stopped me. And I think we can all agree that would be less than enjoyable for all of us—and much harder for your people to cover up from the rest of the citizens. So, talk to me. What did they do?"

Raevyn exchanged looks with Devon, and then uncrossed her arms, pulling the edge of her shirt down over her pants. "CS Sage just informed us that another one of those crafts is landing," she said frostily. "It has the same markings as yours, and the design is identical."

My mind immediately went to Viggo, but with a heavy heart I dismissed the thought. The only heloship my group had was almost out of fuel. I knew he was capable of a lot of things, but manifesting fuel in the middle of a war-torn city was certainly a pipe dream. He would come for me, I knew that… but I also knew there were too many obstacles in the way for him to do it so quickly.

I realized that meant the heloship had to belong to Elena's people. She had ordered them after us—someone had spotted us as we had flown over Matrus! She must've thought her sister and Desmond were still onboard.

Or somehow known *I* was. I shuddered, and lowered the gun slightly. "Listen, the ship after us, it is our people but it's not… they aren't *my* people. I'm from a neighboring country, and I'm falsely accused of a litany of crimes, but really, I discovered a plot…"

I trailed off and sighed, running my other hand over my hair, feeling the odd plastic patch breaking up the growth of hair. "Look, we have problems where I'm from. We're embroiled in a war, and that ship outside is the side that is winning. Only their leader…" I gave a dry chuckle as I realized this was pointless. Nothing I could say was going to come out right, and in fact, saying anything else was probably going to make me look like a criminal.

I sighed and leaned back against the wall, thinking. After a moment, I just shook my head. "Look, all I can say is that *I* mean you no harm. The leader of the other faction, on the other hand—Queen Elena—she's dangerous."

"You just fired a bullet at us," Devon pointed out.

"Not at you, at the ceiling. Believe me, if I had wanted to hit you, I would have. But I really don't want any harm to come to you or your people. And I also really enjoy being alive. I have a future I'd like to get to with a man I love. If you give me to them, you'll be guaranteeing two things. The first is my death, which I get isn't really your responsibility, but it would still be a pretty messed up move for you to let them kill me while I am in your custody."

"What's the second, Miss Bates?" Raevyn asked, pushing off of the wall.

"That Elena will have a way in, and she'll use it. She's devious, a manipulator, and she cares no more for your people than she does for our own. You would represent another thing to control. She might promise not to come back, but she would."

Raevyn absorbed that and looked at Devon, her eyes wary. He too was considering my words, and I felt a burst of hope. If I could convince them that Elena was the bad guy, then maybe I could just….

Do nothing and stay here forever. Unless these people were willing to kill for me, and even then that wouldn't sit right with me. Not to mention, I couldn't pilot my way back home, even if they gave me the new ship.

The door clanged open, and I jumped, my gun immediately going up toward the sound. CS Sage re-entered, a broad smile reestablished on his face. "Alien girl, I do believe we found you an alien boy!"

My heart froze. "Viggo?"

Yes, it was none other than my fiancé standing there, his own gun clasped easily in his hand, his eyes mirroring my surprise and radiating concern for my well-being. I felt myself melt a little as he ducked down to step into the room, feeling the impulse to leap into his arm and kiss him until he understood how relieved I was to see him. How much I had missed him, and…

"Hey, Violet," he said softly. "Want to introduce me to your new friends?"

The elation I felt plummeted as five additional pairs of eyes turned toward me expectantly, and I realized I had just unintentionally lied to them all.

CHAPTER 11

Viggo

The sudden change in Violet's face threw me. Whatever I had walked in on, she was decidedly irritated with it—and clearly tired. But given the two Matrian wardens I had found working on the moderately damaged heloship…

My thoughts faltered. This was all too surreal. When, maybe as a child, I had imagined or hoped there were other people out there in the world, I had always pictured them as a kind of group of nomads, people just scraping by in The Outlands, living primitively, away from the only civilization that had managed to grow in these terrible times. Maybe they would be mutants, barely recognizable as human. I'd never for a moment imagined these hopes were real, or that they could have technology equal to or even superior to our own—yet here I stood in what was clearly a very advanced medical bay, designed and run by other *people*. Not Matrian or Patrian, but still people, with the same general features, and hopefully emotions, that made us all human. It was incomprehensible, yet here we were, face to face with a different culture. My elation was only matched by a strong urge for caution, and, judging from Violet's expression, there was definitely something to be cautious about.

I took a step into the room as Violet frowned and ran a hand over her head. I caught the motion out of the corner of my eye, my focus on sizing up any potential foes, honing in on the tall, lanky man wearing crimson. He stared right back at me, clearly doing the same thing. He maybe had an inch of height on me, but other than that, we were pretty evenly matched.

Violet seemed to recover from her shock, pointing out each of the individuals as she introduced me to them. "HF Hart, CS Sage, KC Alexander, and, uh, K MacGillus—this is Viggo Croft, my fiancé. I…" She stumbled on her words, her voice wavering between awestruck and annoyed. "I had *no idea* he would be able to come after me this quickly. I apologize. I didn't mean to lie to you. I truly didn't think it was possible, given the state we were in when this little adventure began. I was terrified that Elen—that our enemies had found this place. Please believe me when I say that this is not an advance party or even a scouting one."

I keyed in to what Violet was saying, keeping my eyes on the three individuals before me. The older gentleman, CS Sage, gave me a broad smile, his blue eyes twinkling. "Is that true, alien boy?"

My eyebrow raised, and I nodded. "It is," I replied.

"So you're just here on a rescue mission?" asked the woman, her eyes narrowed, not bothering to hide the mistrust in her face. "And we're just supposed to believe that?"

"Look, I have been as honest with you as I could under the conditions," said Violet tiredly. "You can tell our ship is damaged, and two of the three people I arrived with were severely injured in the altercation that took place. CS Sage, am I lying?"

"No," the older man said brightly. "But then again, you're not exactly being truthful. The big man in the back of your heloship has some decidedly interesting mutations in his genetic code, and a severe synaptic imbalance in his brain chemistry. I'm curious, are there more like him where you come from?"

Alarm washed over me, and I looked at Violet, trusting her to take the lead on this, as she had clearly spent more time with the strangers and developed a rapport with them, or at least a semblance of one. I was beginning to realize, from how cagey the group was, that this situation could have devastating consequences if handled poorly.

I needn't have worried about Violet's reaction. She arched an eyebrow at CS Sage, a smile tugging at the corner of her lips. "Much like the mysterious Scipio, this man must remain a mystery."

CS Sage chuckled and then looked at the other two. "I like her. My vote is placed. If you'll excuse me? Her pi-lot"—he pronounced "pilot" as two words, as if he'd never heard it before—"is very unwell."

Violet shifted, and I turned to see the flash of concern on her face. "Can you help her?" she asked.

"I can and I will, young alien lady. Never fear, m'dear." CS Sage tipped an imaginary cap at her and then swept back out of the room.

"Wait! What vote?" Violet called, but the only sound that carried through the swinging door was an amused chuckle.

"We've decided that you should meet the council," said Raevyn, as though some signal had been given, though I could see no sign that she had come by new information. "And give them a full debriefing. If you'll come with us?"

I absorbed that knowledge, suddenly excited by the prospect of meeting with the leaders of this place. This was an entirely new civilization—a conversation with them was a fantastical offer. If it went well, we could come back and maybe start a trade, share histories, learn and grow from each other's inventions… My mind was whirling so fast with the thousands of exciting possibilities about a potential sister city that Violet's reply completely took me off guard.

"No, I'm sorry, we must decline." I cast a look at her, and her gray eyes flicked up to mine, meeting them for half a second. I kept my face blank, concealing the stab of disappointment that went through me, surprisingly strong, at the news. Still, if Violet was saying no, there was a reason. "We need to get back to our ship. Your council can meet us up there, but I said I had an hour, and I meant an hour."

Raevyn frowned. "Very well. Why don't you take a moment to collect yourselves, and we will wait outside to take you back to the ship?"

"Thank you," Violet said, inclining her head. "Or… Tahatlana? May your waters run clear?"

Raevyn blinked, and then her face twisted up into a surprised smile. "Something like that," she chuckled. "You have a good ear."

Violet shrugged, and Raevyn and Devon slipped out the door.

When the door swung closed, I was already moving forward. Violet and I rushed toward each other, and I threw my arms around her, crushing her to my chest and holding her there. She sniffed, nuzzling her cheek against my chest.

"You smell awful," she commented, and I laughed.

"Hey, I had a really busy morning," I replied in self-defense. I knew she didn't care—there had been more than a few times when both of us were less than fragrant, especially after life or death situations. And Violet herself wasn't in much of a position to critique my cleanliness.

She laughed a little and then stopped abruptly, looking up at me with huge gray eyes. "Oh my God, Viggo, how are you here?"

I took a step back. "It's kind of a long story, but to sum up, we used the last of our heloship fuel to take several pilots and pilots-in-training to the Matrian airfield, and we took everything we could, including several of their ships, and then blew up the others."

Her eyes widened, and then a smile crossed her lips. "Seriously?"

I shrugged. "It was Henrik's idea, and it was the best shot at getting to you quickly. Elena was thorough. She disabled the entire Patrian fleet and took *their* fuel before we got to them. There's a chance she stored it somewhere else within Patrus, but we just didn't have time to look."

She nodded, and then pulled me close again. "I was so scared that I'd never get to see you again," she breathed into my chest.

"I know," I soothed her as she trembled slightly. I understood completely—I felt exactly the same way. That fear had been tearing me apart for the last few hours… even now, it scared me more than anything how much sheer luck had led us to find her so quickly. I mean, we'd used what information we'd had, and made some very educated guesses, but luck was definitely a factor. "So, what is the deal with this place?"

Violet exhaled as she gently extracted herself from my arms. "Viggo, there are *people* here. I'm not entirely sure what to make of them, but they're people just like us. Those black stick things the knights are carrying give off an electrical charge, so watch out for that. CS Sage is *ninety-two* years old. And oh my God, look!"

She held up her arm, and I suddenly realized I had completely missed the fact that her cast was gone. I had been so glad to see her alive, I had only given her a cursory glance, making sure she was relatively unharmed, before trying to appraise the situation with the others in the room. I gently took her arm, giving her a questioning look, and she beamed, nodding.

"This can apparently repair broken bones in twenty-four hours."

I softly prodded the plastic encasing her arm, realizing there was some sort of gelatinous fluid inside. "Fascinating. Do you think they will be willing to meet with us again, at a later date?"

Violet hesitated, and then gave a shrug. "I have no idea. They are very suspicious, and I get the feeling they really don't want us to be here. But honestly… maybe? Devon—the Knight Commander—wants to keep us here so he can take apart the, uh, gyroship," she gave me a pointed look, and I caught on quickly, "and reverse engineer it."

"I see. But that means we might have something they would be willing to establish a trade for."

"Weirdly, they also don't know what guns are. They didn't even react to mine until I had to fire it." She quickly explained the circumstances, and I nodded, listening intently, trying to absorb all the new information. After she finished, I frowned.

"That *is* weird. Our history books said that guns were everywhere before the Fall. It seems odd that these people wouldn't even have a record of it."

"I agree, but they clearly don't." She paused, and then looked up at me, the color leaving her face so quickly I almost thought she was injured again. "Oh, Viggo. Jay! I can't believe I didn't ask earlier. Is he—"

"I don't know," I told her honestly, my own heart sinking at the thought of how we'd left the young man. "April was working on stabilizing him when I left. Tim stayed behind to be with him. Morgan also got

Cody out of the water. He's alive, but he was shaken up pretty badly. I don't know how things will go with him if... *when*... we get back." Now wasn't the time to speculate about the young man, and after hearing the new horrors Desmond had put him through, I had no idea what to expect.

Violet exhaled, relief flickering over her face, and then tilted her head up at me. "What about the plant? I know you got the purge to work—but was anyone hurt or... or killed?"

"Gregory didn't make it," I replied reluctantly, and reached out to grab her hand as her face filled with sadness. "A few others. Alejandro's hand got smashed. And Harry's hurt. He got smashed by a door. I'm not sure if he's going to make it. Ms. Dale is fine."

Violet opened her mouth, and I interrupted her, knowing her next question before it slipped through her lips. "Owen is fine. Amber and Logan Vox flew the heloship here—they're upstairs right now. I went ahead and asked them to transfer Solomon to our ship. What about the Matrians? Should we—"

"Offer them a ride home?" Violet considered it for a long moment. "We can, but I doubt they'd take it. Things, uh, weren't exactly copacetic between the three of us."

"Yeah. I was surprised they let you down here on your own."

She grinned up at me, her face smug, and quickly explained what had transpired after Desmond had been thrown from the ship. I felt a stab of pride. "You handled that extremely well—which I would never doubt—but still, getting them to work with you in spite of their Matrian prejudice? Impressive."

"Well, with you and Ms. Dale as mentors, how could I not succeed?" she said, and I felt my love for her deepen, expanding in my chest like a never-ending fountain. Leaning over, I pulled her to me and pressed my lips to hers—just a gentle brush.

"And the award for fiancée of the month goes to..." I breathed after I pulled back, and she laughed a little. "Shall we?"

She checked her watch again and nodded. "We really should," she said.

I took her hand and led her to the door, throwing it open. The two guards outside had disappeared, and Raevyn and Devon were waiting patiently for us. I paused, but Violet was already moving back in the direction I'd come from earlier. She moved quickly, pulling me with her. I followed, trusting her instincts.

Raevyn and Devon sprang into motion behind us after a surprised pause, the sounds of our boots echoing heavily down the narrow hall. Violet led with confidence, and I realized she had memorized the path here. I had done the same thing—naturally—but I still couldn't help but feel proud of her as she moved down the long hall.

The windowpane on the left side of the hall slowed us both as our heads, unbidden, swiveled to take in the view of the buildings inside. Without discussion, we came to a stop at almost the same time. I studied the construction, the lines and angles as well as the practicality, but most of all… the sheer size and scope of it all. It was so dense and compact—and I could make out people from far away—men and women both. It felt ridiculous to have discovered something this big and be leaving so soon, but our own troubles were still waiting for us.

"We really should be going," Raevyn said softly, and I reluctantly started to turn. Violet lingered, her gray eyes darting around as if she were trying to memorize the place, and then turned as well.

She moved a few more feet down the hall, and then turned around the correct corner, moving down the tight passageway toward the door. I moved ahead of her and opened it for her, as Devon's voice carried down the hall from behind us.

"How did you know that was the right passageway?" His voice was sharp, edged with suspicion and mistrust.

"I memorized the route when you guided me here," Violet replied curtly as she stepped through. I held the door open for Devon, Raevyn, and MacGillus, watching them closely as they moved past me. "Just in case you tried anything."

"Smart," said Raevyn. "You'll understand if we continue to escort you, of course."

It wasn't a question, but I replied for us both. "I would do the same thing if our positions were reversed."

She gave me a considering look, then began moving down the stairs. "Never fear, Miss Bates, Mr. Croft—we will return you to your ship whole and in one piece."

I was tempted to say "We shall see," just to test their honesty, but there was no reason for it, and judging by her expressive body language, I was inclined to believe her. We moved in silence after that, with Violet taking the lead. Devon put himself in the rear—something that didn't make me entirely comfortable. Raevyn seemed to have taken up our cause. With him, I wasn't so sure.

Going down the stairs was much better than going up. As much as my adrenaline was holding me up, it didn't mean I didn't feel the aches and pains from the night before. My ribs were still sore, and I was still out of shape from the surgery I had undergone—not long ago, although it felt like lifetimes. I did my best not to let the effort show, keeping a careful eye on Violet. Her injuries were more recent than most of mine, but she seemed to be holding her own just fine.

Violet stopped on a landing about halfway down, turned and looked at the door. "This one, right?"

Raevyn moved past her. "Indeed," she said dryly, pulling the door open and stepping through. The passage was short, and in under a minute, we were back outside. The heat was stifling—I was certain the sweat that had instantly formed all over my body was immediately evaporating under the dry heat.

We made our way across the glass surface—as bizarre as that was—heading toward the damaged heloship. I could make out CS Sage standing by the open cargo bay, tending to the brown-haired woman wearing an olive green Matrian uniform. The tall, broad-shouldered blonde wearing a sky-blue version of the same uniform stood next to her, watching him with her arms crossed.

As we neared, CS Sage looked up, and then patted the dark-haired woman on the shoulder, giving her an encouraging nod. She was holding up her hand, clearly marveling at the plastic now surrounding her fingers.

"That's it?" she asked, blinking up at him.

"That's it," he said with a broad smile. "Just leave it on for a day, and the bones will be completely healed. These"—he extended a hand with a packet of pills inside—"are for your internal injuries. Take one of each, twice a day, with food."

The blonde woman accepted the packet, moving with a swiftness that belied her size. "Thank you, Mr. Sage," she said begrudgingly, and he patted her on the shoulder. Not for long, as she took an alarmed step back, her hand going for a gun at her waist and then stopping halfway when she realized he wasn't actually attempting to hurt her.

"Ah! The alien girl and her alien fiancé have returned," CS Sage announced, seemingly oblivious to the blonde woman's alarm. "Have you told them?"

"Not yet," replied Raevyn from behind me, at the same time that Violet asked, "Told us what?"

"The council has decided not to meet with you after all," Devon drawled, hooking his thumbs through the belt around his waist. "In fact, we have been asked to relay to you that you leave immediately, and never return." He looked at the rest of the group, muttering, "Waste of resources, if you ask me," and Raevyn frowned deeply at him, shaking her head, while Jathem and MacGillus stayed silent but seemed distinctly uncomfortable.

Warning bells went off in my head, but I was still blinking at his declaration—an abrupt departure from what they'd said just moments earlier. What could have changed their minds so suddenly? If their council had such an immediate influence on their minds, it must be a very controlling system. And the idea of such absolute control had never struck me as safe.

"Wait," I tested, unable to really comprehend the decision, "never return? Why? Surely our two cultures could help each other in some way. Even establish a trade of some sort?"

It was Raevyn who answered. "Our system is perfect as it is. We lack the resources to support outsiders. What's more, the council feels that even the knowledge of a society that exists outside of the tower could jeopardize everything, which is why we are going to eradicate all knowledge of your existence. If people learned there was another place they could survive in, they might panic or even try to leave."

"Surely they should have that choice," Violet started to say, and Devon gave her a look so derisive that she dropped the sentence, confirming my hunch—control issues in this society ran mile-deep.

The Knight Commander said archly, "Everyone in the tower has a function, a duty, a service that is essential to the operation of the tower. Ours is a delicate balance, one we cannot compromise on. If people decided to leave, our entire way of life would dissolve. The council has decided that, as advantageous as your technology might be to us, your very existence is a risk, and we cannot excuse your continued presence just because you want to make friends. We've already put ourselves out in order to heal you… I suggest you not waste any more of our time."

Condescension and disdain were thick in his voice, and I fought off the urge to deck him, reminding myself that we *were* on their turf—and we *did* want to leave, after all. I also knew KC Devon wanted the helo-ships. For all I knew, he was trying to provoke one of us into violence so that he could be justified in acting in self-defense in an attempt to secure our technology. His eyes blazed in open challenge. It was probably better for his sake that I wasn't a man who lost his head easily, and I met his gaze with a hard one of my own.

CS Sage looked from me to Devon and back again, the slow swivel of his head catching my attention from the corner of my eye. "Men," he sighed, scratching the back of his neck. "Am I right, ladies?"

His delivery was as surprising as it was humorous, and I heard Violet struggling to keep a laugh from spilling from her throat. I turned away from Devon first to see her hand over her mouth, her eyes sparkling. Raevyn was not as amused: a dour frown hovered on her lips, and her eyes were troubled more than anything, sending additional warning signals to the base of my brain. Maybe it was just because she was used to CS Sage's quirky sense of humor, but I got the feeling that something more was definitely up. But I had no way of knowing what, exactly. For all I knew, she didn't agree with them asking us to leave, but couldn't say anything at this point.

"Anywho, goodbye, little alien girl," CS Sage continued, moving over to Violet and dropping a chaste kiss on her forehead. "If you come back, we're going to blow you out of the sky!"

He held up his hand, his index finger and thumb held up so that they formed two guns, and then he made a *pew pew* sound as he mimicked shooting. Violet's gaze moved up over his shoulder to find mine, alarm filling her gray eyes, and then CS Sage was moving away, Devon and Raevyn moving past us to head toward the door with him.

She turned to watch them go, and I moved up behind them. "I think we should go," I murmured.

"No kidding. Just give me a second to talk to the Matrians, and we'll get going."

"You want me to join you?"

She tilted her head up at me, and then shook her head. "Nope, I got this. I'll see you in a minute."

CHAPTER 12

Violet

I moved toward where Belinda and Kathryn had retreated inside the bay of the repaired Matrian ship. Kathryn saw me coming and gave me a brusque nod. "Seems your people came for you," she commented warily, eyeing Viggo from over my shoulder.

"They did," I replied. It was unnecessary, but it was nice we were keeping some semblance of civility. "You going to try and stop me from going with them?"

Kathryn gave me a stern look, turning her gaze toward Belinda, clearly gauging her reaction. Then she shrugged. "I'm just a pilot. Prisoner acquisition isn't in my wheelhouse."

I smiled. Maybe I had made a bigger impression on Kathryn than I'd thought. More likely, however, she was just as eager to get back home as I was, and didn't want to further risk her life by getting into a shootout.

"Is this thing good to go?" I asked, my eyes moving around the cabin.

"The patch Belinda made isn't pretty, but it'll get us home," she said. "And thanks to the treatment we got from CS Sage, I should be recovered soon. Was that your doing?"

I shrugged, not really certain how to answer or even whether I should tell her the truth. We might be in a better place than we were a few hours ago, but that didn't mean they would take the truth willingly, and they might not even believe it if I told them. Better to change the topic and let them speculate.

"Are you sure you want to take this thing back?" I asked. "Even with the patch, the whole thing could crash."

"What are you proposing?" asked Belinda, breaking her stony silence.

I hesitated at the suspicion in her voice, on the verge of not even extending the offer, but then decided to go for it. "Look, you can come with us. I give you my word of honor that we will deliver you as close to Matrus as we dare."

Belinda cocked her head at me, clearly surprised by the offer. But the mistrust was still there, brewing behind her eyes. Kathryn gave us both a look, and then shook her head. "The repairs are solid," she said confidently. "We can get ourselves home."

The urge to protest—at the very least make a case for it—was strong, but I decided it was a waste of time. I couldn't blame them; if our positions were reversed, I would feel a similar level of distrust.

"Fair enough," I replied. "Good luck."

She inclined her head and then cast another look up at Belinda before nodding. "I gotta go perform a quick check of the engines," she announced. Turning, she moved toward the cockpit and then paused. "Thank you for helping us out. That was… really big of you, all things considered."

Kathryn didn't wait for my reply, just moved forward into the cockpit before I could even begin to formulate a response. Which was good. I wasn't even sure how to respond, considering she had actually thanked me. I was so stunned, I was fairly confident a stiff breeze would knock me over.

"Is that your fiancé?" Belinda asked, and I started and tore my gaze from the door that Kathryn had disappeared through. I saw her looking at Viggo, and smiled.

"He is indeed," I replied.

She scrunched up her face, taking a moment to examine him, and then, to my utter surprise, gave an approving nod. "He's handsome." My surprise quickly evaporated as the large blonde woman met my gaze and grinned wolfishly, revealing a gap in between her two front teeth, as well as a set of cavernous dimples. "Get married before we catch you. It would be a shame to hang you both before you had a chance to proclaim your love. And it's pretty clear that he loves you."

I pressed my lips into a tight line to try to contain my smile, but it was impossible. "Belinda, I had no idea you were a romantic."

The smile slipped from her lips, and she narrowed her eyes at me to the point that she looked like she was squinting. "Yeah, I didn't mean for that comment to be taken as a 'let's be friends.' Because we're not. And we never will be. Best of luck, Violet. You're going to need it."

She abruptly turned on her heel and began moving toward the cockpit. "Hey," I called after her, and she paused, turning her ear toward me. I waited for her to turn, but after a second it was clear that she wasn't going to. "I really do hope your sister is okay. If she is, and we have her, I'll see about getting her back to you. Francis, right? Francis Carver?"

Belinda turned, and gave me a scowl. "How very charitable of you," she sneered. "How very kind. Let my sister go because we were forced to rely on each other to survive, but what about the others your people might have caught? Gonna just keep them as prisoners?"

I frowned and shook my head. "I don't want to keep anyone prisoner," I replied honestly.

"Right. Which was why you kept Desmond a prisoner." I opened my mouth to protest, because that was different, and she held up a hand, forestalling me. "Save it. We were in a tough spot. We helped each other. That's it."

With that, she propelled herself forward into the cockpit, disappearing within. I hesitated, and then turned back to where Viggo was waiting for me at the bottom of the ramp, moving to him quickly.

"How'd it go?" he asked, and I shook my head.

"They're finding their own way home. We should go. I doubt very much the people inside the tower would be pleased with us staying any longer."

He frowned but nodded, reaching out to take my hand. "Let's get you back home then," he said with a smile, wrapping a strong arm around my shoulder. I leaned into his side, suddenly feeling beyond drained, and together we walked over toward the other heloship probably twenty feet away. We might be out of this stew of problems, and it was beyond wonderful to be with Viggo again, but this just meant that I had to find the strength to continue back into the mass of problems waiting for me at home.

As we drew near, a familiar young woman strode down the ramp, a confident swagger in her gait. As the mop of red curls with close-shaved sides appeared, I felt a smile cross my lips.

"Hey, Amber. I heard that you've recently upgraded to pirate status."

Amber placed her hands on her hips and posed dramatically, like a heroine out of one of the graphic novels that were popular in Matrus, and I chuckled as I threw my arms around her neck, pulling her in for a quick hug.

"I'm so happy you're okay," I told her, and her arms came around my shoulders, hugging me tightly back.

"Same here with you, Violet. Don't get me wrong—I love Ms. Dale, but she's old, and Morgan has never been particularly fun. Of course, now I understand. She's a Matrian princess, and it seems those girls are wound up tight."

I snorted. I couldn't help myself, but then I felt a pang of regret at my own humor. Morgan was a princess. Clearly she'd gone rogue or was against Elena, but for what reason? She'd killed her own twin, which meant she could be ruthless, and she was enhanced—likely with the same enhancement Tim had, given the skills she'd displayed last night. Still… I liked her, and she'd risked herself and her cover to help me track down Desmond at the water treatment plant, so whatever her reasons, I was willing to hear her out.

"Hey! Are we leaving yet? This place is really starting to creep me out."

I broke away from Amber in time to see her roll her eyes and then suck in a deep breath as Logan Vox sauntered down the ramp. He was taller than I had realized. Amber's head barely came up to his collarbone. And he was strikingly handsome. Not as handsome as Viggo, of course, but I was exceptionally, unapologetically biased, and maybe some people might have thought the comparison apt. Black hair, short at the back and fashionably long in front, was smoothed over to one side of the pilot's face, and his bright blue eyes seemed to twinkle, as if he were in on some secret joke he wasn't quite sharing with anyone. By the looks of him, he kept himself in good working shape. He looked like a swimmer, lean and athletic, but from how he moved, I could already see that he could be lethal if necessary.

Amber turned toward him, an exaggeratedly slow smile spreading across her face until it became the baring of teeth. "Logan, this is Violet, a very dear friend of mine, whom we are out here to rescue. Do you think you can just… retract the stick in your butt for one minute while I say hello?"

Her voice was saccharine-sweet but also filled with disdain—an unusual combination of the two that I'd never heard from Amber before—yet for some reason all it did was make Logan smile slowly and wink at her.

"Nope. I'm way too jealous."

She sucked in a breath, opened her mouth as if to say something, and then gave an irritated *tsk* and stalked past him, reaching out and shoving him to one side as she went past.

"I'll be in the cockpit," she declared imperiously as he stumbled to one side, chuckling and rubbing his shoulder. He looked around, saw me looking at him, and shrugged before following her into the cockpit.

I looked back at Viggo, who was slowly climbing up the ramp behind me and shaking his head, already answering my unspoken question. "I'll tell you about it later. They've been like that the entire trip. I had to put up with that for *four hours*. Four. So you better love me so hard right now."

I laughed, reaching down and grabbing a fistful of his vest to pull him toward me up the final few feet of the ramp. "I really, really do," I breathed, tilting my head up to him.

"I'm closing the ramp!" Amber shouted loudly, and then Viggo's mouth was on my own, his tongue slipping past my parted lips in a burst of passion so heady I felt my innards become as gooey as the stuff in my new high-tech cast. The kiss ended with him drawing my lower lip in between his teeth, sending delicious shudders through my body, right down to my fingers and toes.

When we broke apart, I felt my eyes slowly open and a wide—probably dopey—grin break out on my face. "I love you," I said.

"I love you too," he replied. "Now let's go grab a seat. Vox was Amber's instructor at one point, and they, uh, tend to disagree on who should be in command. It got a bit rocky before, and we should really... get into a seat. With a seatbelt. Or twelve."

I chuckled, probably too loudly. Maybe I was laughing at everything, even things that shouldn't be funny, but it was uncontrollable: Viggo was here, we weren't going to die... and now we knew there were people. *Other* people outside of Matrus and Patrus. And they were thriving. We weren't the only humans left in the world after all. It was exciting, surreal. I was so tired I was probably delirious.

The deck under my feet shuddered as the high-pitched noise of the engines grew, and I moved toward the cockpit, taking a quick moment to check that Solomon was okay and strapped down for takeoff. He was, and some sort of... pink goo had been applied over the multitude of bullet holes in his gut, presumably by CS Sage. Yet his vitals were strong, and he remained unconscious.

I entered the cockpit in time to see the tower's platform slowly growing smaller. The other heloship was pulling away, and I watched as they headed back down the river—back the way we had come.

"Are we going to follow them along the river to Matrus?" I asked. "Or fly via The Green?"

"The Green," Amber replied, flipping some switches in rapid succession on the control panel, her eyes focused solely on the gauges. "It's better. Elena is going to be pissed after what we did to her airfield, so I wouldn't put it past her to have put any remaining heloships in the air, flying over Matrian airspace, either looking for us or trying to keep away from any more attacks."

"*Unless* we destroyed their entire fleet," Logan challenged. "And it's perfectly safe."

"Don't be dense," Amber muttered, and the man shot her a bemused look. I drew close to the window as the platform dropped away and the river that ran below came into view, the blue of it bright and vibrant against the cracked yellow earth surrounding it.

"Amber, can you turn the ship around for a second?" I asked. "Did you guys notice this?"

"The river?" asked Viggo, and I nodded, my eyes watching the landscape rotate steadily as Amber slowly turned us back toward the tower, angling the nose down slightly. I reached up to brace my right hand on the frame, enjoying the lack of clunky plaster that had made that move irritatingly ineffective in the other heloship, less than an hour ago, and then watched.

As the nose dipped lower, more of the tower came into view, as did more of the platforms—of which there appeared to be four below the one we'd landed on. The area between the tower and the river had been dug out, like the tower was sitting on an additional river bed, and from the side came a swirling, metallic blue liquid that dumped into the churning river waters. I had never seen a color like that. The way it moved and flowed made it seem thick.

"They're poisoning it," I said, confirming what I had already guessed to be true.

"Yeah, but why?" asked Amber, her neck craning to see what we were looking at. "To what end?"

"It could be industrial byproduct," Viggo suggested. "Running anything out here that could let humans survive would probably create a lot of waste. It would have to go somewhere, but that's... a messed up choice, poisoning the river."

"Maybe they just assumed it didn't matter because they thought they were the only survivors," Logan speculated. "That's what we did, after all."

"We don't pollute anything this badly," Amber pointed out, a snide touch to her tone. "We have to tell them, right? They're destroying the river. Making it harder for us to live and survive."

I hesitated, genuinely torn. On the one hand, she was absolutely right: assuming they weren't doing it on purpose, they did need to know that dumping their waste in the river was creating a threat to us. On the other hand, telling them that would key them in to where our societies were located, and that could mean *them* coming to *us*. After all, Devon had eyed the heloship with a hunger that made the hair on my neck stand up. And CS Sage had basically threatened to blow us out of the sky if we ever came back. It was not an easy call.

I looked at Viggo, who seemed deep in thought, considering the problem. "I think we had better…" He trailed off, his eyes going to the tower. "Amber, what is that?"

"Um, hold on a second," she said. I heard her clicking a few buttons, but I was squinting, trying to see what Viggo had spotted. "I got an enhanced image on the holotable, Viggo."

I turned, the holotable glowing brightly as it activated. Then the image of the tower flickered into view, the 3D picture showing a view from much closer than we actually were. I immediately spotted what Viggo had seen, and frowned. One of the platforms seemed to ripple, as if something had just impacted, and a shockwave was radiating outward.

My frown deepened as I moved over to the table. Nothing had hit the tower. There was no impact, no missile, and nobody to fire such a projectile but us. Instead it seemed the panels of glass were lifting up off of the wing jutting from the side of the tower. There were rods attached to the underside of each one, and the dark brown glass shone a bright white as they caught the rays of the sun.

"What is that?" I breathed, repeating Viggo's question. The panels were rearranging into a bowl shape, as the rods behind them reoriented the newly configured… whatever it was to point toward the west.

I felt my stomach drop as, suddenly, the array flashed white under the bright yellow sunlight, catching the rays of the sun so intently the glass bowl glowed with a brilliance that rivaled the river and the sun combined. I wanted to squint my eyes, even looking at a camera feed patched in from the hull of the ship.

"Where's Belinda's ship?" I asked, and Viggo moved over to where an inset keyboard was on the opposite side of the table and clicked a few buttons. The image zoomed up as the outer camera panned, and I could see the other heloship making its way—slowly but steadily—following the glowing blue part of the river back to Matrus. Studying it, I realized the bowl thing was pointed almost directly at them, and I felt the pit of my stomach drop out completely.

"You have to warn them," I shouted at Amber. "Broadcast all frequencies and tell them—"

The glowing seemed to have reached some sort of critical mass, because even as I spoke, a beam of spectacular white light burst forth from the bowl, streaking toward Belinda and Kathryn's ship.

For a second, I hoped that whatever the light was, it would just be some sort of high-technology gadget that didn't cause any harm. A scanning beam. A warning signal.

The next moment, my fragile hope was shattered. I gaped as the beam of light cut through Belinda and Kathryn's ship, slicing it cleanly in half, the edges of where the beam of light had touched bright red even from this distance and clearly melting into slag. The two halves of the ship plummeted downward, each tumbling on an oblong axis toward the broken earth below.

"No, no, no," I gasped, taking a few hesitant steps toward the window, unable to comprehend that they were just... gone. It wasn't fair. We had worked together to save ourselves, and in under a second, our hard-won victory had been ripped away by the people in the tower.

"It's moving toward us," said Viggo, and I turned. Sure enough, the dish was twisting toward us, much faster than it had zeroed in on Belinda and Kathryn, and I felt a stab of anger.

"Amber! Dive!" I shouted, just as the panels on the array began to glow white.

CHAPTER 13

Viggo

Amber was rushing to move the heloship almost before Violet shouted. She threw the control beam forward, her arms extending straight out in front of her, her teeth gritted. The deck dipped, and the view through the bubble was suddenly filled with earth and water rushing up to meet us at a phenomenal rate. I felt myself go weightless, and a high-pitched noise filled the air.

I caught sight of the holotable in time to see the white streak of light filling the screen—then the table went dead, and a juddering, jolting shudder ran through the ship. Something splattered onto the deck, and a klaxon alarm began to sound. Looking up, I could see that a wide strip of the roof grating overhead had turned red hot, and bits of molten metal were dripping down to the deck below, landing with sizzling plops.

Heat blossomed inside the cockpit, and sweat formed instantly across my brow. I pulled Violet away from the dripping wound in the ship, trying to get into a more secure position in the heloship.

"Arm the missiles!" Logan was shouting at Amber. "Shoot the bastards back, dammit!"

"Shoot at a giant beam of light? Are you crazy?"

"Not at the light beam, at the... the weapon!"

Amber's voice sounded dangerously close to hysteria. "If you have time to aim right now then do it yourself!"

Logan lunged at the controls with a grunt, but he stumbled and slid across the cockpit as Amber began to yank back on the helm, shifting us left at an uncomfortable angle. "And get that damn alarm shut off!" she ordered, the muscles in her arms straining as she angled us up and away.

I managed to toss Violet onto one of the built-in seats before the rise of gravity again began to pull me back. My foot slipped out from under me as the deck grew steeper and steeper, and I would've fallen flat on my face had Violet not reached out to grab a fistful of my shirt.

"HANG ON," she yelled, and I wrapped my hand around her forearm.

She looped her other arm through and around the unbuckled harness behind her, gripping the one from the seat next to her, and then she was holding my weight, as I was suddenly dangling from her arm. Violet gave a pained grunt, and her legs came around my chest, hooking behind my back, under my armpits, her hold the only thing keeping me from plummeting into the bulkhead below.

I looked out past her, toward the bubble, and saw the beam of light streaking across it, right in our path. Vox shouted something—it was hard to hear amid the chaos—Amber screamed in reply, and then we were dropping again. Violet and I slammed to the floor in a tangle of limbs as the angle on the deck slid toward ninety once again, but this time we both managed to make it to the seats and strap ourselves in.

"To hell with this," Amber roared, and she pushed one control forward, holding the other one back. We began to spin in the air, the sky, earth, and water pin-wheeling through the bubble at dizzying rates as we dropped lower down, the earth growing larger. Just when I thought we were about to hit, Amber gave an angry shout and hauled back on both of the controls, forcing the nose back up, away from the impending earth.

She stabilized the ship low to the ground, and then began flipping switches. "Find them," she said hurriedly, sweat beading on her fore-head. "If it starts charging again, then we fire."

Logan began cycling through images on the screen in front of her, until they found one of the tower, rapidly disappearing behind us. She watched it for a full minute, her violet eyes searching for any sign that they were firing again, and then sighed, sinking into the pilot's seat.

"We're clear," she announced, flipping a switch and killing the image.

I let out a long breath, and then looked down and realized that I had been holding Violet's hand tightly in my own, squeezing it with a death grip. She and I looked at each other, and I lifted her hand to my lips, kissing the back of it.

"Thank you," I said softly, and she smiled.

"I think we'd better thank Amber," she panted, and I realized she was trembling slightly. I undid our buckles and pulled her into a hug, and she let out a shuddering breath, clutching my arms. "Can we never do that again?"

"I only wish I could promise that, my love. But we're okay. And you're right—that was some spectacular flying, Amber."

Amber swiveled around in her seat to look at us both. "I take thanks in the form of chocolate and strawberries, preferably where the strawberry is covered with the chocolate." Even through her teasing, it was hard not to note her uneven breathing and the pallor of her cheeks.

I chuckled—it was hard not to—and then couldn't resist the urge to tease her a smidge. "Should I also thank the man who taught you?"

"Ha!" Amber scoffed at the same time that Vox said, "Well, obviously. Anybody who could pull off such an impressive move probably had a genius teacher."

I snorted as Amber whipped around to give him a hot glare. "Why don't you go run an internal scan to see how bad the damage was? I think we only caught the very edge of the beam, but..." Her anger seemed to burn out in the face of shock at what we'd just witnessed. "God... can you believe that! How did they even do that?"

"It has something to do with the sunlight, that much is for sure,"

I said, my eyes going up toward the ceiling. The red-hot metal had turned dull again, but the grated ceiling was no longer lying flat. In fact, it had warped inward, in a track as wide as the palm of my hand. "Extraordinary."

Whether they were channeling the sun, or had somehow managed to replicate its heat in order to create a weapon, the implications were mindboggling. If all the panels on the tower could be controlled like that, it made for a pretty formidable defense. Just watching the other ship get destroyed... the ease with which the beam of light had done it... Terrifying. Yet fascinating. Especially now that we were—hopefully—out of range.

"Solomon!" Violet gasped, and she immediately jumped for the cargo bay, pulling away from my embrace. Her knees were shaky. If there was one thing I knew about my girl, it was that she didn't particularly enjoy flying, not since that one time she had accidentally crashed a flying motorcycle into The Green. But of course she didn't let it stop her.

I moved behind her and found Solomon where we had left him on one of the benches in the back, a blanket draped over him, with three thick red strips wrapped around his chest and looped through an exposed support on the bulkhead below, fixing him in place.

"Logan and I strapped him down, just in case," Amber called from the cockpit over the noise. "Is he okay?"

Violet quickly checked his pulse, and then nodded, reaching up to pinch the bridge of her nose and exhale. "He's fine," she shouted into the cockpit, clearly relieved.

"And you?" I asked, taking a step closer. Her silver eyes dragged up to me, and I saw sadness there.

"Kathryn and Belinda are dead," she said. "I'm not even sure how I'm supposed to feel about it, but I feel... I feel..."

I cupped her cheeks between my hands. "Baby, it's okay. Feel however you want. I'm sure whatever happened on that ship between the three of you wasn't easy, but I know you, and you would never wish death on anyone who didn't really deserve it."

"We helped save each other's lives," she murmured. "And now they're gone. If they had only come with us, we could've…"

"Violet. If they had come with us, there would've only been one ship for them to target, and we would've all been dead before we even knew to run."

She nodded, but I could tell that answer didn't satisfy her. It didn't satisfy me, either. It just seemed so wasteful, what the residents of the tower had done. If they were doing it to send a message… it was a cruel one. A shudder ran through me as I realized this was the same thing KC Alexander had said before they'd seen us off—"a waste of resources." Had *this* been what he was talking about? He'd been angry they'd healed us, only to decide to kill us off at the last minute? Anger rose in my gut, but there was really nothing to be done about it, so I let it go.

"Belinda's sister might have been at one of the guard posts," Violet said. "Last name Carver. When we get close enough, can you have Henrik look into it? I… I owe Belinda that."

I nodded, and she seemed to ease up a little bit. Looking her over, I took in the bags under her eyes and the glazed look in them. "Why don't you lie down and close your eyes for a bit? You look like you could use a few minutes' rest."

"You could too," she argued, her words barely distinguishable from the yawn that seemed to catch her unawares. "You've been up just as long as me."

"True, but I got some sleep on the heloship."

"No you didn't," she said, and I shook my head at how well she knew me, but she allowed me to guide her over to one of the benches and sit her down. I quickly pulled out a few blankets and made a makeshift bed for her, complete with a pillow made out of a folded blanket. I helped her take off her boots, and had her lie down on her side, spooning up behind her, knowing she needed to feel some human comfort right then.

It was a tight fit with the two of us on the little bench, but we made do, and within minutes, Violet was fast asleep, her breathing deep and heavy. I lay with her for a few long minutes, absorbing her warmth, and then, before I could fall asleep too, carefully pulled away, moving to the cockpit.

"How bad is the damage?" I asked, closing the door partially to keep our voices from waking Violet up.

Amber flipped a switch, and then swiveled around, her mouth opening to answer, but it was Vox who got there first. "It could've been much worse," he announced, cleaning oil from his fingers with a stained red cloth. "A lot worse. None of the wings were hit, and that area is actually pretty armored for defense purposes. The shaft that controls the wings and the propeller movement is warped, but only slightly, so we have close to ninety percent functionality."

Amber looked at him, her lips pursed, and then she looked back at me, giving me a nod. "What he said."

"How far do you think we are from The Green?" I asked.

"At least a few hours. It'll probably be early evening when we get in. If not later. But we'll get there. You can go grab a few hours of sleep if you want. And maybe use some of those cleansing wipes from my bags. No offense, Viggo, but you reek."

"None taken. I'm well aware," I replied dryly. "But it's been a long… I don't even know anymore. What time unit do you think would be appropriate?"

She gave me a droll look and then turned back to the helm. "Whatever it is, it's been too long," she agreed. "Go get some sleep. Logan, you too. I'll need you to take over for me in a couple hours."

"You sure you want to stay awake by yourself?" I asked. "Everyone's exhausted, and you aren't immune to that either."

"Viggo, I just saved us all from what I am going to call a death ray. My adrenaline is still pumping, and even when that fades, I don't think I could sleep for quite some time after what we just witnessed." Even with her back to me, I could see the slight shudder as she thought about it, and I didn't blame her. Besides, while Amber was notoriously stubborn, she had always proven herself responsible. She'd wake us if her exhaustion grew too severe.

"Okay," I conceded. "Just shout if you need anything."

"Sleep," she ordered. "Both of you."

"I'm going to stay up a little bit longer," announced Vox. "I want to run a few more systems checks, and I think there are a few minor things I can repair before I nap." Amber gave him an irritated look, and he grinned toothily at her. "As long as I have your permission to do so, Captain Ashabee." His tone was teasing and light, but even so, her spine stiffened and she turned away from him.

"Do whatever makes you happy, Logan," she said after a moment.

I bit my tongue to keep from making a comment, choosing discretion and heading into the bay. I pulled out a few more blankets and made them up on the floor next to Violet's bench. It was tempting to climb back on the bench next to her, but it was too uncomfortable, and we both needed sleep. I lay down on my back and closed my eyes.

"Viggo?"

I jerked upright, alarmed and confused. I could have sworn I had just shut my eyes, but it was clear several hours had gone by. Violet was kneeling over me, her small hand on my shoulder, another hand wrapped around a protein ration. I blinked groggily up at her, and then ran a hand through my disheveled hair.

"What time is it?" I croaked, my mouth dry.

Violet checked her watch. "Five p.m. We've been asleep for eight hours. I guess Amber is taking the long way back to Patrus. She said we won't run out of fuel as long as we go slowly and use this tailwind." She reached over and picked up a bottle of water that was sitting on the bench where I had put her to bed what felt like moments ago, and held it out to me. I quickly downed the entire contents of the bottle, feeling exceptionally parched, and then devoured the protein ration, my stomach so empty that I was certain it was wrapped around my spine trying to eat it for the lack of nutrients.

Violet was picking at her own food, playing with it mostly, and I reached out and touched her knee. "Baby, you have to try to eat something. I know it's been a trying day, but I'm sure we're almost home."

The corners of her mouth tilted upward, and she shot me a grateful look. "You're right, but I'm really just not very hungry at the moment. Let's go check in with Amber and see where we are."

I nodded and ran a hand over my face, trying to clear away the grit from sleeping. I craved nothing less than a shower and a bed, in that order. A long night of sleep with Violet next to me would do a lot to help ease the acidic nature of my stomach and the stiff aches and pains in my body, as well as give me time to process the emotional wounds that were there, still bleeding, just under the surface.

Climbing to my feet, I followed Violet onto the bridge to find Amber splayed out on her own mat on the floor, Logan behind the wheel. The sun was beginning to set, but as I moved to the bubble, I could see that we were definitely in familiar territory. The expanse of The Green hung just below us, the river on the right side of the aircraft.

"When did she zonk out?" I asked the man.

He clicked a few buttons and adjusted the controls before answering, his focus on the screen. "About three hours ago. We lost the river for a while, and lost some time in the process, but she wasn't going to go to sleep until she found it again, and luckily..."

"You lost the river?" I asked, frowning.

"It went underground for a while, but we found it, so no big deal. Anyway, I followed the instructions and tried to contact Henrik an hour ago, but no response. You want to try?"

"Sure," I said, taking the headset he offered me and manipulating the buttons so I could speak into it. "Henrik, Ms. Dale, this is Viggo. Are you receiving me?"

I listened intently, watching Violet as she stood by the window, staring down at The Green. There was a pop of static, followed by, "Viggo, is that really you?"

Chuckling at the familiar sound of Henrik's voice, I hit the transmit button. "Yes indeed. What? Didn't think we could make it back from The Outlands?"

"Oh, don't get a big head, kid," Henrik grumped, before letting enthusiasm that would match a youngster's bubble up in his voice. "Did you find Violet? I'm assuming so, or we wouldn't be talking."

"Yeah, I got her," I said, and she flashed a smile over her shoulder at me before turning back to The Green below. "We're all safe. We even got Solomon, and… well… We've got a lot to fill you in on, but we'll do it when we land. Speaking of which, where are we landing? What's the status of Patrus?"

"Well, thanks to the heloships you helped to procure this morning, we were able to remove the remaining Matrians from the guard posts quite peacefully. I can't say I blame them—it's kind of hard to keep fighting with three gunships aiming at you. Drew and Mags took their people into the city to start clearing out the gangs that had formed. We're just trying to get them to stand down, if we can, and if they refuse, well, Mags and her team have started a collection of Porteque gang members, and the ones that did not go peacefully are not happy about their decisions. Alejandro's niece is tough as nails, I'll give her that. We've also encountered only a handful of enhanced people, but Dr. Tierney gave us some tranquilizer guns to help knock them out until we get them secured. We're still working on a long-term solution to that… Anyway, I've got some landing coordinates for you. It's going to be a tight fit, but it was the best place we found inside the city that was big enough to hold everything. Don't worry, I'm sure it won't take you too long to feel quite at home."

He fed me the coordinates, which I repeated to Vox, checking them twice, and then checking my watch. "I think we'll be there in another hour or so, but I'll radio when we get close, okay?"

"Okay. And Viggo?"

"Yeah?"

"Damn good to hear your voice, boy. We'll see you soon. Looking forward to hearing about The Outlands."

CHAPTER 14

Violet

The red-brick, three-story building drew larger as Logan slowly lowered the ship. A tall fence ran the perimeter, creating a wide yard in the front. The space was currently filled with heloships parked wingtip to wingtip, with barely any room in between. It was dark, but I could make out movement down below as people went about their business in between rows of ships.

I felt my breath catch as the proximity alarm went off and I saw how close we were to the other ships, convinced we were going to crash into them. Logan flicked it off, even as Viggo's arms came around me, holding me close to him. The deck shuddered as we touched down, and Logan immediately killed the engine.

"And the crowd went wild," he announced as he dusted off his hands.

"We're not here to stroke your ego," yawned Amber, picking herself off the floor and taking a moment to stretch her back. "You got us on the ground, which was your job, so if you're expecting a thank you..."

"Would it kill you?" he asked, spinning the chair around to look at her.

She met his gaze flatly as she lowered her arms. "It might," she retorted. "Especially before a hot meal and a shower."

"Well, I for one am saying thank you," Viggo said. "To both of you. You are both excellent pilots, and I am grateful for your help in recovering Violet."

He squeezed me a little tighter, and I smiled. "Same here," I told them.

"Anytime, you know that," said Amber. "Now let's get off this thing before the collective might of our B.O. causes it to melt."

I snorted and followed her toward the tail of the ship, eager to get back onto solid ground. Amber hit the button to open the door, while I checked on Solomon. He was still out, but the pink goop that had been placed in his wounds was looking more and more skin-like—like a freshly scarred wound rather than gaping holes. I touched the area around one of the wounds lightly, and the skin felt cool and firm. I wondered about it for a moment, still not really comprehending what had happened at the tower. The miraculous cure seemed like a daydream, impossible to believe, and their weaponized sunlight like a nightmare.

"We need to get him to the infirmary," I announced loudly. "And we should really—"

"Take a break," ordered a familiar voice from below, and I turned to see Ms. Dale standing at the bottom of the ramp, flanked by two people. "Gary, Matthew, can you take Solomon to Dr. Tierney?"

The two men—I assumed they were part of one of the rebel cells— moved up the ramp and began to unhook the wounded man from the straps buckling him in. Ms. Dale followed and stood in front of me, her blue eyes taking me in. I couldn't help it—I rushed toward her and threw my arms around her.

"It's so good to see you," I breathed.

She dropped her arms around me and squeezed back, then let go of me to cup my face, looking me over, even going so far as to take my arm and prod at the new cast.

"Looks like you had a pretty interesting adventure," she said. "And I wish we could spend more time talking about it, but we've been holding off a meeting with Drew and Mags until you, Viggo, Amber, and Logan returned."

Logan gave a little salute as he moved past her. "I assume there's a place where I can grab a shower?" he asked, and Ms. Dale nodded.

"Thomas managed to get the water treatment plant up and running, as well as the power facility. So we've got water and heat, although it's only a short-term fix, and the government will have to put more work into the infrastructure later. Matthew will show you where you and your men will be staying. I assumed you wanted to be placed together."

"That'll work," Logan replied. "I'll see you in…"

"We're giving you all an hour," she cut in. "So you can get yourselves together. I wish we could let you rest, but there's been no sign of what Elena has in store for us next, and we're just moving a bit too quickly to put the brakes on."

"I want to check on Jay," I said. "Is he okay?"

"He's… okay. Quinn and Tim have been watching over him, and Dr. Tierney has him stabilized, but…" Ms. Dale paused, her gaze dropping to the floor as sadness seemed to envelop her. "There's a chance he might not be able to walk again, Violet. The bullet is lodged dangerously close to his spine."

A hollow formed in the pit of my stomach, and it felt like the temperature had dropped several degrees. Viggo was there, helping to brace me, but it didn't stop the feeling of the world suddenly becoming too heavy to even try to hold up anymore. Even though she was dead, I suddenly hated Desmond beyond comprehension. She had caused so much pain, and now, after all of the torture and heartache, her last living son might not ever walk again…

"It's not fair," I breathed, unable to stop a tear from escaping. "Surely there must be something we can do… Maybe… Maybe…"

A random thought occurred to me, and before anyone could stop me, I reached up and began pulling on the tab of the cast they had given me, yanking the plastic off my arm.

"Violet!" Ms. Dale gasped, her hands moving to stop me, but I sidestepped her and held it up.

"Give this to Dr. Tierney," I said. "It's supposed to be used for twenty-four hours, but I've had it on for less than half that, and it repairs injured bones—maybe she can use it for his back. He's got to… I mean… He's too young. It's just got to work."

Ms. Dale sighed, reaching out and taking my hand with her own. "Violet, I have no idea what this flimsy piece of plastic is supposed to do, but I do know that if you remove medical technology designed to help one thing, it might not be the best for another injury."

"But Jay… His back…"

"We don't know anything yet, Violet. The bullet is lodged there, but his spine was not broken. He's young, and also enhanced. Who knows what his body is capable of healing? You can't fix him. You can only be there for him. Okay?"

I nodded, although a dark part of me hated her for saying it. Jay deserved to walk and run and jump and be able to play—he shouldn't be in a hospital bed wondering if he'd ever get to do those things again.

"Let's go check on him right now," Viggo said softly. "It'll be good for him to see you. He was really worried about you."

I let him guide me off the ship, Ms. Dale beside us. The men carrying Solomon had exited at some point when we were talking—I had been so upset by Ms. Dale's report of Jay that I really hadn't seen them leave, and now they were carrying him between them as they entered the red brick building in front of us.

"What is this place?" I asked.

"It's a warden training center," Viggo replied, surprising me. He looked down at me, a corner of his mouth rising up a little. "It's where I was trained when I was a cadet."

"Originally Elena had conscripted it as a place to keep her forces," Ms. Dale said. "But when she had her people pull back and trap everyone inside the city, a few Patrian wardens came here and locked it down, securing it. I stumbled across it after I got into a shoot-out with some Porteque gang members earlier—I hopped the wall after they cut me off from the rest of our team. The wardens inside took me prisoner, I escaped, Henrik showed up, and we talked it all out. They're letting us set up shop and basically take control—pretty much all because we had Maxen, but I'm not looking a gift horse in the mouth."

I chuckled. I was surprised I could find any humor left after news of Jay, but Ms. Dale talked about securing this place for our group so dismissively, as if it hadn't been an impressive feat for what seemed like less than twenty-four hours. But there was also a gem in that story too golden to pass up. "So you're saying that Henrik rescued you?" I teased.

Viggo bit back a smile as Ms. Dale arched an eyebrow. "I escaped first," she corrected me in a firm voice. "He just happened to show up while I was escaping."

I smiled, and the smile faltered and then grew when I saw a familiar lanky shape exiting the building and making a beeline right for me. I opened my arms and was almost knocked over from the force of Tim's arms coming around my waist. He held me tight—I knew it must be hurting him a lot, but he didn't complain, and I held him too, keeping my touch as light as possible.

He pulled back, and I frowned when I saw the bruises all over him. "Tim, are you okay?"

He ducked his head and nodded, his mop-curls bouncing on the top of his head. "Okay," he repeated. "*You* okay?"

"I was only gone for a day!" I protested.

"To Outlands! No one come back!"

"Well, your sister isn't like anyone else," Viggo said. "She's unique."

I felt my cheeks blush as a burst of love came over me. I needed to marry Viggo, just like Belinda had suggested, but this wasn't exactly the right time to bring it up. There was so much to do tonight, and… Well, I was going to take the first chance I could get. I'd bring it up after we got through this meeting. First, though, came Jay.

"Show me where Jay is?" I asked, and Tim gave me a grave look, and then nodded, pulling open the door to the building the men carrying Solomon had entered. The door led to a wide atrium where a picture of King Maxen hung from the opposite wall along with several other pictures of men, a plaque underneath each. There was an office to the right. The door was open, and a few men were inside, playing cards and watching the door. Their guns leaned against one of the walls, and their eyes looked up to check who we were. Ms. Dale raised a hand, and one of them raised his in response before going back to their game.

"Guard duty. They walk the perimeter and then sit inside, in case we have a security breach. Left hallway."

She moved past us, leading the way down a long hallway. "These are the cadet quarters," Viggo supplied as we passed several doors, heading for the door at the end of the hall. "I used to sleep in that room there when I was in training."

"I can't imagine you then... You were a little bit younger than I am now, right?"

"Yup, and probably as much of a handful, much to my instructor's dismay. I—"

"VIGGO! VIOLET!"

I looked away from the door Viggo had pointed out moments ago in time to see Cad and Margot emerging from a door a little farther down the hall, their children Henry and Sarah between them. Henry's face lit up when he saw me, and the chubby little boy broke away from his mom to race over to me. I dropped to my knees and hugged my littlest cousin to my chest as he threw himself at me.

"Mommy was crying," he babbled. "She said you may never come back!"

I looked up at Margot, surprised to see tears in her eyes as she came closer. She didn't even let me get up, just dropped down next to me and wrapped her arms around me and Henry. Sarah and Cad weren't far behind, and within seconds I was being crushed by four sets of arms.

It felt... amazing, and I was surprised to find myself tearing up from the amount of love and concern my family was showering on me. Once again, I felt blessed by the small yet wonderful things this entire adventure had given me, and for a moment, I just leaned into them, happy to feel their warmth.

"I'm sorry," Margot sniffled. "I never should've said anything around him—you know how kids are. I knew you'd come back, I was just..."

"I was, too," I admitted. "But I'm so happy to see you. All of you."

"What was it like?" asked Cad, pulling back. "What did you see out there?"

I opened my mouth, and then hesitated. "Can I tell you about it later?" I asked. "There's so much going on, and I want to check on Jay and… and all the others."

"Don't be silly, of course you can!" exclaimed Margot. "You must be exhausted, and I know they've been holding the meeting to wait for you. I'm just so excited to hear what you saw! We'll talk about it over a hot meal tomorrow."

"No, I can—"

"Tomorrow," she repeated sternly. "Because you look dead on your feet, and I'm not going to let you do anything else."

"Okay," I said with a smile, and we all carefully untangled ourselves. Henry had to be pried off my neck, but that was okay—I didn't mind the little scamp holding on. I felt the same way right now. I didn't want to let go at all.

Viggo held out a hand to me, and I took it, marveling yet again that my arm felt as good as new. Better, even.

"We'll grab you some chow from the mess," said Cad, and Margot rolled her eyes.

"Listen to him using words like 'chow' and 'mess'—thinks he's a real soldier now!"

I chuckled. "Some chow would be great, but you don't have to put yourself out. We'll get some later, after we—"

"We'll bring you something," said Margot firmly. "You need to eat, especially if you're running on empty like everyone else around here is."

She didn't even wait for me to argue or agree, just held up a hand as I opened my mouth. "Nuh-uh," she sang, looking down at her children, and they began to sing *nuh-uh* as she led them down the hall, Cad following with a bemused expression on his face. He gave a little wave and a shrug as they turned the corner, and I couldn't help but laugh.

"Our family is weird," Viggo said. "But a lot of fun."

Our family. I slid my hand into his and leaned into him. "Let's go see Jay," I said, feeling like my run-in with everyone had helped buoy my spirits enough to hopefully pass that love on to him. I knew it wouldn't help him or change anything, but being there for each other in difficult times was what gave us all the strength to carry on. And after all this, Jay was part of our family too.

CHAPTER 15

Viggo

It had been years since I had been in this building, but not much had changed. The same pictures hung on the walls, although there were a few new teachers, some of whom I had served with. Maybe most significantly, unlike other buildings in Patrus, this one was whole and unscathed.

Ms. Dale opened the door at the end of the hall, and I could see that a lot had been accomplished in the last twenty-four hours. Normally there were bunk beds, but they had been pulled apart and then beds rearranged in neat little rows, crammed together as close as possible.

The smell of antiseptic and blood hit my nose as we stepped in, and I could see that most of beds were filled, some with people I recognized, most with people I didn't. The soft noise of talking and murmurs and groans of pain filled the room, and I could see that among the beds, Dr. Tierney and Dr. Arlan were moving, flowing between them and moving from patient to patient, working in tandem.

Dr. Tierney spotted us and nodded us toward a bed, but Tim was already heading in that direction, Violet on his heels. He came around one of the beds and sat down on an adjacent one, and I paused, noticing the crumpled blankets at the foot of the bed he sat on—Tim had been sleeping in the bed next to Jay, probably the entire time we were gone.

Violet sat down next to Jay. The young man's eyes were closed, and an IV line ran from a bag into the back of his hand. His skin was pale, and part of his hair was matted to his forehead from sweat.

"Jay," Violet called softly, putting her hand in his. The young man didn't move, and the hopeful look on Tim's face dimmed slightly. "Jay?" She called his name again, a bit more loudly, but there was no sign of him waking.

I looked around for Dr. Tierney, and spotted her with her back to me. She was treating a patient, but I couldn't tell who and I didn't want to interrupt her in case it was critical. But that didn't mean I couldn't move a bit closer and try to grab her attention once she finished.

So I did. I moved down the row, heading toward her, and two things became clear to me. The first was that the patient she was treating was sitting, not lying down, and the second was that they were being difficult. When I heard the patient's voice, I felt myself smiling, even as Mags hopped onto her feet, her round face red.

"I'm fine!" she insisted loudly, crumpling a wad of fabric in her hands and tossing it back onto the bed. "There are a lot more critical patients here that you should be concerning yourself with!"

She went to move past Dr. Tierney, but Dr. Tierney's hand shot out and grabbed the shorter woman's shoulder. Mags cried out in pain, but Dr. Tierney looked unapologetic about it as she pushed Mags back toward the bed.

"I've had quite enough of your and your family's belligerence today, Magdelena," she said as she forced Mags into a sitting position. "I swear to the mother there is something in the water that gives you lot thick skulls and a poor disposition, but I'm not tolerating it. You will wear this sling until I say otherwise, and if I catch you trying to use your arm during that time, I can and will tranq you, drag you back here, and tie you to a bed. Do you understand me?"

Mags glared up at her, her mouth a tight grimace. I was close enough to see Dr. Tierney's eyebrow lift in daring challenge, and after a long tense moment, Mags cursed and leaned back.

"Fine!" she spat, awkwardly holding out her arm. "I'm fine, though."

"No, you aren't, and firing your rifle today has only exaggerated the bruising on the tendon. If you keep doing it, it will rip, and then I'll have to perform surgery. Given how your uncle reacted to that idea, I shudder to think how you would, so you mind me. Understand?"

"I understand," Mags mumbled, and Dr. Tierney nodded once before helping Mags get back into her sling.

"Smart girl," croaked Alejandro, and I realized he was lying in the bed just past Mags, propped up by a few thin pillows against the metal frame.

Mags rolled her eyes skyward and sighed in defeat. Dr. Tierney glanced over at Alejandro and frowned. "You're one to talk," she said, a mite sarcastically, and Alejandro managed to paint a thin smile on his face before his gaze shifted over her shoulder and met mine.

"Hey-yo, boyo," he said, catching my eye, and I smiled.

"Hey Alejandro—Mags—Dr. Tierney," I said in greeting, moving up the last few feet to them.

Dr. Tierney tied off the sling and then turned, giving me a considering look as her hand disappeared into the pocket of the coat she was wearing. Withdrawing a scanner, she pointed at me and clicked it on. "I'm fine," I insisted as she ran the beam over me. "And I'm sorry to intrude. I just came to find out what's going on with Jay. Ms. Dale said he might not be able to walk?"

Dr. Tierney's eyes were on the scanner, reading the results as she moved it up and down. "I can't retrieve the bullet right now because it's so close to his spine, but it's too early to say for certain what the end result will be. It is a possibility, however."

"Well, Violet has this thing she thinks might help, and—"

Dr. Tierney's eyes shot up, and she cocked her head at me. "What thing?"

"Well, I'm not even entirely sure," I admitted honestly. "All I know is that her arm is healed and—wait a second, doc."

She had started to push past me, but I managed to stop her, and she turned back. "What's going on with Alejandro?" I asked.

"I'm fine," Alejandro insisted at the same time Dr. Tierney said, "It's not good, and not likely to get better until your friend lets me operate!"

I turned my gaze from one to the other and then settled on Dr. Tierney. "What's the problem?"

She sighed and folded her arms over her chest. "Viggo, the metacarpals in some of his fingers are so fractured that I am not going to be able to piece them back together. He's going to lose a lot of mobility in his hand, and each minute we waste not doing surgery, the more likely it'll be that I'll have to amputate instead of trying to repair what I can."

"Why won't he let you operate?" I asked.

"Because there are people in more dire need," replied Alejandro. "I'm fine! I can wait until things calm down. Maybe in a day or so we can—"

"You need surgery now!" Dr. Tierney insisted, and I could tell by the frustrated tone in her voice that this argument had been going on for quite some time. "I'd drug you if I could, but you won't even let me put a damned IV in your arm—"

"Because you'd drug me," he cut in smoothly.

"And you are risking any and all functionality on your dominant hand for no good reason! Earlier we couldn't prioritize you, but now—"

"I'm fine!" Alejandro insisted belligerently, sitting forward. "You just... go check on Violet and Solomon."

Dr. Tierney cast him a glare and then stalked off, clearly unwilling to argue any further. I hesitated, and then hung back, looking into the man's blue eyes. "You need to get the surgery, Alejandro," I said gently. "And if you don't agree to it, I'm going to go hunt Jenny down and bring her here."

Alejandro shot me a death glare, his face already screwing up to tell me to mind my own business, when Mags leaned back in the bed and crossed her legs, smiling like a cat who had just gotten into the cream.

"I already sent some people to pick her up," she declared with an impish smile. "As soon as I heard that he was being difficult."

Alejandro froze, his jaw open, his face going pale. "Oh, nooo..." he groaned, slumping against his pillows. "That woman is impossible when I'm sick, Viggo."

I snorted, not feeling a moment of pity for him, and gave Mags a high-five before moving back over to Violet. Dr. Tierney was showing Violet some images on her handheld. As I came up behind them I could see that they were x-rays of the bullet and Jay's spine, the bullet only a few millimeters away.

"As you can see, it's quite close, but there's no sign that it hit, which is good. None of the organs were damaged either, so once the swelling goes down, I'm hoping to get in there, remove the bullet, and then we'll know for sure how bad it's going to be. But surgery carries risks, and there's a chance that by doing this, I could actually make it worse. He could lose function in one, if not both, of his legs, if he hasn't lost it already. Now, if you're satisfied, may I *please* examine you and your arm?"

I smiled, realizing that Violet had refused to let Dr. Tierney examine her until she knew the details about Jay. Violet nodded, and Dr. Tierney quickly ran her scanner over her, examining the results.

I watched as her face turned from stern, to mystified, to curious and shocked. "The break is fully healed," she exclaimed in awe. "I've… I've never seen anything like this!"

"The doctors at the…" Violet trailed off, and I could see her trying to decide how much to tell Dr. Tierney now. "Well, it's a very weird story, but some doctors that I met—you'll be briefed later—used this," said Violet, holding up the slightly crumpled plastic sheet in her hand. "There's some sort of liquid inside that gets injected into you—although I never felt anything, except my arm feeling a thousand times better."

Dr. Tierney examined the plastic, prodding it a few times. Grabbing a tray off the nightstand, she spread the plastic out and then used a scalpel to carefully cut out a few of the hexagonal shapes and drop them into a petri dish lying nearby.

"I'll see if we can't scrounge up something to do an analysis," she said, placing the lid over it. "In the meantime, do you have any more questions?"

"Only if you've had a chance to look at Solomon. The same group, they put this kind of goop in his wounds, and it looked like it was becoming skin tissue. It might be too late for you to get a sample of what it is, but if we could replicate *that*, it would be…"

Dr. Tierney's eyes went wide, her normally sharp voice rising a bit in intensity. "A medical miracle. I'm on it. Just shout if you need anything else, and… I'm glad to see that you're all okay." She embraced Violet tightly, and then stood, cradling the tray in her hands. "I'll go check on Solomon now and do a small biopsy."

"Thanks. Also… how are you keeping him? I don't want him to wake up tied down, if he doesn't have to."

Dr. Tierney hesitated, and then frowned. "I've got some of the Benuxupane we took off of Cody when Viggo first brought him back. Before you get upset, Dr. Arlan has been toying with it, and I think a small dose might be able to help him be more… level-headed. It's not great, but it'll hopefully keep him from flying off the handle and hurting anyone unintentionally. Would you like me to try it?"

Violet hesitated, and I couldn't blame her. It was a difficult call to make. On the one hand, Solomon was violent, but he'd been showing improvements according to Violet. Yet this was Benuxupane—a drug designed to take away the ability to feel, then modified to also make the taker compliant to all commands, and none of us liked putting a fellow human into that kind of state.

"Can we move him to a more isolated room and just see how he reacts when he gets up?" Violet asked, her eyes wide. "I'd hate to do that to him for no reason, and I'm sure he's getting better. I want to give him the benefit of the doubt without resorting to that."

Dr. Tierney didn't react other than to nod, and then she walked away, heading for a door leading off to the side that served as the bathroom. Likely she had set up a surgical unit inside, as it would be the easiest place to clean quickly.

"Hey, Viggo, Violet," said a soft voice to the right of Jay, and I turned and saw Quinn in the next bed over, a patch over his eye and pink scars crisscrossing his face. "I heard you had quite an adventure! Tell me about The Outlands—being injured sucks so bad, and there's barely anyone to talk to while you all are away." He paused, the hesitant smile on his face flickering in and out. "You have been running around so much, it's hard to even know what's been going on."

"Oh Quinn," said Violet, reaching across the narrow gap to gently take his hand. "I'm sorry, and I understand how it feels to be left out of everything. I'm just glad you're healing up so quickly, and soon you'll get out of here."

He gave her a crooked smile, but it was clear he didn't believe her. Or rather, he knew it was true, but wasn't very excited about the prospect. Not that I could blame him. He had suffered devastatingly under Tabitha's blade, and she had taken so much from him. It was impossible for me not to feel angry with her.

Or wish her back to life so that I could have the pleasure of killing her myself.

Suddenly the door slammed open, and I looked up in time to see an older woman with brown hair, streaked handsomely at each temple, stalk in. She wore a modest dress, collared and long-sleeved, with a skirt that ran down below her knees—the very model of a Patrian female, except for the stubborn glint in her eyes and tilt of her head that said that she would control every room she walked into.

Scanning the room, her hazel eyes lit on Alejandro, and she began to march—not walk, but march—over to him, her arms pumping as she strode. "Alejandro Enrique Simmons, what fool thing did you go off and do now?"

Her voice was stern and filled with irritation, and I couldn't help but smile as I took in Jennifer Wallens-Simmons, Alejandro's wife of three decades. She slowed when she saw me and Mags, a soft, gentle smile wiping away the irritation that Alejandro had borne the brunt of for many years in his marriage.

"Viggo," she exclaimed breathlessly, turning in her trajectory and coming over to me in a few short steps, her hands coming up to pat my shoulders and then cup my cheeks. "My dear boy, we were so worried for you—you barely come by to see us anymore!"

"I'm sorry, Jenny," I said, gently pulling her hands from my face.

"I've been pretty busy."

"Completely understandable, all things considered." She looked me over, her eyes narrowing, and she crossed her hands below her chest, a displeased look coming to her face. "You've lost weight. Have you not been eating enough?"

"I haven't, ma'am, but there's been a lot going on."

She harrumphed, and then turned to Mags, who had come up beside her, her eyes lit up. She embraced the young woman, clearly taking pains not to hurt her. "You could do with some rest, darling. No one wants bags they could practically use to fill a dam under their eyes!"

"Ouch!" Mags said dramatically, but there was a broad smile on her face. "I know, Tía. I'm gonna grab a catnap before the meeting we're having. Let me know how it goes with Tío!"

She excused herself and began walking to the door, a yawn splitting her mouth wide open.

"Dr. Tierney said you needed to stay in bed!" I called.

"She didn't say *where* I had to stay in bed, did she?" she shot back over her shoulder as she made for the door.

Jenny and I watched her leave, and then Jenny turned, giving me her full and undivided attention. "How bad is his hand?" she asked, fidgeting nervously.

I hesitated, surprised she would be asking me this, but I realized she was trying to prepare herself for the worst. "It's not good," I supplied. "Dr. Tierney can explain it better, but he needs surgery—sooner rather than later—and he's being exceptionally stubborn about it."

She *tsk*ed, her eyes drifting over to where Alejandro was feigning sleep on the bed. I could tell he was faking it because periodically one blue eye would open just a slit before slamming closed, the muscles of his face going completely slack.

"That kooky old man will be the death of me yet," she muttered before stomping over to the bed, intent on giving her husband a piece of her mind.

"That was Jenny?" Violet asked after she left, and I nodded.

Ms. Dale, who had been leaning quietly against the wall the entire time, stood upright and smiled. "I like her," she said. "But maybe we don't want to be here to witness whatever fight they're about to have. Your room is only a few doors down; why don't you get washed up and take a few minutes of rest yourself, and then meet us in the main conference room. I assume you know where that is?"

"I do," I said. "We'll see you there."

She nodded and left, following Mags. "You guys should go," said Quinn. "The drugs they're giving Jay are enough to knock him out for hours, and you look exhausted. Tim and I can keep watch on him, and as soon as he's up, we'll let you know."

Violet flashed a grateful smile to him, and leaned over and placed a kiss on his forehead. "Thank you, Quinn," she breathed. "I'm glad to see that the stitches are out."

"Me too—those things itched like hell," Quinn replied dryly, and, having been on the receiving end of stitches before, Violet and I both shared a chuckle with him.

Then I helped her up. We said our goodbyes to Quinn and Tim, and together moved down the hall to go seek out a shower before the meeting.

CHAPTER 16

Viggo

I showered slowly. I knew I shouldn't have, but the hot water felt too good to rush away from as I let it soak into my tired and aching muscles. My time savoring the soothing warmth came to a whopping fifteen minutes, and by the time I made it back to the locker room outside the communal showers, Violet was there, getting into some clean clothes Ms. Dale had given her in the hall.

I averted my eyes as she drew a shirt over her head, and kept walking past her to the adjacent row of lockers, using them to obscure my view of her. I had meant what I said when I told her I was going to respect the sanctity of our future wedding night. It didn't matter to me that I had seen almost all of her body when she was sick; it had been impossible to appreciate in that moment when she was in such pain. I couldn't look at an injured woman, especially one I loved, and feel anything but concern and worry and fear.

Dressing quickly, I was just shoving my feet into my boots when Violet knocked on one of the lockers at the end of the row and then poked her head around.

"Boooooooooooo," she jeered with a smile when she saw I was fully dressed. Her teasing brought a smile to my own lips as I drew the lacings of my boots tight and tied them.

"The towel wasn't enough for you?" I teased back, and she smirked as she leaned a shoulder against the locker.

"Never," she said unabashedly. "But it'll have to do for now."

"That's my girl—taking what she can get." She snorted in response, and I stood up, throwing my bag over my shoulder. "Super fun meeting time."

"And then to bed," she said as I moved past her, pausing long enough to slip her arm around mine. I led her back through the second barracks designed for the cadets—several people were already sleeping in the bunks—and back out into the main hall, two doors down from the room serving as the hospital.

Leading her back up to the main entrance, I went past the office where the guards sat and turned the corner, almost slamming into King Maxen as he came down the stairs. He nearly fell, I startled him that much, and I reached out on impulse to grab his shoulder and stabilize him.

Jerking away from my hand, he huffed and straightened, smoothing down the front of the simple black jacket he was wearing.

He'd shaved recently, his goatee now trimmed and closer to perfect than I'd seen it since we'd kidnapped/rescued him.

"Maxen," I said, refusing to put the proper "King" in front of it. I couldn't. I'd seen the man use unarmed men, women, and children as human shields.

"Croft," he replied, just as bitterly. "I see you were invited to a meeting, while I was not."

I exchanged looks with Violet and shrugged. "You have been in the dark for some time, Maxen. I'm sure it would take too much precious time to catch you up at this point."

"No, this is a blatant attempt to further wrest control from me!" he exclaimed, his voice dangerously low. "By keeping me out of the command structure, you are only further undermining my position as the rightful leader here. I allowed you to sequester me out of the need to keep me safe, but this is an outrage! I deserve to be there, to make my case before that little witch attempts to have her way and oust me!"

I frowned over the "little witch" comment, taking a moment to figure out who he meant before recalling the conference we'd had with Magdelena before we'd raided the city last night. Sweet Lord—had that really all happened last night?

Violet caught on as well and took a step up the stairs.

"Number one: that 'little witch' has a name—Magdalena," she breathed angrily. "Number two, she fought like a Valkyrie for this country and its people, so you will at least show her a modicum of respect."

A growl trickled from Maxen's throat, and instead of responding, he pushed in between us and stalked around the corner, muttering under his breath. I watched him go, knowing that letting him roam free was a bad idea, but one we had to put up with until the imminent danger had passed—especially with five Patrian wardens now counted among our allies, relying on our connection with the king to prove we were on the right side—or we really would look like the kidnappers we probably were. But it was clear that Maxen was not taking the idea of his power evaporating very well.

Whatever. For all of his bluster, the man was ultimately a coward, and I doubted anyone within these walls would help him. Not with so many rebels around.

"What a piece of work," Violet muttered as I led us upstairs into the main command room. In addition to training the cadets, this facility usually received and dispatched all the calls to the wardens on duty and nearby. It was a great learning opportunity, as many of the second-year cadets wound up working in this very room, learning just as much from watching as they did from doing.

It hadn't changed much in all those years, either, but it felt different walking into it, partially because the control center was half-functioning. This was a room that had once had eyes on the whole of the city, and now it was partially—mostly—dark. The workstations where techs would scrub images in search of criminals were intact, but abandoned, as though waiting for someone to return. It was clear the building hadn't suffered any damage during the three-day riot that had ensued after the stadium video, and I was at least grateful for that. This place was familiar, and whole, even if it wasn't fully functional at the moment. It had been a long time since I had felt the small comfort of familiar facilities.

Henrik was standing by the large conference table toward the front of the room, where all the large screens sat, speaking with three men, two of whom I didn't recognize but one I did.

"Mark?" I said, moving closer. I was interrupting, but I could tell they were wrapping things up from the way Henrik was shaking hands and patting shoulders. "Mark Travers?"

A slim man of about five foot eight turned, a broad smile breaking across his face when he saw me. "Viggo Croft!" he exclaimed, taking a step over to me, his hand extended. "I haven't seen you since you brought those so-called prisoners through that checkpoint!"

I laughed, surprised he remembered, and then sobered when I realized why he had. That was the night Elena's plan had really kicked off, and my "prisoners" and I had made off with Maxen. Yup, there was a convoluted history to be sure, but I was just happy to see him okay.

"Yeah, sorry about that," I said ruefully. "I wish I could've explained, but I couldn't trust you would believe me, and we had to get to the king before Elena had him killed."

Mark gave a good-natured shrug. "I get it, man. From what I've heard, you and your girlfriend have been up to a lot trying to stop this madness. I'm just glad you're in one piece."

"You too. Were you one of the wardens to secure this place after the video?"

He nodded, his smile fading some. "We were at the Alberton Memorial Stadium when the video hit. There were about three hundred people in there when we went in, but only ninety-seven got out. After that, with all the chaos, I came here and waited, wanting to see what the Matrians would do. When they bugged out, I got a few of the other guys who hadn't been selected for those work programs and got in here to lock it down. Seemed like the best idea at the time, one that gave us time to think about what we could do—which turned out to be not a lot.

There were only five of us, not exactly a force for change."

"I'm sure you did the best you could under the circumstances. And it's just great we have a place to set up shop. Thank you for that."

"Well, I didn't do it for you, and to be honest, *we* should be thanking *you*. You helped rescue the king and have been trying to put an end to all of this."

I felt a frown cross my face at the mention of Maxen and let it evaporate quickly. Mark was a good man, but he was fairly simple, which meant he supported the power structure in Patrus without question. Chances were that if the vote Mags wanted was held tomorrow—the one deciding whether or not Maxen should be in charge anymore—Mark would definitely vote to keep Maxen in place. And this meant that he and I were going to have to disagree at some point.

"It's the least we could do," said Violet modestly from beside me, and I realized I had gotten lost in my thoughts. I looked around, trying to center myself, and saw Ms. Dale enter with Morgan and Amber right behind her.

"I'm sorry," I said to Mark, "we're a part of this meeting. Can we pick this up later?"

"Of course, of course! I'll see you then."

With that, he and the other two men departed, and Violet and I headed over to seat ourselves at the wide conference table. Morgan met my gaze, giving me a fleeting smile. She looked nervous, and I couldn't blame her... although I was pretty certain her actions were going to speak more to the group than the fact that she was also an enhanced Matrian princess. They certainly had for Violet and me.

I had opened my mouth to reassure her, when the door leading to the server room clanged open and Thomas emerged, carrying a bundle of wires in one hand and flipping through some notes in his notebook with the other. He dropped the length of cable to the floor and then jacked the end of it into the television, turning it on. Pulling out his modified handheld, he clicked a few buttons, and the screen lit up into the familiar display of the handheld screen.

Placing the handheld on the table, he dropped into the closest chair—right next to Morgan—and stifled a yawn before writing a few things down in his notebook. The room was exceptionally quiet, and it was easy to see why. Everyone was exhausted and still coming down from the excitement from yesterday and today, but there was very little end in sight. There was no relief, no one to take over for us while we slept. And so we trudged on, trying to put out fires we couldn't even see yet.

"Well, we're all here," announced a gruff voice from behind us, and I turned to see Andrew "Drew" Kattatopolous, one of the three rebel faction leaders, walking toward the table with Logan by his side. Between them was Mags, still wearing her sling, and she shot me a smile as she plopped into the chair at the far end, opposite Henrik. Owen brought up the rear, and I was surprised to see him there for just a moment—we hadn't had time to discuss or change his station in our command chain before the battle, but it hardly seemed to matter. I was happy to see him; noticing my gaze, he nodded toward Henrik, as though to explain his presence, before sitting down on Morgan's other side. She jerked slightly in surprise, and then seemed to sink farther into her chair, fidgeting with her hands. I didn't even think Owen noticed. He was staring nervously at Violet and me, as if waiting for some sort of punishment. I gave him what I hoped was a friendly smile, but he looked down and away quickly.

Henrik looked up from some papers he had started rummaging through while I was talking with Mark and gave us all a tired smile. He looked pale, and I knew for a fact the man was running on zero sleep, but he exuded control as he leaned forward.

"I know it's been a long forty-eight hours, everyone, but we have some things we need to discuss before we can get to bed."

"Like?" asked Drew.

"Like the command structure, the vote, and our next move," said Henrik, tapping the papers together. "And… a report from The Outlands, apparently." He gave Violet a pointed look, and she nodded gravely.

"I know it's not necessarily about what is happening here," she said, looking around the table, "but you guys will really want to hear this one."

Violet and I had decided that we had to tell the whole group about the tower at once—there was no stopping the questions, and the revelations we'd found out there were world-changing. Besides, we didn't want to have to explain this twenty times within the next week; better to get it over with all at once. I guessed that Ms. Dale had relayed our decision to tell everybody about it to Henrik while we were showering.

Violet's statement was met with raised eyebrows from Drew, obvious interest from Mags, and a curious look from Ms. Dale, who had already seen some of the alien technology.

Henrik nodded. "I have no doubt we will," he said. "Let's just get our command structure straightened out, and then we'll go straight to your report."

"That's easy—" Mags spoke up immediately, looking right at Henrik. "Our new commander should obviously be you."

Drew gave her a surprised look, clearly having expected Mags to try to take command herself, and her grin grew. "I lead only when I have to, Drew. When there's someone more capable, I step aside. Henrik knows his stuff—it was his and his team's planning that made it possible for us to succeed. Even you have to give him credit for that."

Drew looked over at Logan, who gave a little shrug. "I have no problem with it," Logan announced. "I asked around, and Henrik here used to be a warden back in the day—one with a stellar record."

Frowning, Drew laced his fingers across his chest and tilted his head up to think about it. After several heartbeats, he nodded, and I felt a burst of relief, followed by the thought of *We should have more meetings when everyone's tired. It seems to move everything along rather quickly.*

"Well, glad that's over," grinned Henrik, who seemed to have no objections to his new position—and no ego, either. "And I'm grateful for your trust in this. I promise I'll do my best to listen to what you all have to say, but we're all leaders here in one way or another, so I don't expect you to make it easy for me to get my way." He winked comically, and it seemed to defuse some of the strain that had settled into the room. "Violet, I'll hand it off to you now."

Violet took a breath, and I could see her mustering her thoughts, trying to decide what to tell everyone first. Logan and Amber, who'd seen the tower firsthand, looked out at the others with expressions of smug anticipation, which would have been more amusing if I hadn't watched them bicker for an entire heloship trip.

Finally, when the quiet was getting a little jarring, Violet spoke, and I could see she was going for broke. "Guys," she said, "we're not alone out here. There are people living in The Outlands."

The reactions across the table were a mix of disbelief, shock, wonder and curiosity—I could see the idea breaking across people's faces in waves, as Mags's mouth dropped open, Morgan's eyes widened comically, Drew fidgeted uncomfortably in his seat, Owen's hand opened and closed a few times… Henrik stroked his beard, his eyes narrowing in intensity.

"Don't just leave us hanging like that," Ms. Dale finally said, breaking the silence. "Tell the rest, Violet!"

Then the whole story had to come out—and even summarized, it was impressive. The flight with Solomon, Desmond's death, the tense situation with two Matrian wardens who wanted to take her back to Matrus and execute her—it sounded like something out of an action comic, even to me. At Violet's description of the tower, the people and their strange greetings—and then, their horribly powerful light beam that weaponized the sun—people's faces got even more intense. We'd all been tired; but this put new energy in the room, if only for a moment.

"They healed Solomon's bullet wounds?" Morgan said. "Do you think that they… Do you think they fixed his brain, too?"

Violet stretched out her own healed right hand as if considering. "I don't want to dare to hope that," she said. "But if they could heal my arm in 24 hours…"

"What I'd do to get my hands on a weapon like that," Drew said wistfully. "Do you think they are really not open to trade? We could learn so much from another society. I can't believe they'd just let you guys go, frankly."

"Sounds like bad news to me," Ms. Dale said, shaking her head. "We've already seen what one mad queen can do to a group of people.

But forcing them to stay in their tower and never even acknowledging that you were there? That is a dangerous amount of control, and it sounds like a ticking time bomb if you ask me. People can't stay in these kinds of situations forever. They start to want answers. We should know."

Violet nodded, her eyes solemn.

"I regret," Henrik said finally, "to say that we have to move on to the things that are actually going to affect our situation here. While this is all fascinating… fascinating… it's just too big for us to even deal with right now, I'm afraid. So here are our next items on the agenda: one, coordinating a vote to see if the people in Patrus wish to continue letting King Maxen rule over us, and two, the ongoing threat that is Queen Elena."

Slowly, we all settled back into having to deal with the world we faced just outside our doors. "We can't deal with Elena until we have a leader," grumbled Drew. "We need to set up a provisional government and alert the people about it."

"Which is why I think we should table this discussion, for now," announced Ms. Dale, leaning forward. "What you're talking about is going to take a lot of time, and that's something we don't have right now. Elena is coming, and you can bet that she'll be using enhanced humans to try to finish the job."

"She's going to have a pretty easy time of it," announced Mags tiredly. "We haven't completed a full census yet, but a rough estimate based on the numbers we have so far is that there's only about two thousand people left in Patrus—and that was before the groups left to go back to the farms around the city. Not to mention, most of them are women, which means they've had no education in self-defense or fighting."

"Just another way the Patrian… lifestyle has made this fight exceptionally difficult," remarked Amber.

"*I'm* surprised Elena's forces aren't here already," commented Logan. "From what you all have been saying about her, it seems like she would be pressing the advantage. We're not much of a threat at the moment, sad to say, although the fully stocked and loaded heloships will certainly help to act as a deterrent."

"Well, I have a theory on that," announced Thomas. "And that theory is—in the simplest terms—that by hitting that airfield, we may have set her plans back some, which buys us time to think of a solution."

"We might just have that solution," Henrik said. "With young Miss Morgan here."

Morgan started, and then looked around the room at all of us, her green eyes taking us all in, one by one. She swallowed visibly. "You mean a coup, don't you?"

That... wasn't the worst idea I'd heard, but I didn't have enough information. I needed to know her whole story before I could entertain the possibility. For all we knew, she was a criminal to her own people, which would make any claim she had to the throne illegitimate.

Luckily, Henrik had the same idea. "That is a possibility, but before we do anything, we need to hear your story, young lady."

I followed Henrik's gaze over to Morgan again. Her eyes slid from his face to Violet's, and her mouth tightened slightly. She stood up abruptly, and moved over to the large screen mounted on the wall.

"Will this thing be on for a while?" she asked, pulling a chain off her neck. I craned forward, curious as to what she was doing.

"It will. The generators in this building are full for the time being, although I calculate that running every piece of technology in here would eat through the fuel in thirty-six to forty-two hours." A shuffle of papers drew my gaze over from Morgan to Thomas, and he looked up at me, adjusting his glasses. "I gave everyone reports on it." He delivered his last line awkwardly, as if suddenly uncertain whether he had revealed too much, and I couldn't help but smile.

"That's good to know," said Ms. Dale cheerfully. "What are you doing, Morgana?"

Morgan's back was to us, but I saw her spine stiffen. She was silent for a moment before shaking her head and bending over to fiddle with the data chip reader at the base of the screen.

"Much like Amber, I am not the biggest fan of my full name. Morgan is fine." She reached over and hit something on the side of the screen, and it flicked on.

Immediately, blocks of typed words filled the screen.

Morgana, my beloved daughter.

I was reckless. Foolhardy and blind. If you and your sisters were the only good thing to come out of the poor decisions I made, then I consider myself blessed in spite of the suffering I have caused.

Please don't blame yourself, my daughter. You are not responsible for the mistakes of your mother, and I hate the burden my mistakes have become to you. I am doing everything I can to fix it. Believe me, you are my heart, my world... my everything. To have come so close to losing you... I can't even begin to describe the searing pain in my heart... the sickness in my stomach.

I visit you every day, sweetling. You lie in the bed, still as a statue, while machines and doctors fight to keep you alive. I brush your hair and sing to you. Can you hear me? I hope you can... I want you to know you are loved. You were born a fighter, my love. Desmond sings your praises after every one of your training sessions. She says that one day, no one will be able to stand up to you.

That was all I ever wanted for you and your sisters. I wanted to give you strengths and abilities that would keep you safe. It is true what they say. Most men are physically stronger than us. Evolution has made them that way, and I tried to defy evolution, but I see the cost of that every time I see you in that bed.

I will fix it, baby. I will, but please don't leave me.

With love,

Mother

I looked at Morgan, who had moved over to the side of the screen, her hands shoved deep into her pockets. Her back was rigid, her gaze locked on a spot on the wall.

"What happened to you?" Violet asked, the words tumbling from her mouth. I looked over to see the concern on her face, and realized she had come to care about the renegade princess, and I couldn't blame her—there was definitely something about her that made me want to care too. It was just a gut instinct, really, but I had learned to listen to it long ago.

Morgan licked her lips and took in a long deep breath, then exhaled, counting slowly, and I suddenly felt bad that we all needed to hear her story. I could see how hard this was for her.

"My mother and Mr. Jenks"—she said his name bitterly, like a curse—"didn't anticipate all of the side effects that would come from the genetic manipulation they did to me and my sisters. My sisters were born with some... minor problems. Elena suffered from chronic migraines and bleeding from the nose, ears, once from the eyes. Tabitha would go into fits and start slamming her head against the wall.

"Like Tim, my skin hurts when I am touched. I think my pain receptors are even more sophisticated. The softest breeze on my skin would feel like fire, but I could grab a fly out of the air with unerring accuracy. I was a prototype, after all. But where Elena and Tabitha seemed to be able to cope with the... side effects... I was more... sensitive, I guess. *Weak* was the word Elena would use, every time she found me crying. She'd push me, slap me, telling me it would make me stronger, but it never did." She gritted her teeth, and I realized she was fighting back tears. "I couldn't even ask my mother for a hug—because it *hurt* so bad. Can you understand what that's like? Being a little girl who only needs a hug, but, whenever she's touched, would only scream and scream and scream until her voice gave out?"

The words marched out of her, forced between angry teeth and stiff lips, but I felt the anguish brewing just beneath the surface. The memory of a despair so deep on a night so dark, it made it impossible for Morgan to find any source of light.

"Growing up with Elena was hell. She used to call all of us her grand experiments. Tabitha was her first project, obviously, and she learned how to direct her. Selina and Marina followed, and Elena used their codependency against each other, locking them apart from each other when they wouldn't do what she wanted. For a while, Lena and I were a team. We would keep an eye out for each other, help each other if she ever came by, but Elena found a way to get to her. Which was to pit us against each other. Make her hate me. Elena made her choose between us, and, well... It was easy, I suppose. My enhancement was far more advanced than hers, and Desmond would fawn a lot over me as a result. I guess it made all my sisters hate me in a way, but Lena…" She trailed off, her lips trembling. "She said such cruel things to me. Things no little girl should hear, should even think. Once Lena joined Elena's little faction, only Sierra and I remained, and Sierra was still an infant. Once I held Elena's full attention, she was relentless. They'd hold me down and hurt me in every way they could imagine. I won't… I'll spare you the details."

"So, one day, Elena went too far," concluded Ms. Dale. "And you were hospitalized."

Morgan gave a bitter laugh, and shook her head, fighting back against whatever was tearing her apart. "No, I'm sorry to disappoint you, Ms. Dale, but Elena was too smart for that. I… I ended up hurting myself."

Silence met her statement, and she carried on, explaining how she had planned and executed her suicide attempt. She'd snuck into the medical ward and swiped dozens of pills, specifically ones that weren't intended to be mixed together. She'd taken every single one and then fallen asleep, as expected.

"I guess I just didn't ever consider that our mother actually loved us," she said, her throat thick. "She refused to let the doctors give up on me. When she found out what had happened, she began to take steps to… fix her mistakes. That's when she authorized Mr. Jenks to begin experimenting on the boys of Matrus. They expanded the program, started taking boys at unprecedented rates."

"How old were you?" asked Viggo.

Morgan licked her lips again, and met his eyes. "I was ten," she whispered. "Elena was eighteen."

"I don't understand. How did you wind up with the Liberators?"

Morgan faltered, and then sighed. "After Mother found out what Elena had been doing, she told her that she wasn't going to allow a psychopath to become queen. That led to a huge fight, one that for once, Elena wasn't winning. So she agreed to get counseling three times a week, and agreed to get the other sisters to go, too, as well as helping to keep them in line while Mother figured out how to… fix us."

"But she still resented you for even bringing the problems to your mother's attention," said Owen, and Morgan gave another bitter laugh, pressing her back into the wall, as if trying to keep it from falling over.

"Of course she did. Now she had to be more careful. The staff was instructed to report any bad behavior, and the therapists reported only to my mother, as did Mr. Jenks. Elena was furious with me and what I had done. As though I had *planned* this outcome, when I only wanted… I only wanted… Well, Elena doesn't get furious so much as annoyed. She despises delays, and any inhibition to her plans. I had delayed her, and so it was on her to find ways of making me pay."

She shrugged. "Things happened, Elena denied involvement, and my mother couldn't condemn her without evidence—not without having to explain to her subjects what she had done to the royal line. So she had Desmond hide me. At first it was in a safe house, but later Desmond forged papers to have me imprisoned for a while. It was so she could get me credence with the Liberators, and by the time she brought me to them, saying that she had recruited me, I was older—enough that nobody recognized me or connected me to the princess they'd heard was in the hospital in the news. I knew Desmond was close to Elena, but worked for my mother. I knew I could never tell a soul who I really was. She held it over me that she was the only thing keeping me alive—and I was never sure if that meant Elena thought I was dead, or alive and performing some sort of task for her. I even once entertained the small hope that therapy was paying off for Elena and she was getting better. Then, when Mother was murdered, it turned out that Desmond and Elena had been working together behind my mother's back, too."

Morgan trailed off, expelling a shuddering breath. "I had no idea what to do, especially after I found out that's what Mother meant by helping us—using those children to refine us. Strip away the bad so only the good could remain. I never asked her to do that! I didn't find out until after she died. And I was afraid to act. Desmond could have turned me over to Elena at any moment, made me into another of my sister's pawns again. She held that over me, too. As long as I was her good little operative and didn't say a word, she kept me out of my sister's hands. Until you guys came along and blew her cover with the rest of the

Liberators. But you know that part."

She met our gazes, her eyes flashing. "So yeah. That's my story."

I looked around the room, trying to gauge everyone's reactions. I, for one, felt nauseated by her tale. I had never once considered how Elena might have been when she was younger. Truthfully, I couldn't even wrap my head around the idea that she had ever been young. She seemed too sinister to ever have any qualities of childhood ascribed to her, even in her appearance.

"Thank you for telling your story," said Amber. "I know how hard that can be."

Vox straightened in his seat and opened his mouth to say something, but a sharp glance from Amber cut him short. He squinted at her a moment, and then, very pointedly, smiled at Amber.

"It was very brave," he said, an encouraging smile on his face, and Amber's expression went from irritated to considering.

Morgan shrugged and pushed her shock of dyed black bangs from her face. "Thanks, but it's nothing. I'm not the same person I was, and I didn't inherit the 'blindly follow a psychopath' gene, so… thanks, I guess. I mean, you deserved to know, in some ways. Hiding the truth won't make it any less real. It's a thing that will fester if kept inside for too long." She looked around, her voice catching, and then looked back down, and I realized the poor girl had never had anyone to share her story with. She was beyond brave for doing it here and now for the first time—she was fearless. "Never mind. Nothing I told you changes the fact that Elena is out there with something up her sleeve, and we need to stop her."

"I hate to be the guy who asks, but how do we know you don't just want the throne for yourself?" asked Drew, leaning forward. "My country is on the brink of death because of your sister's quest for power or control or whatever the hell she did all this for, and I, for one, don't want to institute a regime change and replace one dictator with another!"

Morgan flushed bright red, her brows drawing together. She opened her mouth to say something, but I wasn't able to keep my mouth shut. "That's not fair, Drew. Based on what Morgan is telling us, she wasn't even *there* when all of this stuff started going down. We can't hold her accountable for the actions of the others."

"For all we know she could've been planted here by her sister! You people cannot seriously be taking her word for what happened! If this is how you've been running things this entire time, you're fools!"

Drew made to stand up, and suddenly Owen was on his feet, slamming his fist into the table, the promise of a fiery death in his eyes. "How *dare* you," he bellowed. "This woman killed her own twin sister to help us! She blew her cover to help Violet track down Desmond. She has every right to be here, in this room, with us, especially after what she suffered at the hands of those supposed to take care of her. Just look at the date stamp on the letter! Do the math! You can't tell me her sister managed to hack into her mother's computer ten years ago to write that letter using her mother's electronic seal, just so that she could have this opportunity ten years later!"

Morgan, still frozen from when I had cut off whatever she was going to say, flushed a deep pink and seemed to withdraw into herself for a moment. It would've been sweet, if we weren't in the middle of an argument about her. Now it was just embarrassing, for all of us, and I was going to make sure Drew saw that.

Drew's mouth dropped, and then slowly closed, disappearing behind his bushy beard. He looked over to Mags, clearly searching for support. "Mags, I—"

"Shut up and sit down," she ordered. "I want to know more about this possible coup."

Morgan looked around the room for a second, having regained her composure after Owen's defense of her. "Before we get to that, may I say something?"

"Of course," Henrik said. "We may still be making our minds up about you, but that doesn't mean we are rude enough to not give you a chance to defend yourself." He gave Drew a pointed look, and then smiled kindly at Morgan. "Go ahead, dear."

Morgan hesitated, looking lost in thought for a moment, and then looked at Drew. "I don't want to be queen," she said coldly. "Never have.

I am the *sixth* daughter. That means that, if I had been a normal girl, I would have been free to do whatever I wanted. I don't want that kind of responsibility! I'm not worthy of it. People deserve someone brave to lead them. Not a coward."

Everyone in the room sat still under the force of her haunted words.

"You're not a coward," Violet said softly, filling the uncertain silence with the warm strength and conviction in her voice. "You were a scared little girl. It wasn't your fault."

Morgan scoffed and shook her head, but didn't reply. It was clear she didn't believe Violet, but she would… with time. At least I hoped she would.

Morgan pushed off the wall and moved to take out the tiny disk with her mother's letter in it. Clipping it back onto the chain around her neck, she moved back to her chair to sit down, biting her lip slightly when Owen slid it out for her before she sat. Drew stood for another few seconds, and then sat abruptly.

"I don't want to rule," Morgan calmly repeated. "Honestly, the only thing I want from this is to get Sierra away from Elena. She's just a little girl, and has no place in all this ugliness."

"So you'd walk away from the power?" asked Logan. "Just like that?"

Morgan's face didn't change as she met his gaze. "Just like that," she agreed.

"Look, I hate to say this, Morgan, but you have to consider the possibility of taking the throne, at least for a short time," said Henrik. "With Patrus so destabilized, we need a stable ally to help us with food and supplies for the winter while we get things together. So… who do you know who could help us? Is there anyone who stands out to you?"

Morgan shifted and let her gaze tilt upward, clearly thinking about it. "Alyssa Dawes," she said after a few moments. "She doesn't hold an office anymore, but she did serve as a special advisor to my mother and grandmother."

"Why?" I asked.

"She was a political activist," Violet said, answering for Morgan. "She caused a lot of social changes, especially regarding Patrian husbands and treating them the same as Matrian husbands."

"If anyone could turn the citizens against Elena, it would be her," said Morgan. "Then you wouldn't even need a coup. The Matrians would take her down on their own."

"And lose a lot of people trying," said Henrik.

"Good," retorted Drew. "Maybe we should even up the score a little."

Violet bit back a growl, her hands clenched, and I could tell she wanted to say something scathing to Drew, probably mixed with a few insults. I was feeling a bit of the same anger myself, to be honest, but now wasn't the time to be getting emotional.

"That's not how we do things here," said Ms. Dale, and I was relieved that she'd been feeling the same way. "No innocents hurt, if we can avoid it. But it seems like this might be a better solution than trying to go after Elena in her palace, so we're going to consider it."

Henrik nodded in approval, and then Violet was standing. "Viggo and I should be the ones to go to Matrus," she said, resting her palms on the table and leaning forward. "We can give Alyssa the information she needs, and that'll leave everyone here free to start working on the other stuff."

There was a long pause, and then Ms. Dale looked at me. "You sure about this?" she asked, and I looked up at Violet for a second.

"Absolutely," I replied. "It's smart, relies on only two agents. Violet and I are great at improvising when things go horribly awry. But best of all, with this solution, you three"—I indicated the Patrian rebel leaders, focusing on Drew, who needed the most convincing—"could work on the provisional government and get it off the ground faster. The people are looking for leaders to trust, and this is the time to show yourselves to them."

"Not to mention, I have leverage on Elena. Leverage I can use to our advantage." Violet looked around the room, her face and body exuding confidence. "If we are torn between these two things, then let Viggo and I handle Elena, while the rest of you take care of this place."

"This is dangerous," Amber said with a grin. "Which is why I think I should be the one to pilot you over there."

"Hold your horses, young lady," Henrik said. "I'm really not sure I like the idea of only a two-man team going into Matrus. We wouldn't be able to back you up if you got in trouble."

"A larger team could be more dangerous," I said. "More chance of getting caught. Just think it over. But we're happy to volunteer."

Henrik sighed and looked around the room. "Any objections?" he asked.

Nobody raised their hand, and I felt a curious mixture of disappointment and excitement. We were so close to doing something about Elena that I could practically taste it.

I was glad Violet had suggested it, but I also knew the odds. I didn't even have to ask Thomas. Chances were if the two of us went into Matrus, we would probably die there. Violet knew this, and still she wanted to go—she was willing to make that sacrifice for the good of everyone, and I was so proud that I could call her mine.

"No objections noted," Henrik announced as the room filled with silence at his question. "Then let's all get some rack time, all right?"

CHAPTER 17

Violet

I slowed to a stop as we rounded the corner at the bottom of the stairs leading away from the conference room, letting my arm stretch out as Viggo continued to pull away, my fingers still laced through his. He felt me stop and came to a halt, turning slowly, his expression inquisitive. I smiled, melting as I looked into the angular planes of his face, trying to make my love for him shine through my eyes.

"Why are you looking at me like that?" he asked.

I had to laugh—he sounded so baffled and confused, and I couldn't blame him. I was acting weird, but… this was the time. It was right now, and it was going to be perfect.

"Because I love you," I said, and he smiled, although the confusion on his face was still there. I'd told him that enough times, I supposed, that it had stuck. I took a step closer to him, holding up our interlocked hands between us. "And I've been thinking about this for a while now. Well, since The Outlands, anyway. I… I want to marry you, Viggo. Now. I can't wait anymore. I am so hopelessly in love with you that it leaves me breathless and shaky, and I feel sick thinking about us not being married. It's time, Viggo. Will you marry me? Today?"

As I spoke, Viggo's face broke out into a smile, and then the smile merged into a thoughtful expression, his lips moving up and down with the gentle rocking of a body of water. When I was done with my proposal, he exhaled slowly.

"Violet, what brought this on?" he asked gently. He didn't say it with alarm, just a genuine curiosity, which was good, because as excited as I was, I was also a little bit nervous.

"It was something Belinda said on the heloship," I said softly, licking my lips. "And I realized she was right. Viggo, I don't want to die having never been married to you."

"Die? Violet—"

"Please don't tell me that we're not going to die. We're going into Matrus. Soon. That's where Elena lives, Viggo. We'd have to be idiots to assume this is anything short of a suicide mission. I am not going in there prepared to die—I am going to fight until my last breath to get us both out alive. But we know the risks, and you know as well as I do that if that's the price we have to pay, then we'll pay it. Just… give me this, please."

"Violet… I want you to look at me." He released my fingers as I spoke, reaching up to touch my cheek and place his other hand on my hip, gently coaxing me toward him. "We're not going to die in Matrus, and this is not a suicide mission."

"I want to believe that. But Viggo, war is—"

"Chaotic?" he cut in with a teasing grin, and I smiled, nodding my head. His expression grew thoughtful again, and he sighed. "Violet, we don't have to rush this. There's no reason to do it right this minute. We still don't even have a fully formed plan yet—we need more intel on the palace, Alyssa Dawes, where Sierra might be. Even with Thomas finally in their system after the heloship raid, it could take days."

"Which are days that I could spend as your wife, not as your fiancée," I replied. "I understand what you're saying, but I've thought about this a lot. I don't want to wait anymore. I told myself I'd find the right moment, and it's now. Not to mention—everyone is here! All of our friends and family, under one roof. I mean, who knows when that will ever happen again, or how long we'll have that for?"

Viggo's face fell, and he nodded. "That's a good point," he said, and from the pained look on his face I realized he was probably thinking about all the people we had lost so far. Those deaths were still fresh, still a hole inside me every time I stopped to look back, and I knew they tore at Viggo every day. Still, he met my gaze and offered me a small smile. "So have I completely shattered my masculine image yet by acting like a nervous bride?"

"You're not nervous," I pointed out. "You're a traditionalist. But these are untraditional times, Viggo, and I'm ready. So unless you're not..."

He gave me a droll look, and then dipped his head down and pressed his lips to mine. "You know I am," he breathed. "But... ask me again."

"Dork," I teased. "So... will you?"

"Marry you?" he questioned.

I pressed my lips together to keep from screaming in frustration and looked up at him, bringing my hands up slowly to his neck and pretending to choke him—just enough to let him know he was driving me crazy.

He chuckled and took my hands in his, removing them from his neck. "Calm down—before I even say yes, which we both know I'm going to, I still want to know who you are planning to have preside over it. I mean... Maxen is really the only officiate who could be legally recognized at this point."

I shuddered, even though I knew Viggo was joking. Taking a moment to consider his question, I finally just shrugged. "I-I don't know. And I don't care. It could be Ms. Dale for all I care. I mean, really, all we need are a few witnesses and an exchange of vows and rings. We got the rings, we can wing the vows—"

"*Wing* the *vows!*" he sputtered, and I fought back a laugh at the alarm on his face. "Violet, the vows are the most important part. What are you planning on saying... 'I promise to share my cookies with you'?"

"Okay, A: I'm not sharing my cookies with you, and B: do you really think I'd come up with something that lame? C'mon, give me a little credit here. I'd at least be generous and say something about massaging your shoulders once a year."

The glitter in his deep green eyes was resplendent with humor, a bemused smile twisting the beautiful lines of his lips. "A year?" he asked. I shrugged, and he shook his head at me. "So romantic."

I gave him the look—an unamused one—and he chuckled, "I'm sorry, love."

"Forgiven. Now are you done stalling? Because I would really like to get married to you."

He snorted and then nodded. "I would really like to get married to you too, Violet."

"Is that a yes?" I needed to hear it, needed to hear the words coming from his mouth.

"It's a yes—I will marry you today."

I let out a whoop and broke off from him, my mind moving rapidly as I began ticking off the things we needed to do.

"Okay, I'll go get a dress, I'll tap Amber to find a location so everyone can be there—we'll probably have to get married in the hospital, so Alejandro, Quinn, Solomon, and Jay can be there—I hope he wakes up, but even so… You'll need to find something nice to wear, too… Oh! And flowers, and some food!"

"Violet, slow down," Viggo called quietly. "We still need to find someone to marry us!"

An idea flicked through my mind, and I grinned. "Don't worry about it," I announced. "You just tell all the guys what's going on, and I've got the girls, okay? Let's meet up in two hours!"

I began moving back up the stairs, excitement coursing through my veins as I realized that in a few short hours, I would be married to Viggo.

There was so much to do before he and I could be… Oh crap— we'd never discussed the names! Oh well. I supposed we could just keep our own (or trade). I certainly wasn't giving up my name… and Viggo wouldn't either. Either way, we'd figure it out, I thought with a grin.

CHAPTER 18

Viggo

When Violet puts her mind to something, she really goes out of her way to make it a reality, I thought to myself as I tugged at the sleeves of the stiff, formal warden's dress coat I was wearing. It wasn't mine, obviously. I had found a storeroom filled with them, and figured they were the best formal option I was going to get in the time allotted. And there was some kind of significance to it, I supposed—given my complicated history with this uniform, maybe it was the best choice after all.

Smoothing the lapels down until I was confident they were regulation, I sat down on the narrow bed in the small private dorm room that was in the opposite wing of the building from where Violet and the women were, and began tugging on the knee-high, perfectly polished boots that completed the uniform. The boots were a bit tight, pinching in the toes, but I could endure them for a few hours.

The door clicked open and I looked up in time to see Owen ducking in, wearing a tight sweater and a pair of black slacks. His blue eyes widened as he realized he was the first in the room, and he hesitated, suddenly nervous.

I stood up, a smile already on my lips. "Owen," I said warmly, holding a hand out to him as I crossed the room. He reached up automatically, and I caught his hand and squeezed, giving him a firm shake. "Thank you for coming. It really means a lot to me."

"Oh, um, sure," Owen stammered, a confused expression on his face. Confused and wary, like I was setting him up for some sort of trap.

I hated that he felt like that, but a part of that was his own fault. He had betrayed us all in his quest to end Desmond's life. What's worse, he had put Violet and her brother in danger while doing so. Violet had begged for us to forgive him instead of simply exiling him from our group, so we had punished him, giving him the task of being Violet's bodyguard. Of course, that had been an impossible task to contend with, and ultimately he had failed to stay with her and keep her out of danger. But he'd certainly proven his loyalty in the attempt.

I could understand his nervousness. "Relax," I told him. "It's my wedding day, not yours."

He smiled—just for a second, but it was there. That old light. I opened my mouth to add something, when the door swung open again, revealing... Anello Cruz. I suppressed a very noisy and very annoyed groan, and managed to plaster a bit of a smile onto my lips as he extended his hand, the bandages and sling that swaddled the arm he'd been shot in notwithstanding. I couldn't completely hate the guy anymore. He'd fought bravely beside us at the water treatment plant, and his quick thinking had helped us get out of more than one tight situation—but he'd never gotten less *irritating*.

"Hey, Viggo, compadre! I heard about your wedding! Congratulations, my friend. Or should I say condolences, eh?"

He pumped my hand as he spoke, and I had to refrain from yanking it back, reminding myself that Cruz was just *naturally* a loud-mouthed, arrogant alpha male. This was really him trying to bond with me, but it didn't make me want to punch him any less.

"You should say congratulations," said Owen dryly. "And tone it down some. Viggo and Violet love each other dearly, so be happy for them or get out."

Cruz blinked in surprise, and then smiled, finally releasing my

BELLA FORREST

hand. "Hey, no offense, mi amigos. I'm just not the 'get married' kind—although for that doctor lady I might make an exception." He adjusted his sling, his smile growing bigger as his expression grew a bit dazed—likely envisioning that scenario—and I seized the opportunity to get to the other side of the room, hearing him ask Owen, "So what'd I miss at the meeting?"

Focusing on my appearance again, I gathered my long hair up behind my neck and wrapped a band around it, running a hand over the sides and top to smooth it out. Once I was finished, I ran a hand over my beard. It wasn't too long, so it didn't need trimming, but a part of me wondered if I should shave it off.

"You should keep it," said Henrik's voice, and I looked over in the mirror to see him closing the door to the hall. He met my gaze in the mirror and gave me a rueful smile. "I wish I could say that it's because you looked better or that Violet likes it, but really it's because we might need to rely on disguise to get into Matrus, and the beard helps with that."

"That's a good point," I said, taking one final check in the mirror. "Anyone hear from Violet yet?"

"No, but I recently overheard Dr. Tierney saying she was running around like a madwoman, trying to set things up," Owen commented, moving over to the bed and sitting down on it, the springs squeaking under his weight. "Amber too."

"Great," I said, fiddling with the uniform in an attempt to try to perfect it, even though it was as close to perfect as it was ever going to be.

Henrik came over and gently pushed my hands away, his eyes taking in the uniform and then tugging a few things here and there. "It's too bad you don't have any insignia here," he said as he brushed off my shoulders. "It would really complete the look."

"I'm glad there aren't any," I said quietly, and he looked up at me in surprise. "That life feels like forever ago... like part of a terrible dream I was half-stumbling through. Violet didn't fall in love with a warden. She fell in love with me."

158

Henrik smiled gently, and nodded. "She's a good woman, Viggo. And soon she'll be your wife, for as long as you both shall live. I'm excited for you both to be getting this start now, instead of waiting. You both need it after everything—"

Henrik's continuing words of reassurance disappeared behind the strange ringing that had started in my ears when he said "for as long as you both shall live." Softly at first, then louder and louder. Miriam's face flashed into my mind, as unexpected an interloper as I could ever receive at this moment, and one that made me feel a stab of guilt, made my heartbeat race and my chest begin to tighten.

I wasn't sure how I managed it, but I somehow excused myself from Henrik and moved to the door in a daze, stepping through it and closing it behind me. In the dark hall, I paced back and forth for a moment, trying to shake out the nervous tension now brewing all along my muscles, before finally coming to a stop in front of a wall, leaning my arm against it, my forehead resting on my forearm.

I struggled to breathe, forcing a slow breath of air past the half-seized up shuddering of my lungs and down deep into my stomach. Except even my stomach felt rigid and unyielding, too small for even the tiniest gulp of air, and I found myself fighting back an extreme urge to put my fist through something breakable.

"Viggo?"

Looking over without bothering to lift my head, I saw Alejandro standing behind me, holding the temporary cast protecting one hand with the other one, supporting it at the wrist.

"Hey," I said, trying to keep my breathing steady and failing miserably. I clenched my hand into a fist. I had to say something… something normal. "No surgery yet?"

"The doc wanted to use some of that special stuff Violet brought back from The Outlands on my hand first. Something about wanting to see if it could repair some of the smaller damaged bones first, because then there'd be a chance surgery would help repair the rest, and I'd get better use of my hand."

"That's great news," I said. I wasn't sure if it was. I had tried to listen,

I really had, but my mind was consumed with Miriam. Our wedding. How we had promised to be with each other forever. Then a stupid fight had led to catastrophe… and now she was dead, and I was about to marry someone else. How cruel I was to her memory.

Alejandro shifted, and then leaned a shoulder into the wall next to me, his sharp blue eyes squinting as he took me in. "You okay, boyo?"

I tried to suck down another breath of air, and shook my head. "I think I'm having a panic attack," I grated out, even angrier for having said it out loud.

"Oh." A pause, followed by, "That doesn't surprise me at all."

I looked over at Alejandro with eyes wide, and he gave me a tired smile. "Is it… about Miriam?"

How well he knew me. I nodded tightly, unable to let her name cross my lips.

Alejandro's voice was full of understanding. "Of course. She meant a lot to you, boyo," he said softly, meeting my gaze. "It's no wonder you're feeling like this. There's still so many lingering emotions inside you, and I'm sad to say this, but they will remain."

I sucked in another breath, rewarded by my stomach easing up a little bit and allowing more air to get in. "I still miss her sometimes," I admitted. "What if me doing this is… being disrespectful to her memory?"

Alejandro smiled and looked around the hall for a long moment, considering the question. "Viggo, you and Miriam were dealt a bad hand. That's a bad way of expressing it, but it's true. You both got unlucky. And it's not because you knew each other or that you even fell in love. It's not that you fought and she left. It was just… bad luck and bad timing. Miriam would understand this. It's only natural to let someone into your heart. She would want it for you. She would want you to be happy. As you and I both know, no man can be an island for too long without sinking into the seas… You love Violet, right?"

"Yes," I said, my breath coming a little easier.

"You'll do anything to keep her safe and happy?"

"Yes," I replied, a little more emphatically.

"Then marry her. You and Miriam had your time, and now you have another chance. Marry Violet, and just... devote whatever time you have left to her, and it'll be a wonderful life, worthy of your attention. You're always going to love Miriam... but that doesn't mean you don't have room in your heart for another."

I hesitated, the fear clutching at my heart feeling oily and poisonous, like the slimy residue from a venomous amphibian that had marched all over it. "I just couldn't bear to lose Violet like I lost Miriam," I admitted, both to myself and to Alejandro. I didn't even want to consider the possibility—getting married felt too much like just one step closer to losing her.

Alejandro sighed loudly through his nose. "Viggo, that situation, the way you lost Miriam, it *can't* happen again. It literally can't. The gender population has shifted in Patrus—women now outnumber men here. That means those women are going to have to have a say in their country, just by the sheer lack of anyone able to handle the role. And that means that all those laws against women are going to change for the better, if not disappear completely."

The tightness in my chest eased up a bit more at his words, until I was finally able to take a deep, steady breath, easing fully into the exhale, letting my anxiety out along with it. Not all of it left—some remained to taunt me, but it was a small voice, one easily overridden by my rational mind. Alejandro was right. There was no way what had happened to Miriam would ever happen to Violet.

Unless, of course, we got caught in Matrus, the small evil voice reminded me—and I decided right then and there to lock it away and throw away the key. No way was I letting my own doubt stand in the way of what I'd wanted to do ever since I'd asked Violet to marry me on that sinking ship.

Alejandro waited patiently by my side, until I pushed off of the wall and gave him a nod, looking into his eyes with all the gratitude I could muster. "Thank you, Alejandro."

"Of course, boyo. It's like that for all of us. You should've seen me before *my* wedding. A stiff breeze could've knocked me over that day.

But trust me, as soon as you see her standing there waiting for you—only you—you'll forget all of your nerves for sure."

I grinned at him, a chuckle escaping from my lips, just as Tim rounded the corner. I stepped out around Alejandro, smiling as the young man bounded over, a lopsided and excited smile plastered on his youthful face.

"Violet ready," he announced. "Waiting for you in hospital. Everyone."

Reaching out, I gently ruffled his hair. "Thanks, Tim. Let me go round up the guys, and we'll be right there, okay?"

"Okay!" he said with a sharp nod. He turned and then bounded back down the stairs, his feet landing heavily on the floor and kicking up a ruckus as he moved quickly to the bottom.

Exchanging looks with Alejandro, I grinned and then moved over to the door, throwing it open.

"It's time, gentlemen," I announced to the men waiting inside.

CHAPTER 19

Violet

My hands were sweating, forcing me to shift the bouquet of flowers Tim had picked for me from one hand to another. The hospital was quiet. People were sleeping, mostly, but Dr. Tierney had helped us—and, I assumed, them—by moving the less-than-critical patients out of the small corner we were holding the ceremony in.

The beds had been shifted slightly, angled in rows to create a wider space between them, as well as in the aisle separating them. A podium had been brought in and placed near the wall. The officiant would stand behind it, while Viggo and I were in front, close to the beds. Our guests would sit in them during the ceremony. Well, some of them would. Quinn and Jay were still lying there, as always.

Solomon had been brought out of his private room for the ceremony. It made me smile to have him here, even if he wasn't awake. He still hadn't regained consciousness, but Dr. Tierney had warned me not to worry yet. If he wasn't up in another day or so, then we'd have to worry. I just hoped it wasn't my fault that he was still unconscious.

Tim entered, flashing me a smile, and I looked over his shoulder, half-expecting to see Viggo on his tail. But as Tim scampered over, I felt a wave of nervous disappointment roll over me, and sucked in a shuddering breath.

"This is so stupid," I muttered as Tim dropped down into a nearby bed, right next to where Jay was still sleeping in his bed. "Why am I even feeling like this?"

"You beautiful," Tim said reassuringly, reaching up to lightly touch my arms. I looked down at the dress I was wearing. It was a simple thing, really, and totally inappropriate attire for winter. The sheer yellow fabric underneath the black crocheted bodice and sleeves was so thin, I'd freeze to death if we were outside. Despite its thinness, it was oddly heavy, which only added to the discomfort of having my legs bare, and the fact that the entire thing was half an inch too tight.

Then again, maybe it was in my head. I'd never been the kind of girl to wear dresses—never had the money or luxury of owning one, really—and I'd usually worn them in Patrus as disguises. At the moment, this one felt no different. I'd traded my good boots for it—at my insistence—to a young woman in Mags' group. Her shoes had been next to nothing, and I just couldn't take the dress without giving her something in return. Yet even after going through all that to secure a dress, I suddenly desperately wished I were in pants and a sweater.

"The dress is okay," I half-whispered under my breath, trying to convince myself. "But my hair is still a half-grown mess, my face is still bruised up… This was an awful idea. I really should go change."

"It fine," Tim said reassuringly. The door opened behind him, and I looked up, my heart in my throat, beating faster than a trapped butterfly. The disappointment I felt as I saw Ms. Dale leading in Logan, Drew, Mags, and Jenny was almost unbearable, and I looked back at Tim.

"I'm getting married in a hospital!" I whispered harshly.

Maybe I was nervous and just needed to complain, or maybe all of this was taking too long. Either way, I just wanted to see Viggo so he could wrap his arms around me and make me laugh about my own silliness. This whole thing had been my idea, after all.

"Thank you for doing that," said a hoarse voice, grabbing my attention. I looked over and saw Jay's eyes open—albeit still looking a little groggy—a half-smile on his face. "Violet," he rasped as soon as his eyes met my gaze, "you look so beautiful." His lips smacked as he talked, and Tim immediately reached for a cup on the nightstand next to Jay, lifting it up to his lips and helping him drink a few mouthfuls.

The move was so careful and practiced that it was clear Tim had been spending every waking and sleeping moment with Jay since he'd been injured. I moved closer and then sat down on the side of Jay's bed, my knees brushing up against Tim's. Jay gave me a sleepy smile, and then yawned.

"Sorry," he said, his voice a little less rough now that he'd had water. "These meds are really good at making the pain go away, but not so good for staying awake." He yawned another time, and then shook his head. "So… you finally marrying Viggo? It's about time."

I looked up as Ms. Dale directed Drew, Mags, and Logan to sit on an empty bed, but only Mags and Drew sat down. Logan moved over to where Amber was sitting, on the bed next to Solomon's, and dropped onto the mattress behind her. He said something, and Amber rolled her eyes silently in return. But as she turned to give him the cold shoulder, I noticed a small smile creeping across her lips.

I wasn't able to comprehend or wonder about their drama right now. I stood back up, unable to sit any longer, and began to shift my weight back and forth, waiting impatiently. Morgan entered the room and made a beeline over to me, a nervous smile on her face.

"Hey, Violet, how are you feeling?"

"Nervous," I replied tersely, shifting the bundle of flowers to my other hand again while I dragged my moist palm down the side of my dress. "You?"

Her green eyes darted around, and she nodded, her smile softening and dimming into a small frown. "Nervous."

"Yeah, well, it's my wedding. Technically I'm the only one entitled to be nervous."

Morgan gaped at me for a second, and then grinned. "You're be-coming one of those bride monsters, Violet," she teased, stepping around me and sitting down in the empty bed behind Jay's. She pulled out a notebook and a pen, opened up to a page, and began reading, her mouth moving softly as she rehearsed whatever speech she had written.

Just when I thought I was going to crack under the pressure of it all, Viggo walked in, and everything just… stopped. It just did.

He looked amazing, with his crisp, perfect uniform and his long dark hair pulled back. For a second I felt like I couldn't breathe—couldn't even think—as I stared at him. Like he'd literally stolen the air straight out of my lungs just with his entrance. It was the traditional entrance for a Matrian wedding: the groom entered while the bride watched. He'd done it for me, without hesitation or any sign of balking, and I loved him all the more for it.

We stared at each other for a long moment, and then Viggo moved purposefully over toward me, his long legs tearing up the floor to be by my side, reminding me of why the women of Matrus wanted their intended husbands to come to them, instead of the other way around. He walked with purpose and determination, no hesitation, both eager and confident to make his way to his soon-to-be-bride, in a way that made my heart pound heavily against my ribcage. As he moved, a thousand images and memories flooded through my head. All I could think was about was how we met—clutching his waist as I rode with him on his motorcycle through a peaceful Patrus, the long night he'd stayed by my side to nurse me back to health after I'd been bitten by the centipede in The Green, the sight of him when he'd opened the door to rescue me from the torture chamber that Tabitha had imprisoned me in when she'd put the knife through my hand. Those thoughts should've assuaged the bats flying around in my stomach, but they didn't—they just made them swoop harder.

The only thing that brought me some calm was when Viggo reached out his hand to me. As soon as his hand was in mine, I immediately relaxed, melting under his steady touch. He smiled at me, giving a nervous chuckle, and I realized I hadn't been the only one feeling that way. Even in separate rooms, across the compound from one another, we'd been having the same anxieties, contemplating this step toward our future together—and I realized that if Viggo and I had gotten through so many horrible things together, we could certainly get through this wonderful one.

Looking around the room, I confirmed that everyone was there: Tim, Owen, Jay, Quinn, Thomas, Solomon, Cody, Ms. Dale, Henrik, Amber, Logan, Drew, Mags, Morgan, Dr. Tierney, Alejandro, Jenny, Cad, Margot, Henry and Sarah, April, Cruz... the Liberators and refugees who had become close to us... and I couldn't help but feel incredibly loved. Not just by Viggo, but by all of them. I was closer to some of them than others, and some of the invitations, like Drew, and Logan, if I were being honest, had been political or polite more than anything else, but still... We had fought together and lost people together, and that was not insignificant to me.

It was so touching to have family there—at a life event I never thought I'd have in a thousand years—and I was surprised to find myself tearing up as I looked at them.

"I'm sorry," I said, my voice constricting a little bit. "I'm not even sure why I'm crying."

"Because this is your last chance to make the right choice and run for your life," Amber declared as she stood up and crossed over to me, passing me a handkerchief that I immediately used to dab my eyes. "You really are too good for this Croft fellow—if that is even his real name, after all."

Amber's catty remark made me laugh through the tears, and I continued to dab my eyes and cry, but I felt lighter on the inside than I could even describe. I pulled her in close for a hug, whispering a thank you, but she didn't reply, just squeezed me a little tighter before letting me go.

"Not nice, Amberlynn," Viggo said, emphasizing her name. "I'll get you for this."

She winked at Viggo, and then patted me on the cheek. "You'll do great at this," she whispered before slipping back toward her seat in front of Logan. "You and him both."

"All right, is everyone here?" asked Morgan, putting down her notebook and dragging my attention over to her. I nodded, and she smiled.

"Then we should get started?"

That earned another nod from me. I was too afraid to open my mouth for fear of shouting "I do!" as loud as possible, just to get it over with.

Morgan sucked in a deep breath, seeming to take a moment to calm herself, and then stood in front of the group, a little set apart, and began to speak.

"So… Well, when I was taught this aspect of Matrian duty, there were some specific phrases and terminologies included that I just… I don't feel capture the relationship between Viggo and Violet at all. Those words were intended for a traditional Matrian/Patrian wedding solution, which I feel doesn't reflect the nature of the bond you two share. So if you'll allow me a little leeway, I'm going to change it up a little bit."

"No objections from us," replied Viggo, and Morgan smiled.

"Excellent." Thumbing through her notebook, she took one last look at what she had written, and then closed the book. "In a time where chaos and violence are pretty much the economy in the world we live, Viggo Croft and Violet Bates have managed to find each other, defying the obstacles in their paths and pushing forward, for each other and for the people they lead. Their love is like a flame, and we are the moths that are circling above it, trying to warm ourselves on the light they produce in each witty joke and each shared smile. Most of us will never know a love like theirs—not as intimately or passionately."

She looked around the room for a moment, her fingers flipping the page, and then she continued.

"Viggo Croft, do you promise to love Violet Bates? Do you promise to always communicate with her, act as her sword and shield, care for her well-being above your own, and above all, treat her as your partner and equal, for as long as you both shall live?"

Viggo's gaze never wavered, but the smile on his lips grew even broader. "I do," he said, his voice rumbling over me.

"Violet Bates, do you promise to love Viggo Croft? Do you promise to always communicate with him, act as his sword and shield, care for his well-being above your own, and above all, treat him as your partner and equal, for as long as you both shall live?"

"I do," I breathed.

"The rings?" she asked, and I turned to see Tim standing before us, his eyes aglow, the open box in his hands displaying Henrik's rings. "Viggo, if you have anything you would like to say to Violet as you place the ring on her finger, now is the time."

Viggo nodded as he picked up the smaller ring between two fingers. "Violet, before I met you, I... had decided to fade into the background. I already felt desperately alone, so why not at least feel alone in my cabin by the woods? Then you came into my life, and it took me forever to realize that you were the little bit of sunlight I needed to actually find some hope and joy in the world. I am so grateful that you let me find it with you."

I was already crying unabashedly by the time Viggo was finished speaking, my fingers trembling as he slipped the ring on my finger. Dabbing my eyes with the handkerchief, I looked over at Morgan.

"My turn?" I whispered, and she nodded.

Picking up the ring, I turned to him, a smile on my face. I hadn't really thought of what I was going to say, but I knew that speaking to Viggo from my heart was always the right way.

"I won't say we haven't had a bumpy road," I said, and there was a collective chuckle in the room. "Our path has always been filled with obstacles—some set by each other, others set up by the world. And yet the best part about being on this adventure—the only thing that gave me strength day after day after day—was you. With you and me together, I found I could believe you when you said things would get better. You gave me hope, Viggo. You showed me a world that could have hope. And even though we are at the darkest point of our adventures together, with you by my side, I know I can do anything. I love you, Viggo."

I slid the ring onto his finger as I neared the end of my speech, having to hurry as more tears leaked from my eyes. I swiped them clean as soon as my hands were free, and I felt Viggo's arm going around my shoulder, helping me to keep upright. Looking up at him, I added, very softly, "And I promise to share my cookies with you. Always."

He laughed loudly, and I felt my love for him grow even more—that I could make jokes with him now, on this very day, and get nothing but the gift of his laughter. I sniffled, even more tears spilling hot down my cheeks. I just needed to keep it together for a few more minutes.

"By the authority of my station alone, as a renegade princess of Matrus, I now pronounce you husband and wife. You may kiss… each other."

I laughed with joy as Viggo spun me around in his arms and then dipped me low, sealing his mouth to mine in a hungry and possessive kiss that made my head reel and my fingers and toes tingle. As he broke it, I felt a delicious and hungry shudder awaken in me at the ravenous look in his green eyes, already twinkling with the promise of our wedding night.

And I simply couldn't wait for it.

CHAPTER 20

Violet

Everyone broke into applause as Viggo kissed me, but I barely registered the crowd. I was lost in the warm glow of happiness as his mouth pressed against mine, his tongue coming out just to tease my upper lip before retreating.

I opened my eyes, dazed, wondering why he'd stopped, and he flashed me a rakish smile. "You know how everyone here likes to talk," he whispered, and I felt my smile shift into a grin. We broke apart—reluctantly—but he kept a firm grip on my hand, giving it a little squeeze as we turned to face the group of our friends, family, and comrades-in-arms.

Amber was already up again and coming toward us, this time with Margot beside her. Margot kissed Viggo on the cheek and embraced me, and then pulled back with a secret smile on her face.

"What's going on?" I asked, suddenly curious. Now that I was paying a little more attention, both she and Amber looked like the cats who had gotten into the cream. They exchanged glances, their smiles growing wider, and then Amber spoke.

"We have a surprise for you," she announced. "Well, for you and for everyone else. It's waiting for you in Command."

"A surprise?" I looked up at Viggo, who gave me a bewildered look and a shrug. "What kind of surprise?"

Amber rolled her eyes and grabbed my hand. "Don't get boring on me, Bates, just come and see."

Then she was dragging me forward, not even giving me a chance to protest. I laughed, caught up with the joy of just… everything, and Amber slowed down long enough for me to get my feet under me, then started propelling me forward again.

"The boys can take *you*, Mr. Bates!" she called over her shoulder to Viggo, and I laughed again, mostly at Viggo's squint-eyed look as he watched Amber and me leave, Margot on our heels.

She led me down the hall and up the stairs, and I paused at the sight before me. The conference room had been… decorated? Well, an attempt at decorating had been made, at least, with toilet paper streamers and a big paper sign that had *Congratulations Viggo and Violet* emblazoned on it in red paint, which still looked a little damp. Desks had been pushed aside, and smaller tables brought in, all with cloths draped over them in a semblance of tablecloths, with candles lighting them. Music piped through some speakers overhead, light and filled with soft violin sounds. A resplendent bounty of food covered a long table against a wall—*real* food, not protein rations. My mouth watered when I saw the cake, three-tiered and spotlessly covered in white frosting.

"What is this?" I breathed, my eyes darting around, trying to take it all in.

Viggo and the others entered behind us, and I heard Viggo's surprised "Oh!" just as Margot announced, "It's your wedding reception."

I looked over at her and the dark-skinned woman smiled, the flash of bright white teeth lighting up her already-charming face. "Amber and I thought of it, although Jenny and Cad helped with the cooking. We procured a few things, and we opened it up to everyone who's on the base—don't worry, we're sharing with everyone."

I shot her a grateful look. She knew me well enough to know that I wouldn't be comfortable if she hadn't invited everybody we'd been working with. Already, people who hadn't been at our wedding were wandering in. The men were shaking Viggo's hand as they went by, offering him words of congratulations or advice. I laughed, reaching out to drape my arms over Amber and Margot's shoulders.

"You are literally the best," I breathed, pulling them close to me.

"Well, to be honest, I think we all needed a party," Amber said after a moment, pulling back. "There's been a lot of stuff going on, and I think we could all use just a little piece of normalcy before... whatever happens, happens."

"That... is a really good idea," I said. "And still, you guys did this in two hours?"

"We did," Margot beamed. "Now if you'll excuse me, I'm going to fetch Henry and Sarah. They're dying to have some of the cake Jenny made."

"And I've got you and Viggo sitting over here," Amber declared, placing a hand on the small of my back as she stepped around me toward a table with some flowers in a vase. They looked suspiciously similar to the flowers still in my hands, and I looked over to see Tim giving me a sweet, smug grin.

I followed Amber as she sat me down at the table, Viggo holding my chair out and then settling into the chair next to me. "This wasn't how I imagined our wedding night starting," he murmured right in my ear, sending shivers down my spine.

I looked over at him, my face flushing beet red, and if anything, it only seemed to make the hunger in Viggo's eyes grow. "I think I can be patient enough for about an hour," he added, and I felt my face grow even redder, if that was possible, the heat spreading across my cheeks until I thought they would burst into flames.

Amber sat something down in front of me, and I looked up, trying to focus on the world that wasn't just me and Viggo, to see a mug filled with something vaguely resembling urine. I looked up at her, questioningly.

"Apple cider," she said. "Still warm and filled with cinnamon. It's an Ashabee family recipe."

I hesitated. "You made this?"

Amber managed to look wounded as well as affronted. "Hey, I can cook *some* stuff, you know. Besides, this is from a cask recovered at the house. All I did was heat it up." She winked, and then moved back to the food table, presumably to grab a plate of food. My stomach growled when I saw a basket of bread rolls, and I turned to Viggo, preparing to ask him what he wanted.

"Oh no you don't," he announced. "I'm now your husband, which means *I* provide for *you*. What do you want from the table?"

"Bread, and whatever that stew is. It smells divine."

He leaned forward to drop a kiss on my lips and then pulled back. "Your wish is always my command," he whispered, standing up.

I wasn't left alone long. Owen found me soon, taking a seat at the table, Morgan next to him, looking unsure but excited in the atmosphere of the party. Ms. Dale and Henrik sat down across from me, and Tim took up the seat Viggo had been sitting in, immediately resting his head lightly on my shoulder. I reached over and took his hand, resting my cheek against the top of his head, and he sighed.

"Different now," he said, a touch sadly.

I looked at him, and then adjusted so I could wrap an arm around his shoulder, taking care to share my warmth but only barely brush his skin. "Why do you say that?" I asked, curious.

He shrugged under my arm, and then smiled up at me, his gray eyes still stormy. "You gone. Married. No room for—"

"You stop right there, Tim," said Owen softly. I looked over at him, and he shifted nervously, pulling on the sleeves of his sweater. "I was an older sibling too, and believe me... there's always room for your brother. Nothing's going to change. Your sister's never going to abandon you, and you will always be loved—by her, by Viggo, and by everyone in the room."

I heard the pain in his voice as he spoke, and started to reach for his hand, but stopped when I saw Morgan already doing so, her hand going over Owen's and squeezing. The blonde man looked up, his blue eyes rimmed with red, and then slowly pulled his hand out from under hers, standing up.

"I'm, uh, going to check out the food situation," he mumbled, before moving off. Morgan followed his movement, her brows furrowing together as her green eyes tracked him, and then she leaned back in the chair with a look of disappointment on her face.

Ms. Dale and I exchanged looks, and Henrik softly announced that he could also use some food and got up. I looked at Ms. Dale, who gave me a shrug, sipping her own mug of tea, and I sighed. Clearly this was for me to handle.

But before I could say anything, another voice beat me to it. "You really shouldn't take it personally, Morgan," announced Amber, manifesting from seemingly nowhere with a plate filled with—heavens, it was fresh vegetables. My mouth watered when I saw the pile of cherry tomatoes, and I looked up at her questioningly as she sat down in the chair Owen had just evacuated. She nodded, and I grabbed one, popping it between my lips and crunching into it, the fresh, distinctive sweetness almost causing me to moan with happiness.

Amber watched my display with an odd smile, and then turned back to Morgan. "By the way, since when do you have a crush on Owen? I've known you both since I arrived with the Liberators, and I never picked up on that."

"Because you never saw us together," muttered Morgan, picking at some lint on the tablecloth—and I noticed she didn't try to deny Amber's realization. "Owen and I never really… got to spend any time together. He was Desmond's number two, remember?"

"Yes, but that doesn't really answer the question, does it?" Amber teased. "Go on, when did you realize you liked him?"

Morgan shifted slightly in her seat and then gave Amber a direct look. "The first day I met him," she replied tersely. "The first day I was in the Liberator base. I was scared and… and angry. Desmond didn't tell me what was going on, I'd been stuck in that stupid workhouse for over a year, and then suddenly I wasn't anymore. It threw me. Anyway, he was running the training the first day I was there, and I didn't want anything to do with it, or him. He comes over, and before he can even say anything, I grab him and throw him across the room."

"You didn't!" Amber gasped, a wide smile on her lips.

"I did," Morgan replied dryly. "I thought he'd get up, scream at me, say something horrible, hate me forever, but instead he held out his hand to me and said, 'You going to be a lady and help me up?'"

I laughed around a mouthful of tomatoes. That sounded like Owen. Good-natured ribbing that helped to defuse difficult or awkward inter-actions was his specialty. Or it had been, at least. After his brother died, he'd been so different… but even now, I could see peeks of the Owen we knew coming back once in a while, and I knew he was healing, if slowly.

"After that I guess I was curious. I'd never been around anybody who could defuse a situation like that. My family, we're—well, I just told you. Everybody turns small problems, these simple little things, into gigantic arguments with pitfalls that are, by design, meant to make you angry and shoot off at the mouth. Then they'd turn all that around and hold it over you, bear slow-burning grudges, before bringing it up in some new argument weeks, even months, later, to repeat the damn cycle all over again. I'd never been just *forgiven* like that before."

Her expression turned deeply inward as she talked, and I could only imagine how much something like that had meant to her. I'd grown up with a lot of the same kinds of expectations, actually—but Morgan's had been multiplied by her unusual family situation and her sisters' en-hancements. Morgan's face turned rueful.

"At first I couldn't understand it. I thought he must be a huge air-head who had never had any real problems. But I asked around, and when I found out about his brother… I don't know, I just thought about how brave he was to still find a reason to laugh, after such tragedy and heartache."

I looked around at the rest of the table and realized we were all hanging on her words, hoping there would be more to the story. "Oh my God, Morgan," Amber said after a moment, her eyes sparkling. "That's the sweetest story ever. Makes Owen seem, well, almost attractive. Which is *gross*." Amber shuddered theatrically, and managed to bring a smile to the other girl's face. "So, yeah," she added, her voice thick with dry sarcasm. "Thanks for sharing. I'll be having nightmares all week."

"Yeah, well, I wish I could just… admit it to him, y'know?" Morgan said ruefully, her smile at Amber's quip dimming slightly as she ran a hand through her hair. "But it's not a good time."

"Yeah, I can see that," Amber said, the sparkle in her eyes going introspective. "But don't give up. There *will* be a good time. Owen just needs a while to deal with everything."

"I thought you were mad at him," I said around another mouthful of tomato, swallowing it and then taking a sip of the apple cider. That was exquisite as well, and I felt my hunger double as I eyed Amber's plate.

She laughed and pushed it over to me, and Tim and I fell on the food like ravenous wolves, using our fingers to grab vegetables and shove them in our mouths. Nothing was as fresh as the tomatoes, and I couldn't help but cram them into my mouth with wild abandon while she continued the discussion as though my brother and I weren't behaving like starved animals.

"Yes, I was mad at him. But that doesn't mean I didn't understand."

"Nobody's mad at him anymore," Ms. Dale said softly, reaching over to grab the last tomato off Amber's plate and popping it in her mouth before I could growl in warning. She gave me a smug smile and half-salute with her mug before leaning back in the chair. "He messed up, made a bad judgment call, but he's doing everything he can to make up for it. Everyone can see that."

Morgan cleared her throat and set her own cup down, arching an eyebrow at us. "Everyone might know that or believe that, but when was the last time any of you told Owen that?"

I swallowed my mouthful of canned asparagus, the slight recrimination in her voice causing me to lose all interest in food. "Morgan, I *do* tell him that. I tell him that all the time." Morgan stared at me for a moment, and then stood up, brushing crumbs off of her pants.

"You're different, Violet. And it hurts him more than you think to know you still have faith in him and consider him a friend. Because he doesn't feel he deserves it, and the more you do it, the more twisted into knots he feels. Not that I'm saying that you shouldn't tell him that, but I wouldn't be surprised if he just disappeared after this conflict was done, if only so he could try to sort through what he's going through emotionally."

Amber leaned back in her chair, tilting it back on two legs and giving Morgan a shrewd look. "You really *do* care about him, don't you?"

Morgan hesitated, and then flushed, one hand running self-consciously over her forearm. "Well, I think we all do, right?"

"Well, yes, but that—"

"Have I ever told you the best way Elena ever ended conversations?" asked Morgan, interrupting Amber. She and I exchanged looks and then turned back to Morgan, waiting expectantly. Morgan opened her mouth, shut it, and then turned and walked away, her head held high and her shoulders squared.

I watched her go, stunned for a moment, and Ms. Dale chuckled. "Well, that certainly is one way to end an uncomfortable conversation," she said with a grin.

I almost replied, but at that moment a plate was deposited in front of me, and I craned my neck back to see Viggo standing over me, a wry smile on his face. "I see you already finished one serving," he said dryly. "And found a new man to replace me. Busy party."

Tim sat up straight and started to move, but Viggo placed a gentle hand on his shoulder as I dug into my plate, scarcely noticing the small conversations going on around me, I was so excited to eat real food.

"Stay there, Tim. I can evict Amber."

"All right, Croft, I'll give you my seat. But it'll cost you." Amber leaned forward, a mischievous glint in her eyes.

"It'll cost me?" Viggo asked. "You're going to deny me the right to sit next to my wife?"

"Well, that's just supply and demand. Don't you want to know the price?"

Viggo groaned dramatically, and I could practically feel him rolling his eyes. I shoveled another spoonful of mashed potatoes into my mouth, content to let the butter dissolve on my tongue and watch the show.

"All right, what is it?" my husband asked Amber.

"First, you have to come dance with me."

"And second?"

"You have to wear these when you do it." She produced a black eye-glass case and set it on the table, sliding it over. Unable to contain my curiosity, I put my fork down for a second to open it, and saw a pair of empty wire frames sitting inside.

"Viggo?" I asked, looking up, and I saw him fighting back a smile, his cheeks burnishing just slightly.

"Don't ask," he growled, snatching up the case and placing the glasses into a pocket in his dress uniform. "And you promised, Amber!"

"Hey, I didn't say one word, did I?" she exclaimed, her hands going up in the air in surrender. "I just gave you my conditions."

"Oh my goodness," Ms. Dale breathed in bemused irritation. "Viggo, give the glasses to Violet and trot Amber out on the dance floor. She really just wants you to dance with her to make Logan jealous. Violet, thank Amber—she just did you a favor."

I gave my former mentor a bewildered look, but she just smiled, taking another sip of her mug of tea.

"No deal," Viggo said, clapping his hands together and then pulling my seat out. "My wife gets the first dance. I suffered one of her traditions—now she'll suffer one of mine."

I smiled and slipped my hand into his, ignoring the wolf whistle Amber was making behind my back. In truth, my eyes were only for Viggo as he led me to the cleared-out space in the middle of the room that was being used as a dance floor.

As soon as we were in the center, nobody around us, Viggo spun me in a circle under his arm, then pulled me to his chest, one hand firmly on my waist. The confidence with which he pulled off the move, as smooth as if he'd been practicing for weeks, left me a bit breathless, my heart once again crashing powerfully against my ribcage. He led with slight pressure, and we began to sway to the music. It was slow, the melody old, simple, and elegant. Violins made up the main part of it, but cellos were present. A single flute, loud and clear, wove counter melody to the stringed instruments, weaving a spell of intimacy around us.

I'd never understood the dance scenes in popular graphic novels; I'd never had time to even try dancing, and the whole thing had seemed kind of silly and clunky. I'd assumed I would be bad at it, to be honest. But now, I suddenly found myself realizing exactly why other girls at the orphanage snuck those romance comics to each other, hiding them under pillows until the wardens took them away or all the pages fell out. I understood why there had always been a dancing scene. They were trying to recreate this feeling—and now I knew no novel ever could.

Everything seemed to fade away, as if the world had just inhaled, and was waiting to exhale. I swore I could've heard a pin drop as Viggo spun me around the dance floor, leading me gently and confidently, so I had no reason to worry about my steps. I gazed up at him, trying to force every bit of what I was feeling into my eyes, certain he could see it there.

"I love you," he whispered softly, his green eyes warm and bright, brimming with love for me.

"I love you, too," I smiled. "Oh man… we're *married*, Viggo! Can you believe it?!"

His lips pressed against the soft shell of my ear. "Just wait until later tonight, Mrs. Bates."

I rolled my lips together, trying to soften a smile that was so grand, my cheeks were starting to ache slightly. "Am I detecting trouble in paradise, Mr. Croft?"

"Not at all… just trying it on to see if I can get used to it. I love the idea of you having my name, but it could be fun to be Viggo Bates. Has a nice ring to it."

I laughed as he spun me out again, then under his arm, turning as he did, so that he could pull me back in against his chest. There was a smattering of applause, and it made me blush, but I ignored it, focused solely on him.

"I like it, but it doesn't have the ring the 'Croft' does."

"True. But neither does 'Violet Croft.'"

"Hmm. We could hyphenate. Or come up with some combination name."

"Oh dear Lord... Crates?"

"Baft."

Viggo threw back his head and laughed at my joke, and it made me happy, knowing that I had made him happy. He pulled me tightly to him and rested his chin on the top of my head.

"We'll figure it out. For now, I'm just happy to call you *my wife.*"

There was a possessiveness in his voice that sent a thrill through me, and all at once I remembered (probably for the thousandth time that day) that we were married, and tonight was our wedding night. Suddenly, I wished we were any place else, so I could finally, *finally* demonstrate my love to him in the most physical way possible.

Luckily, the song ended before my desire for him could flare too high, and he slowly, reluctantly pulled away from me. Everyone was clapping, looking at us, and I had almost caused a scene right then and there. I flushed, and waved an embarrassed hand through the air as I turned toward the crowd of our family and friends, hoping they chalked my embarrassment up to being the center of attention, and not to the fact that I had almost jumped my husband on the dance floor like a lunatic.

Viggo led me back to the table and sat me down. "Now, Amber... I believe it was your turn? And then my wife. Again."

"Oh no—all the unmarried gals called dibs," called Ms. Dale as Viggo held out a hand to Amber, helping her up. He shot her an alarmed look, and she cackled before adding, "And I'm next!"

I laughed, fanning myself with my hand to help cool my heated cheeks, and leaned against Tim. "You are all being really mean to Viggo," I chided, and Ms. Dale laughed, setting down her mug.

"No, we're showing him we care in our own perverse ways. Get him to wear the glasses, and thank Amber in the morning." She winked, and I blushed again, bewildered that I could blush so much in such a short period of time. Ms. Dale stood up and stretched.

"I'm going to go make Henrik dance with me before this song is over," she said, draining the remains of her mug. "Make sure you get in a dance or two before your Patrian drags you off by your hair."

I snorted, sipped my cider, and watched her weave confidently through the crowds toward Henrik, who was standing by the food table, chatting with Alejandro. I watched as she approached, and Henrik automatically held out an arm for her, slipping it around her waist and pulling her tight to him. She smiled and cupped his bearded cheek, giving him a kiss on the lips. Then she leaned her head against his shoulder and just listened as he and Alejandro continued whatever conversation they were having, looking perfectly happy and content.

I smiled. It was good that Ms. Dale had found someone, especially somebody as respectful, wise, and capable as Henrik. If anybody deserved her, he did. Then I laughed, and Tim looked up at me, confused.

"I'm sorry," I said through the laughter. "I just think I might have resigned myself to being that married woman who's trying to get *everyone* married now."

He followed my gaze toward Ms. Dale, and then chortled. "Not possible. Ms. Dale... Henrik... They together because want to be. You did nothing. They get married when they want to. You do nothing."

"Oh, and what happens if I meet a girl I think is perfect for you?" I teased, but Tim seemed to ponder the question for a moment.

"Nothing," he finally said. "I find own girl. Like you find Viggo."

I reached out and playfully ruffled his hair, and he ducked back out of reach, smiling. The song ended, and was replaced by a lively jig, and I looked over to see Margot grabbing Viggo for another dance. Cad watched from the sidelines, and then raised his glass from the table he was sitting at toward me, our gazes meeting. I felt confused as to why he was still sitting at his table so far away, until a few people moved and I saw Henry and Sarah both lying on some chairs, fast asleep, mouths ringed with white frosting. It was odd—neither of the two slices of cake in front of them seemed touched, save for a few small bites—but maybe they'd just been too tired to eat. I smiled and he gave me a droll look followed by a shrug.

"Say what you want about him, he's a good dancer," Amber

exclaimed as she dropped into the seat next to me, her cheeks flushed and her breath coming faster.

"What is the deal with these glasses?" I asked, and Amber flashed me a smile.

"It was part of his disguise when we went into the stadium," she informed me. "Just trust me—and hope that his vision starts going later in life, because he pulls them off *well*."

I snorted. "I feel like I should be uncomfortable with all this."

"Oh, whatever. We all know that Viggo is eye candy, but he's eye candy that only has eyes for you. Your babies are going to be gorgeous."

"Geez, don't say that. We can't even contemplate kids right now, not until this whole mess is over."

"Well, it'll be over soon enough," Amber sighed, and I frowned, the reality of the next few days suddenly hitting me, everything in my stomach seeming leaden while my heart began to race. Amber noticed, and grabbed my hand. "Violet, no. I didn't mean it like that. I'm sorry."

I looked into her earnest eyes and nodded, sucking in a deep breath and slowly letting it out. Amber looked around the room, her scrutiny stopping as she met Logan's gaze, and then she deliberately turned her back to him and cleared her throat.

"What's up with that?" I asked after a moment, nodding toward Logan.

Amber sighed and picked at the tablecloth, her mouth turning down. I almost expected her to clam up, like she had many times in the past, but this time, she started to talk.

"I told you the story about the pilot who trained me, right?"

I nodded. "And I know that pilot was Logan. How did that even happen? The heir to the Deepvox legacy getting hired on as a heloship pilot? I'm surprised he even had to work."

"He didn't," Amber replied honestly. "He did it because he wanted to. He wanted to build a name for himself outside of his father's legacy. It's what made him so attractive to me in the first place. Y'know, a man not letting other men elevate him? Trying to do things on his own, make his own reputation? It was refreshing. And then when I could see he was attracted to me… I sort of played on it to get what I wanted."

"Amber!" I exclaimed, and she flushed.

"Look, I was sixteen, and I did *like* him. I mean, honestly, I really wanted to spend time with him, as well as learn how to be a pilot." She shrugged and took a sip of her cider, her smile catlike for a moment. "I didn't see the harm in doing both."

"But…" I trailed off after she fell silent, her gaze fixed on the drink in her hand.

She blinked and then sighed, setting the mug on the table. "But my father"—she grimaced—"found out. He, uh, caught us making out inside the heloship and dragged me to my room. Locked me in. At first I didn't know what had happened. They sequestered me in my room for three days, only food and drinks and my tutors. Then my father comes in and tells me I'll be marrying Logan. Just like that. No discussion from him, and no conversation from Logan. I was just expected to shut up and do what I was told. Everything was arranged."

"But, if you liked him—"

"Yes, exactly! I liked him—I didn't know if I *loved* him. I was sixteen, Violet! He was almost nineteen. And all I could think to myself once I found out he had arranged our marriage with my father without even talking to me was that… he was just like every other man in Patrus, and to him I was just like any other woman—marry me and keep me in my place. It could have been anybody and he would have done the same thing; preserve his reputation, get a good, obedient wife at the same time—"

She broke off, her cheeks flushed with anger, and looked around. So did I, and I realized her voice had gotten loud enough to draw notice. Glaring at the people who had turned and stared, Amber held their gazes until they turned back to the party, and then sighed, speaking in a slightly lower voice.

"So I snuck out. Jeff helped me, once I explained, and I took one of the cars over to the Vox estate and snuck in. Daddy designed their security system, so it was easy enough to bypass. I got into Logan's room, and he looked at me like I was crazy for being there. We fought, and he just didn't *get* it, so I told him to call off the contract… or have the coroner on standby on our wedding night." She took a sip of her cider, draining it, and set the cup down on the table with a thud. "He called it off. I thought that would be the end of it, until my father informed me he'd found someone three times Logan's age to marry me to—somebody richer, somebody who would pay even more money for me. Only a week later. That's when I realized that was all I was or ever would be to him. So I ran away. I took a while to plan it, and looking back I didn't have any idea what I was doing. But… Desmond found me and recruited me before I could get into any trouble."

She fell silent, and I reached forward and took her hand. "Amber, I'm so—"

"Beautiful tonight," said a deep voice from behind me, and I turned to see Logan standing there, two mugs in his hand. "For the beautiful bride," he said, offering one, and I took it and handed it off to Tim, not having drained my original cider mug. "For the Lady Ashabee."

Amber stared at the mug, and then looked at him. "No one asked you to bring that," she said mulishly.

Logan arched an eyebrow and set the mug down. "It's meant as a peace offering, Amber."

"Peace?" she scoffed. "I don't want peace from you."

Logan's fingers drummed against the back of my chair, and I realized he was leaning on it, staring at her. "And what *do* you want, exactly? Because I just want to talk. Honestly."

Amber's eyes narrowed, and I felt myself becoming distinctly uncomfortable with the position I was sitting in, directly between the two of them. Before she could answer, Logan stopped leaning, taking his weight off my chair, and continued.

"Listen, Amber. I'm this close to using your full name in public where all these lovely people can hear it. So are you going to keep acting like a child who has missed her naptime, or are you going to grow up and come have an adult conversation with me?"

Amber leaned back in the chair and considered him for a long moment while Tim and I shifted uncomfortably. Watching her face changing, I just had to hide a little smile behind a napkin. I liked how Logan was calling her out the same way Amber usually called members of the rest of the group out. We all knew she could be a bit vindictive, and I didn't want her to let it get in the way of things—if Logan Vox could get her to slow down enough to consider that, I would be more than impressed.

After several heartbeats, she snatched up the mug and stood, draining it dry and setting it down next to her other empty mug. "All right," she said slowly. "Let's do this."

Then she moved away to a more private part of the hall, letting him follow her. I watched them go.

"I would not want to be in that hallway," said Owen wryly as he walked up, three plates of cake balanced in his hand. "Here, I figured you and Tim were craving a sugar high." I reached up and took two of the plates, handing one to Tim and placing the other in front of me.

"Thanks," I said, immediately digging in. He sat down with a sigh as I took my first mouthful, and practically died. The cake was simple—vanilla—but oh, so delectable. Within moments, my chunk had disappeared as I quickly devoured it.

Owen watched, his fork hovering between his plate and his mouth, and then pushed his piece over to me. "Here, you clearly need it more than I do."

I laughed, but didn't hesitate, taking another bite and trying not to roll my eyes back in ecstasy. "Honestly," I said around a mouthful, "I don't know why everyone was telling me this was just a simple spread. Everything tastes amazing."

Owen chuckled and reached out and took my mug, taking a sip. "It's because you're happy," he said. "When you're happy, everything is just... better. The weather, the food, the air. How is the air, by the way?"

I took a deep breath and then laughed, waving a hand across my nose. "Smells like men used to live here," I said, and he snorted. We shared a laugh for a moment, and then it dropped off awkwardly.

"Owen, I—"

"Violet, I—"

We both stopped as we stepped over each other's words, and I leaned back. "You go first," I said.

"Well, I just wanted to say... I'm sorry." I frowned, confused, but luckily he continued. "I'm sorry I just left you like that. I mean, what if Morgan hadn't been a good princess? Or one of those berserkers who drank the water at the plant had gotten you?"

I let out a surprised laugh, and then frowned when he looked up at me, his sincerity lying naked on his face. Letting out a breath, I leaned forward. "Owen, you did the best you could under the circumstances. We all did. That place was awful, and nightmarish, and—"

"You shouldn't have been alone on that bird," he insisted angrily, and I shushed him, placing a hand over his.

"Owen, can I say something? I don't want you to take this the wrong way, but you're right." He blinked in surprise, and I continued. "Absolutely right. As my bodyguard, you failed. But, as my friend, who was willing to sacrifice his life so that I could go in pursuit of the woman who had wronged him, you succeeded. And frankly, that's all I want from you, and all I want to be with you: a friend, a comrade, a soldier at arms. Someone who, in fifty years, I can say 'remember when' to, and you'll say that you do."

He sighed, and started to pull his hand away from mine. "Violet, I don't really think I deserve—"

"Oh, pish posh what you deserve," I said, not letting him escape my gentle grasp. "Sometimes even *you* can't see what you deserve, so you need to trust in your friends to tell you. And I'm telling you, I don't bestow my friendship or love lightly. It might seem like it... given all the people here who care about me... but they all won it. Hell, even Thomas has won it, and I hated him when I met him. I thought he was cruel and weird."

A hint of a smile grazed Owen's face for a second. "In your defense, he *can* be cruel, and he *is* weird."

I laughed, but refused to be derailed. "You need to stop being so hard on yourself, and you also need to go over there and talk to Morgan. She likes you. She likes you a lot."

His shoulders hunched, and he cast his gaze over to where the dark-haired girl stood, chatting with Drew. Or rather, it looked like Drew was interrogating her. "She... She likes me? *Likes* likes?"

I blinked, surprised at first by the very childish phrase, and then looked over at Tim, whose face shared a look of bewilderment equal to the one I was sure mine wore.

"You honestly didn't know?"

He shook his head, his eyes wide. "I... I... I just thought she was being nice."

Lowering my forehead to the table was dramatic, but it made him laugh, even as I banged my head against the wood a few times. Sitting up abruptly, I looked at him, and then reached out to cup his cheeks.

"Owen. Go talk to her."

He hesitated, and then smiled, slow and steady. "You know what, I think I will!"

Standing up, he took a minute to run his fingers through his hair, and then moved over toward Morgan. I looked over at Tim, who shook his head at me.

"You right. You *will* be that wife."

I laughed—I couldn't deny it—lightly squeezed his cheek, and looked out at the dance floor. Viggo was now dancing with Ms. Dale, swinging her around the floor while she laughed and then smacked him on the shoulder. They chatted as the music played, something slow and filled with harp sounds, and I smiled. Owen was right. I *was* happy. "Happy" wasn't even the word for it. I could feel everything around me glowing with joy, like it was radiating from my insides, impossible to contain, impossible to stop.

Tim and I sat alone for a few more minutes, just enjoying the atmosphere and being next to each other, and then the song ended. Viggo instantly let Ms. Dale go and moved toward my table, his eyes finding mine. Ms. Dale trailed behind him and clapped her hands loudly. The music played on for a second and then was cut off, and Ms. Dale raised her mug.

"Well, we have a few more surprises for you. We have some gifts, which you can open later, if you want, but there's one very important one that we want to give you now."

I looked around the room, and watched as Amber and Logan stepped up to join Ms. Dale, followed closely by Owen and Morgan.

"What's going on?" I asked, and Ms. Dale smiled.

"We're not letting you go to Matrus alone," she announced as Thomas pushed forward and came to stand next to Owen. "We're going with you."

"And me," whispered Tim.

"And me," resonated a deep, familiar voice, and I looked back toward the stairs and gaped.

Solomon took a step forward, and another, moving slowly and steadily. I saw Dr. Tierney standing behind him, a smile on her face, and then I was moving, standing up and racing across the room. I pulled up short, suddenly afraid to touch him, and he stared at me, his dark eyes glittering. He'd shaved, and his hair had been cut. He was wearing pants and a sweater, but they seemed a bit snug on him.

After a moment in which we stared at each other, my mind trying to find words as the events of the attack on the plant played through it again, he simply pulled me into a bear hug.

"Hey, Violet," he breathed. "Congratulations!"

He lifted me off the ground and then sat me back down, but I kept my hands on his shoulders.

"How... How is this..." The words seemed to dissolve in my mouth, and I looked at Dr. Tierney. "Benuxupane?" I asked, and she shook her head.

"I think... I think they did something to him at the tower," she said. "I can't explain it, but when he woke up, he was speaking and behaving as normal. His readings are good and—"

"He's standing right here, and he wants to officially meet your husband."

I blinked up at Solomon, my smile growing wider and wider until I felt tears beginning to form. "I... Of course... I..."

"I'm Viggo," Viggo said helpfully from behind me, and I turned to see him standing there, holding out a hand. "And as I understand it, Violet and I both owe you our lives. Her twice over."

Solomon took Viggo's hand and pumped it, hard. "It was nothing," he rumbled, but his eyes clouded over, and I realized he was remembering everything that had happened, just as I had.

"Solomon, you don't even know why we're going to Matrus," I exclaimed, and he nodded solemnly.

"I do. Dr. Tierney filled me in. It took a while."

I stared at him for a long moment, then took a step closer. "Solomon, you don't have to do this. You've been through so much. Your mother needs to see you. She's been so worried, and—"

"Do you think I don't know that, Violet?" Solomon announced, softly interrupting me. He lowered his gaze to the floor and shifted. "Violet, I… I remember some of the things I did. Not all of it, and I'm not sure which is worse—the ones I don't know about, or the ones I do. I killed people… and I didn't have any control over it."

"Solomon," I breathed, guilt radiating through me. "Please. It's my fault that you… that you took those pills. It's my fault that you were in this mess. I swore I'd do something to help you, and you're better now. I don't want that to change. I can't bear to see you hurting again."

"Violet, it's not your fault. It's Desmond's. She gave me the pills without knowing exactly what they would do. She used me as her guinea pig, and I trusted her and went with it anyway."

"Yes, but if I hadn't been so—"

"You don't get to be responsible for the decisions I make," Solomon declared, resting his hand on my shoulder. "Violet, I respect your authority here, and I care for you deeply—but don't you see I need this? I… I need a way to strike back at them. To put a stop to any future damage that Elena and Desmond have planned. I need something to *absolve* me of all the things… all of the things I've done. And Violet. I haven't tested it out, but I think that whatever the people who healed me did, they didn't take away my enhancement. I have this power now. I want to use it in a way that is better than I did while I couldn't control myself."

He wasn't angry. Or at least, he wasn't angry with me. There was anger in him, but he kept it tightly leashed, and hidden behind a wall of granite. Even so, there was conviction behind it. I could feel it in his words and see it in how he looked at me. In that moment, I realized that he was right. I didn't get to make his decisions for him, no matter how badly I wanted to make sure he was safe.

"I'm not saying I understand," I said after taking a moment to think about it. "But I know we could really use the help. So thank you."

"Of course, Violet," he replied with a wan smile.

"You're more than welcome to be a part of the process," I said, then turned my attention to the group that had assembled, still standing a few feet away. "But the rest of you should stay here. They'll need all of you in the rebuilding process, and—"

"We don't care," Ms. Dale cut in smoothly. "We're going. Deal with it."

"I've already begun working on the plan," Thomas added with a proud smile. "We can't let you go in alone."

I stood, looking around the room, my eyes tearing up. I had no idea how I was supposed to respond to any of it, so I just hugged Ms. Dale, hard, and she hugged me back just as hard. When we'd held each other for a minute, she pushed me away, smoothing off the front of her shirt.

"Getting me all sentimental," she sniffed, her fingers going under her eyes to wipe away any sign of tears. "Now, you've got some presents to open! So let's open them!"

"Actually," Thomas interjected, taking a step forward. "I was wondering if I could say something." We all looked at the short man, and I watched, wondering what he was up to, as he adjusted his glasses and fidgeted.

"Of course," I said with a smile. "What is it?"

"A speech," he replied absentmindedly, pulling out a small green notebook and flipping it open to a page in the back. Viggo and I exchanged looks, and I took a few steps toward him, my hand extended, reaching for his and finding it.

I looked up to see Thomas watching us, and after a moment, he closed the notebook and put it aside as he began to speak. "As you all know, love is… complicated for me. It is something that adheres to no scientific or mathematic principles—it cannot be measured, weighed, or calculated. As such, it's hard to credit that it even exists. I was certain we could find life in the stars before we could find scientific evidence that love was real." He shifted nervously, clearing his throat softly. "The love between Violet and Viggo has been our cornerstone for a long time; whether we were aware of it or not, their love for each other spilled onto the rest of us. I've run the numbers, and because of their… synchronicity, our missions succeeded when they should have failed. We believed, when we should've called it quits. And we won, when every possible odd was stacked against us. If there were a love that was close to being proven as a scientific reality, versus anecdotal evidence, then it would be between Viggo and Violet."

He finished with a nod, turned to collect his notebook, and then walked away. I watched him go, my heart thudding against my chest so hard I was convinced it was trying to collapse my lungs. How else could I explain the sudden lump in my throat or the inability to catch my breath fully?

"That was beautiful," Ms. Dale sniffed, and I looked over through watery eyes to see her pressing a napkin to her eye. "Downright poetry. Somebody put on some music quick, before *I* break down and cry!"

I laughed, grateful to her for breaking the moment with a little humor, and reached out to take Viggo's hand as he came to stand beside me. The intensity of Thomas' speech had hit me somewhere deep—I'd had no idea that he had any thoughts, inspirational or otherwise, about Viggo's and my romance. I guessed he kept them quiet, but I was so grateful to him for sharing them with us now… and if Ms. Dale hadn't been talking about crying, I definitely would have.

Viggo turned me around in his arms and tugged me close to his chest, touching my cheek and gazing down at me, and I could see in his eyes that he had been moved by the speech as well. The music clicked back on as the party resumed, but he only had eyes for me.

"So our options are presents or dancing," he announced softly. "Or… we sneak out and let them continue the party," he whispered, and I grinned.

"Yes… I like that last one."

CHAPTER 21

Violet

We were halfway down the hall, hands laced together, a giggle at the back of my throat sometimes slipping out—when Ms. Dale's voice brought Viggo and me to a screeching halt. With the nervous tremor of a child getting caught doing something wrong, I turned and saw her, one foot on the stairs with a hand up, something shiny dangling from her fingers.

"We, uh, secured you one of the rooms in the teacher's hall," she said, a knowing smile playing on her lips. "Figured you'd want some privacy."

I blushed beet red, and Viggo stepped around me, hiding me from view as Ms. Dale tossed the keychain at him. The keys jingled as he caught them.

"Thanks, Ms. Dale," he said. "We… appreciate it." Her laughter carried down the halls, the empty rooms reverberating with her delight.

"Go up the second set of access stairs, turn left, second door on the left. Have fun, you two," she drawled, her footsteps loud on the stairs. I waited until they faded, and then rested my forehead on Viggo's back, groaning loudly.

"Could that have been any more awkward?" I asked, my voice muffled by the thick fabric of his uniform. He turned, and as I looked up at him, I could see that Ms. Dale's interference didn't bother him one bit.

"Quit stalling," he grinned, his teeth flashing white as he held up the keychain in his hand. "Let's go check out our room."

His voice was dark, heavy, and I felt something drop in my stomach, and a familiar ache begin below. I let out a shuddering breath as he gave me a hungry look, and I realized that this was it.

This is happening.

"Viggo?"

"Bedroom. Now."

And then he grabbed me, hoisting me up in the air and cradling me against his chest as I kicked and screamed and laughed the whole time. His fingers began to tickle my ribs lightly, and I squirmed in his arms as he carried me past the staircase to the conference room, and to a smaller, narrower set of stairs, taking them two at a time as he carried me effortlessly. He had to duck to avoid knocking his head on the ceiling, and then turned left down the hall, heading to the door.

He dropped the key on my belly and arched an eyebrow. "My hands are full, my love," he said when I didn't immediately understand what he wanted me to do. My hands trembled as I picked up the key, my breath coming a little short. I shifted in his arms, laughing loudly when he grunted and pretended to strain under my weight.

Then, before I could even get the key in the lock, he started tickling me again, and my squirming brought us both down to the ground, laughing hard. We laughed for what felt like eternity—him lying on the floor, me using him as a pillow—until it slowed, then finally stopped. I shifted my head on his thigh and looked up at him, where he was half-lounging on his elbows, staring back at me.

I bit my lip, inexplicably nervous in spite of everything. Viggo's eyes shifted to my mouth, and his lips parted slightly, the hungry expression in his eyes gradually returning. I took a deep breath and then shifted up onto my hands, moving forward to press my lips to his, and he met me halfway.

My mouth immediately opened, and his tongue pressed in slowly, filling me with subtle tremors that raced down my spine, leaving me breathless, craving something more—and this time, I knew that more was coming. Viggo pressed me back, guiding me up while we slowly stood, his mouth never leaving mine. His kiss grew hungrier, wilder, as his arms came around my waist and pulled me forward against the whole tall, hard length of him.

I broke off the kiss, suddenly dizzy, and his mouth trailed down my neck, over my collarbone, his tongue tasting me. I gasped, the tremors increasing, a little surprised when Viggo pulled the key from my numb fingers, his mouth leaving my skin so he could look over my shoulder.

The key scraped off the lock, and he bit back a curse. I smiled, and then he made a victorious noise as the door creaked open. Then his mouth was back on mine, catching me unawares. He pressed the advantage, pushing me forward while I walked backward blindly, trusting him to keep me safe from harm.

I heard the door slam—he must've kicked it closed—and then his hands were on my waist, sliding up. I gasped as his thumb pressed into sensitive flesh underneath the thin fabric of my dress, my head lolling back as his mouth returned to my neck. I clung to him as his hand drew back down, then around. I heard and felt the zipper of my dress parting as Viggo slowly slid it down, and I quivered with anticipation as he began slipping the straps of the dress off my shoulders, his fingers skimming over my bare skin.

He broke off from me, moving around to stand behind me, pressing against my back. He pushed the dress down, off my shoulders and down my sides, leaving it encircling my legs in a pool on the floor, like a trap holding me in place.

But really it was him holding me in place. His breath touched the back of my neck, and I suddenly felt very much like the prey that the wolf wants to play with. Anticipation left me breathless and hopelessly weak as he pressed his lips against one of my earlobes, and even the softest touch was enough to make my eyes roll back into my head, my body wanting to fall backward, into him.

Like always, Viggo caught me, holding me up and using his shoulder for my pillow. His mouth moved again to my ear.

"Violet," he breathed. I felt lost in the overwhelming sensations threatening to tear me apart. I was so vulnerable, and he held me like I was precious, like I was the only thing in the world worth living or dying for. My heart kept skipping beats, and I was powerless to control my breathing.

"Are you certain?" I could barely discern his whisper over the rising tide of my hunger for him, but it broke through, grounding me in the moment.

I turned, my body running on desperate need. "Yes," I managed, my brain still reeling from everything, and I pulled his mouth down to mine. My hands fumbled in vain with the button on his dress uniform, but my fruitless efforts seemed to excite him, and he quickly replaced my fingers with his own, undoing the stiff buttons with practiced ease. He slipped it off, while my fingers worked on the new set of buttons of his shirt.

Our mouths grew eager as we grew impatient, and then, finally, I heard buttons popping, and suddenly his skin was under my hands. I flexed my fingers over his raised pectoral muscles, digging into the solid length of him. I felt his hands on my back, and then my bra fell open, and he was sliding it around and off my body.

I raised my hands to cover myself, suddenly self-conscious, and Viggo stared at me, his green eyes glittering in the moonlight.

"Violet, you're beautiful," he assured me, his hands going to my arms and gently pushing them down. I let him—I trusted him—and I was rewarded with a growl that sent shivers down my spine, refreshing the fire that seemed to be coursing through my veins.

His pants went next, and then he was pulling us both over to the bed—a double, probably a luxury in this setting—setting us down and lying back on the mattress, guiding me until I was straddling him. His hand went to my hip as he gently guided me down, until we were pressed together, only the fabric of our underwear separating us.

I looked down at his face to see the hungriest look I'd ever seen on him. "I wanted to go slow—" he grated, and I saw him fighting for control, his desire for me warring with his desire to never cause me pain.

I met his gaze and smiled, loving him more in that instant than I'd ever believed possible. I leaned down, resting myself against his chest, and pressed my lips to his.

"Don't," I breathed into his ear a moment later.

His response was immediate. The next thing I knew I was lying on my back, Viggo's body over mine, our underwear gone. He hesitated, just for a moment, and as I was about to cry out for him to do something, please, he was suddenly *there*.

The discomfort I felt was quickly lost in the overwhelming sensation of him. I grabbed his shoulders and held on as he made love to me, waves of slow and steady pleasure pulsing through me.

Something began happening, something… incredible. I closed my eyes and clung tighter, trying to urge him to do… something… more… less… I didn't know. Viggo did, however, and continued to take us both higher and higher…

Until everything broke and I was shattering into a thousand pieces of prismatic light, my vision going white as I rode an unbelievable, earth-shattering wave of bliss. Viggo exhaled my name from above me, and I clung to him as I came apart around him, holding him tight as we broke apart on each other, comforted that as we broke, we were also growing back together, only this time inexplicably closer.

CHAPTER 22

Viggo

It seemed as though we stayed there, wrapped around each other, for a long time—long enough that Violet's breathing eased, and the incredible, intense look in her gray eyes softened into pleased exhaustion and she closed them, breaking our shared gaze for the first time. I eased off of Violet, wearied and spent, and so incredibly happy. She murmured something incoherent as I drew away, making a sound of protest, and I smiled as I tugged her closer to me, tucking her in under my arm.

She immediately nestled her head into my shoulder with a soft sigh, her breath coming slow and even as she drifted off to sleep in my arms. I watched her sleep, my hand rubbing soft circles on her shoulder.

I was every bit as tired as she was, but I wasn't ready to give myself over to unconsciousness yet. My heart was still pounding, and, even now, looking down at her as she settled into sleep, a hungry voice was urging me to wake her up gently so that we could begin again. I felt insatiable, still on fire from her hands and soft cries. My name breaking on her lips as she lay beneath me. The trust she placed in me when she gave herself to me completely, trusting me to take care of her.

I pushed the hunger aside, and it went easily enough, the remaining desire I felt submitting to overwhelming exhaustion. I stretched and settled deeper into the bed. Violet made a little huffing sound, and her leg drifted up over my hips, her arms reaching farther across me, snuggling in tighter, almost possessively. I smiled and continued to watch her breathe, matching my breathing to hers. I'd just watch her for a few more minutes, to make sure she was well and truly asleep, and…

A sharp rap on the door jolted me from my sleep, and I checked to make sure Violet was covered. But the sound had awakened her, and she was sitting up, a sheet between her hands, hiding her bare form. It was on the tip of my tongue to tell her that she needn't, that I would make whatever it was go away, when Amber's voice came through the door, muffled by the wood.

"I'm sorry to disturb you guys… but there's a situation with Maxen. We need you down in the conference room."

I groaned and flopped back in bed, running a hand over my face and letting out a sigh of irritation. It felt like I'd only been asleep for moments, but the light outside the tiny window was subtly different, and I realized we must have slept at least a few hours.

"We'll be there in five minutes," I announced, looking over at Violet. Amber's footsteps moved away from the door, and I sighed. "I wonder what the hell Maxen has gotten into now."

"Knowing him?" scoffed Violet, standing up gracefully enough to keep the sheet wrapped around her—though I would have appreciated the view if she hadn't bothered. My imagination immediately flashed to images of me moving up to her and kissing her so well that she dropped the sheet, and then taking her immediately back to bed so that I could have my way with her again. "Who knows? Probably threatened somebody or said something that made someone angry."

I watched her move, a possessive smile on my face. "Maybe we got lucky and somebody hit him. I'm more than happy to pass that job on to somebody else."

The look Violet shot me was half annoyance, half bemusement, and I grinned at her as she pulled some clothes out of her bag. I was surprised to see our things here—I had noticed pretty much nothing but

Violet earlier in the night. Amber or Margot must have deposited the bags here before the ceremony so we wouldn't have to worry about it later. It was a nice thought, and I made a mental note to thank them as I grudgingly got out of bed.

Violet cast me another look, her cheeks flushing, and I smiled to myself, caught up in the memory of last night. It had been… so incredibly worth the wait, but it was adorable how shy she was being. I wanted to tease her. I also wanted to ignore whatever drama Maxen was bringing us and drag her back to bed.

I wisely chose neither, and quickly got dressed. Violet was ready by the time I put my boots on, and I looked over and frowned at the pair of running sneakers she was wearing.

"Where are your boots?" I asked.

She shrugged. "I traded them for my wedding dress."

"As much as I loved your wedding dress and how amazing you looked in it, you really need boots. You know you could've married me in anything and I would've loved it, right?"

Violet put her hand on her hip and arched an eyebrow. "I know that, but the dress felt important. Besides, the woman I was trading with really needed them. I'll find another pair. I'm sure there's a Matrian warden prisoner who is the same size as I am."

I nodded, assuaged by her forethought, and finished tying mine. "I'm sorry," I said, standing up and pulling her into my arms. "I just know that sneakers don't stand up to the kind of stuff we do. Now let's go tend to the errant, soon-to-be ex-king."

She nodded and slipped her hand into mine, pulling us toward the door. We moved in comfortable silence to the conference room—the halls were pretty empty and everything was quiet—and a quick check of my watch told me it was nearly five-thirty in the morning. As if looking at my watch triggered it, a yawn caught me by surprise.

Violet looked over her shoulder at me, a knowing smile playing on her lips, and I resisted the urge to pull her off into one of the side closets and get us both thoroughly distracted. The effect she had on me was palpable—and it hadn't gotten better since I'd actually gotten a taste of what loving her felt like. If anything, the urge was stronger than before.

The conference room was empty, but the remnants of the party remained. Violet made for what had once been the food table, letting go of my hand in the process, and Henrik looked up from whatever soft conversation he was having with Ms. Dale to wave at us.

"Get over here, you two. You're who we've been waiting for."

"What'd Maxen do?" I asked as I moved up to the table, ignoring the grins on Amber and Owen's faces as I yawned again. Thomas sat at the table a few seats down from them, his eyes focused on his modified handheld, his posture tense and threatened, not having even looked up at our entrance.

"Well, for lack of a better word, he escaped," Ms. Dale announced, her mouth tightening.

Thomas didn't look up from his handheld. "With a heloship, several cases of guns and ammo, and—"

"Wait," I said, interrupting him as the seriousness of the situation began to sink in. Amber and Owen seemed to be having a joke at our expense, but now that I noticed it, Ms. Dale and Henrik's faces were grim, tight. They could have gotten even less sleep than Violet and I had. "He took all of that?"

"He also stole several of my data chips with a few programs I was working on," Thomas said, and I felt myself sliding into a chair at the table, too surprised to stand anymore.

"How?" asked Violet around a mouthful of stale bread she'd picked up from the table, rage simmering in her voice. "That man is a complete twit! How did he pull this off?"

There was a pause in which I could feel all the built-up resentment toward the man rising to a boiling point.

"He had help," Ms. Dale said.

Ice flashed through my veins, quickly replaced by the rushing of a dangerous rage.

"Was it one of our—"

"No, not that," Henrik said. "It was the Patrian wardens. One or more of them must have been gathering intelligence for him—studying our programs, the guard patterns, making a plan. From what I've seen, Maxen certainly couldn't have thought this through on his own."

"Do we know which ones—" I began to ask, but Ms. Dale cut me off.

"They all left with him," she said, "so it hardly matters."

I thought of Mark Travers—who had been so glad to see me—and anger churned in my belly.

"I was careless," Thomas said, his voice low and dark, and I realized that the small man was also upset—he rarely showed so much emotion. "I carried on conversations about what I was developing with group members while some of the wardens were listening, instead of insisting they leave. I took a gamble. I thought it might increase their chances of trusting our command if it was clear we had superior technology."

My head was beginning to ache at how much thought Thomas put into almost every action. Henrik waved the man off, and I was glad when he said, "The blame is on all of us, Thomas. We were watching Maxen, but none of us kept as close an eye on the wardens. We assumed they would support us because of the king."

"It's worse than just that," Ms. Dale said. "One of them might have been in contact with the Porteque gang, too."

"I'm scanning the records of our handhelds for unknown numbers right now," Thomas said. "Another thing that I should have thought of—"

"Thomas, nobody is perfect," Violet chided him, sitting down at the table, her bread finished, her eyes sharp and alert with worry. "Why would we think they're joining forces? This still doesn't explain how he escaped."

"We had a patrol heading out at three this morning. They were going to do flybys in concert with a ground unit we've been sending out each night to make sure everyone's safe and no one is trying to loot," said Henrik, the look on his face positively glum. "It was a strong time to make a move—nearly all of our best fighters were taking a break from the last few days, and there was only a skeleton crew on guard."

Ms. Dale picked up the narrative without even seeming to notice that she was finishing Henrik's sentence. "Just when the patrol was changing, members of the Porteque gang launched three separate attacks, at three separate locations, drawing the original ground crew into a firefight and separating them from our heloship team. Thomas summoned another heloship to help put out the fires, and the ship left, but… it didn't get to its assigned destination. We found the original crew tied up and stuffed into a storage room after the ground unit reported their backup wasn't arriving. By the time more of us had woken up to guess what had happened, the king and the wardens were long gone—and the gang members conveniently stopped their assault and retreated very soon after."

"This kind of coordination among factions of the Porteque gang is highly unusual, especially given current circumstances," Thomas said. "The likelihood that their attack was a strategy meant to distract us at a moment when we had the fewest active troops is… Well, I'll say it's very, very high."

I cursed and leaned forward. "What could he possibly be thinking?" I asked no one in particular. The crown had never before allied with the Porteque gang—even the king wasn't crazy enough to support those kidnapping, brainwashing thieves. If Maxen had stooped to using Patrus' most scum-of-the-earth faction, he was more desperate than any of us had given him credit for.

A voice at the door surprised me with an answer to my rhetorical question. "Why should we care?" I blinked in surprise, turning and seeing Mags, her hair sticking every which way and her uniform disheveled, as though she'd just rolled out of bed and come down here. She stalked through the doorway. "Sorry I didn't report sooner," she said, "but I didn't want to interrupt the briefing. Anyway, the king's got what—five men with him? He's not exactly a fighting force. I mean, the heloship is big, but we've got eleven more. He's probably just running while he can, before he gets ousted and has to face the people on the street. He doesn't have a lot of loyal subjects left."

I frowned. A voice in me wanted her to be right, but my gut was telling me Maxen had a plan. He was a coward, and if there was one thing cowards did best, it was lash out blindly when pushed into a corner. But there wasn't much we could do, so we would just have to wait and see.

It seemed the king wasn't keen on waiting: his move came much sooner than any of us could have anticipated, only two hours later. The group of us had had breakfast and too much coffee by then and were deep into discussions about our next move as sunlight grew steadily outside. Drew and Logan had joined us, one coming back from his patrol duties, one from his rest hours—so we were all there when Thomas' handheld made a horrible noise that none of us had heard before.

"What the hell is that?" Logan demanded, slopping coffee everywhere as Thomas stared intently at the screen until the sound shut off.

"It's the default emergency notification sound from my program for broadcasting to handhelds," Thomas said, his voice going even flatter than usual as he turned the screen around to show us. King Maxen's name was flashing on it. Thomas stood up and moved over to the room's large viewing screen, jacking in the handheld and turning on the screen.

Instantly an image of Maxen's face filled the screen, the cockpit of the heloship he'd stolen behind him.

"Well, at least I know my program works," said Thomas ruefully, producing another handheld from his pocket and pulling up a screen full of coding. "He must be using the network I set up."

The king's voice sounded out loud in the room—just when we'd thought we would finally stop hearing it in these rooms—and I could see all of us give a collective shudder.

"My fellow Patrians. I know there has been… some unhappiness with me as of late, and I can't blame you. I have failed you, my people. I failed to see the threat that was Matrus, just like I failed to be there to fight for you when they invaded.

"But I am bound to you through a sacred oath, to serve and protect you, always, and while I have failed at that in the past, I am willing to step up and do it now. My people, we worry about all the things we don't have, the things that at any moment could fail us. Water, food, fuel, power… stability. Well, even as we struggle to rebuild, to bury the dead, Queen Elena of Matrus, the architect of our woes, continues her assault… and now she has resorted to using the mutated freaks that are the fruit of a very tainted womb." He turned, looking to one side, clearly mouthing the words "Switch cameras" to someone off screen.

A second later, the image of a dirt road from overhead appeared on the screen, a formation of black-clad figures marching along the road, the green of the night vision making them appear sinister, menacing, downright evil.

"Viggo, those are the—"

"I know," I said softly to Violet, and she leaned toward me in her chair, her hand reaching for mine. I held it tight, the sense that something terrible was about to happen looming over me, the accompanying queasy feeling coming from a gut knowledge that I had no way of stopping this.

I realized why I thought that a moment later. "That night vision— this video is from at least a few hours ago," I said to the group.

Violet nodded next to me, instantly comprehending what I meant. "Thomas, can you kill the transmission? I think we've seen enough."

The small man blinked, and then his fingers went flying, as Maxen's voice droned on over the video. "As you can see, she's sent some of the very same freaks she tried to turn us into only a few days ago. I was notified of her plans by several informants—the True Sons of Patrus— led by this man, Peter White." I narrowed my eyes, and I heard Violet gasp as the camera changed, and we both recognized Peter. He was a leader in the Porteque gang, and we'd encountered him more than once. Probably *the* leader, now that most of them were dead and gone.

Peter smiled—a charming smile that showed dimples—but the guileless expression was tainted in my mind by the knowledge of what kind of man he really was. There was only the briefest picture of him, and then the view came back to the boys marching, the camera moving in a slow circle around them as Peter's voice presided over the footage.

"Thank you, King Maxen. As you can see, these creatures are well within our borders, an hour or two outside of town, heading for you even now. We've been watching them since last night, and their pace is relentless. They don't seem to need to stop to eat or drink or even to sleep. Luckily, our king has provided us with the weapon we need to stop them."

Violet's face was rapidly turning from worried to downright sick. "The boys have been in the country for the whole night?" she murmured. "Why didn't we know? We could have—We could have changed this—"

"We don't have enough people or equipment to monitor the whole country, Violet," Ms. Dale said, her voice full of regret. "We'd been concentrating on the city… and on you being gone…"

"We missed the country entirely," Mags breathed, finishing the thought. All of us stared at the video, transfixed, and the feeling that something horrible was happening grew in my gut like the anticipation of being punched.

The view changed. It was still aerial, but two heavy machine gun muzzles jutted out into the top of the screen, angled toward the enhanced boys in black. Before I could say or do anything—even cry out in horror—the muzzles began to spin, and then the muffled noise of gunfire erupted through the speakers as bullets began to tear through the ranks. Some of them started running, fast, but the guns followed them until they were all mowed down. Tracking them was clearly a simple task thanks to the night-vision camera.

I looked away for a moment, my stomach churning as a wave of fury seized me, forcing me to ball my free hand into a fist. Those boys were innocent—victims, even—and he had butchered them. Maxen's voice started up again, carrying with it a deep and resolute promise with sincerity that made me want to put my fist through something.

"My people, I will keep you safe from these creatures. I will keep you safe from Queen Elena. Even now, my team and I are planning an incursion into Matrus. The mission will be dangerous and full of peril, but if I am successful, I will bring down Queen Elena and the tyrannical government of Matrus, securing our people's future. Patrus is in a difficult place now, but soon we—"

The sound stopped midsentence, and then the screen clicked off.

Thomas looked up, his cheeks flushed with embarrassment, and I had no doubt that even though he didn't show much else, the video had affected him too.

"That took longer than it should have," he whispered, wiping sweat off his forehead. "Of course, I didn't expect to be hacking into my own program using a remote terminal on a really awful connection… That was certainly difficult, and…"

"You don't have to defend yourself, Thomas," Owen said softly, interrupting the small man's rapidly devolving babble. "You did the best you could." I looked over to see Owen staring at the screen, a dark fury overshadowing everything else on his face.

"How effective is that going to be?" I asked. "I mean, not everyone has handhelds, so surely…"

"We *gave* them handhelds, Viggo," Ms. Dale said after a moment, her mouth thinning. "We tried to hand out one to each group or family. Thomas was working on that mass broadcasting program, and it was supposed to be a way to notify everyone of an emergency."

"I changed my mind," Mags announced grimly. "We have to hunt him down. He's going to be a threat to what we're trying to accomplish."

"I agree with Mags," Drew said. "In fact, I don't even understand why he was allowed to roam free in the first place."

"We couldn't have held him prisoner," Ms. Dale said. "He's a terrible person, but he isn't a criminal. The only reason we took him was to keep him safe from Elena, because his death would help solidify her control, however she decided to play it."

"He just murdered a dozen or so of the boys," Violet grated out. "He *is* a criminal, and he deserves to die for what he just did."

"Unfortunately, the rest of the country might not see it that way," Henrik said gently but soberly, his tone delivering the terrible truth. "All they'll see is enemy soldiers invading their country. To some of them, even knowing that the boys are being controlled, it will seem justifiable as self-defense."

Violet looked away, then up at me, the wounds in her heart plain in those storm-gray eyes. I squeezed her hand, trying to reassure her that at least I felt her pain and understood it. Like me, Violet felt a responsibility to keep the boys safe. This was made harder by the fact that as long as they were under Elena's control through the Benuxupane, they were a threat to us, and to Patrus as well. But Maxen's way was beyond wrong—it was cowardly. And unlike most of the populace, he didn't have the excuse of ignorance.

The silence spread out over the table for a second, and then Henrik sighed, the sound telling us he was about to let out another uncomfortable truth. "We can't waste time trying to hunt him down," he announced grimly. "The biggest threat to us is Elena, and now, it's a race to see who gets to her first."

"Who cares?" Drew spat. "I hope they kill each other."

Mags gave him a warning look and leaned forward, running a hand through the dark mass of her hair. "Why does it matter who gets to her first?"

It was Morgan who answered, her voice soft as she comprehended the situation. "If we want to get the Matrian government to accept the coup we've been planning, then Elena has to be taken alive," she said. "She has to stand trial for what she did, or else… Well, it would look really convenient if she were assassinated, and then all of this information came out accusing her of being a war criminal. The leaders might not be willing to accept it."

"That could mean a civil war in Matrus, which is something Patrus cannot afford," Henrik added. "We're already destabilized, with little to no supplies to carry us all the way through winter. We need Matrus strong, because frankly, we're going to have to rely on Matrian aid to rebuild. It's a hard fact, but it's true."

"Also, if he manages to kill Elena, you know Maxen is going to make a play for the throne," Amber added. "And the people here are scared and want stability. If they found out he actually came through and killed her, they'd rally around him in a heartbeat."

Mags took that in, and then shook her head. "I'm still for hunting him down here. He'd be mad to try to go after Elena with only a handful of men. The palace is heavily guarded, and even we've had a hard time getting anything on it…"

Thomas cleared his throat and shuffled closer to the table. "One of the things they stole from me was a blueprint we recovered from one of the government buildings. It's a map—likely made by a Patrian spy—that details a series of caves under the Matrian palace. The report theorized they were designed to be some sort of fallout shelter. There are several entrances and exits into the castle, and, most importantly, one exit about a kilometer away from the palace, in a wooded area."

Mags fell quiet, fiddling with her sling, and then looked at Henrik. "You're in charge," she said softly, and Henrik nodded.

"We need to maintain order here, and release a statement of our own to the people. I'll let Ms. Dale and Thomas brainstorm something up. Viggo, Violet, we're gonna have to step up your mission. I don't want to take any chances—we need you out of here in case he is stupid enough to try to come back and claim this place first. We don't want the mission to fail because you were caught up in a firefight here."

"We need to question all the guards who were on duty when he escaped," Ms. Dale added. "I need to find out if anyone who wanted to join us is actually associated with the Porteque gang. I wouldn't put it past them to try some espionage."

"How are you going to do that?" asked Logan, and Ms. Dale met his gaze, and forced a smile onto her lips. Logan seemed to need no more information from her. "Right. So what should the ones not going into Matrus do?"

"We need to heighten patrols," said Mags. "If there's a Porteque element still around, we'll need to patrol the streets more, and use two heloships instead of one as support. What happened last night showed us how little it takes to overwhelm our patrols."

"We'll also need to increase guards on this compound," Ms. Dale added. "Even consider moving to another building in another part of town."

"There's not really another good place to store and hide eleven heloships," Henrik pointed out, and Ms. Dale grimaced and then nodded in agreement. "We'll have to stay here for now, but I think we'll be fine.

Maxen is desperate to win back the support of the people, which means he won't start with us... He'll just make us obsolete once we lose their support."

"*If* he succeeds," Mags amended, unnecessarily. "There's no guarantee of that. I'll go get started on the patrols."

She stood up and left, Drew by her side, and Logan a few steps behind—although he lingered for a few moments.

Ms. Dale watched them go, arching an eyebrow. "So I've got to start questioning the guards, provided the meeting is over?"

"It apparently is," Henrik grumbled, and then nodded. "No, it is. That girl knows when it's time to exit and get to work. Viggo, Violet—Thomas is going to explain to you the plan for how to get into Matrus. Everyone else was briefed last night after you two... disappeared." To Henrik's credit, the knowing pause in the sentence was barely noticeable, but I still saw Violet flush, and squeezed her hand again. "Afterward, send me a finalized list of what you'll need, and I'll make sure it's on your bird and waiting for you. All right, everyone. Let's get to work."

Henrik scooped up the papers in front of him and stood up, and immediately everyone leapt into motion—except for Violet, Thomas, and me. Within seconds, the conference room was empty, and Thomas was looking at us, a wide smile on his face.

"I don't normally brag, but I'm pretty proud of this plan," he said, and I found that his enthusiasm was chasing away just a tiny bit of the anger and pain Maxen's actions had stirred up.

"Then tell us," I said, leaning forward, ready to finally put an end to this mess, once and for all.

CHAPTER 23

Violet

Viggo tugged the straps tighter across my chest, making sure I was fully strapped in, and I exhaled nervously. "Why are we doing this again?"

It had to be the fifth time I'd asked the question, but to Viggo's credit, he didn't laugh at me. "Because we have to," he said simply, pulling the strap to tighten it until it was snug against my shoulder.

I looked around the room, needing something to focus on. My eyes drifted over to Tim, and he gave me a thumbs-up. It took me a moment to conjure up a reassuring smile for him, but I managed.

"I think I need you to explain why one more time," I breathed, and the heloship shuddered underneath me, making me grab onto the straps. For the hundredth time, I checked the area under my seat where I'd tied down my bag, reaching out to pat its solid weight. It was loaded down with all my gear and the precious silver egg I was going to have to carry around with me, I hoped, just one last time.

"C'mon, Violet," Amber said over her shoulder, and I looked past Viggo to where she sat at the controls. "You've been flying with me dozens of times."

"Yeah… It's not you, Amber," I said, trying not to panic as the heloship jerked and shuddered again. "It's this plan. Just the first part, really…"

"The machines I saw when I was scouting with the drone are a design of Mr. Ashabee's," Thomas reminded me, his fingers flying over his handheld. He was also strapped in to a hard seat on the side of the ship, but the difference was… he looked indifferent. "It's a defense mechanism that prevents unauthorized ships from traveling into Matrus, and I have to say, it's quite well made. It was designed to pick up on the heat and vibrations of a heloship, and then automatically fire missiles at it—no warning. In order to defeat that system, we have to make it seem like the ship isn't there. No vibrations, no heat. The only way to do that is if the engines are completely cut off."

"There's a bit more turbulence coming. The air up here is getting thin," Amber commented on the tail of Thomas' statement, and he grunted.

"It's to be expected. We're very high up. How are the thermals reading?"

"Outside is…" She paused and whistled. "Negative seven degrees."

"Are we high enough up to, uh, drop?" I asked.

"Don't think about it," Viggo murmured, swinging himself into the seat next to me and starting to hook himself in tightly as well. "Just hold my hand and remember to breathe."

I nodded and placed my hand on his thigh, trying to still the nervous way my breath was coming in and out of me. The cabin was definitely chilly, and even though I was bundled up, I could feel the cold trying to seep in. I knew heloships were designed to go high into the air—Amber had once explained to me that the cabin was pressurized and had an oxygen supply if necessary—but I didn't like the way it just *felt* different up here.

Kneeling at the holotable, which was right now just acting as a regular table, Ms. Dale put down the small mirror she was using, closing the lid on the large silver cosmetics case she'd been fiddling with.

"What do you say, everybody? Have I lost any of my cosmetic skills?"

I stared at her as she packed up the mirror along with the case, welcoming the distraction from the upcoming drop. Ms. Dale had used the time it had taken us to fly to the very eastern borders of Matrus to stuff us into wigs and paint elaborate disguises onto our faces—she was just finishing up the final touches on her own, having made Morgan, Amber, and Viggo into virtually unrecognizable versions of themselves. Now it was her turn, and I stared openly: a black bob wig framing her made-up face, she looked younger by at least ten years—but probably closer to fifteen—and it even seemed like the shape of her face had changed.

"I'd say your skills must have gotten better in your old age," Viggo smirked, teasing her with the compliment like he always did on missions. Ms. Dale *tsk*ed. "Be glad I didn't have to make *you* look any older—your cover would have had to be Violet's father."

"Ouch," Viggo said, feigning chagrin, and I smiled a little, warmed by their friendly banter. With his hair slicked back and tied at the neck, and those infamous wire frames perched on his nose, he was still Viggo—to me—but he hadn't shaved since before the night of the water treatment plant, and now coarse dark hair ran along his cheeks and chin, thick and full. His disguise was meant to throw the Matrians off, although they were more likely to recognize Ms. Dale or me, but I had to admit that the entire look—especially the glasses—had left me feeling breathless when I had first seen it. I sighed, wishing that was the only thing to which I could attribute the butterflies in my stomach.

My own transformation had been more alarming than exciting—and it had been enough to confuse Viggo and Tim for a few seconds, which was certainly a good sign. I looked older, more mature, with bags under my eyes and the hollows in my cheeks more pronounced. I questioned the absence of a wig, but Ms. Dale told me the short hair was a better disguise than she could've hoped for, as no one in Matrus would know I had short hair now. Desmond was the only one who had spotted me—well, the only one who wasn't in a berserk rage—and Ms.

Dale doubted she'd had time to report anything to Elena before her timely end.

"Amber," Thomas said, interrupting the quiet within the cockpit, "when you kill the engine, don't forget to keep the antifreeze pump on, or else this thing will not restart." His voice sounded just as indifferent as before.

"Wait, what?!" I exclaimed, all the calm I'd carefully gathered while contemplating our disguises evaporating in an instant. Ms. Dale reached over and patted my arm as she cinched herself into the seat next to me.

"Relax, Violet," she said. "This is actually going to be a little bit fun!"

I had no idea how to respond to that, so just resigned myself to keeping my mouth shut. Viggo, having finished buckling himself in, took my hand in his, bringing it up to his lips and kissing it.

"We're going to be okay," he assured me, his strong fingers massaging mine, and I nodded.

I wanted to believe him, I really did. Maybe if I had never fallen off a flying motorcycle or tried to maneuver a broken heloship away from a storm, I would have been less conscious of the fact that doing crazy flying stunts could so, so easily get us all killed. It had seemed simple when Thomas explained it to me. Sure, I hadn't liked it, but I was a big girl. I could put away my fear for this.

Now I was on the ship, and rational Violet was nowhere to be found. She'd deserted me and left me zero coping mechanisms to deal with the realization that this plan was *insane*.

Tim caught my eye again, and I noted his concern and exhaled slowly, pushing the panic away. I had to try to stay strong for him and Viggo. At the very least, I needed to keep from having a panic attack while everything was happening. I sincerely hoped I could pull it off.

"We're at 37,000 feet," Amber said, her fingers clicking on the buttons.

"Excellent. Now, we'll have to input these coordinates mathematically. We're so high up that missing our mark could mean the added distance of at least twenty-five miles."

"Please stop reminding me, Thomas," Amber sang sweetly. "I'm ready to input your numbers. You check your math?"

"Always," replied Thomas, clearly missing Amber's joke. "And I ran it through a few computer programs to check it again. It's right."

"Everyone in the cargo bay needs to get up here now!" Ms. Dale shouted loudly.

A moment later, Owen and Solomon appeared from the bay. "We strapped everything down as best as possible," Owen reported. "And the nets are secured."

"Good. Secure the door and sit down. And for the love of everything, buckle your damned seatbelts." Amber cleared her throat. "Start reading me those numbers, Thomas."

Thomas began giving her numbers, and she used the keypad on the arm of her chair to input them while Solomon and Owen got into their seats, one on either side of Morgan. Morgan looked up at Owen as he sat down, and then immediately cast her gaze back into her lap, looking everywhere but at the blonde man.

I had a moment to smile, distracted from my nerves by their awkwardness, and I found myself wondering what had happened after Viggo and I left the party that night. And then the heloship began to move, the entire thing rattling.

"In position in five, four, three, two, stop." Amber clicked something, and we went still again, hovering in place. "I'm ready when you are, Tom-Tom."

Thomas sighed at the nickname, but said nothing as he produced a roll of electrical tape. His handheld had been resting on his thigh, and within moments he had it secured there, wrapped up absurdly with the black tape running around his leg. After a few moments, he ripped off the edge of the tape, setting the final piece down, and nodded. "All right, everyone. This is where things get a bit dicey."

"What are the odds on this, Thomas?" Owen asked, and Thomas blinked and looked up at him.

"The mission or the landing?"

"The landing."

"Good, surprisingly. Sixty-one percent."

"Numbers aren't everything, Thomas," Ms. Dale said sharply. "Are you ready?"

He blinked over at her, and then nodded, his cheeks jiggling slightly. "We're ready. On my mark. Amber?"

Amber exhaled softly, rubbing the tips of her fingers together, and nodded. "Go."

"On my mark—three… two… one… Go!"

I squeezed Viggo's hand hard as Amber leaned forward and flipped a switch.

Immediately the vibrations of the heloship stilled as the engine cut off. There was a moment in which it seemed like nothing was happening… and then we began to fall out of the sky.

Everything seemed horribly weightless, and my stomach plunged with the ship. My grip on Viggo's hand grew tighter, and through the bubble I could see the flat, paper-thin land below start to get closer as we plummeted. The sensation of weightlessness was a lie: we were strapped into the side of a falling ship, and gravity was bringing us down, faster and faster each second.

The cockpit began to shake and shudder, and I was tossed against my harness. "It's wind," Amber shouted. "Just hold on!"

A whimper escaped me as a whistling sound began, all around us, and I heard someone—Solomon—ask, "What's that sound?"

"It's us!" Amber shouted over the growing whistling noise. I looked back at her and saw a wide grin on her face, her eyes narrowed in intense focus while her fingers hovered over a button—presumably the one that would turn the engines back on. She seemed utterly exhilarated, and the glee on her face was almost as nauseating to me as the descent.

"It's okay!" Viggo yelled to me in assurance, but I could barely hear him over the sound of the wind rattling by outside, the whistling growing and distorting until it became a violent roar.

I shut my eyes and tried to keep my breathing under control, but

I was panting. We were going to hit—any minute—and that would be that. I remembered the sensation of falling in The Green, the way I had tumbled through the air with no control, unable to stop myself. My breathing hitched until I was hyperventilating, and every rattle of metal made me cringe, certain this was the last sound I would hear before we died.

"Thomas?" I heard Amber ask, her voice barely discernable over the screeching noise.

"Not yet," he bellowed.

The roaring grew louder, and tears began to leak out from under my eyelids onto my cheeks.

Then Thomas roared, "THREE, TWO, NOW!"

I grunted as gravity returned with a roar, my body still trying to go down while the heloship rocked us up. My breathing was heavy and loud in my ears, and I couldn't open my eyes. My complete belief that we had hit the earth was conflicting with the sudden hum of engines filling the room. I had never noticed before how comforting that sound could be.

There was silence, and then a voice, softly whispering in my ear. "We're fine, Violet. We're okay."

I cracked open my eyes, my heart still pounding in my ribcage, and confirmed Viggo's assertion. We were alive. Although, given that even Ms. Dale looked a little rattled around the edges, I wasn't certain everyone was confident about that.

"I'm setting her down," Amber announced, clicking some buttons. "Seems a shame to leave her abandoned out here, but—"

There was a rattle of the doorknob in the cargo bay, and alarm coursed through me, although Viggo was the first to react by standing up, his gun coming out of the holster on his belt. The door pushed open, and I gaped as Logan strode in, bleeding from a cut over his eyebrow, his hair mussed. "I wish I had known what your plan was coming down," he said, looking around. "Then I could've made a better entrance. Seriously, did we just fall all the way down to Matrus?"

"Logan?" Amber said, whipping around in her seat. "What the

hell are you doing here? You were supposed to stay behind to help Henrik."

"I know. I left my orders with my second in command. I didn't want you coming here without me."

"So you snuck onboard?" Ms. Dale asked dryly.

"How'd we miss you?" Owen added. "We were back there securing the cargo bay for at least twenty minutes."

Logan looked over at us, and then down at his suit, and I realized he was wearing one of the Liberator uniforms. We all were, but we didn't have that many, which meant he must have had to sneak into the inventory room to steal one. And he'd had to keep the suit on for at least twenty minutes—a feat that was impressive, even for somebody like Owen who'd had much more experience. *I* was impressed, at least; Amber didn't look so thrilled.

"I can't believe this," she muttered, clearly embarrassed, turning back to the controls and flipping a few switches, then beginning to lower us down. I took a cautious peek out the window, and it looked like we were already on the ground—but we descended another ten or fifteen feet before the thump that announced we'd touched down.

"Amber, I'm sorry. I just… After we talked last night… How we finished things… And then you were leaving… And it's not that I don't think you can handle it! I do! I just wanted to be here with…" Logan trailed off as she quickly began shutting down the engine, her fingers flying, pointedly ignoring him. As soon as she was done, she stood up and turned to face him.

She was nervous; I could see it in the way she held herself. "Well, it's too late to do anything about it now. Ms. Dale? What should we do with him?"

Ms. Dale looked at both of them, and then over to Viggo, who was finally putting away his gun. He met her gaze, and then shrugged indifferently. "You're correct, he *is* here now." She paused, contemplating him.

"I go where Amber goes," he announced, raking a hand through his thick crop of black hair.

"Clearly." Ms. Dale's voice held the quality of brittle paper. "I don't think we could stop him if we tried."

"Could always tie him up," Morgan said softly, and I looked over to see her standing up. If she was shaken, she didn't show it. "But I think that would get him killed."

"You have enough room in the vehicles," he insisted. "And I'm good in a fight. Amber can attest to that."

"*I* can attest to that," Ms. Dale replied dryly. "Or did you forget you and I were fighting side by side at the water plant? I'll make this short. You can come with us—but you follow every order, every command, like it's life or death. And since I know better than to try to separate you from Amber, I will put you with her."

Amber's eyebrows drew together, as though she were on the verge of protest, but she held it back, giving him another long, hard look. "Am I his superior?" she asked.

Ms. Dale gave the young woman a feline smile. "Of course you are. And if he acts out, I give you permission to shoot him."

Amber continued to stare at the man, her uncertain look quickly turning into an extremely satisfied grin. Logan didn't seem particularly intimidated—he was smiling as well. Then again, I guessed he had just gotten what he wanted: more time with Amber.

That was actually pretty sweet, and I could tell he still affected Amber in some way. Otherwise she wouldn't be acting like this. I just hoped he was patient enough to let her sort through whatever she was feeling and work out what she actually wanted. I of all people knew that forcing a confrontation with Amber would just make her more stubborn.

Ms. Dale seemed to think the situation was handled, because she began handing out orders. "Okay. Men, get the vehicles out and start getting ready. Thomas, explain to Logan what the plan is. Women—and Viggo—let's make sure to touch up those disguises, starting with Amber. Remember, this next part needs to be flawless."

"Roger that," Solomon said, his voice low. He stood up and followed Owen, Thomas, Logan, and Tim to the cargo bay, but was stopped when Logan turned around abruptly.

"Amber?" he asked softly, and she looked up, her face an impassive mask.

"Yes?"

"I'm proud to have you as my superior." With that he turned away, and I was blown away by that shocking display of humility. I found myself thinking he must have much deeper feelings for her than I'd thought, to humble himself like that.

Solomon looked around, moving toward the back along with the young man, and cleared his throat. "I'd be proud to punch you, if Amber asks," he said to Logan in a voice loud enough that the entire group could hear, clapping a large hand onto Logan's shoulder. "But in the meantime, let's go. Time's a precious thing."

I watched as Logan was pushed out by Solomon. The door closed, and I exhaled. I still hadn't even moved since we'd landed, and Logan's appearance had been so surreal, I didn't even have the ability to really register it. I was still shaking from the fall, and now... now was the last moment to stop and breathe before we really started the mission.

And this time, there was no room for mistakes or deviations from the plan.

CHAPTER 24

Violet

The sun had set long ago, and had taken its warmth with it, and yet the sky stubbornly refused to change. The west still held the deep, dark purple of twilight, while behind us the inky black sky shone brightly with stars. Since Maxen's announcement this morning had sped up our timeline, we'd only had the rest of the afternoon to prepare for the mission, and spent the day nailing down the plan and preparing everything we'd need. Now it was night, the time for secret missions, and I could already see the North Star shining above the horizon through the window of the car. We bounced and jostled across the uneven terrain, the headlamps finding no hazards or obstacles blocking our way.

The two vehicles we'd taken with us in the cargo bay of our ship were loaded with all the supplies we'd need. Ms. Dale drove, while Viggo, Thomas, and Owen were squeezed into the backseat of the loaded vehicle, shiny handcuffs around their wrists. Thomas and Owen were disguised too, though not as well as Viggo or the rest of us had to be. They weren't nearly as well-known within the two countries.

I stole a quick glance at Viggo as he looked out the window, his eyes serious behind the spectacles. I appreciated the sight, but I couldn't attribute the hitch in my breath solely to Viggo as we drove across the dark gray and black plains that made up the far eastern borders of Matrus—the direction we had been heading when Solomon had destroyed the controls on Desmond's heloship.

That was an important detail in our story, and I sucked in another slow breath, reminding myself of what I needed to say and how I needed to act.

"Be confident," Ms. Dale said softly as she angled the car toward a fire burning some three or four hundred feet away, right behind a massive metal square that hunkered over the rocky soil. It was the enemy camp, a Matrian outpost manning the anti-heloship guns we'd had to perform the drop to avoid, and from this distance I could make out five or six figures at the post; there were likely more in the green tents pitched a bit farther behind the fire pit. "Remember, you didn't do anything wrong. We're going to get through this."

"I know we will," I said, tugging down the olive-green uniform of a Matrian warden. "Not our first rodeo."

"They're going to ask about the uniform—"

"I know what to say." I stroked my fingers over the butt of my gun as Ashabee's anti-ship missile launcher grew larger. It was much smaller than I had expected it to be. The whole thing sat on four tires that were braced by rocks to prevent it from rolling anywhere. I stared at it, resenting how such a small thing had forced us to perform such a risky move in the heloship, letting the petty anger distract me for a moment from what was ahead.

But only for a moment. Ms. Dale downshifted and began to slow as we neared the encampment. A paved road ended a few feet away, and as if by magic, I could see, down the hill, trees and the tops of houses just beyond the gravel mounds that framed the road.

She brought the car to a halt as motion erupted around the fire at the Matrian camp. I immediately rolled down my window, shouting, "Don't shoot, we're the heloship team that went down the day before yesterday!"

The women—there were seven of them—didn't stop as they grabbed their guns and trained them on us, most of them going to one knee. Only one woman stood, a slender woman whose brown hair glinted red in the firelight.

"That'll be their commander," Ms. Dale said dryly, turning the engine off. "Wait for her to respond."

It didn't take long. "Throw your weapons out of the windows," she shouted. "And come out slowly with your identification papers in your hands, high in the air."

We'd known this would happen, and we were prepared. I tossed the gun out on my side, Ms. Dale taking a moment to roll down her own window and throw hers out as well.

"We have three Patrian prisoners," I shouted as soon as we were done. "Do you want them to stay in, or get out?"

There was a pause. "Get them out—slowly, and their hands better be tied up."

"They are. We're leaving the vehicle now."

I tossed open the door and stepped out, the gravel crunching under my brand-new boots—a wedding gift from Amber that I had discovered when Viggo and I had finally looked at the rest of the presents this afternoon in a mission preparation lull. I kept one hand up, showing my surrender, while I opened the back door for the men.

"Get out," I said gruffly.

Thomas slid out first, Viggo and Owen moving slowly and awkwardly behind him. The sound of heavy and cautious footsteps—several sets of them—moved closer, but I resisted the urge to stop and turn nervously around.

"The second vehicle?" asked the same voice from earlier, only closer this time.

"They can't hear you," Ms. Dale said. "Can I go tell them what to do?"

"Yes, and be quick about it. You—bring the men up to the front of the vehicle."

I looked expectantly at the men, and wanted to applaud when all three of them gave me villainous and murderous looks. After a sufficient pause, I arched an eyebrow.

"You heard her. MOVE!"

I reached over to push Thomas forward, and he jerked away, even going so far as to spit at me. Well… my feet, anyway, but hopefully it was antagonistic enough to be believable. I pushed him forward a bit harder, and then waved at Viggo and Owen.

"You two, move it."

The men came around the car, and I moved past them. "Can I lower my arms please?" I asked the warden in charge as I came to a respectful stop a few feet away. "I'm beginning to feel like I'm the Patrian here."

I saw a few of the women standing on the line smile, but their commander did not. She did, however, nod at me before reaching over to snatch the identification papers I was holding.

"Belinda Carver. Queen's Guard." Her eyes took in my uniform, and she frowned.

"My uniform was in terrible condition after our crash," I lied. "I had to borrow another woman's spare."

"Mm-hm. Well, my name is Captain Amalie Harris, and you will need to answer my questions honestly and to the best of your abilities if you expect me to let you pass. Ms. Carver, how is it that you're coming from the east? Not many airfields out there that I'm aware of."

"We were asked to retrieve Desmond Bertrand from Patrus," Ms. Dale announced as she pushed Solomon forward. Tim followed behind her, his eyes darting around, followed by Logan. "The insurgents were everywhere, but we wound up taking a few prisoners and rescuing a few of our people when we got there. Ms. Bertrand wanted the extra manpower, as we were a skeleton crew, but…" She paused, her eyes drifting down. "But she was killed when this… this monster got on board."

"We were able to put him down," added Amber—though if it hadn't been for her voice, it would have been hard to tell it was her, with all the makeup she was wearing. Somehow Ms. Dale had managed to make her look like a porcelain doll. Her eyes seemed wider and even more luminous, while her mouth seemed smaller, like a dollop of strawberry jam in an ocean of cream. Next to her, Morgan, in her dull brown wig and with way too many freckles dusting her cheeks, looked mousy and shy, nothing like a glorious Matrian princess—a deliberate move on Ms. Dale's part, since Morgan had been the one most worried about having to put on an act in front of strangers.

Amber continued her part of the tale. "But he damaged the ship, and knocked out Kathryn here. We flew for hours before we were able to get her up, and even then, it's a miracle we survived at all."

"The vehicles were on board?"

"No," I replied, taking over the narrative. "Well, yes, but not when we departed Matrus. We picked them up when we went out to search for survivors from the initial attack. But..." I looked down, as if I were suddenly sad or uncomfortable. A quick peek up showed Captain Harris waiting expectantly, and I slowly counted to five before continuing. "The princess didn't make it."

The woman cursed and moved away, her hands going to her hips. She kept her back to us for a long time, and then nodded. When she turned, there was a deep anger in her eyes.

"These Patrians," she spat, looking at our prisoners. "Why would you even keep them alive after what they've done to so many of us? After our queen tried to *help* them?! They should be dead."

Her vehemence caught me off guard, but I corrected my reflexive need to set her to rights and rolled with it. "I know what you mean," I said, pitching my voice lower. "These men killed the princess I was supposed to be protecting, and here I've been for the last two days, keeping them alive." I flexed my gloved hands into fists, my jaw rigid, and then exhaled slowly, drawing from my memories of the real Belinda and her derision for me. "But I can only imagine that the queen wants them—needs them—either to exchange for prisoners or for information. And I don't imagine they'll give it up easily."

The captain caught on to what I was saying, a slow, wolfish smile growing on her lips. "Good."

I had expected her to be more skeptical. After all, our story, while it contained elements of truth, was a bald-faced lie. A bold one, but a lie nonetheless. I was pretty confident that no one here knew Kathryn and Belinda—they had worked in different circles and in different divisions—but there was no guarantee. Morgan and Amber's identification papers were real, unlike mine and Ms. Dale's, taken from Matrian prisoners who were only just similar enough in the face to pull it off.

"Can you let command know we have… Ms. Bertrand's remains with us? We, uh, couldn't leave her there, in the ship."

"You brought her with you?"

"She's in the back of our vehicle," Morgan said softly, keeping her eyes downcast and fidgeting slightly—a good choice for her, I thought proudly. "It seemed wrong to leave her there like that. She gave so much to our people, and they'll never even know."

I was so glad she was the one saying that. If I had tried, I didn't think I could've gotten the words out through my teeth. Maybe it was easier for Morgan because Desmond had kept Morgan alive, even if it was with the threat of Elena hanging over her head. Either way, the commander's eyes grew wide.

"Keep your guns on these men," she barked to her soldiers. "Don't let them move."

One of the women moved up to the six men standing by the front of the car, her eyes narrowed. "We'll watch them, Captain," she said with a smile. Then she drove the butt of her rifle into Viggo's stomach, and he doubled over, immediately wheezing for air.

It took everything I had to remain perfectly still, to keep my face calm even as she reached down to grab his chin and yank him upright, pushing him hard against the hood of the car.

"Captain?" I said, giving her a look. "As much as I want to be in on that, I swore to myself I would see them brought to the queen, intact and whole."

The captain stared at me—long enough for me to wonder if I had blown our cover by saying something—and then, finally, gave a slow nod. "She's right. Stand down."

The woman pouted, but didn't object. She gave Viggo another shove, gentler than the last one, and then let him go, backing away before joining the five women in a line behind her. Their guns had lowered some, in the course of our conversation, and I was beginning to sense that they believed us.

Viggo watched her go, his breath coming in pants as he struggled to stand upright. I knew that wasn't acting. I met his gaze, and he gave me an almost imperceptible shake of his head, warning me not to pay too much attention. He straightened up slowly, fighting through the pain to reassure me, and I loved him all the more in that moment.

Morgan waved the commander over to the second car, and pulled open the back to reveal the black body bag we'd tucked Desmond's remains into. She stepped back as the commander reached over to unzip it. I turned away. Even acting, I couldn't stomach seeing Desmond's remains, as justified as her death had been.

I could hear the captain's sharp intake of breath, and the zipper was quickly pulled closed. "She looks…"

"Those creatures have superhuman strength," Ms. Dale said softly. "It… It wouldn't stop hitting her."

It was a believable lie, considering the remains, and as the captain stepped back, I saw her nodding. "It's a miracle you all are alive," she said. "We heard the reports about those things as well… Can you imagine? Just across the river." She shuddered and fell silent.

"I'm just glad you believe us," Ms. Dale said. "When we landed, we couldn't believe it ourselves. I mean, we were in The *Outlands*."

"Well, your report coincides with the sighting of a loose bird heading that direction, so you're in luck there. Did you, uh, see any signs of life out there?"

Everyone shook their heads slowly. "Just rocks," Amber said. "Lots of rocks."

Captain Harris gave a smile then—just a ghost of one—and then nodded again. "All right. I'm going to call this in to Command to figure out what they want to do, as well as to verify you are who you say you are. You four come around to the front and wait for your orders. You'll get your weapons back when your identities are confirmed."

I licked my lips. If they sent her a picture of any of the wardens we were impersonating, then we were caught. Luckily, we all had weapons hidden on us, so on the off chance we were discovered, we could defend ourselves. However, that route would make our job infinitely more dangerous—if we had to fight this group, and they were able to get word to Elena that we weren't who we claimed we were, things would get hairy very quickly.

I followed the captain around the vehicle, letting Morgan close the back door, sealing Desmond's remains back inside. I came to a stop just past our "prisoners"—a quick scan showed me that Viggo's breathing had normalized—and watched as the captain continued to move past the line of her women. I waited, watching in silence.

Seconds went by, and I changed position, idly moving over to Ms. Dale's side. She leaned her head down to me as I moved up, and I whispered, "Think they're buying it?"

"It's a believable story," she replied quietly. "But you never know. Elena's cagey. Who knows what protocols she's come up with?"

I sighed and turned back around, linking my hands behind my back. The waiting was the worst part of this. There was nothing to do but wonder if this was the part where we were gunned down, our dream of stopping Elena finished before it even really got started.

Seconds grew into minutes, and I could see the captain reading off our identification papers to somebody on her handheld. I drew in a breath and moved over to Amber and Morgan.

"You two holding up?"

"We are," Amber murmured. "But if they start shooting, our boys are right on the front line."

"I know," I said, feeling the nervous tremor in my body start again and firmly pushing it aside. "This is going to work."

As if on cue, the captain turned and began walking back. I held my breath, and then moved forward to meet her. "What are our orders?" I asked as she pushed silently through the line of women. I felt a small burst of hope unfurl—one that continued to blossom as the captain held out our identification papers to me.

"Report to the palace," she said. "Go straight to the garage, and wait for Commander Duvall to greet you. The queen wants the prisoners secured and locked up immediately."

I nodded as I took the papers. "Thank you."

"People are scared, so try to take the quieter streets. The queen doesn't want a lot of attention drawn to your convoy."

"Because of the prisoners," I commented, folding my papers and tucking them into the breast pocket, and she shook her head.

"Because you went to The Outlands and came back. With what's going on in Patrus, she doesn't want anyone knowing that people actually survived out there."

"That's ridiculous," I scoffed. "We only survived because we had supplies on board. As it stands we're almost out of food."

"I agree, but people are scared. Stay off the main streets."

"Will do," I said. "Thank you, Captain Harris."

"You're welcome, Ms. Carver. Please collect your guns and prisoners, and go."

I smiled, and then began shouting orders to everyone. Just minutes later, we were driving again, moving steadily away from the anti-ship missile station, the captain raising her hand in farewell in our rearview mirror.

"Are you okay?" I asked as soon as the group was out of sight, whirling around and reaching for the cuffs around Viggo's hands.

"I'm fine," he grumbled as I pulled the cuffs off. "Not the first time I've been punched in the gut."

I smiled, and suddenly the bumpy ride smoothed out as Ms. Dale pulled onto the paved road. The change felt surreal, and I breathed out a sigh that was half relief and half greater worry. Parts one and two of our plan had been unmitigated successes. I could only hope the rest of it went as smoothly.

CHAPTER 25

Viggo

The streets of Matrus slid by the window as I gazed through it. We were entering the city proper now, and even though autumn was progressing, it still seemed warm with light, calm and peaceful. It felt like so long since I had seen such peace—and here it was, right across the river. I experienced a moment, maybe more than a moment, of jealousy. A pang of anger and resentment burning deep in my belly.

They didn't know, I firmly reminded myself, pushing aside all those petty emotions.

We were heading through the restaurant district. Our first goal, Alyssa Dawes' house, lay somewhere beyond that, buried in the heart of a residential area. The lights here were even brighter—the large glass windowpanes we passed, set back into red brick buildings, were practically white. Inside each bright window was a restaurant, where people sat inside, eating.

As I watched, I began to realize that even though it didn't look like a city at war here, there certainly wasn't a great amount of peace. I picked it up at first when I saw a man walking, his steps hurried, his hands tucked in his pockets and his back rolling forward as he ducked his head—as if perpetually stepping under low-hanging ceilings.

Next I saw a group of women walking together, but instead of appearing relaxed and open, they were pressed together, speaking to each other from behind their hands. They eyed anyone approaching with a general wariness, a deep suspicion, a feeling that, from my observation, seemed shared by others on the street.

Nobody ambled. Nobody laughed. Nobody smiled. Even inside the restaurants themselves. Each one we passed seemed like a snapshot of a room where, just out of the frame, somebody had been murdered, and no one was sure who in the room had done it. It made me feel wary, checking behind us and down the streets we passed, searching for some phantom sign of pursuit.

"Viggo, could you…" Owen hesitated, and then looked away. "Never mind."

"No, spit it out. Could I?"

He gave me an irritated look. "Could you stop twitching? You're making me nervous."

I frowned. Had I been that fidgety? For a second, I considered the possibility that I was being paranoid, that all of this fighting was finally getting to me, and then he added, "These people are already freaking me out."

I exhaled sharply and smiled when I heard Violet do so as well. "*Thank* you," she exclaimed, crossing her arms, just as I said, "I know exactly what you mean."

Violet turned in her seat and we all shared a smile while Ms. Dale *tsk*ed. "Of course these people are feeling tense. Their neighbors across the river have clearly destabilized. The future is nebulous—everyone's mind is running them through every 'what if' scenario humanly possible, or even impossible! It's sad, really. We forget that Elena doesn't really care about her people any more than she cares about ours. They are just a means to an end, and the poor fools don't even know it."

I blinked. Ms. Dale was right, of course. Elena didn't care about anyone but Elena. She was a true sociopath, and a smart one. She knew that she had to pander to the people to keep their support, but she also knew how to lead them, what to tell them to make them believe in her as she made decisions on their behalf. The stories they must've been told about what was happening in Patrus, I was sure, were compelling, filled with alarming battles and noble soldiers.

After all of this, I was beginning to feel that the way people got news shouldn't be in the hands of the government, but rather in its citizens'. The motivated few who could keep tabs on those in charge, and make sure they weren't breaking the rules or abusing their power. Ensure they were doing their jobs, honestly and with integrity.

"There," Violet said, pointing to a spot on the side of the road. Ms. Dale pulled to a stop, Amber stopping behind us, and Violet got out. I watched her go, curious, as she raced into an alley mouth. She disappeared from sight, then returned, holding her hand in a fist against her stomach, long, thin pieces of… *something* clutched between her fingers.

The street was more or less deserted, and she moved quickly, getting back in the car and closing the door.

"Keep heading straight for two blocks," Thomas said. "Go right and then keep going straight."

Ms. Dale pressed her foot on the gas, and we sped off. Violet took her gloves off with her teeth and then began smoothing out the strips of paper she'd collected, using the rolling light of the streetlamps to read them out loud. Tickers—she had found some news tickers.

"Patrians turn on Matrian kindness. Terrorist attacks at the water plant cost the lives of nearly… eighty Matrian wardens. Terrorist attacks are suspected within Matrus from Patrian insurgents. All Patrian males in country to check in regularly with neighborhood warden's office. Failure to comply will result in arrests."

"Dear God," Owen said softly. "These poor people."

"Elena always did have a way with words," Ms. Dale muttered as she took another turn.

"The rest of these are just as bad," Violet continued as she sifted through more ticker tape. She must've dug them out of the trash, so they were a few days old, but still, it was good to know what we were dealing with. "Instability in Patrus and the future of Matrus in question. Biological agents used on Matrian soldiers. Brutal male regime establishing control. War inevitable…"

She looked up from her reading and then crumpled up the strips. "How can we ever battle all this?"

"We can," I said, trying to fill her with confidence. Come to think of it, I *was* confident. Nervous, yes. Worried, of course. But I was confident. "We can, Violet. If Morgan is right, Alyssa's voice will mean a lot, especially because she's established. We forget this, but Elena's new to the people. They're still getting to know her as queen. Their opinion will be easily swayed if there's a more trusted voice telling them the truth."

I finished my impromptu speech and leaned back. The cab of the car went quiet, and then Owen leaned forward to look at Thomas, sitting on the other side of me. "What are the odds for this mission, Thomas?"

Thomas looked up from his handheld and over at Owen, giving him a bewildered look. "The odds?"

"Yes, the odds. And don't pretend you didn't run them. You always do."

"That's true, I do." He turned back to his handheld. "Turn left on the next street."

The silence returned.

"So what are they?" Owen pressed.

"The odds?"

"Of course—don't talk in circles. Are you keeping them back on purpose? Are the numbers low?"

Thomas sighed and turned his knees toward mine, facing Owen a little more directly. "There are three reasons why I might not give you the odds, Owen. The first is that they're dismal, and I recognize that by telling you, I would reduce the chances even more by killing your hope of a successful mission. On the other hand, I might feel I don't have to tell you if the numbers run the other way, and I already know we'll be victorious. Telling you that could backfire into making you over-confident, and therefore turn the mission into a complete failure."

He turned back to his handheld, studying the map. We fell silent again.

"What's the third reason?" asked Violet from the front seat, her voice curious.

"That there are too many working parts in this plan, so the odds are impossible to calculate. Turn right, we're almost there."

Ms. Dale turned right, and I looked out the window, focusing on the scenery again. We'd made it to a residential area, with houses, not apartments, and I could tell this was the nicer, wealthier part of town. The houses were better crafted, on larger pieces of land so they could have a yard or a garden, with fences and security gates in place, keeping them locked away from all the common riffraff. Ms. Dale navigated more confidently—I was reminded that she had probably known about this woman, when she'd been a head Matrian spy—as the streets became tighter, turning into one-way lanes through dark residential streets, houses peeking out from behind the branches of trees, seeming to my nervous brain to watch us as we drove by.

Eventually, Thomas said, "Here," and Ms. Dale pulled to a stop. A brown brick wall, about seven feet tall, ran along the road, and ahead, I could see the break in the sidewalk where the beginning of a drive began, cut off from the street by an ornate wrought-iron gate. Thomas barely looked up from his modified handheld, his fingers moving over buttons as the lines of white code on a black background illuminated his face.

"I'm not detecting any frequencies that indicate cameras or comms, but the gate seems to require a key code."

"How can you tell that?" I asked, and Thomas grinned, not looking away from the screen.

"I can see the box."

I strained my eyes in his direction and saw it—attached to the opposite wall on the other side of the driveway, continuing around the property.

"I should've noticed that," I muttered, and Thomas reached over and absent-mindedly patted me on the shoulder.

"Nobody is perfect. Ms. Dale, could you please drive up to that gate, and I'll hand you the cable to plug into it?"

She put the vehicle in gear and then approached the gate slowly, keeping the headlights off. As she turned, the window was almost immediately filled with the heavy, ivy-covered gates that clearly parted in the middle. Thomas handed Ms. Dale a cable, and she rolled down the window, reaching across and running her fingers over the box until she found a port.

Once jacked in, Thomas hit something, and the green on his screen shifted to red, numbers flying over it, almost too fast to see. After a second or two, they came to a stop, and a four-digit code appeared on the screen.

"Two, two, three, eight," Thomas announced, and Ms. Dale pulled out the cable and input the code. The box beeped, and there was an electric hum as the gates slid apart—just like Ashabee's had. As they came apart, they revealed a circular cobblestone driveway with a fountain in the center. Just beyond that was a modest house, more of a two-story cottage, the cut-rock front and rustic columns resplendent with even more ivy.

Ms. Dale pulled forward, and I saw a light go on through a window on the first floor.

"She knows someone's here," I said. "We need to be careful—we don't want to scare her."

The car stopped, and Ms. Dale killed the engine. "The rest of us will stay on the other side of the cars. You, Violet, and Morgan introduce us."

"Sounds good," I said. "Thomas?"

The man grabbed his handheld and hopped out, and I followed right behind him. I closed the door as Thomas moved around to the other side, where Ms. Dale was. Violet slipped her hand into mine, and we moved to the second car, where Morgan was getting out.

"I should go up there first," she said. "I met her when I was a kid. I mean, she would come by the palace a lot to advise Mother."

"We agree, but we should come with you, so you can introduce us to her slowly," Violet suggested.

"That's a good idea," she said, and Violet chuckled.

"It was Ms. Dale's, of course."

Morgan smiled as she pushed past us, heading toward the house. The light over the porch came on and the door swung open, revealing a very short, slightly stooped old woman wearing an ankle-length white nightgown, her white hair falling straight down her back in a long trail. She seemed frail, her skin translucent and spotted with liver spots, but her hands were steady—and so was the big shotgun cradled in them. She already had the stock on her shoulder, but the barrel was pointing down, for the moment.

"Who the hell are you, and what are you doing on my property?" she demanded in a surprisingly strong and loud voice.

"Alyssa?" Morgan said softly, taking a slow step forward and holding her hands up. "It's me, Morgana. I'm Rina's sixth daughter. Take a minute. I'm wearing a disguise. It was… hard to get here to you. We had to take precautions."

Alyssa blinked and frowned, the lines in her face becoming more pronounced. "Morgana? What are you doing here?"

"You can call me Morgan, please. And I'm here because… because I have friends here from Patrus. We've been on the other side of this war, and we have something big, news that we want you to hear first, before anybody else. We're not here to hurt you. We need your help. Please listen to our story, so you can understand why we chose to come to you."

Alyssa's frown deepened, and her brown eyes flicked to Violet and me, and then past us to the six others standing behind us. "They're all Patrians?"

"Actually, I'm not," Violet announced softly. "I'm Violet Bates—the name might sound familiar to you. This is my husband, Viggo Croft. He is Patrian, but Ms. Dale there isn't. Neither is Owen—he's Matrian born. The others are mostly Patrian."

Alyssa blinked and gave us a hard look. "*Huh*," she said after a moment. "Well isn't that interesting. Come inside. There should be enough seats for you all in the parlor. I'll put on some tea. Just make sure you wipe your feet on the mat."

She disappeared into the house before I could stop her, so I tried to hurry my steps while staying nonchalant, not entirely certain I should let her out of my sight. I hadn't known what to expect from this woman earlier—and I still wasn't quite sure now.

CHAPTER 26

Viggo

For an elderly woman, Alyssa was quick, and by the time I went down the hall and followed her into the kitchen, she was already running water from the tap into a large metal kettle. She shot a glance over her shoulder at me, and then stepped back.

"Do you mind?" she asked.

I moved forward to help and waited for the faucet to finish filling up the kettle. Nodding, she stepped to one side and began reaching into cabinets, pulling out teacups with saucers. Her movements were practiced, as if this encounter hadn't been entirely unexpected.

"I've heard about you," she said as she moved, the clinking of ceramics filling the air.

I shut off the water and picked up the kettle. "Oh?"

"Not very much. I retired when Rina was still queen, so I stopped getting *all* the juicy details quite a while ago. But I have a few contacts in Patrus. I was consulted about the death of your wife, Miriam, actually."

"Consulted?" I turned from where I had just placed the pot on the stove, gaping at her. "You were consulted?"

"Sorry. That wasn't the best term, was it? But yes. I was, for lack of a better word, consulted. Rina had already petitioned the king, as was her diplomatic right as queen, to stop the execution—no official power in that, sadly; it's just a statement in the end—but she wanted my thoughts on whether we should demand an inquiry into the event. To see if there was any foul play on *your* part."

There had been, but it wasn't in the way she intended. "And?"

She looked up from spooning sugar into a serving bowl and sighed, placing the spoon down. "I worked very hard to establish more rights for Patrian husbands in Matrus. It's one of the things that made me popular. Yet as much as I did, it never seemed like enough. So I fought for other things: prison reforms, improving the conditions of work camps, restructuring the orphanages... I've done a lot for Matrus. But one thing I have never, ever done, is take a step into Patrus. Do you know why that is?"

"No, and I'm not sure I'm going to like your answer."

"You'd be surprised. The truth is... my late husband was Patrian, and, much like you, very forward thinking, and he was adamant that I never go. Feared the idea, really. He knew that if I went there, even if only to make him feel more comfortable, I would never be able to adjust to the strict laws the Patrian government had designed to keep women subordinate. Eventually, I would fall prey to something, or say something considered out of line, or... get caught up in a situation much like your wife did."

She pulled out a teapot and set it on the tray, pulling off the lid. She began putting tea into the mesh steeper, her crooked fingers moving with more dexterity than I would've thought possible.

"That's why I tried so hard to change the laws for men in Matrus—not just Patrian males but all men. I figured if I could give the Patrian males fairness in the system, they'd be less inclined to make their wives move, and we could keep our citizens safe. But once they cross that river, their fate is out of our hands."

Her message was clear and painful, but not unexpected. There was nothing *she* could've done about Miriam, either. She finished preparing the tray and looked up at me.

"The water should be hot. Pour some in here, and let's see if anyone was silly enough to sit in my favorite chair."

"How would they know that?" I asked as I began pouring the water, steam wafting up around my head, a few drops of sweat pearling on my forehead.

"Because it's my chair," she said, and I turned, holding out the pot. She shook her head. "Leave the pot over the fire. We'll be coming back for more soon, I bet."

She moved, leaving the tray for me, and I quickly replaced the pot on the stove burner and grabbed the tray, following her as she strode out of the kitchen and into the parlor that sat right across the hall.

Alyssa's parlor resembled a library more than a sitting room. Ceiling-tall stacks of books lined the exposed walls, and stuffed chairs spread out around the room. Violet and Ms. Dale were sitting nearest a wooden rocking chair with a cushioned seat. As soon as I spotted it, I realized what Alyssa meant about it being *her* chair—it stood out alone in the room, much like she did.

She moved to it, sitting and pulling the blanket draped over the back onto her legs, smoothing down the soft fabric. I followed, weaving around a few chairs until I got to the middle of the room. I put the tea set down on a little coffee table, gently shoving aside some books to make room, and began setting out the cups.

"So I hear you have a story for me," she said after taking a few long moments to get comfortable. "Please help yourself to the tea, but talk and drink—I am old."

"Alyssa, thank you so much for this," Morgan said, and Alyssa held up a hand.

"By 'old,' I meant 'impatient and cranky.' Let's get to the point."

I listened as Morgan began telling her the story, starting with the circumstances around her and her sister's enhancements. When she got to Violet's part, Violet took over and began telling our story, starting with her mission to Patrus. I interjected a few times, but mostly kept quiet, listening.

Tim spoke next, filling Alyssa in on some of the more… gruesome details of the experimentation performed on him. It was difficult to stomach, but he spoke with clarity and honesty, his broken words still completely able to convey the horror he'd witnessed. I watched Alyssa's face closely as she listened, and was pleased to see that she was affected by his tale, her color draining slightly as he spoke. He wanted to demonstrate his ability for her with a knife trick involving his hand, but she called him off, telling him that wasn't necessary, and Violet resumed her tale.

Even with only the most pertinent details, it was a long story, and it took the better part of an hour to get out—during which time Alyssa sat calm and attentive, occasionally asking a question, but for the most part silent and thoughtful. Everyone had spoken about something, including Logan, who described life inside the Patrian city before, during, and after the Matrian attack.

After our tale came to a close, Alyssa leaned back in her chair, tapping her fingers against the armrests.

"I don't suppose you have any proof of all this," she said after a pause, and Morgan raised her eyebrows, nodding.

"Actually, we do." From her pocket she pulled a data chip and held it out toward the old woman. "This contains all of the documentation we could recover from the lab in The Green, the raw video Violet took of Tabitha talking about the boys and Elena's plan to kill Maxen, the video we made to show to the Patrian people, footage of the sabotage of the water treatment plant recovered from their security cameras… Everything."

Alyssa leaned forward and took the data chip from Morgan, setting it on the coffee table in front of her. Immediately a green light came on around it, and a screen came up, flat and glowing, right in front of Alyssa's face. She began swiping her hand over it, and I heard Thomas give an excited gasp.

"Interactive holotable," he said in a high-pitched voice, and I smiled at his obvious enthusiasm, even under the circumstances.

She thumbed through files, her expression thoughtful as she flipped from one to the next. "This is a lot of material," she said. She continued flipping for a few more seconds, then dropped her hand and picked up the chip, the screen and table returning to their original state. "What are your intentions here?"

I looked over to Violet and then leaned forward. "Morgan said you might be able to help us. We're trying to stabilize Patrus, but we can't keep doing that as long as Elena is queen."

"So you mean to assassinate her?" Alyssa's eyes were hard.

"No," Violet said quickly. "We intend to have her stand trial for her crimes. The victims of what she's done deserve to tell their stories. Everyone should hear it, and she should be punished."

"She really should be killed," Ms. Dale said crossly. "But Morgan correctly pointed out that her death wouldn't help our credibility."

"It wouldn't," Alyssa said. She opened her mouth to say something, and then shut it, as if reconsidering her words. "These are extremely serious and dangerous accusations, but you're prepared. Very prepared." She looked away, her mouth tightening. "Poor Rina."

"Poor Rina?" Morgan asked, and Alyssa looked over at her, her eyes sad.

"I tried to reach out to her after… well, after you were hospitalized, my dear. She was cold, aloof, isolated. I hadn't realized what she was going through. What she had brought upon you and herself. She reminded me so much of her grandmother—now *there* was a strong woman. Confident in command, downright intractable. I was young back then, and she thought I was amusing. The joke was on her when she had to make me one of her advisors."

She let out a chuckle and then sighed heavily, leaning back into her chair. "This is all so much to take in," she admitted. "I am ashamed to say that I almost don't want to believe you. Then again, I've met Elena. It doesn't take much for anyone to realize that ice runs through her veins."

"So you'll help us?" asked Violet, moving forward in her chair a few inches. "Please. We are running out of options, and the people over there are dying."

Alyssa stared at Violet, her mouth twisting into a grimace. "Look, I have some friends I could get this to who could verify the contents of the data chip within the next few hours. If it is legitimate, then I can make sure it goes out with the nine a.m. ticker blast. Of course, I'll have to paraphrase a lot of it—I'm pretty sure the public isn't going to want every detail, although they will have to be made aware of them."

I blinked in surprise. "You have that much sway with the ticker teams?" I asked. "We actually brought a program that would allow us to override every handheld in Matrus and give out the information that way. We… We figured it would be safer."

"Hmm. It might, but it also might undermine your credibility. I don't know. To be honest, I'm still in a bit of shock here. You have to understand, no queen has ever been deposed before, and I'm not entirely certain how best to proceed. I think—"

"Viggo." Thomas' voice cut me off, and I looked over at him, surprised to see him on his hands and knees, digging around underneath Violet's armchair. Violet started, pulling her legs out of the way as Thomas put his whole head under the chair. There was a ripping noise, and he began pulling out stuffing, muttering to himself.

"What on earth—" Alyssa began, rising to her feet, but she wasn't able to finish her sentence before Thomas said, "There it is!"

The next moment he was standing, a tiny silver bead clutched between his fingers. Thomas looked at me with serious eyes, and then dropped it into a teacup with a plop, splashing some of the brown liquid onto the table, before putting one of the saucers over it.

"What is it?" I asked, feeling my blood starting to rush.

"It's a bug," he announced grimly. "Someone has been listening to us."

CHAPTER 27

Violet

Everyone scrambled. Owen and Morgan immediately moved out of the room, heading for the front doors to get to the cars. Alyssa followed them, but turned to go up the stairs from the front hall instead, and I could hear her footsteps creaking around upstairs. Ms. Dale already had her gun in her hand, and she was peering out the windows.

"We've been here for an hour," she said in a low voice.

"I'm sorry," Thomas replied, his eyes flicking over the screen. "It doesn't emit much of an RF signature. I was just looking through my programs, checking to see if anything had changed, and realized that I was picking up a new signal in this room. I should have thought to check for something like this. I haven't seen any of this design for years—I assume it's very old."

"Old? Then how do we know—"

"It's still transmitting," Thomas said, cutting me off. "If a bug is working, it's better to keep the bug there than risk getting caught replacing it. Ms. Dawes must've been bugged by Rina some years ago, and Elena gained access to it afterward. It's probably voice activated—as soon as she starts talking in close enough proximity, it turns on and alerts someone on the other line."

"Thomas," I asked, "is there a chance that… that nobody was listening? If it was an old bug, how would Elena even know to pay attention to this feed?"

Thomas looked at me, his eyes sharp and nervous. "There's a good chance, in fact," he said. "But we can't afford the consequences if someone *has* been listening in and we choose to ignore it. As far as strategy is concerned, we have to assume we've been compromised."

We all took a moment—but only a very short moment—to let that sink in.

"Someone should be watching Alyssa," Solomon said, gingerly pulling a curtain aside so he could peer out the window. "Maybe she's working with the queen."

"I don't think she is," Viggo said. "We talked in the kitchen, and I'm convinced she is an honorable person. She wouldn't let what Elena's doing go unchallenged."

"This changes things," Ms. Dale said. "We have to go now."

"If there *are* people listening in, why aren't they here yet?" Amber asked. "They've had plenty of time. They…"

"She would have held them off." Alyssa entered the room wearing heavy black slacks, a sweater, and a puffy snow vest around her chest. A scarf wrapped around her neck, and she had a beanie on her head, her white hair tucked in underneath. The fabric seemed like it was swallowing her up, distracting the eye from the shotgun she was once again cradling in her hands.

It occurred to me that I had never seen where she'd put it away after brandishing it at us earlier. She gave us all a look and then nodded toward the door. "She held them off so she could know what the plan was—she knew she had time to hear what you're doing next. If somebody is coming for us, she would have sent them about when I asked what you wanted me to do. So we might have a few minutes."

"She'd have them close—" Viggo said, meeting my gaze.

"But not close enough to tip us off," I finished for him, realizing where Elena had miscalculated—and, probably, where we had. "She assumed we would use lookouts."

"Let's go," Viggo replied, shouldering his bag and rushing everyone toward the door. We exited and ran to the vehicles, Ms. Dale leading Morgan, Tim, Amber, and Logan toward the second car, while Viggo dove into ours, Owen already hopping into the backseat. Thomas and Solomon were right behind me as I came around the back to the passenger side, angling for the front seat. I climbed in, pausing when I saw Alyssa heading toward the gate.

"We'll open it when we're in the cars and leaving," I called softly to her.

"I'm not going with you. For your plan to work, you need me to get that information out." She hunched over, keying in the code, and the wrought iron doors started to swing in.

"What's she saying?" Viggo asked, and I ducked over.

"She's going to try and get the information out. By herself."

Viggo cursed. "She can't go alone. We'll need to send one or two people with her, maybe Amb—"

"No need," Solomon grumbled, already opening his door. "I'll go with her. I'm worth ten of them in a fight, and now that I'm not a monster anymore, I'll have better control over where and when I fight than anybody else they could send at me. I'll keep her safe."

I turned, spearing him with a look. "Are you sure? Elena—"

"You'll get her," he declared, his eyes glistening intently in the ambient light. "I told you I wanted to put a stop to all this. Keeping her safe means the information gets out and the population is informed. You just make sure justice is carried out."

I licked my lips—no pressure, right?—then nodded. "Be careful."

"You too." He looked at me long enough to show how much he meant the statement, then shut the door gently and jogged over to where Alyssa was already moving down the drive, heading for the street. He caught up as I sat down, falling into step with her with what appeared to be little effort, and in a moment they'd disappeared around the curved wall.

Sitting down, I began to buckle up as Viggo hit the gas, heading toward the gate. "Put in the comms," he said, and I reached over and opened a pocket on his vest, pulling out the earbud and subvocalizers. These were the older style, unfortunately. Too many of the gloves Thomas had developed to turn them on and off had been damaged in the fighting at the water plant.

I hooked Viggo's subvocalizer around his neck as he drove, turning it on, and as soon as I slipped the earbud around his ear, his mouth began moving silently, the words hidden from my ears. I quickly put mine in and turned it on, shifting uncomfortably at the feeling of my vocal cords freezing.

—repeat, I am going left. Your team goes right, meet at rendezvous position. My team will be on B channel, yours on A. Touch base if you get in a jam. I'll do the same.

Copy that, Ms. Dale's voice said, and her headlights cut to the right, heading down the same street Solomon and Alyssa were walking down at a hurried pace. It seemed surreal for them to be going out in the city unprotected like that... but maybe they could slip through Elena's defenses that way. The wardens were much more likely to be expecting us in the cars. And Solomon was definitely the best person for the job. I swallowed and kept my eyes ahead, accepting the rifle Owen handed me from our stash of gear in the back. I cradled it carefully, keeping the muzzle pointed down at the floor, hidden behind the dashboard.

Viggo picked up speed as he turned, barreling down the slight incline. We passed by one street, then another, and then I saw another car screech around the corner, heading right for us.

There! I transmitted. If it had been out loud, the sound would've been a shout. As it was, the car was filled with a quiet that was almost worse than the noise of battle—just the wind whistling, the engine roaring beneath us, the whooshing noises of things going by.

Viggo was already braking and spinning the wheels, his eyes focused entirely on the road. I leaned my shoulder against the door as we turned and pivoted in my seat, looking out the back window. At first, there was nothing there, but sure enough, headlights soon appeared in the window, the vehicle growing closer with each passing second.

Hold on to something! Viggo transmitted, and I spread my legs wider, bracing them on the frame of the vehicle and grabbing the handle above the passenger side window. Viggo cut the wheel hard, yanking the emergency brake with his right hand, and our center of gravity shifted suddenly as we rounded a sharp corner in a squealing slide. He downshifted and slammed the emergency brake off, releasing the locked wheels, then hit the gas, and we jerked forward.

They shot right past us, Thomas exclaimed, and I turned and saw the flash of red light as the other car's brake lights lit up the lane in front of us.

Yeah, but they'll be right back, I said. *We need to get off this road.*

I know, Viggo said, but we were in an alley that seemed to run between the backsides of houses. There was no break in the brick walls, save for small doors leading in and out of backyards and gardens.

He accelerated, and I clutched the handle overhead as though it would help us, my heart pounding wildly in my chest as he continued to race down the narrow street, garbage bins and little windows blurring past far too rapidly. Viggo looked over at me—just a quick glance—and then smiled… and suddenly, for a moment, this was exciting. It reminded me of the first time he'd taken me for a ride on his motorcycle. How exhilarating it had been with him in control.

I trusted him implicitly.

They're catching up! Owen shouted, the tone of the shout carrying even through the subvocalizers.

The roof, I said, looking up.

This set of Ashabee's vehicles were equipped with a moon roof—we'd chosen them for the mission partially for that reason. Reaching up, I yanked at the handle, sliding open the small window, just wide enough for one person. I passed Owen my gun as I stood up, hunched over so as not to give away my position, rocking with the motion of the car. I peeked over the edge of the roof and saw the other vehicle, thirty feet behind and closing, just as Owen gave me back the gun.

Then I stood fully, the rifle braced to my shoulder, and fired at the vehicle, the weapon's loud retort rudely interrupting the silence of the road. As expected, the bullets ricocheted off, but the car jerked back and forth for a second, backing off a few feet as it narrowly avoided jerking into a wall.

There's an intersection fifty feet ahead, Thomas transmitted, and I dropped down into my seat, yanking the belt over my body. Viggo pulled the emergency brake again, and we turned left—just as I saw another SUV barreling toward us down the road and shouted Viggo's name.

He pulled the wheel hard, and we spun, doing almost a 360-degree turn. I could barely see what was what as the world whirled around us, and then I felt Viggo hit the gas, flooring it. The car jerked as he released the brake again, and then we were out of the SUV's way, Viggo dodging the second car as it exited the alleyway.

Hell yes, Owen shouted as we headed down a clear path, the two vehicles behind us having to slow down to turn around and avoid hitting each other. Then, from the road on the right, another patrol car barreled toward us, forcing us to cut to the left.

C'mon! Viggo groaned as we entered yet another alley that ran between backyards.

Viggo, this neighborhood was built oddly—there's a five-way intersection coming up. If we can get a bit of a lead on them, we can lose them, Thomas transmitted sharply.

You're in their systems; can you tell where all the enemy cars are? Are they being tracked?

They are, and I can, but only for small increments of time, or else the people tracking them on their side will notice something's up, and that'll give our location away.

Okay. Hold this one until we lose them in the junction, okay?

Roger.

Viggo's eyes darted up to the rearview mirror, at the third SUV in pursuit.

Viggo? Ms. Dale's voice buzzed in my ear. *We seem to have slipped out of their net. Where are you? Do you need any help?*

Give me a second, Viggo responded as he upshifted, coaxing even more speed from the vehicle. *Owen, get a flash grenade ready. We're going to blind them just before this intersection.*

I'll transmit our location to the other car, Thomas said.

Owen immediately produced a metal can from our bags and moved up to the moon roof, keeping his head low.

How far, Thomas? Viggo asked after a moment in which the smaller man's voice was absent from our channel.

A heartbeat passed, then a few more.

Thomas, how far?

Two hundred feet and counting! Thomas' voice came back onto the line.

Owen—now.

Owen stood up, his hand on the grenade, his body moving as he let it loose and then immediately ducked back down. I kept my eyes lowered as a brilliant flash lit the night behind us, and Viggo surged ahead, while all we could hear was the long screech of brakes. He slid through the intersection, following Thomas' advice, taking the third road from the left, and didn't stop until the pursuit fell from sight behind us.

There was no sign of headlights behind us for a whole minute, and I let out the breath I had been holding.

That was close, I said, and Viggo and I exchanged a smile.

Thomas? Figure out our best path, Viggo said.

Already pulling up their system. I... He paused, staring at the screen, and then looked up. *Viggo, we're already surrounded,* he said, turning the handheld around and leaning forward to show us the various cars moving along the streets, searching for us. I scanned the map, trying to find a way out, but couldn't—the net they had set up was too well spun. We were going to get caught. It was only a matter of when.

Viggo? What do you need?

Viggo frowned at Ms. Dale's voice, and then looked around the car, almost apologetically. *I guess you tuned in to hear we're surrounded. We need for you to get to the caves and get to Elena. We'll try to distract them, keep them busy for as long as possible.*

What? No! That's risky. How do you know she hasn't just given a kill order?

We don't, Viggo replied, throwing the car into gear and moving us forward. *But we'll just have to hope she hasn't. Complete the mission. Maybe rescue us if you can find the time.*

There was a long pause and a burst of static, followed by, *Roger that.*

Viggo, take this road and get to the intersection of Burberry and Olwent, Thomas said. *There are two cars waiting for us there, but maybe we can use them against each other. We have some grenades.*

How far away is it? Viggo asked, shifting up and gaining even more speed.

Head this way for two blocks, take a right for another five, and then another right, and we'll be there.

That's really close to the city center, Owen commented. *Are you sure?*

It's their weakest point—all the other cars are patrolling the streets, but there'll be a window in which these two cars will be on their own. If we can pull them after us and then pile them up... it might work.

It's as good a plan as any, I added.

A car suddenly rounded a corner behind us and accelerated hard, bumping into us.

Who is that? I asked as I pulled up the rifle and unbuckled my belt. *They weren't on the map!* The vehicle accelerated behind us, and I was thrown forward into the dashboard—not hard, but enough to be rattled. I climbed up to the moon roof again, pushing the rifle out first.

I don't know! Thomas replied, plainly irritated. *Maybe a car that doesn't have a tracker... Does it really matter?*

I tuned out his voice as I drew the rifle smoothly to my shoulder and began firing, the shots ricocheting off the hood and windows. This driver didn't panic, just accelerated again, jolting me into the side of the roof. My hip hit hard, and I sucked in a breath, pain radiating from the spot, and then fired again.

The stock shook my shoulder from the recoil, but I continued to fire, going for their weak points. They were too close for me to get a shot at their tires, but as I saw the grill on the front, an idea occurred to me.

Ducking down into a squat, I ejected the magazine, taking the new one Owen handed me and slapping it in.

I stood, firing at the grill, expending the magazine into it, hoping for a one in a million chance. I ducked back down, almost disappointed—but then smoke began to pour first from the front of the car, then through the cracks in the side. The pursuit car immediately dropped back, slowing down. Viggo sped away, and I pulled my coat around myself and exhaled.

Great shooting, Violet, Owen praised, and I smiled grimly as I ejected the second magazine. He passed me a new one, and I slapped it in.

We plowed down the street and rounded the corner, and another vehicle appeared behind us, the headlights already angling toward us. I cursed and started to stand up again, when Viggo's arm shot across my chest.

Hold on to something, he ordered, and the next thing I knew, everything jolted as Viggo took the car up over the curb, driving down the sidewalk.

There weren't many people in the way, but the few who were out walking scattered to avoid us in a panic. I had a moment to spot a newspaper stand ahead—and then Viggo hit it with Ashabee's reinforced vehicle, catching the inside of it and pushing it out into the road with a bang. The vehicle behind us, still on the road, swerved to avoid it, but kept pace, coming up on the curb right behind us.

Viggo grinned, and I hurriedly put on my seatbelt, my hands going to the dashboard.

Viggo? I said as I saw the columns of a nearby building in front of us, the ones being used to support the second-story balcony. And then he crashed into the first one.

I couldn't believe how easily it fell apart. I jerked forward against my belt, and then we hit the second, shattering it in a plume of dust and stone. He jerked the wheel to the right and we came back on the road, just as a corner of the balcony began to break apart. I turned, searching it for people, and was relieved to find none—it was too chilly to be eating outside.

This is the intersection! Thomas announced as Viggo darted through it, and two more vehicles joined the first, still trailing dust after escaping the collapsing balcony. I groaned and began to unbuckle the belt, when Ms. Dale's voice cut across the comms. She must have been listening in on our channel the whole time.

Viggo, turn right.

He immediately swerved to the right, then cursed and violently jerked the wheel. Just where we'd been headed, I saw a flash of my mentor standing in the middle of the street, a familiar-looking tube thrown over her shoulder, a smoke trail billowing out from behind it as she braced herself against the kickback of a shot.

The rocket caught the lead vehicle behind us right underneath the engine, and the SUV flew into the air and rotated, the tail end coming forward until the entire thing was upside down. It landed with a crash, crumpling the cab, as Viggo slammed on the brakes and came to a halt.

I blinked, trying to clear the dizziness caused by our spinning retreat, and looked back to see Ms. Dale picking up a second launcher and firing it. The shot caught the second car in the side, and it rolled, slamming into a building.

Ms. Dale tossed down the second tube and raced toward us, the third and final vehicle slamming into the burning wreckage of the other two cars and flipping onto its side.

Are you crazy? Viggo demanded as she opened the back door and climbed in.

Coming along on this mission was my bloody wedding gift to you, she practically snarled as she slammed the door. *To keep you safe! I can't do that if you won't let me.*

That's no excuse to—

Shut up and drive already, Viggo, she ordered, her eyes narrowing. *You can bitch at me about the mission after we get to the palace.*

Viggo opened his mouth and then slammed it shut, putting the car into gear and driving off.

There was a long period of silence, and then Thomas cleared his throat. *It's, uh... It's all clear ahead,* he announced awkwardly.

CHAPTER 28

Violet

The streets were darker now, lights shutting down overhead as it grew too late in the evening for anyone to be out. Businesses were closed, everything shuttered and eerily quiet.

I felt more exposed like this, like someone could see us easily, and Viggo dimmed the lights as we drove. I looked out the window as the streets curved around, staring at the buildings and down the alleys that periodically broke them apart, their edges lit by the silver light of the moon.

It was full tonight, illuminating everything in pale blue tones with highlights of white. That was what allowed me to see the palace through the buildings as we flew down the road. Lights were on, giving it a warm and approachable feeling, but I knew what lurked inside. That mad chase through the city had only been practice. *This* was where everything got really dangerous.

Viggo drifted right as the road forked, and the buildings went away as we moved down a slight incline, suddenly surrounded by trees and vegetation. The road rolled underneath us in a slow S curve, then leaned slightly more to the right, until it ended rather suddenly at the edge of a wide meadow.

Morgan, Amber, Logan, and Tim were already there, unloading their car. We pulled up next to them, and Viggo shut the car off and climbed out. The rest of us followed suit, and Owen and I moved around to the back to start pulling our gear out. Who knew how long we had to get ready before they found us? We worked quickly.

One by one we stripped down to our Liberator suits, moving silently. Our bulletproof vests would be worn underneath them tonight so that they wouldn't show when we used the cloaking function, but there was nothing we could do about our bags or guns, other than put them down or try to stand behind something, using that to hide what we were carrying.

Viggo was busy as we got ready—he and Thomas were setting up a transmitter and pointing it toward Patrus, trying to boost our subvocalizer transmission so we could check in and update Henrik. I grabbed my husband's (my *husband's*!) gear and moved over, intent on getting him in it as he transmitted.

He nodded at me as I approached and then sat down, allowing me to unzip the top of his suit and maneuver the vest over his head, making sure the straps were well on. It was a clunky move and added time to our stop here, but we hadn't been able to make up a plausible excuse to tell the Matrian guards why our prisoners needed bulletproof vests, so we'd had to go without protection during the earlier part of the plan. This part relied much more on stealth—if we got caught, there was no feigning innocence or talking our way out of it, and we would be needing these vests. I noticed that Morgan had already dispensed with her wig, complaining that her head itched.

"It's ready, Viggo," Thomas said. His subvocalizer was off, I assumed so as not to get in the way of Viggo's transmission.

Viggo nodded. *Patience, this is Harbinger, come back.*

I squinted at Thomas, mouthing the word "harbinger" at him, and he shrugged. "Good names fill people with confidence," he mumbled, and I smiled.

This is Patience, Henrik replied. *Listen, there's no time to talk. I don't know where you are with Silver Fox*—I looked at Thomas, and he mouthed Alyssa's name at me—*but we got problems here. More boys have been spotted on roads leading into the city. We've fortified our stronghold and ordered people to draw back to defend it, but it's only going to be so long before someone starts firing.*

We're moving on to the second protocol, but they know we're here. They're expecting us, Viggo replied.

Then I hope you give them hell, Harbinger. And get us out of this before we have to start killing these boys.

Roger that.

Viggo nodded at Thomas, and Thomas shut off the long-distance transmitter, moving swiftly to break it back down. I heard one of the vehicles start and looked over in time to see Ms. Dale driving it toward some trees growing in a tight cluster, followed by Morgan starting hers up as well. The only thing left inside was Desmond's body, and if we died inside the palace, it could be a few days before anyone found the vehicles. We wanted to make sure of that, at least.

I shuddered and stepped back as Viggo pulled up the sleeves of his suit and zipped it up. He smoothed his hands over it, and I handed him his bag.

"That should be everything," I said, turning off the subvocalizer for now. If only for this moment, I wanted to hear my husband's voice responding to mine. "You have ten pounds of semtex with detonators, a mask in case there's any tear gas, a knife, the tranquilizer gun with five darts for Elena or any boys you encounter, waterproof bags—" He let out a surprised laugh, and I shot him a look as I continued, "The special canteens that pull water out of the air, some rations, extra magazines... Have I forgotten anything?"

He bent over and placed a kiss on the top of my head. "Of course not. Best wife ever," he said in a low voice in my ear, and my stomach dropped a little, my body growing warm with desire and anticipation. I somehow managed to take a slow breath and push the feeling down— now was not the time for me to be lusting over my husband. Even if he did look amazing in his Liberator suit and tactical gear, with his long hair gathered behind his neck and the spectacles still perched on his nose.

He moved over toward where Owen was now helping Thomas get his gear on, and I trailed after him, bending over to scoop up my own bag and weapon.

"I really want to tell you about the notebook and stuff I brought, Owen," Thomas was saying as we walked up. Owen was focused on trying to cinch him into his bulletproof vest. Unfortunately, I could immediately see what the problem was: Thomas' belly was a bit too rotund for the strap to slip through and then double back to cinch down on the other side.

"Suck it in, Thomas," Owen grated, tugging hard at the strap, and Thomas yelped in pain. Owen made a frustrated noise and let go of the strap. "This isn't going to work," he announced.

"Then let me leave it off," Thomas replied, shifting his shoulders. "It's heavy and hot and itchy, and I'd rather not. Besides, I really need to explain the system I created here, so you can use it as effectively as possible in the event I—"

"Knock it off, Thomas," Owen growled, raking a hand through his blonde hair. "You're starting to make me nervous."

"What?" Thomas blinked, his face reflecting his surprise. "No, I just wanted to prepare you on the off chance I—"

"*Knock it off, Thomas,*" Owen repeated, slightly louder this time, and Thomas sighed.

"All right, Owen. Here, help me get this off."

"Hurry up, you two," Viggo said as he bent over and picked up Thomas' handheld. "How do I search for RF waves again?" he asked.

"Left column, third one down. Sniffer.exe. Just hit it, and the modifications I made to the handheld will be red on the screen. Red blobs indicate where the activity is concentrated."

Viggo began to move the handheld around as Owen helped Thomas pull off the vest. Thomas zipped his suit up quickly, and bent over to pick up his bags.

"Anything?" he called, and Viggo shook his head.

Thomas moved over, his short legs moving briskly, and plucked the handheld from Viggo's hands. He adjusted a few buttons on the screen and began swinging it around, whether nervously or just plain impatiently, it was hard to tell. After a moment, he smiled, and nodded.

"Over there," he said, pointing.

Viggo moved over to it, Thomas and the rest of us behind him. Tim nudged his way over, and I reached out to tousle his hair.

"Do you have the serum Dr. Tierney gave you?" I asked, and he nodded.

"In bag. What now?"

Viggo kicked the ground a few times, finding one place that seemed more disturbed than the rest, and one kick reverberated slightly. Squatting down, he felt around in the dirt, and then pulled back handful after handful of wet grass and earth, until he seemed to find something about half an inch down. He pulled a few more handfuls away, and then dug his fingers into something, and a square bit of earth bounced up half an inch at an angle. He pulled it open, revealing a flat door with a keypad on it.

"We're going down there," I told Tim, and he gave me an annoyed look.

"I know. You be okay? You hate tunnels."

I shrugged. "Not as much as I hate falling," I replied, and he smiled.

"Maybe you go first," he said with a wink, and I resisted the urge to push him. Instead I turned toward him and checked his uniform.

"Are you wearing your vest?" I asked, and he nodded. "Have you tested the suit yet?"

Tim hesitated and then nodded again.

"Hurts," he informed me, and I frowned, a pang of fear going through me. If he couldn't use it, then that meant he could be exposed and vulnerable in a fight.

I couldn't think about that now. Viggo had told me about Tim's abilities in the field. I had to trust that my brother was more than capable of taking care of himself.

"You'll be okay," I said quietly, sensing that he needed my

reassurance. "Tim Bates—unstoppable ultimate warrior."

He gave me an incredulous look and shook his head, his gray eyes returning to where Thomas was now hacking into the door, trying to get it open.

"Don't like fighting," he said after a minute. "Too much sad people. Too much crying."

My face fell, and I nodded. "I know, Tim. Believe me, I know."

Morgan jogged over, finished with hiding the car, and looked around. "How are we doing?" she asked, her eyes moving over to Thomas and Viggo, crouched over the door.

"We're in," Thomas announced—whether he had heard Morgan or was just informing the rest of us, I wasn't sure—and there was a sharp hiss as the door was pulled open. Viggo turned on his flashlight and shone it into the hole below, revealing metal rungs embedded in the rock, the ladder running down a stone tube that was maybe three feet wide.

I swallowed as I looked at it, and then put the fear aside, reminding myself that it was better than falling. It was strange, but the thought comforted me. Viggo swung in first and began moving down the ladder, seemingly unbothered.

"You don't think we'll encounter anyone coming up?" asked Amber, and Morgan shrugged.

"I doubt it. The entrances to the caves were sealed up by my mother. I wasn't even sure where all the doors were."

"Neither was the spy who got the plans," said Thomas as he slipped his backpack on, his trusty handheld secured around his wrist by a tight black cloth with a bit of fabric cut away in the middle, revealing the screen. "The map only shows the tunnel systems and which doors lead to the palace. Where each door opens in the palace is a complete mystery. *Subvocalizers on.*"

He began moving down the tunnel as he spoke, following his own order and switching to transmit his voice into our ears for the last of the sentence. I followed suit and watched, my heartbeat rising in tempo, as Logan entered, followed by Amber and Ms. Dale—then, finally, I was up, taking a step onto a lower rung and holding the sides of the passage until I was far enough down to grab one with my hands. Tim and Morgan followed me, and I bit my lip when Morgan closed the heavy door above us, cutting off even the starlight.

There was a bit of light coming up to me from below, probably Viggo's flashlight, but the tunnel was still so dark. Dark and tight. I paused, taking a moment to grab my own flashlight, turn it on, and slip it into my mouth.

We descended in absolute silence, but our movements and steps in the tunnel generated enough of an echo to worry me. At one point Tim stepped on my hand, and I cried out—my voice was silenced by the subvocalizers, but transmitted to everyone else. I heard my own hiss of pain distorting over the line, followed by Tim's un-subvocalized apology echoing off the walls, and I shook out my aching fingers and continued to move, allowing a bit of a lead to grow between me and Ms. Dale.

The way down was long—long enough for me to start thinking uncomfortable thoughts. If I fell, would I kill everyone below me? I stopped myself before going down that road. I was being morbid.

To take my mind off of the stress of being in such a tight space, I began to count rungs as they passed under my hands. I was at two hundred and fifty-eight when Viggo announced, *I see the bottom,* and I narrowly avoided shouting "Yay!" into the comms channel. After another fifty rungs, I was at the bottom too, shaking out my aching legs and forearms, straining to catch my breath.

How far down are we? I asked as I shone the light around the wide room, the minerals in the walls glittering. The cave floor looked to be dry, but stalagmites grew in tight little bunches from the floor, with a smooth path cutting through them. I looked around for an explanation for this marvelous path, and noticed that the stalactites above had been cut off over it, left broken to prevent anything from growing beneath. It must have been designed and shaped by human hands—though how they'd accomplished that feat, I had no idea.

Three hundred feet, give or take, replied Thomas, pulling out his handheld and moving it around the room. *Got a reading up ahead.*

Viggo, Ms. Dale called sharply, and I turned to see her pointing at a sign on the side of the cave wall, with two phrases inscribed on it. "Escape Route" was the top one, and it had an arrow pointing up, I assumed to indicate the direction we'd come from. "East Lab" was the second one, and it pointed to the right, the same way Thomas was directing us.

A lab? I asked. *Is it possible Mr. Jenks did his research here?*

That makes sense. It would have been close to Elena to monitor the pregnancies, and no one would bother him down here. Ms. Dale followed Thomas as she spoke, her flashlight panning around, and I followed, the group of us forming a single-file line to make our way down the narrow passage. *Morgan?*

He was there a lot when I was a child, so that seems likely enough, she said, flipping her dark bangs anxiously. *I'm just glad he never brought me down here to study me.*

Yeah, this cave doesn't exactly scream happy childhood memories, does it? Owen added dryly, and I smiled in spite of myself.

I got a door, Thomas announced, cutting through our small talk, and our line of people paused and flattened out against one of the walls. I stuck my head out slightly and saw the door—then paused, alarm bells going off in my mind.

It looked just like the ones we'd seen at the Facility and the Liberator base—both designed to keep out the toxic environment of The Green.

CHAPTER 29

Viggo

can't see any cameras, I said after studying the intimidating airlock ahead of us, my voice instinctively down to a whisper even though we still spoke through the subvocalizers. Thomas shifted next to me, grunting slightly.

I'm getting a reading for one. It could be inside the door. There's a keypad, right?

Yes, that's the only thing that makes it different from the doors we saw in The Green. Why would it be down here?

He gave me a look and shrugged. *If this is supposed to be a last measure against biological attack, then the system would need to be enclosed and self-contained.*

It's a lab, Ms. Dale said, as though the answer were obvious. *It's for keeping whatever they're working on from getting out.*

So there could be biological agents in there, I said, and everyone fell silent.

It's possible, Thomas said. *But we all brought masks, so we'll just put them on in the airlock.* He turned and fixed me with a look. *Or do you want to come up with a better way to get into the palace?*

I still don't understand why we aren't just letting Alyssa handle this, Logan grumbled, and Morgan bit back a growl.

Because my eight-year-old little sister is up there with Elena, she said, *getting fed who knows what propaganda, and every minute Elena is given to run around and set her plans in motion is a minute that will cost countless more lives.*

Amber gave the man a look through her lashes and shook her head, joining in the argument, much less heatedly than Morgan. *You know why we need to stop her. Your men are over there in Patrus getting ready to fire at the boys. You said you wanted to be here—are you having second thoughts?* For once her voice was carefully modulated; she sounded more concerned than angry. I listened in mild surprise.

Logan hesitated, and then frowned. *You're right. I'm sorry. I just... I don't like this laboratory thing. No one knows what we'll find inside.*

Maybe we'll get lucky and it'll be a fallout shelter, Violet commented, leaning forward again to check the door. *For now, Thomas, I assume you have a way in?*

I do, I do, but I need Owen.

Me? Owen looked up from the back of the line, and then shrugged. *What's up, Tom-Tom?*

Not you too, the short man sighed, but that was his only protest, and he was soon focused again as he pulled out a small flat box attached to several cables. *At the bottom of the keypad will be a port matching one of these heads. Find the one that matches, plug it in, hit this button, and wait.*

That's easy. Why can't you do it? Owen reached for the device as he asked the question, and Thomas sighed.

Because I'm not as good with the suit as you are, Thomas said simply, zipping up his bag. Owen smiled and unzipped a suit pocket, slipping the device inside and reclosing it.

I always like hearing that, he quipped, and then he disappeared in front of our eyes.

I always hate seeing someone do that, Ms. Dale said, and Owen chuckled through the comms.

The reappearing is worse, Amber replied. *One time Quinn got the drop on me—the little imp hung on some pipes for two hours waiting for me to come down so he could scare me.*

Did he scare you? Logan asked.

He got a black eye, so what do you think? Amber retorted, and shared a smile with Violet.

I smiled, easily picturing the scene, and waited, trying not to dwell too much on what was coming ahead of us. It crossed my mind that I should cut off nonessential little conversations like this, but I let it pass. The cave was dark and unknown, but we weren't in immediate danger, and the talk helped take everyone's minds off the fear of anticipation. Besides, if Ms. Dale was allowing the distraction to go that far, then there was a reason.

It's in, Owen reported after a minute, and I looked over and saw the device floating off to one side, seemingly suspended in midair.

If the camera sees that... I trailed off, warning in my voice.

The only camera is in the airlock, Thomas replied, his fingers on the handheld as lines and lines of code ran over it. *I'm putting it on a loop, but...*

He fell silent, his brows furrowing while he read the lines of code as they drifted by. *This system is hack-proof,* he said. We all looked at him at once, and he blinked. *No, I don't mean I can't hack it—what I mean is I can't get into their system from here using what I brought. I need access to a terminal that's hardwired in. I can trick the doors one at a time, but without that... I won't know how to stop anything if it is used against us.*

Like what? Owen asked.

Like, I don't know, Owen! Thomas exploded irritably. *For all I know, there could be man-sized murderous robots on the other side of the doors! That ride unicorns! And kiss you to death! That's what I'm trying to say— there's a computer system there, but I can't crack the firewall without three days of prep. Each security system we run across I can jack into and take over, but without a direct line into their system, I can't do it in a way that will let us know what's ahead of us.*

Calm down, Thomas. No one expects you to be a superman, I said soothingly, and the little man seemed to deflate somewhat. *Now, is this door hackable?*

Yes, they all are. The door's already open, and the camera is now set on a loop. So if anyone's watching, they won't see us.

Perfect. Owen, will you kindly open the door for the ladies?

I heard the hand wheel spin and the door creak open, the hinges slightly rusted, before Owen's hands began to appear again holding it open. I led the way around the corner, stepping inside what was, indeed, an airlock. Two doors that shut tightly enough to create an airtight seal, ventilation ducts in the top for pressurizing or detoxing the air, a panel with lights and buttons that controlled those ventilation areas. I'd kind of hoped never to see one of these again, after all the troubles we had gone through every time we'd gone into one... *Maybe in another life-time,* I thought ruefully.

A sign on the opposite door caught my eye. "Danger: Toxic Environment Ahead." Several more signs were posted along the walls, all reminding workers to put their masks on.

Well, Violet said wryly through the comms, *it's a good thing some-one reminded everyone to bring their masks.*

I shot her a glance, and saw her smile as she pulled her own mask out of her bag. Everyone dutifully fished through their bags to find their own, and I saw Logan looking around frantically for a moment, and then reaching over and pulling one from a case on the side of the wall.

Looks like they put some out for us, he declared triumphantly, slip-ping the straps over the top of his head and pulling it down over his face. He probably hadn't thought to carry one in the pack he'd brought... *Another good reason not to sneak along on sensitive missions,* I thought to myself.

When we were all geared up, I pulled my pistol out and began screwing the silencer in. *Just because we didn't see any guards outside doesn't mean there aren't any inside,* I said, turning to face the group. *Be careful and keep an eye out. Remember your suits will help hide you—we want to avoid detection for as long as possible. If we get caught here, the whole plan falls apart.*

If we get separated, fall back on our contingency plans, Ms. Dale continued for me from where she knelt on the floor, pulling grenades out of her bag and clipping them onto her belt. *Logan, whoever you end up with, you're following their orders, so try to stick close to Amber, or else there's no telling where the two of you will shake out once things are said and done.*

Awesome, Logan replied dryly, bringing his rifle around to face forward. Behind him, Owen was slowly pulling the door closed behind us. He quickly turned the hand wheel, and there was a soft hiss that went silent as the seal moved into place. Flashing me a thumbs up, he pulled his bag back onto his shoulder and slipped his gun out of its holster.

Thomas, open the inner door, I said, and Thomas nodded, clicking a button. A red light next to the door began to flash, and immediately a white mist began to pour from the vents above, filling the room. I reached out and ran my hand through it, pulling it back to see if it would irritate my skin, but it didn't.

I focused on the flashing red light, waiting for the room to pressurize. It turned green a few short seconds later, and I moved to the door, cranking the hand wheel. The door swung open, revealing an interior just as foggy as the airlock, and I stepped in.

Even though the suits regulated our temperature, I could tell the room was warm and humid. I stepped out of the airlock, my gun out but lowered, and was surprised to feel that the floor was… soft. Looking down, I frowned when I saw a blanket of thick green moss.

Everyone followed me out of the airlock, and as Thomas closed it, I realized this side of the inside door was covered in moss too.

This is… This is The Green, Violet whispered, her silver eyes darting around, searching the mist for any sign of life. *Why is this here?*

Who knows, Ms. Dale said, her voice containing a brittle edge. *It does no good speculating. Thomas? Do you detect cameras in here?*

No, and I doubt they would put cameras down in these areas.

Why bother? asked Amber, seeming to understand. *If they're just studying the ecology, then they wouldn't care. Maybe they were trying to figure out what was causing the poison or changing the atmosphere?*

At that moment my ears caught something, and I turned, taking a few steps forward with my flashlight held high. There was lighting overhead, but the mist obscured a portion of it. It was difficult to see how large the room was or what could be out there just a few feet beyond us, so I was relying mostly on my ears to tell me that things were safe… and this didn't sound quite safe. The mist roiled angrily as I passed through it, following the sound.

It was so soft at first, I couldn't be sure I had heard it, but as I drew nearer to the source, I frowned at the familiarity. I waited for my brain to find the memory—and then, in a flash of adrenaline, I realized why the buzzing of thousands of wings was all too hauntingly familiar.

I stepped forward, trying to wave tendrils of mist out of the way. There couldn't be… Surely not here…

I managed to blow some of the mist away enough to see the source of the noise: a huge glass tank filled with thousands of familiar insects, their red bodies pushing up against the glass toward us. Violet let out a surprised sound from behind me, and I turned to see her drawing close.

Red flies? she whispered as she stared at the tank, and I could see the shudder running down her spine. She shook her shoulders, trying to clear the feeling, and I couldn't blame her. The things had nearly killed me, Ms. Dale, and her more than once. *How are they still alive?*

I swallowed, wondering if I should even mention it. *Alejandro told me that they cannibalize their own when they lack food. The females target males first, mate with them, and then consume them, lay eggs, and tear each other apart. The new generation arrives to finish off the old, and the process continues again.*

Her eyes drifted down to the bottom of the tank, and I followed them, seeing there what was clearly the cannibalized remains of thousands of flies as Violet's mouth turned down in disgust.

Oh, she said after a moment. *Are we safe?*

Perfectly safe, Thomas assured her through the comms. *Except that their cage's functions are controlled by a master computer.*

I've got another tank of red flies over here, but there are animal remains at the bottom of it, announced Ms. Dale from somewhere off in the mist.

There's another one down here, but these flies aren't red. They're green, added Logan.

Green? I asked, turning around.

Yeah. There aren't very many of them, though. I can only see about seven of them in this thing.

That's nothing, said Morgan, her voice soft and low with something that sounded like awe. *I just found the river.*

What? asked Violet, turning around and heading back into the mist toward where we'd last seen Morgan. I followed behind her, making sure not to lose her in the mist as we slowly pushed through it. And then suddenly the mist parted, revealing a tiny stream of the familiar bright blue, glowing water as it fed through a channel carven in the cave ground, flowing at a moderate rate. I saw Morgan standing a few feet away, moving up and following the small trickle.

She disappeared into the mist, and a moment later, her voice was back on the line. *It's being fed in through a hole in the wall.*

They probably have it hooked up to a pump, Thomas mused.

Let's move on, Ms. Dale said brusquely, and I reluctantly admitted to myself that she was right. We couldn't let our curiosity about this bizarre place keep us from the mission. *Thomas, where are we going?*

Now that I'm down here, I can finally orient this map. I can't believe they didn't include a compass on this. One second. There was a pause. *Okay, check your compasses and head northwest. Only one way in and out of this cavern.*

The horrible buzzing of the flies continued as we moved, growing louder as we approached more of the vats and quieter when we moved away from them, and I ignored it, focusing on the path ahead. This place was creepy, and I had a thousand questions about it, but we had a lot of ground to cover if we were going to get into the palace.

CHAPTER 30

Viggo

Violet followed me closely, and every time I turned to look at her, I saw her eyes darting around, taking everything in just as I was, not missing a detail. The buzzing faded away after a while, and the passage narrowed considerably, until we were moving through it in single file. I was in the lead, with Owen bringing up the rear.

The tunnel continued narrowing, forcing me to duck low to avoid scraping the top of my head, and then widened up again, admitting us to a new area—I assumed we'd found our way out of the first cavern into another set of rooms. The mist was continuous and thick, making it difficult to see, but I held my flashlight up, trying to illuminate the area. This chamber was quieter, and I heard the familiar trickle of water.

There's another stream in here, I announced. *Be careful not to fall in—that stuff is concentrated.*

According to this map, there are several other doors ahead, Thomas reported through the comms. *I'm trying to look for the right one now.* It was hard to make out which dark form was his, but I thought he was standing next to the Owen-shaped blob, a few blobs down. This was beginning to grow ridiculous—but I had to wonder if the tainted water was the reason why the mist was so thick.

All right, fellow non-scientists, I said as I pushed forward. *Does this effectively confirm that the environment of The Green is caused by the river?*

It does and it doesn't, Owen said. *Because The Green is wide, and runs for miles in either direction on both sides of the river... but then we have Matrus and Patrus. Why would it be concentrated in one area but not affect things farther downstream?*

Two potential reasons, replied Thomas. *The first is that the area The Green encompasses is actually a lower elevation than where we built our city. That creates a pocket just outside of the extreme cold of the mountains, and after years and years of being there, it has created its own thermal pocket to thrive within.*

What's the second? Amber asked.

That the area of The Green sits atop a water reservoir that has been contaminated so badly, that everything around the area is affected by it.

Does that mean our water supplies will eventually be contaminated? I asked, mentally wondering if that was one more thing we needed to deal with in our countries' futures.

Well... maybe, but probably not. I, uh, I guess you didn't see that report I left for you and Violet in your debriefing packets, huh?

I blinked and panned my flashlight around, looking for a sign of something through all the mist. To be honest, I had focused on the overall mission, and not the various technical details Thomas had included. He tended to over-report things, and at this point, it had become second nature to skim and move on. This particular packet had been thick, jammed full of reports that had been made in our absence, and I... I was a newlywed. Still, it bothered me that I had missed something, and I wasn't afraid to ask.

Sorry, Thomas. I guess we didn't. What did I overlook?

That King Maxen's grandfather basically created a way of filtering out all the toxins in the water, and had been secretly using the river to supply all of Patrus with water for drinking, bathing, swimming, and growing our food. That was the real purpose of the water treatment plant. We only discovered it after the raid, after I recovered more information from the computers in the plant itself.

Wait, so he could've—

I shook myself, suddenly floored. That was a big shock—just one more thing to shake the foundations of our world. The implications were stunning; we would have to put some thought and effort into that when we got back from—

I was so absorbed in what Thomas and I were talking about that I almost missed the trench that loomed out of the mist beneath me, glowing blue with the contaminated water. I would've stepped right into it, but Violet grabbed my arm and pulled me back before I could even contemplate how badly it was going to hurt. I stumbled back, a few steps away from the group, and my back came in contact with something hard.

Whirling around, I saw fangs and an open mouth coming right for me, and I shouted and ducked down, raising my gun and freezing with my finger on the trigger as I comprehended the glass in front of me. I had run into a tank, and as I watched, the massive silver python hit the glass, its open mouth smashing into it with a thump. It reared back, black tongue flicking out to taste the air, and the huge head turned, its beady eyes spearing me with a look. It nudged the glass again with its nose, thumping against it, and I slowly straightened as Violet came out of the mist, looking concerned.

I'm okay, I said. *My new friend here gave me quite a scare, though.*

Guys, this room has tanks with silver pythons in them, Violet reported on the subvocalizer, and I turned my back on the snake—as much as it made my skin crawl—heading back toward the manmade river.

Viggo, this mist is making it impossible to stick together, Ms. Dale said, just as I almost slammed into her as I moved. My hands went up to catch her shoulders, and I grunted.

Sorry, I muttered, taking a step back. *Point taken. Everyone link up. We're forming a human chain.* I held my arm out to Violet, and she slipped her arm through it, locking us together at the elbows, and then followed suit with Ms. Dale.

Everyone call it out, I said, and after a moment, everyone checked in that we were linked to someone in our long line. When Tim called in, his voice coming strangely through the mist now that I was used to hearing things in the comms, I regretted for a moment that he would have to be touching somebody—and that the similarly afflicted Morgan would have to do it, too, for that matter—but I knew this discomfort for him was infinitely preferable to his being lost in the damn mist.

I began to move again, stepping over the small channel of water, alerting everyone to its location. We walked for several minutes in silence, more thumps sounding in the room from other tanks containing more giant snakes, which were knocking their noses against the glass in attempts to strike at us as we passed. I ducked down low under a stalactite, and my flashlight caught the cave wall in front of me.

I stopped short and started to adjust, when Tim's voice carried through the cave, slightly muffled by his gas mask. Of all of us, he was the only one who couldn't use the subvocalizers, although he had the earbud. The subvocalizer caused him too much pain, so we had decided he would do without. But it meant he couldn't notify us of anything when he saw it, not without using his voice.

I could tell he was whispering to whoever he was holding on to, and then Morgan's voice came on. *Viggo, there's something different in this tank back here. Tim wants you to come look at it.*

I exchanged a look with Violet, her eyes widening at mine through the clear panels of her gas mask, and then let go of her arm, moving carefully back down the line. Tim was bringing up the rear, and I saw him before I saw the tank. I was moving close to him when the mist suddenly parted, and I recoiled, unable to fully comprehend what I was looking at.

Fur that was coal black and deeply matted ran across the creature's huge, four-legged body. It sat like a dog, hunched over, the head and mouth wolf-like—but the tail was monkey-like, twitching as the creature stared at me through golden eyes. A pink tongue lolled out of its mouth, drool dripping in thick globs down to the floor of its cage, and its teeth were jagged and yellow.

It closed its mouth, the head cocking back and forth as it seemed to study me. Then a paw—scratch that, a *hand* came up and pressed against the glass. The palm of the hand was long, the bones between the joints in the fingers longer still, and the tips seemed curled. It studied me for a moment longer, seemingly waiting for me to do something, and then presented its back to me, shaking itself and then lying down on its belly.

"What that?" asked Tim, his eyes wide and alarmed.

I hesitated, and then shook my head. *I have no idea. I've never seen it before.*

The paws... Did you see that? Does that mean it can open doors and... use weapons?

I looked over at Morgan, and shook my head again in answer to her question. I was baffled. If this was a creature from The Green, it was one that neither I nor Alejandro had come across. There was a gleam of intelligence in its eyes that gave me pause, a predatory patience that made me wonder if there would be a way to kill the denizens of these tanks before they got out and got to us.

Viggo? Violet's voice was a welcome distraction from a conversation that was leaving me feeling a bit more nervous than before.

Yeah? I replied, turning to face the front, where her figure was now completely obscured behind the mist.

I think I'm hearing voices coming from ahead.

Alarm coursed through me, and I moved as quickly as I dared, following the line of people back and linking my arm through Violet's. I strained my ears, and I could definitely hear... something. It was barely discernable, but certainly human in origin—comforting, in this environment, but only slightly.

I pressed forward, following the sound, and soon it became clearer. It was difficult to tell their gender; their voices were intentionally pitched low, in an effort to disguise their location, but that probably meant they couldn't hear each other well, either. Avoiding that issue was half the reason we'd brought the subvocalizers. Slipping my arm out of Violet's, I moved forward a few steps and shut off my flashlight, following the voices.

Stay there for a minute, I ordered the team. The mist roiled as I drew nearer, and as I pushed through it, I almost impacted with the cave wall. In the dimness I could see a narrow passage, much like the one separating the two chambers we'd just come from, cutting into the wall a few feet away, the voices echoing from within it. I leaned my back against the left side of the wall and began easing myself around the corner and down the passage, picking up each foot deliberately, trying to make sure I didn't give away my presence.

After a few seconds, I was finally able to discern actual words among the echoing sounds of the conversation carrying through the mist.

"I'm really not sure this is the right data chip, sir."

"Keep trying. One of the ones we stole from that… Tyler fellow has got to work." I froze when I recognized that voice, an icy stab of rage cutting through my gut.

"His name is Thomas, sir."

"I don't care what his name is, I'm ordering you to open the door!"

"Trying, sir."

Maxen and whoever was with him fell silent, and I heard the sound of footsteps echoing through the chamber. At first I thought they were heading toward me, and I drew back, keeping my gun at the ready. But then I realized the moving person was pacing the confines of the chamber they were in. I pushed forward again and looked around the corner, risking a glance inside.

The mist seemed to be thinner in there, almost non-existent, and I spotted Maxen, Mark Travers, two of the other Patrian wardens, and… Peter of the Porteque gang. He was flanked by two of his men, and I could pick out the triangle tattoos displayed proudly on all three of their faces.

Mark knelt on the floor in front of an airlock door, fiddling around with the keypad, while Maxen impatiently paced the cavern floor.

We've got a problem, I transmitted to my team as I pushed back, moving away from the area as quietly as I could. *Maxen and Peter and some of their men are in the chamber in front of us. They're trying to use one of Thomas' stolen data chips to get in.*

What? Thomas exclaimed, his alarm coming clearly through the subvocalizer, and the mist broke enough for me to see him working away at his handheld. *That's insane. They can't just stick random data chips in it and see if it'll work. They'll set off the alarms!*

As though his words had been the cue, a klaxon alarm began screaming out overhead, loud enough for me to clap my hands over my ears and frantically search for the source of the sound so I could silence it.

You had to say it, Amber muttered through the link. There was a howling snarl from behind us, and I pushed Violet ahead.

Thomas, Violet, Owen, get in that cavern and get that door open, I ordered as I moved back down the line. *Try to disarm them if you can, but there might not be time. Priority is the door. Tim and Ms. Dale, you're with me.* Tim and Ms. Dale stayed behind as everyone surged forward.

I heard Violet's voice, her subvocalizer turned off, ringing out in the cavern, ordering Maxen to stand aside and let them open the door.

And then one of the monkey-like creatures bounded out of the mist, heading right for me. It happened so fast that I almost tripped in my mad scramble to get away, and Ms. Dale and Tim both opened fire at it. It soared over me, missing me by inches, and landed behind me, its black body quickly turning back around. I didn't know how it had gotten out—but I had a sinking feeling that whatever chip Mark had inserted into that door, it had done more than set off a klaxon alarm.

The beast lifted its lip, revealing the jagged teeth again, and I fired right at its head. I expected it to drop—I'd hit it right between the eyes—but it just looked at me, long tail twitching. We were frozen for a long moment, staring at each other. Then it surged forward, teeth snapping. I rapidly backed away, looking for something—anything—I could use to kill this thing. And suddenly Tim raced between us.

He tossed something dark from his hand, and the wolf creature's tail snatched it out of the air. For a heartbeat, I thought it was going to throw it back, but then it opened its mouth and snapped it up, swallowing it whole. Tim seamlessly adjusted his trajectory, spinning around and coming right back for me. He tackled me just as the creature's head exploded with a loud, messy bang that reverberated through the caves. I landed hard on my back, the breath coming out of me in a giant whoosh.

I panted, and then gently pushed Tim off of me and stood up, looking at the bloody mess that was all that remained of the creature's body and trying to shake the ringing out of my ears. I looked down and realized I was covered in blood and charred bits of the creature. I grimaced.

How'd you think of that? I asked, and Violet's brother shrugged.

"Someone feeds… it catches."

I chuckled, and reached over to rest my hand against his shoulder. *Thank you.*

Save your thanks, Owen said. *Door's open and creatures are getting out in the lab. Move it.*

Ms. Dale, Tim, and I exchanged a three-way look as a long howl sounded from behind us, just close enough to a human wail to make the hairs on the back of my neck stand up. A chorus of similarly eerie howls joined it, making a bizarre harmony, and we took off down the corridor, following it around as it curved. The tunnel ended in the small chamber I'd first seen Maxen in, barely five feet across, with a door just off-set from the tunnel on the right.

It hung open, Owen with his hand on the inside wheel, urging us in. Inside, Morgan, Amber, Vox, and Violet had all their various weapons trained on Maxen and his team, while Thomas was fumbling with his gear, clearly the one responsible for the open door.

I got inside first and immediately turned to help Owen close the door. Tim slid in after me, followed closely by Ms. Dale, and I heard the sound of teeth clacking together as something tried to get her by her ankle, narrowly missing. Owen and I heaved, and between the two of us, the door swung quickly inward.

Something made for the gap, trying to find its way in, but got caught in between the door and the wall. There was a yelp, like a child's shriek, as the door bounced back outward a few inches, and then Owen and I slammed it shut, spinning the handle as fast as we could and sealing all of us in. The door thudded violently, jerking slightly in the frame, and

Owen took a slow step back.

The room immediately began to decompress, but over the hiss of the air I could hear whatever was on the other side slamming against the door, trying to get in. The door began to shudder near the hinges that held it together—it was clear that the creature was targeting the weakest part of the door. *How would it know to do that?* I wondered, alarm racing all over my body.

"Open the door," Violet loudly ordered Maxen and his group as the hissing sound of the pressure equalizing died down, and I heard the hand wheel of the opposite door spinning as the group opened it up. Everyone stepped through quickly, and Owen and I brought up the rear, swiftly closing the interior hatch door and sealing it.

One thing was immediately apparent: the air here was clear. No sign of the cloying mist. I ripped off my mask and sucked in a deep breath of air, and then switched off my subvocalizer and nodded to everyone.

"Air's clear, but keep an eye out for dangers in this room."

Then I stared head-on at Maxen, never taking my eyes from his face as he slowly took off his mask, my hand curling into an involuntary fist.

"What the hell are you doing here?" I demanded.

CHAPTER 31

Violet

I tore off my mask with one hand but kept my gun pointed at Maxen. We were in some sort of monitoring station—screens hung around the ceiling in long rows, but right now they were dark. A series of desks made a circle in the middle of the room, terminals placed inside the tiny cubicles that separated workstations. The terminals were also dead, but Thomas was fiddling with one, unscrewing the back and plugging something in. Unlike the last room, this room had not two, but three airlock doors—the one we had just come through, and two others. Those two were located on the opposite side of the room from the entry door, approximately to the left and right of its position, angled to match the walls.

The king still held his own weapon. There hadn't been time to disarm his group, with the sounds coming from behind us in the tunnel. I was pretty certain both groups were too scared to think about anything but getting through that door.

Luckily we had caught them unawares, so only Maxen and Peter had their weapons readied. Everyone else's were holstered or tucked behind their backs. They were smart enough to realize they wouldn't get to their guns before the shooting began. And we would go for the armed ones first—which included the king.

Who was currently glaring daggers at my husband.

"What the hell we are doing here," the king pronounced, "is the same thing that you're doing. Taking down Elena. Taking control. Getting rid of the monsters."

Viggo's voice came out as a growl.

"That's not what this is about," he said. "We're here to take a criminal to trial for committing crimes against humanity and end this war. And I suggest you get out of the way before you get hurt. I'm not going to harm you unless I absolutely have to—but Elena, her wardens, and the creatures inside these labs will have no such qualms."

I had to hand it to Viggo. Even furious and in such a compromising situation, he hadn't lost his sense of justice. I was already biting back threats to the king of Patrus. I'd been done with his arrogance, terrible decision-making, and selfishness for a long time, and now the temptation to just shoot him was stronger than ever. But that wasn't how we had chosen to go about this fight.

King Maxen looked back and forth between his group of men and Viggo. He still hadn't put down his weapon, and he raised the gun now, as though to point casually at my husband.

"Mr. Croft, I think your days of threatening your king are over. It's your group who should stand down and let the real authority take care of things."

I couldn't hold my tongue at that one.

"You lost any authority you had the day you used women and children as human shields," I snapped, twitching my gun to remind him that I already had a bead on him. "Put the gun down, Maxen."

"Your group would be nowhere without us anyway," Viggo said. "You wouldn't have found this place without stealing intelligence from us. Your group doesn't know all the facts, and you don't have what it takes to finish this mission safely. You need to leave now, before more people die."

"Thanks for all your help, by the way," Peter said, speaking for the first time, his voice just as arrogant and needling as I remembered it. We'd tangled with this man before, and he'd been left with the very raw end of the deal. I knew that incident was still in his mind as he eyed me, and it was going to make this encounter even harder than it already was. "Without your careful planning we never could have gotten into this place. All we had to do was take a boat across the river and wait for you guys to start causing chaos. We were able to drive through this precious little city without any of the... sweet ladies noticing at all. Oh, and that program your beta male made? Great. It's too bad none of you thought to use it to its full potential."

I heard Thomas take in a sharp breath as it was clear that Peter was mentioning him, and let my eyes flick to the side, where I saw the rest of our group. Owen took a careful step away from Morgan, into the shadows, his face thunderous. I realized what he was going to do in a moment—and I had to assume that Viggo knew, too.

"His name is Thomas," I snapped, putting the full weight of my anger into my voice and willing them to look only at me. "And he's a genius, so you'd better be respectful. Now put down your weapons—"

"And we'll let you get out of these caves while you still can," Viggo finished the sentence.

Indecision flickered in King Maxen's eyes, but Peter's voice made it die out.

"No way in hell. We're not going to let you replace one psycho bitch with another." He raised his own weapon, and I saw the barrel aimed straight at me.

If Viggo's presence had been dominating the conversation before, now it seemed as though his voice filled the room.

"Reconsider where you're pointing that gun," he growled. "You're pointing it at my wife."

"So you married her?" Peter scoffed, shooting me a lecherous look. "Did you have an enjoyable honeymoon? Is there a chance she could be pregnant?"

I felt my face flush and a wave of sheer rage crash through me. Viggo's voice snapped out like a whip.

"Don't you dare talk about her like that!"

A smirk spread across Peter's face—but before he could speak, Owen appeared behind him, his fist in mid-swing. The Patrian crew all jumped, twitching toward Owen, and I seized the opportunity. I lunged forward and spun, lashing out with my foot, catching the king's hand and knocking his gun from his fingers.

I completed the spin in time to see Peter crumble, Owen standing over him, shaking out his hand, his face businesslike and hard. Peter landed in a pile on the ground, groaning softly, and Maxen scrambled across the floor, trying to open the door behind him—the one on the left.

"Don't," I said, the sharp edge of warning in my voice, and he stopped, looking at me. "We don't know what's on the other side of that door."

The king immediately let go of the wheel and turned around, scowling at me. Like a true coward, however, he turned and began yelling at his wardens rather than addressing me directly.

"How could you just let them get the drop on us? I'm your king! It's your duty to keep me safe!"

Mark, Viggo's former second in command, turned away and looked at us.

"We have this handled," he stated flatly. "And the king needs his weapon if he's going to survive in this place."

He stooped over to pick it up, and Owen reached over the clearly dazed Peter to grab his arm. His face was filled with warning, eyes flashing with violence.

"Don't do it."

"What are *you* doing here, Mark?" Viggo asked, taking a step forward, his voice softer now, almost concerned. Mark shot him an angry look.

"The same thing you should be doing," he retorted, pulling his arm out of Owen's and taking a step back. "Following our king's orders."

"Mark..." Viggo said, trailing off, clearly at a loss for words.

Viggo, I'm in the system. Thomas' voice only buzzed in our ears, and as one, we turned to look at him. Mark's eyes flipped between us, unable to hear what we were saying but watching our attention move. Thomas continued to speak, his mouth moving but producing no sound, except in our earbuds. *This is a really good system. Really good. Like... it shouldn't even be in this antiquated terminal, sort of good.*

Tell me something worth knowing, Thomas. I realized Viggo had turned his subvocalizer back on. Mark stared at him a moment, watching his mouth move, a scowl twisting his features.

"What are you doing?"

"None of your business," I said. "Stay quiet until we decide what to do with you." The man glared at me, but didn't say anything else.

While Viggo and Thomas talked between themselves, I kept a close eye on Maxen and his group. Peter groaned loudly again, and Owen took a step back. Thomas continued to speak as if he hadn't noticed the tension in the room.

Well, I've found an itemized species list, he said. *The next room is a botanical one, attached through a long tunnel to something containing...* He paused, looking at a list. *Some sort of spider species, and centipedes.*

I shuddered at the thought of centipedes, my skin already beginning to crawl from the feeling of a thousand phantom legs running over me. Panic almost swallowed me right there, the sensation was so real in my mind, but I managed to refrain from dropping my gun and batting at myself. I still had nightmares about getting bitten or being buried alive in dirt that turned into thousands of wriggling bodies.

Violet, Ms. Dale's voice came through the subvocalizer, and I jerked my mind from the dark place it had gone. *While Viggo is busy, let's start tying the king's group up. Make them go to the corner of the room—we can leave them here if we have to.*

Following her cue, the rest of our group advanced on the king and his men, all our weapons trained on them. I spoke for our side, knowing that most of my companions' subvocalizers were still on.

"All right, guys, you're going to move to the corner of the room. We don't want you to have to get hurt."

Dammit, Thomas said, as the group of them begrudgingly began to shuffle toward the corner.

What is it? Ms. Dale demanded.

I can't get control of their system, he replied. *This system is flawless. Apparently there's a master computer in one of these workstations located closer to the palace, and that's the one we would have to use to take control. There's nothing I can do about—*

He stopped as the screen went dark. A second later, Elena's smiling face filled it, and a pang of fear shot through my gut.

"Attention, intruders. Perhaps you felt as clever as a cat stalking a mouse in a cellar, confident of your dinner for the evening, but allow me to twist this little scenario for you and invite *you* to be the dinner."

The screen turned off, and I heard the sound of all of the airlocks hissing, as the light on the inside began to flash yellow. The wheels began to turn without the aid of human hands, and I shoved my gun into my pocket, suddenly unable to worry about the king and his crew.

"Masks!" I shouted, and pulled my mask out from under my arm, fumbling with the straps but managing to get it on.

The moment our guns were no longer trained on them, the group of wardens scattered, picking up weapons and grabbing gas masks from where they had set them down. Mark scrambled forward, and before I could do a thing about it, he'd snatched up his gun and handed it to Maxen, helping the king pull his mask on before pulling his own on over his face.

"We have to run!" the king shouted through his mask, clearly in a panic, and for a bare moment I felt relief that they were clearly too worried about the escalating situation to be able to try to win back control of the room from us.

"No—Mark—stay here," Viggo pleaded his former comrade, abandoning his argument with the other man. "We're safer in numbers."

"You don't get a say," Mark said frostily. "We are following the king. If you'd like to remember your duties and join us, by all means do so, but—"

"Line up at both doors and try to keep anything from getting through them!" Ms. Dale shouted, her voice ringing loud in our ears, interrupting Mark and pulling her rifle out while adjusting the strap over her shoulder. "No need for silence now."

I slid my pistol into the holster and drew my rifle around my body, moving to a spot between the two doors so I could turn and fire easily. The outer set of doors hadn't opened yet—the wheel was still spinning, slowly enough to let the fear within my gut blossom into terror that I held at bay with action.

I dropped down to a knee, and within seconds Mark and the other wardens were moving over to me, temporarily accepting our truce, taking up positions in front of the left door, while Tim, Amber, and Logan took up positions at the right. Maxen slipped around us until he was behind me, but as I turned, I saw Thomas pointing a gun at him, waving him back toward the line. He frowned, and then moved next to Mark. Viggo, Owen, and Ms. Dale stationed themselves at the other door, with Thomas lurking in between the three groups—all of us with pistols drawn.

The outer doors started to swing open, my eyes snapping to them, and I pulled the stock of the gun up to my shoulder, bracing myself. Viggo and the others did the same, and as the doors opened fully, mist curling out of them, I held my breath, waiting hopelessly for something—anything—to stop them.

I heard Viggo shout in warning and turned, seeing a flash of something silver, and Viggo opened fire as a silver python slid in from the door behind us. I noticed the fat lump squirming within its belly, just a few feet under its head—likely this was the monkey creature that had been in pursuit of us—and a nauseated feeling grew in my stomach as the people defending that side of the room pelted the creature with bullets. Its body jerked as Viggo fired, and then everyone on that side was firing into the wide-open door. I returned my gaze to the other doors, searching for movement in the tunnels ahead and finding none.

A quick glance at Viggo showed me that Ms. Dale's plan was working. Already the bodies of pythons littered the floor, silver coils blocking parts of the entrances. Owen tossed something out the door, and an explosion followed. I looked back toward my door. It was still clear.

"Viggo," I shouted. "This door is clear. We should start falling back to—"

Something detached from the ceiling on the right and swung in, landing in a crouch in the area between the two lines and coming up swinging. One of the Porteque men on the left caught the blow, and there was a sickening crunch—and then his body fell to the ground, the straight line of his neck interrupted by an obvious break. A young man wearing black pants, a black sweater, and a black balaclava mask twisted around to face us, his hands still in fists.

Elena had sent the boys to fight us.

Before I could even react, Maxen began firing at the boy, catching him in the shoulder and chest. He went down, and Maxen shouted, "Let's go!" before darting through the door on the left. The Porteque man closest to me started to turn toward me, bringing his gun around, and I shot him without hesitating, dropping him to the ground. Tim raced past me toward the fallen boy, moving to check his pulse.

The others began to follow Maxen just as something dark and huge exploded into the room on the other side, clawing its way over the body of a python with a hunting howl. The fear that sound sent through me was nothing, though, compared to something I almost felt before I heard—the sound of buzzing.

"Run!" Ms. Dale roared, and I saw her toss something at the monkey-wolf creature as Tim came to push me up, shouting for me to move. I didn't even catch a glimpse of which door we went through, just scrambled through the airlock, trying to avoid the explosion.

There was a loud bang as Ms. Dale's grenade went off. My ears rang from the force of it, and we all stumbled. I shook my head to clear it, climbing back to my feet and helping Tim up beside me. I moved over and did the same for Morgan, the haze that had drifted into the room through the open airlocks making it difficult to see anything. The buzzing grew louder.

"We have to go!" Morgan said, and she grabbed my hand, dragging me with her.

Then we were running, out and away through another cave, running from the buzzing of the red flies. They'd have plenty to feed on in that room with all the bodies, and I fervently hoped that would buy us a little bit of time, just enough for all of us to get out safely. I ran as fast as I had ever run, scanning wildly through the mist with my flashlight.

The ground was uneven, and I stumbled and stubbed my toes and should've fallen a dozen times—but somehow I was still up and moving. I drew to a sudden stop when I almost impacted with a wall, and took a few steps back, breathing heavily and listening for sounds to tell me what was happening and where the next door was.

Looking around, I gasped and almost dropped my flashlight when I saw Morgan appear suddenly out of the mist, my hand twitching for my gun. I could see her eyes darting around, looking for others, and I shook my head. I turned on my subvocalizer.

Viggo? I wheezed into the comm-link. There was a burst of static, and then nothing. I tried it again, several more times, each time growing a little more frantic.

"It's no use," Ms. Dale's voice came out loud as she approached, much like Morgan had—seemingly from nowhere—giving me the cut-off signal with her hands. "We're either being jammed or the rock is interfering with our signal. Either way, I haven't seen anyone else. Have you?"

I shook my head and straightened up, realizing I was shaking, though I didn't know whether it was from adrenaline or from rage.

"No. And Maxen shot that boy and got away. We need to—" I stopped as a shadow emerged from the mist behind Ms. Dale, my gun going up and firing a warning shot near it. The shadow shifted and quickly drew away as Ms. Dale whipped around, her gun raised.

For several moments everyone was still, waiting and watching. Then Morgan moved past us, slowly, pushing slightly into the mist. She stood very still for a second, and then turned.

"It's gone," she whispered, moving back toward us. "I think you scared it, but it can't last long. What were you saying?"

It took me a moment to remember what I had been saying. My heart was still pounding, and the adrenaline rush was making my skin tingle with alertness.

"That we need to find Maxen and get him off the playing field."

"Wrong," Ms. Dale said, shaking her head. "My first priority is to get to Elena. Let's stick to the plan." I rubbed my forehead.

"You're the primary for this mission," I said, and she nodded. We'd ranked everyone on the team from primary to tertiary, so in the event we got split up, those who were of the highest rank would take control over the others and lead them on the next part of the mission. It was to ensure that we had a backup plan, and that both of our objectives were achieved. "So this is team 'stop the queen.'"

Morgan swallowed. "We were all assigned to that mission anyway," she said, her face rueful, and Ms. Dale smiled wanly.

"What are the odds of that?"

"That we got separated right into our mission group… or that all three Matrian women are going after the queen?" I asked, and she blinked, and then gave a ghost of a smile.

"I didn't even consider that last part. I was going with the first."

"Well, my answer is, who cares?" I replied, shouldering my rifle. "We need to get moving. If we can, we need to find a way to get her down here and closer to us, where the playing field is less to her advantage."

Ms. Dale had opened her mouth to reply—then she seemed to spot something on the wall behind me, and moved toward it instead. The mist billowed and shifted around her as she moved, and I saw a cabinet on the lab wall, filled with several familiar canisters. She pulled them out, five in total, and passed two to me and two to Morgan, taking one for herself.

"Good times," I said when she handed it to me, unable to stop myself from thinking of the time Ms. Dale had taken me into The Green for training, before I entered Patrus. Ms. Dale smiled wryly.

"Good times, indeed," she replied. "Let's move. We don't have access to Thomas' map, and this place just got worlds more dangerous."

I nodded and began walking, keeping a hand against the wall and following it, trying not to jump at the various growls and sounds erupting all around us. Maybe, just maybe, we could get through this one unnoticed and unscathed.

CHAPTER 32

Viggo

When all hell broke loose and the buzzing started, my first thought was to chase Tim as he ran after Violet, leaping over the Porteque man she'd shot, my legs moving furiously. Then I caught a glimpse of Peter moving through the door on the left, and something took over—a snap decision, an instinct from deep within. All I knew was I couldn't leave that man running around the caves. He hated Violet, hated me, and he would hurt her to get to me. The thought of him and her ending up in this horrific place together after I'd let him pass by was unbearable.

The mist was dense, but I followed the dark shape of his shadow, my gun still in my hands, my feet pounding on the uneven ground. Without missing a single step, I ejected the magazine and slammed in a new one, continuing my pursuit. I kept his form in my sights through the swirling mist, but always felt one step behind.

Someone's scream lanced through the cave, and I paused, my ears straining. Sweat had accumulated on my brow. I wiped it off impatiently, my chest heaving. The scream stopped suddenly, and I heard growling and the wet snapping of teeth, but the sound was muted, seemingly coming from somewhere in the distance.

Licking my lips, I looked around, my listening hard for any sound of Peter's footsteps but finding none. I moved forward. I had been running for at least a minute, maybe closer to two, and I still hadn't hit the edge of this cavern. It must stretch out widely, and the lighting had changed to the soft blue of ultraviolet light, making the fog glow an eerie green.

I moved forward through the mist and stopped again when I heard a grunt, somewhere off to my left. I took another step forward, and then froze when I saw a dark orange vine cutting across the moss just inches from my left foot. My heart pounded as I slowly withdrew my foot to avoid contact with it, Alejandro's warnings ringing loudly in my ears. The orange vines were attached to a carnivorous plant, one that used the vines to ensnare prey.

"God, what *is* this?" somebody muttered, and I immediately recognized Peter's voice, a rush of cold rage going through me. I stepped over the vine and kept an eye out for any more. The mist swirled and spun as I stepped through it, and I waved a hand in the air, trying to get it to settle. It thinned some, and I could make out someone struggling a few feet away.

I stepped over another vine, keeping a healthy distance from it, and then I saw him. An orange vine was wrapped around his leg, steadily moving up to encircle his torso. The man was bent over, fiddling with his shoe, while the vine was already excreting slime that acted as a digestive juice. Eventually, according to Alejandro, the vine would drag Peter back toward the heart of the plant, where he would be deposited in a giant pod and left to be digested, the plant growing stronger as it fed on his remains.

As I watched, the vine flexed and grew tighter around the man's midsection, making him cry out in pain. The slime was covering his torso now, his clothes beginning to disintegrate. He continued to struggle, which only caused it to exude more digestive slime, and I hesitated.

This man was about to die, either by my bullet or the plant's slime, and for a long moment, I considered just walking away. It would be a painful, gruesome death, but one that he deserved. He was a monster who tormented women. Surely he deserved this. I should just walk away.

Yet as my conscience was decrying those dark, hideous voices crying out to leave him, he stood up victoriously, a satisfied smile on his face and a knife in his hand. Before I could even shout warning, he began cutting the vine.

You should never ever cut an orange vine, Alejandro had told me.

At first, nothing happened as he sawed into the fibrous vine, trying to cut it off.

"Stop," I said, stepping forward through the fog. Peter paused only for a moment, looking at me like he didn't even register my presence, before he began to cut deeper. The plant flexed under his hand, and white, milky liquid began to ooze from the cut. At first it only dripped, but as he sliced deeper, it sprayed out, catching him in the face.

Peter's skin erupted in burning blotches, and I could actually hear the sound of his flesh sizzling. The fiery rash spread rapidly down his neck, chest, and arms, and he opened his mouth to scream before collapsing on the ground in agony, his body jerking and flopping around as he tried to tear at his flesh.

Alejandro called it the "orange vine's revenge," but it was far more gruesome than it sounded. The liquid would burn through his skin, right through to his bones and vital organs.

I stared, the sight too hideous to turn away from, and then lifted up my gun, firing a shot and ending his thrashing. It turned out that I couldn't let him suffer after all, no matter how much he deserved it.

Turning away from his disintegrating corpse, I looked around, realizing two things. One, I had lost Violet—everybody—in the mist, and two, I didn't even have a map.

Violet? I said cautiously into the comms. There was a burst of static, followed by... nothing. I tried a few more times, tapping the comms, and then gave up. We were either being blocked or the walls were interfering.

I turned off the useless subvocalizer and slowly moved forward, searching for a wall. I kept a sharp eye out for orange vines, taking care to step over them. I was damned lucky that I hadn't come into contact with one while I was chasing Peter.

I was so preoccupied looking for a wall to orient myself and avoiding getting caught in the orange vines that I didn't notice the toe of a boot peeking through the mist until it was too late, and I slammed into the person on the other side of a thick curtain of mist. That person made a startled noise, and a shot rang out, almost right next to my ear, making my ears ring from the proximity.

"Thomas!" I shouted, and the flailing next to me stilled.

"Viggo?" he asked, squinting up at me from where I had knocked him to the ground. I quickly checked to make sure I hadn't pushed him into any vines, and then helped him stand upright.

"I'm sorry, I didn't know you were here."

"He is," came Owen's voice, and I saw a dark shape approach and then step through the mist as though parting a curtain. "So am I. The comms aren't working."

"I know," I replied, looking around at the group I'd found myself with and feeling glad we'd developed a contingency plan. "So it's time to move on to our backup plan. I wonder how Ms. Dale and Henrik knew there was a chance we were getting separated."

Thomas seemed not to notice my sarcasm. "The probability was too high to ignore," he said. I looked at Owen, amused, and he shrugged.

"Your mission is my mission?" he asked, and I smiled.

"Don't let my wife hear you say that. She might think we're in love," I quipped. "And yes… I think I'm the person with standing orders here, so you're following me."

"Please. *You* aren't my type either."

"My wounded heart," I said, then shook off the levity. "Ms. Dale isn't here, and I know she was going to cover the queen—so we're sticking with my mission. Find a way to stop the Matrians from controlling the boys."

"All right," replied Thomas. "But I also need to get to the terminal that controls the computer down here first. I have a program specifically for finding out where the highest traffic concerning transmissions is located."

"Well, let's get you to that terminal," said Owen, pulling out his compass and looking at it. "Where's the nearest door?"

Before either of us could answer, a growl reverberated in the room, trickling out slow and lethal. I motioned for silence, peering into the mist while Thomas looked at his handheld for the maps he had downloaded there, his focus unwavering as he searched for the nearest door. The mist roiled and moved, and I found myself despising these caves and the monsters inside. How shortsighted it had been for anyone to bring in creatures from The Green. If one got out, if it made its way into the palace… it could cause untold havoc.

Owen reached out and tapped me on the shoulder, and I turned to see him pointing toward Thomas' shadow, the smaller man having already gotten his bearings. I nodded and began to follow him, keeping my footsteps light and continuing to search the mist for any sign of our growler.

After a while, the mist began to thin, and we came to a tunnel that was completely free of the blasted stuff. We moved down it, and relief streamed through my chest when I saw the massive airlock door at the end of it—and this one was closed. Apparently Elena hadn't opened everything up in her mad gambit to rid herself of intruders.

Thomas knelt down and pulled out the same little box with the cables he had handed Owen earlier. I shone my light through the door's small window, while Owen took position by the tunnel entrance, keeping an eye out for anything trying to get through.

The room beyond was slightly wider than the last chamber with an airlock door, but the walls were smooth and worn. I continued to look around, searching for any sign of movement, and felt a prickle of alarm go up my spine. I had an uncanny feeling that I was being watched.

The instinct was too strong to ignore. I turned around to face the tunnel again, and tightened my grip on the handle of my gun. I lifted it and my flashlight higher. The light hit the mineral-rich wall, chasing away some of the shadows, and I panned it slowly left and right, starting closer to the bottom and moving up.

About six feet up, the light cut across the toe of a boot, casting a shadow behind it.

"Viggo?" Owen's voice was hushed from the other end of the tunnel, but it reached me as I slowly swung the flashlight farther up.

A leg came into view, covered in webbing, and I took a step back, my skin beginning to crawl. This caused the light to move up another foot or so, and three large arachnid legs—long, thin, and covered in coarse hair—came into view, draped over a man's chest.

I became aware of a soft scratching sound, and lifted my flashlight higher, to find the giant spider crouching over the man's face, its mandible tearing the flesh off in small rips and tears. A multitude of black eyes glittered from the top of the head, and it moved slightly, its fat, heavy body settling in place over its kill.

I fought back the urge to vomit, yanking my pistol up and firing round after silenced round. The bullets sank into the spider's fat body as easily as cutting butter. Its prey fell from its legs, and the spider dropped onto the floor, rolling onto its back with a thump, its legs curling up and twitching. Immediately I heard something rustling overhead.

"Viggo?"

Ignoring Owen, I pulled the flashlight up and over, trying to track the source of the noise, and found two more sacks hanging from the tunnel's walls—one with red organs already spilling out, but the other one moving under all those fine, delicate strands.

"Help me," I said as I hurried over to the cocoon, pulling my knife from my boot. I began to cut the webs away, but could only reach up halfway to the man's thigh due to the way he was hanging. Owen's knife moved on the other side, and then we grabbed his ankles and began pulling.

The silk was strong—frightfully so—but with our combined strength, we managed to wrest the still-living man away. We caught him, and I sat him down as he frantically reached up and began peeling the webbing from his face.

Maxen's blue eyes met mine as he peeled more of it off, and then he sucked in a deep breath, as if he had been suffocating, and began coughing.

"There's two," he wheezed, and I stepped back, redrawing my gun and looking around.

Owen caught my eye and wet his lips.

"Viggo, these are the spiders we harvest the silk from for the suits," he said, his voice low and steady. "They're normally quite shy, but if they're starving, they're deadly. We almost never discovered them or what their webbing could do, because—"

Something rippled into view behind Owen, and I fired without thinking, catching the spider with three bullets as it leapt through the air toward Owen. He flinched and ducked, turning back, and I heard him swallow audibly.

"They use it to hunt," he finished.

"I'm not going to die in here!" Maxen screamed, ripping his arms free and running for the airlock door. I had time to wish we'd left him in the cocoon before I looked up to see a wave of spiders—the smallest one the size of a ten- or eleven-year-old boy, the largest bigger than a horse—dangling from strands of silk attached to the ceiling, watching us. As soon as my light cut across them, they vibrated slightly, and the next thing I knew they had disappeared. I began blind firing at where some of them had been, and Owen stepped up next to me.

"HEY!" Thomas shouted.

I turned to see Maxen, who had pushed his way through the door Thomas had gotten open, and was now trying to slam it shut. Thomas was wedging his body into the opening, struggling against the king.

I moved to help when a spider fell on top of me, dropping me to the ground. Webbing, hot and slightly damp, began to shoot onto me from its backside. I struggled to bring my gun up, and then the creature went flying as Owen kicked it off of me and pulled me up. He gripped his rifle to fire a spray of bullets around the room, the sound reverberating loudly in the tunnel. As if the sounds had a physical effect, the spiders began to flicker in and out of visibility, the ones Owen caught in his spray falling dead to the floor or dangling ominously on their silk strands. The shots had obviously stunned them, but there were too many clinging to the walls. We needed to run.

"Damn you, MOVE!" Maxen roared, his shout punctuated by a deafening gunshot just as Owen's gun clicked empty, filling the room with silence. The spiders scattered for the moment, seeming to decide that there was too much noise. I turned and saw Thomas stumbling back a few steps, his breath coming in pants, as Maxen turned the air-lock wheel and sealed himself inside.

"Thomas!" Owen shouted, and Thomas shook his head, as if suddenly becoming aware of himself.

"Owen?" he called in confusion, slowly turning toward us. "Owen, I'm sorry. I tried to hold the door."

I fired at a spider as it materialized out of thin air behind Thomas, ejecting the clip as the creature curled to one side and died.

"*Thomas!*" Owen shouted in alarm, and I looked up from sliding in a new magazine to see the blood now soaking Thomas' abdomen, around a clearly visible wound, staining his clothing in seconds.

The little man looked down, his face morphing into an expression of surprise as his hands hovered just over the edges of the wound.

"Oh," he exclaimed softly. "He shot me." The words were so simplistic, so hollow, that I felt my alarm turn to full-blown panic as Thomas listed to one side, toppling over like a building being knocked down.

We both rushed toward him, but Owen managed to catch him before he hit, his hands cradling him and gently lowering him to the floor. Heartsick, I looked up through the door's window to see Maxen already pushing open the door into the next observation station and disappearing within. Then I turned back to the gloomy room, searching for any sign of the spiders.

CHAPTER 33

Tim

When Violet said to run, I ran, my legs pumping as I sprang over the body of the Porteque man. I wasn't sad to see him dead. I was angry—Maxen had killed one of my brothers. Again.

I wanted him dead so bad I could taste it, but I couldn't find him, even though I looked. I wasn't sure which door he'd run out of or whether I was going in the right direction, but it didn't stop me from looking. I ran and ran, skipping around obstacles that loomed out of the mist. Enhanced reflexes were awesome for avoiding bullets, but they didn't help me track people, and after a while, I realized I was alone.

I stopped and peered around the mist, looking around for any sign of life.

My hairs stood up on end, just in a small spot—on the side of my neck, low, almost where my neck met my shoulder. I followed my instinct and surged forward, easily avoiding the silver python's bite. I felt the snap of its jaws in a little pop of air behind me, pulled my gun, and fired a single round over my shoulder.

I heard the satisfying sound of a thump as the snake's body landed. I waited, and then began to run again, trying to think as I moved. I could feel rather than hear movement coming from my right, like something was trying to keep up, and from the soft slapping sounds of their feet, I realized it was those weird dog things.

Suddenly I missed Samuel. But he had bonded with the other children of the refugee camp, and I'd had to let him go. They needed him more than I did, and the field was no place for a dog. I just wished I'd had more time with him. I'd felt like we were in freefall ever since Violet had found me.

Violet. We had just found each other again, but now it was different. She was married now. I loved her, loved Viggo, but I knew that it meant it was time for me to move on. Be a grown up.

I just wished I knew how to do that. Did I have to find a girlfriend now? How would that work, with my skin always hurting, aching, burning? Clothes itched, no matter how soft they were, and the suit...

Stopping mid-motion wasn't easy, but I had perfect balance. All the time. I stopped, just as the black wolf-monkey went flying at my face, its teeth snapping as it slid by, missing my position by inches. I ducked its tail, and it smashed against the wall with a yelp. I stared at it, watching as it picked itself up, staring at me through those little yellow eyes the entire time.

It started forward, just as I'd known it would, and I charged it. Surprised, the thing took a few steps back, a growl of warning erupting viciously from its lips. There was... something in the mist behind it, and I feinted again, slowly pushing forward, driving the thing back a few more feet.

The python waiting in the mist snapped its jaws, catching the wolf-monkey around its midsection and lifting it up. The python shook it back and forth in its mouth, the wolf-monkey's legs kicking out as it whined, and then, with a gruesome crack, the smaller creature stopped moving.

I watched the snake lower it down to the ground and begin swallowing it, fascinated by the way it could open its mouth wide enough to engulf the creature whole, and then turned to begin running again.

I loved running. It filled me with a sense of freedom unparalleled.

When I had been trapped in that cell, I'd never been able to run. There was no room to move in that tiny, suffocating space. Running felt like freedom. Obstacles just made the experience more fun. I never knew where they were, but I was never afraid—I was too fast for them to slow me down, and I could use them to my advantage. I liked jumping over things, and flipping was amazing, but launching myself even higher in the air so it felt like I was flying… That was the best.

I needed to find Violet and Viggo, but as I ran, I began to realize the caves were too big. I stopped again, trying to pull my mind out of the pure joy of movement and think. I knew we had to get to Queen Elena… but we were also supposed to free my brothers. Both were important, both I wanted to do…

I stopped, not really to catch my breath, but to think. We'd known we could possibly get separated, so there were people whose parts of the mission were supposed to override others so that we could work with the groups we had. But I was alone. Did that mean I should keep at the mission originally given to me? Probably.

But I didn't even know where I was going in the caves—and other people had had the same mission as me. It was probably already getting done without me. I'd been on my own before, but then I was just taking care of myself. This time, I wanted to know what to do that would work best for the mission.

It wasn't the solution, but I found myself reaching for a little pocket in my sleeve, where a small envelope was tucked. Violet had given it to me before we'd gotten onto the heloship. She'd made me promise not to open it unless something horrible happened. Unless she got hurt or… or… I cut that thought off. I knew my sister wasn't dead. But I needed to open her letter now.

Reading was difficult for me. I had learned in the orphanage—Violet had helped me—but after I fell into the river and was taken to the facility, I hadn't been allowed to read. Well, there was nothing to read, really. Sometimes I wrote Violet's and my names into the window when the condensation got high, but that was pretty much the only chance I'd gotten to practice.

It took me several seconds to puzzle through the small script.

Dear Tim, it began. She didn't bother saying a bunch of things about what might have happened to her. I read through it, and though my hands never shook, I felt light and strange inside.

Among everything she'd written—and it was a lot—some phrases stood out to me:

I know we've only been back together for a short while, but it has been worth all the times I've searched and waited for you to have you back with me.

I've watched you grow so much since we rescued you from the Facility.

Viggo and I are married now, but that doesn't change my feelings for you one bit. You've always been my family, and you will always be my little brother. If something happens to me, Viggo will always be your family now, too.

I know you'll make the right choices.

I'm so proud of you.

It didn't help me with the mission, but it helped.

I looked back down at the note, and frowned when I saw a few letters printed facing me. I had folded it so the words would be inside, like wrapping them in a blanket. Curious, I unfolded it and realized there were words on the other side, too.

I love you, Tim, it read. A secret message within a secret message. I felt warmth growing inside me, even in this horrible place.

Refolding the paper and stuffing it back into the pocket of my suit, I took a few steps forward and then sidestepped the python that had been waiting for me to move for several minutes. I wasn't sure if its vision was bad or what, but as its jaws snapped closed on nothing, I leapt back over its coiled body, and then began to run again, trying to give it the slip.

I thought as I ran. Violet's letter hadn't changed the situation, but it had filled me with more confidence, like a hug from her—always worth it, even though it made my skin ache—or laughing and joking around with Jay. I would follow the mission I was given, unless I had to improvise.

It turned out to be a good decision. I found a passage and took it, the steady sound of the snake slithering behind me filling my ears. Then I rounded a corner and came to a sudden stop, regardless of the creature chasing me.

A group of boys were standing in the chamber, right in front of an airlock door, as though they had just come through. My brothers, wearing all black and horrible masks that covered their faces, making them into blank-faced soldiers.

Without thinking about it, I tensed my muscles and activated the suit.

Fire exploded over my skin, and I clenched my teeth together as I tried not to cry out. Now my hand did shake, uncontrollably—I could feel it, not see it—and I felt like I was going to die.

The serpent slid in beside me and then reared back, its head moving up in the air and hovering at least six feet over my own, seeking back and forth. Somehow I managed to take a few steps out of the way, and then the other boys swarmed it. Some of them leapt up in the air, while others went low. Two grabbed it and began pushing it back, their legs and arms straining against its muscular body.

One boy lashed out with his foot, kicking it in the jaw, while another pulled out a gun and began firing at its head. The snake started to coil around one of them, opening its mouth, when a fourth boy leapt up and, without apparent effort, thrust his fist right through one of the snake's beady red eyes. His arm disappeared into the eye, and the snake writhed back and forth as he jammed his arm even deeper. Then the beast started to fall. The boy leapt off of him, landing in a crouch, his arm soaked with blood. But he just stared at the snake, motionless, not even bothering to wipe the blood away.

I fought to breathe through the pain as the snake collapsed, trying to think about what I could do as the boys began standing up. I needed to get through that door to…

My legs were beginning to tremble from exertion. I paused, and, slowly, each movement adding more fuel to the fire burning across my skin, I reached into my pocket and pulled out the vial Dr. Tierney had given me.

Liquid to gas, she had said… Were those black masks that left only their eyes exposed gas masks, too? But they wore them all the time… even in Patrus. The greater visibility in this room meant that the toxic mist was much thinner here. Had Elena sent them into the caverns without any protection?

My whole body was shaking now—a sensation I hadn't felt since some of the tests I'd been given in the Facility—and I couldn't spend any more time contemplating. I could run if I needed to. Back into the mists.

Hoping it would work, I tossed the vial into the middle of the room, retreating. The glass broke, and several of the other boys turned toward the noise, converging on it. They raced to the spot, and then paused, their masked heads cocking back and forth. I had time to wonder whether Ms. Dale and Dr. Tierney had tested the serum, which was supposed to negate the effects of Benuxupane in the bloodstream within moments.

Those closest were the first to fall, but after a few moments, they had all collapsed.

I relaxed, letting the suit's cover disintegrate, and sucked in a deep breath of relief as the fire faded to a tingle, like a thousand pins and needles were using me as a pincushion. I shook out my arms and legs and proceeded to the middle of the room, first to check that each of the other boys was okay, and then, one by one, to take off their masks, removing the camera headset combinations underneath and breaking them apart. I recognized quite a few of them from our time in the Facility together. It filled me with feelings—some sad, some angry, some that I didn't have a name for—to see my brothers lying there, their faces weary and dirty. Maybe now they'd get a chance to rest and heal.

There were ten boys in total. Four of them were older than me, in their early twenties, at least. I supposed I should call them men. The six younger ones, however, were the first to start to wake up.

I stood in the center of the room, waiting as they slowly climbed up to their feet. Some of them were looking around, confused and bewildered, while others were rocking back and forth, shaking and crying as if they were in pain.

"Who are you?" Colin demanded, and I remembered him as one of the boys who had turned quickly on Viggo.

"Tim," I replied simply. "We brothers."

Colin sneered and looked around, squinting as though just waking up.

"How did you get us here, traitor?"

"Not traitor," I informed him. "I Tim. Your brother."

"No!" another voice shouted, and I turned to see a boy named Matthew pushing forward through the small group now standing up and milling around, his eyes dark and angry and confused. "You tried to hurt Desmond. She helps us! She gives us medicine so we—"

"She dead. And she lie."

Matthew flushed red, his hand balling into a fist, and I took a step forward, my gaze menacing.

"Queen using you," I announced in a low voice.

"No!" insisted Matthew, his face going red, and I took another step forward, crowding him.

"Desmond using you. She work for queen. You work for queen. She send down here—no gas mask. Danger. Queen don't care. You tool. Just like gun. You kill for queen. You die for queen."

"You're a liar," Colin screamed, and I felt his movement and turned, elbowing him in the jaw and knocking him down, the momentum of his charge at me carrying him a few feet away.

"How you get here?" I asked as he slowly picked himself up. "Where you one hour ago? Who you with? What you eat? Can you 'member?" More than anything, right now I wished I could talk as quickly and easily as the other boys, but the words… still weren't coming to me. I pushed the frustration deep down. My words would reach them. They had to.

Colin looked at me with anger as he slowly picked himself up, but Matthew was looking around the room in alarm.

"I don't remember," he said.

"Because Benuxupane," I told them. "Tamed you, make you like dog. We not dogs, we people, and we not slaves. I show you, we—"

Just then one of the older boys sat up, so suddenly it was like someone had put a coin in him to play music, like the jukebox I'd seen once—a long, long time ago, before Violet had tried to smuggle me to Patrus. The young man's head jerked around the room, and his gaze landed on us. He stared for a moment, his expression shifting from blank to very angry, and I took a step away from him as he climbed to his feet, his breath coming in long, slow growls.

"We help you," I said, but the growl grew louder and he simply swung at me. It was easy to dodge him, and he stumbled past me, clutching his head and moaning... but the four other older boys on the ground were getting up in a similar fashion. Slowly, their eyes clouded with pain and anger.

I knew then that I wouldn't be able to convince those boys... those men. I could see in their eyes that they just wanted to hurt everyone around them. Just like the wardens at the water treatment plant. I looked around at the younger boys, who were also gazing on their fellows with confusion and panic, and shouted, "That way!"

Then I planted my feet and turned. I could buy them time to run away. I sidestepped an incoming blow and landed a kick to the closest one's shoulder, knocking him to his knee, his hand coming down to stop him from toppling over.

Jumping up, I stepped on his back and spun off it, extending my leg. A shudder ran up my leg, letting me know I had hit my target, and I landed on my feet. The second boy was down, grabbing his jaw. The third boy grabbed me—too much was happening at the same time for me to react to everything—and I gritted my teeth as I felt his grasp through my suit, trying not to scream in pain as his hand tightened around my arm, making it feel like someone was dragging a knife across my skin.

My free arm snapped out and I poked him in the eye, a sharp jab, and he dropped my arm, screaming and grabbing for his face. I couldn't even feel relief for a moment as the fourth man stepped around him. I expected him to punch at me, but felt his leg move like a brushing against my skin. I dove and rolled over the leg sweep he performed, my back erupting in agony as I rolled across the floor and back onto my feet, heading after the boys where they had moved down the tunnel.

Keeping up with them was easy. They were shouting to each other loudly and in a panic as they moved, and I followed their voices.

"Don't go in mist!" I shouted ahead to them. "Dangerous! You hurt!"

Roars erupted from behind me as I ran, and I picked up the pace. The wall and voices ahead continued to curve around, and eventually led to another tunnel, which forked. On one side I could see a gathering of creeping mist as it went down, and the other fork seemed to rise out of it. I hoped the younger boys had taken my advice.

Listening for the roars coming down the tunnel behind me, I steeled myself and went invisible one more time, biting my lip as the pain and the tremors came back, worse than before. I crouched down, my legs already burning, and fumbled on the tunnel floor for a rock. Or a dirt clod. Or a shoe. Anything.

The pounding footsteps of the older boys came closer, then closer still. I tried to feel where they were even through the ache burning over my skin—the timing needed to be perfect...

I wasn't sure it was perfect, but I was improvising. When the noises reached a critical level, I threw the dirt clod in my hand down the misty fork of the tunnel, aiming for the walls. It made a loud clattering noise just as the berserkers rounded the corner—and I saw them all turn, like animals seeking prey, and take off after the noise.

I didn't wait to see if they would turn around. I took the other tunnel, relaxing my body out of invisibility and letting out a shaky breath. I followed it through to another airlock, where I was relieved to find the younger boys standing in a confused huddle. Far behind us now, a few roars sounded, faded and muted, and didn't grow louder. I hoped that whatever was in the toxic mist would knock them out or drive them away soon... rather than killing them. But there was nothing I could do about that now. We had to fix things to keep more people from being hurt. I tried to focus on that.

"I trick them," I said shakily to the younger boys. "Us—quiet. Don't know if they come back."

They all looked cautiously up at me, seeming to take things in.

"You stayed behind," Matthew said softly, and I shrugged.

"You brothers. Keep safe."

Matthew and Colin exchanged looks and then turned away, gathering the other four boys into a small circle. I heard them whispering furiously amid their huddled group, and felt a nervous tremor run through me, knowing there was nothing I could do about it. It was up to them whether or not they'd trust me.

The whispering died down after a short time, and they turned to look at me.

"Can you prove it? About the medicine and Desmond?"

"Now?" I asked, and they nodded solemnly. I shook my head. "No data chip. But... you help me. I show you queen using you. If wrong, you kill me. Deal?"

Matthew and Colin exchanged looks, and then looked around at the other boys. After a moment, they nodded.

"Deal."

My smile grew, and I nodded approvingly. "Good. Now... who open door?"

Colin looked around and then moved over to the door, taking a moment to shake his shoulders before placing his fingers against the door's lipped overhang. I studied this for a moment, and then shook my head.

"Wait," I said, walking near to him, remembering how those monkey things had gone after the door. I moved him over to the other side of the door and pointed at the hinge. "Pull out here—weakest part of door."

Colin examined it, and then nodded, and several of the other boys raced over to help as he began to pull and strain, trying to remove the hinge. On the other side we'd have to punch through, but it wouldn't be so hard with all of us working together.

All I could think was that Violet was going to be very surprised when she saw how we were going to help her take the palace.

CHAPTER 34

Violet

Ms. Dale led the way, her flashlight barely cutting through the mist. I moved behind her, gun drawn and ready to fight, but it seemed everything had died down a bit since the earlier frenzy. Still, I knew now what was lurking in these caverns, and it didn't set my mind at ease. And the mist certainly wasn't helping. Maybe the horrible creatures we had seen and heard weren't chasing us because they had our teammates cornered somewhere and… I shut the thought down. There was no way of knowing. We had to keep to the plan.

We eventually found one of the long, thin tunnels that connected caverns and often led to airlock chambers. It did indeed lead to an airlock door, and I stared at it, realizing that without Thomas, we couldn't get through it.

"We should head back," I said. "We might have these orders, but—"

"I've got it," Ms. Dale said, unfastening a pocket on her sleeve and pulling out a data chip. "Thomas gave it to me. It's a crude hack, according to him, but now that Elena knows someone's here, we can only be stealthy for so long."

I frowned and watched as she knelt down, plugging the chip into the port.

"Why would Thomas give that to you?" I asked.

She looked over her shoulder at me and sighed, turning back to the door. Blue lines were pulsing on the data chip, and she stood up and crossed her arms over her chest, watching it.

"Thomas and I had a very frank discussion before we left for this mission," she announced softly. "You know that we… developed contingencies."

"I know that," I said, narrowing my eyes. "Unless… Were there other contingencies, not just the ones that we all discussed? Why? What for?"

"Keep your voices down," Morgan whispered, and I turned to see her at the entrance of the tunnel, peering out into the mist, her posture alert and wary.

"Sorry," I said, lowering my voice. "That still doesn't change my question."

"Violet…" Ms. Dale said, her voice tired. "We didn't want anyone to be unduly concerned. We just figured when things went wrong, we'd need to control where the pieces landed."

"What were you expecting to go wrong?" I asked, but I was afraid to know the answer.

Ms. Dale looked at me, and then smiled.

"I'm proud of you. You know that, right?"

I blinked at her, baffled by the way the conversation had shifted. It unbalanced me.

"No," I said, deciding to turn into the skid. "But what does that have to do with anything?"

"Violet, you were one of my best students. You trained harder than the rest, had more fire and determination in your eyes, and I knew that you would be a great warden one day. But the girl who stands before me makes the Violet I trained pale in comparison. You're fierce, yes, but more than that—you care. You care so much and so deeply that sometimes I hurt for you, knowing the burden that rests on your shoulders."

She paused, and I could tell she wasn't finished, so I waited.

"I promised myself that I would do everything in my power to keep you and Viggo safe. So that when this was all over, you and he could be together, in love. In order to keep that promise, I realized the odds of your survival were far greater apart than together."

I was taken aback by her words, but it still didn't make sense to me.

"What does that have to do with anything? Viggo and I are a great team." I'd assumed that she and Henrik had asked us each to do separate parts of the mission because of our specific skills—not because of some secret strategy discussion about us endangering each other.

Ms. Dale ignored the question as she moved around me, and I turned and realized the data chip was now glowing a bright green, a four-digit code in the door glowing. She hit a button, and then began turning the wheel.

"That's very true," she said. "But the chances of us surviving and accomplishing our mission also dictated that you needed to be separated."

"I know that," I grated. "There's no reason to be secretive about that. But you're acting like… You're acting like you guys planned for one of us to *die*. Without talking to the rest of us."

She pulled the door open and called to Morgan, and I stepped into the airlock, feeling a bit dazed. Morgan stepped in behind me, and Ms. Dale came around the door, tucking the data chip back into her sleeve.

"We had to consider possibilities, Violet," she said evenly, but her eyes only met mine for a moment. "I know I should apologize for not being straightforward with you both." I turned around as she talked and grabbed the hand wheel, pulling the door closed to seal us in. "I considered it for a long time. But with your marriage… Thomas said newlyweds were thirty-two percent more likely to sacrifice their own lives for each other, and predicted you and Viggo were actually at a higher percentage of doing so, as if all of us didn't know that already. But he had a—OW!"

My head snapped up to see Ms. Dale slapping her forearm. The door was still a few inches open, and as she pulled away her hand, I saw the crushed body of a green fly pressed against her suit. She shook her arm, dislodging the body, and then quickly pulled the door shut, sealing us in.

Immediately, all thoughts of annoyance at Ms. Dale for withholding her reasoning from us fled my mind.

"Let me look at it," I said, but she brushed by me and hit the button on the door, pressurizing the airlock.

"Let's get inside first," she said, her voice unconcerned as she stared at the blinking red light on the door. As soon as it turned green, she was rotating the wheel and moving inside the darkened lab.

I quickly moved in behind her, checking the room for any sign of movement and finding none. The small room was constructed similarly to the last one—workstations in the middle, forming a circle, screens lining the outer walls. There was only one door this time, still sealed. Pulling off my bag, I opened it and began searching the contents for my first-aid kit. I pulled the egg out and sat it on a workstation. It was so cumbersome, things had a tendency to drop under it.

Ms. Dale rolled up the sleeve of her uniform, a knife already clenched between her teeth. The bite mark was visibly red and swollen, and Ms. Dale, barely flinching, ran the knife over the top of it, opening it up. Immediately a thick yellow pus ran from the wound, tinged red with blood, and I felt an urge to gag as I watched it.

"That's never a good sign," Ms. Dale muttered as she grabbed the kit from my hand and opened it up.

"You know, I couldn't be certain the intruders down below were you, especially after Maxen gave that delightful little speech about coming to take me down. And you were so clever about overcoming the locks and the cameras that I never would've known... until this last one, that is. It was forced open in such a hurry that the cameras were overlooked. And imagine my surprise to see you, my dear annoying Violet."

A chill ran down my spine as I heard Elena's voice, and I turned, feeling considerably exposed for such a small room. Morgan reached out and touched my shoulder, and I turned to see one of the workstation screens lit up with Elena's face looking out expectantly, a cruel smile playing on her lips.

"Elena? Can you hear me?" I asked, taking a moment to steel myself before moving in front of the screen. I looked over at Ms. Dale, and she nodded, mouthing the words "keep her busy" at me as Morgan cleaned her bite wound.

"I can indeed." She smiled, her teeth gleaming unnaturally white on the bright screen. "Are you alone?"

I considered lying, but then realized that she must've seen us in the airlock. Were there cameras in this room?

"I'm with Ms. Dale and Morgan."

"I saw that you brought Morgana. Come to seek revenge, little sister? Kill Ms. Dale and Violet, and I'll let you come back home. I'll even let you see Sierra."

Morgan gave me a look, her face reflecting how repugnant she found that idea, and I smirked.

"She can't come to the terminal right now," I said sweetly. "I'll give her your message."

Elena's smile grew wider. "Is that all of you?"

"It is. Viggo is back home trying to stop the boys from killing everyone."

"Liar," she replied, and the screen changed, showing me a picture of Viggo and Owen battling against something to close the door, while Thomas lay on the ground behind them, his hands on his stomach, as if he'd been shot. They'd just managed to shut the door when the screen cut out, and Elena was back.

"Where are they?" I asked, unable to stop the cold swoop of terror that had sunk into my stomach at the image.

"Oh, Violet, like I'd ever tell you that."

Ms. Dale waved her hand at me, and I looked at her. She pointed two fingers at her eyes and then pointed up toward the ceiling, and I nodded at her.

"So, uh… Does this mean you're watching us right now?" I asked, letting out a breath through my teeth, my terror turning into anger. I made a crude gesture with my finger and held it up to the screen.

"I am," Elena replied smoothly, without even a quirk of her lips. If she knew what my middle finger was doing, she gave no sign of it—and I'd tangled with Elena enough at this point that I knew she wasn't expressionless. I would take a gamble on the fact that she couldn't see me. In fact, I was already doing it. I felt a cold smile come across my mouth and nodded silently at Ms. Dale, giving her a thumbs-up. She hopped on top of a workstation and pressed the tip of her knife into a screw holding one of the roofing vents in place. I sighed when I realized where we were going next, and turned back to distracting Elena.

"I showed you that so you can understand something. I hold the cards—at any moment, I could open the doors to the observation lab you're in, or he's in, if I wanted to. I could come to you, if I wanted to. You are finally at my mercy, and it is very tempting to open all the doors inside and let the specimens eat you. But honestly, I do so love this idea the best."

As she spoke, Viggo, Thomas, and Owen flashed onto the view screen again. The two men were hunched over Thomas, frantically trying to stem the flow of blood that I could now see seeping out from Thomas' stomach. There was no sound, but Thomas' mouth was moving, as was Owen's. Thomas was wide-eyed and scared—I could see it plainly on the screen—his hands shaking as he tried to say something to Owen. My heart began to rebel in my chest, and the cold sensation in my stomach was back... I had almost thought Elena was playing that video to trick me, but this... This felt real. I felt tears forming in my eyes and prayed that Thomas was okay, that Viggo and Owen would patch him up and get him out of there.

As if she knew my thought, Elena continued to talk as the video played.

"I'm going to make you watch your friends die one by one, Violet. First Thomas, then poor Ms. Dale. She won't be long for this world—not after that green fly bit her."

"Is there an antidote?" I asked, looking over to where Ms. Dale was handing the now freed grate to Morgan. She looked over at me, and I gave her a thumbs up, motioning for her to head up.

"Oh, Violet," Elena breathed wistfully, an amused smile on her lips.

"There is, and I do have some. But you? You have nothing I want."

"I wouldn't say that," I said. "Because I have the egg. The real one. Right here with me at this very moment."

"You're a liar," Elena said confidently. "Eyewitness reports said you blew it up with my sister."

I smiled. It was unfortunate Elena couldn't see it, all my rage and worry for Thomas' wound, from being stuck here negotiating in this lab of horrors, scrolling across my face at once.

"There were two." I bit out. "One was the first prototype in Mr. Jenks' lab in the Facility. The second was the real one. I gave your sister Tabitha the fake and blew her up with it."

Elena went quiet, her face thoughtful. That might be the only reaction I was going to get when she realized I had had one up on her all along—but it was so, so worth it. After a moment, she looked back at the camera.

"Go into the airlock," she said. "I want to see it."

"I knew you didn't have cameras in here," I said, perhaps a bit petulantly. But it was worth the annoyed expression that drifted across her face. "And no thanks—you'll lock me in there."

"I won't strike any deal unless I can see that you have it."

I hesitated, and saw Ms. Dale helping Morgan up into the vent, sweat dripping down her forehead.

"I'm going to prop the door open," I said. "One minute."

I moved over to the airlock door and pulled it open, wedging one of the chairs from the workstation into the opening. Inside the chamber, I held up the egg toward the camera for a moment, slowly moving it around so I could change the angles. After a few seconds, I lowered it and stepped back into the lab.

"Satisfied?" I asked as I thrust it back into the bag.

"What are your terms?" she asked, and I wondered if I was imagining that her voice was colder, darker than before… that she knew I'd had her fooled.

"Sierra, and the antidote for Ms. Dale. First aid for Thomas. Safe passage for all of us." I stated the demands while Ms. Dale pulled herself completely into the vent.

"Fine. I'll send a warden down to retrieve—"

"No deal," I said. "I'm dealing with you, and we're dealing here, in the lab. The creatures in this place will keep us all honest."

"I'm not going down there—that place is suicide." Her face looked rather smug at the thought. "There's a lab close to you. Lab 3C in the level above. Go out this airlock and look for a ladder leading up in the next cavern. You'll have to find it after that, but I haven't released anything on those levels yet. I'll come down, we'll do the exchange in the airlock, and, as a gesture of queenly goodwill, I'll even let you leave unscarred."

I highly doubted that, but then again, I had no intention of meeting Elena at Lab 3C. At least, I had no intention of being where she expected me to be—so I guessed we were dealing on the same level.

"Fine," I replied.

"If you try anything, I *will* know," Elena added, and then the screen went dead. Her warning echoed in my ears as I climbed up onto the desk and held my bag, the egg back inside it, up to the vent. I was waiting for Ms. Dale to grab the bag, but also, I needed an excuse to take a moment before climbing through another vent.

CHAPTER 35

Viggo

I kicked a spider that suddenly appeared looming over Thomas, sending it flying, and grabbed Owen.

"We need the code!" I shouted as I shot another spider shimmering into view.

"One... three... three... eight..." Thomas wheezed, his blood-stained fingers reaching up for the door. "I can... get it."

"I got it," Owen said, his fingers dancing over the keyboard. The door clunked as the locks released, and Owen began spinning the wheel while I covered our backs. The spiders were still coming, in greater and greater numbers, and I knew that if I didn't do something, we'd never get the door shut—I had no idea how many more were out there.

Grabbing at my belt, I shouted, "Grenade!" and hurriedly removed one, pulled the pin, and tossed it into the room at the approaching spiders. I knelt down and shielded Thomas' eyes as the flash grenade went off behind me, the white phosphorus light flashing red behind my eyelids. I gave it a second before I opened my eyes and turned to look over my shoulder. The spiders were wobbling around, mostly visible and clearly disoriented, and I pressed the advantage.

I grabbed Thomas under the armpits and began to drag my friend through the gap in the door as Owen fired rounds at the closer spiders. I pulled Thomas in and set him down as gently as I could, though I could see him wincing, and moved to help Owen close the massive door. The door swung inward slowly—too slowly—but the spiders were still stunned. We had time.

I reached the door and began to pull, straining against the weight to make it close faster, when a hairy leg slid in through the ever-narrowing gap, hitting me in the knee. It didn't hurt, but my knee folded up under me, and I fell, thrusting out my arms to catch myself. Still, my chin struck hard on the door, my teeth feeling like they were going to be jarred out of my head, and I fell to my knees.

Looking around, dazed, I saw Owen yanking on the door, trying to close the gap as the hairy legs scrabbled to pull it back out toward the lab. He had let go with one hand and was firing at the legs sticking through the gap, blocking them from moving. Two more appeared, higher up, and Owen dropped his gun with a yelp and grabbed the door with two hands, pulling against the combined strength of the two arachnids—and losing as the gap grew wider.

I scrambled to my feet and grabbed the wheel, pulling hard. The door resisted for a second, and then there was a sickening crunch, and I felt something hot spray against my arm and neck as the airlock slammed closed. Owen broke away as soon as the door was closed, moving toward Thomas while I turned the wheel, sealing us in. There was a click as the door sealed tight, but relief was impossible to find.

Turning, I saw Thomas panting hard and Owen kneeling over him, hands pressed to the wound on Thomas' stomach, trying to staunch the blood still flowing from the wound, fast. I dropped my bag and tore it open, searching for the first-aid kit that had shifted to the bottom of the bag.

"Tell me what to do, Thomas," Owen said, his voice holding a frantic edge.

Thomas continued to pant, clutching at Owen's hands, his eyes wide, terrified, tearing up.

"I knew this would happen," he stuttered out, each word punctuated by a short gasp. I felt the hard case of the first-aid kit and pulled it out, my fingers suddenly feeling nerveless.

"Shut up, Thomas," Owen told him. "You have to save your strength!"

"Eighty-six percent probability," Thomas nodded. "I knew it. I tried to warn you... tell you... the code."

"No!" Owen said, spotting the kit I was holding out for him and snatching it. "Dammit, Thomas, you weird little man, don't give up!"

"Bag... Notebook... Instructions," Thomas wheezed, ignoring his friend's protests. His face was brimming with unconditional affection as he looked up at Owen, the edges of his mouth curling up in a sad smile. "Thank... you... for... being... my friend."

Then his breath gave out, soft as a baby bird, and he went still.

Owen stared at him, the first-aid kit hanging open in his hand.

"Thomas?" he rasped, his voice breaking.

My heart suddenly felt like it was trapped in the vice-hard grip of one of the berserk wardens we'd fought at the plant, stuttering in my chest. Owen shuddered and leaned over Thomas, his breath coming in gasps.

"*Thomas?*" he said again, emphasizing his name more.

"He's gone," I said, hating myself for saying it. God, how my heart ached. Thomas was gone, stolen from us by Maxen in a cowardly act. It had been senseless, cruel, and vicious—nothing worthy of our friend at all. It took everything I had not to break down and cry, to remember the mission... If I couldn't keep going, this all would have been in vain. Centering my thoughts around that, I was able to build a dam between my heart and the flood of emotions threatening to break me down.

I leaned over and pulled Owen against me, hugging him for a moment or two. The man sniffled, and then jerked away from me, his face hopelessly lost.

"Everyone I love is dying," he croaked.

"Not true," I told him, my voice strong and certain. "You know that's not true."

Owen sniffled again, and then took a deep breath, pushing the mountain of pain back and nodding, the clarity that came into his eyes frightening.

"Maxen."

It wasn't a request, and his jaw was set, a searing hatred burning in his eyes.

"Okay," I said with a nod. "Grab Thomas' bag."

I stood up and moved over to the other side of the airlock, hitting the button to detoxify while Owen grabbed Thomas' bag and handheld.

"We left that lock pick thing outside," he said, pulling out a little green notebook and opening it up as the chamber began to filter out the toxic air. "Hopefully he has a backup, or we'll be trapped in here."

"We won't," I said, watching the light that indicated contamination levels. "We've got semtex."

"Fun." Owen studied the pages. "He really thought of everything," he whispered, his resolve clearly threatening to break again.

I looked over at Thomas' still form, felt the dam in my heart buckle and then hold, and nodded.

"He was good at that." My voice came out harsh and wounded, but it didn't change my resolve.

The light turned green, and I cranked the wheel, tearing the door open. I stepped in, Owen behind me, and quickly closed the door. The lab beyond was fairly small, yet identical to the last ones—workstations in the middle, screens around the outside edges, dark and deserted. I moved through it toward the only other airlock door in the room. I saw the outer door hanging wide open through the small window on the inner door—a clear sign that Maxen, useless as he was, had come through here. I looked at Owen, and he studied the airlock before we moved into it and he pushed a button.

The door started to swing closed, gears whirring to turn the wheel and secure it. We waited impatiently, seconds ticking by. Once it was shut, we opened the inner door and waited for several more seconds. As we waited, I realized we hadn't even stopped to take our masks off—not that it ultimately mattered.

"We need to find a ladder up," Owen said. "The upper labs are where we can find the master terminals, according to Tho—his notes." He sniffed again, and let out a slow breath. The light went green, and I opened the next door, pushing through. Owen tucked Thomas' notes and handheld away and stepped out behind me.

It was another contaminated study chamber. The mist was less thick in this room—whether it came from the expansive size of the room, or the fact that the stream here was a much smaller trickle than in the other rooms we'd seen, I didn't know. What I did know was that this chamber's ceiling was almost forty feet up, and there were several palm trees growing huge inside. Tall grass filled the chamber, taller than me, and I could see the grass moving, hear it rustling, all in the dimly lit chamber.

I took a few steps forward and saw the slightly bent grass where Maxen had pushed through just a short time ago, and nodded to Owen.

"Be on your guard," I told him, and he nodded, his gun already in his hand.

We pushed through the grass, following his trail. It was impossible to move silently—the grass was too thick and tall to prevent it from making noise as we passed—so I moved quickly instead, trying to keep an ear out for anything approaching.

There was a chittering sound, like someone coughing softly several times in rapid succession, and it was greeted with a gurgling yowl from the other side of us, somewhere ahead. We froze for a second, and then Owen said, "*Run,*" in a low, urgent voice.

I waited for a single heartbeat, and then ran, tearing through the grass.

"That's the sound the Goliaths make," Owen shouted from behind me. "They are lizards—well, like a cross between a serpent and a lizard—and they're incredibly dangerous!"

Everything in here is. Before I could turn that thought into words, a dark shape crossed overhead, and without thinking I fired at it. It landed with a thump somewhere in the grass behind us, and I continued to run. I heard something thrashing through the grass, moving in tandem with us, angling *toward* us—and then, through the waving and shifting grass, I saw Maxen.

He spotted us, his arms pumping, hair plastered to his sweat-drenched forehead, and then veered ahead, sprinting like his life depended on it.

Behind him, something large and low to the ground raced by with a serpentine swish, legs barely touching the ground, the rustling of the grass marking its passage. There was a sudden break in the grass, and we returned to mossy terrain. The transition was so sudden that I almost slipped on the soft slope, barely catching my balance. I slowed in compensation, but Owen raced past. I steadied myself and looked up, seeing that he was aiming for a ladder at the top of the hill.

Something scrambled through the grass, long nails clicking on the rock just below the moss, and I looked over my shoulder to see a long neck rear up about four feet off the ground, squat legs practically springing up the slope, long tail whipping back and forth. Atop the long neck sat a triangular head, wide eye sockets containing red and yellow eyes with a slit running down the middle.

The creature's jaw dropped open, and something oozed out, a thick, yellow, viscous fluid that seemed to come out of the gums surrounding tiny rows of small pointed teeth. It reared back, a hissing sound escaping it—and then Owen's gun went off loudly, the bullet cutting through its open mouth, nearly separating the jaw from the rest of the body.

The goliath slumped over and rolled, its momentum still carrying it forward, and I picked up the pace, not wanting to get entangled.

"Don't let them spit on you!" Owen had slowed to fire his gun, so we were running side by side again, the ladder looming closer.

Owen sprang up it first, scaling the rungs quickly. I was fast behind him, my hands grasping the metal, and I climbed without looking back, knowing it would only slow me down.

A quarter of the way up, I heard a shout of *"Wait!"*

Looking over my shoulder, I saw Maxen racing to us, and realized he had somehow gotten behind us—gotten attacked or turned around—and had just found the mossy patch. He emerged from the grass, and I saw three moving trails converging behind him. I wrapped an arm around the bar and pulled my gun.

"Don't," Owen said harshly, and I looked up to see him turning away from Maxen, continuing up the ladder. I hesitated, and then thought of Thomas, lying all alone in that airlock by himself. He would never talk about percentages again. Never again have an awkward social faux pas in one of those uniquely *Thomas* moments that, despite everything, I had come to enjoy about him. The king of Patrus hadn't thought about him as a person at all, even though he'd had plenty of time to get to know him. He'd shot him when he was defenseless, his only crime trying to keep the door open for me and Owen.

I'd ignored Maxen's cowardice before, time and time again, protected him in spite of it. This time, I turned away as Maxen slipped and fell, hitting the mossy ground with a whump. The clicking of talons on rock sounded, and Maxen groaned—and then began screaming. I steeled myself and didn't look back as the Goliaths began chittering again, Maxen's screams still audible over the sound until we reached the top.

Owen reached the hatch ahead, cursed when he saw it was locked, and shoved a data chip he had pulled from Thomas' bag into the lock's port. I paused beneath him, trying to shut out the screams that were still coming up from behind me, reminding myself that the king had shot my friend in cold blood to save his own hide.

The door beeped, and Owen removed the data chip and pushed it open with a groan. As he did there was a loud crunch, clear even from this far away, and Maxen's screams went quiet. I wasn't ashamed to admit that I was relieved when he finally died.

He had gotten what he deserved.

I climbed through the hatch and closed the door behind me. Looking over at Owen, I saw a grim, satisfied gleam in his eyes.

"Did Thomas give you any instructions on how to override security protocols?" I asked as I straightened up to look at the room, finding it similar to the ones we'd been through before, with two doors, still empty and desolate. The only notable thing was a sign that said "Access to Palace" next to the left door. That would be the one we'd be taking.

Owen pulled out the notebook, flipping it open to the first page and studying it. I looked over his shoulder and saw that the page he was perusing was an index. After a brief pause, Owen flipped to a page and nodded.

"Yeah."

"Does this room contain the, uh, master control computer, or whatever it's called?"

"Master terminal," Owen said, sitting down at a workstation and powering the terminal on. "Let me check." He referred to Thomas' notebook, and then reached into the bag Thomas had given him, pulling out handful after handful of data sticks and sifting through them. "I'm looking for number twelve," he told me, running a hand through the pile to spread them around.

I began sifting and found number twelve within seconds. I gave it to Owen, and he plugged it into the drive, turning on the terminal. He sat down in a chair, propping up Thomas' notebook, so he could follow the directions. A black screen opened up and filled with lines and lines of green code, illuminating Owen's face, making him appear almost sickly. He nodded.

"It's a master terminal. What do you want me to do?"

"Our team is down below with who knows how many doors they need to try and get open. Let's clear a path for them—open all the doors and hatches. Including the ones that lead to the palace."

"All of them?" he repeated in question form, his eyebrows going up. He blinked, and then a slow smile grew wide on his lips. "You're gonna cause a little chaos, eh?"

"Hell yeah," I replied, crossing over to the sole terminal in the room, and then paused. "They'll be all right," I stated, more for myself than for him.

"Of course they will," he replied, tapping out a series of commands on the terminal. "Besides, they can't open the doors safely without drawing attention to themselves, so it's better this way." He hit enter, and immediately code began to run across the screen, ones and zeros scrolling by faster than I could process. Then the screen froze. For a second nothing happened. And then it went dark as both of the airlock doors in this room began to swing open at the same time. Immediately I could hear the sounds of The Green pouring in through the door on the right, opposite the door leading to the palace, and it was noisy. We maybe had minutes before something got in here to get to us. Maybe less.

I went back over to the hatch and hauled it open, leaving it standing upright on its side, and then grabbed my bag as Owen swept the chips back into his. I exited and stepped out into the cavern beyond. Once we were both a good distance away from the airlock door, I ripped off my mask and took in a slow breath, checking the air. As I suspected, the atmosphere from the simulated version of The Green wasn't persistent.

"We're good," I told him, stuffing my mask into my bag. We followed the cave as it led up, slowly tapering in and curving around at a meandering pace. Eventually, we came to a door built into a wooden frame, and I slowed to a stop. It didn't look automatic—maybe that was why it hadn't been opened like the lab doors—but Owen stepped forward and twisted the doorknob, and it opened with no noise, no alarm, no problem.

I pulled up my gun as we got our first glimpse of the darkened room within. Pulling my flashlight out of my pocket, I clicked it on and stepped inside, shining it around the room and revealing a small library, with elegant sitting furniture positioned in the center of the room. Owen stepped in behind me.

Hello? came Amber's voice through the earbud, and I jolted in surprise at the unexpected sound. *Is anyone receiving me?* she asked.

I turned my subvocalizer on. *Amber? Is that you?*

Oh, Viggo. Thank God. She paused to breathe out noisily, and then continued. *Who's with you?*

Owen, I said. *Thomas... Thomas didn't make it.*

No, she breathed, and her mic cut off suddenly.

A second later Vox's voice filled the silence.

Viggo. It's just us here, so we were going to follow Amber's mission of working to save the boys.

That's what we're doing too. Is Amber okay?

She will be, but she's... She needs a minute. There was deep concern in Vox's voice, but also confidence, like he knew whatever she was going through would last only moments, yet ached that she suffered. I wasn't sure how I had realized that. Maybe because Violet was the same way... But I was just glad he was there for Amber.

Have you heard from Violet? Ms. Dale? Morgan? I left Tim out, but I worried about him. Without a subvocalizer, he couldn't respond to us, so it would be useless speculating. I just had to hope he would be listening to us to figure out where we were, and try to meet us en route.

No. We exited the lab on the south side of the palace. Amber mentioned that when you guys escaped here last time, Owen and Ms. Dale got into the security room to shut their transmissions down while you and Violet escaped?

Owen met my gaze.

We did, he said into the subvocalizer. *And I know where it is. Meet us at the east stairwell.*

There was a long pause, and then Amber returned, her voice low and urgent.

Go without us, she said hurriedly. *Guards just found us.*

Her mic cut off suddenly, and my ears were left in silence once again. I involuntarily tightened my hand against my gun. There was nothing we could do to help our teammates other than fulfill our part of the mission.

Change channel to F frequency, I transmitted to Owen. My heart was heavy, but keeping our communication safe was of utmost importance. Owen gave me a thumbs-up and clicked over a second before I did. Then I took one last look at the doorway leading back to the caves before nodding at Owen, signaling for him to open the door that would lead us deeper into the palace.

CHAPTER 36

Violet

I followed Ms. Dale as Morgan led us through the rectangular ducts, the thin metal rattling loudly as we crawled. We paused for a moment, and then moved forward, and I realized the duct had stopped and turned sharply upward. I panicked at first, before realizing there was a ladder. I guessed I wasn't the only one who went climbing around in ducts—maintenance had to get up here sometimes.

Ms. Dale climbed rapidly, Morgan somewhere ahead of her, her feet making almost no noise. I followed, trying not to think about how far down the bottom was steadily becoming. We climbed for what felt like forever, but was probably less than a minute, before stopping again. Morgan whispered something, but Ms. Dale's body blocked most of the noise, making it indiscernible.

There was a rustling sound, and another long pause.

"What's going on?" I whispered, slightly on edge.

A sharp beep sounded, muted but recognizable, and then something shifted, light spilling through a hole at the top of the shaft. Morgan pulled herself up and then leaned over to help Ms. Dale out. She was panting, but she heaved herself through.

I climbed quickly, my nerves starting to get to me, and pulled myself through as fast as I could. I dragged my legs out, and Morgan put the metal floor plate down. My eyes soon adjusted to the new light as I stood up and looked around.

"Where are we?" I asked, knowing there was no real way to answer that question. The room looked exactly like the other workstations we had seen; the only difference was that we had entered it through a ventilation duct. It wasn't one of the misty rooms that simulated The Green, but a group of computers and darkened monitoring systems.

Ms. Dale, as always, was quick to correct my assumption that there was no more information to be had, even if she was unaware I had made it.

"Second level," she said, her breathing harsh and heavy. I looked up and saw that sweat was pouring from her forehead, and then my gaze dropped to her arm, noticing the fabric of her Liberator suit was stretching tight over her forearm.

"Ms. Dale…" Her eyes met mine, and she shook her head.

"I'm fine," she grated out, reaching to grab a desk and pulling herself up. "We need to head up another level."

"How do you know that?" Morgan asked, standing from her squat.

"I memorized the map," Ms. Dale said softly, her eyes moving around the room. "Also, the labs have designations."

She pointed to something on the wall, and I noticed a sign like the one we'd encountered at the entrance to the caves. The top one was the lab name—2A—and the second one read "Access to 2B." I looked across the room at the other airlock, and saw "Access to 1D." I felt like an idiot for not noticing those sooner.

"We need that one," Ms. Dale said, gesturing to the one labeled "1D." "Here, Morgan," she said, holding out a data stick to her.

Morgan accepted it and moved over to the door to hack it, and I approached Ms. Dale.

"Ms. Dale… what do you want me to do about your arm?" I asked, and she shook her head, finally seeming to catch her breath.

"Nothing," she replied. She met my gaze, and her face softened slightly. "It'll be all right," she reassured me.

It didn't work—I was worried about her—but there was nothing we could do about it, and that was probably what Ms. Dale wanted me to understand. For half a second I considered meeting Elena at the lab and honoring our arrangement… but I had to toss the idea aside again, needlessly reminding myself that she would never honor any deal I made with her.

"Violet!" Morgan called, her voice slightly panicked, and I turned to look at her as she stepped away from the door. Through a window in the airlock wall, I could see the outer airlock opening up, and I quickly yanked my mask from my bag.

The inner airlock door began to open by itself, the hand wheel turning without anybody's aid, and I slipped the mask over my head. Ms. Dale was still fumbling with hers, her swollen arm trembling slightly as she tried to grab the straps. I reached over and plucked it out of her grip, slipping it onto her head and pulling it down over her face.

She shot me a grateful look as she sucked in a breath, and I turned to see Morgan backing away from the door a few steps, her mask once again on her face. It swung open, as did the ones behind us, and then… nothing.

We exchanged looks.

"Why did they suddenly open?" Morgan asked, and I shook my head.

"No clue," Ms. Dale said. "Still, this might make things a little easier for us. We just need to find the ladder leading up to the third level."

"All right," Morgan replied, shaking out her shoulders. "That should be easy en—"

An angry bellow drowned out the rest of her words, and I turned to see a black-clad man racing toward us through the airlock. I leapt back, dragging Ms. Dale with me as he charged into the lab. I let go of Ms. Dale as he swung between us, trying to knock both of us down with a single blow, and he missed, stumbling forward a few steps.

He caught me as he stumbled past, though, and I spun, hitting the ground hard, pain erupting in my shoulder and hip from where I hit the floor. I couldn't wait the pain out—I picked myself up to see Morgan stepping under a wild haymaker thrown by the man, who'd ended up closest to her.

Then Ms. Dale pushed off the wall to deliver a sharp kick to the back of his knee, and he tumbled forward, hitting the floor hard. I pulled out one of the tranquilizer darts from the sheath inside my suit. The young man—he could only be one of the enhanced boys—levered himself up with his arms as Ms. Dale moved past him, out the opposite airlock. I ran to him, jamming the needle into his side as he started to pick himself up.

He didn't seem to notice as I leapt over his legs, and I looked over my shoulder as I ran through the airlock to see him weaving back and forth, struggling to stand. Relief passed through me, but it lasted only until I heard two more angry bellows from the open doors, following me as I ran across the mossy floor of the cave we'd entered.

Ahead of me, I spied Morgan as she suddenly ducked low, and I followed suit, narrowly missing a tree branch obscured by the mist. She dodged right, and I followed her up a steep incline, my thighs beginning to burn. The mist started to dissipate as I climbed, and I could make out Morgan, and even Ms. Dale, more clearly.

Behind me, I heard the thudding of heavy feet, and glanced back to see two more older boys in black charging after me, maybe twenty feet behind. I poured on the speed, a stitch forming in my side, and Morgan glanced my way and then started to drop back.

"What are you doing?" I asked, and she looked at me, just as Ms. Dale shouted, "The ladder!"

I looked up to see a long ladder running down from the ceiling of this chamber. Ms. Dale was already at it, leaping to grab a rung farther up, while the footsteps behind me grew closer. Morgan gave me another look as I passed her, and then she turned and leapt into the air. I didn't see what happened as I ran, but there was the sound of something hitting something, and I looked back to see one boy on the ground, the other swinging at Morgan as she easily avoided him.

I almost plowed into the ladder, I was moving so fast, but

managed to stop myself short by catching the rungs. And then I was climbing. I moved quickly, my hands and feet flying, trying to give Morgan some room, and turned back in time to see her leap from the ground and plant her foot on another boy's shoulder, kicking off it and twisting in midair. She landed just below me on the ladder, shouting, "Climb!"

I moved, spurred by the angry noises coming from below us. Above me, Ms. Dale was closing the distance to the hatch secured in the ceiling, and I was halfway down when the ladder shook violently in my hands. My heart lurched as I heard a metallic groan, and I felt the ladder move a solid inch to the left. That sensation was like a nightmare.

"GO GO GO!" Morgan yelled, her hand pushing roughly at my backside in an effort to get me to climb faster.

I did, fear of falling lending another boost of adrenaline to my already flying limbs. Ms. Dale was pushing the door open, and the ladder jerked back to the right, the boy below angrily trying to dislodge us. I kept going, my mind on the bars ahead, and suddenly Ms. Dale was helping to pull me through.

I turned around to help her grab Morgan, latching onto one arm. She gave a yelp, and then I felt all of her weight transfer to me, and I realized the ladder had been torn out from beneath her. I grunted, taking a moment to readjust my body weight and brace her better, and then Ms. Dale and I began to pull her up, until she was lying on the floor, panting.

We stayed like that for a heartbeat or two, just trying to catch our breaths.

"You know," Ms. Dale wheezed, breaking the slow silence that had formed, "I'm pretty sure adrenaline is bad for the bite."

I shot her a sharp glance and shook my head at her, unable to find the humor in her statement.

"They ripped the ladder right out from under me," Morgan whispered with a shudder.

"I guess it's better than thinking to climb up after us," Ms. Dale muttered dryly.

I sat up and looked around the room. Like the floor below, the air-lock doors were open here. Unlike the other floors, the sign on the left door read "Access to Palace" with an arrow on one side. The one on the right said "Access to 1C." If we wanted to get to Elena, we would go that way, through another section of the artificial Green contained within.

Even if I had actually planned to meet Elena, I wouldn't set foot in it.

"Do you think Thomas got all the doors open?" Morgan asked, and I felt my heart sink, thinking about what I had seen on the screen earlier. I hadn't had the heart to bring it up with them yet.

Now, it seemed, was the time, but the words were hard to form.

"Thomas... I-I think we've lost him," I said softly. "I'm not sure how, but he was bleeding from a stomach wound, and from the video Elena showed me... it really didn't look good."

At the time, I'd forced myself to be optimistic, trying to believe Viggo and Owen would fix him somehow. But now that I replayed the dire scene in my mind, I found it all but impossible to see how Thomas would get out of this wild place alive. He'd been bleeding so much.

As I spoke the words to Ms. Dale and Morgan, a wave of pain crashed into me hard, making me want to cry. Thomas had been my friend. Weird, yes. Eccentric, yes. But in spite of the cold, analytical façade he wore as an outer shell, Thomas was a deeply caring individual. I couldn't even comprehend the idea of losing him. It was just... too much.

Ms. Dale closed her eyes, her face sorrowful, and then, even as I watched, she pushed it aside. Morgan, on the other hand, removed the mask and scrubbed at her cheeks as tears fell from her eyes. She let the tears fall, and then donned her mask again, her eyes red.

"We need to move," she muttered. "Elena will be waiting for us."

I nodded and picked myself off the floor. There would be time to grieve after. If we survived. I knew what we had to do, and it was time to get started.

"If we follow this tunnel to the palace, can you figure out where the entrance would be for 1C?" I directed the question to Ms. Dale, and she nodded.

"I can."

"Then let's go."

I shouldered my bag and began heading toward the airlock door, toward the cave. Together we moved, keeping a sharp eye out for anything behind us. After we were some distance away, I took the mask off, took a deep breath, and waited for a wave of dizziness to hit me.

It didn't, and I gave Ms. Dale and Morgan a thumbs up, indicating they could take off their masks. Behind us, I began to hear sounds—chittering… buzzing… hissing… and wondered if the creatures inside were tracking us somehow. We still had our suits, which meant we could, if we wanted to, go invisible and avoid them. Maybe. Without knowing all the creatures that could be behind us, we had no way to tell whether they had other ways to track us besides sight.

I wondered if they could even survive in the oxygen-rich environment, then decided I didn't care. If they got out and wreaked havoc in the palace, it would only draw attention away from us and maybe give us a fighting chance. We skirted the new cave, the sounds growing distant behind us, and made our way to the walls, searching for the exit.

Morgan found it first—a flat piece of rock with a perfectly rectangular seam carved into it. Kneeling down in front of it, I slid my lock-picking tool out of a pocket on my thigh, and put it in the small hole carved into the middle of the slab, hoping this would work. I hit the button, and the device whirred, but it didn't even seem to have to work before the door clicked, and the device shut off quickly.

"Huh," I said. "I guess this one was unlocked too."

We didn't have time to dwell on that mystery. The door pressed inward, the gravelly sound of rock scraping on rock filling the room, and then it stopped, an inch deep, no more. I slipped the tool back into my pocket and put my shoulder to the slab.

I pressed with my legs, and the rock began to slide forward, slowly, but easily, rolling in and revealing a hardwood floor. The slab stopped a

few feet in, and I stepped around the exposed sides to find myself in…
an office. Backing away, I looked at the secret door I had just pushed
open, and realized that when the door was closed, it blended in with the
wall, a massive floor-to-ceiling mirror mounted on it. On either side of
the mirror were bookcases, and on the left side of the room was a desk,
two soft chairs in front of it and a massive stuffed chair behind it.

"This was Mr. Jenks' office," Morgan said as she stepped out from
around the wall, her green eyes growing wide. "It was always such a hike
down here from the nursery, and I hated it."

"The tunnel in the castle that grants entrance to Lab 1C is two hundred feet away to the east," Ms. Dale said, resting her back against one
of the bookcases and wiping some of the sweat off her face. "And the entrance there is two floors up in the castle proper. What would that be?"

Morgan tilted her head, thinking about it for a moment, and then
nodded.

"Somewhere in the servants' quarters," she announced. "But I'm
not exactly sure where. I was never allowed in there."

"I've been there," Ms. Dale said, pushing off the wall. "I have a
rough idea."

We gathered our stuff as Ms. Dale peered around the door, checking for any signs of guards. Then she pulled it open and stepped out,
looking in the opposite direction.

"It's clear," she whispered, and her finger flickered to her throat to
turn on her subvocalizer.

Shouldering my bag, I followed her lead. We left both doors open
as we exited, knowing that eventually, something would find its way out.

I just hoped that whatever it was did it soon, and didn't kill us in
the process.

CHAPTER 37

Violet

Morgan ran through the channels, testing things, and discovered our comms were active again—at least, we could contact each other—as Ms. Dale led us up a set of stairs. She didn't stop between floors to check the doors, just continued to move with certainty while I called the names of our missing teammates over the link, trying to reach them. Static met my entreaties, and as we neared the third landing, Ms. Dale gave me a look and reached for the collar around her neck.

"We have to change channels," she said softly but aloud, I assumed so nobody listening in would realize.

I wanted to protest. If we changed channels, Viggo would never find me, not without cycling through all the channels and listening in. But we'd done it this way deliberately—we didn't want to risk anyone getting captured with knowledge of what comm channels we were on. We all knew the brutal reality of how cruel Elena could be, and even though Tabitha was dead, I didn't doubt the queen had another sadist squirreled away, intended for a violent purpose. So I just nodded.

"Channel J," Ms. Dale told me, and I turned the small dial embedded in the collar, counting off the tiny jolts that were transmitted to my neck as I changed the channel.

Seconds later I said, *Violet, testing channel J. Confirm?*

My mouth moved, no sound coming out, and a moment later, Morgan replied.

Confirmed—Morgan.

Confirmed—Ms. Dale.

Comms all set, Ms. Dale immediately turned toward the handful of steps remaining, climbing them quickly and stopping at the wooden door at the top. More stairs led up, and I recalled that this side of the palace was taller than the rest because the royal quarters were above.

She pushed the door slowly, eyeing the hallway, and then swung it open fully and stepped out onto the hardwood floors, checking the opposite side of the passage. We walked through the door, and Ms. Dale began leading us, checking doors as she passed them. We turned down another series of halls, and I marveled once again at the size and the scope of this palace.

Then I realized the people in here—ordinary people who lived and worked in the palace, most of whom were probably asleep right now, unless the palace had been evacuated—were at great risk from the monsters below, and I felt a wave of guilt. I hoped the wardens would do their job and push whatever we had unleashed back before anyone was fatally injured… but regardless, I had a mission to consider.

It was a hard reality, but one I accepted. I would feel guilt for it later, of that I was certain, but for now, I had to be hard. If we finished things tonight, nobody would have to suffer in this war again.

Where is everyone? Morgan asked suddenly.

It's the middle of the night, Ms. Dale said. *They might have been evacuated, or they're downstairs dealing with whatever is coming up from the caves. Or they're asleep.*

We turned and headed down a long hall, Ms. Dale's pace picking up slightly.

We're getting close, she announced.

And then one of the heavy doors in this passageway creaked open, emitting a bleary-eyed maid carrying a stack of folded sheets before any of us could even think to use our suits. The woman came to an abrupt stop, her eyes trained on us. Ms. Dale lunged for her, but she tossed the sheets up with a shriek and began to run.

"HELP!" she screamed.

The next moment, two wardens appeared ahead, and I dodged down the hallway to the right, Morgan following suit, while Ms. Dale went left.

"It's on this side," she shouted to us. "I'll give you covering fire… one at a time."

I nodded and rose to a crouch, facing Ms. Dale. She nodded too and then turned down the hall, using the corner as cover and firing at the two guards. I ran, and gunfire erupted loudly down the hall, drowning out the relative quiet. I made it safely across—they were aiming at Ms. Dale, who ducked back, ejecting a magazine and pulling out a new one. Her hand shook, the swelling having reached the palm, but somehow she managed.

Morgan caught my eye, and I watched as she backed up a few steps and then raced for us, her legs blurred. She dove, arching her back like a swan taking flight, and then curling seamlessly into a roll as she landed on our side, propelling herself right back onto her feet.

There was a delayed burst of gunfire, and then Ms. Dale tugged a grenade off her belt, pulled the pin out with her teeth, and tossed the thing haphazardly down the hallway.

I was already moving with Morgan down the hallway, Ms. Dale close behind me. We were about ten or fifteen feet along it when the grenade went off. The floorboards shuddered underfoot, and a blast of heat tore down the hallway, dissipating only slightly before it reached us—small patches of fire burning behind us and a haze of smoke surrounding us. Morgan led the way through it, her gun drawn and her eyes wary.

Well, they definitely know we're here now, Ms. Dale transmitted. *They'll be coming.*

Are we close?

Ms. Dale hesitated.

I'm not entirely sure. Two hundred feet is hard to gauge. We're in the right—

A burst of gunfire sounded from behind us, and Ms. Dale grunted and fell forward into me, dragging me down. Morgan stepped to one side, her body reacting before she could stop, and her arm went up, firing two silenced rounds behind us. I heard a thud as a body hit the ground, and looked to see a woman down, another woman ducking back around the corner. I fired a few shots at the wall near her, keeping her back.

Ms. Dale cursed a long string of obscenities into the comms, and I turned to see her on her side, her hand on her lower back just below the bulge of her vest. Blood streamed steadily from between her fingers.

Help me move her, I shouted to Morgan, and together, we dragged her into a side room that turned out to be a cupboard of some sort, Morgan keeping her gun trained down the hall.

We can't stop for first aid, Ms. Dale gasped. *Just pick me up—they're going to be closing in.*

Let me get a pressure bandage on it at least, I urged, pulling my bag around. I froze, forcing myself to stop what I was doing, when I heard shouting carrying down the halls. It was muted by distance, but not by much. Morgan was already picking Ms. Dale up, throwing her arm around her shoulders. Coming around to her other side, I took her other arm and wrapped it around my neck before placing my hand over her wound.

She gasped, and then gave me a nod.

Let's go, she said, her face strained and tight with pain.

I moved back to the door and pushed it open with my toe, my gun in the hand supporting Ms. Dale, trying to ignore the sensation of blood creeping under the fingers of the other one. Ms. Dale moved forward, but there was a hitch on the side the bullet had gone in, her leg moving awkwardly, and with her head so close to mine, I could hear how strained her breathing had become. Morgan and I held a portion of her weight as she struggled to keep up.

We turned down a long hallway just as the sound of running

feet drifted toward us from up ahead, and the three of us took an immediate right, trying to bypass the guards. We had passed through a kitchen and into a dining hall when Ms. Dale sagged in our arms, her breathing coming in sharp pants.

Set me down, she managed, and Morgan and I carefully positioned her on a bench. She sagged against it, listing to one side, and I noted the paleness of her face.

Adrenaline patch, she said. *Two blood patches and a pressure bandage.*

I quickly retrieved my first-aid kit and began doctoring her, applying the blood patches first and then the pressure bandage. Morgan moved over to the door behind us, checking the hallway.

We got a problem, Violet, she transmitted.

My hands were shaking. I tore off another strip of tape with my teeth and placed it over the cotton I had put over the wound.

What? I asked.

Guards are in the hallways on either side of us, she said. *They're checking rooms... It's just a matter of time.*

We'll use the suits, I said.

You'll use the suits, Ms. Dale corrected, her hands pushing mine away as she sat back up. Color was slowly returning to her cheeks, but not enough to indicate she was out of the woods. Then again, until she saw a doctor, I didn't think she *was* going to be out of the woods.

She pushed off the bench, forcing herself onto her own two feet and hissing in pain.

Take a cube of the semtex and a detonator out of my bag, she ordered, and Morgan immediately stepped around her to get into her bag.

What are you planning? I asked, now picking up on the sounds of doors being opened and closed near us.

I'm going to be a distraction, she said, swinging around her rifle and checking the magazine. *You two are going to get to Elena.*

What? No—they'll kill you.

They better hope they do, she said, a wicked gleam in her eyes.

Because I'm going to kill them.

Ms. Dale, just use the suit, and they'll—

She can't, Morgan said, cutting off my words. I looked at her, and her face was apologetic. *The gunshot probably damaged the suit. There's a chance it'll injure her, or worse.*

Violet, Ms. Dale said, stepping over the tail of Morgan's words, and I looked at her. She lowered the rifle onto its strap, and reached over to cup my face, hers softening again.

This is what has to happen. I'm slowing you down, and I'm a liability. But this? I can do this for you. I can buy you a chance. Elena's probably moving now. If you can intercept her, follow her... you stand a chance. She'll try to run—if she does, get to the roof.

There was a loud bang from very near the doors, and I knew the kitchen was next—then us. Unless the ones in the other hallway got to the other doors first.

Ms. Dale speared me with an intense look, then smiled, looking unconcerned.

This is karma, Violet. I did something... something unforgivable to you, and now I can finally repay that debt I owe you. When you're ready... when you think you can forgive me... ask Viggo, and he'll tell you everything. I love you, brave girl.

Her words were like stones in my heart, sinking to my shoes and holding me in place. I watched as she hobbled over to the door, somehow moving quickly in spite of the pain she must be experiencing. She kicked open the door we had just come through and tossed out a grenade. There was a bright flash and a loud bang, indicating she had used a concussive one, and then she stepped through, her rifle firing wildly.

Wait! I cried out, knowing she heard my words through our comms. *I love you too! Please don't—*

The suit, Violet! Morgan interrupted, and I looked to see Morgan's body already shimmering out of existence—I was still too stunned by what I was witnessing to really comprehend it. It was unfurling before me in real time, Ms. Dale's mouth opening in a shout as she fired down the hallway, the door swinging closed. Morgan's invisible hands shook me hard, and then struck me across my face, and I jolted back into myself.

I stared at the empty air where she should be for a moment, and then dropped my bag on the floor, clenching my muscles and letting the discomfort of the suit sink into my skin, drawing strength from its pins and needles. It did nothing to match the ache in my heart as the door between me and Ms. Dale slammed shut, her shots moving away and becoming more muted.

We'd only moved a couple steps before the doors to the opposite side burst open, and six wardens raced across it. Ms. Dale's bursts of gunfire continued down the hallway across the room from them, and they didn't do anything more than glance right through us and then move through the doors, chasing her.

I relaxed my muscles, and a moment later, Morgan did as well, reaching over to grab my bag and hold it up to me.

I'm sorry I hit you, she said softly, and I took the bag into my numb hands, trying to think of something to say. I slipped it back on, and she reached out and grabbed my wrist.

Violet, we have to complete the mission, she said evenly, her eyes placating.

I nodded again, and then forced myself to move through the doors the guards had just run through, the doors that weren't ricocheting with fading gunfire. I turned my subvocalizer off long enough to whisper, "Change to channel K," and turned left down the hall, following it, my gun drawn and my adrenaline surging.

Morgan, checking in on channel K.

Violet—confirmed.

Our words were mechanical, automatic. We were halfway to the next junction when I felt the floor and walls shake hard, a smattering of dust exploding from the junction in front of me and scattering all over the place. I stumbled and caught myself on the wall, and then felt despair crushing into my heart.

She can't be gone, I thought to myself, my heart aching, agony in every beat.

I thought of her, and then pushed the thought aside, straightening. It was too much to think about it right now.

C'mon, I forced myself to say, allowing rage to bypass my despair. For the moment, fire consumed my sorrow, filling me with something I could use.

CHAPTER 38

Viggo

I slowly cracked open the door to the palace, peering through the slit. The hallway was clear from that side, so I pulled the door back fully and stepped out into the hall that was revealed, my gun raised. The corridor was empty, silent, and still—no sign of any danger.

I motioned Owen out, and he scanned the hall.

How do we get to the east stairwell from here? I asked.

He checked Thomas' handheld.

This way, he said, pointing to the left. *Fifty feet and turn right.*

I began moving down the corridor, keeping my footsteps light and my eyes alert. I felt dangerously exposed in the hallways. Elena had cameras, and that meant we were on them. Getting Owen to the security room was a priority—he could shut everything down using Thomas' instructions, which would help keep Violet and the rest of our group safer, too.

It occurred to me as we checked the next corner that we should go invisible, before I remembered we couldn't really go invisible. We had backpacks and Thomas' bag—gear we needed for this mission. It would be very conspicuous if there were floating bags passing by the camera.

I was torn between wanting to ransack the palace in a hopeless search for Violet, and knowing Henrik and everyone back in Patrus was relying on us to stop the boys before they started killing.

If they hadn't already started. It made me heartsick to know my wife was somewhere in this maze of danger without me, but I knew her. Even if we were on different missions, she wouldn't want either of us to break from them. There was too much riding on this. Too much at stake.

I was deep in thought, but not so distracted that when a pair of wardens rounded the corner from the junction ahead, I didn't go into instant fight mode. But they'd spotted us the moment we'd spotted them.

The four of us froze, and the wardens got to their weapons a heart-beat before us, leveling their rifles right at our chests. They were only ten feet ahead. If they fired, we would probably be dead even with the bulletproof vests. I looked over at Owen, who slowly began to place his gun on the floor in front of him, his free hand held high in the air. He shot me a look out of the corner of his eye and nodded.

Picking up on his beat, I too slowly lowered my silenced pistol to the floor.

The two women exchanged glances, and the one on the left pulled her rifle tighter to her chest.

"Lace your fingers behind your head," she said, her voice quiet but holding a bite of iron.

I raised my arms and did as she ordered, watching her body language closely. She exhaled slowly and then moved forward, the other woman a step behind her.

"Turn around," she commanded, gesturing with her rifle.

I exchanged a glance with Owen and then began to turn. The quiet one moved forward as I did, the muzzle of her gun going down as she reached around to grab her handcuffs with her other hand.

At that moment, Owen's sharp elbow caught her in the nose, and I planted a kick toward her chest, shoving her back a few feet into the one who had spoken.

They both grunted as they impacted, and stumbled. I moved

quickly, grabbing the woman on top and delivering a sharp blow to her chin, Owen a heartbeat behind with a boot to the other woman's face.

They both went down in moments, and I shook my hand out. I hated hitting women, but it was better than killing them.

Owen and I breathed in relief, and then grabbed the women, depositing them into a nearby room and tying them up. We needed to be careful. Any loose end would raise the alarm, but there was no doubt in my mind we were already being hunted.

Stairwell is up ahead, Owen said, and I nodded, exhaling to calm my nerves and focus.

Right. Let's go.

I pulled open the door and let Owen take point, checking over my shoulder to make sure our rear remained clear. Ahead was a door—plain and wooden, with no special signage that told us of its significance—but Owen made right for it, grabbing the doorknob and then placing his ear to the door.

I waited, keeping my back to it and an eye out on the hallway behind us, and then he cracked it open. A second later he tapped my shoulder, and I slipped in behind him while he held the door open.

Up we go, he transmitted, and moments later we were climbing the stairs.

We moved rapidly—any minute now wardens would likely be barging in, looking for us, and we needed to get up several flights to one of the higher sections of the palace.

A rattle of gunfire brought us up short, and my heart leapt in my chest as I angled my head so I could see the door on the next landing.

It could be Violet, I said over the link, and Owen surged forward toward the door. He moved to the other side of it while I pressed my back to the wall. Another burst of gunfire sounded, and I reached over and grabbed the doorknob, opening it a crack so that Owen could peer through it.

He shook his head, and I opened it more, and then he jerked back as a single shot went off, gasping as something pinged into the stairwell, setting off sparks. I slammed the door shut and rushed over to him, ducking as a rifle went off, bullets tearing through the wood like rocks through wet tissue.

I was low enough that none of them caught me, and that was very lucky. Owen was leaning beside the door, his back to the wall, his eyes wide.

Are you okay? I asked, and he nodded, his jaw set hard.

It didn't get me—it was just a ricochet. I don't think anybody was even looking in my direction. But it was close.

I went to the door and pulled it open, taking control to give him a moment, just as a dark shape passed by at a sprint. There was a shout, followed by the sound of two people colliding. I opened the door to see one warden down, Amber engaged in hand-to-hand combat with another, her hands flying to block incoming blows. She landed a sharp jab, and the warden stumbled back a few steps, dazed. Amber took a slow step forward, and the guard moved quick as lightning, her hand pulling out her gun and shooting Amber point-blank in the chest before I could stop her. The redheaded woman crumpled to the floor.

"NO!" Logan's voice howled from down the hall, and he raced by just as I was leveling my gun at the warden. He blocked my view of her with his body. I eased off the trigger as Logan slapped the gun out of the woman's hand, a round discharging into the floor as he did. His second blow was delivered right to her throat, and I heard her make a choked sound before doubling over, clutching her neck.

He drew back a fist, slamming it down into her cheek, and she dropped to the ground. But Logan wasn't finished, and as I watched, he knelt over her and began delivering blow after blow to her face. I stepped out into the hall, intent on checking on Amber, when her still form suddenly moved.

She groaned, and picked herself up as the other sounds faded away. The sound of Logan's fist on the warden's face was the only noise in the hallway. Amber's breathing was strained, and I didn't doubt she was in a lot of pain. I exhaled again, realizing her bulletproof vest had saved her life. But stopping a bullet from a powerful handgun such a short distance away wasn't easy, and I was sure she would carry the bruise for a week.

Amber made it to her hands and knees, her eyes squinting in pain, and then turned.

"Logan," she called softly, her voice hoarse, and he froze, then turned, his eyes staring at her. His anger and dismay melted into relief, and he crossed over and dropped in front of her, pulling her tight into his arms and cradling her against him.

"Thank God," he breathed, and suddenly I felt very awkward standing there. Neither of them had noticed us yet, and now I felt like I was witnessing what should be a very intimate moment between them. Owen and I exchanged uncertain looks.

"It's fine," Amber said roughly. "I'm fine. Logan... I'm okay."

"Dammit, Amber. I was so scared." His hands started smoothing her hair as he held her. "You know I—"

Owen cleared his throat loudly, and Logan whirled, drawing his pistol and pointing it at us, still on his knees. He stared at us, Amber giving us a surprised look from over his shoulder, and then lowered his gun.

"Hey," he said, so casually that it was as if he hadn't been about to declare his everlasting devotion and love to Amber.

"Hey," I said, fighting back a smile as Amber began to blush, hard, suddenly realizing the intimacy they were displaying.

"Let me go," she ordered, her violet eyes lowered, and Logan took one arm from around her but kept the other there, helping her to stand. She didn't shrug him off, just shook her red curls over to one side, then nodded and stepped away from the helping hand.

"Hey, guys," she said, waving a hand in the air. "We, uh... We broke free of the guards."

"So I see," I replied, turning off the subvocalizer for the moment with a smile. "Are you okay?"

She nodded and then looked around.

"Uh... so... Operation Free the Boys?" she asked, leaning over to pick up the bag and gun the guard had confiscated from her.

Owen and I exchanged looks, and I nodded, turning back to meet her gaze.

"Yeah. Let's, uh... Let's do it."

"Two floors up," Owen added, taking a step back into the stairwell and pointing up.

"Cool," Amber said, shouldering her rifle and taking her pistol out. She moved past Logan, who still stood motionless in the middle of the hall, staring at her, and toward us.

I looked at Logan and smiled. "C'mon."

We climbed the steps quickly, syncing our channels and going back into silent communication. When we found the area of the security room, we stopped out of sight of the guards and began pulling off our gear, hiding it in one of those curtained alcoves I remembered from my escape from the palace... It felt like years ago, but it hadn't been all that long.

The plan was simple and relatively straightforward: use the suits to get in, and then take control of the station. We had an advantage, even if they were expecting us.

When all of us were ready, Owen moved toward the door to the security room and went invisible, the rest of us following suit. I did as well, and suddenly remembered why I didn't really like using the suit—it was worth it to be invisible, but only just.

I'm going in now, Owen declared. The door opened slowly—just wide enough for him to slip in—and then remained still. *I got two guards waiting for something to come through this door, one at nine o'clock, the other at three, but they're distracted by the reports coming in from the main room. The main room has four more people watching the screens and giving orders.*

Thanks to Owen's intelligence from inside, it was easy enough to slip by the first two guards and knock them out before they realized we were there. They had increased security, that much was certain, but with the four of us working in tandem and using the suits, we were able to take them out quickly and efficiently. We didn't kill any of them, and within ten minutes, we had tied them up and tossed them into a side room. Soon, Owen was deep in the computer system, trying to use Thomas' chips to determine how we could cut off Elena's communications with the boys, while Amber, Logan, and I developed a plan.

Or rather, Amber did, while I listened to her reasoning for staying behind.

"I'm a woman," she insisted. "I can radio the Matrians and send them on a wild goose chase. If I do it right, I can take over the command center here, and they'll just think the shift changed. They might not even notice the cameras are under our control—it'll keep up our cover for longer. That will buy us time for you guys to get to the control room, and—"

"The control room—transmission room—whatever you want to call it—isn't here," Owen announced at that moment, his voice glum. "It's… I think it's being patched through here though? I'm not really sure what I'm looking at."

I looked over and saw him thumbing through the pages of Thomas' notebook, his eyes searching for something. Then he frowned and looked over at me.

"It seems like Elena's set up a relay station between here and the… people feeding the boys orders."

"Okay… so we can't stop the people who are giving them orders?" I asked, my stomach plunging. He hesitated, and then shook his head. All this work… it couldn't be for nothing.

"Maybe not, but we might be able to get them to stall," he said.

"What do you mean?" Logan asked, and he ran a hand through his hair.

"Someone *here* has to be giving someone *there* orders, right?"

"Not necessarily," I replied, trying to understand what he was getting at. "Elena could've given them the orders before they left."

"No," Amber said. "A small sub-section of the Matrian governmental code is that no operation can legally be carried out without having constant communication with the palace." She exhaled, and looked at us, her eyes wide. "It's a small law, but an important one, drilled into the wardens. The fear was that if anything changed during a time of war—say, a treaty or peace—they needed to be able to contact everyone to make sure it was enforced."

Logan gave her an incredulous look and shook his head.

"Who comes up with this? That's ridiculous."

"It's not," I told him. "Not when you consider what the Matrians stood for before Elena assumed control. None of them wanted to fight. They wanted peace from their neighbors, not war. You don't leave an active weapon out there without a way to get them to stand down. Amber, how do *you* know that?"

She shrugged. "Desmond had us learn stuff like this in case we had to impersonate a warden."

I smiled, appreciating the irony. "What's the protocol if they lose contact with high command?"

"They are to stand down operations and wait. After four hours, they are to break down operations and return home to assess what has happened."

Logan chuckled, and we all looked at him. "Bless those Matrian peace-makers," he said with a grin.

"Wait," said Owen, turning around and away from the terminal. "Wouldn't Elena change that?"

"She might have. But it's a chance we have to be willing to take," Amber replied. "It's really our only option, short of finding their location and going there to take them out."

"So wait—what do we do?" asked Logan, looking around. "I mean, can we stop them from getting orders?"

"We can," Owen replied. "We just need to take out their transmitting antennae on the roof. If we do that, we can take out all communications through the palace's official channels... and then there's a good chance they'll stop the attack with the boys."

That was a solid plan, and I took over the rest, signaling my approval.

"Amber, you and Logan stay here and keep them off our backs for as long as possible. Give us a couple blocks of your semtex and extra detonators, and then block yourselves in. Owen and I will go blow their communications array sky high."

Amber arched an eyebrow and exhaled a sharp breath.

"That's no small order," she said. "But we got your back. Good luck."

"You too," I said, chambering a round into my gun and moving toward the hall. "You too."

CHAPTER 39

Violet

The hall before me was filled with doors and hallways leading to who knew what. I saw a sign that said "Servants' Kitchen" heading left down a hall, and pointed to it.

Here? I asked Morgan, still entertaining the secret hope that Ms. Dale would answer, having miraculously survived all the guards, patched herself up, and found our new channel... It would be just like her, wouldn't it?

It's about right, Morgan replied, and I nodded, pushing away the stab of disappointment when hers was the only voice coming through the comms, focusing instead on checking both sides. I ducked back around the corner into the hallway we'd just left, motioning Morgan back as a regal voice became audible, instantly recognizable. My back to the wall, I used a trick Viggo had taught me and held a mirror down low, peering down the corridor and seeing, in the tiny glass, what was clearly Queen Elena's figure, flanked by several guards. From the quick glance I got, they were striding toward us, Elena giving orders.

I looked over at Morgan and nodded toward the door a few feet behind her, and she nodded back and moved over to it, keeping her steps quiet. I followed in her footsteps as we slipped through the door into what appeared to be a closet. I held the door slightly cracked and tried to calm my heartbeat enough to hear what the queen was saying in the corridor beyond.

"—tine has been broken," she said imperiously. "They're getting into the palace. Where are the bloody torch units I ordered? They should be here by now. It might already be too late. Sierra and I may need to evacuate while this problem is resolved."

"My queen," another voice replied, growing louder as the group passed by. "I do not want you chased from your home! We will put an end to this, you have my..."

I couldn't make out the rest, the words lost to the chaos of the entourage stomping by behind her. My eyes watched through the crack as *sixteen* wardens walked past, and I looked over at Morgan.

We have to follow her, I said. *And she has a* lot *of guards with her.*

Morgan gave a tired chuckle, shaking her head. *Well, good news—Elena is definitely afraid of you. But we can't take on that many.*

We don't have to. All we really need is Elena neutralized for a few hours while Alyssa gets the word out. We cloak, follow, and use the dart.

Morgan stared at me, and then nodded. *Your bag—they'll—*

You'll have to guide me, I said.

Her eyes widened, and she stood, quickly tucking a few grenades into the pockets of her suit. It looked odd and bulky, but they would go invisible with her, and she'd still be armed.

I pulled my bag tight around my shoulders and watched her disappear eerily from view—it never felt any less strange. A moment later, there was a ripple by the door as it was pushed outward. I sat my rifle down and went invisible as well. The bag still showed, and if anyone came up behind me, it would be a dead giveaway. But maybe it would surprise people just enough...

From around the corner where the retinue couldn't see my floating backpack, Morgan fed me instructions. I followed, my path surprisingly free of any people. Maybe it was because the queen was moving through, but it was definitely eerie. I could hear her talking ahead, but

I couldn't make out her words as I crept along the corridor, adrenaline pumping in my chest.

It felt nerve-wracking, just plain wrong. I kept expecting a trap, or somebody coming around the corner, but there was no one. Certainly they had installed thermal cameras. Morgan might be close enough to look like a stray guard in thermals, but if they showed the live footage of the hall at the same time, it would become obvious something was up. The palace had to have noticed by now… So where were they?

My muscles burned and began to shake as I continued to follow the processional, close enough to hear it, but not so close that I could see it. I knew I didn't have long before I would have to stop—my stamina for using the suit wasn't even close to what it had been before my fight with Tabitha. We needed to get there soon, or I was going to give everything away. The people watching the cameras weren't so incompetent that they'd miss a girl dressed all wrong running around the halls this close to the queen.

Violet, they're slowing down. There's a room off to the right side of the hall, the door slightly open. I'm in there. Morgan's voice came suddenly, but I felt a wave of relief as I picked up the pace a little. It was risky—once again, the bag was visible—but my control over the suit was going to give out. Soon. The pins and needles in my muscles were being replaced with straight up loose numbness. Never a good sign.

I kept moving straight, and then stepped into the room. I held my muscles tense for a few seconds more, slowly pushing the door closed but leaving it slightly ajar. I heard Elena's voice through the crack, still muffled, and then my control gave out.

I reappeared instantly, my arms and legs burning fiercely as the feeling returned to them. Exhaling, I began shaking my arms and legs out, turning and looking around the room. Morgan appeared behind a wooden desk and looked at me quizzically.

Are you okay? she mouthed, her voice buzzing through the earbud.

I should be asking you that question, I replied, wiping my forearm against my forehead and grimacing when it came back slick with sweat.

Her face was exceptionally pale, right down to her lips, but she didn't miss a beat as she began pulling objects from her pocket.

I'm fine. It was a transparent lie, but I understood it. *This is the nursery, and we're right outside the safe room. She's got Sierra in there.*

And sixteen guards, I reminded her. *You want to use the concussive grenade and go in shooting?*

She hesitated. *It could work... but we can't risk Sierra getting hit by the blast.*

I really don't see any other way, I replied honestly. *Do you?*

Morgan hesitated a moment more, and then nodded grimly.

With my enhancement, I should be able to direct everything away from her. Desmond used to train us for scenarios like this. Just keep an eye out for her, too, please... I couldn't bear it if anything happened to her.

I thought of Tim, then of Morgan's past, and knew what the young woman must be feeling.

Of course.

Then we have to move now. She's got an escape plan, and if she and Sierra manage to get out of here...

She trailed off, but I could finish her sentence for her: If Elena got out of the palace before we could get to her, then she would win. If she escaped, she could pull back and muster her forces to crush us, using the boys as the final insult and injury all at once. We were running out of resources, and morale was low. There was no way Patrus could mount an offensive sufficient to stop her. This was it.

Let's do it, I said, and Morgan nodded. We moved back over to the door, and I began to push it open.

Then a familiar roar bellowed down the hallway, and I froze before quickly ducking back. Heavy footsteps pounded toward us, and I closed my eyes, praying that the berserk boys from below didn't have a way of tracking Morgan and me.

Suddenly the footsteps doubled, and then tripled, and I heard a lower roar sound out as the fast-moving footsteps raced by, a shadow cutting over the crack in the door so fast it looked like a bat hunting insects in front of a lamp, always too fast to clearly spot any discernable features.

A heartbeat later, gunfire erupted loudly from the next room, and one of the berserkers—if that was what they were—gave a throaty roar of rage. Screams and shouts echoed out amid the gunfire, and Morgan and I ducked as a bullets cut through the wall to the left of us. The bullet holes were several feet away from us, but it was still unnerving enough to make us stay down.

We stayed like that as the sounds of panic increased, Morgan's grip on my arm tightening as the altercation gave no sound of stopping.

Sierra! she transmitted as I turned to look at her.

She stood suddenly, gun in her hand, and pulled open the door, stepping through and going invisible. I watched for a moment, and then shook away the surprise the boys' entrance had caused, rising to follow Morgan.

The gunfire had all but stopped at this point, and as I swung around the corner, I could see why.

One of the boys was down, blood pooling around him as he twitched on the ground. Another was obviously wounded, but seemingly oblivious to it, as he continuously drove his fists into the pulped remains of a warden's head. I shuddered and averted my gaze, following Morgan's footsteps as she moved fast across the wide antechamber, heading for a large metal vault door that hung ajar, as though its hinges had been damaged somehow.

The still-standing boy almost plowed into me to get to a warden missing a leg and trying to drag herself away, but a different warden lying on the ground just behind him lashed out with a foot, catching him in the back of the knee. He fell, and she leapt off the ground onto his back, wrapping her arms around his neck and squeezing.

I didn't want to leave her to face the boy alone or vice versa, but I couldn't risk her stopping us, so I dodged it all and darted by.

I'm entering the vault, Morgan announced, and I waited a moment before slipping after her through the crack in the vault door.

My momentum carried me a few steps forward, into the vault before I had the thought to stop. Morgan was already as still as a statue, suddenly visible, tension radiating off of her like a furnace.

I could see why she had given up all efforts toward stealth: it wasn't going to help her here. Elena's face was impassive as she looked back at us from behind thermal goggles, one hand on a little blonde girl's shoulder, the other hand pressing a gun to her head. The little girl's eyes were round with terror, confusion, and pain as she looked around, fighting back tears.

"Elena, why are you—"

"Shut up," Elena ordered, shaking the young girl by her arm. "And Violet—drop it."

"Who are you—" Sierra said, her sentence cutting off as I let go of my control of the suit. Sierra took a cursory glance at me, and then her attention waned, her focus solely on Morgan. "Morgana?" she said uncertainly, staring at the girl next to me. "Why—who—"

"Sierra," Morgan breathed. She'd turned her subvocalizer off, and I reached up and did the same. Morgan's head snapped up to look at Elena. "What do you want?"

Elena arched an elegant eyebrow, but her expression didn't change.

"You really have to ask?" she replied, before looking at me. "Egg."

"We didn't even bring it up from the labs," Morgan began to lie, and in a fluid motion, Elena moved the gun and pointed, pulling the trigger. The shot went off, and I flinched slightly as something behind me dropped to the floor.

Looking over my shoulder, I felt sick to my stomach when I saw the still form of one of the berserker boys, his hand outstretched just a few inches from my foot. I turned in time to see Elena smoothly put the gun back to Sierra's temple, her face never moving a muscle.

"The egg," she repeated. "Or I let whatever comes in next tear you apart limb from limb."

Morgan turned her gaze toward me, her face configured in a silent plea, but I was already opening my bag. I pulled the silver case out and held it up, and then placed it on a table that separated us from Elena. She watched me, her eyes gleaming with warning as she grabbed Sierra's hand, jerking her forward. I took a slow, healthy step back, shooting a glance toward the still-open vault, checking for the other berserker.

Turning back, I realized Elena was staring at the egg. She did that for a long moment, and then blinked, her gaze suddenly returning to me.

"The key?"

I glared back at her, irritation at the smug look on her face warring with my concern for the terrified little girl. After a pause, I reached up and tore the chain off my neck. I held the key out, dangling from my fist, and then put it on top of the egg.

Elena's lips curled up, and she met my gaze. "Thank you," she said, her smile growing, and getting crueler, a fraction at a time.

I realized it had gone very quiet in the room behind me, and turned in time to see the third boy, reaching for Morgan. She leapt suddenly, but it was the wrong direction, and he caught her with his wild, artless blow, low and in the side.

Morgan went flying through the air, impacting on a bookcase with a thud and sliding to the floor. I followed her trajectory, when a movement from the corner of my eye caught my attention. Turning, I saw Elena moving toward the open door, the egg tucked under one arm, her hand tight on Sierra's wrist as she dragged the little girl from the room.

Then the boy stepped in front of me, and I barely had a moment to register his swing. I dodged it without even thinking, and then scrambled back as he pressed the advantage. He swung at me again, and I darted out of his way, barely avoiding blows and well aware of my limited abilities against him.

"They're getting away!" Morgan's voice, rough and out of breath, came desperately through the room.

I couldn't shoot him, but I needed to get to Elena, and fast. The gun was still in my hand—Elena had never ordered us to put our weapons down. She had counted on us not wanting to risk Sierra, and had gambled correctly. Yet even though the boy threatened my life, I couldn't— wouldn't—pull the trigger.

A thought occurred to me as I ducked under a wild haymaker, and I sprang forward, rolling between his legs and coming out the other side. I reached into the pocket on my thigh and pulled out a tranquilizer dart—I had just two left, but I only needed one for Elena—and ripped the cap off with my teeth.

He was turning around to hit me, but I ducked low and jammed the needle into the meaty part of his thigh and then moved away. The young man looked down at the tranquilizer dart, then back up at me as I slowly retreated, his eyes dark and wild with rage. He bared his teeth and snapped at me with a vicious snarl. I moved back more quickly, trying to search for anything I could hit him with while he advanced—one step, two—and then he toppled over, glancing off the table and dragging a chair down with him. It smashed on the floor as he let out a long sigh, his eyes drifting closed.

I exhaled sharply in relief, and took a moment to collect myself, not even bothering to think about how close I had come to death—again— then rushed over to Morgan. She was already picking herself off the ground, her breaths tight, sharp gasps, her eyes watering.

"Okay," she wheezed, swatting my hands away, and I was reminded for a brief moment of Tim. "Did you see where they went?"

I didn't have to ask to know that she was talking about her sisters.

"Out through the back door," I said, ignoring her hands and helping her up. "I need to check under your vest. You could have internal—"

"Go," she said, pushing me roughly before stumbling to one side. "Roof... Left... Straight. Door."

"Morgan, I can't just leave you—"

"*Go.*" Her eyes were hard, and the look she gave me promised the harsh side of her anger if I dared to protest.

She was right, of course, and I turned and went, moving at a fast run and hoping Sierra was throwing the mother of all tantrums and buying me every second I could get. I was going to need it.

CHAPTER 40

Violet

Morgan's instructions were easy enough to follow, but the hall I found myself in was long, and every foot I went made me suddenly doubt whether I had actually followed her directions, wonder if I had already lost Elena. I tried to listen for the sounds of Sierra crying, but they were lost in the general sounds of chaos and gunfire now erupting all over the castle.

I stopped short as a warden went across the hallway ahead of me, barely sparing me a glance, and then quickly activated the suit when I saw one of those monkey-wolf things chasing after her, terrified it would spot me and distract me from my purpose. It stayed focused on its prey, and I quickly shed the backpack, no longer needing it, and moved forward, willing my aching limbs to keep working with the suit.

The door to the stairwell finally came into view, and I breathed a sigh of relief as I saw it. Why, I didn't know—maybe just at the reassurance that there was still a chance to put an end to this. But the sight didn't stop that icy hand of fear from suddenly seizing my heart, or the wave of panic that threatened to overwhelm me as I reached for the handle.

I couldn't deal with those emotions right now, so I ignored them both as I yanked the door open and hurried up the concrete steps that led to the roof.

A wave of déjà vu struck me hard as I emerged out in the open. This was where Lee had landed, right before he had killed Queen Rina and Mr. Jenks and tried to leave me behind. Did things always have to end here?

Not much had changed, and I could see the heloship docked a few hundred feet away, its running lights spilling out onto the dark rooftop. Elena was already dangerously close to it, ready to take off into the starry night beyond and turn this mission into a failure. Neither Sierra nor the egg was with her—had she already loaded them up? How long had I been following her? It felt like it had taken ages to find her, but it had probably only been a few minutes.

The full moon had sunk significantly since our drive through the city, now it hovering near the horizon, but with the moonlight and the small spotlights that occasionally lit up the edges of objects on the roof, I could see a small group of black-clad figures waiting between Elena and the heloship. Most were shorter, younger, but there were a few taller figures interspersed between them. They stood at the ready, masked faces watching as Elena approached.

I started to run, knowing I was making noise but hoping they wouldn't hear me until it was too late. If I could just reach Elena, then I could take her out. Hopefully the boys wouldn't attack me without an order. I just had to reach her.

I focused on Elena as I moved, somehow managing to keep my muscles tensed for the suit, when one of the boys stepped up to the queen, pointing in my general direction. The next moment I recognized the strange protrusions from his mask as thermal goggles, and my heart sank as Elena turned in my direction, her own goggles pulled back over her head. Her mouth moved.

An instant later a boy was in front of me. I reached for my gun, knowing I'd never reach it in time, and something hard slammed into me, sending me flying a few feet across the roof. I landed roughly on my back, muscle memory causing me to slap the ground with my hands and tuck my chin to my chest, breaking the fall and protecting my spine. My control over the suit went out immediately, and the fire that filled my limbs just added to the pain of the blow.

I rolled several feet, sharp pebbles and stones tearing at my suit and skin underneath, scraping me. My adrenaline was pumping too fiercely for me to black out, and I climbed back onto my feet, watching the two boys staying warily close and blocking my way to Elena, keeping just out of fist-reach.

One of the boys moved again, really just a blur, and I dove to the right. I was too slow, and he caught me midair, slamming my legs down. The roof whirled around me, and I slid to the ground.

My hip throbbed, and I groaned, managing to somehow climb into a sitting position, but I found myself leaning against a cobblestone chimney. I grabbed the edge, hauling myself up.

I barely had my feet under me when a strong hand gripped the back of my neck, squeezing hard and hauling me the rest of the way up.

Roughly, the hand pushed me forward between the two boys, barely keeping me steady as I tripped over my own feet, reeling.

"Stop playing with her and bring her over!" Elena shouted.

Immediately I was pushed forward. I glanced over my shoulder to see the tall boy behind me, his eyes dark and unreadable through the holes of the mask. He propelled me closer to Elena, and I used the momentum to weaken his hold, my hand going for my gun while I distracted him with my struggling.

I didn't have to shoot the boys anywhere lethal—I just had to disable them so I could get close to the queen. Provided I didn't miss and hit a major artery…

It didn't matter. As soon as the gun was in my hand and coming around, another of the boys to the side blurred over, and I felt my weapon ripped violently from me, my fingers going numb and then burning as I realized it had scraped the skin. The gun skittered across the roof and came to a stop some distance away, and I stared at it as I was shoved forward.

Elena was within spitting distance, and, with no other resources left, I lunged for her, rage coursing through me, trying to swing. The boy holding me hauled me back and kept me from striking at her, and then threw me forward onto my knees. I clenched my teeth to keep from crying out, and reared back to look up at her.

Elena stared down at me, her face implacable. Then she smiled.

"You had every opportunity to let it go, Violet. I'm confounded as to why you couldn't, but frankly, I won't even try to understand your reasoning. I'm sure it is something sentimental, but I really just don't care." She simultaneously shrugged and nodded, before pulling her gun up, aiming directly for my head. "It'll be better this way. It'll be faster, and you'll finally, *finally* get to have a little peace and quiet. Just give up."

I glared at her.

"Never," I whispered, looking up at her only to see the end of a barrel, a bullet inside with my name on it. "I'll never stop trying to stop you. You don't care whose life you ruin in your mad quest to do… whatever it is. As long as there is breath in my lungs, as long as you use people to hurt others against their will, I will fight you."

Elena's smile deepened. "Well you certainly won't have that breath in your lungs for long," she breathed, pulling back the hammer. "The boys are now mine, thanks to the Benuxupane sample you got us, and they will be forever. You've lost, and I get to sleep tonight knowing I pulled the trigger." She began to tense her finger, and then stopped. "You know… I think I might actually come to miss the chaotic element you added to my life, Violet. Without you, all this would've seemed so… boring. Easy. Not a victory worthy of my talents. I suppose I should thank you for that, but… I have a heloship to catch."

Viggo's face appeared in my mind as Elena's finger tightened on the trigger. I closed my eyes.

Viggo, I love you.

Just then, an explosion rocked the night, and the rooftop beneath us shuddered.

My eyes jolted open, my heart beating wildly as I instinctively threw myself to the ground at the noise. In front of me, Elena still held the gun, but she was looking to one side—the side from which the lower rooftop extended beneath us—as the noises of shouts and gunshots filtered up from below.

"What was that?" she snapped, her voice low and dangerous.

In that moment, when her guard was down, I struggled to find the energy in my legs to move, to crawl backward, to attack her—and then a dark figure blurred into motion in front of me, the queen's face snapping forward again with a gasp just as the gun was knocked from her hand, clattering metallically onto the roof beyond.

Elena took one step back, and then another.

The blur stilled, resolving into the boy who had been roughly shoving me moments ago, his body positioned between me and the queen. Elena held her wrist gingerly, squinting at the boy in front of her.

"Stand down," she ordered.

The boy cocked his head at her and then shook his head.

As soon as he did, some of the other boys began shaking their heads, turning toward her as well. They broke rank, reaching up in unison and pulling the masks off, and I looked at my savior, my mouth falling open as his mask came off too.

Tim was standing there, protecting me from Elena.

Elena took another slow step back, and another. She looked at the group of mask-less boys, seeming to latch onto the ones who still wore their masks... who were now behaving oddly too. They looked around, tapped their ears, stepped back out of their neat ranks, looking around as though they'd just woken up.

Elena, in turn, muttered something into a comm unit on her neck. She tapped it twice, then shouted, "Don't just stand there! Apprehend her!"

The ranks of boys did nothing. The unmasked ones continued to advance, and the ones in the masks stared at her, some of them swaying on their feet. I found myself watching from the roof as if spellbound, transfixed by the scene.

Elena stood where she was a heartbeat more. Then she turned and broke into a run, racing for the heloship—and everything seemed to move at normal speed again. Some of the masked boys scrambled away, while the rest were already on their feet, moving to stop her. I started to haul up my aching body to go after her, but my brother held out an arm to stop me.

"Revenge," he said, watching as she began climbing the ramp to get into the heloship—only to come to a complete stop halfway as the boys at the foot of the ramp began to move up it.

As I watched, I realized there were more black-clad figures at the top of the ramp—clearly what had made her pause—and she turned around, warily looking at the oncoming boys.

Tim turned and looked at me, his face apologetic.

"Sorry for hurt. Played part. Had to trick her."

I turned to him, still baffled by the sudden shift in events. I had expected to be dead by now, but I was alive, watching as the boys Elena had exploited slowly converge on her.

"They're not going to—"

"No," Tim said, shaking his head and smiling. "I know. We need alive. More valuable."

"More legiti—" I stopped, my blood running cold, when I saw Elena reach into her pocket and pull something out. Her hand went to her mouth and back down again. "Wait. Tim, call them ba—"

Then Elena fell to her knees, screaming. She clapped her hands over her ears, her mouth gaping wide, her voice coming out in an agonized screech. There was a ripple of uncertainty in the boys as they watched her scream, and they hesitated, looking around.

"Grab her!" Tim bellowed. I was too focused on Elena to say anything. What had she just done?

Moments later she slumped onto the ramp and began to roll down it, her legs and arms moving limply. The closest boys backed up a few steps as she came to a stop, visibly baffled, and I lost her behind the crowd.

"Get them away!" I told Tim, starting to push through the crowd.

Elena slowly stood, swaying back and forth, her back to me.

The rooftop was silent and still for a long second, and then she turned, her eyes burning hotly as she met my gaze full on.

"Clever Violet," she said after a long moment, her voice raw from screaming. "You thought to trap me. Don't you know… I always have a contingency plan."

One of the boys broke through his confusion and raced for her, but she casually reached her arm across her chest, bringing the back of her hand down on his face. Instead of simply stumbling back, the boy went flying through the air, disappearing over the edge of the rooftop with a scream.

"Run!" I yelled to anyone and everyone, retreating, and Elena advanced, death in her eyes and a sadistic grin playing at her mouth.

CHAPTER 41

Viggo

The hallway we had found ourselves in ended abruptly at a door, and without waiting, Owen and I pushed through it, knowing we'd reached the door that led to the roof. The cool night air engulfed us, and we found ourselves standing before a narrow set of exposed stairs, winding up one side of the palace. Owen started moving up them, but I grabbed his shoulder and held him back, taking a moment to close the door behind us and break the lock.

We should hurry, he transmitted, but I kept a firm hand on his shoulder.

Careful. I moved up the stairs first. This roof was lower than the one to our left—that one went up three more stories, the two uppermost having rows of windows, but I couldn't see any sign of danger lurking from above. Most of the windows were darkened, only a few emitting a glow of light into the night. The rest of our roof was wide and low, with ventilation shafts poking up and out of it, as well as massive heating and cooling units that seemed to eat up the open space, creating dozens of barriers and shadows. Just above them, I could make out the dim shape of something jutting up from the far corner beyond.

Are those the antennas? I asked, pointing to the equipment on the far corner of the roof, which looked from here like a tangle of metal silhouettes surrounded by a tall barbed-wire fence.

*Yes. We should—*He started to move again, but I pulled him back down, and he gave me an incredulous look.

Why are you being so hesitant? he demanded. *What are you seeing that I'm not?*

Nothing, I replied, shaking my head. *But that is critical equipment. Would you leave it unguarded?*

He opened his mouth, and then shut it with a snap.

That's a good point. Amber?

Just at that moment, Amber's voice came through.

Viggo, there's some sort of fire below in the labs. The electrical systems are pretty much melting, and we've lost many of the cameras. I'm diverting a lot of the guards out of the area—mostly I'm telling them to help evacuate the servants—but things got out of the lab, and—

We let them out, I told her grimly. *Just do what you can to help preserve their lives as well as ours. We'll take care of the communications antennas.*

I slid off my backpack and motioned for Owen to do the same.

What supplies do we really need to take down the antennas? I asked.

Semtex, detonators—we won't need it all unless you want to destroy this part of the palace.

I do not. So...

There was a flash of a smile on Owen's face as he pulled a tube of the metal-melting chemical from his bag, along with a few more clips of ammunition. I fished a rope out of my own pile and added it to the collection.

Rope? he asked, raising an eyebrow as he picked up the rope and tugged on it. *Really?*

We're on a roof with limited access. I want a backup plan. He laughed bitterly through the link, and I frowned at him. *What?*

It's just nice to hear you have a plan for once. You know, just when

I've finally decided, what's the point? Plans, no plans... everyone dies just the same.

I pulled out my gun and checked the magazine, counting the bullets through the holes on the side.

Owen, stop it. Give me the bag. I'll go first and you follow behind, in case anyone is lurking out there.

I looked again, studying the long, dark shadows draped across half the roof, searching for any sign of movement in the relative quiet of the night. There was nothing, but I was on edge, alert.

I should go first, Owen said, already hefting the bag over his shoulder.

Owen, you're better with the suit than I am. Give me the tube and the gun and run interference for me.

Owen frowned but passed it over with a nod.

Let's just get it done so we can find everyone else.

Thinking about Morgan? I asked as I put on the bag. He smiled, but the expression evaporated quickly.

That's none of your business, he transmitted, before slowly disappearing from view.

Well, be prepared for it to be everyone's business, I replied, taking a direct path toward the structures on the corner of the roof. They slowly became more visible as I moved toward them, and I realized there was a massive satellite dish in the middle, but around it were straight, long metal frames, towering into the night, nearly as tall as the adjacent rooftop. The metal mesh fence surrounding it was, I realized as I neared it, marked with a sign announcing 10,000 volts of electricity was coursing through it.

Violet and I have stood up to our fair share of teasing.

I knew I should be focusing on the mission and only talking about critical things. But Owen's tone when he'd mentioned giving up on all plans... I suspected he was in that dark place again, the place that made him do irrational and painful things, and I hoped maybe, just maybe, a little reminder of something good in the world might shake him out of it.

Yeah, but you and Violet are so confident. I'm... I'm not so much. I mean... I didn't even realize she was into me until Violet said something. His voice didn't sound as heavy as before, but it was still loaded with some kind of worry. It was eerie talking to a vanished man, knowing he was near me somewhere while we were talking about this but feeling like it would be no different if he and I were on opposite sides of the palace.

Oh God, I said with a smile as I approached the fence. *Please tell me my wife isn't becoming one of those wives.*

Owen's chuckle in reply made me feel a little better as I stopped just short of the fence. A slight hum emanated from it—a tiny sign of the 10,000 volts—and I reached into the bag to pull out the tube of solvent.

Maybe she is, he said, *but can you blame her? She's ridiculously in love with you, and—*

Did you just call my wife ridiculous? I teased as I unscrewed the tube. *Because I'm sure she'd love to know you said that.*

Isn't that the point of love—to be ridiculous with, to, and for each other? he shot back, and I paused in my careful application of the black, tar-like goo I was pressing against the point where the fence wires overlapped. The goo itself didn't transmit electricity—that was one of its selling points—but I had to be careful that neither the tube nor my fingers touched the metal.

I should've gotten you to write my wedding vows, I said after a thoughtful moment, resuming my work. *I gotta cut a hole in this thing, in case you haven't noticed. It's electrified.*

I have, just hurry up. It's making me nervous how quiet everything is up here.

I agree, I informed him as I slowly drew the tube down, applying the substance liberally. Overhead, wisps of smoke were appearing, and molten metal began to drip down as the chemicals did their job. *And I'm not even the one using the suit.*

I gave you that option, he coolly replied. *And don't worry, I'm watching the doors.*

That will only last as long as it takes me to get this fence down. I moved my hands up to start dragging the tube across the top and back down the other side, creating a four-foot-long, three-foot-wide door where the section I'd separated would fall out. *Once we're in there, we aren't going to have a good view.*

I know. I wish I knew how to help Amber get the cameras back up.

Well, unfortunately for Amber, the redhead's voice cut in, reminding us nothing we had said was private, *Thomas' manual didn't cover electronic meltdown.*

Any chance we can just pull back? I asked, taking a step back to admire my handiwork and wait for the solvent to finish melting the metal. *I'd love to lounge in that control room.* I tried to keep my tone light, but Owen seemed to have gone even stiller than before at the mention of Thomas' name, and I was still worried about him.

They know something's up, Logan said, his voice a tight whisper. *I'm not sure how much time we have before someone's back up here. The room had four people manning it, Viggo. Four. She's just one.*

I'm a very convincing liar, Amber replied, seeming unimpressed with Logan's concern for her. *Anyway, to answer your question—no. Sorry. You gotta take the antennas out. Then we can talk exit strategies.*

I sighed—her answer wasn't unexpected—and then kicked out with my boot, impacting the impromptu door I had created. My boots also shielded me from being electrocuted, if there was still a charge in the partially severed mesh, and the piece I had carved out went skidding across the rooftop and came to a rattling stop.

That wasn't exactly stealthy, Owen said sourly, and I ducked through and moved around the base of the satellite dish. I sat my bag down beside the concrete block from which the dish jutted, pulling out the cubes of semtex and placing them on the ground.

The blonde man appeared next to me a second later, studying the dish and its mount.

We'll need to really control the explosion, he said, kneeling and producing a knife. He cut through one of the semtex cubes, halving it and then quartering it again, as he spoke. *We don't want to bring the roof down on the upper levels, but at the same time, we have to damage the equipment enough to make sure they can't repair it quickly.*

What do you recommend? I asked, taking the quarters and rolling the clay-like material into a ball.

This size, maybe even smaller. I'll climb up the dish and put it on there, but you'll have to climb the antennas.

I hesitated, wiping my hand on my thigh, and shook my head.

Too exposed. If anyone comes out or looks in through one of those windows, we'll get—

Viggo, I just saw a group of wardens heading your way, Amber cut in. *In one of the adjacent halls. I can't be sure they're after you, per se, but—*

Thanks. It was rude cutting her off, but I didn't want to waste a second. *What's the messier way to do this?*

Owen hesitated, then slapped a ball of explosive onto the concrete wall holding up the dish.

Let's hope they didn't skimp on the contractor they hired to build this, he muttered. *Every three feet one of these goes down. I'll move behind you and put in the detonators.*

I picked up the balls we had made, cradling them in my hand, and returned to the front of the equipment tangle at a jog, sticking them to the side of the wall while Owen planted the detonators. We had three quarters of it set up when I heard something—a slight scraping sound—and froze.

A heartbeat later I moved behind the large radio tower, using the metal frame as cover, and looked out onto the still rooftop, searching for any sign of movement.

Viggo?

I didn't reply to Amber's voice. I didn't have time—bullets pinged off of my cover, and I ducked under it as the gunshots sounded.

I counted four muzzle flashes! Owen, can you confirm?

Six… no, eight! What do you want to do?

I was already smashing the remaining six or so balls in my hands into one large one and planting it haphazardly at the base of one of the legs holding the radio tower up.

Toss me a detonator, I ordered, and Owen's hands moved, something small arcing through the air toward me.

Reflexively, I caught it and pushed it in before moving over to the other side, keeping low. The gunfire had cut off unexpectedly, but I could hear whoever was out there scrambling around, searching for a better position.

Rope! I shouted.

Owen looked up at me from across the narrow divide that separated us, and then pulled the coil we'd dragged with us into his hands, tossing it to me. Someone fired at it as it flew through the air, interrupting its trajectory and pushing it back in midair, and it landed a few feet from either of us. I cursed, preparing to lunge for it, when Owen darted out, shimmering from view.

Owen! I shouted as the coil began to move. Gunfire exploded all around us, and Owen grunted, reappearing suddenly in the middle of tossing the rope over to me. He slid through the gravel after it, his hand going to his side and coming away wet with blood.

It's just a graze, he said. *But the suit's damaged.*

Growling, I went to my knees and fired a few shots toward our attackers. I was firing blind, but hopefully it would buy us a few seconds.

We're pinned down, he said as he dropped, looking at me with a blind, desperate determination in his eyes. *My suit is gone. Leave the detonator with me.*

He held out his hand, and I gave him an incredulous look.

I'm not doing that, I informed him, ducking as sparks shot off overhead, probably a bullet ricochet, and then rising back to a knee and firing. I saw a shadow peel away from a cluster of shadows creeping around on our right side and realized the door I'd cut into the fence was on that side.

I fired a few rounds near the first approaching warden, and she danced back a few feet, giving me a little time.

Viggo, can't you see? Owen grabbed my arm and gave me a look, broken and angry, that sent a clench of fear through my heart. This was what I had sensed in him earlier—the despair that made him want to do stuff like this. *I have to do this! I can… finally make up for all the wrong I've done you and Violet. I can finally see Ian.*

A sharp pain tugged at my heart as he spoke, but… I couldn't let it happen. Not so close after Thomas. This wasn't the time or the place for a sacrifice. Not one I could prevent.

I'm sorry, I said, pulling out the length of rope as my bullets whizzed by overhead. *But I can't let you off that easy.*

Viggo, I—

NO! I said, activating the suit so I could quickly loop the length of rope around the leg of the tower closest to the edge. *I'm getting us out of here.*

Owen groaned, and I looked over in time to see him lifting his gun up to his shoulder, firing at the mass of wardens now closing in on us.

You stubborn, egotistical jerk! he shouted as he fired. *Don't you know you can't control everything?*

You're still up and moving, Owen, I retorted, looping the opposite end of the rope into a makeshift harness and getting into it. He fired another couple of rounds and then pulled back, gasping as his hand went back to his side.

Doesn't mean you get to decide how I die, he said, his voice harsh with pain. *I have to do this.*

No, you don't, I said angrily, moving over to him and grabbing him under his armpits, intending to drag him if necessary. *We need you, Owen. Morgan needs you to come back and support her. Violet and I need you to help us rebuild. Thomas sacrificed his life so we could do this and get out alive. So you get to die on this roof the exact second after I do, or not at all!*

Owen looked up at me as I dragged him closer to the edge, a wry, bitter smile on his lips, but at least he didn't resist.

What would Violet say if I let you die?

She would understand.

There was a rattle, indicating that the group of wardens had finally reached the fence, and I handed Owen the detonator as I pulled his back tight to my chest, wrapping my hand around his waist. I wrapped my other arm around the rope and took us over the edge, and then began to rappel down using my makeshift harness to slow us. We were a third of the way down when I heard shouting above, and as I kicked off the side of the building, I ordered—*Blow it.*

I heard the click right before the explosion, so loud my heart felt it, and an orange-red ball of fire erupted above us with an angry roar. We fell away from it, arcing back toward the building. My feet impacted the side, and I kicked off again, releasing more line so fast that the rope sounded like a zipper. We dropped another thirty feet, landing heavily against the side, my ankles and knees bearing the brunt of Owen's and my combined weight.

Even though my muscles were burning, I kicked off again as bits of flaming debris began to fall all around us. The rope continued to unravel as I let it out, and then suddenly it was burning through the glove I was wearing, cutting into the flesh of my hand with all the bite of a dull knife. I yanked it away, and then we were in freefall. I wrapped both arms around Owen, my feet around his thighs, knowing when the rope caught us we would jerk, and he might fall.

There was a sharp and sudden tug as the rope ran out, and my shoulders and waist screamed in protest as the rope tried to cut right through them, but I kept a hard grip on Owen.

You're insane! he shouted as we bounced upward a few feet.

We fell back down, the rope tightening again. Then there was a loud creaking sound from above, and I looked up to see the top of the radio tower wobbling, the rope wobbling with it. There was a sharp, metallic twang, and suddenly gravity was pulling us back down.

We landed hard in the bushes below. For a second, I just lay there—gnarled branches and twigs digging into my flesh—staring uncomprehendingly at the roof dozens of feet above, and the tower jutting off of it at an angle, bobbing up and down a few times before going still.

Owen? I asked, sitting up and then stopping as a wave of intense pain radiating from my shoulder warned me not to move.

Looking down, I saw a broken tree branch jutting through my shoulder, right above my collarbone. As if looking at it suddenly made me feel it, I grated my teeth against the fresh wave of pain that seemed to be exploding all around it, but there was very little blood. A good sign.

Owen, I gasped, looking over to my right. *Are you okay?*

I'm here, he replied softly. *Bushes broke our fall. I'm still... You* threw *us off of the* roof.

I did. Can you—

"NOBODY MOVE!" a female voice bellowed, and I tilted my chin to my chest to see a dozen or so wardens—one of them holding a flame thrower, of all things—standing in a semi-circle around us while fire and smoke wafted up from the rooftop. I lifted my uninjured arm, straining against the pain, flicking off my subvocalizer while I was at it, and put on my most congenial smile.

"We have important information about Queen Elena that shows she's a war criminal," I announced very slowly, wincing as the pain in my shoulder continued to grow.

"Tell it to the brig," one of the women snapped, coming around and hauling Owen up. Then it was my turn, and before I could point out the branch, I was hauled off of it, the branch yanked out. My vision went white as the pain took me over, and I felt myself being dragged away.

Please, I thought to myself, *let Violet be okay.*

CHAPTER 42

Violet

Now that Elena was on the rampage, the boys moved—some of them much faster than others, some running away, some attacking, the difference between the ones in masks and the ones not blurring—but I looked away and down, searching for the gun Tim had pulled out of the queen's hands. I could hear the sounds of fighting, Elena grunting, but I focused on finding the gun, knowing the boys were protecting me, giving me a few extra seconds.

"She fast!" Tim warned from behind me, and I looked up to see several blurs moving across the roof, barely ducking in time as a boy was flung over my head, landing a few feet behind me. Tim raced over to help him, and I continued my search, keeping an eye on the fighting.

"She must've taken pills for speed and strength at the same time," I shouted back, spotting the gun a few feet away and making for it.

I was halfway to it when Elena's face was suddenly in my vision, just inches away, the smile on her lips growing wide, until her teeth were bared like a snake's.

"I never imagined I could feel this way," she said softly, stepping forward, forcing me to step back. "I knew I wanted you dead—but that was practical. Now I want you dead because... I think... I think I *hate* you. Isn't that weird?"

She spoke in low, lethal tones, her voice pleasant, and it sent a wave of apprehension through me. Looking over my shoulder, I tried to spot something—anything—that would help me stop her, and I realized some of the boys were down, the others missing. She had torn through them so fast. It was horrifying.

Elena gave me the chance to look, her face softening a touch.

"You are really pretty, aren't you?" she said, reaching out with a hand, then snatching it back. "I think I hate that too." Then she giggled and turned away, spinning around in delight before stopping and looking up at the moon.

"They told me I shouldn't take all the pills, y'know," she said softly, and I got the feeling she didn't care who was listening, she just wanted to speak. "Said it would cause problems, but I can't tell what they are. I can't even remember. All I feel is this... tightness in my chest when I look at you. It sets my teeth on edge. Makes my head hurt. What is that?"

I exhaled softly and reached into my pocket, pulling out my last and final tranquilizer dart. Her back was to me right now. If I could keep her distracted, maybe I could just... slide it in.

"It's anger," I told her, taking a step closer.

"Anger. Huh. So this is what Tabitha felt all the time." She continued to look up at the moon, her voice serene, as though she had not a care in the world. I reached over, intent on driving the needle into her back—and then Elena blurred out of view, and the next thing I knew my hand was twisted up behind my back, the dart falling from my nerveless fingers.

She managed to catch it with her other hand and held it up in front of me, pressing her cheek to the back of my head.

"Right now it feels like fire under my skin," she hissed into my ear. "Like there's something toxic coursing through my veins, and the only cure for it is to see you lying so still, so silent—the stillness only death can bring."

I struggled to break her hold, but she held me tight, seeming to anticipate my moves. Her hand went up to my throat, catching it in a terrible grip and squeezing so hard my vision went gray. My lungs kept trying to expand for more air, but nothing could get past her rigid hand.

"ELENA!" a voice screamed, and suddenly I was on my already-battered knees, coughing and sucking in precious gulps of air. I managed to scramble around to face the roof access door, and saw a small figure standing there at the edge of the steps—Morgan, lit by the moon, challenging her sister.

Elena moved away from where she had dropped me, toward her younger sibling, and Tim raced over to me.

"Violet?"

"I'm fine," I wheezed. "Help Morgan."

He nodded and darted off, while I climbed back to my feet, trying to figure out where the gun had gone.

"Morgana," Elena seethed, moving over. "I'd hoped those psychotic young men would deal with you."

Morgan smirked, but the expression looked pained. "Your hopes were in vain."

"I wouldn't be so sure about that. You look awful."

"Then maybe you'll finally be able to beat me," Morgan replied. "But I doubt it. Mother always said I was the best fighter in the family."

"Be sure to tell her that when you see her again."

A deadly silence followed Elena's statement, and I whirled to see her blurred form racing right for Morgan. But Morgan took a step to one side at precisely the right moment, and Elena pressed forward too far, now unbalanced by Morgan's disappearance. The blurred lines of Elena came into focus as she slammed into the handrail, so I could see the surprised look on her face as she crashed to the ground a few paces past it.

Morgan chuckled dryly as she painstakingly turned.

"I could never understand your obsession with strength and speed as the better enhancements," she announced, her green eyes watching Elena as she picked herself off the ground.

"This is nonsense," Elena growled, dusting off her pants as she righted herself. "Let's end this so I can finally get around to killing Violet."

She moved toward Morgan—not at a run, but at a sedate, almost relaxed pace—and pulled back her fist as she closed the distance. Morgan smirked at her, easily evading the blow, moving back a few feet and coming to a stop. Elena again raced in to hit her, and once again, Morgan sidestepped.

"I don't think it's nonsense," she said, continuing to evade Elena's blows with graceful skill. "I genuinely want to know. I'm betting you only used those two pills, in fact. You always did value martial prowess over the ability to dodge bullets or evade blows. But really—and maybe I'm a bit biased—but really I always thought enhanced reflexes"—her fist lashed out, hitting Elena square in the face, and Elena moved back a few steps, clearly dazed—"was the better power."

Elena raised a hand to her stunned face, touching her lips. Even from there I could see the glisten of blood on her fingertips. She stared at it, her face intently focused on it. Then a laugh escaped her, soft and surprised, followed by another, then another, until she was laughing wildly.

I looked over at Morgan and saw her looking at me, alarm on her face, and I renewed my quest for the gun. I spotted it as the tide of laughter began to dwindle, and began moving slowly, trying to angle around Elena to reach it while her attention was focused on Morgan.

Then Elena blurred, moving toward Morgan, and Morgan stepped to the left—but Elena's trajectory shifted, the blur changing angles just a fraction.

I could hear the impact that followed. Elena stood—foot and fist forward—as Morgan flew backward, landing hard on the gravel. She was still for a moment, and my heart pounded, horrified at the way she lay like a corpse. But then she let out a choked groan, and began to move around.

Elena pulled back her fist, a crooked smile slashed across her face, and then she blurred again, just as Morgan reached her knees. There was a wet crack, and Morgan flew back a few more feet, rolling on her side. She coughed, the sound wet with blood, and Elena moved to her form, bending over and grabbing her younger sister.

That was when Tim appeared from nowhere, halfway in the air, his boot extended. His foot planted square in Elena's face, followed immediately by his other foot as he flipped over, landing precisely in the gravel between Morgan and Elena. Then he vanished again, before Elena could even stop grabbing at her face to see what had hit her, only to reappear right behind her, landing a high kick to the back of her head.

I raced for the gun, sliding painfully to my knees in my desperation to get to her. Elena had regained her footing and was looking warily around. Her thermal goggles were no longer on her head, and I hoped they'd gotten knocked off in the fighting.

Every instinct in my body was screaming in alarm. I had to kill her—I had to. If I didn't, she would kill all of us one by one. There was no reasoning with her; her mental state was rapidly deteriorating, and if she killed us, there would be no one stopping her from killing every man—every person—who remained in Patrus.

I raised my hand, bracing it, and took aim, my hand steady and my heart sure—when Tim reappeared again. Once again he was in the air, a kick directed at the queen, but she blurred, and the next thing I knew Tim was flying toward me.

I stood to catch him, but he hit a few feet ahead of me with a thud. I met Elena's eyes as I raced forward to him, my heart in my throat at how still my brother was. She smirked, and then beat me to him, using her enhanced speed to get there, her enhanced strength to haul him up by the throat, and… after what I had just seen… her enhanced reflexes to dodge the bullet I sent flying at her in a panicked rage.

"Put him down," I screamed, fear grasping at my heart as my little brother's legs kicked in midair, a choked sound escaping him.

"Oh, all right then!" Elena smiled, and stepped back toward the side of the building, keeping Tim between us. I shifted, circling to try to draw a bead on her, but every time I did, she would reposition him so that he was between us. Tim frantically clawed at her wrist, trying to break her grip, but I could tell his strength was fading.

"DON'T!" I cried, my heart breaking as she brought him ever closer to the edge. "*PLEASE!*"

I was begging, and I hated myself for it, but I couldn't let her kill my brother. I would go crazy.

"Violet, I'm just doing what you asked," she taunted cruelly. "I'm going to put him down, and then I'm going to *rip* your throat out and *bathe* in the blood!"

I squeezed a shot off, going for her foot, desperate to stop her. But I missed, and she flung my brother to one side—right over the edge of the building. I saw him falling and screamed, firing wildly. Elena blurred, dodging the bullets.

The gun was knocked out of my hand with such force that I spun around, my arm aching and throbbing angrily, reminding me that it had been broken until recently, and then what hair I had was yanked sharply in a fist as Elena started to drag me over to the edge.

"Time to join your little brother," she crooned as she hefted me up by my hair. The pain was agonizing, but not as awful as the look on her face as she gazed at me. "Goodbye, Violet," she said, her grin turning victorious.

I grabbed her wrist, trying to break her grasp—or hold on, or take her down with me—as she swung me around. Then, suddenly, she stumbled back, and I fell to my feet again, only inches from the edge of the roof. Dazed, my head throbbing, I looked over to see someone on Elena's back, holding her firmly across the chest and then hauling the surprised woman back to the edge.

Ms. Dale gave me a wan smile—her face pale and covered in blood—and I saw the detonator in her hand as she tipped Elena and herself over the edge.

"Some people deserve to die," she said, and then they were gone.

I raced over to the edge, needing to stop it, but the force of the explosion that came a moment later drove me back several feet, my hand going up to shield me from the flames. I fell to my knees.

Tim, Thomas, and Ms. Dale were all gone—I had no idea where Viggo was—and our plan with Alyssa was in tatters. Everything welled up in me like a tidal wave of anguish. I began to sob, uncontrolled, unable to see anything, my own gasping, choking breaths the only sound I could hear.

Hands pressed against my back, surprising me, and I jerked back, turning to see... Tim. His hands were scraped up, his throat already ringed with bruises from Elena's hand, but he was there... alive and whole.

"Tim... how?" I breathed as he sank down beside me.

"Easy. I grab wall. You okay?"

There was a shout on the roof, and I turned to see a flood of wardens racing through the doors like bees swarming from a hive. I had no fight left in me. We had no exit plan. Slowly, wearily, I began raising my hands.

"Ms. Dale..." I said softly.

Then the guards were there, and apparently they weren't taking any chances. The last thing I saw as they drew near was the butt of a rifle, aiming for my head. Then I saw nothing.

CHAPTER 43

Violet

I opened my eyes and then immediately closed them, the obnoxious bright white light causing my head to throb. Lifting my hands to block it out, I heard someone say, "She's awake," and slowly tried to sit up, in spite of everything.

Letting my face flop into my hands, I winced and pulled my hand away from the tender area on the right side of my head.

"What's happening?" I asked, trying to peel back my mutinous eyelids.

I finally succeeded, and was greeted by three walls comprised of bars, concrete ceiling, and floor. The awful white light filled the cell from overhead.

"Violet, baby?" I turned toward Viggo's voice like a thirsty person hearing the sound of running water. He was peering at me through a set of bars that separated us, his hands wrapped around them. The weight of his concern for me was pressed into the lines of his face, and without even thinking about it, I twisted on the cot I found myself on and reached for him.

"What happened?" I asked, relieved as my fingers stroked over his.

He reached out and grabbed my hand, pulling it through to his side of the bars and pressing it to his lips.

"I don't know," he replied, moving closer to me. "But everyone's here."

Everyone who's left, I found myself thinking, and I swallowed and looked around. Sure enough, there was Owen, Amber, Logan, and Tim—all ensconced in cells like mine.

Tim was the first team member my eyes sought after Viggo, and I immediately noticed the dark purple bruises on his face and neck, so purple they looked like they had been painted on. He waved at me as I noticed him, and I waved back, offering him a nebulous smile.

Owen sat across the hall from Tim. His face was scratched, and there were bandages on his side and shoulder. He sat with the wall at his back, his expression unfocused, lost in thought. He blinked after a few moments and looked over at me, offering a tremulous smile of his own, but he looked downtrodden and raw. I could tell he was hurting over Thomas, and felt my own pain flaring up in my chest in response to his.

Amber was pacing the tight confines of her cell looking extremely frustrated, and I noticed she was favoring one side, as if the other side of her body were bruised and tender. There was also a dark bruise forming around her left eye, causing it to squint almost shut.

Logan was next to her, her cell sandwiched between his and Owen's, and he sat on his own bed, watching Amber pace back and forth. He looked fairly well, besides a bruise on his face. I suspected when the wardens discovered the two of them, they had been less than gentle taking them in. Much like they'd been with Tim and me.

Amber continued to pace, then suddenly kicked one foot out, rattling the cell door.

"We saved you from Elena!" she bellowed angrily, clearly addressing some unseen guards or cameras, and I flinched at the loud noise. "The least you can do is give us a proper room!"

Her voice reverberated down the halls, but other than that, there was no sound.

"Amber?" I whispered hoarsely, pressing the heel of my hand to my eyebrow. "Can you give me... an hour or two before you do that again?"

"There's food on the floor, Violet," Viggo said softly, pointing to a tray in front of the door. "It was hot, but now, uh, probably not. Also water. You need to eat."

I shook my head, a wave of nausea hitting me, and lay down instead, curling up toward him. His bed was directly on the other side of the bars, and he lay down next to me, his hand reaching out to take mine.

"You need to eat," he insisted.

"In a little bit," I replied, tears beginning to prick my eyes. "Viggo... Ms. Dale... She—"

"I know," he said, his face forlorn. His eyes were red-rimmed, and I could feel the pain radiating off of him. He clutched my hand a little tighter. "Violet... Thomas... He—"

"I know," I whispered back, and then suddenly I couldn't stop the tide of tears as they tore through me. I felt the loss of Ms. Dale and Thomas like a knife through the heart. Something special had been taken away, and I felt its absence, my world diminished, two people smaller, and that was a lot.

I cried for a long time. Viggo whispered to me and comforted me all the while, and I hated the bars that separated us. I needed to feel his arms around me, holding me when he said everything was going to be okay, even though none of us could be certain. We were in a prison, after all.

Once the tears had passed, I looked around and sniffled.

"Where's Morgan?"

"We don't know," Owen said, his back to the bars and to me, but his voice carrying his concern. "Tim said she was carried away and they were giving her medical treatment, but then they knocked him out, so..."

I looked over at my little brother, still relieved to see him alive. He was sitting, his back pressed to a wall, on the other side of Viggo's cell. I grimaced when I once again noticed the angry, deep purple, almost black bruises that seemed to cover his whole throat from when Elena had held him over the edge of the building. He scrubbed his eyes when I looked at him, fidgeting with obvious worry.

"Morgan pale. Breathing not good. They say intubate. That's tube—"

"Down her throat," Logan said irritably, and I felt a moment's levity at the sight of Amber reaching through the bars to smack him on the head.

"Don't take this from Tim. Let him talk," she chided, and Logan glared at her, rubbing the back of his head. A moment later her hands went back through the bars and pushed his aside, feeling his head for injuries. "I didn't actually hurt you, did I?"

"No," Logan said, leaning into her touch with a sigh, his long hands coming back to wrap around hers and pull them to his shoulders. "And I deserved it. Sorry, Tim."

"Is okay," Tim replied with a shrug. He met my gaze and sighed. "Last I saw. Sierra okay, but… other boys taken away too. Somewhere different. Don't know more."

"None of us do," Amber said sadly, pressing her face between the bars. "We don't know anything that's happening."

"How long have I been unconscious?" I asked.

"It's one o'clock in the afternoon," Viggo informed me, and I turned my attention back to him. "You've been out for almost twelve hours. They checked us all out—" He rotated his shoulder with a wince, and I noticed the edge of a bandage under his shirt, my eyes flicking back up to his with questioning concern.

"I'm fine," he insisted. "I'm going to have a pretty cool scar though." He held up a bandaged hand and looked chagrined. "And one here too," he added.

"That you got from jumping off a roof you were trying to blow up with crap gloves and not enough rope!" Owen barked, his voice rueful. I looked over at him, and he shook his head at me. "Your husband is insane."

The corner of Viggo's mouth quirked up and then dropped, and I could understand. Our hearts were heavy—too heavy to enjoy our usual banter, even with Owen's joking words or with the realization that we'd ended up together again after everything. Elena was dead, her plan thwarted, as far as we knew. Presumably Viggo had done something to stop the boys, but that didn't mean anything. We had no idea what was going to happen now, who was going to be in charge… or who the population was going to believe.

As it turned out… right now, *nothing* was going to happen. Or later. Or even later. We kept waiting for someone to come down and explain what was happening or tell us we were being convicted of regicide, but the only person we ever saw was a portly woman who delivered our food. She wasn't a warden; or at least, she wasn't wearing the uniform.

She was a good deterrent against our escaping while she served us. She was older, her hair streaking white, and walked laboriously with the rolling food cart. There was no way we would attack an elderly woman to escape, which meant our options weren't good. The beds were welded together, as were the hinges. Owen, Viggo, and Logan spent the first two days halfheartedly trying to figure out a way to break through the door, but never succeeded.

In truth, maybe we just didn't have the energy to break out. The women who had tormented us and hunted us were dead, but so were two of our closest allies and friends, with others back home in uncertain conditions. All of us were exhausted and heartsick and tired of fighting. Maybe, since we were together for once, able to keep tabs on our closest family, we all knew in our hearts that we would just have to wait and see what fate had in store for us.

For three days we were confined to our cells, going stir crazy, just waiting. The woman never answered our questions. I was beginning to think she was hard of hearing, or even mute, because she never said a word. The only solace we had was in each other, so we talked. We talked about all sorts of things—speculating what was happening with our group of rebels, the boys, Morgan and Sierra, Matrus. Then we talked about all the things we had to do when we got back to Patrus. Then the cycle began again.

At night, Viggo and I would lie next to each other with only the bars to separate us, and talk about what we would do if we got out of here. Nothing to do with the war or the rebuilding—we talked about where we could put our home, what we wanted it to look like, what kind of motorcycle Viggo had been hoping to buy, whether I could start a self-defense center for women in the hills of Patrus... There was even the slightest mention of children. Our children. The speculation, cut off from all politics and current events, helped, even if it was bittersweet. It was tantalizing to think about this whole thing in terms of being done and over with. To think about the life we might have, if none of this were burdening us anymore.

On the morning of the fourth day, I woke up and saw the old woman standing on the other side of my cell door, looking at me intently.

Rubbing my eyes, I sat up, then reached my hands through the bars to wake Viggo.

"Yes?" I asked, my voice cracking with a yawn. "What is it?"

The woman smiled kindly and waved her hand at me.

"You and your friends are to accompany me."

She nodded and took a step back as two wardens appeared and unlocked our cells. They held open the doors, and I saw Amber and Logan peering at us through the bars of their own cells, looking groggy.

Tim snored on, oblivious to the change in our status, while Owen watched warily from his own cell. I exchanged a look with Viggo and then stood, stepping out into the hallway. Viggo did as well, and after a long pause, I moved over to him and took his hand.

"Who are you?" I asked the older woman, and she clasped her hands behind her back.

"Edith Carmichael," she replied. "Warden High Commander, retired now, of course. Edi for short. You and your people will be escorted to some better rooms, where food and fresh clothes await you. Would you like a moment to prepare before you meet the queen?" As she spoke, the two wardens began unlocking the others' cells, releasing them.

"It depends," Viggo said cautiously. "Who's the queen now?"

Edi just smiled and slowly turned away, lapsing back into her staunch silence and moving down the hall at a sedate pace. The wardens opened the other cell doors, letting everyone emerge as Viggo and

I moved hand in hand down the hallway.

The older woman led us through the control room for the prisons and up a flight of stairs, and I could hear hammering and sounds of construction coming from the doors.

"The palace has suffered quite a bit of damage," Edi said dryly. "But most of it was superficial."

I thought of Ms. Dale going over the side of the building and the explosion that had followed, and leaned into Viggo. We continued to follow Edi, and she continued to lead us up, until she stopped at a landing and opened the door.

"Your rooms are here. Everyone has their own except for Mrs. Bates and Mr. Croft. I understand that they are married."

"We are," Viggo said, and she nodded and pushed open a door.

"This will be your room. Mr. Bates," she said, addressing Tim. "You are across the hall, and everyone else can pick their own room. I'll give you an hour to shower and change, but the queen will only be speaking with Mrs. Bates and Mr. Croft."

"Why?" Amber demanded. "You've locked us in here for three days. We deserve answers."

"And you'll have them," Edi replied acerbically. "Now, go rest in some nice rooms with much better food than what you were getting in the prison, and be patient for just a little bit longer. We don't want to stress the queen with too many visitors at once. Mrs. Bates and Mr. Croft will fill you in."

Owen was the first to accept her decision—he simply lumbered silently by, heading to a room down the hall and stepping into it. He shut it with a click, leaving us all standing in the hall.

"Let it go, Amber," I said softly. "Let's just see what happens."

"I can stay with you," Logan added, a slow smile tugging on his lips. "Make sure you're safe."

Amber looked up at him, her answer evident in the fact that she said nothing at all, and then moved down the hall, past Owen's door and into the next room, shutting the door as well. Logan watched her go, bemused, and then went to the room across the hall.

"Good luck," he called as he stepped into it, leaving the four of us alone.

"More sleep," Tim yawned as he opened the door, wincing a little as his neck stretched. He shut the door with a click, and I looked at Viggo, who shrugged.

"See you in an hour," I informed Edi, and she gave me a wry grin.

One hasty lovemaking session in the shower and a hurried break-fast coupled with frantically getting dressed later, we were five minutes late getting out the door, and I was completely okay with that. Viggo had made love to me like the world were caving in around us, as if I were his only safe place. And in those minutes, he was mine. We took shelter in each other's arms and solace in each other's touch, and for a brief moment, I felt a spark of hope that maybe things were going to get better—and clung to it, for the both of us.

Still, I could tell Edi was perturbed at our tardiness as she led us down the hall, grumbling under her breath. I didn't care. They had locked a pair of newlyweds apart for several days. It was really their own fault.

The door she led us to was nondescript, and she pushed it open and stepped inside. I went in first and immediately saw Morgan lying in a hospital bed, Sierra sitting next to her. She looked at me curiously when I stepped in, and then reached over to gently touch Morgan's shoulder.

"They're here," she whispered, and Morgan's eyes opened. Her face was horribly bruised, her left eye almost swollen shut, and I could tell when she tried to sit upright that more than a few of her ribs were broken.

"Hey, guys," she whispered harshly, her voice coming out raw, and Sierra grabbed a small plastic cup from the table next to the bed and handed it to her. Morgan took a sip and then handed it back, groaning.

"Morgan!" I said, taking a step toward her, relieved to see her alive, when Edi loudly rapped her knuckles across the door.

"You will address her as 'Queen Morgana,'" she said primly. "Of Matrus, of course."

"Edi, you old windbag, lay off them." Morgan coughed and then shuddered, her hands going to her sides. "I'm really tired, Edi, and I just want to let them know what's going on. So back off—they aren't enemies or subjects. They're friends."

Edi sighed and nodded.

"A queen should have friends... I just wish they weren't the same people who killed the *last* queen." She shut herself on the other side of the door as she spoke, ensuring her words were the final ones in the conversation, and I smiled.

"She's interesting," I said, and Morgan gave a half-hearted chuckle.

"Don't make me laugh," she wheezed in pain. "I broke six ribs. One of them punctured a lung and I had to have surgery. It's why you guys were in prison for so long."

"Morgan was sleeping for a long time," Sierra added, her voice high and whisper-soft—the first time I'd heard her speak since she'd been in the safe room with Elena's gun at her temple. "I was very scared for her. I told the tribunal about your brother and his... friends helping me. But it wasn't enough to let you all go."

"Sierra, you should let me fill in the blanks," Morgan chided, but there was a fond look in her eyes when she looked at her little sister. "Suffice it to say, a lot has happened. I technically couldn't pardon you because, while I am the heir apparent, you can't legally crown someone while they are unconscious, and you certainly can't act on orders from them, so... it was a bit of a legal snafu."

She rolled her eyes, and I smiled. "How are you feeling?" I asked.

"This too shall pass," she said, leaning into her pillows. "Seriously though, I don't have a lot of time before these painkillers kick in, so I want you to listen. An inquiry was led by Edi and Alyssa into the entire thing. Evidence was logged, testimony was given—not by you, of course, because Alyssa was speaking as your advocate—and the investigation has been ruled upon, signed by me, and sealed. Elena was found guilty of war crimes, despite being dead. Our government is willing to give reparations to Patrus, to help stabilize them. Everyone—you, Viggo, Amber, Owen... *everyone* has been given a blanket pardon, and you are all considered state heroes, free to come and go as you please."

I blinked, momentarily speechless. "That's a lot to take in," I breathed.

Morgan grimaced. "Don't get excited yet—that was the good news. There's more."

"Bad?" asked Viggo. Morgan gave a small twitch in her shoulders.

"Just listen. There are two things you aren't going to like. The first one is regarding the egg. It was on the heloship, and survived unharmed—those things are damn near indestructible. The council met and decided they weren't going to destroy the egg."

"But you're the queen," I said. "That egg is the result of cruel genetic testing done on the boys!"

Morgan gave a self-depreciating laugh and shook her head at me.

"They added another law in the charter," she said. "The council can, with a unanimous vote, overrule a queen's orders or commands. They don't want to risk another Elena ever again. But… they want to study the egg."

"No, they can't! It's—"

Viggo placed a hand on my shoulder and looked at Morgan.

"We won't argue," he announced, and I blinked up at him in surprise, wondering what he was planning. "But I think we should stipulate that the Matrians have to share any and all discoveries made, experiments done, and research, with Patrus. And access to any medicine developed as a result."

Morgan smiled at him for a long moment.

"You might just be the man to make that request," she announced finally, and he blinked.

"What do you mean by that?"

"She means you're in charge of Patrus," announced a masculine voice from behind us, and I turned and saw Henrik stepping in. He looked… weathered, tired, and as if the world had just ground him down using the heel of its massive boot.

I immediately turned and wrapped my arms around him, hugging him close.

"I'm so sorry," I said, my heart breaking for Ms. Dale all over again.

He didn't say anything as I hugged him, and as I pulled back, I saw him wiping his already red eyes with a knuckle.

"I can't talk about it," he said hoarsely. "I just... I can't. But... I want you to know she loved you both... very dearly. She wasn't so good at showing it, but... she did."

I sniffled, tears beginning to fall from my eyes again, and Viggo pulled me into his side, sheltering me from the pain.

"Thank you, Henrik," he replied softly. "How did you get here?"

"I got a call from Ms. Carmichael asking me to testify. I wanted to know what happened to you, so I came. They wouldn't let me see you—not until the trial was finished—but..."

"They never even questioned us," Viggo cut in, and Henrik sighed.

"They didn't need to. Now, can you let me get out what I came here to say? I'm... I'm tired. And there's a lot to do over in Patrus."

"I'm sorry. What did you come here to say?"

"We finally got a provisional government in place. It was quite a little event, but since I know you're dying to know, I think first we should start with the boys. They were pressing in, and we were about to give the orders to fire, when they just... stopped. Almost as if someone had flipped a switch. We followed them back when they started to leave and tracked them to the place they'd obviously been kept. We then collected their handlers. The boys are safe, and Dr. Tierney is working to get them off the Benuxupane, although we are having to keep the older boys on it for now—they are too unstable.

"Now, onto the other bit of news, and why I'm really here. Mags, Drew, one or two of the old Patrian politicians who have come out of hiding, and I have created positions, and a scaffolding of rules and laws to hold them in place. But the people demanded a leader, and you're it until a proper election. I hope you don't mind, but we took the liberty of changing the official title to 'Chancellor.'"

For a moment, I got to experience the strange sensation of watching my husband freeze in complete and utter shock.

"That's... That's crazy," Viggo said after he'd found his voice, but Henrik shook his head.

"It was delightfully simple," he replied. "Your legend has grown, young man. People have noticed your bravery and willingness to save people. We even held a second election to make it more democratic, and we handled it as simply as possible: one leader collected the votes with guards to make sure there was no tampering. There were many other candidates, but Jeff, Mags, and a couple of Drew's men campaigned hard for you. So you're it, provisionally. That is, until new elections in the spring, which was when we'll hopefully have ideas about term limits and elected positions." He ran a hand through his hair and sighed softly. "I have a heloship on the roof, ready to take you back to Patrus—but we've been invited to stay the night in the palace before going home. I would take them up on it. There isn't much luxury on the other side of the river, unfortunately."

He moved toward the door.

"Thank you for coming, Henrik," Morgan said softly from her bed, and Henrik slowed, but didn't stop.

"Yes, thank you," added Sierra formally. "My sister and I will be in touch in a few days to help figure out what your people will need, but we already decided to load your heloship with food, water, medicine, blankets, and fuel."

"Thank you," Henrik replied, pulling the door closed. We fell silent, and then I turned to Morgan.

"Morgan, you said there were two things I wasn't going to like. What's the second?"

Morgan sighed and shifted.

"Ms. Dale has been found guilty of matricide. She won't be recognized as a hero due to her actions. She... The only way to keep it from looking like an assassination plot was to censure her to spare you."

"What?" I breathed, my stomach dropping out from under me and the world suddenly lurching off the tracks. "How could you..." I paused, unable to find the words, staring at Morgan. Try as I might, I couldn't keep the disbelief and anger from showing plainly on my face. "You *signed off* on that?"

"I had to," Morgan snapped, her shoulders hunching guiltily, then a wince of pain going across her face. "The only way to keep you guys from getting caught up in Elena's *murder* was to tell them Ms. Dale acted of her own accord. Which is *true*, I might add. I... I didn't like it, but I thought of Ms. Dale, and what she would've done, and I knew she wouldn't care if she were called a villain if it meant keeping you safe."

Her words, no matter how true, felt like someone was dragging a rake across my heart. It wasn't fair—Ms. Dale had been with Viggo and me almost since the beginning. She'd fought this fight as hard as anyone, harder than most, and she'd given her life to keep all of us safe from a psychotic despot.

Viggo grabbed me and pulled me hard against his chest, and I realized I was shaking so hard the tears spilling from my eyes were jolting on my cheeks.

"This isn't right, Morgan," he growled. "Elena was psychotic and killed a lot of people. It was self-defense."

"I *know* that, Viggo. Believe me, I don't like it either, but in the eyes of the public, their queen was murdered. *Before* she was legally convicted. They weren't just going to let that go. I really hate it. But I did what I had to do—and what Ms. Dale would've done—and you both know that. Just know too... she will always be a hero in my mind. Always."

Her voice wavered, and I looked over to see Sierra handing Morgan a tissue. The new queen immediately swiped it across the corners of her eyes, inelegantly wiping her nose on it afterward. I knew, could see in her eyes, that this did hurt her. And somehow, that made me feel slightly better about the situation. Slightly.

It would take a while, I decided, but I could let this go too. Because Morgan was right... This was what Ms. Dale would have wanted. For now, I'd allow myself to feel the anger and resentment that came with it. I just wouldn't direct it at her.

"This is... too much to take in," I said softly, after taking a moment to collect myself. "Half of it feels like a dream. The other half feels like a nightmare."

"I'm in too much pain for it to be a dream or a nightmare," Morgan replied tiredly. "But I understand what you mean. You should go and get some rest in a comfortable bed for a while. Process things. Edi will take you to your rooms. These drugs are kicking in, so I'm going to go to..." She didn't even get to finish the sentence. Her voice got slower and slower, and she trailed off, her eyes drifting closed.

"She drops in and out," Sierra explained softly. "You should go. We'll reach out in a few days."

"Okay," Viggo whispered. "Thank you, Sierra."

The little girl smiled up at him, a dimple forming in one cheek, and then turned back to her sister. Viggo and I left the room and followed Edi, who had waited for us in the hall. She led us to the rooms.

"I trust you won't mind if I post guards outside your door?" she asked primly, giving us an expectant look. "It's protocol whenever we have visiting dignitaries—for both our protection, of course."

"Of course," Viggo said. "I trust we'll be able to move around freely?"

Edi's smile was nothing short of bemused. "Of course. With an escort, mind you."

"Why'd you convict her?" I asked suddenly, the words spilling out of me. I looked at her, realized I was tearing up again, and fought it back, forcing the words through my constricted throat. "Why'd you do it?"

The bemused expression left Edi's face as she looked up at me.

"Melissa Dale was a dedicated spy and recruiter," she said softly. "I knew her. Her loyalty was unwavering, until she took up with you. Do you know what that tells me?"

"What?" I snapped, still angry enough not to care that I was showing open hostility to an ally. Viggo certainly didn't stop me. If anything, he stood behind me, an unwavering pillar of support. He wanted to know as well.

"That you were the cause she thought was worth dying for," Edi replied simply, her tone calm and knowing. "She didn't deserve what we did to her, but if she was willing to sacrifice her life to keep you safe, then I would honor her death by doing the same. Even at the expense of her memory. Rest assured, many will question it as the stories persist, as they will, and Ms. Dale's legacy will not be forgotten by anyone. Including me. Now, if you'll excuse me, I'll leave you alone—I know you must want to fill your friends in on everything. I'll have dinner sent to your room."

The conversation with Morgan had been hard; telling everyone turned out to be harder. I knew Tim was sleeping, so we began with Owen. His surprise, awe, and pain at the proceedings mirrored mine; I could see the relief plain on his face when we told him about Morgan's new status and all our exonerations. But when I got to the part about Ms. Dale, I found I could barely get the words out. Viggo had to take over for me, and seeing Owen's reaction to the news only made me feel worse.

At the end of the story, I made to go find Amber, but Owen shook his head at me.

"Do you want me to tell the rest of them?" he asked. "I know... I know this is hard for you. Let me share that load a little."

I looked up at Viggo, who was nodding.

"That's really generous of you, Owen," he said, and the two men shared a look of understanding and companionship that warmed me to see. "Thank you. Violet, he's right. You should rest."

After that we were finally able to make it back to our room. When Viggo closed the door and pushed me gently toward the bed, I just lay down without speaking, and he pressed himself behind me, holding me close.

Only then did I break down fully, sobbing uncontrollably at the injustice of it all, and the bitter truth of their words. The loss of Ms. Dale was too fresh for this as well, but there was nothing I could do to change it. Still, I let myself wallow in my grief, using Viggo as my anchor and spinning out into the void. Missing her voice, her confidence, her wry wit. There was a permanent hole in my heart, an absence of her, and I felt every millimeter of the wound, feeling it bleed out.

Viggo kept it from festering—he mourned with me, but not as deeply, knowing that now, more than ever, I needed him to be strong for me. He held me tightly, whispering to me reassuringly, long until the sun had drifted low into the horizon. He made me eat the stew they brought down for dinner, making me focus on something practical and ordinary. I was glad the fare was simple—I didn't think I could hold much else down. Later, he helped me bathe.

He took such gentle and tender care of me throughout it all, never complaining or growing angry at me. Viggo let me grieve, and it made everything, even in this dark, horrible place of loss, so much more okay. By midnight I slept, and for once, I did not have nightmares.

By morning, I felt better. Tired, but better. I woke, rolled over, and saw Viggo looking at me, exhaustion evident on his face.

"Did you stay up all night?" I asked softly, my voice still rough from crying the night before.

He nodded and reached up to touch my face. "Of course I did. I was worried."

"I'm sorry," I breathed, looking down. "I just…"

"I know," he replied. "It isn't right. I hate it too, but it's too late to do anything now. We'll… We'll just have to move past it."

"What do you think the others think?" I asked.

"We should ask them. The guard who delivered dinner said breakfast would be communally served down the hall. Feel up to going down there to see who's there and getting their input?"

I nodded and drew my tired body up, slipping from the bed. Viggo got up as well, and within a few minutes, we were dressed. I held his hand as we left the room, following the guards as they led us to the dining room.

I was surprised to see that almost everyone in our group was inside. Then again, there hadn't been very many of us on the mission in the first place… and there were fewer of us now. I felt like I was never going to forget that fact. Of the survivors, the only one not at breakfast was Tim, but that didn't surprise me. He was still at the stage of wanting to sleep the day away. And, in my opinion, he'd earned that right.

"Hey," Owen said from the buffet-style table, smiling gently at me, a heaping pile of toast on his plate. I saw it and my mouth watered—but then I thought about the people in Patrus, and how they were probably dining on protein rations, and my appetite deserted me. I helped myself to a small bowl of cereal and some tea, sitting down at one of the four small circular tables where Amber and Logan were already sitting. Owen finished loading his plate up, while Viggo got a cup of black coffee and sat down next to me.

"So," I said, breaking the strained silence. Amber looked up from where she picked at her own food, her eyes blank and empty.

"Ms. Dale?" she asked, and I nodded.

"It sucks," she declared, pushing her fork away and crossing her arms. "They didn't even take our statements!"

"Alyssa acted as our advocate," Viggo replied. "Morgan backed her up in that she told the truth—it wasn't our intention to kill Elena, but Ms. Dale went against the plan and killed her."

"I would have done it if she hadn't," I said numbly. "Do you think they would've executed me?"

Viggo reached out and took my hand.

"Over my dead body," he said evenly, squeezing my hand.

"Ms. Dale would've wanted it this way," Owen said after a pause. "Put yourself in her shoes. You're saying you wouldn't have done the same thing for all of us? Even if it came at the price of a tainted memory?"

I stared at him blearily, trying to decide whether I should feel angry. It took me the length of that stare to process what was going on in my heart, but eventually I sighed and placed my hands in my lap.

"I already thought of that," I admitted. "And you're right. It wouldn't matter to *me*, and if it could keep all of you safe, I don't think I'd care."

"Exactly. Besides, that makes Ms. Dale a hero twice over: not only did she stop Elena, but she spared us from getting executed for regicide."

I exhaled slowly. "It still hurts," I said numbly.

"That's because Ms. Dale was a hell of a woman," Logan said softly, and I looked at him. He gave a sad smile. "I know it's not really my place to say it—I didn't know her as long as you all did—but I could pick up on it the moment I met her. She was just... calculating and fierce, y'know? I haven't met many people like that in my life, man or woman, and... I kind of admired her."

"Me too," said Amber, her lips quirking. "Not just 'kind of.' Hell,

I want to *be* her. She was so pragmatic, but underneath that hard spy exterior, she had a heart. A living, feeling heart."

"She was courageous," Viggo added with a nod, and I smiled. "When she found out the truth, when she learned what was really going on? She decided to do something, even if it meant going down as a traitor. That made her brave, and that made me respect her."

"She never let us down," I whispered. "Not once, not ever. I'm going to miss her guidance."

"We all are," replied Viggo. "But we'll remember her like this. Not how they tell everyone else to remember her, but how she was. And we'll tell our children the truth about her."

I sniffled and smiled, his words like the first bit of sunshine poking through a mostly overcast day. I rested my head on his shoulder and slid my hand under his, lacing our fingers together.

"Oh God. Henrik," Amber breathed, and instantly that moment of joy vanished, deflated under a heavy stone. "Do you think he knows?"

Before I could tell her about our conversation with him yesterday, the man's own voice cut through the silence.

"He knows," Henrik said gruffly, and I turned to see him leaning on the door, watching us—and my heart gave a leap to see Solomon standing solemnly behind him.

Henrik's eyes were rimmed red, and he still looked exhausted. The two men moved into the room, and I once again threw my arms around Henrik. He accepted the hug stiffly, with a soft pat on my back.

"I'm okay, Violet."

I let him go, but only because I needed to move on to Solomon, relieved to see him well. He was already hugging Amber, patting her gently atop her red curls. I thought about waiting patiently, then thought *Screw it*, and simply threw my arms around both of them.

I felt Solomon adjust his grip to include me as Amber and I squeezed him and each other, then eased back.

"I'm so glad you're okay," I told him. "I figured you would be, but…"

"I'm okay. Alyssa's friends took care of us. We didn't meet with much resistance—I assume you all drew them off…" He trailed off, then looked away, swallowing hard. "I… I regret even going with her. Maybe if I had been with you, we could've…"

"Don't," I said sharply, shaking my head. "We have no idea how you being with us would've changed things, and it's pointless to dwell on it. What happened," my voice caught, my mouth suddenly dry, "*happened.*"

Solomon's expression did not lighten, but he nodded sadly. "I know. I was just supposed to do something useful."

"You did," Amber replied. "You were a part of getting Alyssa to help us. You kept her safe. That was important."

He hesitated, and then sighed. "Yeah. I guess you're right. Is it all right if I join you?"

Amber and I both nodded, and Solomon dragged an empty chair over to the now-crowded little table, Henrik following suit. He moved slowly, almost plodding, still favoring his injured side.

My fear and anguish for him must have shown on my face, because he picked up a fork and said, "Violet, you don't have to worry about me. I know the score. I made my peace with it."

"Just like that?" I asked, unable to stop myself, and he speared me with an angry look.

"No, not just like *that*," he said bitterly. "But I'm an old man, Violet. And I'm tired. There's been so much hatred, so much death… I just don't have room for any more. Losing Melissa broke my heart. Is breaking my heart. Yet in spite of that, I can't go on feeling angry for something she wouldn't care about anyway. I don't have the time left to waste on it, and I suggest you don't waste any time on it either."

"I'm sorry, Henrik," I replied, contrite. "I didn't mean it like that. I just… I wanted to know if there's a trick to it."

Henrik sighed and reached over to touch my hand.

"No, *I'm* sorry, Violet. I'm still a bit… raw." He withdrew his hand to run it over his face, tugging on the edges of his beard. Leaning back in his chair, he looked at us. "I also wanted to let you all know that I'm staying here. I asked, and Morgan is allowing me to take over training in Ms. Dale's old studio."

"But why?" I asked, shocked by his revelation.

Henrik gave me a kind smile. "I've been told it hasn't been changed, and I don't want to change it. I want to spend the rest of my life doing what she did before all of this, if only so I can feel closer to her. They're even letting me take over her apartment. Her things were boxed up after her defection, but Morgan is letting me have them. I know it sounds strange, especially since I've been working so hard to change Patrus in the past few days, but... I'm so tired of it all, and it's time for me to let you kids take the reins for a bit. This is how I want to spend my remaining time on earth."

My heart twisted, and I offered him a shaky smile. "I understand, but... we'll miss you, Henrik."

"I'm not going either," Owen blurted, and I looked at him, my eyes going wide. He fidgeted, looking down, and, even in the midst of all this sadness and worry, I wondered if I could see a bit of pink tingeing his cheeks.

"I'm sorry, but I need to make a fresh start. I really feel like I could do some good over here—maybe even start training to be a Matrian diplomat and change some of the antiquated laws regarding males. Besides, Morgan hasn't been here for a while. I figure she could use a friendly face. And with Thomas..."

He trailed off, and we all fell silent, and I felt a pang of guilt. I'd been so wrapped up in the injustice of what happened with Ms. Dale that I had... Well, it wasn't that I had forgotten him, but I had prioritized her, and I was fairly certain that made me an awful person.

"Owen—God, I'm sorry," I said, and he gave me an incredulous look.

"Why?"

"Because! I spent all this time dwelling on Ms. Dale and how unjust it was, that... well... we didn't talk about Thomas like we did Ms. Dale."

"Thomas would've found that sort of thing in poor taste," Amber announced, picking at her food again. "We talked about it once—I can't for the life of me remember how we even got there—and he said it was the worst part of funerals. Everyone crying about who they lost and why they were important... It just wasn't Thomas' way."

"Doesn't mean I'm not going to miss him," Viggo said softly, and I looked over at him. He met my gaze, his eyes still red and filled with grief. "He saved all of our lives, and gave us every opportunity to put an end to all this madness."

"Him and those damned odds," Henrik said, tugging at his beard. "He and Melissa both… They just wanted to keep everyone safe, no matter what the odds. When they put their minds together…" He looked up, his eyes bright with unshed tears. "They were impossible to argue with."

"Thomas was my best friend," Owen added. "I could never understand why, but I… I loved him. And God, I miss him."

"We all do," I whispered. "Even me. I know he and I didn't get off on the right foot, but…"

"He respected you a lot, Violet," Owen interjected with a sniffle. "He might not have always shown it, but… We all know how he felt about emotional displays."

We all chuckled, but it was a somber, short laugh, because it came coupled with the knowledge that we were never going to see Thomas again, never hear him quip about the flaws in our plans or the problems with emotional decision-making.

I exhaled sharply and leaned against Viggo, needing to touch him, to feel comforted. He leaned back into me, and we supported each other.

"Besides," Owen added after a long moment, a gentle smile coming across his lips, "I feel like Thomas wouldn't want us to dwell on the past. He'd instead want to bring up the future of Patrus, and want to know what the new chancellor has planned."

"Oh God," Viggo groaned, placing his face in his hands. "Why did you have to remind me?"

"I'm so sorry, Viggo," I breathed, appalled that my grief last night had eclipsed that turn of events, but he shook his head at me. "Have you thought about it at all?"

"I did. Last night. I'm just… I'm still not sure what to think about it. I don't think it's right that you can get elected when you're not even there."

"I think it's great," Amber said casually, taking a sip from her mug.

"I mean, I would've much preferred Mags, but seeing as we can't break Patrus from its patriarchy too soon... you're my second favorite."

Viggo smiled at her. "Does that mean you're coming back with us?"

"Of course! I'm not missing my opportunity to get in on the ground floor of a brand new government! I'm aiming for Spy Master."

"You can't just declare that loudly in front of half a dozen witnesses," Logan laughed. "It kind of defeats the purpose."

"Yeah, yeah. So what do you say, Viggo?" she asked, leaning forward on her elbows and giving him a wide smile.

"I'll have to think about it," he replied, and I felt a smile bloom on my lips—a real one. It was a moment of normalcy in the wake of turbulence, and I embraced it. Soon we'd be back in Patrus, ready to roll up our sleeves and put the country back together brick by brick. And with a little luck and a lot of love, we'd build something new and improved, ready to stand the test of time.

It was all we could do.

EPILOGUE

Violet

One Year Later

"Aren't you ready yet?" shouted Viggo from the closet, and I ignored the question, staring at myself in the full-length mirror and adjusting my dress. I turned to one side, then the other, and sighed, running a hand over my stomach and pulling the loose yellow fabric down so that the small bump was more noticeable.

"Honestly, Violet, we need to be in the car in ten—" I looked up in the mirror and saw Viggo emerging from the closet, his hands busy tying a black bow tie around his throat. He smiled fondly at me and dropped the untied ends of the fabric, crossing over to me. I exhaled and leaned into his chest as his arms came around mine, his large hands pressing against my stomach.

"You look beautiful," he breathed in my ear. "And frankly, I love that you're starting to show. I couldn't be more proud."

I smiled and tilted my head to one side, and he planted a soft kiss to my cheek.

"I love you," I told him.

I felt his smile as he pressed his lips to my cheek yet again. "I love you."

He slid around to my side, pulling us together and looking at the image we presented in the mirror. It was hard not to see the subtle changes in both of us. We were both a little fuller—even though this past year had been rough—and a bit more rounded out. I had more flesh on my bones, but I was still fit, just… healthier. My skin was better, my hair growing in thick and shiny, my gray eyes luminous.

It didn't change the fact both of us still had nightmares that would tear us from our sleep in a panic. But we talked about them, described them to each other, and it helped soften them over time.

The last nightmare I'd had was when I found out I was pregnant. I had been too stunned and surprised to bring it up with Viggo immediately, and had fallen asleep waiting for him to come up from one of his late-running council meetings.

In the dream, I had been back in The Green, lying there, unable to move as all the creatures closed in. And then pain began radiating from my abdomen, and when I looked down, my stomach was flayed open, with massive black centipedes that somehow bore resemblances to Tabitha, Elena, and Desmond climbing out of my womb and heading out into the world, beginning a whole new cycle of destruction and terror… and it was all my fault.

I woke from the terror with a cold sweat drenching through my clothes, feeling frozen to the core, afraid to look down at my belly in case I would see that my nightmare was a reality. But Viggo had been there. As always, he was right by my side to comfort me and chase away the shadows.

It hadn't exactly been the ideal way to tell him about the baby, but, of course, he had made it feel perfect, soothing me with his words and his hands.

A sharp rap on the door leading to the hall jarred me out of my recollections, and Viggo shouted, "Come in," as his hands went back to the tie.

"Everyone is waiting for you and Violet, and I'm afraid they're growing quite impatient," Jeff announced as he stepped in. "Should I tell them you are ready, or will you need a few more minutes?"

"We're ready," I announced to Jeff with a smile. He gave me a small bow, and I resisted the urge to shake him. "Jeff!"

He smiled, his eyes twinkling. "So sorry. Habit, you understand."

"It's been a year, Jeff, and frankly, I still feel weird about you serving as our butler," I told him. "You're not our butler, you're our friend."

Jeff's face softened as his lips curled up into a smile.

"Violet, I'm not merely your butler—I am your secretary and bodyguard, and I consider it a distinguished honor to serve you in that capacity. Besides, this is my skillset. And, may I remind you, I would be hard-pressed to find a position better suited to my own needs in my field. So please, I beg of you, allow my attempt to preserve tradition."

I glared at him, but I couldn't shake the smile from my lips.

"Fine," I said in mock exasperation. "Keep bowing! At least tell me—"

"Tim and Jay are both waiting for you in the atrium," Jeff answered me smoothly. "I'll be coming behind with the other state officials, but you have to be there first, Violet. You're in a critical role."

"I know, I know," I breathed. "Viggo?"

"I'm ready," he announced as he turned, bow tie neatly tied. "Let's go."

He took my hand, and the three of us exited the bedroom, heading down the hallway toward the stairs. Morgan had changed the palace quite a bit in the year she'd been queen—for the better, I thought. The carpets were a deep blue, while the walls were painted a bright, warm yellow. It seemed like nothing bad had ever happened here—it *felt* like nothing bad had ever happened here. It was only when I thought about it too much that a pang of loss caught me off guard.

I missed Ms. Dale and Thomas. I thought about them every day, and I remembered every day what they had sacrificed so that we could change our world. I still wasn't sure it had been worth it to lose them, but our world *was* improving. Especially after the harvest this past autumn—we'd had more than enough fresh food to feed Patrus and Matrus both, and Viggo had worked out a great trade agreement with Morgan.

We followed Jeff outside to the car that was waiting for us. The city streets slid by as we headed for our destination, the sun still out but hanging low in the sky, giving us a brilliant view of orange and pink skies over Matrus.

Viggo shuffled through some papers next to me—it seemed like he was always working these days, and the reports were endless—and made a pleased noise. I looked over at him.

"What is it?"

"It's Alejandro's report on The Green and the effectiveness of the filtration device we created for the river."

"Oh?" I sat forward, instantly excited. "And?"

He gifted me an exuberant smile. "It works—King Patrick's filters can effectively remove eighty-nine percent of the toxic materials, even upriver in The Green, where the toxicity is greater. Unfortunately, we don't currently have a delivery system big enough to accommodate the whole river, and we will definitely need to set up two facilities to ensure that all the water is treated, which would mean another adventure with the MPJC."

I grinned at the groan in his voice. Even though it had been his idea to form the Matrian-Patrian Joint Council, he couldn't stand it now. Mostly because it would be him and Morgana ready to get it done, while fifty statesmen and -women argued this way and that, and, more often than not, devolved the conversation into insults and name-calling. Progress, right?

I, however, was relieved by the news, and intended to let him know.

"That's fantastic! Does that mean we're scrapping the plans to go back to the Tower?"

Viggo's forehead wrinkled.

"Maybe… I'd like to send an envoy on a peace mission, but with their defensive capabilities, it seems unwise right now. I'm still entertaining Amber and Logan's crazy idea to take a heloship and explore the world around us a bit more—and they don't necessarily have to get near that place. They are really chomping at the bit, and I can't blame them.

But we barely have our feet under us—we should learn to walk before we can..."

He trailed off as he changed papers and continued to read, another sigh escaping him. This one was heavier, reflecting his exhaustion. Luckily, by now we were both used to the highs and lows as information came across Viggo's desk; for every good thing, there was always something to chase away the elation, some new problem or trial that needed to be faced.

"What?" I asked.

"Nothing—Drew wants us to be more aggressive in our demands to send a few of our own scientists to the lab where they are working on the egg, but I'm going to deny him."

"I'm sure if you just asked Morgan, she'd be more than willing to do that," I replied.

He gave me a look and smiled. "I know, but it isn't a good way of showing we trust our neighbors."

"Viggo, you and I both know resentment still runs deep," I replied, feeling saddened by my own words. It was true—there was a lot of mistrust of the other side in Patrus, even after Morgan and the rest of Matrus had made amends and continued to be helpful and accommodating at every turn. Everything Morgan had done had borne the risk of her hurting the Matrians to help the Patrians, and just like in Patrus, a small group of people complained. Although, to be fair, a small group of malcontents in Patrus complained about Viggo just as much, and often questioned Maxen's death in the caves, calling Viggo an assassin. Luckily, it was a small part of the population, but I knew personally how much trouble a small group of people could cause when they put their minds and wills to it.

"It will take years before everyone can ease up," I told my husband. "Until then, let Drew have this, and just ask Morgan. It'll be all right."

"You're right, of course," Viggo said with a sigh. "I just hate that I have to be the one to go to her asking for more when she's gone above and beyond helping us. Our economy is still fragile, and with how low our population is... she saved us."

"Because she wants to show that the petty differences that held us apart are a thing of the past. But that takes time, and it takes her giving in to us every now and again. Especially where the egg is concerned. The public knows too much about it to feel comfortable with them handling it alone. As much as I hate to admit it, Drew's right—even if he's being obstinate about it. Just ask."

"You sure you don't want to do this for me?" he asked, giving me a look from under the spectacles perched on his nose. He needed them for reading now—we weren't entirely sure why—and I never complained.

"I'm just your bodyguard," I replied. "You got elected chancellor—you even got to run in the official election! Clearly, you wanted the job."

He smiled, taking off his glasses and putting the papers down, sliding over to close the distance between us.

"Want me to quit?" he asked as he drew closer, his voice a low rumble that still had a devastating effect on me. I let out a shuddering breath and turned toward him, my hands going to his shoulders as he leaned closer.

"You're going to wrinkle my dress," I murmured, and he smirked.

"Good—you shouldn't look so gorgeous in your dress. You're going to take everyone's attention off the main event, and if I know Morgan, she's not going to like it."

He took my hips and pulled me over, his mouth dropping to my neck and placing soft kisses against my sensitive skin. I couldn't help it—a moan escaped me, and I flinched when I saw the driver's eyes flick to the mirror and look directly at me, before turning back down.

"Viggo," I giggled and squirmed, pushing against his shoulders. "Please! The driver!"

He grumbled and pulled back, an irritated expression on his face.

"I never should've become chancellor. We could be alone in our mountain cabin right now, minding our own business and—"

"Oh, come on, you know you love this," I chided him. "Not being in charge—but you like helping people, and this is the best way of doing it. So calm down, my love. Besides… we'd still be here today, even if you weren't the chancellor."

He opened his mouth, and then shut it. "Fair point," he said, returning to his seat.

On impulse, I leaned across the seat and grabbed the lapels of his suit, pulling his face to mine for a slow, loving kiss.

"I do wish we were in the cabin too, though," I murmured softly, for his ears only, and I was rewarded with a smoldering look, promising that when we got back to our rooms later that evening, we were going to finish what he had started.

The rest of our drive took place in comfortable silence, and I started collecting my things as the car turned and began heading up a slight incline, the houses and shops stopping a few hundred feet away from the entrance of the temple.

I didn't wait for the driver to let me out—I never did—and came around the car to Viggo's side just as he was stepping out. Even though he didn't like it, I was still his bodyguard. I was going to be his bodyguard for at least another month or two, before my pregnancy became too obvious and the council put in the request for me to go on leave. But that was for another day.

It didn't matter—I was also his wife, which meant I went with him everywhere. I was the best suited to keeping him safe for that reason alone, and they would just have to deal with the fact that I was more than comfortable in both roles. And when I became a mother, I would be comfortable in three.

Viggo took my hand as I slid around the car, and we walked up the smooth stone steps toward the cave mouth. We were early, but people were already forming in massive crowds. I kept close to Viggo, my eyes scanning the crowd, looking for any sign of hostile movement.

My gaze passed over a familiar face in my scrutiny, and I paused, dragging my gaze back over and staring. It couldn't be her.

Then she saw me looking, and her eyes went wide, a broad smile crossing her freckled face. She lifted her hand slightly, and I couldn't stop myself.

"Josefine?" I said, taking a step over to where the crowd of people were standing behind a cordoned-off line. The general masses would be let in soon, but for now, only state officials and royalty were allowed into the caves.

"Violet!" she shouted, and after a moment of hesitation, she ducked under the rope and raced over to me.

I heard one of the wardens shout in warning as the young girl raced over, and I quickly held up my hands.

"IT'S OKAY!" I shouted loudly. "I know her!"

A man and a woman were calling Josefine's name in panicked tones, but she ignored them, her small shoes clicking against the stone as she approached.

"Violet?" Viggo asked, giving me a questioning look.

"It's Josefine," I reminded him. "She was... a girl I knew at Merrymount Mill. I didn't think I'd ever see her again."

Josefine stopped just short of me and pushed a hand through the curly ginger hair on her head. Her bangs had grown out, and she was definitely taller. She cast a glance up at Viggo, a polite smile on her lips, and then stuck out her hand.

"My name is Josefine Rankin, Chancellor Croft," she said formally. "And I'm so happy you are here! I hoped you would be! Oh, Violet!"

I smiled at her enthusiasm and reached out to place a hand on her shoulder.

"It's awesome to see you again. Are you waiting to get into the temple?"

She nodded, her face beaming with joy.

"Yes. Me and my parents are... That's my dad."

I looked up to see an auburn-haired man with his hat in his hands, turning it nervously between them as he watched me and his young daughter. I glanced at Viggo, who shrugged, and then looked back at Josefine.

"Would you... Would you like to come into the temple a little early? You can return to your parents before the ceremony."

"So I can meet Morgan and Amber?" she asked, her eyes growing wide.

I suppressed a groan as I recognized the hero worship.

Someone—and by someone, I meant Owen—had turned to art and taken to making our story into an adventure comic, one distributed in monthly episodes on both sides of the river. It was accurate, mostly, but definitely designed for children, a move I understood, but still resented in some ways. It had glossed over the violence and the pain, making the story seem more whimsical than it actually was.

"Queen Morgan," I corrected her, needing to put a wedge between the image of Morgan from Owen's comic books (and it was *very* flattering) and the real person I knew. "She's your queen, remember."

"Not for much longer," Josefine said with a cheeky smile. "Papa accepted a job in Patrus to help in the construction. Soon, you and Viggo will be our king and queen."

"Patrus is no longer a monarchy," announced a steady voice from behind us, and I turned to see Mags moving toward us, her thick hair braided on top of her head and then artfully disheveled. She was wearing black slacks and a white dress shirt. A vest pulled the outfit together beautifully, and she smiled as she saw me. "Hey, Violet, aren't you late?"

I looked at the watch on my wrist and sighed. "I am, but I'm waiting for Josefine's answer."

"She can go," her mother announced loudly, and I looked up and saw her smiling at me. Beaming, really. "You're her hero," she added.

I felt the pang of guilt, knowing Owen's stupid comic books had once again been blown out of proportion, and sighed.

"I get that a lot," I commented as I reached out a hand to the young girl. "Shall we?"

"Mags will escort me down," Viggo said from behind me, and I raised my hand as I continued up the steps. Mags *would* escort him down—she was the head of his wardens now, a bold and stunning move for Patrus that had been one of the first positions he had announced.

Oh, there had been pushback, but it didn't matter, because it had the intended effect of recruiting women to the wardens when Viggo had opened up jobs to both genders. No Patrian woman had believed she would get a fair shake with a male in charge, and the rest was history.

"Was that really Magdelena?" Josefine asked, her eyes widening.

"She stopped that revolt six months ago. With the Porteque gang. Without a single shot fired!"

I smiled. She talked about it so casually, as if there hadn't been several lives threatened. She was right—Mags had handled the situation beautifully, planning and executing the rescue operation down to every minute detail, but it didn't change the fact that the gang members had taken an entire school hostage for forty-eight hours in an attempt to draw Viggo and me out.

"That was her, yes. Head Warden Magdelena."

"Oh wow," said Josefine wistfully. "I'm just so excited to see you all. I hoped I would. I wanted to tell you how—"

"Excuse me, Mrs. Bates?"

I turned away from Josefine to see an olive-clad warden climbing the steps leading down, one hand on the wall, and I recognized Edi immediately. I checked my watch and winced.

"How mad is she?" I asked.

Edi gave me a weathered smile and shook her head.

"She's not mad, she's… concerned. Will you and your guest accompany me down?"

"Duty calls," I announced in a conspiratorial whisper to Josefine, and she giggled. "We're on our way down, Edi."

The elderly woman nodded and peered over my shoulder.

"Where's that eye candy you call a husband?" she asked, her eyes gleaming, and I rolled my eyes.

"On his way with Mags," I informed her, resuming our descent down the steps. "He's cutting a dashing figure in that suit he's wearing—just remember, he's *my* husband."

"I'm too old for that sort of thing," Edi called after me. "I just enjoy looking."

Josefine flushed as I shook my head with a chuckle, continuing down the stairs toward the temple.

"I get that a lot," I told her, and she looked up at me, a shy grin on her face.

"I can't believe you're letting me come with you!" she squeaked.

"You really... I mean... You're sort of my..."

I let her stammer for a second, and then paused on the steps and turned to face her.

"Josefine, you were my friend before all this happened. Can't I persuade you to be my friend again?"

Her eyes grew large as she considered it, and then nodded slowly.

"I guess I can? I mean... we only knew each other for a short time, and then you were gone. I thought they were going to execute you."

"They tried to," I replied. "In their own way."

"But you didn't die! You refused to give up! You were so brave!"

"I was afraid," I told her bluntly. "All the time. Every choice, every decision... it meant the possibility that someone would die. People did die. What I did... it wasn't anything special. You could've been right there too, if circumstances had been different, but I'm glad you weren't. When did you get out of Merrymount?"

"Shortly after you left," she replied. "But my mom was still in prison, and they wouldn't let me go to my dad once... once everything happened. I was so scared he was dead. The way the ticker made it sound, it seemed like he could've been."

"But he wasn't, and now you have a family again, reunited and whole."

She smiled up at me. "That's why you're my hero," she said softly. "You and Owen both—you changed the laws, and now my family is together again. Mom got released after the bill you both wrote forgiving her and all those like her for their crimes. Y'know—the Broken Homes Act?"

I grinned at her. "I remember," I said dryly, moving farther down the steps. "It took three months to write, another three to get ratified by both governments, and was a blinding migraine on both sides. That's..." I paused and looked back up at her. "That's why I'm your hero? Because I co-authored a law?"

To be honest, the only reason Owen and I had gotten roped into it was because of our experiences on both sides, and our connections to the leadership. Because it was going to be the first law to be enacted by both countries, Owen and I (and a team of lawmakers) had sat down and hammered it out as the first bi-national cooperative effort. It had been rough, and it wasn't what we had originally wanted, but it was… better.

"Yes," Josefine said, breaking me from my train of thought and reminding me I was in a conversation. "I mean, I read those comics, but I remember what happened at Merrymount, you know. I know a lot of the story is left out. I went to the library and checked out the transcripts from the investigation, as well as the oral history project you and the chancellor started. I accessed those and listened to what everyone on that side of the river went through. It was awful."

I licked my lips, my mouth suddenly going dry.

"That's, uh, pretty impressive, actually. I don't think *I've* listened to all of that." And there had certainly been some content that would be heavy for a… I wracked my brains, trying to do math… an almost ten-year-old girl.

Josefine looked up at me, her gaze heavy, and I was reminded that she had always seemed more than your average child. Growing up in the orphanages did that to some of us. But even so, I was beginning to suspect that Josefine was a very special case.

"Probably because you were there," she said. "It was easier for me because I wasn't, and even then, it was still painful. What was… What was Ms. Dale's secret that she hid from you?"

I felt myself start to break, and I looked away, fighting back the tears.

"I never asked," I admitted, cursing myself for even including it in the recording. It had felt important enough to include… but now everyone wanted to know. "Viggo offered to tell me, but… I never wanted to know."

"Why not?"

It was a simple question, but there wasn't a simple answer. How could I explain that I didn't care what wrong she had committed against me? That it ultimately didn't matter, because she was dead and all this was over? What would the knowledge change, save potentially tainting a memory of her that I wanted pure and pristine and whole? It didn't matter—she was gone, and all I had was a memory of a woman willing to sacrifice herself to save me and both our worlds. Surely that more than made up for any past transgressions.

"We should go," I said after a moment. "Morgan's going to *kill* me."

"Oh. Of course." We resumed walking, but now the silence between us was a bit strained. I wanted to assure Josefine that she hadn't upset me, but I *was* upset. It wasn't her fault—she had just been curious—but every time I thought of Ms. Dale, I felt more than my share of melancholy. I wished she were there so I could ask her how long it would hurt for, but she wasn't. And I felt that.

"Violet!" I looked up as we came down the last part of the stairs and saw my brother moving toward me, pushing through several official-looking people to reach me.

"Tim? I thought you were in the atrium."

"I got bored," he said. "Besides, Jay wanted to come down early to see if any... if *there were* any pretty girls."

"I was just telling Tim it looked like a bust," announced Jay from behind him, and I looked up to see him wheeling himself across the mosaic floor in his wheelchair. "But then you walked in." He grinned smarmily at me, and I gave him a dry look. "My name is Jay Bertrand," he said, holding out his hand to Josefine.

"Of course! You're Desmond's so—" Josefine broke off, her eyes drifting back to the wheelchair he was seated in, awkwardly pausing as she recalled who had put him there.

"Son," he finished for her, his smile never wavering. "And yes, her parting gift to me was less than pleasant. But the ladies really dig the wheelchair."

"No, they dig all the muscles," Tim said, slapping him lightly on a solid shoulder. It was true—Jay may have lost the use of his left leg all the way to the hip, and his right leg all the way to the knee, but he kept active, and his chest and arms had grown significantly during his convalescence. With his enhancement, he could do pretty much anything with his upper body alone. What was even more incredible was how well he had taken everything, all things considered. "I stand next to him, and I can't even get a hello!"

"You're Tim!" Josefine chirped excitedly, a wide smile on her face. "Your speech has gotten much better than in the comics. Oh. Wait… Should I say hello?" Tim flushed bright red, looking mortified.

"No!" he said, clearly uncomfortable with the young girl's faux pas. I bit my lip, trying not to laugh at his obvious embarrassment and subsequent backpedaling. "You're too—I mean… What I mean to say is…"

"That he is looking for a girlfriend, but us injured guys get all the attention," came Quinn's voice, and I saw him turning around to face us, an eyepatch over one eye. His scars had faded significantly, but were still there, making his face resemble a patchwork quilt—and a messy one at that—but the impish smile remained. "Cry me a river, Bates. I'll take whatever help I can get." He squatted next to Josefine. "He might seem like boyfriend material, but trust me—you can do much better."

"You're a little old for her, grandpa," I pointed out, though I couldn't help but smile at the way they were all joking around just like ordinary boys… and how Josefine didn't seem to be bothered in the slightest.

"Oh my God, you're Quinn!" she exclaimed. "You're…"

"The genius behind creating a linked network between Matrus and Patrus?" he asked, anything but humble. "Yes, I know. I built an informational bridge between our two countries, and gave everyone free access to it."

"Settle a bet for us, Violet," said Jay, ignoring Quinn's bragging. "What do ladies like better—charm, smarm, or farm?" As he spoke, he pointed to himself first, Quinn second, and Tim third, and I cocked my head at him.

"Why is my brother the farm?" I asked.

"Because he's just got that good ol' farmer thing down, all shy and nervous. Not to mention, all of those speech classes go right out the window when he sees a pretty face. Goes right back to how he was before."

Tim rolled his eyes theatrically behind Jay's back, and Josefine's hand leapt to her mouth as she covered her smile.

"I'm not answering that question," I announced, fighting back a laugh of my own. "You three will just have to figure it out for yourselves."

"Yeah, whatever, Violet," Quinn quipped, his hands moving to his hair and mussing it slightly. "I just spotted the next target of my affections. Wish me lu—hey!"

"All's fair in love and war," Jay replied as he wheeled past Quinn, heading toward a pretty young woman wearing a soft coral dress—and not-so-accidentally running over Quinn's foot in the process. I rolled my eyes. This was their latest pastime, competing for feminine attention, and I wanted nothing to do with it.

"I don't know about you, but I think they need some alone time together," I said to Josefine. "Maybe it'll remind them women like more than confidence or arrogance—they like to be treated like people and not prizes."

Quinn flushed bright red, stalling. "God, are we really doing that, Violet? Why didn't you say anything sooner?"

"Because I love you and I know you didn't mean any harm by it. But I really have to go—Morgan is waiting for me. Think you can tone it down some before we get back?"

"I'll make sure they do," Tim said, crossing his arms across his chest. "You and Josefine go. We'll see you soon."

I looked at my watch and cursed. I was now fifteen minutes late. Grabbing Josefine's hand again, I began to push through the crowd. I spotted the small side tunnel that ran left of the fountain—the same one Elena had been in when we had supposedly thwarted the bomb meant to kill her—and moved into it, Josefine keeping up behind me.

It curved right and then left, ending in an archway that led into a smaller rounded cavern. I could hear Amber speaking softly as I approached, but I couldn't make out what she was saying, just the tones she spoke in—calming and supportive.

"Is she freaking out yet?" I asked as I stepped in, Josefine in tow, and Morgan scowled at me through the mirror she was standing before.

"You're... late..." she panted, and I realized the young queen was in the middle of an anxiety attack. Her hands gripped the wooden vanity she was hunched over—the mirror attached to the front—while

Amber fanned her with a stiff piece of paper. Still, she looked beautiful. Her white dress was perfectly cut, cinching her waist and exposing her shoulder and collarbones. A simple black ribbon wrapped around her waist, forming a small bow on the front, while her skirt was full and voluminous.

"I'm sorry," I said, letting go of Josefine's hand and heading right over to her side. "What's wrong?"

"Nothing. Something. Oh, mother… Am I *really* doing this?"

I smiled and placed a hand on her back, rubbing small, gentle circles.

"I understand. I felt the same way when Viggo and I were getting married."

"Oh?" She looked up at me, her eyes glittering with curiosity as she fought to catch her breath. "Really? I thought… you were… pretty composed."

I laughed and shook my head.

"Is that really how I looked? I could've sworn everyone could see the whites of my eyes with how I was feeling inside."

"Why were you scared?" asked Josefine.

"It was just nerves," I replied, turning to her. "I was second-guessing everything, and frightening myself in the process."

"How did you fix it?" Amber asked, looking pointedly at Morgan.

"I didn't. Viggo did. The instant I saw him walking into the room… everything just settled. My heart went still. Everything fell out of focus. Everything except him. And in that moment, I just knew what we were doing was the right thing."

"Problem solved, then," Morgan said under her breath as she turned toward the door. "SOMEONE GET MY FIANCE IN HERE!"

There was a rustle behind one of the curtains, and a sky-blue warden stepped out from the alcove behind it. "Yes, my qu—"

"Ignore that order," I said with a laugh. I knew I couldn't *actually* order her, but there was a quick flicker of relief on the warden's face, and she hesitated, looking at Morgan. "You're not supposed to see him before the wedding—you'll piss off the chamberlain lady."

"Oh God," Morgan said with a shudder. "She's right, cancel that order. I'll just go to him!"

"You *can't*," Amber said in exasperation. "They've only just started letting the public in. The wedding's not for another hour!"

Morgan narrowed her eyes at us, her jaw set at a mutinous angle. "I'm the damn queen," she snarled. "And it's my damn wedding. They'll get over it."

Her spine straightened as she spoke, uncurling and becoming rigid. Unyielding. Commanding.

I looked at Amber and shook my head. "Can you let the chamberlain know the wedding has been moved up by fifty-five minutes? Tell the guards up top to use the Patrian wardens with us to help search bags for weapons, but get the public down here in a hurry."

Amber gave me a dry smile. "Think you can keep her here for five minutes?"

"We need to double check her makeup is perfect. That'll be at least a few minutes."

"Why?" gasped Morgan, turning around toward the mirror. "Did you see something wrong with it?"

I gave Amber a pointed look, and nodded.

"I'll relay the orders," she said as she moved down the corridor. Turning to Morgan, I coaxed her into a sitting position.

"Calm down," I urged her. "And focus on something else."

"Like your new friend there?" she asked, her eyes flicking to Josefine.

"Old friend," I said, carefully reapplying some of her makeup. "We were at Merrymount together."

"The work facility?" she asked, blinking in surprise. "You met her there?"

"She did, but she wasn't there long. I'm surprised she remembers me, to be honest." Josefine's voice ended on a diminished note, and I turned toward her.

"I could never forget you, Josefine. You were kind to me in a place where kindness didn't exist. It meant more than you could possibly know."

"But it's my fault," she blurted suddenly. "It's my fault you went after Dina! That you... That you... killed her."

"What?" I asked, my eyes widening in surprise. "No it's not."

"It is! I should've been braver! I should've fought Dina harder when she came in. If I had, maybe she would've run away, or—"

"Or she would've killed you," I exclaimed loudly, cutting her off. "Her braces were *removable*, Josefine. She turned them into a weapon and tried to use them against me. That's why I—Why she died. She tried to kill me. I killed her first."

"It was self-defense," Morgan said softly, and I shook my head.

"No, it wasn't," I breathed sadly. "I went into her room looking for a fight. I wanted to hurt her—and all she'd done was tear up Tim's photo. In retrospect... that seems a very petty reason for someone to die."

"Violet..." Morgan trailed off, her hand reaching out and taking mine. "It's over now. There's nothing you can do but find some way to move on. You saved our worlds—we are fundamentally changed in extraordinary and unprecedented ways. You've done great and amazing things for the people here."

I smiled. Morgan had misunderstood my melancholy over Dina's death. I just didn't dismiss it easily. I carried the guilt of that memory within me so it could temper my anger, hone it and contain it, until I was certain it was pointed in the right direction.

"I'm fine," I told her. "And it's *your* wedding. Josefine, you didn't do anything wrong, and you aren't responsible for any of this. Morgan, your soon-to-be-husband has probably been rushed to get ready and is feeling pretty uncertain. Shall we?"

Morgan smiled and nodded. I helped her stand up and held her train as we moved over to the door.

"You should go find your parents now," I whispered to Josefine. "I'll make sure you have an invitation to the reception. I want to see more of you, especially if your family is moving to Patrus."

"Of course," she breathed. "I'll let them know!" She turned to run off, and then paused, turning back. "You also did great and amazing things for the boys," she added, and it took me a minute to put the comment into context. By the time I had, she had already disappeared, and I smiled at the sound of her feet carrying down the tunnel.

"You have a fan," Morgan said as she ducked under the archway. "And she's right, you know. The boys are all thriving now."

She wasn't wrong, but she didn't give herself or Viggo enough credit. If anything, the project was their brain child; I was just one of the only people who had enough free time to oversee it and make Viggo's ideas reality. It made me happy to shoulder the load, not only for him, but so that I could spend time helping them. The program at the school we'd established in a secluded area in the Patrian farmlands included therapy, education, medication, gene therapy for the more extreme cases... even outpatient counseling and a housing and foster family program—anything the boys might need to start building lives from the wreckage Desmond and Elena's plans had left for them.

Morgan's scientists had discovered a number of things from combing through Mr. Jenks' research—one of the biggest ones directly affected Morgan and Tim both, a welcome relief that had come as a complete shock to the two of them. They'd been able to uncover the reasons that they, and some of the other boys as well, were so sensitive to touch, and a drug to deal with the problem had been developed shortly afterward. Now both of them could experience human contact in a way that had been denied them their entire lives. I was thrilled beyond words for them—it was hard to imagine Morgan going through with a wedding without the new drugs.

Beyond that, Cody was more stable too. He'd chosen to live with Morgan in the palace, and she referred to him fondly as her little brother—and she had just finished establishing a sister school in Matrus, so the boys could decide where and how they were going to live, and hopefully be reunited with their families.

"I'm just glad I could do something to help them," I replied. "And Josefine isn't a fan, she's a friend. One I'm happy to see alive and well. She suffered greatly under the past regimes. Her father was Patrian, her mother Matrian, and the law broke them apart."

"Really? Then it's a good thing she got to meet the woman who was directly responsible for making a lot of those changes. Y'know, before she got so famous."

"Ugh, that really is Owen's fault," I said with a chuckle.

"He took to art. It… It helped him to draw it."

"But those books are so topical," I insisted as we walked down the long tunnel. "They skip over the horrific stuff."

"He painted the horrific stuff too," Morgan said quietly, her gaze directed far away for a moment. "All of it. The pieces are in a studio if you want to see them—he won't go in there though. Once he paints them, he never wants to see them again."

I felt my heart clench in my chest. "Oh."

"He doesn't like to talk about it. I can imagine you don't like to talk about it either. But please tell me you at least talk to someone about it."

"I talk to Viggo. We share everything, including each other's nightmares." I thought about it for a long moment, and added, "And there was the oral history thing. I included an audio file. It was… cathartic, actually. It hurt, of course, like tearing duct tape off of my heart, but afterward, everything felt a little better."

"Good. I worry about you sometimes."

"You could pick up a handheld and call," I replied tartly, and she chuckled.

"You know the council hates that," she replied. "They don't like the idea of me having so many direct conversations with various people in Patrus, actually. They prefer to work as intermediaries. Maybe it makes them feel important?"

I chuckled, but a pang of sadness washed over me. She was right, of course. We were friends, but we were citizens—no, not just citizens, *leaders*—of two different countries, and unfortunately, there was always going to be someone upset with the status quo. Someone who wanted to change things or interfere with what we had built.

And who knew—maybe that change could be good. All I could do was hope and pray that for now, our way was working, and would continue to work for as long as possible.

"How do I look?" she asked, and a peek over her shoulder told me we were near the main chamber. There was a murmur of voices coming from it—a soft din of hushed conversation that was happening everywhere and nowhere at the same time.

"Perfect," I replied as Amber pressed by, followed by Meera and Dr. Tierney. I smiled as I saw the two other women, and moved back a few steps to let Meera go first—she was the matron of honor, after all. Sierra took up the front as Morgan's family member, consenting to the union, just as Cody did for Owen on the groom's side.

"I'm really sorry I couldn't ask Margot," Morgan whispered from ahead.

"Don't worry about it," I said. "Henry has the flu anyway. They weren't going to be able to make it." Especially since Margot was pregnant with baby number three, but it wasn't my news to announce, especially not right now.

Not to mention, my Aunt Sarah and Uncle Kurtis were spending time with their grandchildren. We still hadn't really formed a relationship, although to be honest, they didn't seem particularly interested. Neither was I, for that matter—their behavior after I rescued them from Tabitha hadn't really bred the happy warm feelings of family between us. Then again… I had all the family I could possibly hope for, so it was a moot point. If they didn't want a relationship with me, I could accept that. Even if it drove Cad crazy.

A hush filled the hall, and I heard the strong voice of the chamberlain filling the room.

"We are gathered here, in the eyes of the Mother, in the home she provided us, to unite our queen and her chosen in a bond of love, honor, and respect. A united front to stand as both shield and sword against all foes and evils that would do their people harm. As per the queen's wishes, they will co-rule Matrus with a strong and united rule, further cementing the queen's belief in a better and brighter future. Will the petitioners of this union present themselves?"

"That's me," Morgan said excitedly, stepping forward. I waited for Meera to move, then a heartbeat longer, and followed. The room was quiet, reverent, as Morgan stepped through the archway, shimmering in her white, gauzy gown.

From the other side of the room, I saw Owen stepping out from his own archway, Cody leading the way with a familiar wooden box in his hands, his face a bright smile. The box was the same one Henrik had given Viggo and me, but the rings were different—Morgan had wanted something special to carry them in, and I had thought this would be perfect.

Viggo stood directly behind Owen, and I smiled at how amazing he looked in his formal attire. Then I heard, rather than saw, Cruz—also in the chosen's wedding train—speaking in a loud whisper that echoed throughout the cavern.

"But Viggo, I'm telling you, reinstating the Power Fight League could really be—"

"*Anello!*" Dr. Tierney whispered indignantly from behind me in the procession, and Cruz blinked and then immediately looked contrite.

"Lo siento, mi amor," he whispered. Dr. Tierney gave him a pointed look, then looked at Morgan and Owen. "Right—so sorry, Owen. Queen Morgan." He fell back in line, trying to look inconspicuous, and I caught Viggo shaking his head.

As the wedding procession moved along, I saw Henrik stepping up after Cruz—in fact, I was pretty sure Cruz was supposed to go at the end of the line, judging by the way Henrik grabbed his shoulder and stepped past him to move behind Viggo. Following Henrik were Cody, Solomon, Jay, Quinn, Tim, and Logan—and Logan waited for Cruz to regain his spot just in front of him before continuing the procession. It was all I could do to keep from laughing, but I was pretty sure Owen and Morgan didn't care.

"My man should've cut," Amber whispered up the line, and I grinned as I saw Logan rolling his eyes at her from behind Cruz's back.

Owen and Morgan noticed none of this, or maybe just ignored it, their eyes solely on one another. Their eye contact never broke as they drew together, coming to a slow halt.

Owen reached out with his hand, and Morgan settled hers on top of his in an almost ritualized way. Then again, the chamberlain had made them practice more than a few times. I waited as they moved forward together, up to the lip of the pool, where the chamberlain waited.

The chamberlain's hair was free, her dress a simple white frock, her arms and legs bare.

"They stand here as equals—partners—their duties to each other as well as their people. Does anyone object to the union of the two before us?"

Silence met the question, and she smiled serenely.

"Recite your vows," she commanded.

I looked at Viggo as Owen began to speak, staring at him across the small space that separated us. He grinned at me while Owen recited his vows—the very same vows Morgan had made us recite—and I returned the smile, pressing my hand to my stomach, right up against where I hoped Melissa (or Thomas, if our child was a boy) was settling in for the night. I recalled the moment of our wedding, the vows sounding comfortingly familiar, and I knew they were still as true for me and Viggo as the day we'd said them. I knew as long as Viggo and I had each other and our family, we could face whatever tomorrow brought, for good or for bad.

And the bad was disappearing, slowly, one day at a time.

What's next?

Dear Reader,

I hope you enjoyed the conclusion to The Gender Game series. It's been an incredible journey and I want to thank you for accompanying Violet and Viggo til the end.

Saying goodbye to them and their group is both sad and bittersweet—their story will always hold a deep place in my heart—but I'm also looking forward to a new adventure.

This book marks the end of Matrus and Patrus's story, but not the end of the world that surrounds them.

If you're curious to know more about the mysterious Tower civilization Violet came across in this book, keep turning the pages to read 3 early sneak-peek bonus chapters from *The Girl Who Dared to Think*—a book that continues the story of Violet's greater world.

The Girl Who Dared to Think releases very soon: August 9th, 2017.

Check out the breathtaking cover, and keep turning for the bonus chapters:

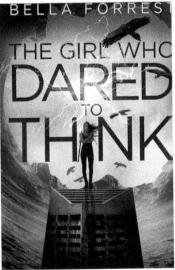

Thank you, once again, for reading, and I cannot *wait* to see you there!

Love,

Bella x

Blurb:

How do you fight an enemy when they're inside your mind?

A gargantuan glass-walled tower looms over a deadly wilderness. They say it's all that's left.

The Tower's survival is humanity's survival, and each must serve it faithfully...

Twenty-year-old Liana Castell must be careful what she thinks. Her life is defined by the number on her wristband—a rating out of ten awarded based on her usefulness and loyalty to the Tower, and monitored by a device in her skull. A device that reports forbidden thoughts.

Liana is currently a four, the lowest possible acceptable score, and despite her parents' perfect scores of ten, she struggles to increase it. Rebellious ideas come all too easily, and resentfulness seems part of her being. She is an Knight-in-training, but her future will be dark if she cannot raise her worth...

Threes require drug treatment.

Twos are isolated.

Ones disappear.

When Liana's worst nightmare comes to pass and she drops to a three, desperation spurs her down a path few dare to tread. A chance encounter with a cocky young man whose shockingly dissident attitude toward the Tower couldn't possibly have earned him the perfect "ten" on his wrist, sets her on a trail to save herself—even at the risk of dropping lower.

Stalking the young man seemed like a simple enough task, but after events take an unexpected twist, Liana finds herself taking a treacherous dive into the darkest depths of the Tower... and the decades' old secrets buried within.

In a society where free thinking can make you a criminal, one girl dares to try...

An unforgettable tale brimming with suspense, mystery and romance—*The Girl Who Dared to Think* will thrill fans of *The Gender Game...*

CHAPTER 1

Before the Tower, humanity dreamed of flying.

We made great machines to lift us away from the earth, roaring on engines that growled with noxious fuels, then rockets that shot us into space. But once we were there, we realized it wasn't enough. We grew restless. We waged war. We won, and we lost, and we brought the earth to its flaming knees. The sun tore open our irradiated, weakened atmosphere, and life dwindled to ash.

And now, nearly three hundred years after the end, we survived. Hidden behind the thick outer walls of the Tower, we served the monstrous structure that was both our salvation and our prison.

Once, we had dreamed of flying. Now, we didn't seem to dream at all.

"Squire *Castell.*" Gerome, my commanding officer, snapped me out of my musings, and I cringed. I'd been daydreaming again, and not about productive things. That was not in service to the Tower.

I turned away from the window I had been gazing through and, forcing an apologetic look onto my face, met my mentor's mildly disapproving gaze. Gerome's dark eyes reflected nothing, but his face reset to its normal stoic expression. After a moment he gave a barely perceptible nod and turned to the man next to him, the thick fabric of his crimson Knight's uniform creaking slightly, the sound magnified by the narrow concrete walls of the service hall we were standing in. "As I was saying, this is Squire Castell. She will be accompanying us, Mechanic Dalton."

Dalton, a 'seven' from the Mechanic Department (or Cog, as we referred to them), glanced pointedly at Gerome, and even out of the corner of my eye I could see the look of disgust he was shooting me. No doubt he had seen the number on my wrist and condemned me—which meant today was not going to be the brand-new day I had promised myself it would be.

No—it seemed both of us were destined for mutually assured sniping. Dammit.

It wasn't either of our faults; whenever any department needed to use a Knight's equipment, our protocol was to provide them with an escort—and these occasions were typically used as training for Squires like me, so we could learn our future duties when we became full Knights. This time—like most times—we needed to go outside to repair a few of the solar panels on one of the Tower's outside branches.

Dalton shot me another irate glance and I realized he'd said something and I had missed it. *Strike two,* I thought to myself. Gerome was turning and moving down the passage away from us both, heading toward the elevator just a few feet down the hall so I realized Dalton must have told him the level we had to get to. I moved to follow, but Dalton held out a disdainful arm, blocking my path.

"You'll come up after us," he said with a sniff. "I don't want to risk the psychological contamination."

A twinge of anger ran up my spine, but I looked away, biting my tongue.

As always, the narrow passageways in the shell were practically deserted. We were in its depths so there wasn't much to look at—just pipes and concrete and steel walls.

"I can't believe they sent a *four,*" Dalton muttered as he turned toward the elevator. I couldn't control myself this time. I opened my mouth to say something when Gerome shot me a look over his shoulder, his message clear. *Stay back—do not act.*

Yeah, okay. Fine.

The two men stepped forward onto the elevator's exposed steel-gray platform. Several beams of blue lights shot out from the platform and I heard the computer begin chirping out their names, identification codes and rankings as they began to rise. I watched as they were quickly lifted up toward the next floor, disappearing from view. I wondered if the system ever failed. Gerome was okay but I felt Dalton could benefit from a long fall to a cement floor.

You're part of his detail for today, I scolded myself. Gerome would have been disappointed; my thought had been dishonorable for a Squire—or anyone, really. Besides, Dalton's dislike of me was for a reason. A stupid reason, but one I was not helping with my negativity right now.

Level 173, Squire, Gerome's voice buzzed in my ear.

Sighing, I pressed the button, watching as a new platform slid out of the wall and covered up the exposed shaft the elevator ran through. Taking a deep breath to mentally prepare myself for the scan, I stepped inside and waited. Almost immediately the lights came on, and I felt a dull pain in the back of my head as the neural net surrounding my cerebral cortex buzzed with activity and the computer ran its scan of my credentials.

"*Identity verified: Squire Liana Castell, designation 25K-05; you are cleared for elevator use.*"

I fruitlessly prayed for that to be the end of it, eager to get moving. The computer, however, was not done with me.

"*Your number is currently four,*" its artificially rendered feminine voice chirped. I scowled, and once again felt a throb in the back of my head. It was bad enough that Dalton disliked me because of my number; for a stupid *computer* to remind me of it was just downright depressing. I leaned against the wall of the shaft and waited for it to finish the worst pep talk in history. "*For a Squire of the Citadel as well as a citizen of the Tower, it is recommended that you—*"

"Seek Medica treatment," I recited along with the machine, the speech ingrained. It lectured anyone ranked five or lower—but the lower you were, the more the computer had to say. "Yeah. Got it."

"Your well-being is for the well-being of the Tower," the computer said. *"Remember that, as a Squire, it is your duty to—"*

I knew the rest of its speech by heart. The damn thing regurgitated it every time I so much as breathed too close to a high-security area. *Your number is too low. Have you considered Medica treatment? Maybe it's time to find new friends!* I made a face and then uncrossed my arms, pushing up off of the wall as the platform began to move, my eyes watching the painted numbers on the walls glide by.

A four. I was a lousy four, and the end of my Knights training was drawing near. If I didn't raise my number before then, I'd fail to meet the ranking requirements to be a Knight. Consequently, I'd be dropped from my department, and essentially become homeless, doomed to try to find another department to take me in before my number fell to a one and I got arrested. All before I turned twenty-one. My parents would make a case for me and get me extensions, I was certain, but they could only buy me so much time. Not very much at all.

My eyes caught the number 150 as it slid past and I turned, a trill of excitement interrupting my bleak thoughts. I waited patiently until, like dawn breaking, I was greeted with a section of glass paneling. Here, the elevator shaft was now exposed to the inside of the Tower behind a glass tube that ran up and along the walls.

The walls of the Tower were actually a shell—one that was, by design, for defensive purposes. It contained two layers—the outermost layer holding the hatches into and out of the Tower, with a grand set of stairs inside, wrapping around the Tower, and seemingly endless. The innermost layer contained hundreds of floors that held a collection of things—service tunnels and quarters mostly—but the floors of its lowest section housed the machines that kept us alive. The lowest floors were also the densest floors, as they bore the weight of the entire structure.

As a result, not all of the elevators connected with the floors at the top; they typically stopped at the highest available level, meaning the citizen inside would have to walk to the next elevator if they needed to go any higher. The lift I was in, however, and a few just like it, ran all the way up the interior walls.

My eyes soaked up one of the more beautiful sights in our Tower (beautiful sights were few and far between, after all): the artificial light emitting from the walls was set to 'morning' and rays of bright light were beginning to cut into the shadows of the dim nighttime lighting, revealing three structures dangling from the ceiling. Their bases were massive at this height, and from this angle I had a full view of all three of them, gleaming in the artificial morning light. The glowing white walls of the Medica's smooth-sided cylindrical structure were closest on this side, the white almost too bright to look at directly. Circular walkways girdled the giant cylinder—one for each of its sixty floors. The walkways were thin and white, interrupted only by steps that ran up and down between floors, and the bridges that connected the structure to the rest of the Tower. Opposite the Medica was the Citadel, with its black-and-crimson-lit arches, dark steel edifices, and stylized walls, borrowing heavily from Gothic architecture to distinguish its cylindrical shape. Between them dangled the luminescent blue-and-black cone-shaped structure of the Core. Its circular levels were stacked, the widest level connected to the roof. Each level below was slightly smaller than the one above it, making the whole thing appear like coins of different values stacked together from largest to smallest. The Core was the heart of the Tower and the heart of Scipio... *Our benevolent computer overlord.*

The net in my head buzzed, warning me that it was detecting a strong spike of negativity, and I quickly broke the thought apart and shut it away. "Stupid," I muttered, catching a flash of my scornful amber eyes in the glass as I spun away from the view to face the wall. I glanced down at my wrist.

The band wrapped around my bronze skin was made of black microthread, a smooth material that was thin but practically unbreakable. Mounted atop it, the digital display that showed my number was glowing a soft, irritated orange—our overlord's little reminder that I wasn't good enough. Scipio, the great computer that monitored the nets in our heads and used the readings to determine our worth, had never liked me. Supposedly he didn't have emotions, but I had long suspected that he took some perverse pleasure in my failings. He'd never had any faith in me. Then again, neither did my parents. Or my teachers. Or anyone really, except for my friends and my brother Alex.

Alex had explained that the number was a representation of the concentration of positive versus negative thoughts in your brain. The net couldn't exactly read direct thoughts but it read the feelings associated with them and, through some sort of complex algorithm, could perform an ongoing risk assessment on the citizen in question, to determine the likelihood of dissidents. The thing was, I didn't consider myself dissident. In fact, the most aggravating thing about my existence was the number itself, which seemed self-defeating.

The elevator slowed as it approached Level 173, where Gerome and Dalton were waiting. It halted at a cut-out section of wall, and I stepped out quickly. The elevator hovered for a moment behind me, awaiting new orders, and then sank back into a slot in the wall to await its next rider. I was halfway down the ramp connecting the elevator to the floor when the tip of my boot caught on something—my other foot, of course!—and I pitched forward, starting to fall. Gerome moved quickly to steady me. Being a confident man, he used his right hand, which meant I caught sight of the number there: a cool blue-colored 'ten' shimmered against his pale skin as he grabbed my upper arm. A perfect citizen. Gerome was a prime example of how being perfect could make a person boring.

I straightened and shot a glance at Dalton. He was standing a few feet behind Gerome; he tilted his chin away from me, refusing to meet my eyes.

I clenched my jaw. It was beyond unfair. Dalton's ranking of seven was so average that the typical citizen of the Tower wouldn't bat an eyelid. Since we had met, however, he had looked down on me. The way he was acting, you'd think we were here on a secret mission sent straight from Scipio, not to fix malfunctioning solar panels, and that I (the lowly four) was his lone obstacle, rather than his escort. The worst thing was, he could get away with it; he obviously knew from experience that the odd spike of righteous superiority on his decent track record wouldn't lower his number. It made my blood boil.

"Peace, Squire," Gerome said, clapping a massive hand on my shoulder. "Cogs have never been the most social of our departments."

I grunted in response.

Gerome looked at me. His face resembled the holographs we had of the ancient Greeks: chiseled, each feature designed as if by an artist. His thin, distinct eyebrows rose up under hair that had just begun to go silver at the temples, and his cleft chin jutted toward me like an accusation.

"We don't want you slipping any lower," he said, his voice devoid of empathy. "Your number is low as it is. Have you considered—"

"Medica treatment?" I muttered, looking at the metal flooring so Gerome wouldn't see me rolling my eyes. Dalton moved down the service hall ahead of us, and I moved quickly to follow, hoping that walking would keep Gerome's lecture brief. "Yes. My parents have been talking about it quite a bit."

Gerome caught up to me with one swift step. Up ahead, Dalton had begun climbing a steep set of narrow stairs toward a rectangular access hatch. As he pushed it open, I saw the black outer walls of the shell waiting beyond.

"Your parents are good citizens," Gerome said. "Strong. Capable. Champion Devon made them Knight Commanders for a reason."

I grimaced, looking away. "They're very perfect."

They had wanted me to be, too. They'd been disappointed.

Gerome stopped at the foot of the stairs, and the way he snapped his heel against the floor made it clear that I was meant to halt as well. I did so, wondering if I had gone too far. Gerome hated sarcasm like a cat hated water.

"Lord Scipio spared you," he needlessly reminded me in that soft patronizing tone I got from nearly everyone. "You were a second-born twin, illicit and undeserving. Your parents yielded your life to his judgment, and he deemed that you would live. Must you continue to throw these… tantrums?"

My face grew hot and I curled my hands into fists, feeling my nails biting into my palm. In a way, he was right. Each family was allowed two children by law, but my parents had given birth to my older sister Sybil before I was born, and even though it was by seconds, I was younger than my twin brother. My mother, overflowing with maternal instinct, had been willing to kill me right then and there. Excise the excess, so to speak. Scipio, however, ordained that I would live. For a time, my parents had thought that made me special. A chosen child, destined to lead the Knights into a glorious new era.

When Sybil died unexpectedly when I was five, grief only inflated their opinion of me. As I grew a little older, I began asking questions about Sybil's death, trying to make sense of it. It came to a head when, at the age of seven, I made the mistake of asking why Scipio hadn't prevented Sybil's death, and my mother had responded by slapping me across the face and hissing words I would never forget.

"He chose you over *her*," she had spat, her eyes glittering with tears. "You have a destiny—but when you ask questions like that, it makes me wonder if he made a *mistake*." Her number had dropped to a nine that day—the first and only time I ever saw it happen. Of course Scipio didn't choose me over Sybil; the computer couldn't prevent death and Sybil's demise had nothing to do with Scipio having allowed me to live. But that was the day I learned to never question Scipio's decisions out loud.

Eventually my parents' grief faded, and they turned their attention fully on me and Alex, trying to make us into carbon copies of them, essentially. They wanted so badly for us to carry on the family tradition. Which was why they were astounded when Alex, upon turning fifteen, defected from the family profession—he was recruited from school into the Eyes, Scipio's private order of engineers and residents of the Core. After that, all expectations fell firmly on me.

As for the destiny my parents had hoped for? Well, I found out a year after Alex defected that it wasn't even true. The only reason I was alive was because another child had been stillborn. I wasn't special.

Scipio hadn't cared about me; he had been correcting a population imbalance.

"I can't help how I feel," I muttered.

Up at the access hatch, Dalton had turned and was shooting fiery looks in my direction. I found myself suppressing the urge to throttle the man.

"You *can*," Gerome said, his tone firm. "You just *won't*."

When we finally topped the stairs, Dalton was practically frothing at the mouth with impatience. He muttered a few words in the Mechanics' tongue, a language unique to his department, as we stepped out onto the landing. I stared at the massive staircase heading down, the ensconced lighting making the stairs appear to extend for eternity into the darkness, pressed between the scorching heat outside and the confines of the Tower.

"Are you quite ready?" Dalton asked in the common language.

I tried not to glare at him. Really, I did. I concentrated every ounce of effort I had on keeping my face still. But I could feel my lips twisting, my eyebrows shaking. Before my expression could grow any more gruesome, I turned away.

Gerome gave me a disapproving look as he gently set down a bag he had been toting on his shoulder. "Squire—can you please help Dalton into the lash harness and give the safety briefing?"

I nodded and squatted down to open the bag, pulling out the harness with its heavy black dome set on the back. Locating the top, I picked it up carefully and turned, holding it out to Dalton. The man screwed up his face in the now familiar look of disdain—but because Gerome had ordered me to do it, he had no choice but to obey. He held out his arms and allowed me to help him put the lash harness on.

"These are the lashes," I said as I helped him settle into it. I began pulling on straps, tightening the harness around his shoulders and chest. "When used correctly, they can prevent you from falling. Where would you like them fed through—your arms or your waist?"

"Arms," Dalton said bitingly, and I blinked but wisely kept my mouth closed. Arms were fine, but only if you needed to move fast. The waist was better if you had work to do, but it wasn't my place to question a seven, so I didn't.

Coming around behind him, I felt around the base of the case and grabbed one of the two metal ends at the bottom, pulling out a long line and threading it through the small loops in his uniform, underneath his arm, and finally through a small eyelet at the bottom. I repeated the process on the other side and then began double-checking each strap, to make sure the harness was secure.

"Okay," I said as I worked, not wanting to waste any time. "The tip of the lash is designed to absorb ambient static electricity as it flies through the air, building up a charge so that it will bond with anything it touches—metal, glass, you name it. To use it, simply—"

"I know how to use it, *Squire*," Dalton practically spat, his patience apparently coming to an end. "I'm a seven, and the Cogs designed and built them for the Knights, if you'll take a moment to remember."

"Of course," I said, trying to remain patient. "But I'm supposed to—"

"I'll be fine." End of discussion, apparently. I took a deep breath in, trying to calm some of the resentment that had boiled up in my gut.

"Ready when you are, Cog Dalton," I said, trying to make my tone as cheerful as possible.

Dalton sighed, then looked over at Gerome, who had rethreaded his own lash to come out from the small eyelets over his hip, just above his belt. Lashes were standard equipment for Knights, so our harnesses were worn under our suits, the lines running through internally de-signed channels. I had configured mine that morning, knowing we were going outside, in an attempt to prepare beforehand. Apparently that ef-fort was going to go unnoticed.

"Does she have to come?" Dalton asked as he approached the exte-rior hatch—the only one that led onto the branch. "I would feel much better if it was just you, Knight Nobilis."

And I would feel better if you slipped off the branch, I thought, then flinched. Bad thoughts. I was having a really hard time controlling them today. Well… every day, really.

Gerome's voice was patient as he spoke. As if he'd had this conversation too many times before. "She's my Squire," he said. "She needs training to be a productive member of the Tower. She'll be no trouble. I stake my reputation as a Knight on it."

Honestly, if it had been up to me, I probably would have just stayed in for the day. Going outside the Tower was always something of an ordeal, and one look at Dalton's sneering face had told me how much more unpleasant the excursion was going to be. Still, it was my duty as a Squire to follow Gerome around and do what he said. And besides, if I *didn't* do it, my parents would probably have me executed or something.

Dalton bit his lip and then sighed in defeat. "Fine," he muttered.

He shoved the exterior hatch wide open and a blaze of bright morning light slashed in. We'd chosen this time of day so as to avoid the intensity of the sun; it would take some time before it started heating the night-cooled air. All the same, I could feel the warmth of it prickling against my skin as I looked out over the solar branch.

The branches were beautiful, in their own way. Massive slats of solar panels spread some three hundred feet out from the Tower, forming a full platform one could walk on. I hopped out after Dalton, watching as he fidgeted with the lash harness. The things weren't standard issue for mechanics, and, despite his claims to the contrary, he didn't seem to know how it worked. He pulled the cable from its wrist holster and stuck the glowing tip to the ground. It fizzed, and I winced.

"You'll want to be really forceful with those," I called. It was a novice mistake; lashes were designed to be flung with speed and force to absorb the friction in the air and form a static burst when they connected.

Dalton looked up.

"The lashes," I said, tugging one of my own out. The tip shone with blue light. "You have to really slap them on."

Dalton stared at me for a moment, then turned away without a word. He stepped away, using his cable to lower himself off the edge of the solar branch and down the side.

"He really should be more forceful with that," Gerome said, peering out beside me.

I felt a small stir of pride at that. Gerome, like most people aside from my weapons trainers, rarely told me that I'd gotten anything right. Even this wasn't praise per se but at this point in my life, hearing that I wasn't a *complete* colossal failure was worth *something*.

I peered out over the edge and watched as Dalton slowly descended, the feed in his suit lowering him down. The view was breathtaking; the vibrant green of the river below, coupled with the brighter yellow desert—a desolate wasteland. Coincidentally enough, it was called The Wastes. The sky was already a bright blue, even though it was early morning—but there was nothing to diffuse or block it with. There was rarely a cloud in the sky, and the mountains in the distance were barely visible on the best of days—the heat from the desert acting as a mirage to hinder the view. But on nights when the full moon was out, they could be seen, sitting very small, to the south. Everything else was vast, empty and devoid of life.

Gerome slapped down his lash with a forcible *tink*, the electricity pulsing in a small series of arcs around the impact point, and began to rappel down slowly, following Dalton. Without wasting another moment, I moved to one side and stepped off, not bothering to throw my own lash until I was plummeting. It hit the side of the branch with a click and the harness arrested my fall by feeding out more line to slowly catch me. I braced my feet on the side of the glass, taking care not to damage the solar panels, and threw my second lash down. It stuck firm, and I released the first line as I kicked off, dropping down a few more feet and coming to dangle from the very bottom of the branch, my heart pounding.

As cocky as the move had been, my stomach lurched. The Tower was over a mile tall and the sides were sheer. I could see the world splayed out below me, and the massive wall of the octagonal Tower. The thing was flawless and brown, the perfect form broken only by the great solar branches jutting out of and around the gargantuan block. Hanging in thin air from the side of the monstrous edifice was terrifying. And exhilarating.

Gerome dropped beside me, beating Dalton down. Gerome, of

course, had attached his lashes the proper way, and his descent was a bit more controlled than mine.

I scrutinized Dalton's faltering progress above. The mechanic was *slow*. His every movement was so plodding that I wished I could do the job myself. It would have been one thing if he had been doing it safely, but he didn't even seem to know how to use the tools correctly. He was handling them like they were going to *break*. He placed his free lash so gently each time, letting it lower him down before he gingerly placed the next one to repeat the process. It would have been comical if it wasn't also deeply dangerous. All it'd take would be one failed connection and Dalton would get to do his best bird impression for over a mile-long drop.

Then again, it wasn't really his fault. Despite his proclamations, he was using Knights' equipment. The Knights were very protective of it—lashes included—which was why whenever anyone from another department requested their usage, they got a pair of Knight escorts with it, to make sure their equipment got returned in working order. I just happened to be one of the escorts today. It also wasn't his fault he was out here; it was common for sevens and sixes to get selected for the more dangerous work—they were of a high enough ranking to be reliable in their duties but a low enough ranking to be expendable.

I scanned the underside of the branch and quickly identified what we were there for. A clump of wiring had fallen loose, spilling out through a break in the metal plating. It happened sometimes—the air was still right now, but winds whipped by at high speeds and would cause shearing to some of the plates, until they broke off or the screws came out.

I threw out a hand, letting another lash fly, pulling me in closer to the damage. Dalton was just reaching it as I did, and began lashing himself over quickly—so quickly, in fact, that I paused and allowed him to go first, which earned me a sullen, angry look as he lashed by. I waited before I resumed my movement, careful to stay far enough away so that the man wouldn't feel inspired to actually start talking again.

Dalton drew himself in close to the exposed wiring. I winced as he used his fingers to connect his lash to the metal surface above, not even watching for the flash that confirmed its attachment. He then began fiddling, tugging a wire this way, then that, and I relaxed a little—his lash was holding. I let out a yawn, releasing the lashes with my hands, trusting my weight to the harness and settling into the lines. Some might have felt worried, hanging that high up. Me, though? In spite of any trepidation I felt at the height, I always felt more at home on lashes than I did on the ground. They were my wings.

"Watch him carefully," Gerome said, coming to my level.

I glanced at Dalton. He definitely didn't strike me as the criminal sort, but then again I was a four. According to Scipio, I was pretty rife with dissident urges of my own.

"If it was up to me," Gerome muttered, "a seven would have no place here. It is a respectable number, but the branches are too valuable to risk. There are nines among the mechanics. I would rather they do it."

I felt a spark of irritation.

"And a four?" I asked. "Where should *she* be?"

Gerome shook his head. "You're different, Squire. *And* you aren't touching any of the machines directly."

And there's the truth of it. So long as I wasn't actually doing anything, Gerome would overlook my number, for now.

I looked back at Dalton and paused. The man had given up on sorting through the wires and was now poking at the branch's wall with one of his lash cables with increasing desperation, the other one holding all of his weight—one had disconnected. I raised an eyebrow. It looked like he couldn't get the thing to reconnect.

"Gerome?" I said. The way Dalton was handling the lash wasn't just unsafe; he was going to—

There was a flash of blue light and Dalton's only connection broke. The lash tore free. He attempted to turn in our direction and had just enough time to reach out a hand to us before gravity began its deadly pull.

Gerome let out a shout of surprise and I saw his arm moving, a cable spinning from his hand to strike the metal surface beside where

Dalton had been hanging, but Gerome had always been cautious, precise, professional with his lashes. Dalton was plummeting, desperately throwing lashes in all directions in a futile attempt to save himself.

I didn't like Dalton. He was a pompous ass, cruel to those he viewed as inferior, and smug in his assurance of his technical knowledge. But I couldn't let him die. I began retracting my lashes as I spun upside down on them, letting the slack pull in before I kicked off the bottom of the branch to send myself torpedoing earthward. In an instant, I was staring at the ground, over a mile down, the sheer brown expanse of the Tower rushing by my side.

He's a jerk, I thought as I fell. He'd been nothing but abusive. But, hey, here I was, falling through the air. And there he was, plummeting down just feet below. What choice did I have, really? My body moved on its own.

I pressed my arms and legs together to move faster than Dalton, and tore through the air toward where he was flailing about. I felt the pressure of the wind against my body, the air blazing against my suit. I gritted my teeth, pushing forward, and with a guttural yell I reached out and grabbed one of Dalton's flailing lashes by the cable, avoiding the tip—that would have hurt like hell and the shock through my suit could knock out my own lashes, which would be bad. I pulled the line to tug us closer together until I could get my arm around his waist. He clung to me, and I could feel him vibrating with terror as we dropped.

I whipped my head around to stare at the Tower as it streaked by. To Dalton's credit, the shot *was* tricky. Estimating the angle to throw at and the drag on the line, the shot needed to be precisely and forcibly executed. I sucked in a breath, paused for an instant, then fired the lash.

It struck the side of the Tower and rebounded, the tip sparking angrily. I cursed, glancing down. Another branch was hurtling toward us, solar plates glinting like teeth. In my arms Dalton was thrashing about like a panicking fish. I was sorely tempted to hit him upside the head, but instead I turned back to the Tower. One more throw.

I threw. The lash spun through the air, colliding with the side of the Tower. It buzzed and then, with a flash of blue, it stuck. I felt the jolt in my arm as our fall was slowed, and then we were swinging, our feet practically skimming the lower branch before we hit the side of the Tower. My legs were already braced for the impact, and I managed to catch our collective weight with a grunt.

"Hold on to me," I ordered, and I felt the terrified Cog wrap himself around me as the mechanisms in my harness helped pull us up. My arm now freed, I threw a second lash through the hole in my uniform at the wrist, arcing it so it landed fifteen feet above us, and I slowly began to pull us back up to the branch where Gerome was still hanging.

Dalton was still flailing about like he was going to die. I shot him a look. "Would you *hold still*?" I snapped. "I really don't want to drop you."

A lie—but hey.

Back inside the Tower, I reached up and ran a hand through my black hair, panting but flushed with triumph. The cool air washed over my skin, and in that moment I could have kissed the nearest air circulation unit. At my side, Gerome actually gave an approving nod.

And then I looked at Dalton.

The mechanic was staring at me. I expected gratitude, or at the very least some joy at being alive… but instead I found nothing but hatred.

"What makes you think," he said, voice soft, "that you can just… handle me like that?"

My stomach dropped and for a moment my mouth didn't seem to work at all.

"I… *What*?" I managed.

"I was fine," Dalton snapped insistently. "I was fine, and you felt the need to—"

"You were *not* fine!" I retorted, taking a step toward him and suddenly aware of the baton I wore at my side. I wondered if a sharp blow to the side of the head would improve Dalton's temperament.

"My lashes were fully operational," he replied. "I was entirely capable of saving myself, and certainly didn't need a *four* to come to my aid."

"Well, excuse *me*, Mister Seven," I said. "It looked to me like you were falling to your death. Maybe next time I'll just let you get on with it."

"Liana." Gerome's voice held a note of warning, but I didn't care. I was too frustrated to apply any sort of brake to my mouth.

"Maybe you should!" Dalton sneered. "The idea of a *four* thinking I needed saving, of laying hands on me! I have a family, you know. I can't even imagine what my wife would say if she knew."

"She'd probably rather have you saved by a four than have you come back in a bag, Cog," I hissed. "Or, you know, not in anything at all. It's hard to get bodies back when they've fallen off the damn Tower."

"*Liana.*"

I turned sharply, glaring at Gerome. "And what do *you* want? Are you going to scold me, too? I saved a life—and even if he won't admit it, you know I did. Was it *wrong*? Was it *bad*? *What*?"

Gerome's features were somber as he reached out, seizing my right arm and lifting it so that I could see the dial on my wrist. Tears pricked my eyes as I stared at it. It couldn't be right. It couldn't be. The number shone hot and red, though. *At risk.*

"Oh, dammit," I breathed.

CHAPTER 2

I stared, stomach churning, at the dial on my wrist. A tremble rolled through me. Being a four had been bad enough as a Squire. But no matter what department you were from, once you hit three, Medica treatment was no longer just recommended; it was *required*. If you were a two you were placed in confinement on your floor and sent to mental restructuring, a rigorous process of intensive drug cocktails and heavy indoctrination designed to raise a person's number by completely re-writing their personality. If I dropped to a two, I would be automatically expelled from the Knights. Ones disappeared into the dungeons of the Citadel—I wasn't even sure what happened to them.

"A *three*?"

I looked up, my whole body numb. Dalton was gazing down his long nose at me like some kind of pompous vulture, thin tongue darting out to wet his lips. I tried to press down a surge of disgust at his pres-ence. Such thoughts were not helpful right now. I could practically *feel* Scipio leafing through my emotions via the net in my head.

"Liana…" Gerome began, but I turned away.

"It's fine," I said, not sure where the lie came from. "I—I'll get it sorted out."

"The Medica will sort you out, you mean," drawled Dalton. "At least *I* won't have to deal with you again."

I glanced back as Gerome turned on the engineer, his eyes flat as stone. "She saved your life, Cog."

Dalton stood up a little straighter. "I still had my lashes. I was perfectly capable of—"

"I have been training with lashes my entire life," Gerome said matter-of-factly, "and Liana is already twice as talented as me. I respect your loyalty to the Tower. I respect your commitment to its values. What I *cannot* respect is your flippancy toward its Knights. Unless you're trying to mar your record and bring your number down, I suggest a change of temperament."

Dalton had gone pale, and now he nodded shakily.

I glanced at Gerome. The speech had been defensive, but it wasn't meant as complimentary. How very Gerome: the facts, flat and simple, with no emotions or loyalties beyond himself and the Tower to get in the way. I appreciated the support, but sometimes I wished the man would show me something that resembled actual kindness—not the damnable cool statement of facts.

"Liana," he said, and this time it was not a tone that allowed me to ignore him.

"Yes, sir," I said, shoulders slumping.

"You will be required to visit the Medica tomorrow," he said. "They will give you what you need in order to be a productive member of this Tower."

My gut clenched. "Yes, sir."

"For now," he said, "I think it would be best if you—"

A low buzzing cut him off, coming from the net in my head. The vibrations seemed to flow together, until my eardrums rattled with sound that wasn't there. I bit my lip; direct messages had always left me with a vague sense of vertigo.

Squire, a voice said in my head. I recognized Scipio, and shivered. The programmers had chosen a soft, male voice for him, and for some reason whenever he spoke I imagined a young man, blond, sitting upon a throne, sword across his lap. He was regal, condescending, and completely at ease in his power. I wasn't sure if I hated, loved, or feared him. He merely was what he was.

There is an incident that requires your attention. A 'one' has appeared in the Water Treatment facilities. You are to assist in apprehending him. Immediately.

Scipio's words rang in my ears, and for a moment I stood, frozen in shock. I had expected a reprimand, not a call to duty. I watched as Gerome's iron façade twisted. He turned away.

"Something has come up," Gerome said. "I need to—"

"I got it too," I said hurriedly.

Dalton's stare darted between the two of us like we were mad.

Gerome stared at *me*.

"Confirm to me what you heard," he said.

I looked at Dalton, not particularly wanting to give the man the gossip that he wanted. The communication had been for Knights only. All the same, Gerome wanted an answer.

"A one has appeared in Water Treatment," I said. "I am to assist."

Dalton let out a gasp but Gerome just nodded.

"We're taking the plunge," he said.

Dalton, predictably, gasped again. I, on the other hand, offered the first genuine smile of the day.

The plunge was a sheer shaft that ran almost the entire length of the Tower, from the ceiling to the lower levels. Unlike the elevators, this tunnel was narrow and didn't always run in a perfectly straight line. For an experienced Knight, lashing your way down the plunge was simple, but, much like the drop outside, my stomach never failed to lurch when I leapt out into the empty air. The narrowness and random changes in the tunnel meant there was little room for error. It was one of the faster ways of getting to a lower floor, but at least one Knight a year died due to a mistake that sent them slamming off wall after wall in free fall, often getting no time to place new lashes before they hit the bottom of the passage. Seeing the deadly shaft of pipes and exposed beams, and leaping into it was as thrilling and terrifying now as it had been the first time I'd done it.

I'd be lying if I said I didn't love it.

Gerome leapt into the narrow shaft first, and I managed to last three whole seconds before I followed, a mad grin on my face. I placed my foot into nothingness and then allowed gravity to take me, throwing my lashes at the last possible second to arrest my descent down.

Gerome stared straight forward, his short hair barely moving as we hurtled toward the ground. His approach was methodical: a flick of the wrist here or there to keep himself perfectly centered as he shot downward. By contrast, I was a meteor. I spun and whirled, dancing about him as I let my feet clip the walls, grinning in spite of my mentor's disapproving glances. My teachers had always been very firm on the fact that the plunge was for emergency transportation only, but they had been forced to remind me several times over the years. Something this wonderful couldn't just be for when things were bad.

"When we arrive," Gerome shouted, his voice barely carrying over the wind roaring in my ears, "you are to stay with me. We'll search the perimeter indicated by Scipio while others search the interior."

I shot out a cable and yanked myself away from where a beam cut across the path, slipping my slim form through the narrow gap between the beam and the wall, leaving the wider space for Gerome's muscular form. Once I was past it, I took the time to answer. "Wouldn't it be more efficient if we split up?" I yelled back.

"We're not splitting up."

I winced, and for a moment I was all too aware of the low number on my wrist. Of course Gerome wouldn't want me to go off on my own now.

"Yes, sir."

Coming to a halt in the plunge was never easy, but Gerome managed it nicely, throwing a hand in either direction so that the lashes he shot out caught the walls simultaneously, at the same elevation. He came to a halt just above the exit we needed to take, which was little more than a door-shaped hole.

I speared one lash to the top of the exit and shot past Gerome through the narrow space, throwing another lash up and back to catch the doorframe as I passed through. I eased the latch and the cord gave a gentle pull at my wrist, slowing me until I landed, feet skidding along the ground.

Behind me, Gerome eased himself through the doorway. "Being flashy will get you killed," he grunted. "We have procedures for entering and exiting the plunge for a reason, Squire Castell."

I wanted to make a face but held the impulse in, opting for a curt nod instead. It never seemed to matter that I could do things nobody else could. My expertise, and what I could accomplish with it, meant nothing in the face of the immutability of the Tower. It was all I could do not to scream sometimes.

Gerome strode off and I fell into line behind him, my boots slapping moodily against the floor.

"So, what do we know about this guy?" I asked, trying not to think about the fact that my own dossier had just been flagged and passed on to the Medica. Gerome would have the information on the individual we were looking for—sent along with our orders.

Sure enough, he pulled a small, pen-like device from his pocket and held it up to one side. An image flared into view over it: a picture and several lines of text.

"Grey Farmless," he said, reading off the information. "Citizen designation 49xF-91. Looks like he was initially raised by the farmers but his parents petitioned the Department Head to drop him and they did."

I blinked, looking at the face with renewed interest. Getting dropped by your parents was a rare occurrence, but it did happen. When a parent simply couldn't take their own child's presence, or else thought them a bad influence on their floor, they could "drop" the child, essentially rendering them homeless to go find a new floor. It was extremely rare for any Hand to drop their own children, which made me curious.

In the picture, Grey's mouth was twisted into the smallest of frowns, his soft, dark brown eyes staring intently toward the camera. His hair was a light brown or dark blond—it was hard to really tell—and his square jaw framed lips set at a slight scowl. He wasn't classically handsome, but there was something sultry in the dry disdain of his features that made my heart skip a beat, and I quickly pushed the feeling back—it was woefully unprofessional. There was something else stamped into his features. It was subtle, but there: a *bitterness*—that I couldn't help but recognize in myself.

"What did he do?" I asked.

"Hm?"

"Why did they drop him?"

Gerome scrolled through the notes.

"Doesn't say," he replied eventually. "I do see that his number dropped before it happened, though. Might have just been natural prejudice against a dangerous element." I shoved my right hand behind my back, biting my retort clean in half. Picking a fight with Gerome about calling the lower numbers "dangerous elements" made about as much sense as saving Dalton had, and I was done doing stupid things today.

The search proved boring. Water Maintenance was a fascinating process, or so I'd been told. Intricate, delicate, and deeply scientific, the mesh of vein-like pipes kept the Tower from dying of thirst, grew our crops, and provided energy. This floor, however, held nothing of the supposed majesty of the profession. Everywhere I looked it was pipes, pipes and more pipes. Some glass, some metal, they tangled together into complex and intricate knots with only sparse room left for walkways to wind between them.

"Why would someone even be *in* here?" I asked, using a lash to tug myself up and over a particularly large pipe that had been built directly across the footpath.

Gerome pulled himself up over the same pipe without so much as a grunt.

"It makes sense," he said. "Good place to hide. Not to mention, these pipes go into the Depths."

I cocked my head at that. The Depths, as the council had taken to calling them, were a series of caverns and maintenance shafts at the base of the Tower. Supposedly they had become too irradiated to inhabit, but sometimes people would talk about *undocs*, the undocumented citizens of the Tower, hiding down there. It didn't seem likely to me. If there were people down there, surely the council would have done something about them by now. Besides, there was nothing to live off of in the dark, under-powered floors that made up the Depths.

As I was contemplating the idea of someone actually trying to live down there, a figure emerged from behind a nearby pipe.

I froze, looking him up and down. He was taller than I'd imagined from the picture, and better built. Also, his hair was a little lighter, and he looked more rugged; a layer of stubble had grown along his jaw. All the same, this was our guy. I raised a hand, but found myself momentarily speechless as his intense brown eyes locked with mine.

As he shifted, his wrist came into view. His band glowed hot and red, like an angry burn.

"Gerome," I finally blurted.

My mentor turned, and I could feel his eyes zoning in on the young man. Gerome wasted no time.

"Citizen Farmless," he said, advancing, one hand unslinging the stun baton from his waist. "You are hereby placed under arrest by the order of the Knights. Should you fail to comply, you will be—"

Grey didn't even wait. He turned with alarming speed and darted back the way he had come. Gerome cursed and broke into a run. I took off after him into the maze of pipes.

The guy was *fast*. He swung under and over pipes, his feet never missing a beat, never faltering for an instant as he sprinted ahead. Within moments he had a sizable lead. Growling, I thrust a hand forward and sent a lash spinning out. It collided with a pipe, and with a flex of my wrist I let it surge me forward at a breakneck pace.

I was almost near the fleeing man when I saw a familiar grayish tube just beyond him. An elevator.

That's fine, I thought. The scanner would read his number. The elevator would hold him in place—like any other person with a ranking of one attempting to use them—and we could just grab him when it refused to move.

That was what I was telling myself as Grey stepped onto the platform and the blue lights erupted from the bottom, moments before it began to lift him upward. I nearly slammed into a pipe as I gaped, dumbfounded, at the machinery. It hadn't even chirped out his ranking, and it *always* recited rankings if anyone lower than a nine was present on the platform.

Grey had the nerve to grin and actually waved at me as he disappeared behind the wall. I felt a burst of annoyance at the odd sense of pleasure his acknowledgement brought me.

Gerome entered the room just as I seized on that annoyance, racing up the ramp and onto the platform that slid out of the wall to support me. I didn't break my movement as I flung the lash up, attaching it to the underside of his elevator and letting it haul me up as I dangled in the shaft. Below me, the blue lights of the computer flashed red in warning—indicating that someone (me) had broken protocol.

"Liana!" Gerome bellowed, as I disappeared into the shaft. "Get to C-9 and head him off! I'll come around the other side."

His voice carried after me as I pulled myself up toward the panel above, reeling in so fast the line seemed to whistle. I couldn't stay under here for long—it was too dangerous.

The elevator began to slow and I waited until it had almost stopped before disconnecting my lash. I fell a few feet down, and flung out both lashes so they attached to either side of the shaft. The lashes fed out as I continued to fall, and at the last possible moment I reversed the feed and had them reel me back up—faster than was safe but I needed momentum. As I shot past the lash points, I disengaged them, angling my body up and through the now exposed doorway. I landed with a hard thud of my boots, a few feet behind Grey.

Grey froze and turned, his eyebrows jacking up into his hairline as he gazed at me in surprise. On impulse, I raised my hand and waved at him. He blinked, and then ran.

I felt a smile bloom on my lips as he sprinted, and flexed my shoulders, suddenly confident. *This* was what I had been made for. I felt my worries slipping away, my concerns staying far below with my supervisor as I lashed my way after him—through the pipes that crisscrossed the room, skimming surfaces as I shot lash after lash, in pursuit of Grey.

Because of his speed, and the pipes being so dense, I lost him behind a few, overshooting his location, too fast to stop. I swung back around, letting the swing of the last lash carry me back in a reverse trajectory and releasing it at just the right moment so I could land on an outcropping of pipes. I stared at the floor below, trying to find him.

The room was silent—only the occasional sound of water gurgling or steam escaping could be heard. My eyes scanned the piping he had disappeared behind. After a long moment, I lashed down to the catwalk below, looking for any sign of the man.

He hadn't disappeared after all—but had come to a stop by a junction of pipes and was now hunched over one, rooting around like a farmer planting seeds and not a man being pursued by the Knights. I coughed as I unsheathed my stun baton, releasing a menacing hum of electricity.

"So," I said, drawing out the syllable, "are you going to introduce yourself, or...?"

He spun around, his dark blond hair mussed and touching the sides of his face. His eyes found mine immediately, his muscles surging and tensing beneath his clothes. He didn't exactly look like a villain to me. Then again, I was a three, so maybe villains were just my type.

I tapped the tip of my baton against some of the piping, letting a thin tendril of power curl lazily up from it.

"Awkward silence works too, I suppose," I said, taking a step forward.

I failed to anticipate his speed, though, and he moved close, grabbing my wrist and attempting to break my hold on my baton. Alarmed, I reacted instinctually, striking a low blow with my foot in an attempt to get him to move back or upset his balance. His foot came up to block my blow, and I froze as he kicked it away.

I launched another kick, which he blocked as well, his hand still firmly wrapped around my wrist. We stared at each other, tension radiating from both of us.

"How do you know to do that?" I asked after a pause, looking at his feet.

He smiled, a flash of white straight teeth. "You're pretty, for a Shield," he said, referring to the Knights by their nickname.

I glared at him then thrust out my arm, my fist clenched, intent on knocking the smug look off of his face. He blocked the blow with his forearm, and then slid his arm around my waist, pulling me tight against him. I flushed and looked up at him, extremely uncomfortable at his proximity and the way his brown eyes lit up as he looked down at me, that cocky smile still clinging to his lips.

"Let go of me," I said, forcing air back into my lungs as I tried to fight my way out of his arms.

Grey smiled a slow, arrogant grin. "Let go of a pretty girl in the middle of a dance? My mother raised me better than that."

"Apparently not, *Farmless*," I spat, and was immediately mortified by my own words. They sounded harsh and cruel—spoken out of a nervousness that stemmed from the feeling of being trapped.

Grey's jaw twitched and he abruptly released me, keeping cool despite the simmering anger burning behind his brown eyes. He sucked in a deep breath as he took a slow step back, creating a little bit of room between us.

"Liana!" I heard Gerome's voice from the tunnels behind me, clearly looking for me, but I ignored it, keeping my eyes on the oddly untroubled fugitive in front of me.

"Citizen Grey Farmless, designation 49xF-91—to be precise," Grey informed me, his tone exasperated and curt. "May I ask why, exactly, you feel the need to brandish a weapon at me, Squire?"

I gave him a confused look and he gestured to the glowing display on his wrist. "I already know your number," I informed him, baffled by his odd behavior. "It's a one, Citizen Farmless. I've been given full authority to take you into custody."

I slapped my baton against the ground, forcing a shower of sparks, in an attempt to re-establish control of the situation. He seemed to be having a hard time getting it through his head. I wondered whether maybe that was because he was off the medicine handed out by the Medica for all twos and ones. *The medicine I would soon be taking*, my mind reminded me, and I pushed the thought away. Now wasn't the time.

Grey lifted his arm, turning it to display his number.

"Not a one, Knight. Sorry to disappoint."

I stared. The end of the one seemed to have gotten lazy, curled around, cooled to a soft blue.

"A six?" I said, dumbfounded.

"Nine, actually," he replied with a suffering sigh, "but who's counting?" He looked pointedly at the three on my wrist, one sandy-brown eyebrow slowly lifting.

"You were a one," I insisted, trying to force the flush from my cheeks.

"Well I'm not now," he replied. "Funny how the world works."

"I can't just let you go," I said. "There's no way that—"

"Squire Castell."

I turned and saw Gerome approaching, his own baton held loosely in one hand. He moved straight toward the young man, who took a step back and lifted his arm again.

"I'm a nine!" he announced. "There's been a misunderstanding."

Gerome paused, then turned toward me. His slate-gray eyes seemed to stab clean through me.

"This *is* the same man, isn't it?" he asked.

"Yes, sir," I answered, somewhat unsure of how that was possible.

I shuffled uncomfortably, glaring at the man's number. It couldn't be right, could it? But to think otherwise would be to assume that Scipio was wrong, and if I wanted to start claiming that, I might as well arrest myself and spend the night in a cell.

Gerome looked at me, then at the man, his hard eyes seeming uncertain. "Very well, then," he murmured after a pause. "We cannot arrest those in Scipio's grace. The Citadel apologizes for any inconvenience you have suffered, Citizen."

Grey gave him a shrug, donning an expression of mock sincerity. "That's no problem," he replied. "I just want to help the Tower run as *smoothly as possible.*"

I stared at him. His words were dripping with sarcasm, his eyes glinting with amusement. How the hell was he still a nine? It didn't make any sense.

"You were a one!" I erupted, gesturing at him. "You fled from Knights of Scipio's order!"

Gerome's baleful gaze fell on me this time, and I shrunk under it. "You know as well as anyone that Scipio marks criminals with a one, to make their capture easy and assured. If he is not a one, then he has committed no crime."

"But—"

"We're done here, Squire," Gerome said, his voice gaining a hint of steel as he turned and walked away.

I could only stare at his retreating form. It seemed that Gerome was as indifferent to crime as he was virtue. Actions didn't matter to him, or to the other Knights. It was all about Scipio and the number you happened to have flashing on your wrist. They were off the hook for everything else. Gerome was too indifferent to even admit there must have been some kind of mistake. But I couldn't exactly blame him, either; this was the only protocol he knew.

I, however, couldn't stop thinking about it. In all my years of having my accomplishments ignored, I hadn't really stopped to consider the things a high number could get away with. Now, my mind was abuzz. This *couldn't* be right, could it? And yet, it was happening.

I shot a lingering look back at Grey. He was lounging against a pipe, his eyes bright with quiet amusement. As I turned to follow Gerome, Grey gave a mocking salute, a smug smile tugging at the corners of his lips.

Oh, I'm going to figure out exactly *what you're doing.*

CHAPTER 3

I followed Gerome along one of the many bridges that connected the shell to the entrance of the Citadel, the Knights' headquarters. The giant cylindrical structure was dark and foreboding, stylized with great arches and loops of metal tempered to look like stone. The level we approached had high, towering walls, and lining those walls were gargoyles set upon platforms. Blue-and-silver banners bearing Scipio's insignia (a tower wreathed in lightning) hung from the structure, and high above I could hear the whoosh and snap of Squires and Knights lashing between the arches of the Citadel, practicing their art.

Reaching the looming front doors, Gerome was waved through, while I was brought to a stop, a crackling baton barring my path. I looked up and met the eyes of Lewis, a Knight who had sparred with me once. I had even thought of him as friendly.

"Nobody below a ranking of four is admitted here," he said, his voice unyielding. "You may take the residents' entrance, as you still live with your parents."

I looked to Gerome, but the man just shook his head. I should have expected the reaction, to be honest. Gerome would have arrested his mother and spared the devil based on the number on their wrists. I bet the devil was good at cheating the system too… maybe I could find him and he could give me some tips.

"Go home, Liana," he said, rubbing at his brow. "You need to speak with your parents."

I bit my lip. "What about my report, sir?"

"I will handle your report," said Gerome. "I was there. At any rate, the testimony of a three is inadmissible in the records. Dismissed."

He never said "goodbye" like a normal person might have. So I shouldn't have been surprised when he turned and disappeared into the darkness of the building beyond without another word. In front of me, Lewis continued to hold his baton, eyes level with mine.

I swallowed hard as I stared at the man. It wasn't even that I liked giving the reports, but it was my job. To be disallowed from even doing paperwork somehow felt like a bigger slap in the face than anything else I had experienced.

What am I going to do—write a treasonous report? I thought bitterly. Then I tried to catch the sour thought, bundle it up and send it to some part of my brain where it wouldn't be noticed. I couldn't allow myself to fall to a two. Happy thoughts.

Hey, you okay? a soft voice in the back of my head asked.

I jumped and stared at Lewis. He just brandished his weapon again, apparently concerned I might try to force my way in. I took a step back and exhaled, looking around. It hadn't been him talking, and there wasn't anyone else around, which really only left me with one option: my dear brother, with his personal access to Scipio's communication networks.

"Alex?" I muttered softly, knowing the implant in my ear would pick up the sound and transmit it back to him.

Literally and metaphorically coming at you through your thoughts, buzzed the voice in my head. *I went to check in on you and saw your number had dropped. What's going on?*

I smiled and walked away from Lewis to settle down on a bench. Alexander had always been the first to ask what was wrong. I rarely heard from him these days, except in a crisis. My parents hadn't taken kindly to his decision to leave the Knights, even to directly serve Scipio, and as a result he never visited. I missed him, truth be told. There was something earnest and good in Alex that was hard to find elsewhere, and it often made me wonder just how he had come to work with Scipio.

"It's nothing," I said. "Stupid run-in with a moronic Cog."

A pause.

Your ranking has slipped to a three, Lily.

I scowled at both the patronizing voice he used, as well as the nickname. He was the only person who called me that and I wasn't fond of it. "So?"

So, three is when compulsory Medica treatment kicks in. Not to mention, your apprenticeship is nearing an end. They could drop *you.*

I let my head fall into my hands, a wave of defeat rolling through me. Alex had never been one to mince words, and he knew me well enough to know exactly what I was afraid of. My number had fallen because I couldn't stay positive, keep my thoughts in a good place on a consistent basis. The Medica was going to fix those thoughts, whether I liked it or not. And I had to do it, or risk losing my department forever.

"Maybe it's just a bad day," I muttered. "Maybe it'll be better in the morning." Using the net to communicate was weird; it always looked like someone was talking to themselves, although everyone knew they weren't. Or at least hoped they weren't.

It won't be.

"Gee, thanks for the reassurance."

A soft chuckle. *Would you rather I coddle you with lies?*

I watched as a pair of stiff, straight-backed Knights in crisp, crimson uniforms strode by, heading toward the building. Everything about the place was so rigid. So stiff. Was this really all there was to life? Rules, and grappling with your own brain out of the terror of ever, even for a moment, thinking something bad?

"What's it like, working for the Eyes?" I asked, partially to distract myself.

Alex sighed. *Work, work, and more work,* he admitted. *But it's fascinating. The sheer amount of data we have access to, you wouldn't believe it.*

Data, he'd said. People's emotions screened and compiled into a revolting blob of *data.*

Did I say something?

"No."

Your negativity concentration—

"You're reading me!?" I cried, jolting to my feet and causing a nearby Knight to shoot a disparaging look my way.

I'm just watching your screen while we talk, Alex said hurriedly. *I like to keep an eye on you.*

"Alex, that's…"

Would you rather I didn't?

I paused, considering. "No," I said eventually. As invasive as it was, as bizarre as it was to think that someone always knew my inner state of mind, it was comforting to know that someone cared enough to look. To look at that negativity and not just slap a number on it but ask *why* my thoughts looked that way. Alex had always been different like that, and I adored him for it. It gave me hope, knowing that someone like my brother worked with the Eyes.

The net in my brain continued to buzz, but Alex didn't speak for almost a minute.

Things are changing, he finally said.

I tilted my head up, looking at the Core. The great computer was located somewhere in there, but the Eyes never let anyone other than other Eyes inside. Even their trainees, called Bits, weren't allowed inside, until after they had passed copious screenings.

"How so?"

I can't say. Or maybe I'd simply rather not—I don't know, he replied. *Just… get your number back up, and stay away from any more moronic Cogs. Or just Cogs in general.*

I chuckled at the tone of his voice—it was dryer than the desert outside. Eyes and Cogs were notoriously bad at getting along, and it seemed Alex had picked up that characteristic as well.

So it is possible to get some positivity out of you after all, he drawled. *Anti-departmental humor works like a charm every time.*

"Seriously, though, it's creepy for you to just… read me like that."

He was right, though; I was smiling.

You sure? I thought it was endearing.

I laughed. "Pretty sure you don't have any idea what's endearing about you."

There was a silence, then a sigh. *I have to work.*

"I know."

You going to be okay?

I stared down at the number on my wrist. "I don't know," I replied honestly.

Another silence.

I'll do what I can, he said.

The buzzing in my head cut out, and just like that Alex was gone. With the noise, and my brother gone, I abruptly felt very alone. I thought about going home. About seeing my parents. But they didn't care about anything more than the number on my wrist, and now that I had finally dropped—as they expected me to—I suddenly didn't want to. The only thing that could possibly redeem me would be if I went off and managed to catch an entire gang of criminals—and even then it might not work. Both of them were Knight Commanders, the highest rank in our Order without becoming Champion, and that seat was held by Devon.

I realized that I didn't want to go home. In that moment, perhaps it was more that I couldn't. I turned, moving back across the bridge, intent on finding an elevator to take me back to Water Maintenance.

The elevator decided that the three using it needed an insultingly long lecture on immorality in exchange for travel back down to Water Maintenance. I waited, stewing in sullen silence, for it to finish and deposit me where I needed to go. I quickly went back to where I'd confronted Grey. He, of course, was long gone, but the pipes along the wall still bore the faint black mark where my baton had struck as I flew out of the sky to arrest him. Flew out of the sky and saw his wrist.

A nine.

I gritted my teeth as I walked forward, scanning the area for something, *anything* that might indicate what had happened. He had been a one. I had seen it, and even if I hadn't I would have known. The easy smiles, the spark of character in his eyes; those things died when someone's number got higher. Even aside from that, why would he have run if he wasn't a one?

I moved up to the place where he had been hovering, but there was nothing obviously different about it. Uncertain, I lowered my hand into a gap between the pipes and rooted around in the little pocket within.

"So, Grey Farmless," I muttered. "What were you rooting around for over here, huh?"

It was a stupid venture. Grey was cleared. Even if I had found a bloody knife and a confession to murder, the man would have been free to prance about the Tower while people looked at me like I was going to burn the place down. To the eyes of the world, a nine was all but infallible, and a three was just waiting to explode. Still, something drove me. I needed to know the truth.

Just then, my fingers brushed against something. It was small, smooth, and the contact sent it rolling away from me. I cursed, scrabbling for a moment, and just managed to close my hand around it before it got away. Yanking my hand out, I held it before me, then slowly opened it.

It was a pill. And while Medica pills were brightly colored and well labeled, this one was a nondescript white, the sides completely blank.

Hello… What might you be?

I rolled the pill in between my fingers, thinking. *I ought to take it to Gerome* was the first thought that came to my head. This was important. Significant. As I thought about it, though, I pictured Grey. Cocky, self-assured, and so… *himself.* So much more himself than anyone I had ever known—and so unafraid to be so. He didn't act like someone worried their number would fall. He didn't act like someone who was worried about their number *at all*.

I stared down at the three on my wrist. Medica treatment. Mood-altering pills. Liana—vanished.

I shoved the pill into my pocket.

Ready for more?

Visit: www.bellaforrest.net for details on purchase.